ON THE EDGE OF THE GREAT RIFT

Paul Theroux was born and educated in the United States. After graduating from university in 1963, he travelled first to Italy and then to Africa, where he worked as a Peace Corps teacher at a bush school in Malawi and as a lecturer at Makerere University in Uganda. In 1968 he joined the University of Singapore and taught in the Department of English for three years. Throughout this time he was publishing short stories and journalism and he wrote a number of novels. Among these were *Fong and the Indians*, *Girls at Play* and *Jungle Lovers*, all of which appear in this volume, *On the Edge of the Great Rift* (Penguin, 1996). In the early 1970s Paul Theroux moved with his wife and two children to Dorset, where he wrote *Saint Jack*, and then on to London. He was resident in Britain for a total of seventeen years. In this time he wrote a dozen volumes of highly praised fiction and a number of successful travel books, from which a selection of writings were taken to compile his book *Travelling the World* (Penguin, 1992). Paul Theroux has now returned to the United States, but he continues to travel widely.

Paul Theroux's many books include *Picture Palace*, which won the 1978 Whitbread Literary Award; *The Mosquito Coast*, which was the 1981 *Yorkshire Post* Novel of the Year, joint winner of the James Tait Black Memorial Prize and was made into a feature film; *Riding the Iron Rooster*, which won the 1988 Thomas Cook Travel Book Award; and, most recently, *The Pillars of Hercules*. Most of his books are published by Penguin.

Fiction

Waldo
Jungle Lovers
Saint Jack
The Black House
The Family Arsenal
Picture Palace
World's End
The Mosquito Coast
The London Embassy
O-Zone
My Secret History
Chicago Loop
Millroy the Magician
and
On the Edge of the Great Rift (*containing* Fong and the
Indians, Girls at Play *and* Jungle Lovers)

Travel

The Great Railway Bazaar
The Old Patagonian Express
The Kingdom by the Sea
Sunrise with Seamonsters
Riding the Iron Rooster
The Happy Isles of Oceania
Travelling the World
The Pillars of Hercules

PAUL THEROUX

On the Edge
of the Great Rift

Three Novels of Africa

PENGUIN BOOKS

PENGUIN BOOKS

Published by the Penguin Group
Penguin Books Ltd, 27 Wrights Lane, London w8 5TZ, England
Penguin Books USA Inc., 375 Hudson Street, New York, New York 10014, USA
Penguin Books Australia Ltd, Ringwood, Victoria, Australia
Penguin Books Canada Ltd, 10 Alcorn Avenue, Toronto, Ontario, Canada M4V 3B2
Penguin Books (NZ) Ltd, 182–190 Wairau Road, Auckland 10, New Zealand

Penguin Books Ltd, Registered Offices: Harmondsworth, Middlesex, England

Fong and the Indians first published in the USA by Houghton Mifflin 1968
First published in Great Britain by Hamish Hamilton 1976
Published in Penguin Books 1992
Copyright © Paul Theroux, 1968

Girls at Play first published in Great Britain by The Bodley Head 1969
First published in this edition by Hamish Hamilton 1978
Published in Penguin Books 1983
Copyright © Paul Theroux, 1969

Jungle Lovers first published by The Bodley Head 1971
First published in this edition by Hamish Hamilton 1978
Published in Penguin Books 1982
Copyright © Paul Theroux, 1971

Published in one volume with a new preface in Penguin Books 1996
Preface copyright © Paul Theroux 1996
All rights reserved
1 3 5 7 9 10 8 6 4 2

Set in 10/12pt Monotype Sabon
Typeset by Datix International Limited, Bungay, Suffolk
Printed in England by Clays Ltd, St Ives plc

Contents

Preface

'There is a crack in the earth which extends from the Sea of Galilee to the coast of Mozambique, and I am living on the edge of it, in Nyasaland.' I was writing in blue ink on a sheet of school foolscap, in my little house in the bush near Soche Hill. It thrilled me to be so far from home, and to be able to make a statement like that. It was the hot season, known locally as 'The Suicide Month', because of the suffocating and depressing heat. But that was a settler expression, and most of the white settlers had bolted from the country when the Africans took power.

'The crack is the Great Rift Valley,' I went on. 'It seems to be swallowing most of East Africa. In Nyasaland it is replacing the fishing villages, the flowers and the anthills with a nearly bottomless lake, and it shows itself in rough escarpments and troughs up and down this huge continent. It is thought that this valley was torn amid great volcanic activity. The period of vulcanism has not ended in Africa. It shows not only in the Great Rift Valley itself, but in the people, burning, the lava of masses, the turbulence of the humans themselves who live in the Great Rift.'

I went on writing, describing my school, my students, the villages nearby. It was a letter from a distant place, where I felt I had arrived, and I knew I was happy. When I published this 'Letter from Africa' in an American newspaper I had a distinct sense that I had fully embarked on a writing career.

At the age of twenty-two, hoping to avoid being drafted into the US army, but also wishing to see the world, I joined the Peace Corps. When I went to Malawi in 1963 it was called the Nyasaland Protectorate and was administered by Britain. In rural areas, women and children dropped to their knees, out of respect, when a white person went by in a Land-Rover. African men merely bowed. The country became independent in July 1964, and four months later there was an attempted *coup d'état* – sackings, shootings, resignations. People were arrested for repeating rumours, charged with 'creating alarm and despondency' – how I loved that expression. The President-for-life, Doctor Banda, had spent much of his working life in Britain and did not speak any African language well enough to give speeches in anything but English. He wore three-piece pinstriped suits and a Homburg hat and had an interpreter for talking to his people. It was, for some months anyway, very cold in the country. Many Africans I met were pious members of the Church of Scotland, but they also believed in ghosts and witches. There were stubborn, moustached English settlers who said they would never leave Africa; and nuns, lepers, guerrillas and runaways. Malawi had a once-a-week newspaper and a terrible railway station and steam locomotives. It was a country of constant rumours. In the deep south of the country the Africans often went stark naked; in the north they wore English flannels. This was not the Africa I had expected. I think my contemplating its oddness from my isolation at the edge of the Great Rift helped make me a writer.

I remember a particular day in Mozambique, in a terrible little country town, getting a haircut from a Portuguese barber. He had come to the African bush from rural Portugal to be a barber. It went without saying that he would only cut the hair of white people. Mozambique had been a colony for hundreds of years – the first Portuguese claimed it in 1505. This barber did not speak English, I did not speak Portuguese, yet when I addressed his African servant in Chinyanja, his own language, the Portuguese man said, in Portuguese, 'Ask the *bwana* what his Africans are like.' And that was how we held a conversation – the barber spoke Portuguese to the African, who translated it into Chinyanja for me; and I replied in Chinyanja, which the African translated into Portuguese for the barber. The barber kept saying – and the African kept translating – things like, 'I can't stand the blacks – they're so stupid and bad-tempered. But there's no work for me in

Portugal.' It was grotesque, it was outrageous, it was the shabbiest, darkest kind of imperialism. I could not believe my good luck. In many parts of Africa in the early 1960s it was the nineteenth century, and I was filled with the urgency to write about it.

After my two years in Malawi I went to Uganda and signed a four-year contract to teach at Makerere University, at the time considered to be one of the best universities in Africa. V. S. Naipaul was for a time a visiting lecturer. My friendship with him, and his close attention to my writing (often he would go over something I had written word by word) had a profound influence on me. Uganda was a green wilderness of great beauty. I was self-sufficient, and I had fallen love with the English woman whom I was to marry. I felt different from everyone I knew, and yet I had found a place for myself in Uganda. In this mood, I began writing about the Chinese man who ran the grocery store around the corner from where I lived in Wandegeya. This neighbourhood was famous for the thousands of bats which hung in the branches of the trees and took off in a black cloud at sunset to hunt for insects. The Chinese man, his grocery store, his Indian competitors, his African customers – these were my characters in *Fong and·the Indians*. I had written two novels before this, but *Fong* was the first piece of fiction that satisfied me.

My future wife taught at a girls' school in Kenya. While I was writing this novel, I courted her by driving hundreds of miles on rutted roads, from Kampala to her bush school north of Nairobi. Kenya had been heavily colonized by unsubtle and presumptuous white people with sharp elbows; so the atmosphere – different from that of Uganda – interested me, and a girls' school seemed to contain all the contradictions and snobberies and class distinctions of imperialism. My writing method, then as now, was to write a book in notebooks (first draft); and copy it out in longhand on sheets of lined paper (second draft); then type it myself (third draft), before correcting it and turning it over to be retyped by someone else (fourth draft). I was typing *Fong* when I began to write the first chapters of *Girls at Play*.

It became clear to me, writing *Girls at Play*, that I was privileged to be living in an African world that had not been written about. This was not the Africa of Conrad, or Karen Blixen, or Hemingway or even Laurens van der Post. No one had written about this particular Africa. That, I think, was my good luck. It was for me to describe this unknown time and place. There was a colonial hangover, and Africans were now being uncomfortably accommodated in the white clubs; but I was not a member of any club, I did not go on safari. I came to be fascinated by this Africa of hilarious dancehalls and village feasts and bush schools. There were crazed politicians ranting all over the countryside, and yet there was a power vacuum in which most Africans, rather enjoying the anarchy, felt free. In a cheerful, scribbling and self-deluded frame of mind, in this in-between period that occurred after colonialism and before politics and soldiers put the screws on, I felt safe.

Jungle Lovers was the result of my departure from Africa. In 1968, after five years in Malawi and Uganda, my wife and I were attacked by rioting students in Kampala. After that, I lost my will to teach any students; my confidence was gone. I said to my African colleagues: 'You do it. I have no business here.' I decided to leave for good and took a job teaching in Singapore. The Singapore authorities had got wind of the fact that I was a published author and, taking the philistine view that writers were troublemakers, they insisted that I sign a paper saying that I would not write or publish anything about Singapore while I was under contract. They also put me on the lowest salary scale. I wondered what they were trying to hide.

I discovered: nothing – or very little. Singapore was a small humid island-city that called itself a republic. It was dominated by puritanical overseas Chinese who were growing rich on the Vietnam War. My students said they wanted to emigrate to Australia. I taught courses in Jacobean literature. I questioned whether I was cut out to be a teacher in the tropics. Of course, I wasn't, and I saw writing as liberation.

Forbidden to write about Singapore, I wrote about Africa – in *Jungle Lovers*. The weather was very hot – I could only work at night or on weekends; I kept my writing secret from my employers;

and in the middle of writing this novel I contracted dengue fever. It took me more than two years to write *Jungle Lovers*. When at last I had finished and sent it off, I left Singapore (and teaching) to write my Singapore novel, *Saint Jack*. I never took another salaried job.

That was in 1971. Now, rereading *Jungle Lovers*, I am struck by its peculiar humour and violence. Some of it is farce and some tragedy. I suppose the insurance man and the revolutionary were the two opposing sides of my own personality. I had gone to Africa believing that political freedom would create social change. Five years did not change much, and now more than twenty-five years later this novel of futility and failed hopes seems truer than ever. That was my mood on leaving Africa. I was younger then. Now I should say that it takes a long time for change to come about, and change ought always to come from within. Outsiders, even the most well-intentioned in Africa, are nearly always meddlers.

Nowadays, people my age are asked: '*Where were you in the sixties?*' Americans went various ways. They clung to universities, or dropped out and became part of the counter-culture; or they were sent to Vietnam. Some, like me, spent the sixties in the Third World – it was a way of virtuously dropping out and delicately circumventing Vietnam. I was in my twenties in the sixties, and I think my African novels are very much of their time. Many African countries had just become independent; colonialists were going home; volunteer teachers – and insurance agents and revolutionaries – were arriving and wondering what would happen next. No one realized that the darkness they found was the long shadow of Africa's past.

FONG AND THE INDIANS

For Anne

'... The entry of the Asiatic as labourer, trader, and capitalist into competition in industry and enterprise not only with, but in, the Western world is a new fact of first importance ...'

– Winston Churchill
My African Journey
1908

Part One

I

The grocery store on Uhuru Avenue (formerly Queensway) was owned by Sam Fong, a Chinese immigrant. They called him an immigrant; actually he had lived in East Africa longer than the Prime Minister, who was an African. But to be one Chinaman in a country of seven million Africans is not easy: you stand out; the East cannot save you; you remain a visible immigrant all your born days and so do your children, and so do theirs.

On the window of the store in white irregular letters was written FRIEND FROCERY POP IN PLEASE FOR BETTER PRICE ANYWHERE IN AFRICA. Some Swahili progress slogans had been written on the window but were now scratched out. Four years after independence Sam Fong discovered that the less said about progress the better. The slogans antagonized his customers and often got him into ideological hot water. Take ONE MAN, ONE VOTE (a stick figure with a ballot between its fingers illustrated this slogan). Many Africans came into the grocery store and said, 'Big words, big vote. Where this thing vote? You tell me.'

'Like the Holy Spirit' – Fong was a Catholic – 'the vote is everywhere. But you can't see it, that's all,' said Fong, grinning and thinking how much better the sentence would have sounded in Chinese than Swahili.

'These bloody fool politicians,' the African would answer. 'There is no vote, just their fat asses in big cars for ever. Finish, that's all. Give me the British any day. At least they don't talk through their ass. Those British they say what they mean. If they think you bloody baboon they say straight out, "I think you African chaps are bloody baboon." British are too honest, you

7

know. That's why everyone like them *kabisa*. But these politicians are bloody sheet.'

'Be patient,' Fong would say. This he had been saying nearly every day of his thirty-five years in East Africa. When he realized that the progress slogans upset his African customers he scratched them off the window.

In spite of the fact that many of Fong's white customers might say (and often did say), 'The Chinese are born grocers,' Sam Fong was not a born grocer. It should have been clear to anyone standing in the grocery store that Fong's real genius was in carpentry: the hardwood shelves covered every wall from floor to ceiling; bins, vats, counters, stools – all mortised and tenoned (not a nail in the place) – were everywhere, unbreakable, sturdy, hard, with chamfered edges and smooth surfaces. But on the formidable expanse of shelves were only a few cans, a few lonely packages of tea and hair straightener and skin lightener. On the smooth counter, as big as the Congo, was a tin receptacle containing stale bread and a few old cream buns; in the bins some onions were starting to shoot green stalks into each other; in the vats maybe a dozen handfuls of rice. Speaking plainly, there were no groceries in the grocery store. The only piece of grocery-store furniture that appeared to be fulfilling its design and justifying its labour was the stool Sam Fong's wife Soo sat on, week after week, smiling at the empty shelves beyond.

Sam Fong *had* been a carpenter. The grocery store came after independence when necessity forced Fong to learn a new profession. He had been a foreman in the carpentry shop of the Ministry of Works when East Africa was a British Protectorate. Shortly after independence an Englishman came up to Fong and asked, 'In point of fact, I want you to tell me straight out, Fong, who would you say is the keenest chap in the workshop? I don't want a dogsbody, you understand.' The Englishman bared his teeth. 'I want someone terribly keen.'

Sam Fong thought a moment and then pointed to Mohinder Singh, chief *fundi* of the workshop; Singh was gnawing a dowel that he found too large for a hole.

'No, no, not a *muhindi*. I want a native, an African chap, you see? A black one.'

'Take anyone,' said Sam Fong.

'Are they all that keen?'

'No. They're all the same. Useless buggers,' said Sam Fong in Swahili. 'Buggers', he said in English.

'I'm afraid I can't agree with you there, Fong. No sir, I can't. You give these people half a chance and there's no telling what will happen. Oh, I know, we're not in charge any more, but that's hard cheese; we'll just have to live with it. Now for goodness' sake, Fong, point me out a keen chap. I'm a busy man.'

Fong shrugged in the direction of an African man in rags sawing a board. The man sawed very quickly with one hand and picked his teeth with the other hand. The board was held firm by the man's toes, which curled round the edges and prevented it from moving. 'Keen chap,' said Fong, 'like the rest of them.' These words were Sam Fong's undoing.

The next day the Englishman appeared again and handed the African an envelope. The African, who was working on his back under a table at the time, glanced over and took the envelope firmly between the large and second toes of his right foot.

Sam Fong looked on in horror. He half expected the African to rip open the envelope with his toes and hold up the letter with his left foot for all to see. The African did not do this. Instead, he just raised his right foot a few inches, holding the envelope above the sawdust, the wood shavings and spittings, and continued drilling the hole under the table. Neither the Englishman, nor Sam Fong, nor the envelope moved for a full five minutes. The African put down his drill and moved out from under the large table sideways, like a crab. He passed the envelope from his foot to his left hand, and, squatting on the floor, opened it. He looked at the Englishman.

The Englishman's face brightened and twisted itself into a smile so large that it was almost not a smile; the Englishman's eyes popped and he clasped his hands behind his back and rocked on his heels. He turned his face to Sam Fong and continued rocking and grinning, although Fong remained horror-struck, yellow, his eyes and mouth only slits in a lineless face.

The African looked bewildered, almost harmed. He walked up to the Englishman and said softly, 'I'm going to England.'

'You deserve it, son,' said the Englishman, bouncing once on his toes. 'You're a keen chap.'

The African went over to Sam Fong. 'I'm going to England,' he said.

'May your misbegotten children die diseased in a whore-house there. I hope you never come back,' said Sam Fong in Chinese. He grinned and then uttered a Swahili proverb.

The small, barefoot African and the large Englishman, bags under his eyes, bags in his trousers, his paunch-tightened shirt bursting over his belt, left the workshop arm in arm, and walked down the driveway to a waiting Mercedes with *Department of Technical Assistance* written on the door. Before the Englishman got into the car he stopped, looked up the driveway to Sam Fong, winked and erected his thumb in what he intended as a gesture of mutual triumph. Sam Fong raised a ripe middle finger to the man, something he had not done since he was a very young boy in Central China.

Sam Fong's curse was not as powerful as the will of the Department of Technical Assistance. The African came back six months later. He had gone on a carpentry course in Birmingham where he found out about drill presses, steam drills and table saws that could do the work of ten men. If Fong had been in the habit of going to the movies he might have seen, in *News from Britain*, the face of the African he cursed being shown around the Birmingham Technical School by a man in a white smock. Looking on were two Nigerians, a Zambian, a Ghanaian in a robe, a Sudanese in a fez and a Kenyan in a three-piece suit carrying a fly whisk, which he flicked at giant whirring machines. Sam Fong's keen chap was wearing real clothes and even a pair of shoes, and later in the film operated a drill press while the six Africans and twenty white Birmingham Tech. students applauded and waved into the camera. At the end of the film, while the narrator said, '. . . but it's not all work and no play for these keen carpenters . . .', the Africans were shown riding a red double-decker bus, eating a meal of fish and chips topped off with large helpings of jellied eels, being shown what looked like a museum by a bald man with a thick gold chain around his neck, and ('. . . there was lots of merriment in store for these keen craftsmen in wood . . .') dancing with large-chinned and flat-chested English girls from 'right across the High Road at Birmingham Domestic Science College, where five Zanzibaris will finish their course this year'.

When Mohinder Singh came to work the next morning and described *News from Britain* to Sam Fong ('. . . dancing with a *mzungu* girl and goodness knows what . . .'), Sam Fong wept. His tears were scarcely dry when the African showed up and announced, with an official letter of appointment as proof, that he was foreman. Fong was given a drill. He handed his pencil and clipboard to the African and, cursing in Chinese, took his place under the half-made furniture, on his back, 'like a whore in Shanghai,' he reflected.

The African now wore suits, bought a motorcycle and a fountain-pen and carried a humming transistor radio with him wherever he went; he showed up to work late and drunk, called the other Africans bloody baboons and useless natives and began saying to Sam Fong, 'Carry on then . . . I'll leave you to get on with it . . . Pull your finger out . . . Belt up or I'll sack you off . . .' One day, about a month after Fong gave up his clipboard, the African foreman said, 'Carry on, you bugger, or I'll buy one of those super drills that does do the work of ten fat men!'

Sam Fong sighed. 'What do you want, *bwana*?'

'I am asking you are you knowing what the drill is this side?'

'This is the drill,' said Fong holding up his drill.

'Are you being cheeky with me?' asked the foreman angrily. 'I can have your bloody job if you act *kali* . . .'

Sam Fong stood up, brushed off the wood shavings, looked at the foreman, said 'You belong in a tall tree' in Chinese and then '*Kwaheri*, bye-bye.' He mounted his bicycle and pedalled quickly out of the Ministry of Works compound, away from the Work for Progress posters and the shrieks of the foreman who was attempting to disperse the crowd of workmen that had gathered.

Sam Fong never went back. On the way home he made three resolutions: never trust a white, never trust a black, never be a carpenter; as he repeated these resolutions to himself he saw a sign reading STORE FOR HIRE APLY FAKHRU ENTERPRISES LTD, and later that afternoon signed a ten-year lease with a pyjama-clad Ismaili who demanded £50 in advance for a mouldering empty shop at the lower end of Uhuru Avenue. In the contract was a clause which read, 'And I promise to buy all stocks and stores and goods from the above-named Hassanali Fakhru at prices to be agreed upon so help me God.' Only later, in the heat of argument, was this pointed out to Fong. The lumber for the shelves and counters, the bins, the vats, the scales, the light bulbs, the plate glass, were also bought, again under protest, from Fakhru. Twice a day, in Chinese and Swahili, Sam Fong said to Fakhru, 'I hate you, I hate you . . . You're a bloodsucking Indian, and if you did this in China the Emperor would cut your tongue out, your hands off and he would wisely make your penis into sausage for the dogs!'

Hassanali Fakhru listened to the jerky Swahili, smiled and answered, 'The trouble with you foreigners is you're not interested in building a nation. You have no spirit of *harambee*. You just make money and then go back where you came from and leave our poor African brothers with nothing. Now me, I can tell you I am interested in developing this country and building a multiracial society and I have to deal with shit like your kind to do so. The contract was finalized long ago so there's no need crying over spilt milk. Buggers like you make my job very hard, let me remind you, and give Asia a bad name. Now piss off, my friend.'

Sam Fong would utter a vile Chinese oath and make his way, past hand-coloured portraits of the Aga Khan with a garland around his neck, to the door. With a belch, and smoothing his pyjama top, Fakhru would return to his papers. It happened twice a day. There was no need, he felt, for either party to get excited: such was business. During these first six months Sam Fong worked on his shelves, and even taking into consideration the tyranny of Fakhru, Fong considered the six months to be very happy ones. He worked all day and far into the night sawing and sanding and banging pegs into the shelves and counters; he did not have to draw plans. He had a good eye and could measure anything by merely looking at it. He was foreman, workman and customer. He was alone in his work and very happy with his tools and wood. He worked steadily, and the shelves in the shop in his mind soon became the shelves in Fakhru's hired *duka*. They were lovely large shelves, very strong and smooth, braced and solid. Fong knew they were beautiful, but still he remembered his resolutions and refused to do any carpentry for anyone but himself. He vowed never to allow himself the humiliation of being an employee ('Get on with the job or I'll sack you off!') or even a confidant ('Tell me, Fong, who's the keenest chap in the workshop?').

As the weeks passed he grew more and more worried about the prospect of becoming a grocer, while still resolved that he would never be a carpenter again. Being a grocer frightened him, opening his own store frightened him, and soon all this fear transformed itself into rage at night and he started beating his wife to calm himself. His wife, Soo, understood and received each beating on good faith. It was just another wifely burden. Many times she had to remind herself of her obligation to shriek.

Two days before the opening Soo stayed in the shop and busied herself with white paint and a large board. At the end of the day she showed Fong the sign: FRIEND FROCERY POP IN PLEASE FOR BETTER PRICE ANYWHERE IN AFRICA. She smiled. 'This is your sign. This is your store, noble husband. You are now a grocerman,' she said in Chinese. Instead of being pleased Sam Fong felt only fear, and for her sign and her words Soo Fong was so severely beaten that she was unable to attend the Grand Opening.

'I am abundantly heppy – overjoyed I should say – to be the honoured patron of this Grand Opening Day of the Sam Fong grocery *duka*,' Fakhru said to his brother-in-law, Sam Fong and the five African stragglers who had caught sight of the ribbon across the door of the grocery. Fakhru's speech, written by his son, who had been directed, 'Big words in this or I'll kick your ass to Zanzibar,' took well over thirty minutes to deliver. Fong agreed to the speech only because his own English was faulty; in fact, his entire English vocabulary consisted of nouns for food and perhaps ten verbs which he always used in the present continuous tense. He felt humiliated and helpless; his bitter enemy and master, Hassanali Fakhru, stood in the doorway and spoke. But it was only temporary, an hour at most, and then he would be free.

Fakhru referred to Sam Fong's perseverance and high values, Asian values, tried and true. He went on to speak at length of how he, Fakhru, had started out from just such humble beginnings. He spoke of the necessity for lifting oneself up into the world by one's own bootstraps. Snatches of the Koran, progress slogans and parts of pop songs ('As our friends the Beatles say, money cannot buy us love . . .') were also part of the speech, and he finished by saying, 'I do believe I have covered up all the major points . . .'

Soon it came time to cut the ribbon. Sam Fong held out a pair of Mother's Own Cutting Scissors (Fakhru Enterprises Ltd, four shillings sixpence), and Fakhru and Fong, each with his thumb in a metal loop, began sawing away at the ribbon. The leverage was wrong and instead of the blades working against each other they were far apart. A good minute passed and the ribbon was not even frayed. Fakhru lost his temper, pulled Fong's thumb out of the loop and threw the scissors down. Then he lifted the ribbon, and chomping down once with betel-stained teeth, tore the ribbon in half. 'That's how we do such things where I come from,' said Fakhru, holding the two ends of the ribbon. His brother-in-law snapped a picture.

Sam Fong stood impassive and stiff. The people on the sidewalk clapped and then went away. Off in the distance Soo moaned.

'And now for the Grand Opening,' said Fakhru. 'I shall be your first customer.'

The two men entered the store. Except for the carefully made furnishings the store was almost bare. Sam Fong went behind the counter and folded his arms.

'If you please, kind sir,' said Fakhru showing his teeth, 'I would like a becket of tea.'

'Big-big or small-small?' inquired Fong, now leaning on the counter gingerly in the manner of a grocer.

'Bit smaller,' said Fakhru.

Fong went to a corner of the store where on a large shelf sat a tiny box of tea. He placed the box of tea in front of Fakhru.

'You see,' said Fakhru, 'it's not that I am not liking tea. I'm crazy for tea. But I am having lots of tea beckets already. I just want to be your first customer. I'll take it.'

'Two shillings only,' said Fong.

Fakhru slapped his fat palm against his wide perspiring forehead and made a meaty *plop*. 'You said *two shillings*?'

'Right. Now I grocery man, you customer. You pay, I take money.'

'You buy this goods from me for sixpence, you sell to me for two shillings. You call that business?'

'What you calling it?'

'When I have to pay you one shilling sixpence to be first customer I rather be second customer and save money. I call it robbery.'

'You stealing from me, I stealing from you. That business,' said Fong.

'I give you ninepence only. If you refuse I give you broken arm quick,' said Fakhru, throwing two coins on the counter. 'That the thanks I get for being first customer.'

Fakhru spat a long stream of betel juice through the notch in his front teeth. The juice landed on the floor like a red bubbly snake, a bad omen suddenly materializing out of thin air. Clutching his tiny box of tea in his hand, he stormed out of the shop with a swish and flap of his large pyjama trousers. His jaw was moving back and forth rapidly, kneading his betel for another go.

With Fakhru gone the shop was in silence. The two Grand Opening ribbons fluttered when Fakhru brushed by, but now hung limp. Sam Fong stared past the empty door. From the woodwork came a slow wail: Soo in pain several rooms away. Fong dropped the two coins into a wooden box, leaned against the counter, took a deep breath, sighed, and four years passed.

2

There were three more children now, and none seemed larger than a frog; the older children – two of them – would have helped their father, but there was nothing for them to do.

In four years all that Sam Fong had managed to do was to perfect a tight grin which he was able to switch on and off. He had never grinned so much in his life. As a carpenter he did not have to grin at all. As a grocer he found that he spent most of the day grinning. He would not have noticed it except that it made his face hurt, and it was only much later (perhaps two years) that he could grin painlessly. On the other hand, his wife, who had very large teeth, found it a great relief to grin. All of this, Fong reflected, was business.

The carpenter in Fong did not die. Fong continued to hammer, saw and plane; when the counter got very dirty or the shelves very greasy it was the carpenter and not the grocer in Sam Fong that took charge. Instead of washing the counter he sanded it down; if there was a lot of grease on the counter it was planed. When a feeble African woman dropped a whole bottle of vinegar on the floor one day Fong rushed into the back room, grabbed his crowbar and hammer, tore up the floorboards and fitted new ones. After these carpentry exercises, done at top speed, Fong felt very well; it was a much better feeling than he got from beating his wife. Hammering helped him fight his moments of depression, though after four years – spent mostly leaning against the counter – Fong felt like throwing up the whole business and walking away. His moments of remorse over quitting the carpentry job were quickly dispelled, if not brightened, by the memory of the African at the Ministry of Works telling him to carry on, that keen chap who tormented the carpenters and who, if given a second chance, would make Fong's life miserable. Fong remembered his resolution and went back to hammering mindlessly on the counter; at other times he would go to see Fakhru and buy what Fakhru called 'Stocks and Stores'.

The largest selling items in the store were the five kinds of skin lightener (three for women, two for men). Sam Fong thought it was odd that there should be only one kind of bread, one kind of matches, one kind of cigarettes, one kind of ketchup and *five* kinds of skin lightener. He made up a joke which he told to everyone who bought a tube of the skin-lightening cream: customer walks in; customer asks for skin lightener; Fong gets skin lightener and hands it to customer saying, 'Now you be Chinese like me.' No one thought it was funny. Once, when he asked an African what he was going to do with the cream, the African said it was good for the cold weather, it prevented lips from getting stiff and (this was the African's exact word) 'unsightly'. With each crate of skin lightener a poster was enclosed: Fong studied these carefully. There were always four characters in the picture – each a different dusky shade. Fong's favourite was the airplane poster. On this one the four people were deployed around the movable stairs of a just-arrived plane. A shiny purplish man oiled a tyre, a man with a dull, carbonized face wiped the rail of the stairs, and both men looked blackly upon their shabby tasks; their coveralls were soiled with blotches of soot and finger-wipings of plane grease. Standing on the runway was a mocha air hostess greeting a prosperous quadroon-yellow African carrying an attaché case. A sizzling parting had been burned across one temple, and a thought bubble at the side of his head contained the following: 'Boy! She sure is some dish! I am sure glad I bought that extra tubel!'

This yellow African with a slightly oriental look about him stuck in Fong's mind and would not leave. And though none of his customers saw the humour in it and went on believing privately that even a small tube of skin lightener could squirt them surely into the middle class (whiteness being the confessed aspiration of many of them), Sam Fong persisted with his joke: 'Now you be Chinese like me.'

When Fong went to buy 'Stocks and Stores' from Fakhru he made up his mind that he would buy only the necessary items; inevitably he came back with much more than he wanted, though much less than he bargained for. On paper what he bought looked like a great deal; when it was delivered in the rattling, grey Peugeot van that bore Fakhru's name, it looked like very little. These sessions with Fakhru wore Fong down and caused Soo Fong many days in bed recovering from the bruises which the enraged and humiliated Sam Fong inflicted on her. The beatings were, as before, accepted by her with great forbearance; 'welcomed' is perhaps the wrong word, though there was more than mere acceptance in her attitude towards the beatings, and often she was pleased in the knowledge that she was fulfilling a useful function. (There is more than a smattering of masochism in any folk culture.) In order for Fong to get what he wanted from Fakhru he had to agree to buy other things.

Fakhru had introduced Fong to the fascination of black market merchandise. 'You know bleck market?' Fakhru had asked. Sam Fong stared. Fakhru translated into Swahili.

'Yes,' said Fong. 'In town.'

'Where in town?' asked Fakhru.

'Where they sell the bananas,' said Sam Fong.

Fakhru smiled and wiped his whole sweating face on his pyjama front, which he lifted with two hands. He spat. 'Not *that* market. Now I tell you about real bleck market,' he said.

He told him. But after two transactions in the Congo (one in Kinshasa, one in Lubumbashi) Fong was lost. He never understood why the border guards should be bribed; he never fully comprehended the smoked fish thrown on top of the merchandise, the exchange control shell game in which the Congolese francs were converted into salt, then into ivory, then into cigarettes and finally, at some equatorial out-station, into shillings and at some future date (this last transaction known only to Fakhru) into rupees. Fong nodded. 'Now I know black market.'

Black market with its elaborate ritual of almost religious propor-
tions, came to be synonymous with high quality and instant
wealth. Sam Fong accumulated mattresses, yards and yards of
Belgian cloth, galvanized pails and dozens of other items which no
one bought, but which Fong thought useful to have around the
store in case a customer should come into the store with more than
a shilling. At the start of the bargain, when Fakhru would mention
an item, Fong would recoil.

'Good recapped tyres just arrived.'

'Don't want tyres,' Fong would say. 'I selling grocery food.'

'Good recapped tyres you don't want,' Fakhru would say. 'Sal
right with me. Everybody wants those tyres, those *bleck market
tyres.*'

'You say *black market tyres?*'

'That is what I did say.'

And Fong would buy a dozen. Eventually he would sell three and
the rest would be used in flower beds for planned but unfinished
gardens; one hung by a rope would become a swing, others would
be cut to pieces to be made into sandals.

With the exception of some tea, sugar, matches, rice, patent
medicine ('Samson Blood-purifying Lozenges' 'Uncle Pompey's
Gripe Water'), hair straightener and skin lightener, the goods that
Fakhru fobbed off on to Sam Fong – and in particular, the black
market goods – rarely sold. If they did, they yielded no profit.
They were usually too big to be displayed, and so the store always
seemed uniquely bare. Soo thought of taking down the grocery-
store sign every time Fong bought a new black market item. When
he bought mattresses Soo imagined a new sign: SAM FONG MAT-
TRESS SHOP; or the tyres: SAM FONG TYRES FOR ALL OCCA-
SIONS, but always he would sell a few and permit the rest to be
transmogrified into sandals, flower pots, etc. The mattresses that
were not sold were torn apart by a cripple who, for two shillings a
mattress, made each spring into a coat hanger. The coat hangers
did not sell either, but when Soo pointed this out to Sam Fong he
replied, 'Yes, I know, Africans don't want them: no coat, no coat
hanger. But they're easy to store, no?'

A system was inevitable, it was the difference between life and death, and after four years Fong had worked it out in detail. He made lists of the things Africans bought and had a final list of high-priority items: cigarettes sold singly, matches, blood-purifying lozenges, fruit salts, sugar, hair straightener, skin lightener, aspirin, kerosene, unrefined Nubian gin, tea and a few other things. The dust-covered canned goods he learned never to restock; they had been on the shelves since the Grand Opening Day. Among these were ten cans of Spam which had been packed in Austin, Minnesota; thirty-five cans of Australian processed cheese from Melbourne; and about a gross of cans with no label except the following scrap, sometimes studied by Fong, stuck to one of the crates: 'The ruddy-bright delicious juice of fine tomatoes – excellent for any meal or as a between-meal refresher and a terrific source of Vitamins C and A . . . [the next part was illegible, then] . . . *Serving Suggestions* . . . Serve chilled as a beverage; hot as a soup or beverage; or use it for making aspic salads, sauces, stews, etc. Drink it morning, noon or night . . . *Quick 'n' Easy Appetizer or Snack Idea* . . . With your favourite crackers add one three-ounce package . . .' The rest was torn. Sam Fong had stopped dusting the cans and had given up trying to fathom the writing on the crate. To open one of these label-less cans was to throw three shillings to the wind, for whatever was in cans Fong did not like. At first he had said to his customers, 'Just arrived from Minn – nice good meat in very strong can' or 'Honest better price for this sent today by my brother in Australia . . .' or (in the case of the gross of unmarked cans) 'What is inside is secret – only three shillings to have secret revealed . . .' No one bought the cans; this ceased to worry Sam Fong and even pleased Soo Fong. No grocery store was complete, she felt, unless there were cans on the shelves. Empty shelves upset her. It is perhaps in the nature of every grocer to develop a weird anthropomorphism for groceries: Soo felt sorry for the tiny stack on the large shelves; to stare at a pyramid of three small boxes of tea, alone in a corner of the store, untouched, caused her genuine pain. She averted her eyes from the pathetic little piles of unsold merchandise in the grocery store.

Life went on. Somehow Fong managed a small profit, but nearly all of it was spent in rent, 'Stocks and Stores' and overhead expenses. Some he put in the bank, but only as a gesture, for he never banked more than a few shillings. The last week of the month – the week before Soo took her abacus down from the shelf and began flinging the beads to and fro as her husband barked his cheek-tightening Chinese at her – was a terrible one: the tea was watered to a sickly urinous colour, meat did not exist, no one used soap and grasshoppers caught under the streetlights at night and fried were the main course at every meal. The children sat in their corner of the back room and grumbled over their grasshoppers. Sam Fong would silence the complaints with: 'Eat these nice fat insects. You are lucky to have them. In China they are a delicacy.'

Often Fong regretted having made his resolution about never being a carpenter, but the resolution was irrevocable. The other two – never trust a white man, never trust a black man – also caused him considerable anxiety. His customers, when they appeared at their infrequent intervals, were either white or black. If a white man bought something (the whites never bought much more than cigarettes, but they always bought the whole package of twenty and never asked for only two or three), Fong felt he was being cheated or spied upon. Africans made him nervous as well and many were the times when an African in a clean shirt and tie, perhaps even wearing a suit, walked in and awakened fear in Fong, the helpless fright that envisioned the African announcing that he was the new owner of the grocery store and that Fong should pick up the bundle of papyrus and begin sweeping the floor. This, in four years, had not happened; but the anxiety, together with the knowledge that the Africans were in power and he himself was 'free' (the image of a man splashing in a wide muddy river occurred to him), prompted another saying which he repeated incessantly to his wife: 'A man who is free to feed himself might choose poison', and sometimes worded as 'When people are free anything is possible, even tyranny'. The African who, in six brief months, became foreman of the workshop also became the symbol of what Fong imagined would be inevitable frustration and eventual failure.

He trusted no one except a fellow Chinaman who ran a camera shop and spoke of going to Canada. There were, he had heard, three other Chinese in the country, but he had never seen them. They lived in the bush. His dealings with whites inspired less anxiety than his dealings with Africans, but much more futility, for he was certain that the whites were responsible for his ended career in carpentry. His resolutions did not cover brown men; he continued to do business with Fakhru, and, with more rage than anxiety, more insolence than fear, get cheated. He knew he was being cheated by Fakhru and he explained this in another proverb: 'Behind every dark man there is a white man making money.' This became to his wife and him, crouched in the light of an oil lamp over their fried grasshoppers and urinous tea at midnight on the last week of the month, one of his wise sayings.

Fong was more worried about being cheated than he was about making money. Cheating made him squirm; it made him nervous and murderous. Making money was not one of his dreams. He did not sit in his store and dream about Nubians carrying trays of fried pork and jugs of rice wine, tall black men in silk wearing gold daggers and waiting on him, cooling him with feathery fans. He did not imagine himself sitting in the back seat of a Mercedes shouting for his driver to turn left, or, with the car radio blasting, drawing up to the Nile Villa Hotel while dozens of curious and greedy onlookers asked, 'Who is that wealthy Chinaman?' and stared. These were Soo's dreams, two of them at any rate, and she stopped speaking of them to Fong when quite in earnest he beat her unmercifully for repeating them to him. He had explained to Soo that this was another world, her world of fantasy, and it was not populated with people like Sam or Soo Fong. The idea of wealth was not just unattainable, it was unthinkable; when the thought was uttered he ridiculed it. He was meant to serve, to work; and lately his preoccupation with being swindled prevented him from having time even to ridicule the thought of wealth.

Sometimes he thought of happiness. This idea of happiness was set among wood shavings in a noisy workshop. Table legs were being turned on a lathe, drills scraped against wood and bored into the centre of thick boards, gouges turned up long curls on doors that would be graceful, and muscular men pounded pegs into joints while Sam Fong, like the leader in a Chinese musical revue, directed the busy men with a little lemon branch, his nostrils full of sawdust. No one was paid, no one cheated and lovely smooth furniture bounded out of the workshop on short hard legs, like indestructible little men, sturdy and mindless. This could hardly be called the dream of a voluptuary, but this was Sam Fong's dream, based on his happiest days in Africa when there was no money and when he had plenty to eat. He had renounced it, but because he had renounced it as a way of life it became sacred to him; he would see it after death. The workshop in this other sphere was bathed in a rosy glow from the lumber room; each naked man acted on his command and was dwarfish and serene in his industry. Money had nothing to do with it, though cheating certainly did; he knew for the time being he had been cheated out of it all.

He narrowed his eyes at the empty shelves and sold an African a two-ounce tube of skin lightener and three cigarettes. Though the tube cost three shillings sixpence and the cigarettes tenpence, he took the African's twenty-shilling note, and, without blinking or moving his head, or even without looking at the man, gave him the exact change. On this day, more than four years after his shop was opened, Sam Fong became a *dukawallah*.

3

Sam Fong heard something inside his head rattling; it was like the loose bolt in an old ripsaw handle that only an unskilled carpenter could tolerate, someone who knew nothing about tools. He pressed the side of his head, as if that might tighten up the bolt. Nothing happened. The noise, clank-clank, continued. Fong looked towards the front of the store and saw that the real cause of the noise was not a loose bolt but rather a white man. The white man was picking up and dropping little cans on one of the shelves. The white man was also talking out of the side of his mouth to a man next to him who was not white, but not black either; and when Fong stared at him he realized that the man was not brown, and not yellow. Next to the white man the other man looked simply non-white, and this man listened intently to the white man, who was still dropping the little cans on the shelf and talking in a language Fong had never heard before. The noise, the men, the foreign language caused Sam Fong's groin to ache and become very cold. For a moment Fong felt like killing both of the men, or, at the very least, beating his wife to a pulp.

Fong turned to Soo and shouted at her in Swahili.

Soo stared at him wonderingly, as if he had just struck her. She did not move; her intent gaze made her look as if she were leaning towards him softly. She was still a pretty woman. Even after eight children, many beatings, large helpings of grasshoppers and hard work, she retained a definite facial beauty, and her hands were like small new plants. She had married at twelve and was now not much over thirty. The marriage had been arranged by mail. Bundles of twenty-shilling notes wrapped in a greasy letter written by the Chinaman in the camera store had been sent to Hong Kong, and from there to Soo's father. At first Fong thought he might have to go all the way back to Hong Kong or Shanghai to get her. But with the help of an Armenian rug merchant who was fleeing for his life and his millions, Soo's father put her on a ship, and she was on her way to Mombasa with an envelope of rose petals, incense for the bridal bed and her maidenhead intact, before her twelfth birthday. Sam Fong took the train to Mombasa, where he slept among cotton bales, dodged Arabs at night and sweltered during the day among foul-smelling Bajuni sailors; and one day the ship arrived. When he saw her, Fong was surprised by the smallness of the girl – no one had ever mentioned that she was twelve years old. Fong took her up-country on the train, through the bush and past the grass-grown volcanoes to his little hut on the equator, and once back, treated her like his daughter for one year. He bought her sweet cakes and bracelets, took her for walks, bought her cloth, sang her songs of boatmen and people playing in paddies among new blossoms; he held her gently and let her snore innocently against his chest, and at the end of the year, and the end of his vow to the quaint Chinese custom of waiting, and, needless to say, at the end of his wits he dragged Soo into his bedroom one noon, threw her on the bed and fell on top of her. It was like a huge farm implement ploughing up one pale flower, not quite crushing it. Soo said nothing. Her face expressed only one emotion well: wonderment. And so when Sam Fong screamed at her in Swahili she looked at him with every inch of her lovely lemon face showing wonderment.

'I am very sorry, dear husband and master,' said Soo, 'but I have not enough knowledge of this tongue to understand what you are saying.' She spoke in Chinese.

Sam Fong nodded and captured a whiff of air in his mouth. He exhaled the following in Chinese: 'You see those white men there playing with those cans? Serve them or I'll choke you like a hen!'

Soo looked at the men and then at her husband, and then back at the men. One was still talking and fingering cans; the other listened. Sam Fong felt uneasy; he expected them to come over and ask him who was the keenest chap in the store. For this question, and for a long time, Sam Fong had the carefully rehearsed answer: 'Me.' But saying it was something else. It nerved him up.

On the other hand, the men – one white, one not white – looked odd to Fong: while one was as white as the Englishman with the bad news, he was dressed quite differently. Both of the men in the store were dressed the same, with straw hats and flowered shirts, sunglasses and large watches; they did not wear trousers but rather something Sam Fong recalled as looking like foreshortened Chinese pyjamas, striped in bright colours. They wore high socks and had the largest pairs of shoes and, by implication, feet, Fong had ever seen. Fong had seen men dressed just like this on the golf course near the bypass road, striding along followed by a pack of little African boys towing gleaming wheeled carts; the word 'golf' was not in Fong's vocabulary, the activity was unknown to him (he imagined the men walking in front of the wheeled carts to be hunters). The two men in the store bore a definite resemblance to those others, in the same clothes, on the grassy meadow. What was especially strange about the men near the shelf was their short hair; their heads seemed shaven (several times they had doffed their hats to wipe their foreheads) and they were both round-shouldered. They were the healthiest men Fong had ever laid eyes on. He had a feeling of what was coming. The white one would come up to him, smile and introduce the non-white one. Then the non-white one would say, 'This is my store now' and the white one would wink. Next day the non-white one would come in drunk and fat, bully Fong, tell him this was not his country (it happened – these words – three or four times a week as it was) and that Fong should start sweeping the floor. He shouted again at his wife. He could shout without opening his mouth, like a ventriloquist.

'Find out what they want and send them on their way! They are mixing up all my nice cans with their damned drop-drop!'

Soo approached the men. The men reduced their talk to a whisper and leaned against each other. The non-white one started looking around and smiling, but kept his ear close to the white one's mouth.

Even if Sam Fong and Soo had understood English well, which

they didn't, it is doubtful that either of them would have been able to grasp the full meaning of the heavily breathed monologue that was taking place near the Spam. It went something like this:

'You take your average run-of-the-mill Chink and what do you do with him? You stick him in the middle of your biggest continent and you say, "Smile, be nice, and don't forget there are seven hunert million jest like you that'd give their eye-teeth to be in your place." Then you leave him there for fifteen, sixteen, give or take a few years, and what happens? I'll tell you what happens. Sure, he doesn't know beans about upward mobility, but he scores. How does he score? I'll tell you how he scores. Because he gets a lot of plain outright cooperation from your average national, African, say. Why? You got *me*. That's one for the books. If I knew the answer to that I wouldn't be in this racket . . .'

The man who was speaking looked over at Soo and stopped talking; then he smiled and turned to Sam Fong, who smiled back and, almost against his will, bowed slightly in the direction of the two healthy men. Sam Fong's right hand was still, as it would be for the next ten minutes, unknown to himself and unseen – because of the beautifully large counter, and probably because he had been a long time in Africa – wisely on his fear-frozen groin.

Fifteen minutes after Soo had approached the men and the men had begun talking in a hoarse whisper, one broke away from the shelf of Spam, walked directly – almost quickly – up to Sam Fong, whipped off his straw hat, twisted his whole face sideways, raised his hand up out of his pocket and poked it, open and obvious, over the counter into Fong's gut and said, nodding his shaven head once, '*Hi!*'

4

Fakhru was having a bad day. He had failed miserably in an attempt to persuade a Goan shopkeeper to buy a shipment of canned milk. The milk had been canned in Switzerland under the auspices of the Milk for Moroccan Mothers Crusade; machinery, tins, paper for labels and the milk itself had been donated by several large firms in France, Italy, Austria and Germany. A famous French artist had designed a label free of charge and lent his name to the crusade. Diverted from Rabat by some Congolese, the shipment of milk was stored in a Kinshasa warehouse for a year; Fakhru did not hear about the milk until it had reached Katanga, but by then Fakhru was on bowing terms with the UNICEF representative in East Africa, who graciously provided trucks to ship the milk overland. Fakhru told him that the milk was intended for the Fakhru Famine Fund. He would distribute it. The trucks arrived in front of Fakhru's door late one night; Fakhru gave each driver 100 shillings and some worthless Belgian Congo francs for the 'mission of mercy', the milk was unloaded, new labels were gummed on by his wife and children bearing the name Fakhru Enterprises Ltd, and the crates were put up for sale. But there were no buyers.

The Goan shopkeeper said the price was too high. Fakhru said it was real milk from England. The Goan said that he did not care if it was horse piss from Lisbon; the price was too high. Fakhru said the cans were strong and would last for ever and ever. The Goan said, 'Good, then you can sell them in ten years' time, isn't it?'

Fakhru started to leave the store. He paused and turned to the Goan and said in Hindi, 'Any day now that big milk train from Nairobi might be derailed off its tracks. In this happenstance, faithful friend Lobo, these white ladies would pay anything for

29

milk. You know they have no breasts – you see them, don't you? They would pay you shillings thirty a can and you would become very rich. For this you would thank your friend Fakhru.'

Lobo stood firm. He did not want the milk. Besides, the milk train had only been derailed once and that was in 1943 by some idle Boers in the Highlands who hated the British and thought Hitler was nice. They had since packed their wagons and moved to South Africa.

Fakhru got similar answers from six other shopkeepers including – and this was heartbreaking – an Ismaili who claimed that the time for milk-buying was not ripe; it was an inauspicious time for a big deal. At noon Fakhru was so angry that he went to the nearest slum and tried to get some out-of-work Africans to derail the train. He saw this as a way of getting even with everyone, especially if the Africans were arrested for it.

'No one gets arrested,' Fakhru explained to a languid African lighting a thick tube of Indian hemp. 'Just a little spill milk, nothing to cry about. What do you say?'

'How we go do dis?' queried another African, accepting a pinch of hemp from Fakhru.

Fakhru shrugged. 'Easy. Few rocks on the rails, couple log and *ptooie* the train go down and all the milk she get spill, isn't it?'

The Africans (there were five of them) were not interested. It sounded big and dangerous. Someone might find out. One was not feeling well; he said he had a fever. Another said he had a sore finger. One of the hemp-smokers came straight out and said he thought Fakhru's price was too low.

'That's my price,' said Fakhru.

'She too small,' said the hemp-smoker.

'Thank you *please*,' said Fakhru sarcastically, baring his betel-stained fangs. 'You want to get rich quick-quick and you don't want to do anything. I ask you to kick Patel. It very difficult to kick Patel because him fat. You kick Patel. I give you shillings fifty. I say punch up Ali the Toothmaker when he call my mother bad names. Ali have big knife from Mombasa. You punch him up. I give you shillings fifty. Now,' Fakhru sighed, 'I ask you to derail little small train from Nairobi. It too easy – my wife Shoogra would do it if she didn't have so many kids to take care of. Now I ask you this easy thing and you sit there smoking my *bhangi* and tell me to bugger off. You wonder why this country don't develop like UK, eh? I tell you why – because you're all bloody lazy!'

With that he stormed away. He moved fiercely among the decrepit houses in his white pyjamas like an angry prophet. He had told the truth; he was honest and he had bathed with sweet soap and smelled clean. The smell of the decaying slum, the postures of the squatting people cooking over charcoal in doorways angered him. Nearly everyone had let him down. The only ones who had not let him down were the UNICEF people, but even at that he had had to bribe their drivers.

Still in anger Fakhru went to an eating house, and while his brain squirmed in his head trying to conceive a profit amid the clutter of a whole shipment of unsold tinned milk, took his wrath out on the enamel plates of lumpy food. He snatched and spooned lentils, boiled cabbage, chillies and sticky globs of rice into one large bowl and covered this with a dumping of yogurt; this he squeezed quickly and stirred with the tips of his fingers. And then he ate it. He kept his mouth open during the whole meal; he bent over the bowl and threw the squeezed mixture down his throat with a squelching, scooping motion of his fingers. He refused to look up. It was almost as if he were fanning the food into his mouth, so quickly did his fingers move through the mixture; and he did not stop to lick his fingers until he had eaten the last squashed and sodden grain of rice. When he was finished he threw his head back and belched one prolonged roar which began somewhere in the bulge of his pyjamas and ended high above his head at the brownish photograph of Gandhi supping with the king. He scraped his chair back, rose noisily, threw four shillings at a Dravidian hunched against the wall and then bought some *pan* – betel nuts and pungent seeds wrapped in a betel leaf – threw that into his mouth and chomped down once. Almost immediately he had a gob of betel juice ready for the nearest wall, and as the glugging in his stomach started, a plan began to take shape in his head.

The yellow one, thought Fakhru, and then laughed. Sam Fong amused him. Fakhru's rage disappeared as his belly rumbled and he staggered towards the grocery store. Fong was not capable of cheating anyone but himself. He worked hard, stayed open at night, keeping the store candle-lit when he thought that the number of customers might not justify the burned inch of wick in the hurricane lamp; he did not drink, smoke or go screaming around the brothels with his pants down. What fascinated Fakhru was that in spite of the fact that Fong was compelled to buy everything from him, Fong still managed to swell his bank balance, which he never touched – not even at the end of the month when he handed Soo the bags bulging with large green grasshoppers. ('I thought only Africans ate those bugs,' Fakhru had said to him.) Fakhru knew the banking habits of everyone he did business with: he had a relative in every bank in town whom he got information out of as easily as he got gobs of red juice out of a dry betel nut. Fakhru knew Fong to be an unshrewd, incautious businessman, gullible and not very bright, but one that still made a profit by a means which Fakhru had never before considered and, when he knew the means, deemed inhuman. By starving himself, keeping his children naked and all feet in the family unshod; by not using things like soap, combs, hair oil, mirrors and so forth; by not smoking, by gluing crumbs together with fat to make cakes, by throwing away nothing (least of all empty tins which became cups, orange crates which became chairs and insects which became rare food by Fong's performing no more complicated an operation than uttering the words: 'This is a cup', 'This is a chair', 'This is a delicacy'), Sam Fong managed a profit. He swindled only himself and his unsuspecting family. It also allowed him to be foolish and incautious about what he bought. Fakhru knew Sam Fong would buy every single can of milk.

5

'Name's Newt, Bert G. Newt, Jr,' said the man to Fong, replacing his straw hat. 'This here's Mel Francey.'

'Hah!' said the man called Mel Francey in greeting, showing Fong his fine set of teeth. 'Ah'm an Afro-Amirican and I wanna tell you, friend, the Amiricans's really cleanin up their own back-yard. Why, back in the States the white min pick up the trash. Ain't that right, Bert?'

'Sure is Mel, sure as yer standing there. Jest wanted to tell the gemmun what's we're doing in the field of civil rights . . .'

'Civil rights!' said Mel Francey, slapping his thigh. 'Why we got Jiminy on the moon and freedom at home. We got every damn thing, scuse me ma'am, we desire, really and truly.'

'Creepers, Mel,' said Bert Newt. 'Ain't nothing really . . .'

'Creepers, nothin!' said Mel Francey. 'My ole Granny's seveny-eight next week and she got her own special wheelchair with an engine, nice little house, people runnin about gitten her every damn thing. Call that nothing?'

'Well . . .' Bert Newt wagged his head.

'Kids go to the best schools, ride the best buses, get free dental care, the whole shebang. Call that nothin?' Mel Franccy shook his jowls and said, 'Heh! You show me another country where Afro-Amiricans are better off than they are Stateside . . .'

'Another country?'

'Ain't none,' said Mel Francey emphatically. 'Ain't no other country that'd happen in. You go ahead, smart guy, and tell me one – just one is all.' He took Bert Newt roughly by the front of his flowered shirt and shook him. He said, 'Hell man, you go on tell me! *Tell me!*' Mel Francey was now worked up; his anger was

33

genuine; beads of perspiration clung to the hairs on his arms. He glowered at Bert Newt.

'Well,' said Bert Newt, 'They say lotsa countries Afro-Amiricans got better rights . . .'

'Rights, hell!' shouted Mel Francey, now dropping Newt and stamping on the floor. 'I got more damn rights than I can shake a stick at!'

'What ain't you got, man?' asked Bert Newt.

'I ain't got nothin!' This was shouted.

Both Bert Newt and Mel Francey burst into laughter, slapped each other on the back, shook hands and continued with their very loud *haw-haw-haw*. They seemed oblivious of Sam Fong and Soo.

Sam Fong dropped the meat cleaver he had picked up when the man said 'Hi', and now he stood gripping the counter watching the two men (Were they madmen? If so, why were they dressed so well?) wiping their eyes, still laughing.

Little wonder that Sam Fong was frightened: his encounters with white men had been anything but cordial. Whites were sinister bastards and they talked too much. Fong understood neither their language nor their disgusting habits. As for their desires, their yearnings – who could understand? Beating Africans, locking them in iceboxes one year; hugging them and popping their eyes out at them the next. One year caning them, the next year patting them on the back and saying, 'You deserve it, son.' One year picking their pockets, the next year putting it all back, and more. Fong had actually seen a red-faced white man stuff about thirty shillings in the pocket of a black policeman, for which the white man was returned a snappy salute. The emperor would not have stood for it. These were things that Fong had witnessed over a period of thirty-five years in Africa. There were times when these whites had screwed up their courage, come straight up to Sam Fong and asked where opium could be obtained. At first Fong had not understood, but once the loud snuffling was translated into Chinese by the man in the camera store who had overheard the request and knew English, Fong was astonished by the depravity it signalled. In China they had taught him the catechism, baptized him, told him to be a good Catholic and fear God. They had even started teaching him English, nearly all of which – with the exception of the few verbs in the present continuous tense – he forgot; on the other hand, the request for opium was made so frequently that it became one of the few English sentences that Fong knew. But what kind of person would want opium? Only a very rotten idle son of a whore; and this, Fong decided long ago, was what every white man was. It was not until the African in the workshop was sent to England that Fong made his firm resolution; the resolution was formulated not so much from this single instance of white cruelty, the demotion, the loss of his job, as from the resulting wisdom of this long accumulation of disgraceful episodes with whites.

It is one thing to make a resolution; it is quite another to throw money away. Fong was not irrational about making a profit – he did not connive; he did not make a practice of rubbing his hands and bowing; he did not stand on the sidewalk and drag people into his store. But he knew that if he did not make a small profit he would, quite simply, die like a dog. He decided that when the two men stopped their talking and he ventured into Swahili he might come out a few shillings the better for his patience. What he did not understand was, why all the talk? Why this noisy kowtow and dumbshow? What were they shouting about and in what language? Fong was consoled by the fact that they were arguing with each other, perhaps arguing over the ownership of the store. It was certainly true that the non-white one bore more than a passing resemblance to the keen chap in the workshop who had come back drunk and disorderly and well-dressed from England to snatch his job away. The argument had alternated between war and song; Fong could not tell if they loved or hated each other, though he finally decided on the latter. There was no denying that these men were enemies, but it was also true that they did not seem to have weapons, and, as the proverb has it, yuan from a coolie are as welcome as yuan from a prince. That was why Sam Fong dropped the meat cleaver.

Soo had not stirred. From time to time she had winced. Once she saw the men had no intention of speaking to her she crept back behind the counter, stayed there silent and yellow and continued to peer at the two loud men.

She saw the two men turn away from each other and start talking to her husband. She was afraid, although she was not sure who would get the worst of it.

'We're not here to sell you America,' said Bert Newt.

'No sir!' said Mel Francey.

'You buying nice bread?' Fong asked. This was almost the limit of his English. He added in Swahili, 'Good, good bread, baking yesterday.'

His words went unheard.

'Fact is,' said Bert Newt, 'we're not here to sell you a thing!'

'Not a damn thing,' said Mel Francey.

'You buy good tea, better price anywhere in Africa,' said Fong, exhausting his English.

'All we want to do is get acquainted, get on a hand-shaking, how-are-you, face-to-face relationship, a first-name basis, you know what I mean? I want you to call me Bert. This here's Mel . . .'

The two hands were again extended. Fong did not see them. The hands were withdrawn.

'Point is, we want to leave all our differences aside. Oh, I know what you're saying to yourself. You're saying: Who those two Yankee big-mouths think they are, banging into my store and shooting their mouths off! Their country is damn rich and big! You're thinking we're just two gung-ho guys . . .'

Recognition flickered across Fong's face for a moment at the utterance. He said nothing.

'. . . I know you're thinking of the Iron Curtain and the Cold War. Well, let me tell you, just between you and me: that's for the big fellers in Washington and Peking. You and me, we're the little fellers . . .'

'Yeah!' boomed Mel Francey. 'That's raht!'

'. . . We got no grief with you just cause your eyes are different and your skin's yaller . . .'

'Colour of a man's skin don't mean a damn thing!'

'. . . We come here into your humble little store,' said Bert Newt, apparently winding up, 'to extend the hand of friendship across the ocean and across the sea. We want *you* to come to *our* little houses and homes to have a modest but nourishing meal someday. And let me repeat, we don't come as Americans, we do not come to sell America . . . Jeepers creepers, try to *forget* that we're Americans! Just call me Bert and I'll be happy as a clam . . . I'll tell my wife . . .'

Sam Fong saw that the talk was about to end; the voices were getting softer, though the words no more intelligible. He leaned towards the men and very quickly, in Swahili, English and Chinese, repeated a list of the items that could be had: 'Bread, butter, egg, hair straightener, buns, juice, bread, potato, rice, razor blade, sweet, rice, recapped tyre, soap, egg, bread, smoking, nice tea . . .'

Bert Newt and Mel Francey smiled.

'See you around,' said Bert Newt.

'*Sayonara*,' said Mel Francey, clapping his hands together in front of his face and bowing, as he had once seen Marlon Brando do.

They began backing out of the store.

Sam Fong looked dejectedly at them; they were smiling at him and still backing out. Fong did not hear Bert Newt say to Mel in a whisper, 'Now you see what the State Department is up against. These guys won't budge an inch. You go on and tell me our work isn't cut out for us . . .' And Mel answered, 'I know just what you mean, brother . . .' They were still backing up and smiling. Mel Francey still had his hands together in front of his face.

Outside the window Fakhru swung down the sidewalk. Sam Fong experienced an odd sensation on seeing someone he had always thought to be his enemy. He waited for hatred but felt only joy when he saw Fakhru. *He can save me, he will know what to do.* It was the feeling of relief that the farmer in his filthy hut, beset by mysterious strangers, has for the fat landlord rolling up in a great golden carriage.

Fakhru turned to splash a gob of betel juice into the gutter, but he was still walking briskly, and when he turned to wipe his mouth on the back of his sleeve, he crashed into Bert Newt and Mel Francey.

'Sorry, *bwana*.' Fakhru was the first to speak. He spoke to Bert Newt.

'Name's Newt. Bert G. Newt, Jr. This here's Mel Francey . . .'

'*Hah!*' said Mel. 'I'm an Afro-Amirican from Alabama where they say we got a lot of trouble, only we don't, that's all. Your average newspaper's a damn liar!'

Fakhru extended his hand: 'Hassanali Fakhru of Fakhru Enterprises Limited.'

'Chalk one up,' Bert said under his breath. They shook hands.

'Welcome to this humble grocery,' said Fakhru. 'I hope from the bottom of my heart that you have been treated as a brother.'

'This your store?' asked Bert.

'In a manner of speaking, yes, please. But I am compelled to add that it is currently leased to my old friend and colleague, Sam Fong, the yellow one there at the back.'

'Frenayers?' asked Mel Francey.

'Beg pardon?'

'He said, *is this man a friend of yours?*' Bert was eager.

'Most definitely he is, although as you can see he is quite obviously a *kaffir*. But this is no matter – we are here to build a multiracial society with *harambee* and Africans and goodness knows what . . .'

'I'll shake on that,' said Mel Francey, pumping Fakhru's hand.

Sam Fong watched closely. Fakhru knew how to handle these people; there was no question of that, Fong felt safe with Fakhru in the store. He saw the three men move towards him.

'What do they want?' asked Fong in Swahili when the three stood before him.

'You understand this language of Swahili, of course,' Fakhru said laughing.

'Hell no!' said Mel.

'I know *jambo*,' said Bert.

'Well, that's a good beginning,' said Fakhru, and then in Swahili he said to Fong, 'Me know what they want? How am *I* to know what they want? This is your store, not mine!'

'I listened with both ears but understood nothing of what they said.'

'Did they buy anything?'

'No.'

'Did they sell you anything?'

'No.'

'Did they give you anything?'

'No. Ask them where they're from.'

Fakhru asked.

The Americans brightened and both started talking at once, interrupting each other and gesturing.

'They say they're from America.'

'Why don't they speak English?'

'They do, but it's different English. Anyway, friend Fong, what makes you a *fundi* on English?' Fakhru giggled, then turned to his new friends. 'Is there anything at all you would like to communicate with my old friend Sam Fong?'

'Tell him we want to be frins, that we come in peace and don't mean no harm,' said Mel.

'Beg pardon?'

'He said, tell the man we want to be his friend . . . *We just want to talk to him!*' Bert spoke loudly, thinking that if he spoke loudly he would be better understood.

Fakhru turned back to Sam Fong. 'They say they would like to talk to you at greater length with a view towards selling you, at extremely low prices, goods from American bleck market.'

Sam Fong smiled. It was the first emotion he had shown since the Americans entered the store. Bert Newt and Mel Francey saw him smile. Both reached over the counter, dragged his hand out from behind and shook it vigorously.

'He says he's ready to talk any time. He wants to be your friend.'

6

The Americans went away at peace with themselves and making plans.

'You're very lucky,' Fakhru said to Sam Fong, still in Swahili. 'These people want to sell you good merchandise, *American* merchandise from American bleck market. That is a very bleck market indeed. Americans have even been known to lend money at low interest if they like someone . . .'

'I do not need money,' said Fong. 'But a little black market merchandise is always welcome, no?'

'Interesting that you should bring up that subject. It happens that I have just received a shipment of *number one* canned milk all the way from the *world famous* UNICEF dairies in England, United Kingdom . . .'

It took just ten minutes to convince Sam Fong that he should buy all the cans. They were black market cans, which was assurance of their high quality; and who could tell, Fakhru's argument ran, the milk train from Nairobi might be derailed any day, that is, knocked off its rails by unfortunate happenstance. The white women who had no breasts, as any fool could see, and therefore were incapable of suckling their children, would pay anything for this canned milk. When it came to children, Fakhru said, white people acted very strangely indeed.

Once again Sam Fong felt a kinship with Fakhru. When they were doing business and Fong knew he was being swindled, he had nothing but bald hatred for the Ismaili. Yet as soon as white men were mentioned, as soon as they entered a business transaction, Fong felt that it was he and Fakhru against them all: whites were the real enemy. And, since independence, by an odd quick process which Fakhru said in English was known as getting 'jumped-up', the Africans had taken their place as second enemy, and Fong felt the same uneasy awe for their sudden power ('I can have you deported tomorrow, you bloody bugger') and boundless contempt for what he felt to be their true instinctive existence: a daily filthy slumber in the shade of the nearest tree, then a rapid roll in the mud with their reeking women, their lives dominated by bananas which could be had by stretching out their long arms. It was a lifetime of spear-throwing and sleeping and sweaty small moments humping their women like hares until a white man came by, gave them new clothes to cover up the dirt, gave them police protection and power and jobs they did not deserve. The white man's most evil deed was clothing the African. The clothed African was dangerous: he had pockets, and these pockets the white man stuffed with twenty-shilling notes. No clothes, no corruption, Fong had reasoned: how do you go about bribing a naked man? But now the African and the white were good friends, they loved each other, and the white man made a lot of money in this. The African was happy in his dirt, eating dung and throwing his spears – why should he complain? He had lost nothing. Sam Fong and Fakhru were left, the only visible immigrants, surrounded by enemies, and Fong felt very close to Fakhru.

So close, in fact, did Fong feel that when he gave Fakhru the cheque for the milk he knew he was swindling him. The milk cost 1000 shillings; the cheque was made out to Fakhru Enterprises Ltd for 1000 shillings; Fong knew perfectly well that he had 632 shillings ninepence only in the bank and that the cheque would bounce. But by the end of the mouth, when the long rains started, the train from Nairobi would be derailed and, by then, Sam Fong would have much more than the difference in his account. In a way, it was the first time that Sam Fong had given a serious thought – by planning ahead – to making a profit. He was sure it would pay off. In the meantime he could use 632 shillings ninepence in his account as an emergency fund, as he always considered it.

There had been only one emergency in his life: buying the merchandise, leasing the store and becoming a *dukawallah*. Since those first anxious days there had been no threat to his calm. The bank balance assured him of continued calm. Shortly after he arrived in East Africa he saw Africans as enemies and realized that he had seven million of them. As calm as he felt, he was still realistic in believing that it could not last and that he would most likely be deported. And Fakhru was in the same boat: calm because he was prepared for the inevitable disaster.

Feeling almost brotherly towards Fakhru, Fong handed over the cheque that he knew would bounce. He did it with the grim smile of the entrepreneur. It was the only way he could get the milk.

'You will not regret this,' said Fakhru in Swahili. And in Hindi: 'Blessings on your house; may it be kept safe from Africans . . .'

'When will the goods be delivered?' asked Fong.

'Straight away,' said Fakhru. 'Which is to say, now-now.'

He left.

Sam Fong looked across the counter to Soo and said, 'I am happy.'

7

Fakhru was not surprised when the bank teller informed him that the cheque could not be cashed as there were insufficient funds in the account. He did feel let down, for he had decided – absurd thought – that the Chinaman was honest, that he swindled only himself. Fakhru also thought of himself as a good judge of character and prided himself on knowing 'the native mind'.

It was not the first time someone had pulled this shoddy *dukawallah* ruse. How many others had there been? Hundreds, thousands, and not one of them with sufficient imagination to try a really extravagant swindle. This petty cheating depressed Fakhru; he knew full well he would prevail over the felony, but this was no test of business prowess. What Fakhru prayed for was a gigantic swindle for which he could summon all his powers, and which, by a counter-swindle, would make him the wealthiest man in East Africa (donations to His Highness's favourite charity; painless bribing; a coffee estate; an American car). Fong's was an ordinary slimy trick, ludicrously small, and, worse, Fong wrote so big that it was impossible to alter the cheque.

'You can't give him overdraft?'

'No,' said the teller.

'He's not bleck, you know. No worry about a little overdraft.'

'Sorry,' said the teller.

'He's almost white – yellow to be exact. How about an overdraft? Little bit, not so much.'

The teller was silent.

'Yes, but certainly there must be some mistake. Bye-bye,' said Fakhru bowing, withdrawing and pulling his empty leather

43

briefcase off the counter. He hurried back to his cluttered office to think.

Rubbing the picture of H.H. the Aga Khan for luck, he dialled his cousin Goolshan at the bank.

'Goolshan, my flesh and blood, son of my mother's noble brother now dead, alas, and unable to see what a success his son has been – didn't I see you on the evening of the great and auspicious Gurpurb Celebrations at a tiny but very comfortable bar outside town with, if you will pardon an unsolicited compliment, an exceedingly charming African girl in a rather tight dress? Or did my eyes deceive me? Allow me to praise your discretion, not to mention your . . . what's that?'

The voice at the other end of the line barked something hoarsely in Hindi.

Fakhru laughed, winked at His Highness and said, 'The yellow one whose father's name is Fong . . .'

After a few moments Fakhru said, 'Yes', listened, then, with elaborate thanks and an apology for having mistaken some profligate for his upright cousin Goolshan, rang off. He looked at Fong's frayed cheque, spat, did a little figuring on the back of an envelope he rescued from the wastebasket, took his own cheque-book, called his houseboy (an elderly man in shorts) and set off for the post office.

Fakhru did not like to wait in line. As soon as he arrived in the post office he directed his houseboy to the correct line, pressed threepence into the old man's hand and went over to lean against the wall. Mehboob was there; so were the three Patels, Visrani, Mehta the barber, Mistry the carpenter; and, off to the side, Ali, the half-caste butcher, whose shop was not far from Sam Fong's. They traded agonies. Visrani adjusted his dhoti and said that business was very slack; the rest concurred: business was in a terrible slump. 'We'll be eating shit very soon,' offered Mistry. From this they went on to the rupee, which they discussed for a full ten minutes. Tenderness entered their voices; it was as if they were talking about an old friend. One of the Patels said it might be devalued. 'The poor rupee; it's the fault of those people in India –

they don't know what life is about,' Mehta said. 'No one here knows either,' another Patel said. 'The world is out of tune,' said Visrani, chewing. Mistry said that there was a strike in the workshop across the street, 'and the winds are starting to blow in the direction of my own workshop.'

Fakhru agreed with everyone, excused himself and went to look for a litter basket. He found one attached to the wall near a long table; it was half-filled with crumpled, scratched-out cable forms. He took aim and spat. Then he unfolded his cheque book from his pyjamas and wrote a cheque for 368 shillings and made it out to Sam Fong. He looked for his houseboy; the houseboy was still far from the window.

When he returned to the group he asked them what they were doing. They said they were either buying stamps or registering letters or posting parcels; that is, their African assistants were doing these things. In the line closest to the wall were the nine khaki-clad, barefoot Africans holding envelopes and papers and talking. They were enjoying themselves immensely; the lines were all very long, and it was cool in the post office. The majority of those waiting before the windows were Africans wearing khaki office uniforms; there were also a few pot-bellied American women with cork helmets, suede boots and clean bush jackets, on which were sewn rows of cloth loops for shotgun shells but no shotgun shells. Some Germans with over-large knapsacks and beards stood in a group and shouted loudly at each other; they clutched postcards. A small lady pushed a stack of Christmas cards under one clerk's wire mesh; she said she was sending them by surface mail to the Hebrides. From time to time the Asians lining the walls glanced at their deputies in the stamp queues.

'The little blecks,' said Fakhru, using the Hindi diminutive, 'they love to stand in line.'

'It's their line, it's their country,' said Mehta with gloom in his voice.

'If we really wanted to,' said S. R. Patel, 'we could take over this whole filthy place.'

'Who wants it?' said Mehta lugubriously.

'I'll tell you a sad story,' said J. H. Patel. 'You know I'm running a wholesale place – just like yours, brother [he nodded towards Fakhru]. I sell the usual: razor blades, Madrassi towels, nice fabrics, good-quality American-type soap, a little bit of coffee and the rest. So this African woman [he said this in English, pronouncing it *Effrriken vhooman*] is buying lots of goods from me. I put this down in my book. Then she buys rice in large bags and some bread, *daily* you understand. I put this in my accounts and I deliver it all in my pick-up. The last trip I make – this has been going on for about three weeks – I give her the bill. She says she has no money, but her brother, maybe I should see him. She gives me his name, address in the Parliament Office Building, in the Ministry of External Affairs. Why is this brother of hers in the Ministry of External Affairs? There is a very good reason for this: he is the big minister. Off I go to see him. His secretary, a fat and very pleasant *muhindi* tells me to wait. I wait. Then she tells me to go in. I go in. When I enter I see the minister brother sitting at a big desk. He tells me to take a seat, then he says to me, "What's your problem, my good man?" Very British, these blacks . . .'

Mistry laughed, the rest nodded and took this pause as an opportunity to spit.

'. . . I say to him, "Let's call this *our* problem, not my problem." He says, "Es you vish." I say, "Your sister owes me 1500 shillings only." He says, "So what?" I say, "So I want my 1500 if you don't mind, good sir; my family likes to eat now and then." He says, "You *wahindi* are all rich and you give us hell of trouble – what's 1500 to you? My sister" – he continues – "she's just new at this sort of thing; give the poor girl a chance. Don't you know we Africans believe in African socialism? We always pay. Everyone is brothers; *she* your brother; she'll pay you." I say, "if you don't mind I am taking the liberty to correct you: *she said you pay me*. She said I must see you." "She gave you my name?" asks this big black. I say, "Yes, indeed." "Did she say I was going to pay you?" "Not exactly," I say; "she just gave me your name, she wanted me to see you." "Take a look," says the black; then he says, "Now you see me – are you satisfied? Give my sister whatever she wants; we

Africans are poor; this is a poor country, a *developing* country, dirty and poor, and you are wasting my time. Our colonial masters just stole like hell from us, but now most of them see the error and sinning they did on us." He keeps talking: "These white men wouldn't come in here and say what you're saying – they know better than that. They know all kinds of problems we have, even some we don't know and myself, some I don't know, and I'm a minister. Now take my advice," he says, "I'm a busy man, my sister she's also a busy woman, and we can't be bothered with your financial problems; as for me, I was born in a mud hut with no clothes and had to shit in the grass, so don't try to tell me your family is hungry . . ." Then this black says that he has to meet the Prime Minister, so I better go home and stop troubling. I go home and what do I find? I find the sister in my shop. She needs more fabrics . . .'

'That *is* a sad story,' said Fakhru. And he thought, Yes, that is a sad story indeed.

Mehta said that the same thing happened to his cousin in the Congo. A big *bwana* in the government said his cousin had to supply fresh meat every day or they would kick him. 'Only pretty soon,' Mehta continued, 'there was no government, at least no *bwanas* giving orders up and down; no big *bwanas*, no problems, business she keeps going on. That's how it was in the Congo,' he said.

'What are you going to do?' Visrani asked J. H. Patel, ignoring Mehta's footnote.

'What is he going to do! What do you think he is going to do?' Mistry shouted, grinning for no reason at all. 'He's going to give this black sister what she wants! No, J. H.?'

'What else can I do?' said J. H. Patel. 'I'm a poor man.'

All smiled and stroked their chins.

'These Africans,' said Fakhru, 'they want everything free, if you ask me. They have no business sense. They are killing us.'

'They don't know what business is,' said S. R. Patel.

'No, man,' said Ali the half-caste, in his one offering to the group.

47

'And we get blamed for everything,' said Fakhru.

'Just bloody swindlers, that's all,' said Visrani. 'These blacks. They should be kicked *kabisa*.'

Fakhru looked over and saw that his houseboy had got the stamps. He excused himself, offered his condolences to J. H. Patel and went to the opposite side of the post office. He watched a well-dressed African opening his letters. The African tore them open and sighed, threw the envelopes into the wastebasket and lumbered heavily out. Fakhru went to the wastebasket and poked around with his finger. He turned up two nice envelopes; on each one the address was written in very small letters, and neither of them had its flap gummed. Fakhru put a filled-out deposit slip inside with the cheque for 368 shillings, crossed out the address, added the address of the bank and affixed the stamps which had been bought (and moistened) by the houseboy. He dropped the envelope into the box marked *Local Letters* and looked at his watch: it was nine thirty.

Fifteen minutes passed. An African with a big canvas sack came over and opened a small door at the bottom of the letter box. Gathering up the letters in his two hands, the African stuffed them into the sack and then threw the sack over his shoulder and lugged it into the sorting room. Fakhru went outside and found the bank's post office box. It was number 250. While he watched it half an hour passed; beggars had gathered and were bleating around his knees. For luck Fakhru dropped threepence into a leper's cup, and at that moment an African wearing a grey uniform and a red fez shuffled up to the box. Fakhru pulled out his own key and pretended to be opening the box just above that of the bank. He glanced down and saw his letter, crossed-out address and all, in the bank messenger's hand. The messenger removed his fez, then slowly knelt and peered into the box; when he was satisfied that it was empty he creaked the rusted door of the box very slowly shut, played with the key for a while and then shuffled back to the bank. His bare feet scraping on the gritty cement pavement made such an unpleasant sound that Fakhru decided not to follow too closely.

At typewriters and adding machines in the large walled-in area of the bank, thirty Asian girls pecked at keys, flipped through thick files and sipped at cups of tea. Fakhru watched the fezzed messenger distributing the envelopes among the girls. He looked at his watch again: it was quarter to eleven.

Fakhru knew that the cheque had to be cleared through his own account; he had purposely written a cheque on the account he had in that bank so that the process would be simplified. He allowed fifteen minutes for this. The cheque would then have to be passed to whomever handled Sam Fong's account, another ten minutes, and finally it would have to be added in and computed on the balance sheet, another fifteen minutes. By eleven thirty Sam Fong would have 1000 shillings in his account; by eleven thirty-five Sam Fong would be penniless.

All the calculations were correct. Fakhru went to the teller at eleven thirty and presented Fong's cheque. The teller scribbled on it and passed it to another red-fezzed African; when the cheque was dropped before the teller again there were more initials on it.

'How do you want it?' asked the teller.

'Five hundreds, 300 in twenties, 100 in tens and the rest in fives,' said Fakhru, opening his old leather briefcase.

8

'These Chinamen only understand one language,' said Bert.

'Killin, burnin and violence,' said Mel with conviction.

'No,' said Bert, 'Chinese. You know, we didn't say a straight word to him the whole time.'

'Easy does it,' said Mel. 'This here's gonna amaze the shit out of the old man.'

'You're telling me.'

'A real honest-to-God Chinese. First one I set eyes on this side of the Chu-Chin-Chow in Mobile.' Mel shook his head. 'But you know what? They look the same wherever you go and that's a truth.'

'How about that smile?'

'How about that! Did you *see* him? We had him in the palm of our hand. Him and ... and ... What was the other one's name?'

'Dunno. Got it here somewhere.' Bert Newt lifted his flowered shirt. Underneath, attached to his plaid belt, was a small tape recorder. A thin wire leading from the tape recorder was adhesive-taped over the bulge of his abdomen; a tiny microphone dangled near his navel. Newt unstrapped the tape recorder and peeled the tape and wire from his skin. He placed the box on the table and allowed his thick fingers to puzzle over it like hairless creatures eager to devour it; they hovered close. With a quick gesture Newt held the box fast with his left hand and squeezed a plastic rectangle with his right. The tape recorder squawked.

Mel Francey put his head close, just in time to hear the loud noise of Fakhru bumping into them, and then:

'. . . *Sorry, bwana . . . Name's Newt. Bert G. Newt, Jr. This here's*

Mel Francey . . . Hah! I'm a Negro from Alabama where they say we got a lot of trouble, only we don't, that's all. Your average . . .'

'What about the hands?' Mel reached for the tape recorder.

'Wait a sec,' said Bert, snatching it away and winding it forward.

'*. . . Hassanali Fakhru of Fakhru Enterprises Limited . . . Chalk up one . . .'*

There was a little slap on the tape, the handshake, barely audible.

'That's the baby,' said Mel.

'Yeah, lemme play it again,' Bert mumbled.

He wound the tape back again. Again the handshake was played, this time louder, a little *pip*, like a dung beetle releasing a pellet on to a hard surface. Mel Francey beamed and demanded to hear it several more times.

'*Pip . . . pip . . . pip.*'

Mel said the old man would eat that one up. He sat down and fanned himself with his hat. 'How was I?' he asked.

'Beautiful, great.'

'You think I was okay? I mean, did I hit him hard enough with the Alabama business?'

'Terrific. I seen a lotta guys come through this office, Mel baby, but believe me, you got every one of them beat by a mile. You can take that from me, and I been in this racket one hell of a long time.'

'Think so?' Mel Francey shook his head. It created an odd effect, because, as he shook his head, he still fanned himself with his straw hat. He looked at Bert Newt and said, 'Course, you didn't do so bad yourself, brother.'

'How about that *jambo* bit?'

'Nearly cracked me up, that's all. Wow,' said Mel, 'we got 'em by the ass.' He squinted: 'Say, Bert? Where *did* you get that *jambo* bit?'

'Book,' said Bert fiddling with the tape recorder. 'It's *howsaboy* in Kiswahili.'

'I liked that a lot.'

'Think the old man'll like it?'

'*Think!* I *know* it's gonna amaze the shit outta him!'

'What about a CFFRR on the thing?'

'Sure,' said Mel. 'I'll get the card.'

Mel Francey went to the file cabinet and took out a rectangular card. At the top of the card was printed: CONFIDENTIAL FACE TO FACE RATIO RATING.

'Lessee here,' said Mel. He read, 'Christian names, other names, address, tele . . . What'd that guy say his name was?'

The tape was played again.

'Now which one you suppose is his Christian name?' Mel inquired.

'The one he said first. That's usually the case.'

'Ginrilly,' said Mel. He mumbled slowly as he wrote: 'Christchun nayum. Has-san-alley . . . Oth-er nayums Fakroo. There we are.'

'What've we got next?'

'Verbalization rating.'

'Give him about sixty. We got well past Hi.'

'Six-ty,' said Mel, writing. 'Motivation?'

'High.'

'Response reinforcement?'

''Bout seventy. He smiled, remember?'

'Yeah. Big shit-eatin grin.'

'Let's do the Chinaman,' said Bert Newt.

9

At roughly the same time as Fakhru was standing in the bank dealing the careful final blows to Sam Fong's account, Fong found himself counting out wrinkled five-shilling notes to a man of about forty, barefoot and in rags except for a new red shirt. The man said he was a Young Pioneer; he carried a knobbed stick painted with the colours of the national flag. He said that unless Fong gave him fifty shillings his windows would be broken and, adding a euphemism in the vernacular, his wife would be 'handled'.

Sam Fong had stared at the Young Pioneer and said nothing. He went to the back room, took a brick out of the wall and from the opening withdrew all that was there in the cobwebs and mould; a damp fifty shillings. It was all he had.

The Young Pioneer leaned his stick against the counter and took the money with both hands cupped, in the traditional manner and not without grace. He reminded Fong that this was the African way and said, 'Thank you, brother.' Fong dipped his head in the direction of the Young Pioneer.

'I know you only come here to make money. You send money to white banks overseas and you don't care if we cope up at all.' The Young Pioneer leered at Soo. 'Then you don't want to marry Africans and I don't know why. You just want to stay with your own people. You don't care about us . . .'

'I just gave you fifty shillings,' said Fong.

The Young Pioneer looked at the crumpled bills in his hand and said, 'Yes, *bwana, you* didn't give us any trouble. We like people that help us, even the bloody Communists if they help us we say thank you. But if you businessmen don't want to help us we don't want you here and I don't care if . . .'

'Thirty-five years in this country,' Sam Fong said smiling, gesturing around the shop, at his wife, and nodding towards two of his small children, who were playing on the floor and croaking.

The Young Pioneer raised his arm stiffly in a mechanical salute and shouted, 'Forward *ayver*, backward *nayver*!' Then he tossed a little card on the counter, picked up his knobbed stick and left. Outside, he climbed into a new minibus. On one of the seats, his bulk and the fact that no one sat with him testifying to his importance, sat a man in a fur hat, leaning on a beaded cane. On the other seats were more men wearing red shirts: they were crammed in, five to a seat. On the side of the bus was written in yellow:

DIES IST EIN GESCHENK DER WESTDEUTSCHEN
BEVÖLKERUNG.
THIS IS A GIFT OF THE PEOPLE OF WEST GERMANY.

The minibus lurched away.

Soo took the card. She stared at it a full minute and then translated it into Chinese: 'Now you are a non-transferable membership card of the People's Congress Party. How much did it cost?'

'Fifty shillings, which means no more money behind the brick.'

Soo clucked.

'These Africans have an odd way of collecting taxes,' said Fong.

Money had been collected from Fong many times before, and each demand for money was matched by something tragic happening. The first tragedy Fong remembered was in 1960. A fat man, an African, had come to the carpentry shop together with a white man wearing glasses and dressed in shorts. They wanted chairs, they said. But once in the workshop they assembled all the workers and gave speeches. They said that the day was coming when all the people of the country would break off the chains of slavery; everyone would soon be free and the snakes would be driven out. The white man – this surprised Sam Fong – not only spoke in Swahili, but he also said that white men had enslaved the African from the beginning of time; the guilty ones were the whites, said the white man. He went on to say that the whites were thieves and hyenas. The fat African who carried a fly whisk shouted, 'Yes, yes!

But the dawn is breaking and we will no longer be slaves,' and the white man added, 'Long live the black power of the People's Congress Party!' At this point the two men collected money from all the workers; Fong had looked dolefully at the ragged workers emptying their pockets into the fur hat of the African. Sam Fong had contributed three shillings sixpence to the cause. The white man and the African went away, the workers went back to their hammering and sawing, and then the tragedy occurred: the country became independent. Taxes were raised, soldiers suddenly popped up everywhere, the workers were frightened, and many resigned and went back to their villages where there were no soldiers and no taxes. Sam Fong saw the fat face of the African in the newspaper every day; the white man's picture also appeared once in a while. Shortly thereafter another white man had inquired, 'Who is your keenest chap?' and six months later Sam Fong was out of a job.

The money-collecting always seemed to mean that trouble was not far off. A year after independence there were rumours that two ministers had resigned from the government and were campaigning against the Prime Minister somewhere in the bush, giving speeches in banana groves. Sam Fong did not believe the rumours until the Young Pioneers showed up with their hands out demanding money; the rumours proved correct. It was about this time that Fong – under pressure from his customers – scratched the progress slogans off his storefront. His African customers said they were fed up; there was no freedom.

Except for the money contributed on these two occasions and the loss of his job, Fong did not suffer physical attack; no one 'handled' his wife, and independence and freedom seemed simply more expensive than what existed before. 'Run for your life! Everyone is being beaten up,' the rumours sometimes said, but Sam Fong in four years as a shopkeeper in this free country had never seen anyone beaten up. As far as he was concerned this was the problem: the British had made a regular practice of beating people. The results had been amazing; the protectorate had prospered. Sam Fong believed privately that there should be public whippings, that incorrigibles should be locked in iceboxes to suffocate now and then. But it did not happen. Nothing happened. The government wanted money or anything else it could get, taxes, presents, free food, bags of rice, goats, songs. No one 'handled' Fong's wife, no one kicked in the window of his store, no one laid a finger on him; business was awful.

'So this is freedom,' said Sam Fong to Soo. 'They take your money and *pftt* you are free. And now there are no shillings behind the brick.'

But the feeling of impending disaster persisted: if they are collecting money something is going to happen. When there is a revolution, the people leave town and the streets are deserted; when there is a revolution it is the grocer who suffers most.

The arrival of Fakhru's van the next day put these morose thoughts out of Fong's mind or, rather, converted the gloomy thoughts into hopeful business prospects. This canned-milk transaction was Fong's first genuine deal, assuming, as Fong did, that there must be something fundamentally dishonest about every business deal. If there was trouble, Fong now reasoned, the milk train from Nairobi would not get through.

Fong had never seen so many cans. For the first time in four years Fong felt as if he truly was a grocer, and his mind started using that perverse logic that is characteristic of small grocers: Fong felt as if he were getting the canned milk free. By the time the trouble came, the train derailed, the milk sold and the money deposited, there would be ten times as much in the bank as was there originally; he would never miss the small investment – he would have a great pile of shillings instead. Fakhru's driver panted and huffed as he dragged the boxes into the store; he heaped the boxes against one wall. At first Fong was going to help unload the boxes from the van, but when he remembered that the boxes had yet to be sold and that he had no money stuffed behind the brick, he suddenly went limp, unwilling. He stood quietly and watched the boxes being unloaded. He counted twenty-seven of them. Each time the African driver slammed a box down, Fong's head moved slightly.

'We can call it Sam Fong Friendly Milk Store,' said Soo from the back.

'Don't be a fool,' said Sam Fong.

Hearing this, Soo came forward. Fong slapped her. She withdrew.

What am I getting excited about? Fong thought. The cheque bounced, I have money in the bank, Soo can make a sign: SAM FONG FRIENDLY MILK STORE. If money is being collected there is going to be serious trouble. Many people will leave town, but whites will not leave town. Whites will stay; everyone loves them. Their children drink a lot of milk, cow's milk, which is why they sometimes have a bovine look about them. Whites are not frightened by revolutions. They will buy this mountain of canned milk. The money will come, I will deposit it, Fakhru will cash his cheque. And Fakhru will appreciate my method of operating because has not Fakhru on many occasions swindled me?

He shouted for Soo. Soo entered the shop from the back again and stood bravely before Fong, expecting the finale to the beating.

'Get a board,' said Fong.

Soo went outside and got a thick board. He never hit me with a board before, thought Soo.

'Not big enough,' said Fong when he saw the board.

That man is very upset, thought Soo, heaving the largest board she could find.

'Now your brush,' said Fong, satisfied with the board.

A new torture, thought Soo, remembering stories of chopsticks that had been pushed through the ears of the unlawful in her native land.

'Some paint,' said Fong.

I am finished, thought Soo, he will kill me with the materials that would have gone to mock him; that's what I get for opening my mouth. But she could find no paint. She found only half a pint of turpentine. She presented this to her husband and said, 'This will have to do. I assure you that it will be an equally painful substitute. When you have beaten me with the board and inserted that pointed brush into my ear and pushed it to the other side it will make no difference if you cover me with paint or turpentine. In any case, I shall die, as I deserve to.'

'Are you out of your mind?' Fong said. 'I want to make a Sam Fong Friendly Milk Store sign. Now where is the paint?'

Soo looked in the back room and found only mice; Fong looked in the shop. The can of paint was not to be found anywhere. The last sign Soo had made was the Friend Frocery sign; Fong had suppressed – either through mockery or beatings, or both – all Soo's attempts to make any other signs (SAM FONG MATTRESS SHOP; SAM FONG TYRES FOR ALL OCCASIONS) and somewhere in the course of four years the paint had been lost. But Fong did not give up the search. He was still on his hands and knees combing the trash near the baseboard, the large dead roaches and mango peels. So absorbed was he that he did not see two figures enter the store until he came upon their shoes. He scrabbled and flung refuse this way and that and finally he turned his eyes upward. Above him were two Chinamen in white starched shirts and wide trousers.

'Comrade,' they said as one.

Fong stood. He was fascinated by them. He did not bother to brush the dirt off his knees. His head tilted to the side in amused bewilderment. He greeted them as masters and said that it was a blessing that they should enter his shop; it was God's wish.

The small triangular faces of the two men seemed to get smaller. Their mouths fell involuntarily open and showed decaying teeth.

'We were driving by,' said the taller of the two, 'and I saw your sign. I said to Comrade Chen, "That is a comrade; we should greet him."'

'When did you leave China?' asked the second.

'The Year of the Dragon, nineteen thirty,' said Sam Fong.

'That was a good year for us – big campaigns in the middle Yangtze in the summer, victory over two reactionary divisions in the winter, many defectors to our side . . .'

'Many people left then, too,' added the taller one slowly.

'I left,' said Fong.

'Whose side were you on?'

'There were so many sides, I could not make up my mind – I was on no one's side. I was a carpenter in our small village workshop, making excellent cupboards of our rare and wormproof teak. One day my father said to me, "Son, the Manchus are gone for ever and from now on it seems to be every man for himself . . ."'

'You joined Chiang Kai-shek?'

'No, we walked to Foochow, got on a boat and here I am. My father died while on the boat, God rest his soul.' At this point Fong made the sign of the cross slowly and mumbled a little prayer. When he emerged moist-eyed from his little beatific reverie he looked at the two men and asked, 'Who is the emperor now?'

The Chinamen looked at each other, almost sadly.

'You remember Mao, of course,' one began.

'The library assistant fellow? They were offering 50,000 yuan for his capture the year I left – 20,000 for only his head! Now there's a *real* troublemaker, my father used to say.'

The faces of the two men seemed to become yet smaller. In a new tone of voice, restrained, though shriller than before, the taller one said, 'He is Chairman now and we are bathed in the light of his glorious thought!'

'So they didn't catch him?'

'They couldn't. The peasants were ripe for revolution.'

'Well, as I said, my father and I were in Foochow at the time, just leaving.' Fong laughed – barked, rather – but he was alone in this.

A customer entered the store. It was Margerine, an old, greying African man wearing broken eyeglasses mended with bits of Scotch tape; he had been given his name by an English memsahib who was unable to pronounce his clan name M'gheren'he, and said she thought it sounded terribly like Margerine. He often ran errands for Fong in return for jelly beans or small cubes of greasy homemade soap. Today Margerine had twopence. He wanted a cigarette.

'One cigarette, twopence, and a match for nothing,' Fong said cheerfully, lighting the cigarette; Margerine held the cigarette at arm's length over the match and did not put it into his mouth until half of it was in flames.

Fong was glad to see Margerine as he once was glad to see Fakhru. The conversation with the Chinamen was getting nowhere. He asked Margerine how his family was getting along, how the beer was doing and whether the bananas were ripening. These were the safe topics of conversation: Fong thought of the country privately as 'Bananaland'.

'Just this morning I gave fifty shillings to the Party,' said Fong.

'What's the sense?' shrugged Margerine, puffing and then squinting through the smoke. 'The Prime Minister – that monkey – has locked up five of his cabinet ministers. These ministers are all Dada and as you know the Dada people are the most fierce and primitive *savages* [he said this in English] in the country. There will be too much trouble, sure.'

'We wait and see,' said Fong, remembering the milk, the paint, the unmade sign.

'What is there to see? Just more trouble,' said Margerine. 'Remember in nineteen fifty-six when the Queen came? A nice lady, the Queen. We were all happy. Then in sixty Philip [he pronounced this Philipy] took the flag down; bye-bye, I said. I felt like crying. All my friends were happy. We're free, they said. I said to them, you *buggers* wait one year and you will be crying too.' Margerine shook his head and looked at his cigarette; he squeezed out the glowing tip, put the butt inside his rags and went out.

The Chinamen had watched it all with respectful awe. 'You speak that black language?' asked the taller one.

'Oh, yes,' said Fong. 'I can even sing hymns in Swahili.'

'That man is your friend?' asked the other.

'They're all my friends,' said Fong. 'When you're a grocer even one enemy is too many.' Well put, he thought.

The Chinamen were impressed. 'That is very good, you know. We have a little present for you.' The taller one reached into his briefcase, took out a pile of books and magazines and placed them on the counter. 'These are for you, comrade. Read them. If you want more we will gladly provide them. Show them to your friends, our black brothers. In any case, we shall come back and talk to you. You have no idea how great your country has become.'

'There is going to be a lot of trouble,' Fong said. He had such conviction in his voice that the two Chinamen began speaking at once.

'That is a filthy lie spread by capitalist lackeys and warmongers!'

'The dogs in America say that! Do they know that spindle production has risen 300 per cent in the past six months?'

'I am sure there is going to be trouble. I've been hearing rumours, and just this morning I was forced to pay . . .'

'Don't believe a word of it!' shrieked the taller one. 'Don't worry, comrade, these rumour-mongers are paid by American dogs and cats. Chairman Mao just last week swam fifteen miles – now you stand there and tell me there's trouble!'

'Chairman Mao?' Fong frowned. 'I don't know about Chairman Mao. I mean this country.' And he added in Swahili: 'Bananaland.'

The Chinamen smiled, patted the magazines, reminded Fong that he should read them and noiselessly left the store. Outside, one turned to the other and without moving his lips, said, 'Talk about lackeys!'

Fong put the magazines in the window and yelled again for Soo. She was in the back pulling the wings off grasshoppers. She appeared at the doorway.

'What about the sign?'

'We have no paint,' said Soo. 'If you gave all the money to the black boy with the big stick then we have no money either. How can we buy paint?'

'I'll write a cheque,' said Fong.

'But we have never before taken money out of the bank.'

'Let me worry about that,' Fong said, smiling. He took his cheque-book from inside his shirt and wrote a cheque for two shillings. 'Go buy some paint,' he said, 'quick.'

Sam Fong was not alone on Uhuru Avenue. It was the longest street in East Africa and crammed with people and shops. Take an average day, average except for the worried-looking Chinese woman running from the lower end to the junction, dodging idlers and paper sellers, with a cheque for two shillings inside her dress and her hand flat against her dress, holding the cheque in place as she runs. She runs slightly stooped, her feet slapping against the pavement; it is clear from the inexpert running and the number of people she bumps into that she is not used to running on the Uhuru sidewalk. A side street, perhaps, but not the main street of the capital.

At the lower end the street is narrow, pitted with ant caves; near the junction at the centre of town an island begins abruptly in the middle with a broken KEEP LEFT sign, with palm trees, flower beds and people squatting or sleeping on the neatly trimmed grass. One fellow is roasting corn cobs over a charcoal stove. Those who live on Uhuru Avenue see nothing – they sell, they sleep, they haggle on the sidewalk, they buy one newspaper a day and ignore the stack of literature that is yellowing and curling upon the sidewalk near the paper seller. Only the tourists notice the completeness of the stack of booklets: *China Reconstructs*, *Yugoslavia News*, *Soviet Woman*, *Key to Your Stars*, the suitable-for-framing hand-coloured portraits of President Kennedy and Patrice Lumumba, pamphlets of Gujarati love songs, *Machines that Made America* (Students Edition), *Peking Review*, *Reader's Digest*, *Ebony*, *The God that Failed*, J. V. Stalin's *The Foundations of Leninism* and V. I. Lenin's *Imperialism: The Last Stages of Capitalism*, these last two both low-priced and austerely printed but none the less suffering the effects of being too long in the sun and dust; comic books with John Glenn in a space capsule saying 'We did it!' and two-colour pamphlets showing gross-booted Negresses smiling in Red Square and many more, all unsold, doing nothing more than drawing attention to the smudged daily, the typeface askew, the captions reversed but the headline still legibly exulting *COUP IN ALGERIA!*, while beside it and beside the inflammatory literature the paper seller slumps in a cretinous doze (his gaping mouth could be mistaken for a smile). There are people hurrying by who have better things to do than read: they are on twenty-minute coffee breaks, pocket-picking missions, they are begging and buying; and one, no longer yellow in the bright sun and seen only by those she barges into, is off to buy a can of paint.

In twos the whores march out of step wearing extravagant wigs wisped and spun with jet-black horsehair mounted high and looking like charred beehives; their protruding bottoms bulge shiny against their bright dresses which, decorated with swirling metallic patterns, sparkle in the equatorial morning sun. They are the only ones who look at ease on the sidewalk; they alone are not hurrying; they ignore nothing, no one, take long, patient, undisturbed looks at men racing the engines of their cars at stoplights or men in shirtsleeves shielding their eyes from the sun. They are trailed by little dirty boys who nudge each other and imitate the girls walking. The high heels, the tight dresses and heavy purses of the girls give them a strange halting gait that is half ass and the rest purse as they clomp along Uhuru to the walk-down bars. What is oddest is that they are not black – their faces are brown mostly, some are quadroon yellow like that man alighting from the plane in the skin-lightening poster in Fong's shop; the Congolese girls have long lateral scars on their cheeks, the Sudanese have symmetrical rows of bumps across their foreheads, others have claw marks raked parallel to their eyes. As they walk along they pat and adjust their wigs. Under their wigs their heads are shaven.

New to this crowd the Chinese woman pushes past two of them, and one of them smirks; it is a big, deliberate smirk and it takes up nearly one whole side of the girl's face.

The Chinese woman dashes past the National and Grindlay's Bank where resting Hindus take refuge on the shaded wall, symbolic meeting place for a thousand Asians on an East African Sunday afternoon; past the now green statue of George V, crowned and hugging a sceptre to his robes streaked with bird-lime; past the basket market and six ladies wearing (as they were directed by a brochure) simple, comfortable, low-heeled shoes, sensible dresses, roomy cotton brassières and stupid-looking straw hats; past Cashco, the only supermarket in the country, air-conditioned to a dull chill seasoned with the dust of imported packaging; past the Mercedes agency where twelve lion-bearded Sikhs are goggling at their turbaned friend behind the wheel, his bracelet clanking on the dashboard, his dagger stabbing the upholstery, all bumping turbans and saying *yah-yah!*, and one African quietly, corpulently, kicking the tyre of a huge new model and enquiring, How much is that in shillings? She goes past a jeep loaded with soldiers who are giggling at one of their number who has chosen to amuse his comrades by aiming his air-cooled machine-gun at passing cars; past the trophy-laden windows of the safari outfitters, two tusks framing rifles, bullets, bush hats with leopardskin sweatbands and one grinning head of a stuffed lion; past a *Wir sprechen Deutsch, Nous parlons français, Hablamos español* curio shop with zebra handbags, reedbuck rugs, ivory Christs, Zanzibari chests, legs of waterbuck made into lampstands, hoof ashtrays, elephant-foot wastebaskets, lion-tooth rosaries, hippo-tooth brooches; past six coffee shops, three of which have Hindustani jukeboxes and so have a score of Pakistani boys combing their hair in front and tapping their pointed shoes to the screech and clang of the latest hit from Karachi; past a bar which intrudes on the sidewalk with men hunched in circles around little tables, each table holding the quart beer bottles of whichever race that table happens to be occupied by: Italian contractors at one, Greek bakers at another; two dark-suited Africans and a bespectacled American in native dress – flowing robes, rough sandals, an elephant-hair bracelet, a broadsword – at a third, semi-integrated table; five Englishmen, each wearing white shoes, long white socks, white shorts and white shirt and sporting a pink face and big ears at a fourth table; Indians sipping orange squash at a fifth, and so forth; past LAL SHETH TOOTHMAKER, FAZAL ABDULLAH KITCHENWARE, BOMBAY BAZAAR NICE TEXTILES; past RAHEMTULLA FUNSTORE, filled with slot machines and Africans, FANCY PAN-WALLAH, filled with betel nuts and Indians, NEW GOA GROCERY, filled with Goans and groceries and managed by Lobo who refused to buy Fakhru's canned milk. Uhuru Avenue is now a two-lane thoroughfare, with men in rags, and some not in rags, snoozing near the trunks of the palm trees planted in a row down the grassy islands; while the Chinese woman, who has not yet blinked, crosses the island and dashes in front of a dozen quickly braking cars lurching around her, and into a side alley to MEHBOOB PAINT SUPPLY where, four years before, she had gone to buy the paint she needed for her first sign.

She points to a small can. It is handed to her by Z. F. R. Mehboob. She pulls the cheque out of the neck of her dress and smoothes the little cheque flat against the counter. Z. F. R. Mehboob smiles at its smallness, mutters, 'Two bob only,' wraps the can of paint in an old newspaper and jerks his head sideways in thanks.

The Chinese woman is out flapping down the street as Z. F. R. Mehboob hands the cheque to a small boy to deposit. Down the main street she goes, faster than she came, past the palm section, past the section that was paved for the Queen's visit, past the post-independence sidewalks – useful most of all to the beggars who now have a kerb to sit on, and, as a bonus of progress to this city in a now different Africa, something entirely new, alien at first, but now serving necessity's perverse demands: a gutter.

All is blurred to the woman; she sees nothing because she knows she has no business on the street, she does not belong there and yet she knows she is running full tilt through colour and noise, unseen herself possibly, except by beggars. And at the far end of the street she begins to slow down at the section without sidewalks, home of HASSANALI FAKHRU ENTERPRISES LTD, ALI BUTCHERY, J. H. PATEL DRYGOODS, some tin-beating Africans in a vacant lot, a bar with no doors, a prostitute with the face of a pangolin leaning against a wooden shack, the taxi rank, a quagmire of battered Volkswagens. Now she is panting, the can of paint in her hands, and she enters the last shop of the street with a gasp.

11

'Indeed,' Fakhru was saying, 'he can be very difficult to deal with, but if you will excuse me for saying so, I am sure something can be arranged . . .'

Fakhru was at ease, he was happy and he was about to express his willingness to help. These feelings of generosity were inspired by the Americans who had done nothing more – but indeed it had taken them nearly a whole day – than follow the Rule Book and learn to say Fakhru's name. They cared. Fakhru was ready to help and had a feeling that, with his generosity, he could make a little money on the way.

Bert and Mel cocked their heads closer and tried to follow the Ismaili in his description of Fong. They had sent the office boy out for beer, but Fakhru had refused it; they had each offered Fakhru a cigar, and Fakhru had turned down the cigars as well, politely; Mel, who made a practice of putting the refused cigar in the man's pocket and saying 'Keep it for later', discovered that Fakhru's pyjama suit had no pockets. In frustration Mel went to a cabinet, took two fistfuls of Kents and dumped these in Fakhru's large soft lap. Fakhru did not smoke but said he would give them to his cousin who did. 'Course we got no bidnis givin 'em to ya, but a body can't buy Kents *nohow* these parts,' said Mel, and this caused Fakhru to smile and say thank you a third time.

Unbribed and looking reasonably comfortable in the chair, Fakhru continued to talk: about being brown in a black country; how His Highness had said this or that; how he himself, a humble tradesman, saw Africa as a test of his devotion, like a long exile with the usual temptations and hardships, as the Prophet himself had endured in the desert. East Africa could be a jolly place, he said, but – and here Fakhru looked frankly at Bert Newt – something had to be done with the blacks.

Bert said that scads of just plain vital little Africans had gone to the States, where they had verbalized all their conflicts *vis-à-vis* the new developing nations in transition; the flap and feedback had been very good, generally speaking, although Bert said that he could not be more exact because he was not near the figures.

Fakhru shrugged and produced another smile. He went on, 'And this yellow man Fong . . .'

There was a series of barely audible clicks in the room.

His tongue working behind his teeth to produce some very thick *p*'s and *t*'s, Fakhru warned the two men who were now anxiously nibbling at ball-point pens that they might have trouble understanding the curious language that Fong spoke and that, in any event, Fakhru himself would be glad, 'more than heppy', as he put it, to act as interpreter. When Bert replied that they were ass-deep in liaison men Fakhru asked if they knew Swahili of the upcountry variety. No, they said, they didn't, but added that they were sure someone did and thought privately that this someone, whoever it might be, could always use a little extra money; it was a poor country. Fakhru lectured them on the difference between Swahili as it is spoken by the devout on the coast and the kind uttered by the *muntu* trader a thousand miles inland. (This adjective made both Americans very uncomfortable.) Fakhru said he knew both kinds. Bert Newt, to shake off his discomfort, said, 'Chrissakes, there are two kinds of *jambo*!'

Fakhru moved on to Sam Fong; he said that although Sam Fong had said he wanted to be friends, there were few people Fong trusted and this seemed to be a characteristic of the yellow race: they were excessively difficult to know.

'Thass puttin it mahldly!' said Mel.

'You can say that agin!' said Bert.

Bert had a feeling that the whole approach might be misunderstood. He assumed a kindly look and spoke out of the corner of his mouth, like a farmer, or at least the way he heard the farmers in the movies talk. He wanted to get to know everyone, he said, on a face-to-face basis. Of course they had scholarships, cultural exchanges and what-have-you for African students; but nothing, it seemed, could put them in touch with the grass roots, as it were. 'Your average grass-rooter is a tough nut to crack – takes a lotta finesse to know 'em good,' said Bert. Sam Fong was a good man to know, he knew 'Your Average African', and Fakhru knew Fong. 'We just wanna be friends,' said Bert. 'Who cares what colour he is? Life's too short to start fretting about colours.' He wagged his head.

'Amen, brother,' said Mel Francey.

Sam Fong, thought Fakhru. He had never in his life seen two men so eager to do business. What did this yellow man have that they wanted so badly? Did he possess some great secret? Was he a criminal on the loose? Fakhru reflected and as he did, Sam Fong ceased to be a man; very soon he became, in Fakhru's mind, a valuable commodity, like the UNICEF milk or free fly spray that had to be taken over and given a price, hustled out of the country and hawked to Sudanese farmers in order to be fully appreciated and used. As long as these things were free – like Sam Fong staring at the open doors of his shop from behind the far counter, like the milk or fly spray being tossed free of charge off donated trucks to tribesmen who hardly cared and who did not pay – as long as these were free they were without importance; they had no value and would fail precisely because they were gifts. Since people of different colours could never be friends, there could never be anything like an exchange of gifts; there had to be trade, and this commerce could be as meaningful as love. That was the way life went on. If this was never mentioned in the Holy Koran it was not the Prophet's fault, for he never had a family to support.

Fakhru grew silent and meditative; Mel Francey rose, winked at Bert and slipped out the door.

When Mel was gone, Bert looked at Fakhru and said, 'See, this here's a great little country and we want it to stay that way. You remember what happened when the Chinese invaded India? Must have broke your heart . . .'

Bert continued. Fakhru repeated 'Of course, of course' at intervals and thought to himself: This bloody man thinks I'm a bloody Hindu.

'. . . And the same thing could happen here. Why I've seen it happen with my own eyes in a slew of other countries.' He drew close to Fakhru and said, 'Confidentially, it's happening right next door . . .'

Fakhru tried to think which of his friends owned the shop next to Bert's office. He could not think clearly so he smiled, looked at Bert and said, 'In brief, as I understand it, you want to chet with my yellow friend, Sam Fong.'

'That's all. No reason to get long-faced about it. We'll just debrief him a bit and shoot the bull.'

'I must therefore warn you that he is, as you say, stubborn as a jeckess. He might have to be, as you say, helped along . . . somehow . . .'

'We're all human,' said Bert. 'I mean, Jesus Christ!' He laughed instantly and very loudly and then stopped. In embarrassing seriousness he continued, 'See, this thing is my headache. I got your peri-urban minorities to deal with. Mel, he's your African man, your national; he's the right colour, if you see what I mean.'

'Of course,' said Fakhru. 'But the yellow one . . .'

'You let me worry about him. You think he'll talk really . . . ?'

'As I say, he might need, as you say . . .' Fakhru produced another smile.

'Yeah, yeah,' said Bert. 'But I want you to know one thing: you're swell to help us out here.'

'I try my best,' said Fakhru.

This was not the end of the conversation. Though Fakhru would have been very happy to leave, his politeness forced him back into his chair, and he added what he thought were appropriate remarks. Bert talked about Africa again, in general, and then about America's role in it. Fakhru was growing irritable; he had not had his morning tea and now it was almost lunchtime. He knew he would gorge himself on curry and *dal* and then want to sleep. Another day would be gone with only the beginnings of a very uncertain transaction made. He heard Bert say Africa a few more times and when Bert paused, Fakhru suggested that Africa was filled with monkeys.

Yes, Bert agreed, he had gone to the game parks with his whole family; he had seen them. He proudly pulled out baby pictures which he showed to Fakhru, very slowly and with many comments. In the background of every picture was a different facet of American life which, along with the weight and age of the baby, he described to Fakhru: a car, a typical house, a strong bicycle ('they don't come any better'), a set of golf clubs and so forth.

'You have an abundance of children,' Fakhru remarked.

'No, I don't,' said Bert, 'only one, but he's healthy as a horse!'

'You have an abundance of sneps, then,' said Fakhru.

'Yeah, sure, lotsa pictures. But it's the same kid.' He smiled fondly at the snapshots.

The morning was gone. Fakhru was now very angry; he had had a dozen things to do and was not even sure if he had done one of them – who could understand what these Americans said? Fakhru made up his mind that if it was the yellow man Fong that the Americans wanted, then he, Fakhru, would put his best efforts into selling him, at a reasonable profit. And at the moment, Fakhru's hunger was so strong, his boredom so intense, he felt that the Americans would have to pay a high price for him. The British were right; Americans really didn't have any manners. He watched Bert Newt rise and he resolved again to make him pay; that's all he would understand, that's all any white man would understand: money. It was the only reason Fakhru had not gone out in a rage earlier in the discussion as he often did with Africans who squandered fortunes and hoarded trifles; like, though the comparison hurt him, his own children, to whom money was nothing and a little green worm was treasure. He had no patience with them either. It made Fakhru sick to see people misuse money. Yes, that was the only reason he stayed; with men who seemed to know so little about Africa, the profit was sure to be great. The published fact that the living prophet, H.H. the Aga Khan, not only had many stables of race horses but also owned vast tracts of Europe and America was of great solace to Fakhru. One had to be realistic in matters of money, and the Americans would soon learn the wisdom of paying and making others pay.

Bert put his arm around Fakhru and led him to the door. He started saying, 'I want you to know I think you're really swell . . .' But Fakhru's face was ashen and Bert felt his Khoja friend go limp.

Over the door was a picture of the late President Kennedy. It was a good photograph: his perfect teeth, the knot in his tie out of place enough for all to know that he was just like everyone else, basically; his lovely brushed hair, the easy smile of a man who knows what he is doing, the face that all can love, young, even handsome, not unlike that of His Highness.

'Jeck,' Fakhru blubbered with emotion.

Fakhru's face remained ashen, his eyes cast up at the late president. His blubbering died to a sniffle, which he trimmed with his sleeve. But the tears continued to flow from his cast-up eyes, down his grey cheeks to his loose shirt. He removed his round beaded cap and held it chest-high, slowly squashing it in his grief-stricken fingers.

'He was a great man,' said Fakhru, still sniffing. 'A great *bwana.*'

'Yep. Sure was,' said Bert Newt sadly, making wet noises with his lips as he stuck and unstuck them in his own grief. Bert did not know what to say. Like so many Americans, he was rendered helpless by death or great emotion. It was not a coincidence that the astronaut who was shot to the brink of the stratosphere in a giant rocket, gasped and said into his radio, as he gazed – the first human being to do so – at the twinkling mystery of the universe, 'Wow', was an American, like Bert. The death of the great prince made Bert helpless and sad, all the more sad since – like all the millions of others who stood mute after the murder was performed – he knew he had to be mute because now there was no one he could call on for help.

'Everyone loved him. It was a real love, for he was kind man, good man, honest man and too young . . .' Fakhru did not know what to do. He felt it would be rude to leave, and yet the man, the

American at his side, as if anxious to leave, had released his grip on Fakhru's shoulder and was shrugging silently and digging his toe into the carpet.

For a brief moment all Fakhru's anger was gone; his strong desire to cheat Americans was gone; no longer did he wish to help the Americans swindle Sam Fong (or whatever it was they planned to do). For a few seconds, before the picture of the late president, Fakhru achieved absolute peace: he loved all men and saw the wisdom in death, giving without asking why, and begging in rags with a wooden bowl and he saw the gift of innocence in all African countries, and the simple people who must never be harmed. Goodness illuminated all his thoughts and such a glow, such radiance, that no man had a colour and all men were equal and good. And goodness was continuous until the end of time because man was and God was, as the Prophet truly said.

Then the moment passed. Outside, traffic moved noisily down the street, there were yells, a sound truck with loudspeakers played a party song, and somewhere in town someone was counting a large square pile of worn but negotiable hundred-shilling notes, wetting his brown finger in a sponge and making the old bills snap . . .

Fakhru replaced his beaded cap, and without glancing again at the portrait said, 'Cheerio, *bwana*,' to Bert Newt. At lunch Fakhru told his own assembled, munching family how the late President Kennedy came from a humble and wise, but extremely wealthy and shrewd family.

12

'You have chitted me!' shrieked Z. F. R. Mehboob. He began running feverishly towards Sam Fong's *duka*.

Africa makes her visitors very nervous, for it is only her visitors who do business, and business entails dangerous postures. Z. F. R. Mehboob's private fantasy of Africa was of a vast, a mountainous dark sow, bristling with old hairs and with a multitude of dugs for her piggies. She slumbers; the sun beats down on the piggery; from afar others come to suck. With a yawn and a groan the dark sow rolls over the sucking piggies. Some survive; those that do get very nervous, and understandably so.

Z. F. R. Mehboob came to Africa a quiet man, gentle in all ways, generous, given to prayer and impulsive acts of goodness. Four public declarations of bankruptcy and a near-revolution (the sow rolls over her farrow), the presence of black people everywhere who never smiled at him, turned Mehboob, in eight years, into a rumour-mongering bundle of nerves and a Persian. He was a Moslem South Indian; but the kinship between Dravidian and Negro was too close for Mehboob to bear and literally overnight he became a Persian.

Eight years in Africa had refined Mehboob's techniques of raving and taught him courage. Now he would quite shamelessly run out of his shop and rave on the sidewalk, something that was not normally done by members of the Asian community. Shop-keepers and their families were seldom seen outside their shops. His wife, for example, only went outside the shop on Sunday after-noon to sit for one hour on the wall in front of the National and Grindlay's Bank; she was always accompanied by ten other women. But raving took no courage in Mehboob's eyes.

Typical of what Mehboob considered a courageous act was his monthly drive up-country to sell wholesale goods to bush *dukas*. Nothing extraordinary in this, one might suppose. But Mehboob had dreadful thoughts as he drove up the narrow mud tracks lined with high, dense elephant grass: naked warriors watched him, savages who, if so inclined, could crush him. These fierce men were at the summit of every hill, behind large boulders which they could roll on to his van, his goods, his head; it was said that these tribesmen slept in the warm mud puddles in the middle of the road, indolent prey for the passing 'Persian' who, when caught at the next village for the murder of the tribesmen, would pay the maximum penalty, a punishment verified by his half brother's friend's cousin, a cotton-ginner in Burundi at the height of the Bahutu uprising against the Watutsi. The punishment consisted of cutting off the offender's feet and ordering him to stand on his stumps (raucous laughter as he falls), then cutting off his legs to the knees and making him stand again, and so forth . . . It was too much for Mehboob to think about; only the thought of it made deep dread. Mehboob considered the seven million Africans around him to be capable of it, but still he made monthly trips up-country in his van, alone except for his servant, who rode in the back; he felt that at any moment he might be dismembered or crushed. Enemies were everywhere (sometimes pygmies stopped him by gathering in droves on the road – they beat on his car and sang until he agreed to buy a few poisoned arrows); even taking into consideration all the craziness that courage involves, and all the paranoia that the Asians in East Africa were heir to, some threats were real: a trip up-country was an act of boldness.

Raving on the street? Yes, although Mehboob did not think it very serious, even that required some courage. And here he was, Z. F. R. Mehboob of Mehboob Paint Supply shouting in a shrill Madrassi voice, 'You have chitted me! You have chitted me!' to the blue African sky, uncluttered by clouds. He dashed, as the day before the yellow lady had noiselessly dashed, the length of Uhuru Avenue and into Sam Fong Friend Frocery.

Sam Fong greeted him with a nod and a grunt.

Z. F. R. Mehboob rushed up to Sam Fong and almost burst into tears; his face contorted and for a few moments he thumped the counter and was speechless. Then he shrieked, 'You have bounced a cheque at me! You are a yellow thief!' This was repeated in Swahili.

'I have done nothing,' said Sam Fong in Swahili, in order to clear himself and also to signal the fact that he could not understand Mehboob's accusation in English.

'Is chitting me nothing? Do you think I am a *mshenzi* fool? I am a poor man, my friend! And you have chitted me, you thief!'

'I pray for you to stop shouting in *Kizungu*,' said Sam Fong, now distressed. He had seen Indians get excited before; he had seen one go mad and act like Mehboob, accusing everyone in sight of horrible crimes. Fong did not take Mehboob seriously; he simply wished that Mehboob's brothers would show up and drag him off as, fifteen years before, that other Indian was dragged into the bush and beaten insensible by his brothers until he became manageable enough to send to Calcutta. Fong made a new proverb, which in its rough state ran something like 'Never listen to the madman, but watch him closely'.

When Soo Fong entered the shop Mehboob showed his teeth and snarled in the censorial way that dogs do. This angered Sam Fong but he realized that Mehboob did not know what he was doing. He folded his hands and asked Mehboob what he wanted.

'So you want to know why I came? Oh! If you would be so kind as to look at this please!' said Mehboob, mixing pleasantries with hysteria.

Mehboob took some scraps of paper from the folds of his clothes. There was Sam Fong's cheque, apparently uncashed. A little note was pinned to it.

'This is your signature?'

Sam Fong looked at the cheque. How inferior his signature looked in English; how lovely it would have looked in Chinese: two bold characters, each like a painted jewel box.

'Yes. That is my name. Sam Fong.'

'Read this.' It was a note pinned to the cheque; the name of the bank was printed at the top. There was a typewritten message centred on the sheet.

'Soo, read this paper,' said Fong.

Soo took the paper. First she read it aloud in English, barely moving her lips, '. . . Leglet there are insufficient funds in the account to pay the above . . .' She translated the sad phrases into Chinese.

'I am a pauper,' said Fong in a whisper.

'I want my two shillings and I want it now! If I don't get it I will ring for a constable or the nearest *askari* and you will end your days in prison.' (Mehboob pronounced his last word 'brison'.)

'I had almost shillings seven hundred only in my bank.'

'You have nothing in your bank now. You have no bank!'

'And there is no money in the store,' said Fong, violating his proverb, listening and believing instead of just watching the madman. 'The young boys collected all my shillings from me to give to the government. I have sold nothing for two days. We are eating locusts again. If what you say is true, then I am a pauper, I have nothing . . .'

Z. F. R. Mehboob wailed again, agonizing, throwing his head back; this wailing after a few moments turned into plain dry baying.

Sam Fong looked up at him. He was sad. Madness in an acquaintance is unpleasant, but one's own poverty is unspeakable; it means indignity and an inauspicious death.

Fong was wondering whether he should throw himself at Mehboob's feet and beg for mercy ('I will ring for a constable') when Fakhru walked in. Fakhru saw Soo Fong in the corner, the dirty-faced children peeping around her legs and holding to her long skirt; he saw Sam Fong, silent, with folded hands; he saw his friend Mehboob, face upraised and baying at the empty top shelves.

'I greet you all. *Salaam*, Mehboob,' said Fakhru. 'What is the *monena*? Are you unaware that quite a large crowd has gathered outside to listen?'

'My cheque for two shillings has bounced, *kabisa*,' said Fong.

'Calm down, Mehboob,' said Fakhru placing his hand on

Mehboob's shoulder. Mehboob stopped baying and faced Fakhru; his eyes were red and his jaw was slack.

'I am robbed, and you tell me to calm down!'

'To be robbed of two shillings is to be blessed,' said Fakhru. He took two shillings from his purse and placed the coins in Mehboob's hand.

Mehboob looked disappointed; his whole face relaxed into regret. He had made up his mind to be offended. He felt doubly cheated. He had been eager to continue baying. 'No Persian would stand for this insult,' he grunted, feeling the money. 'You may tell the yellow one that if he sets foot again in my store he will be asking for a beating.' Mehboob left, snarling and pushing his way through the crowds of Africans that had gathered at the entrance.

'Your cheque bounced?' asked Fakhru.

'Yes. Only two shillings and I do not know why.'

'Have you forgotten the one you gave me?'

'Yes. No.'

'That one did not completely bounce, let us say. But you are in my debt for shillings three hundred and seventy only. This includes Mehboob's two.'

'It is true. I am a pauper.'

One tear ran out of the right eye of Soo Fong and down her cheek.

'What are we going to do?' There was no emotion in Fong's voice; he meant what he said. For the first time in many years – almost since the time, thirty-five years before, he had walked to Foochow with rags on his feet and eaten an occasional rat – he had nothing. What was left on the shelves would not keep them alive. One does not eat aspirin and skin lightener and grow fat. The situation was desperate and because it was desperate Fong could not afford the expense of getting excited, of beating on the counter and weeping until another crowd gathered. He appeared very calm. But the words he was speaking to Soo in Chinese were of darkness, poverty, slavery, humiliation and, without resorting to ambiguity of proverbs, death.

Soo Fong said nothing. There were several more slow tears, but no sound came from her lips.

Fakhru seemed to understand. He waited until Fong stopped speaking in Chinese (Fong had not turned his head; he appeared to be praying to the empty air in short lunatic syllables), and then leaned forward and said, as sympathetically as he could, 'I think you should see the Americans.'

Part Two

Part Two

13

Fong's guess was correct. The Young Pioneer who had dropped into the grocery store to extort money from him *had* been a bad sign, like the obnoxious winged demon in African superstition who shows up in a person's head shortly before a tragedy and flaps foolish signals that only a witch-doctor can fathom. The Young Pioneer never came again; no one came to the shop for a long time. There was trouble.

The Prime Minister, as Margerine had reported, had thrown out more of his cabinet ministers, all Dada. They had been criticizing him, people said. They were fed up, one high official was reported to have said. One of the cabinet ministers had been seen in town, drunk, saying that the country was bankrupt; no one had actually seen or heard him, but many heard that he had been seen.

The full story of the dismissals was told to Fong by Margerine. It ran as follows: The Prime Minister invited all his ministers to the State House to discuss the rumours. ('Let's be English about this,' the Prime Minister was supposed to have said; to the press he said, 'Mind your own business. This trouble it is just a family squabble because I am fed up of this disloyal and stupid cabinet.') When the ministers had arrived and were seated and drinking in the mansion, the army drove up, handcuffed six of them who were pointed out by the Prime Minister – a careful sign from him, perhaps a gentle nod – threw them into the back of a truck and took them to a detention camp.

At the moment of his arrest, one of the ministers (he happened to be the Minister of Finance) suddenly produced two fistfuls of American dollars from beneath his traditional costume (long robes embroidered with lovely designs, and a peaked cap that made him look like a sorcerer). He waved these two crumpled bouquets at his colleagues while frantically repeating that he had lots more for anyone who would help him. He was seized by three soldiers. The remaining cabinet members pretended not to see him until the trucks were out of sight. Then they made a dash for the money that had been knocked out of the Minister of Finance's hand. This they divided equally.

It was a simple operation, the six arrests, and this might have been the end of it had the whole affair been kept as quiet as the Prime Minister requested it should be. But one hour after the last minister was tucked struggling into the back of the army truck, rumours began to fly about town. That was when Margerine told Fong the story in detail, breathlessly, glancing around as he whispered.

In each shop on Uhuru Avenue a similar scene took place: the owner of the shop listened carefully to the worried whisper of an African ('It's their country,' said Fakhru to his wife. 'They should know.'); the African, in return for the information, gratefully received a free cigarette which – since it had to be smoked in the presence of the shopkeeper – extended the story of intrigue and allowed the African to add details of the arrests as well as a bit of background material, tribal wisdom and warnings. Sam Fong and the Indians closed their shops. Those that had iron gratings locked them across the plate glass. Trash barrels, bicycles and laundry were brought inside. The streets were deserted, empty in the sunshine.

The rumours were contradictory. But the existence of rumours indicated that something was seriously wrong; it did not do any harm to close early and take a holiday and stay off the streets. The rumours each started off truthfully saying that the ministers were taken to the State House to discuss a problem of national interest. At this point truth lapsed and fantastic savage descriptions took over; these descriptions may have indicated to a certain extent the sincere wishes of many who were spreading the rumours. The dominant story was that the ministers had been tied up on the floor, their hearts cut out by the Prime Minister and his chef and these organs distributed to the remaining ministers – some of whose teeth *were* in fact filed to sharp points – who ate slabs off the still pulsing things, for strength in battle. One rumour had the Minister of Health washing them down with the blood of one of his former colleagues. Other rumours told of the ministers roasting on spits, tortured with heated spears and disembowelled. And there were many hints of sexual violation. The news on Radio East Africa said nothing of the arrests, but listed a number of people going on courses to England; the major news item was of a man in New Jersey who had a plastic stomach grafted to his innards, the point of the story being that in his old, ulcerous stomach-sack two buttons, some paper clips and the US equivalent of fifteen shillings was found.

When the rumours reached the relatives of the luckless ministers, some of the relatives had their lawyers prepare habeas corpus briefs to be submitted to the courts, and others paid nocturnal visits to witch-doctors for medicine strong enough to destroy the Prime Minister. Other relatives of the arrested ministers gathered in groups to begin sabotaging the government. This last alternative was by far the most popular. It became even more popular and more violent when the government passed a law in Parliament (this was two days after the arrests) making it illegal to carry weapons and a criminal offence to spread rumours. Old ladies with bundles of firewood in their arms were arrested for possessing dangerous weapons; several men with walking sticks were charged with treason, attempting to overthrow the government by force. As soon as rumour-mongering became a criminal act rumours began in earnest, and everyone was now firmly convinced that the ministers had been killed and devoured, with relish, *in camera*.

The terrorist gangs blocked roads and tore up hunks of pavement, pulled down power lines and beat up tourists. They roughed up twelve Germans so thoroughly that the Germans, who were by no means of slight build, were rushed shrieking to the hospital. The German Ambassador's picture was in the paper the next day gloomily pointing to twenty-six broken cameras. The government said that this incident proved that the arrested ministers deserved to be in jail; their constituents and henchmen had no regard for human life or anything decent. In the meantime, an English tea planter was hacked to death, an up-country surveyor's wife was sexually outraged by three men, and a rural sociologist was set upon and his glasses smashed. ('Your goggles are finished, ha-ha,' the attackers said, according to the sociologist.) The terrorist gangs worked busily, efficiently; it was almost as if it had been planned months in advance. They beat up a few Africans whom they called 'stoogies', burned a few grass huts and then with methodical passion began breaking the plate glass of Indian shops and tormenting the Asians. One Indian girl was raped with such insistence that she had to be sent to Bombay on the morning plane. In protest her father closed his shop and said he would never open it again. Many Asian boys were stripped naked and made to run home. If silence can be taken to mean a certain deep understanding, the Asians seemed to understand perfectly why their community was being attacked. For the time being the ministers were forgotten.

The rumours now said that it was all part of an Asian conspiracy to take over the country and outbreed all the Africans. The little Indian girl that had been raped and sent to Bombay was accused of enticing Africans to sleep with her in order to get information from them; caught in the act she had screamed to make it look as if it was defilement instead of sabotage. She lost all African sympathy, and the next day the Asians suffered a renewed attack from larger numbers: more shops were broken into and looted; two were burned to the ground; the flower beds of Uhuru Avenue were trampled. Fakhru and his family moved into a cement room at the back of the house. Sam Fong nailed his children into a packing crate and he and his wife rolled themselves into reed mats, in which they stayed for most of the day, like pastries. Detail was added to the conspiracy rumours: the Asians, it was said, were breaking into their own shops, burning and looting them so that they would win the sympathy of the government, which would in turn punish the Africans; at the same time the Asians would be collecting insurance on the damages.

The government did nothing. From time to time statements were issued saying that no rumours should be believed, and that anyone who believed them would be dealt with severely. The Minister of Information said on a special radio broadcast that he had heard many rumours to the effect that people were believing rumours and spreading lies that he personally was satisfied were untrue. He further implored the Asian community to calm down and not to cause any further disturbances. Nobody had anything to worry about. He explained that really nothing had happened, no one had been arrested − certainly not the cabinet ministers; the whole mis-understanding was the fault of a few rumour-mongers and 'some people who don't mind stealing and sucking blood from the Africans, but aren't men enough to take out citizenship because they don't have any guts at all . . .' The broadcast finished with the Minister of Information saying over and over again and even into the fade-out, 'Things are back to normal, I tell you. Things are just back to normal . . .'

This was followed by more attacks on the Asians. Fakhru looked down from the window of his cement room and pleaded with the gangs of boys to stop breaking his windows 'Why are you doing this to me?' he moaned. 'Because you're not having guts,' was the answer. Sam Fong suffered no damage, but he re-mained in the back room rolled in a reed mat with his eyes shut just the same.

Then, mysteriously, the attacks stopped. Mehta explained this by saying that since all the stores were empty and there was nothing more to loot, the Africans were merely giving the Asians a little time to stock up with more merchandise from Nairobi. When more goods arrived there would be more stealing, he said. But this was not the reason. To Mehta one terrorist looked very much like another; in fact, each arrested minister had his own terrorist group, and the terrorist groups had now started to ignore the Asians in order to effectively terrorize one another. They continued in this for a week, until one group had subdued all the others; with the help of the groups that had been subdued, the dominant group directed all its rage against the government. The terrorists broke windows of trains and cooperative societies, raided police stations, tipped over a bus, broke into several schools and destroyed equipment, burned down the house of one minor politician and raped another's wife.

The army was called in. The army was composed almost entirely of one particular tribe, loose-limbed, tall, muscular men with purplish skin, graceful necks and small, closely set eyes. They had a loping, pigeon-toed gait and handled their rifles like walking sticks, now clomping them on the pavement, now swinging them, now pointing them – all done with simple-minded ease and great strength. Their lips were genially everted, their heads perfectly formed – rounded in every plane – and their ears were small, tightly rolled and very delicate. Although they were widely reputed to be cowards, most people had seen at least one soldier bullying or beating someone, and no one openly defied the soldiers.

In a very unsystematic way the soldiers began appearing in bars and on the streets; they leaned against the posts of shop verandas and sat sullenly in doorways. More than one white housewife gliding through the supermarket searching for a broom handle came upon these large armed men idling near the Coke machine at the back, their rifles with bayonets fixed resting against the kitchen utensils. On a dozen kerbstones the soldiers sat, rifles across their thighs, their legs sticking out in two directions, their heads lolling over heavily in sleep. The presence of the soldiers caused considerable alarm – it was more than their size, their purplish faces, their uniforms; it was, in fact, their sub-machine guns. In a country with little experience of armies it is fear rather than anarchy that is inspired in people who see soldiers among them. To be anti-military is a complicated reaction for a naked man facing an armed man. For the naked man to be scared out of his wits is simpler and, from the government's point of view, more convenient. The terrorist groups faded out of sight. The soldiers were offered no resistance; the Asians opened their shops and joshed them with generosity.

COTTON PRODUCTION UP 1000 BALES THIS YEAR! or TRIBAL CLASH IN TOGO or US TO BUILD SCHOOL OF DOM-

FONG AND THE INDIANS

ESTIC SCIENCE were the headlines in the newspaper. No deaths –
nor even the presence of the soldiers – were mentioned. A State of
Emergency had been declared the day the soldiers appeared; the
announcement was made once and never repeated. The Asians sat
in their shops behind shuttered windows and watched the empty
sunlit avenue. The shelves were bare. Africans began drifting into
the streets. There was now a fatigued panic, a disordered anar-
chism, which showed itself in totally aimless drunkenness, casual
abuse and fistfights that ended abruptly and without a victor as the
fighters suddenly dropped their arms and walked away. It was an
orgy of not caring that even the Minister of Information was
unable to soothe, directed against no one, purposeless, hardly
serious and almost not harmful.

It was at this time, a month after the arrest of the six ministers,
in this period of shambling chaos, that the Prime Minister gave
one of his sermons. He came in convoy to the main stadium; in
front were the motorcyclists waving people off the streets and stopping traffic; behind the Rolls Royce were truckloads of market
mammies singing party songs and chanting his name over and over
in singsong. The melodies of the political songs were those of
hymns; the words had been altered. One, to the tune of 'Moses
Hath Deliver'd Us The Promised Land', had been adapted by sub-
stituting the name of the Prime Minister for Moses and Af-ri-ca
for Pro-mised Land. The Prime Minister carried a fly whisk and a
cane and wore a three-piece suit. His bodyguards and his mistress
accompanied him to the platform where he sat glowering through
dark glasses at the audience squatting in the dust. As he rose he
lifted his arms and his jacket was removed; the cane and fly whisk
which he casually released never hit the platform floor: they were
caught by cabinet ministers to his left and right, and returned. The
Prime Minister belched into a lace handkerchief and began speaking over the slow chanting of his name. He spoke with many pauses
so that the translator at his right could convey the message in the
vernacular. The rings on the Prime Minister's fingers glittered as
he spoke.

'Brothers!' he shouted, 'God has seen fit to make me your Prime

Minister and I thank His Great Wisdom and Mercy for giving a humble man this chance of a lifetime! I am a simple African. You are simple Africans. Your parents and their parents before them were simple Africans. Your children are simple Africans. We are all Africans. Africans are black, unlike Englishmen who are white. We think as Africans. We play and work as Africans. I speak to you as an African when I say unto you, God has seen fit . . .'

Sam Fong sat with his whole family, seven yellow, sallow people, small and neat, almost lost in the grandstand in the sloping pudding of black nationalists and rags. He had been awakened at five that morning by a Young Pioneer who ordered him to go to the stadium at once; and there Sam Fong sat for four hours, waiting for the Prime Minister to show up. Neither Sam nor Soo nor the children stirred; they tucked their hands up their sleeves and hunched over. Their faces were turned without expression upon the Prime Minister, who continued to shout 'Brother this' and 'Brother that' and to repeat his black incantation whenever he seemed at a loss for words. The translator had a high voice, it was almost a screech; he shook his fists and bounced on his toes and at the end of long sentences he asked for applause: 'Now *clap!*' The audience clapped.

The speech contained very few different words, but the words were said over and over in many patterns as if they were not part of a speech at all, but rather magical syllables which became weighted with more magic in their repetition. The Prime Minister said 'Poverty, ignorance and disease are our greatest enemies' five times; then he said, 'I say unto ye the ministers I arrested are nothing but stupid enemies and skunks.' For 'skunks' there was no word in the vernacular; he changed this to snakes, for which there was a word. After this he repeated 'poverty, ignorance and disease' several more times, amid cheers, and followed it with an appeal to the Young Pioneers to find every disloyal citizen and bring him to justice for punishment. Yells from the Young Pioneers assembled around the platform encouraged the Prime Minister. He said that from that day onward the Young Pioneers would be his personal spies ('I baptize you *The Black Guards!*' he shrieked) and that everyone – including the Asians, the vandals and the troublemakers – would have to step lightly.

He said that perhaps he would be accused of being too harsh. He didn't care. 'I'm not going to play second or even third fiddle to the Chinese or the Yankees . . .' No one understood Africa, he said, even Winston Churchill didn't understand Africa. '. . . And sometimes even I, an African, do not understand Africa! So are you going to turn around and tell me that some stupid fool who isn't even black is going to tell *me* about Africa? I was in Chicago, Las Vegas, Wales, Rome, Waco, Texas, and even in Frisco, and I didn't tell anyone how to run their affairs. I kept my big black mouth shut . . .' There was an uneasiness in the audience, the applause had become noticeably less and there was a slight murmuring; the Prime Minister quickly began speaking in a very high voice, dropping definite and indefinite articles, with a bush accent: 'I am not communist man, not even democrat or fascist man. What do these *kizungu* words mean to me? As you jolly well know, we all being simple Africans from dirty villages. Communist and democracy these are big words from big book. What are book anyway I ask you. These things they call book are just crushing out our brains to hell . . .' There were loud cheers. The crowd was won over. It was as if he had crooned them a song.

'No, I say unto ye, I am African and I am Prime Minister and God help the false friends who try to overthrow me – I will throw them straight away to the crocodiles!' The Prime Minister sputtered and shook his fly whisk at the audience: 'Now you know there has been a little family squabble down at State House. Pay no attention to it, don't worry about it, don't think about it. Go back to your banana groves and be quiet; plant more seeds this year, use fertilizer. I warn you that if you get mixed up in this unhealthy business, what I call family squabble, you will not live to squeeze your handfuls of porridge. This is especially a warning to our friends the Asians . . .'

As the Prime Minister said these words a thousand brown men in the stadium stiffened, closed their mouths and allowed their heavy lids to droop. During the next part of the speech these men appeared to darken a bit, go browner. Even Sam Fong, who was sitting very near to the Asian section, seemed to become unmistakably swarthy as he listened.

'I will say this only once and I hope your ears are wide open. We will not tolerate people who smile and then go ahead and take money out of our pockets. This is what I call cat and mouse friendship because you're running with the hare and hunting with the hounds and I hope that is abundantly clear especially, I repeat, especially to our very good friends the Asians, who had better walk on tiptoes from now on . . .'

The Prime Minister accepted the applause. The Young Pioneers – 'The Black Guards' – were not sure whether they should stand to attention to show how well disciplined they were or whether they should cheer and sing to show how much they loved the Prime Minister. About ten stood still; the rest whooped and hollered the Prime Minister's name. The Prime Minister flapped his fly whisk at them and left the stage. The entire audience stayed at rapt attention while the last part of the speech was translated into the vernacular. It was a difficult translation. There were no words for pockets, cats, hounds and tiptoes, just as a bit earlier there had been no word for second fiddle. When the translator finished (with considerably less hyperbole in his words) – the Prime Minister had long since driven away – it was clear to all the Asians that the crunch was coming and that they were being held responsible for the family squabble. They filed out of the stadium in groups of ten, for safety. Sam Fong joined the Asian groups not so much because of the safety they offered, but more because (this thought made him very tired) he was a debtor and he felt obliged to follow them, at a decent distance.

14

Sam Fong kept his shop closed. The job of boarding up the windows gave him enormous pleasure: a whole platoon of the army could not have broken through those neatly sawed and joined boards. He fed his family on food from the cans. He did not really want what was in the cans, but they had rusted, the labels had mildewed, and they were unsaleable: the cans of Spam from Minnesota, the processed cheese from Melbourne and the shiny unlabelled cans which, without emotion, Fong discovered to be tomato juice tasting strongly of steel. Sometimes at night, as he huddled with his family in the back of the boarded-up store, he heard the *pop-pop* of gunfire. It was a small noise, like a fire-cracker, and not the cannon noise he had imagined it would be. He also heard voices, again just mumbling voices, small, not screams; he heard people running down the street, their bare feet slapping on the pavement, and then the sound of boots and heavy puffing, a voice, *pop*, a sigh – none of it loud or even scary, but more like the sound of a radio playing a thriller two large rooms away.

The noises were not loud; their ghostly smallness did not frighten. Yet it was clear to Sam Fong that he should not go outside or answer the door after dark. These long nights in the ripe dank of the store, in almost dead silence, caused in Fong a religious fervour that was awakened slowly, as the nights passed, in oddly shaped memories. He was like a man piecing together a long silent dream. He recognized it as fervour immediately, but it did not become religious until the memory was nearly complete. He stopped telling his children stories of the emperor and the rice paddies and the streets of Foochow that were crammed with rick-shaws. There were no more stories like the one he had told of the tiger he had once seen in a thick cage, near his village, guarded by a black Indian who, for rice and meat, would bang on the bars of the cage with a stick and make the tiger open his mouth wide. There was once astonishment, even savagery in his stories; now there was a gentle solemnity. Fong told about little Jesus helping his father in the carpentry shop; the murder of the innocent children (not bloody; it was their souls which mattered and these ended up in heaven) by the bad King Herod who wanted Jesus but never found him; the guardian angels whose wings ('bigger than that counter there') protected all those who loved God. Fong told his children the few Latin phrases he could remember and the way to say the rosary. They said the rosary, fingering the beads, ten Hail Marys, one Our Father, ten Hail Marys and so forth into the long night until, with the muffled sounds of the people running and the *pop-pop* of those in pursuit outside the strongly boarded shop, they all dropped off to sleep, their rosary beads still clutched in their hands.

There was another story that Fong had lately become skilful in telling, also religious in its way, the story of a search. Fong squatted on the floor, his back straight, his small hands raised, making quick gestures as he spoke. It was about a man who left his family and wandered through the world, across the ocean and desert and in the dense banana groves; he was punished by fearful winds and storms, by black people, brown people and white people, by earth rumblings and wild beasts. God sent these things to him because the man did not understand them; God wanted to make sure the man was sincere and good – good enough so that he could finally love what he did not understand. Sometimes the man almost gave up, but when he remembered that it was God Himself sending troubles to a very little man he realized that there was order in the earth. At the end the man was poor; he was very upset and almost broken, but he did not lose his faith. He triumphed because he was in a strange land and he knew how to be patient and how to pray.

With this new fervour Sam Fong passed his nights peacefully with his family and was so engrossed in his piety and gentleness that he did not notice how short his supplies were getting. When he finally realized this there was almost nothing in the store: there were some onions, there were two unlabelled tins, there was a handful of rice and perhaps a pound – if one included their inedible wings and legs – of grasshoppers. The cans of milk were there in crates, but for Fong they did not represent food; he did not drink milk and he discouraged the rest of his family from doing so. The cans, furthermore, did not represent the promise of money, for the shop was closed and there was no telling when it could open. Standing in tall piles, gathering dust and harbouring roaches, the crates very rapidly became a symbol of helplessness, for his piety calmed him but it did not fatten him, and now he was nagged by hunger. The children cried easily and it became hard to tell them even a simple tale. There was no money, not even a halfpenny. Soldiers shuffled on the street. Fong took a mystified look around the dark, boarded-up shop; what seemed most strange to him was that so much time, so many years could have passed and now, old, with children scuttling around his ankles, in his closed grocery store he had a dumb lonely vision of all those years in Africa.

The vision was foreign, plainly odd rather than shocking: he lacked what the Chinese call 'the necessary grains' – he had nothing; he was among neither friends nor strangers, but enemies; and worse than not owning anything, he was himself owned. This last thought almost made the meditation painful, but when Fong recalled the story of the man who was sent great suffering, he reached the conclusion that only very few are sent great suffering, and pain is a blessing when it is sent by God. Fong knew it was a gamble which in a moment of weakness he could lose completely; everything could be gained as well if he were strong. Another look at the empty shop, now buzzing with one underfed fly, and it came to him again: *I have nothing, I am owned, I am a slave in a strange country*. Fong remained in the grocery store and prayed. His prayers were pure: they were praises; they contained no threats, no requests, no bargains; they asked nothing and offered everything.

*

Fakhru was all smiles and had his son by the throat. It came to him that he was thoroughly enjoying throttling the little boy, that it was doing him, Fakhru, a lot of good. He let the boy drop to the floor. He rushed away in a rage of disappointment. Earlier in the day he had been on the verge of stabbing his houseboy (the houseboy was against the wall, Fakhru's knife was very close to his ribs, having already pierced the front of the houseboy's uniform), but reason prevailed: he kicked the houseboy in the shins and was done with it. He knew he would be hanged (he, a civic-minded person with a sense of values and fair play) if he stabbed the houseboy (a dung beetle, a man to whom a kick was sound advice, a black man *and* a Christian). The houseboy had dropped a cup. Fakhru's son had said that someday Africans and Asians would marry each other and when they did there would be no colour difference: Africans would lighten a bit, Asians would get darker. Fakhru had not hesitated a moment. The thought of his empty unprofitable shops, the Prime Minister's speech about 'playing cat and mouse' and picking people's pockets had removed the domestic pretence of Fakhru's patience, that slight pause of natural politeness before insult was uttered. He wrapped his fingers around his son's small neck and a thought came to him which he said aloud: 'You are an Asian because I am an Asian, and you are my issue. No one cares about us because we are Khojas and know the value of a shilling. If I kill you no one will care, no one will hang me, for you are an Asian. I am doing this country a service by ending your brown life. The Queen might give me an MBE . . .' He smiled; he was not excited, he spoke calmly, realizing that he could rid the world of one renegade and not be blamed for it, and as he spoke, smiled and realized this he tightened his grip and squeezed harder. Shortly after, he dropped his little boy and stopped smiling. The boy's colour was now green, but he was alive and rubbing his neck. It came to Fakhru that he had tried to kill two people that morning and it was still not time for lunch.

He clasped the photograph of H.H. the Aga Khan and held it before himself so that he could see the face of H.H. framed by his own puffy, sweaty jowls mirrored in the glass. He loved the tragedy of it: the brooding red-eyed Fakhru tormentedly showing over the serene Aga Khan, bestower of good will, with soft doves in his breast. I must calm myself, he thought; I can't go around attacking the houseboy, my own family. He looked at the young Aga Khan and had two quick thoughts: one was *He has very white teeth, which means he does not take betel*, and the other was *Does he know what a trial these blacks are?* He thought of the Prime Minister's speech, of the empty shops – *his* empty shops – and winced. The blacks were getting restless; he could be asked to leave the country tomorrow. In a couple of hours he could be sitting in the dust, penniless in Pakistan or wherever the blacks shipped him. He had thought of this before – scores of times. He knew he could be deported with no warning at all; he also was well aware that, forty-one years before, he was born in a country which now he had no memory of. Fakhru complained incessantly of Africa, like Mehboob, but he knew it would be deadly to leave. He was prepared to leave, however, and assumed – as most of the Indians did – that he would be on the plane for Karachi or Delhi the next day.

It is always prudent to buy off one or two of them, Fakhru thought, and then he quickly reconsidered. He would give them nothing: Bribes are expensive, I am a poor man, I may even be a madman, but I am not mad enough to give away my money to these monkeys! The doleful purspiring face continued to stare out from behind His Highness. Fakhru thought again of his own property, now idle, not earning a penny; he thought of the many rents which, because of road-blocks and soldiers, could not be collected; other stores burnt, looted of all merchandise. The thought of rents and shops and things he owned brought him to Sam Fong. From there it was, mentally, a very rapid transit to the Americans.

Mel Francey had taken to calling them 'Injuns'. 'What the Injuns up to today?' he would inquire of a shopkeeper. Or, 'You Injuns better keep your heads down for a bit,' he would say in discreet warning. After the Prime Minister's speech, all of which was recorded on the spot by Mel and Bert's secret abdominal tape recorders, Mel had said, 'Them pore Injuns gonna get their raggedy asses kicked straight out of this place!' Mel had not made up his mind about the Asians. He knew they were dirty and threw things on the lawn and did not eat with their left hand for a very good reason; he was quite sure they swindled Africans, but – and this was the real problem – he did not know whether he had made up his mind about the Africans. He was not crazy about the Africans; he found it hard to say two words to them without them asking for a free trip to the States, and recently he had noticed that the Asians laughed good-humouredly when he squeezed their hands, winked and said, 'What's new with mah ole pals the Injuns?'

Mel went to the window. The orange dust was rising in a cloud as a dozen fully armed warriors with bells and feathers and leopard-skin loincloths jogged towards the Nile Villa Hotel where fifty Rotarians from Cedar Rapids – on their way around the world – were expected to be lunching; old men in short pants languidly pedalled their bicycles; urchins played in the bubbly filth of open drains. Mel felt odd; he was in a foreign country, away from home.

Being away, that was a new one. He used to think of Africa as home. The previous year, his first, he had stood in the very same (air-conditioned) spot and looked down; he had just arrived from Washington where, at the airport drugstore, he had been racially abused by a drunk in overalls: the man had called him (he winced inwardly) a 'no account coon'. But Mel's own inner resources, coupled with the knowledge that he was going to Africa and, more than that, was an Afro-American, helped him to be tolerant and walk away from the man and, with dignity, board the plane for East Africa. He had arrived in Africa – it had long been a dream of his: Mel Francey, Afro-American, good-will ambassador, in his own sweet land. Louis Armstrong had done Ghana; James Meredith, Nigeria; Cassius Clay, Egypt; Martin Luther King, Liberia; and Mel Francey, East Africa. He had, that year before, looked down at the people shuffling slowly on the baked and littered African street, one of the first main streets he had ever seen with rocks and boulders strewn on it, and said to himself, *these are my people.*

That ended. A new feeling (it used to be cruel but recently had stopped being cruel and become dull) was of remoteness and being among strangers. He did his job, an easy one; it merely required his vigilance and a surrender of will, and when he did think private thoughts he thought of Alabama and being away. Even in his worst persecuted moments, when he felt what he was doing was obviously wrong, a betrayal, and that he should get himself back to Mobile and quietly sit at the front of a bus with his eye peeled for those who might call him an 'uppity no account coon', even in those awful moments he did not look at the tangle of sleepy bodies ambling down the street and think, these are my people. A year before he had, but that year had changed him, eliminated the sentiment and made him a perfect stranger.

He seemed to be dozing off, until he saw two figures dodging the tiny cars in the street (everyone had a small car; the cars were like little toys). One figure was clothed in white and wearing a beaded cap and wide flapping trousers; the other was small, wore a white short-sleeved shirt and a huge cork helmet. Mel got his binoculars out of his desk and peered at the two men. It was them; they had come.

Relief was one of the sensations Mel felt when he saw Fakhru. This was unexpected – the feeling of relief, not Fakhru. (Fakhru was long overdue; the State of Emergency had interrupted what Mel thought would be a fast contact.) It was as if, in the middle of all the East African heat, he felt cool ginger ale materialize in his mouth. The State of Emergency, rumours of a coup, a countercoup and soldiers deserting by the hundreds, atrocity stories ('You won't believe this, but they took this little girl . . .') and, especially retailed by the American community, the stories which began, 'When I was in Uttar Pradesh . . .' and ending 'Boy, it was touch and go for six solid months', had punished his patience and fatigued him. What upset Mel especially and often made him angry was that his colleagues were fond of telling him about what they called 'your African'. 'Your African,' they would say, 'according to your best authorities, has this tiny little gland that squirts smelly juice over his skin to scare your moskeeters away. And man, your

African has a shit pot full of aggression and no more sense of decency than a hound dog . . .' Mel could not help but feel that it was not the granddads in short pants, the warriors and pygmies getting their pictures taken by Rotarians or the scores of gland-secreting terrorists, who seemed to drop, silently in droves, out of the trees at sunset when everyone locked themselves in their houses; no, not 'your African' – they weren't talking about him. They were talking about Mel, and he didn't like it one bit. Not only was it the stupid and thick-headed racism in the statements that he knew so well and despised; more than that, each state-ment indicated plainly that Mel (and family) were no different from those people down there on the street, pissing against the side of the National and Grindlay's in full view of everyone; Africans, whom he had grown to dislike so much. He was just like them, the colour kinship, that's what everyone thought, and he was getting damned tired of it in a quiet way which he expressed only in sighs.

Fakhru and the Chinaman paused to let a car pass. Mel put down the binoculars, dashed to his desk and buzzed Newt. He returned to the window and saw the two men enter the building. Mel felt relief. He was worthwhile and doing his job; he was of some account; he had scored.

'Now how's mah ole frins the Injuns?' said Mel when Fakhru and Sam Fong were seated, surrounded by free cigarettes, Pepsi-Cola ('Your Moslems are by and large teetotallers,' the chargé d'affaires had said; he had spent a little time in Cairo), copies of *Why Vietnam?* and, safely out of their wrappers and tubes, some Havana cigars.

Fong was tense. He sat uncomfortably in the huge chair, his cork helmet in his lap, his feet dangling, not touching the floor. He was hunched over, unblinking, attentive and uncomprehending, as he had been at the Prime Minister's rally, as he had been indeed ever since he lost his job at the carpentry shop in the Ministry of Works. He glanced at Mel and Bert from time to time, but kept his eyes mostly on Fakhru, who giggled, clucked and tilted his head in affirmation and respect. At intervals Fakhru asked permission to translate into Swahili ('I will put our yellow Chinese friend into the picture, please'): 'You see, these Americans know their business', 'It is a nice place – free Pepsi-Cola and everything', or 'They are going to start talking business any minute now . . .'

'Let me put it this way,' said Bert, coming to the point after twenty minutes of how hot the weather was, how it was muggy, just like Baltimore in the summer. 'Does he know what the score is?'

'Most assuredly,' said Fakhru, 'but as I have perhaps mentioned before, he wants to know exactly what it is you want him to do.'

'Reason we ask,' said Mel, 'is that we want him to know that we're behind him all the way . . .'

Fong looked at Fakhru and gulped audibly to call attention to himself. Fakhru turned and said, 'Negotiations proceeding well. We will proceed slow-slow. Quick-quick makes bad luck.' To Mel he said, 'My friend understands you but does not wish to comment. These are hard times. We are beset, if I may say so, and are suffering dearly – blamed, I would say – for the present unrest. Many of our shops have been broken out of and our community has been attacked by His Excellency, the Honorable Prime Minister. These harsh words and also sticks and stones. Sticks and stones may break our bones, but names will never hurt us, as the noted proverb has it. It is the stones which worry us greatly indeed thank you please.'

'Sheer thing,' said Bert. 'But your average newly independent country goes through your usual . . .'

'Many of our number have disappeared, many injured. An abundance of shops burned. My windows broken. Sheth's daughter molested and sent to Bombay.'

'. . . phases of growing pains . . .'

Mel sighed.

'Yes. Well, life is not without peril. We hope for the best. But, if you will allow me to say so, my yellow friend has undergone deep tribulation and humiliation. His modest grocery shop has been plunged into ruin by the present state of affairs, in which the blacks are killing each other, not to mention members of our own community. My friend Fong's business is finished, *kwisha*.'

'Washed up, eh?' said Mel, but not kindly.

'Yes, please. One might put it that way.'

'You tell him he doesn't have a thing to worry about,' said Bert. 'Understand?'

'They are being difficult,' said Fakhru to Fong. Fong looked at the Americans.

Bert grinned at Fong and nodded his head and, exaggerating the words with his mouth, hissed, 'Yesssss, yessss, yessss.' He also rolled his eyes as he hissed the words.

'What are they saying?' asked Sam Fong. He spoke his Swahili quickly; the Chinese intonation added a dull metallic note to it and so his sentence came out *cluck-cleek*.

'Patience,' said Fakhru. 'Leave everything to me.'

Bert Newt coughed. 'I mean, we're always glad to help friends in need. That's what makes the world go round. Last year foreign aid amounted to billions of dollars – *billions!*'

'Good heavens!' Fakhru exclaimed. 'The yellow man Fong is in very great need. Poverty is a dreadful thing; it makes one lose one's dignified, well-being and estimation. Observe this poor damaged man. He is thin as a snake and quiet as a mouse. He suffers, you see. And yet, as I have told you, he is not an easy man to deal with. Perhaps this is why he has no estimation and is poor – because he is filled with stubborn.' Fakhru looked at Fong with pathos; his own English was going to pieces; a *billion*, he thought.

Mel looked at Fong and saw only the enemy. Sam Fong threw grenades, sang stupid songs, made pig iron in his back yard, marched idiotically and held up a little red book called *The Sayings of Chairman Mao*, wore a shapeless wrinkled uniform with red stars on it and a cloth cap like Barney Oldfield's. Sam Fong raped nuns on tables, burned pagodas and produced children like they were going out of style. He infiltrated and sabotaged African countries. Mel was getting edgy. Sam Fong, the Chinaman, had spoken only once, in Swahili; he was not responding to good will; he sat breathing slowly through his nose. He made Mel so nervous that Mel, a non-smoker, snatched up one of the Havanas, bit the end off and began chewing it unlit.

'Tell him we don't want anything from him,' said Bert, wiping his mouth with his handkerchief. 'All we want's a chance to do him a good turn.'

'They appear to be giving in,' said Fakhru to Fong. 'Now we will eventually strike a bargain. They have a very wide selection of merchandise,' he added brightly.

'I am your slave,' said Fong. 'I have nothing to say except my freedom from your debt is very important.'

'You want to starve?' asked Fakhru.

'A happy man cannot starve. I was happy today until I remembered that you owned me.'

'This transaction will make us both free,' said Fakhru. 'You free and me free.'

Sam Fong blew a sigh.

'What did he say?' asked Bert eagerly.

Mel wheezed, crossed his legs, uncrossed his legs, bit his cigar, spat out some strings of tobacco and wheezed again.

'It is his habit to be difficult,' said Fakhru. 'He said that customarily one does not get something for nothing. Of course, I don't agree, but he says . . .'

Bert leaned over and said, 'Tell him . . .'

'*Tell him to cut the crap!*' shouted Mel. 'We get his ass down here and tell him we want to be *frins*! We tell him fifty times we don't want him to do anything, just take our good will is all – and this is the thanks we get! Well, you tell him to *loosen up*, hear? Cause if he don't loosen up he can take all our good will and shove it!'

'Mel,' pleaded Bert.

'I'm sick of this blah-blah-blah jive. Why don't he jess take our good will and forget it? Huh? Is it cause we too damned nice or what?' Mel slowed down. He looked at Fakhru. 'Fakhru, I like you boy. You're a square shooter, and you and me, we got something in common: you nowhere and I'm nowhere. But you tell this guy if he don't loosen up then I'm gonna jess write that bitch off as a loser . . .'

'What Mel means – and you can correct me if I'm wrong, Mel . . .'

'You wrong, boy,' said Mel quickly. 'You dead wrong! Now you let *me* handle this.' He turned full upon Sam Fong.

Fong had listened to the outburst without moving; now he inched slowly backwards under Mel's gaze, like a yellow cat who sniffs danger coiling up on a chair.

'You tell him *first* to cut the crap,' Mel said, now calmly, with reason in his voice. 'Then you tell him we're not gonna pussyfoot around the place – no sir, not when we're fully prepared to finance his business and get him back on his feet and out of the red.'

Out of the red, thought Bert. Good title for our report.

'You mean money,' One of Fakhru's eyes seemed to come unhinged. It lolled sideways.

'I mean *money*,' said Mel. 'What's the use of playing games?' he explained to Bert, who was as stiff in his chair as Sam Fong.

The next exchange was in Swahili:

'I think we are making progress.'

'What is all the shouting about?'

'They are simply listing the products they are prepared to sell us. And at a very good price. Too good.'

'What's the word?' asked Mel.

'He is still reluctant. He wants to know what he is wanted to do.'

'Tell him . . .' Bert began.

'Tell him he's jess yaller!' shouted Mel. And then Mel's expression changed: it glowed and widened; he laughed, too loudly, repeated what he had said and laughed again, and now his laughter closely resembled hooting.

Fakhru looked at Mel and Bert. Mel was still grinning and emitting hoots at greater and greater intervals; Bert was immobile and seemed to be in a state of shock. Mel's eyes were red; Bert's were glassy, pearly. Mel was loose, Bert starched. For the first time since he had entered the office Fakhru felt the moment was right for a move. The two men had eased themselves, one by shouting, one by silence, into a position where they were incapable of bargaining sensibly. Sam Fong did not have the slightest notion of what was happening. Fakhru made his move.

'The yellow man's business is very modest' – pause – 'but it has big possibilities.'

'Now thass what we like to hear!'

'He is a clever man as well' – pause – 'but then so are we.' Fakhru winked.

'Damn right,' Mel winked back.

'Mmmmmm,' murmured Bert.

'They have a shipment coming in very soon,' said Fakhru in Swahili.

'Who cares?' said Sam Fong.

'He is seeing it our way,' said Fakhru in English.

'Now you're talking,' said Mel.

'He is used to dealing with his own countrymen,' said Fakhru. 'He is unaccustomed to American generosity.'

'We'll show him what America's prepared to do,' said Mel.

'They have a lot of bleck market merchandise. *American* bleck market. Smile,' said Fakhru in Swahili.

'I am your slave,' said Sam Fong. He smiled.

'Now we're getting somewhere,' said Mel.

'He wants a cheque,' said Fakhru simply, in a small voice.

'Tell him to name his price!' shouted Mel with exuberance.

'*Mel*,' said Bert. There was agony in his voice, but still he did not move a muscle; he said nothing more.

Mel put his face next to Bert's. 'Look, Newt, you want this creep or don't you? Say so now or shut your fat honky trap.' This came out in a hoarse voice that was intended to be a whisper.

'They are being difficult,' said Fakhru in Swahili. 'Nod your head up and down two times.'

'Money enslaves,' said Sam Fong in Chinese. He nodded his head up and down two times.

'Grin.'

Sam Fong grinned and showed his bad, grasshopper-nourished teeth.

'Only 50,000 shillings,' said Fakhru.

'How much is that in *real* money?' asked Mel.

15

One day later, when everything seemed quiet, and the sun was shining on the thick blossoms that littered the island of palms on Uhuru Avenue, and only the soldiers gawking into store windows or ambling along in twos and threes indicated that something might be wrong, J. H. Patel, V. R. Gupta, Z. F. R. Mehboob and a young man known as 'Dino' Raheem were served with deportation orders and given twenty-four hours to leave the country.

The official statement to the press said that the four 'acted in a manner that was disloyal and disaffected towards the government'.

Fakhru learned of their impending deportations while he was standing in line at the bank, where he heard most of his news (it was the one place where he did not give someone a penny to stand in line for him). He knew the four very well; he had done business with Patel and Mehboob; Gupta was well known; and he had often seen Raheem combing his hair before shop-windows.

With the American cheque duly – even gladly – endorsed with Fong's signature, Fong thinking the whole time that it was not a cheque (it bore no tax stamp and was larger than the East African ones) but an invoice for American goods, Fakhru was almost as conspicuous in the bank as the deportees getting their last traveller's cheques. Fakhru had three Nubian bodyguards who wore flat First World War helmets, bamboo shields and wrist knives. They each carried a long spear, one a wrench, another a bayonet and the third a broadsword with half the blade missing. Except for their weapons they were naked. When the cheque was cleared Fakhru withdrew 25,000 shillings in twenties. His briefcase proved too small to hold all the notes. He asked the bodyguards to put some in their pockets; they shrugged and raised their weapons, exposing their sleek nakedness. The deportees, however, were settling their affairs in the next line; they were each allowed to take only 1000 shillings out of the country. Fakhru suggested they get their allotment in hundred-shilling cheques, put these in their pockets and sell him their briefcases. To console them Fakhru said, 'I am thinking that you will not be needing these any more, especially if you are bound for our motherland.' The briefcases were handed over. Of the remaining amount, Fakhru deposited 300 shillings in Sam Fong's account and 24,700 in his own.

Business over with, his five briefcases bulging with hard bundles of new notes and his bodyguards hovering around him, Fakhru went to the Foreign Exchange counter where a large Asian crowd had gathered. He listened to the details of the deportations and offered his condolences.

Later in the morning Fakhru detoured over back roads to his house. He put half the notes into his safe and hid the rest in his mattress, behind the Queen's picture, in pots and pans and in between the pages of a number of holy books; then he hurried off to tell Sam Fong of the 'first transaction', the 300 shillings and the unfortunate fate of the Asians.

The boards were still across the front of the grocery store. Fakhru rapped on the boards for several minutes before he realized that he was the landlord; he went around the back and opened the rear entrance with his own key. Inside, Fong and his family were crouching, pale and unarmed and expecting the worst.

'It's not the soldiers,' whispered Soo in Chinese.

'Don't be so sure,' murmured Sam Fong, eyeing Fakhru.

'Brother,' said Fakhru, 'you will thank me in profusion when I finish speaking . . .' He told Sam Fong that he had during the night received and sold some American merchandise on behalf of the grocery store and had deposited the money in Sam Fong's own account. 'Not much, but slowly by slowly makes a big bundle, as our friends the Africans say.' There would be more, of course, when 'a few more details can be finalized'.

'We have money in the bank,' said Fong to no one in particular.

Soo screwed up her face. Then she got the cheque-book.

Fong asked if he could write Fakhru a cheque there and then for 100 shillings, 'or is this a trick?' Fakhru assured Fong that it was no trick, that with things in the country as they were they had to stand shoulder to shoulder; he accepted the cheque and gave Fong five twenties, which were passed to Soo.

Soo ran out of the shop to buy food. Nothing more was said between Fakhru and Fong until Soo returned, prepared the food and everyone had (ravenously, deliberately, chewing rapidly and not speaking) eaten. Belching into his empty plate – with disgust Fakhru had watched Fong lick it with his pink pointed tongue – Fong said simply that he had not had solid food for a week. He was not complaining, he said, and it did not worry him; not only was there a State of Emergency and no business, it was also Lent. 'And man does not live by rice alone,' said Fong.

'Most certainly,' said Fakhru, thinking Fong had said 'rent'. He smiled, then told Fong what he had heard about the deportations. Fong listened with interest. Deportation was something that he dreaded; his overriding fear, above that of African violence, the occasional earthquake, the dry spells, paganism, new taxes, hot weather and the frequent changes of government – each new government arriving with screams, shooting and mobs of rock-throwing people – was the fear that he would be sent away. Where would he go? He had no idea. China, he felt, might not after thirty-five years be the same place. More than anything, Fong wanted to know the reasons for the deportations: 'What kind of men are they?' he asked.

'Patel is a Gujarati Hindu from Baroda; Gupta is a Bengali, a Brahman, or so he says; Raheem is a Punjabi Muslim; and Mehboob, whom I had thought to be one of ours, a Khoja, Ismaili, turns out to be a Moslem South Indian, Dravidian perhaps, almost a *karia*, a black. But the minister says,' Fakhru took out a newspaper and read, ' "They are Asians, known for their wily ways and tight fists, and all are cut from the same cloth, in this case cheap Asian cloth." Bad joke, I would say.'

'No Chinese?'

'You are the only yellow man here, my friend. When a Chinaman goes, it will be you.'

He is telling the truth, thought Fong. He pinched his face at Fakhru. Fakhru was being a friend. Sometimes he was an enemy. But friend or enemy, Fong still knew that Fakhru was the only man he could talk to, he was his only link between the grocery store and the world that lay outside his boarded-up windows. It had been that way for over four years. Sam Fong did not at the moment consider the fact that his debt to Fakhru was unpaid, that none of the canned milk was sold and that he had no choice but to listen to Fakhru and do what he was told. He was so moved by the act of kindness in recognizing that he too had no place in East Africa ('we have to stand shoulder to shoulder') that he completely forgot that he owed money and was virtually owned by the man in the pyjamas, whose gob of betel juice was now running down the wall of his back room. He was a kind man, a brother; *no, not that*, thought Fong, *but kind, yes*. 'What did they do to get deported?'

'They're not deported yet, not until tomorrow. They have been told to *bugger off*' (this was in English) 'in twenty-four hours. You ask me what did they do? I will tell you. I know all of them very well . . .'

He started with J. H. Patel. Patel's crime was selling dry goods at wholesale prices to the sister of the Minister for External Affairs on unlimited credit. When the bill became large Patel visited the minister, but was turned away; the minister told him he was being greedy and that a white man would never come in and act that way. After the visit, the sister got more than ever in debt; the amount owed was now huger and more hopeless, the chances of repayment nil. The State of Emergency put an end to the sister's purchases – Patel's shelves were empty – but she had got so much merchandise from him that she had no place to store it. She asked Patel how much he wanted for his store. He said, 'Why do you ask me how much when you know you have no money to buy it with?'

'You're just saying that because I'm an African,' said the woman.

Patel protested. 'No, I'm not a racialist. We are all brothers – even Mr Nehru said that. But I am a businessman as well as a brother. I say you have no money because you have no money. You owe me shillings eighteen thousand six hundred forty-two only, which I know I will never see . . .'

The sister of the minister called Patel 'a tightfisted bloodsucker' and said that she was going to tell her brother how the cheeky Asian had insulted her.'

'Now Patel is leaving. The sister has two stores, lots of merchandise and no debts. Nice, you see?' said Fakhru.

Mehboob was the most innocent of all. He just happened to be noisier and more conspicuous than the rest of the traders; it was unfortunate that his shop was in the centre of town where everyone could see him, but that could not be helped 'because it was his father's and his grandfather's shop as well,' said Fakhru.

There were various accusations against Mehboob. First, he was an Asian and therefore looked down upon Africans, the Africans said. It was also said that when he got drunk he shouted for all to hear: 'When the Asians go, so does the economy! Long live *wa-hindi*!' He kept his daughter chained in the back while he 'went about with African women who painted their lips and burned their hair'. He made Africans drink from a cup which he refused to touch. (Fakhru explained to Fong that Mehboob did not even use his wife's cup because it was 'unclean', and made his wife bathe before she prepared food.) The Africans said that Mehboob was discriminating against them; although he liked Africans, 'We know what he is really thinking: he is despising us!' The head of the Young Pioneers said, 'He thinks he's special! Well, we'll show him how special he is – we'll kick this rogue back to India!' Fakhru said that ever since the Prime Minister's speech in the stadium the Young Pioneers had been shouting this on the grass outside Mehboob's paint supply store. Even the police were getting tired of hearing the noise, and when they asked the Young Pioneers to stop it, the police were threatened with violence and told to mind their own business. To simplify matters and set an example, and also to keep the peace, the police decided to tell the government to serve Mehboob with a deportation order. 'Easy, no?' said Fakhru.

V. R. Gupta was a nationalist whom Fakhru disliked intensely. ('If ever there was a troublemaker it is V. R. Gupta.') Gupta spoke four African languages and knew most of the tribal customs; he once alienated a roomful of Indians who were discussing the viciousness and chronic thievery of a certain Nilo-Hamitic tribe by saying quite simply, 'It is because they are a pastoral people; agriculturalists are more concerned with property.'

He was born in East Africa in 1906 and resembled a *saddhu*, bony and wrinkled, leathery but with a warm light in his grey eyes. Throughout the colonial era he had struggled to bring independence to East Africa. He organized and consolidated African opposition to the British colonial government; he let Africans use his back room as a secret office, started and edited a newspaper (later banned by the Colonial Office) in which nationalists wrote about how they only wanted to live and work together as equals and build a society for all races to share as equals and have a voice, and so forth. When the Africans were jailed Gupta hired lawyers for them. He often said, 'I was born in Africa. Africa is my home. I am an African . . .'

Fakhru did not think Gupta was in his right mind. Gupta *was* an African; that was the trouble with the little Hindu. He spoke nonsense ('It is because they are a pastoral people') and formed the first political party in the country, financed the party and advised the party leaders, who were all Africans, on constitutional matters. When the party won the first election Fakhru suspected that Gupta had a motive and was perhaps cleverer than any other Asian in the country; but Fakhru was tired of hearing him accuse the Asians of not cooperating with the Africans. 'You will pay for this in the end,' Gupta warned.

He did not have the majority of Asian support, but he had a great deal of sympathy: the land laws were discriminatory before independence, only whites could own land and grow cash crops. But he made enemies quickly among members of his own community by saying, 'in the eyes of the whites you are also black men.' He had no desire to chase the whites out of the country or to terrorize them. He said that the Africans must have what was rightfully theirs in order for all the races to settle things lawfully and fairly. Mahatma Gandhi had been an encouragement to Gupta's father (the great man paid his father a visit on the East African coast at Lamu in 1893); Gupta himself had the personal support of Mr Nehru; but in spite of the fact that Indian nationalism was an inspiration to him and his African colleagues, Gupta said, 'when someone calls me an Indian my heart is heavy'. Gupta was the first Indian to have an East African passport and said he was proud to be a citizen of East Africa. 'In America aren't the Italian immigrants called Americans? America is a nation of immigrants – I quote the late President Jack Kennedy – all of them Americans. So let us all be Africans . . .'

Three communities spat in unison at Gupta's suggestion. Gupta did what he could to bring the races together, but none would budge. Fascist sentiments, put forward as 'realistic' by the leaders of each community, were agreed upon in a hapless sort of way by everyone except Gupta. Leading African businessmen saw Gupta privately and told him he was wasting his time; 'Let's face it,' these men said, 'Africans *are* dirty, they *do* smell – I'm an African: I know. And they're happy where they are, isn't it?' Gupta sighed and attempted to reason with them. He spoke of the brotherhood of man. The British said, 'Yes. Hm. We've got quite a mixed bag here. But masses of complications, if you see what I mean . . .' The Asians repeated the proverb about its being impossible to take the curl out of a dog's tail, even if you bury it in the ground for weeks. The one time Gupta saw Sam Fong, Fong told him the Chinese proverb, in Swahili, of the monkey you could teach to ride a horse, but the monkey's hands were still hairy. And everyone went on buying and selling.

Gupta turned back to the government. He studied the parliamentary reports closely after each session ended. It was obvious that things were not going well (one member of Parliament suggested that a law be passed to limit the size of Asian families). Perhaps, Gupta thought, there was not a constructive and vigorous enough opposition. He saw value in his supporting the Opposition party: it was a legal party, the members seemed honest, their spokesmen only needed encouragement in being active in parliamentary debate. Gupta helped the Opposition party to grow and at the same time saw it as a moral duty not to withdraw his financial support from the ruling party.

This was his mistake. Word got around that Gupta was masterminding the overthrow of the government through the Opposition party, so that the Asians and their African 'stooges' could take over. All the back-benchers in Parliament were locked up along with the six ministers at State House. The imprisoned politicians were said to be in collaboration with 'The Leech', as Gupta had come to be called by the government. The Prime Minister's speech in the stadium had been directed against Gupta; 'the cat and mouse friendship of running with the hares and hunting with the hounds' was a reference to Gupta's support of both parties. Gupta was 'disloyal and disaffected towards the government'. There was documented evidence in Gupta's own handwriting to the effect that elections were a year overdue and it was 'time to ask the common man, in a democratic manner, if he wanted a change of government . . .'

'Only troublemakers want elections,' said the Minister of Defence.

Gupta surrendered his passport and agreed to leave the country within twenty-four hours; he knew enough of constitutional law to see that in a flash he had been made stateless.

'A fool, in other words,' said Fakhru.

Sam Fong stared. He looked for a pattern in the deportations but saw none.

'Now Raheem . . .' Fakhru explained that Raheem would be a liability to any society. He had no job, but always had money 'because he is in the habit of pinching tyres and then selling them back to their owners'. He slept with African girls and introduced a number of perversions to his circle of friends; he drove too fast, he chain-smoked and ate pig; he was indiscriminate in telling people – African, Asian and white – to fuck off. He had respect and admiration only for Americans, and his one wish was to marry an American girl who looked like Shirley MacLaine ('That broad has class,' he said). Because he went to the movies every day he picked up a strong American accent and a number of slang expressions.

His nickname, 'Dino', was given to him by one of his own seedy admirers (he had a gang) one day when Raheem leaned against the fence at the cattle market and, tossing his head in the direction of the Wambugu Fishnet Factory where many young girls were employed as stitchers on the machines, said, 'At least we're where the action is.'

He had started to believe that he was Dean Martin. He and his gang saw all the Dean Martin movies, and afterwards the members of his gang said, 'You were super today, Dino.' 'Yeah,' said Raheem, 'they can't screw me.' He did not have an objectionable voice. That day at the bank, while the mob of Asians told Fakhru the details of the deportations and got their traveller's cheques, 'Dino' Raheem looked at his reflection in the glass wall at the Foreign Exchange counter, and, ignored by the babbling Asians and tossing his head, sang:

> It was just one of those things,
> Just one of those car-azy things,
> One of those bells that now and then rings
> Just one of those things . . .

And when he finished the song he turned to the Asian mob and said, 'Okay, cats, let's get this show on the road . . .'

Fakhru confessed that he understood only Patel and Mehboob. Sam Fong said he understood none of them; he thought privately that if they could be deported, so could he. He thought of China: his village, the huts, the cows, the sun setting on the paddy fields.

'They're leaving today?' asked Fong.

'No. They have twenty-four hours. They're going tomorrow.'

16

The Prime Minister was also leaving. He was going to his farm to work on the soil, he said: 'Planting has to begin even when you're a prime minister.' He had to get his mealies planted before Parliament was called, 'and my advice to all you *bwanas* is to forget about politics and do the same.' But the general feeling of the Asians was that the Prime Minister was taking no chances and that several attempts had already been made on his life by supporters of the arrested ministers. Among the Asians it was whispered that the Prime Minister's 'farm' was in London.

The Prime Minister's departure on the same day as the deportations was a stroke of luck for the Asian community. It meant that the Asians could go to the airport without being accused of saying good-bye to (and therefore sympathizing with) 'the disloyal blood-suckers'. V. R. Gupta, 'The Leech', was seen as especially dangerous, 'a stoogie who should cast the moat from his eyes', as the editorial in the weekly of the ruling party described him. Any demonstration of sympathy towards Gupta was sure to mean trouble for those who sympathized. For twenty-four hours the Asian community practised caution; they avoided Gupta altogether. His packing was done in silence, alone, in his office, the old *saddhu* shuffling among his tables littered with papers and the autographed pictures of well-wishers: African nationalists and American political scientists.

Fakhru persuaded Sam Fong that it would be very wise if he also went to the airport, 'not to see these bloody *wahindi* leave, but to make the old man's departure more auspicious'.

Fong did not see the logic in this. He reflected that there was very rarely logic in these moves, or if there was he could not understand it. He could only ask God's guidance and large protective beard. (Fong had thought from his earliest days that the faithful, the devout, were allowed to hide in God's bushy beard; this was simple because: Q. *Where is God?* A. *He is everywhere*.) What Fong had not considered was that Fakhru's offer had a great deal to do with the Americans. This was not anything very sinister on Fakhru's part; but Fakhru's friendly visit and affectionate bursts of betel juice on the wall of the grocery store were all prompted by his special deputation as guardian of Sam Fong. ('Keep an eye on him. You take care of him and we'll take care of you, Fakra.') As he had agreed to this and accepted the cheque on behalf of Sam Fong, he had to make sure that the Americans got their money's worth, that Fong became friendly, that his store reopened and prospered, that he was grateful to the Americans and seen regularly with Fakhru, in whom the Americans had placed much of their trust and a good deal of their money. It was no effort for Fakhru to do this, for to keep Sam Fong at his command he knew he would only have to prevent him from ever being able to repay the 370 shillings that Fong owed. With Fong's shop closed this hardly required any effort; in fact, Fakhru realized that the danger was not in Fong's paying the money back, but rather in the strong possibility that Fong could very easily starve to death. By depositing small amounts of money in Fong's bank account Fakhru knew that he could keep Fong alive and in his debt until the end of time, and could please the Americans. ('Smile.' 'I am your slave.' A smile.) There was no logic in it, but there was a degree of order, and it was from this order, created by Fakhru, that profit was born. Fong did not see the logic because there was none; the fact of his debt to Fakhru kept him from ever seeing that his poverty had been ordered by Fakhru. If Fong had detected this he would have thrown Fakhru out the moment the first gob of betel juice hit the wall.

Fong agreed to go to the airport to see the Prime Minister off. Fakhru picked him up in the grey van; in the back of the van were the three Nubian bodyguards who were not only armed as before with knives, arrows, spears and the broken sword, but were now decorated with little bows (on the arrows, around their biceps, trailing from their waists in fluttering skirts) in the national colours: gold, red and black. The bodyguards peeped out from the back of the van as it drew up to the grocery store. Sam Fong got in front with Fakhru.

The airport road was jammed with vehicles – cars, buses, bicycles – and people walking in groups. It was a narrow road; many dangerous curves caused it to be called 'the road to heaven'. Even now, a full hour before the Prime Minister's departure and the deportations, several accidents had occurred. At Milestone Two a bicycle lay twisted in the road; twenty feet away the rider sprawled, his feet and one of his arms turned unnaturally back to front – like a dropped doll – his face against the street, flattened, glued with blood. Cars detoured slowly around the man. 'When the Americans get to the moon they will find there a black riding a bicycle,' said Fakhru as they passed the corpse. Farther up the road two cars had pulled off; the rear of one was crushed, the headlights of the other were smashed. Standing in the shards of broken glass were the drivers, smoking cigarettes and taking turns yelling. Sam Fong counted two dogs, a cat and four snakes squashed flat and seeping innards on the road, all delicacies, the whole lot (with rice and vegetables) enough to feed the average Chinese family for a month.

There were Asians in most of the cars, men in the front seat, women and children in the back; the rear window of each car displayed seven or eight heads of long braided hair gleaming with coconut oil.

Fong did not speak. He looked with regret at the dead cyclist and the squashed animals. Death upset him; he saw nothing more. A month after he arrived in East Africa he stopped seeing mud huts, women pounding peanuts in large wooden mortars and naked children tending cows, prodding them with long poles; he did not see the activity along the road, only the death, although the simple items of equatorial life, the activities of tribesmen, were all there unchanged, existing as they had existed thirty-five and even 350 years before. Fong was startled by the screaming of the police sirens. About a dozen white-helmeted policemen on motorcycles roared beside the line of traffic, waving their arms and making gargling noises.

'He is coming,' said Fakhru. And without another word he pulled off the road and came to a dead stop.

The cars in front did the same, pulled into banana groves and beside fruit stalls, leaving a wide corridor of road without a single thing moving on it. Five minutes passed and several police cars careened by; long black arms swung threateningly at the parked cars. It was against the law to be moving when the Prime Minister drove by. While they waited at the side of the road Fakhru told Sam Fong stories of people – mostly arrogant Greeks from the Congo – who had not obeyed this law, and how they had been kicked by the police.

After eight minutes the Prime Minister himself, standing like Father Divine in a red open-topped Rolls-Royce, his lion's mane fly whisk aloft and snapping in the breeze, zoomed past; the tyres sucking at the hot soft tar made the only sound. Behind him were 'his women' – in another Rolls – and behind his women were three truckloads of singing youths, the Black Guards and one busload of market women clapping their hands and singing the song about the Prime Minister, 'who showed us the Promised Land'.

The Prime Minister's procession was made up entirely of Africans; they stuck their knobby heads out of the cars and grinned when they overtook the parked cars, the Asians. When the procession had passed, the women who had stopped pounding their peanuts lifted their heavy pestles once again; the little dusty boys resumed poking and kicking their cows; men in doorways tilted gourds of beer up and took long swigs; radios were flicked on; and out of the fruit stalls, turn-offs, driveways, side roads and banana groves wheeled the Asians, gunning their engines and roaring back on to the airport road, swerving and jockeying for position among the cows and goats.

The parking lot at the airport was full. Fakhru, however, merely hunched over the wheel pretending he was one of the Prime Minister's functionaries. He followed the Prime Minister's procession to the front door of the main lobby, where he deposited, for all to see, Sam Fong. One of the bodyguards, at Fakhru's signal, opened the door for Fong and stood, helmeted and armed with a sword and covered with coloured bows (but otherwise naked as a jaybird), while Fong clambered out and winced at the large crowd.

'I will join you straight away, my good fellow,' said Fakhru in English, for the benefit of the people standing near the Fakhru Enterprises Ltd van.

Sam Fong shrugged and ducked into the crowd that filled the lobby. The Prime Minister had entered a few minutes before and was in the VIP lounge making a statement to the press about the necessity for using lots of fertilizer on the tung trees this year. One journalist asked him about the deportations and he replied, 'I don't know a bloody thing about these deportations. I am a simple farmer, I tell you.' Fong was being crushed; he fought for air and wriggled through the crowd until he saw an empty space near the weighing-in counter; several Asians milled around near the counter showing passports and exchanging Hindustani words in soft voices.

Above the murmuring of the crowd in the lobby burst one angry nasal voice; Fong listened but did not understand a word of it.

'Tell these gringos I don't dig people pushing their lousy mitts all over me!' said an Indian in a pink shirt, pointing a comb and sneering at two huge black policemen.

The angry Indian with the comb stalked over to another Indian at the counter who looked at an air hostess, his mouth set in a grin of pain; the air hostess said that he would have to weigh his camera. It was J. H. Patel. He looked at her, held tight to his camera and said nothing.

'Hi, you little pastafazool, how's yarass?' said the Indian with the comb, rolling his eyes at a small, sleek, Indian girl standing at the edge of the crowd, her eyes downcast; she adjusted her sari on her shoulder and continued to stare at the floor.

'Yes, I am J. H. Patel. That is correct, I am being deported. You will observe my British passport,' said the Indian with the camera, still grinning in pain at the air hostess.

'Let's hit the road, Jack,' said the Indian with the comb.

'My name is not Jack, it is Jayantibhai, and I wish you would go away, Raheem.'

'I *am*, Dad, I'm being deported. Wow!' said Raheem, slipping the comb into his back pocket. He no longer appeared to be angry. He snapped his fingers and said, 'We're swinging!' to Sam Fong, who turned away so quickly that he nearly knocked Fakhru down. Fakhru had spotted an American and had crept up behind Fong, intending to put his arm around him.

Gupta sat on his cracked, weather-beaten valise, his head in his hands, waiting his turn to have his ticket seen, his possessions weighed. There was a wide space around him occupied only by a small boy playing with a large dead bug; a few Indians eyed Gupta from the safety of the crowd, tilted their heads and clucked. Fakhru took Sam Fong by the arm and backed towards Gupta, all the while pointing at the ceiling – distracting the policemen – as he dragged Sam Fong backwards. Soon Gupta was directly behind Fakhru.

'Friend Gupta, how goes it?' asked Fakhru.

'This is a sad day for me, an old man leaving for a strange country,' sighed Gupta. 'But it is also a happy day, for I feel that by leaving I am also serving.'

'There is no money in India,' said Fakhru.

Gupta ignored the remark. 'The Lord Krishna says that the river never stops and that we must never be at rest. Perhaps now you will see that there is a greater need than ever for us to educate and love the African who has given up part of his homeland that we may prosper . . .'

'We?' asked Fakhru sharply. His back was still to Gupta; he spoke smiling to the crowd across the lobby.

'We are one people,' said Gupta. 'All men are broth –'

'Businessmen,' said Fakhru. 'Except you, Gupta, my friend.'

'You are very narrow-minded,' said Gupta. 'Though I am sorry for this unkindness.'

'Soon you will be in India or elsewhere,' said Fakhru. 'Since you have already abused me, then I do not mind saying: *Soon you will be very hungry*. That's what you get for hugging the blacks.'

'My mistake is the mistake of us all. I did not love them enough. The *Gita* says . . .'

Fakhru walked away, dragging Fong with him. 'That man is a bloody fool,' he said. 'I'll bet he cannot even count to a hundred.' He stopped ranting about Gupta when he spotted Mehboob wedged between two policemen and a customs official. The customs official was explaining that Mehboob was sixty shillings over the allowed limit. Mehboob was pretending not to understand and asked the African official if perhaps he could explain the snag in Persian.

Two hundred Indians, all relatives of Mehboob, kept their distance. A little courage, thought Fakhru, and I will be a nawab. He moved closer to Mehboob, pushing Fong ahead of him; when he spoke he did so without moving his lips, hoping that if there were any difficulty the customs official and the policemen would think it was Fong who was speaking. He pressed Fong close to Mehboob and spoke.

'Little trouble?'

'Blacks,' was all Mehboob said.

'And Mehboob Paint Supply? Paint, I know I do not have to remind you, dries up very rapidly when it sits idle on shelves.'

'You will not let it dry up.'

'I am a very busy man,' said Fakhru.

'The store, the paint, many good English paintbrushes, some good quality sun-goggles, ladders, few all-purpose display cases – the whole *shauri* for 4000.'

'Shillings?'

'Pounds,' said Mehboob.

'I can pay you in dollars.'

'Where?'

'Karachi, Calcutta, Delhi, you name it.'

'It's a deal, then?'

'Three thousand five hundred in dollars, 500 more in rupees.'

Mehboob turned away, looked into the face of the customs

official and made his calculations by drumming his fingers quickly on the ticket counter. 'That is 25000 shillings or 1250 pounds. I asked 4000. I will stick to my price, thank you.'

'Karachi is a long way from your paint store, brother.'

'Fifteen hundred,' said Mehboob.

'All right, but only half in dollars. The rest in rupees – and I might throw in a few escudos. You never can tell when you might be in Portugal.'

'I am giving it to you free,' said Mehboob. 'We are being drummed out by these blacks.'

The policemen stood closer to Mehboob, confused by the mumbling, the drone that seemed to be coming from Mehboob's direction. But Mehboob, like Fakhru, had not moved his lips. The customs official repeated in Swahili, English and in sign language with impatient gestures that Mehboob would have to surrender sixty shillings.

'Sixty shillings!' shouted Mehboob. 'Would you deprive a poor man of sixty bob?' To Fakhru he said, 'You're robbing me, but what can I do? I am in no position to argue. *Acha*, 30000, half in dollars, some rupees and as many escudos as you can manage. Thirty thousand.' Mehboob said the numbers slowly, sadly, in Hindi.

'You will get your money in a week, in the land of our fathers. Allah be praised.'

J. H. Patel paid his overweight charges and glanced across the lobby at his relatives, none of whom stood near enough to exchange a word. They fidgeted; most did not look. An old woman wept.

Fakhru edged over, with Sam Fong, towards Patel.

'This is the end of your coffee growing, one would presume,' said Fakhru.

'There are my sons,' said J. H. Patel. 'They will see me through this hardship.'

'Are they seeing you through now?' said Fakhru gently. 'They are afraid even to whisper to you. Look at them standing there, frightened as mice. Oh yes, they are good people, but will they fetch good prices – will they dare market this year's crop? They will think of what happened to you and hide under their beds. Of course, I don't blame them. But I will feel sorry for you, in Bombay, perhaps living in a doorway, licking the raindrops off motor cars and chewing on rags for nourishment. You cannot make chapatties out of dirt, I will assure you . . .'

J. H. Patel looked at his relatives, all silent except for the wailing granny, bunched together, their dark eyes expressionless, helpless, uncomprehending, twenty feet away.

'The blacks will nationalize your coffee and let the berries rot on the ground.'

'I'll sell you half,' said Patel, still looking at his relatives.

'How many acres?'

'Six hundred at £500 an acre. That is pounds sterling.'

'Give me 800 at 425.'

'Seven fifty at 440.'

'All right. I know I'm being swindled but I try to help people out of trouble,' said Fakhru. 'And your pickers. Sign them over.'

'You can have 2000. They are very healthy, as you know.'

'I know they had a strike last year. Give me three,' said Fakhru, looking away.

Patel's eyes were on his silent relatives. 'I will not argue; my plane is leaving. Listen carefully. I want to be paid 400 shillings a man, in Geneva, in German marks. Is that clear? I do not want rupees. This will be confirmed through my brother, S. R. You know him? Good. I will send him a letter of agreement. You will have to see him . . .'

Patel was handed his boarding pass.

> *Yesssss, it's witchcraft*
> *ca-razy witchcraft,*
> *And although I know*
> *It's strictly tabooooooooooo.*

'Dino' Raheem was snapping his fingers and doing a little bobbing and weaving dance for the tearful relatives, the wives and children of the deportees. In the empty space between the deportees at the ticket counter and the relatives, a space created by caution and fear, Raheem had ample room to dance.

Patel muttered and said that Raheem was a foolish Moslem. Fakhru heard the remark, but said nothing; he preferred not to ruin a good business deal with petty religious differences. And when Patel repeated the remark, this time rather loudly, Fakhru said, 'Indeed. Quite right,' in English.

'Look what I've done here! I give credit to the blacks and lose two *dukas*, gifts for charity, coffee for the Five-year Plan, donations to the Party, the use of my trucks for the singing market mammies – and *this* is what I get for it!' Patel held out his boarding pass, the cardboard crumpled in his brown fist.

'Blecks,' said Fakhru hoarsely, calculating the annual coffee yield set against 750 times 440 plus 3000 times twenty, in German marks, at the present rate of exchange . . .

'These blacks,' said Patel. 'They turn us upside down and shake the money out of our pockets. Then they tell us to go away . . .'

'What's that again?' asked Fakhru.

'I said these bloody blacks they turn us upside down, shake out our money, then throw us out.'

'I will see your brother, S. R., later,' said Fakhru rapidly. 'You will like Geneva – His Highness has a home there and speaks very highly of it, and you know what the Lord Krishna says.' Fakhru hustled Fong to the front door of the lobby; he told Fong to find his three bodyguards and tell them to meet him immediately at the side of the main building, near the runway.

Two planes stood on the runway, an Air India jet and an East African Airways Super VC-10. Facing these planes, on the upper viewing deck, stood 5000 silent Asians. On the runway were the police band, ten ranks of Black Guards, some soldiers, the singing market women and what was left of the cabinet. The Prime Minister was just leaving the lounge.

In silence, four figures (one tap-dancing) made their way across the blazing tar of the runway. When they reached the metal stairs of the Air India plane three of the men turned and waved, one bowed and blew kisses with both hands. The crowd of 5000, composed entirely of brown faces, was impassive; several handkerchiefs appeared from the midst of the faces and then, just as quickly, disappeared. It was as if the 5000 had come to the airport for some other purpose – the sun perhaps – and, caught by surprise, saw some vague acquaintances leaving, whom they dutifully, tolerantly, watched, almost sullen in this obligation, since only the fact that it was unexpected and obligatory – not racial or political, but simply social – gave it any importance.

When the jet engines revved up on the Air India plane, the Asians on the upper viewing deck began speaking in a babble of voices that could not be heard above the roar. And after the plane sped down the runway and was in the sky, a renewed silence fell upon the Asians. The eyes of the Asian crowd returned to the runway, where the following spectacle was taking place.

Fakhru was being carried, slung by his wrists and ankles like the carcass of a goat, towards the Prime Minister; Fakhru's three Nubian bodyguards did the carrying. Fakhru's face was turned up and his feet, soles to the sky, were on the shoulders of the Nubians.

The Prime Minister stood on a red carpet which led across the runway to the plane. One of his soldiers leaned forward and whispered to him; the Prime Minister shook his head.

Fakhru was brought before the Prime Minister. For a moment he was held, and then he was ceremoniously placed at the feet of the Prime Minister. The soldiers standing near bent closer and cocked their rifles. Fakhru rolled over on the rug, like a hound, and touched his forehead to the glossy shoes of the Prime Minister.

From the upper viewing deck a heavy stillness was breathed forth; all eyes were upon the figure of Hassanali Fakhru, face down, prone on the carpet, in his familiar white pyjamas.

Either sensing what was about to happen or else out of exasperation, the Prime Minister swished his fly whisk at Fakhru's head. Fakhru's buttocks rose up, then his shoulders, until he was on his hands and knees. He paused this way for several seconds; then slowly his whole body inched backwards along the carpet. When he was about ten feet away he raised his eyes to the Prime Minister. At this gesture, the three Nubians came over, seized his legs and held him upside down.

It was a quick motion. In a matter of seconds Fakhru was hanging vertically in the air before the Prime Minister, bobbing up and down, his clothes and arms flapping loosely; and from his pockets fell two-shilling pieces, half crowns, enormous pennies clanking like doubloons and tightly wadded notes of every denomination. It went on for a full minute. As soon as the first coins hit the carpet and rolled on to the runway, a cheer went up – first from the ministers, then from the singing market women, then from the Black Guards, then from the soldiers and finally from the 5000 Asians on the upper viewing deck. The police band played the national anthem.

Fakhru was still being shaken, but now nothing fell from his pockets. His arms shot out to the side and he was dropped. The Prime Minister flicked his fly whisk, this time with conviction, briskness; Fakhru grinned broadly, squatted and, bowing towards the Prime Minister's shoes, showed his empty palms. The Nubians seized him again, this time almost roughly, and he was carried off in the direction of the Transit Lounge, as before, like a dead goat.

The Prime Minister raised his arms and received the ovation. His arms dropped; he shouted something and the cabinet ministers fell upon the money, which they scooped up and stuffed in a box embossed with the national coat of arms and carried by the Prime Minister's private secretary. Without another word the Prime Minister walked towards the waiting plane, down the carpet, up the silver stairs. On the top step he turned towards the Asians on the upper viewing deck and raised his arms again stiffly as if to say, 'You are forgiven.' And the deafening cheer which rose from the upper viewing deck was so shrill in its determination that it could have signalled joy or pain.

17

Sam Fong had watched the whole scene from the upper viewing deck by peeping out from behind the sari folds of a very large, curry-scented Indian woman. She was with her family: pot-bellied husband (Fong was amazed by the size of the man's bare feet which distended his rubber sandals) and three thin-legged boys. While the four Asians walked mournfully across the runway the woman was dishing food out to her family from a basket, which she held tightly. In between furtive waves with small handkerchiefs (which they also used to dab their lips), the family gobbled dripping brown sweets the shape and size of golf balls, brittle wafers and glistening yellow objects composed of knotted tubes of juicy dough. When they had wiped the stickiness from their fingers and mouths they looked in the direction of the Air India plane, wagged their balled-up handkerchiefs and sighed.

At first Fong was not sure whether the man prostrate before the Prime Minister was truly Fakhru or not. But certainly the Nubians were Fakhru's – the coloured bows and the broken sword were unmistakable. It was at the end, when the man squatted and showed his empty palms, a characteristic gesture of Fakhru's ('I am a poor man – not having money, I tell you') that Fong was sure. That was all Fong saw; he never saw the Prime Minister raise his arms, for just after the money fell the Indian family started on vegetables, and the activity that accompanied this blocked Fong's view.

But he heard the cheers. Staring up at the large Indian man and woman, he was impressed by how loudly they could cheer with their mouths filled with cabbage. As the cheer went up, once, twice, from all the Asians around him, Fong felt as if something had just come to an end. It was a definite signal, a deep sigh, meaning things would now be different, perhaps better, the Black King appeased by Fakhru kneeling before him; perhaps he would now be able to open his shop. It was an expression of enormous emotion, but still he could not decide if it meant something good or bad was happening. For a clue Fong searched the Asian faces as they cheered, but this did no good because the Asians appeared able to cheer without smiling; they merely opened their mouths and yelled, and the more they yelled the more vacant their eyes became. Gloom seemed to descend as soon as the cheering stopped. Were they happy? Was there a reason for his feeling that something significant had happened, caused by Fakhru and evident in the long silence in which they munched sweets or the deafening cheers in which whole gobbets of the portable dinners were spat on to the runway? Fong could not tell. As the Asians filed out their faces were expressionless, some masked and made inscrutable by heavy eye-narrowing jowls, others shrunken, lined long ago with permanent wrinkles of pain or grief. They all had adjusted their clothes, plucked damp cloth away from sticky flesh, fanned themselves and walked with their feet apart, saying *he-hi-hee-chay-ha-hay-hee* without pause and without emphasis.

Fong found Fakhru outside, giggling in the van. They drove home in almost complete silence. What happened on the runway was not mentioned. The only reference was a brief one, very oblique, by Fakhru: 'These *blacks*! These *wahindi*!' And then laughter and a genial shaking of the head. Just before they turned at the clock tower on to Uhuru Avenue, Fakhru said, 'And *these Americans*! – May I be blessed with a long life . . .'

The grocery store did reopen. There did seem to be fewer (and, for some reason, smaller) soldiers on the street. The Asians did seem to be, at least for a time, off the hook. And Sam Fong was reasonably happy.

Most of all he was happy because the shop was open; that meant the canned milk could be sold. Fong did not have business schemes or an income outside the grocery store. He had

passed from the hold of a Chinese freighter to the inside of a
carpentry shop, and from there to the grocery store, without
once intentionally standing in the sun or looking at the huts or
walking in the jungle that sprouted only fifty yards from his
store. That there were possibilities for income outside his store
was irrelevant because of the danger implied in walking into the
unknown. For Fong anything outside his store, the territory
beyond the shelves, was spooky, dangerous, murderous. It did
not frighten him because he knew he would never have dealings
beyond the walls of his store. For a long while now, the shelves,
the counters, the empty bins, the mountain of canned-milk
crates had been as much a part of Fong's household – his whole
world – as the children's low wooden beds or Soo's shiny-seated
stool. Now the boards off the front windows allowed sunlight to
enter his store, his life; the mildew and cobwebs that had
accumulated during the State of Emergency were swept away. Some
cans of milk were put on the shelves and their crates made into
chairs. Fong believed that he would have a chance to control his
life, to repay his debt and to not have to suffer the humiliation
of Fakhru's commands ('Smile.' 'I am your slave.' A painful
smile.), for as low as he felt Fakhru's canned-milk counter-
swindle to have been, he knew it could only be reversed by a
suspension of milk deliveries. He maintained his belief in – and
even prayed for – the milk train's imminent derailment, followed
by a mob of white women at his store demanding the cans of
milk and paying high prices.

On the day the grocery store reopened most of the shelves were
filled with cans of milk, many of the bins and vats were filled and
even the large counter had a pyramid of cans on it. The skin
lightener, hair straightener, blood-purifying lozenges, muscle tonic,
fat, tea, matches, soap, rice, onions, cigarettes, Chinese magazines
and plastic wallets were squeezed on to one small shelf. And so
they had to be, for no longer did the sign in front read FRIEND
FROCERY POP IN PLEASE FOR BETTER PRICE ANYWHERE IN
AFRICA. The new sign read SAM FONG FRIEND MILK STORE FOR
ALL YOUR MILK NEEDS. Soo had done this herself, her tongue

protruding in concentration, while Fong and the children stacked the shelves with the cans of milk.

There were memories: the paint and brush from Mehboob, the terrifying scene with Mehboob accusing Soo of having cheated him and now Mehboob elsewhere; the State of Emergency almost at an end, no more nocturnal patterings of feet and gunshots; like an old brown snapshot, cracked and frayed, the memory of the small deathly noises at night during the first days of the emergency, the family sealed in the store, eating locusts and listening; the milk swindle that backfired.

Sadly, the memory of the milk – the reminders covering most of the shelves in the store – ended all reverie and brought Fong around to the cold thought that 370 shillings were still owed to Fakhru. Until this was paid Fakhru was at liberty to tell him to smile, nod or follow him. Even a small weakness enslaves: Fong chewed on his own proverb and stared into the stillness of the store.

The milk was on the shelves, most of it, some was still in the crates; the sign was up, the floor swept; there was nothing more that could be done. He could not drag the white women off the street; he could not – as Fakhru had once tried to do – pay someone to derail the milk train. All that he could do was all he had ever done since he became the owner of the grocery store: wait. He wanted to do more, but it was not possible; he had learned that the *dukawallah* keeps his elbows on the counter and his eye on the door. He smiles. He tries not to eat his stock or, once it is arranged in stacks, interfere in any way with the merchandise. For him, being present is a skill. He stands guard over his stock and waits for money to drop into his biscuit tin so that he can pay his debts and die in peace.

But his debt remained unpaid. The thought of it made Fong's stomach sour and heavy. Fakhru did not threaten him with imprisonment, though once in a while he reminded him of the debt in an offhand way: 'I tell you this government owcs *millions* – you owe me shillings three seventy only – but this bleck government owes *millions* and I am quite certain . . .' Fakhru had not asked any more favours of Fong. The store was open. The shelves were almost filled. Sunlight splashed through the front window. Everything was fine except that Fong was not making any money.

Fakhru's recent gentle attitude towards Fong developed from the thought Fakhru had that his Chinese friend, so earnestly desired by the Americans, could die of starvation without a murmur, and leave Fakhru stranded. Fong was that sort of fool, a silent and inactive Gupta, seeing nothing, caring about the wrong things, with no sense of values. Several times when Fakhru had this vision of Fong dying without sufficient advance notification he ran to the store and peeked in: each time the Chinaman was leaning on the counter, saying his rosary and smiling into thin air.

Something had to be done to make sure that Fong did not die. Fakhru proposed a plan: Sam Fong would be the agent of Fakhru Enterprises Ltd. The cans of milk took up most of the available space in the store. It was not possible to stock anything else worthwhile – there was no room for it. But Fong could take 'orders' for other things and there could be a weekly retainer for this service, plus a commission for anything Fong might sell. Soo was brought into the discussion and together the Chinese couple tried to think of loopholes in the agreement. There did not seem to be any, but that did not mean that there were not any; in a way it meant that there were many large ones. But both Soo and Sam Fong knew, with what approached horror, exactly what had been sold since SAM FONG FRIEND MILK STORE opened: two razor blades, an onion, eleven cigarettes (four filtered, seven plain-tipped – the plain-tipped were a penny cheaper) and one box of matches. Two weeks' sales. The milk train showed no signs of derailment. There was not enough money coming in to stay alive on; a fresh crop of locusts would not appear until the rainy season began, and that was months away.

Fong agreed to be Fakhru's agent, and as he agreed, signed the paper, shook hands, uttered a proverb and listened to Fakhru saying, 'You're doing us both a big favour, friend Fong. I am believing that you will get rich in this way, as Christ is my witness . . .,' he felt sure that he was being swindled. He would accept the swindle. But he would get his weekly shillings and would be able to buy rice and bean seeds and would know exactly how much he owed, to the penny. That he would pay when his lotus bloomed or, rather (Fong quickly corrected the image), when his milk train was derailed.

'These are the American goods for which we negotiated some time ago,' said Fakhru, handing Fong a handbill on which were listed about fifty items. 'You take no-risk-free-trial basis and sell when you can. I am very busy with my new coffee *shamba*, paint store and whatnot.' Fakhru promised a weekly retainer of ten shillings, the subsistence allowance, plus 500 free handbills which read as follows:

SAM FONG FRIEND MILK STORE
Agents for Fakhru Enterprises Ltd
Plot 34/DP/67/Z
Uhuru Ave.

Dear Sir/Madam,

May we introduce ourselves as one of the leading Grocer, and stocklist, of AMERICAN Household & Kitchenware. We are advised to approach you for business relations.

Our Prices are competitive and we accept Bulk Orders & Party orders on sale or return basis. We shall be very oblige if the Reader would humbly give us a chance to serve your Needs, and also please ask you friend & Neighbour to take advantage of us.

We are pleased to inform you the arrival of the following goods *first class*: Buckets & Basins, Pedal dustbin, Lavatory brush & holders, Bread Box, Fridge box, cup, saucer, Schoolchildren, Bottles and Sandwiches Box, Petrol cans, cutlery Trays, Cake and Flour containers, glasses wine, glasses beer, mugs, jags, crokery, teasets, Cup, Fire King Cessaroles, SanckSets Handy.

And also Spoon Knife fork frypan saucepan broom Brushes & Water Filters, Pressure Lamp, Torch Batteries, Torches,

Glasscloths, dishcloths, floor, yellow dusters etc, etc, and many more Articles for your Family and Fried.

We are pleased to accept your Requirement. Your visit to our shop saves time and Trouble for Your Daily 'Needs'. Visit to shop will be Highly Appreciated & most Earnestly Desired by,

Yours faithfully,
S. Fong, Mgr.
for Hassanali Fakhru Ent. Ltd.

Soo translated what she could of it for Fong. Fong said, 'What about milk?'

'No milk here,' said Soo.

'Write milk,' said Fong.

Across the bottom of each handbill, in blue pencil, Soo wrote *Milk.*

The handbills were given to Margerine who, instead of slipping them under the doors of white households as he had been directed, brought them to a nearby slum where, to his relief, all 500 were eagerly taken by an Arab butcher who promised to distribute them to his customers. He did this by wrapping flyblown joints of goat meat in them.

Fong expected hundreds of white women to respond. He was ready for them: he put his rosary away and watched the door. Each time a white woman drove by (none walked) Fong assured himself that she was looking for a place to park. But the only white woman that entered the store went away empty-handed; she had said what she wanted (to Fong it sounded like '*Nyagah, nyagah*'), and when Fong said, 'American goods? Milk?' and held a can in each hand, the woman became angry and shouted, '*No, Nyagah!*' 'Nice milk. Good nice milk. Too good nice milk,' Fong said. He was still saying it with repetitions and variations as the woman, sighing, walked out of the store.

Three weeks after the handbills were distributed Fong had sold none of Fakhru's goods and none of the milk. He was now certain that Fakhru had swindled him with the American merchandise and the talk about getting rich. The tiny doubt had been dispelled. Fakhru was a crook. Fong wondered why there had been any doubt at all about Fakhru's intentions. Fong had received thirty shillings and had spent it on food. He knew he now owed 400 shillings. He knew the milk deal was a swindle, the handbills another fraud. But his faith in the train did not waver. He knew it would crash one day; he knew the white women would come. So sure was he of this that he had refused to sell any of the milk to Africans. Margerine had asked for, but was refused, a can. Another week passed, another ten shillings from Fakhru, no business and still the feeling that very soon something good was about to happen. Fong braced himself against the counter; he prepared himself for the onslaught of white wives, like the stranger who pauses in a forest and knows very well that there are savage animals and deep holes all around him, but gold and jewels as well; the man who stands silently in the darkness with one hand over his groin and the other hand outstretched waiting for it to touch gold or be bitten off. It was that kind of risk. And one day there was a noise at the door, the sound of clothes, the scuffle of shoes; Fong looked up sharply to see, not the big-nosed face of a white woman at the head of a charge of housewives, but instead a thin yellow one, almost familiar, unsmiling, and saying. 'You are a running dog.'

18

The talk about Asian bloodsuckers and leeches had ceased with the Prime Minister raising his arms to the Asians on the upper viewing deck at the airport. Now the Asian community was largely ignored. Where before there had been insult, now there was nothing. Before the Asians had suffered persecution, now they were suffering nothingness, some more than others, but all felt it, for the suffering was actual. The inattention, the nothingness, the neglect hurt them deeply.

S. R. Patel expressed it to Fakhru by saying, 'At least before we knew where we stood. They called us bloodsuckers. We called them baboons. They raped up Sheth's daughter. We gave them few kicks. Gupta waves his arms and says, "Help the poor blacks." We say no. We make a little money on the black market. They chisel us out of Party donations and free credit. We swindle them. They break our windows. A fair fight – everybody knows what the sides are, everybody knows what's going on. Now,' he sighed, 'they deported J. H. and the rest of them. You make a big *shauri* at the airport. Nobody calls anybody bloodsucker. Nobody says nothing. Nobody even gets deported again, no broken windows, no more kicking houseboys. Business as usual. Nobody knows what's going to happen next. I'm bloody sick of it, man.'

Fakhru made sure the papers for the coffee *shamba* were in order. He had the signatures of V. B., M. K. and R. H. Patel as witnesses. He sipped his tea and sampled some *laddhu* and then, swallowing, he shook his head and spoke.

'That's a nice speech and some of it is true. But don't you see,' he said, 'they are still baboons?'

'How are we supposed to know that?' asked S. R. dejectedly. 'They don't call us leeches.'

'We were never leeches!' said Fakhru sharply, grinning. 'They were always baboons.'

To prove his point, Fakhru told S. R. a story. A sahib up-country was on his veranda drinking one afternoon; it was a lovely day and the man was lucky enough to have a large mango tree in the garden. 'What nice chutney I could make from those mangoes,' the sahib said. He went over to the tree and peered up into the branches. He was astonished to see his houseboy curled up and dozing on a branch, his arms hanging down, his cheek against the bark of the branch. 'Hello there! What are you doing?' shouted the sahib. 'But sah,' said the houseboy, 'I thought you gave me home leave.'

'So you see,' said Fakhru, 'there's nothing to worry about. They are the same.'

'Fakhru*bhai*, I tell you it would make me very happy if they were out on the street there throwing big stones through my windows! I like things to be normal: they throw stones through my windows; you ask me who is doing such a dreadful thing; I say *blacks!* Who are you? you ask. I am S. R. Patel, I reply. Hah! Such a thing is not possible now.'

S. R. was getting excited. When he described the Africans throwing stones through his windows he had a crooked smile on his face; his voice was louder than was necessary, shrill, and it cracked as he grinned and gulped through his description of the African rock-throwers. Fakhru looked concerned; he did not consider S. R.'s reaction to be a healthy one.

'You have a little *duka*, don't you?' Fakhru began.

'Little *duka*, medium-size, yes.'

'You selling a little housewares, few dry goods, so forth?'

'Indeed. And the coffee *shamba* . . .'

'You make a little . . .' Fakhru pursed his lips and looked down; he pretended to be counting money by a rapid motion of his fingertips.

'Little bit,' said S. R.

'So what you worrying about?' said Fakhru in irritation.

'I worrying about . . .' S. R. did not finish the sentence; it was as if he could not think of what was worrying him, although Fakhru gave him time to think and did not interrupt. Several full minutes passed; S. R.'s mouth was open, but he did not speak. Still he looked very worried.

'Africa,' Fakhru said, breaking the silence (he hoped to bring S. R. around; S. R. looked as if he had just been kicked out of the world), '– it's no place to raise kids. Of course, I have my own solution. If the blecks get in my way I just *kick* –' Fakhru kicked some sawdust on S. R.'s floor. 'That way they respect you. They like big *bwanas* – they don't like some little chap weeping and crying. You must be firm and tough with them. *Hoot* at them! Even strike them, my friend. Just yesterday I had to . . .'

S. R. turned his eyes upon Fakhru; they were veined red like bad yolks, like the eyes of a religious fanatic. His lower lip trembled; it was perfectly dry. 'I can't sleep,' said S. R. 'I'm not ashamed. This is true. I don't know what is going to happen to me. I can't take food, maybe little bit *dal*, few rice. I *worry*, I *suffer*. I say to my wife, "Let's we go to Canada. Ramesh is in Canada – we have nice time, no worry." She asks me is Canada near Abyssinia. I can't explain it. Where is the world? I feel like a radio – nice clean Japanese-type, shiny good batteries . . . but . . .' S. R. looked down and groaned, '*But no programmes*. No programmes, nothing but wires inside me, no programmes, no talking in here, you see what I mean?'

'You suffering, isn't it?'

'Too much,' said S. R. He breathed a sob.

'My advice to you is, *Go to Canada*. And if you're looking for a buyer for your little *duka*, household wares, so forth, you can count on me. I gave J. H. a fair price for his coffee. I do the same for you . . .'

'Publicity American-style!' said Fakhru foolishly, handing Mel Francey ten of Fong's handbills for inspection. Mel fingered one of them, wrinkled up his face and looked at Fakhru.

'Sam Fong Friend Milk Store,' he grunted. 'What the hell kinda store is *that*?'

'Milk store. Like shoe store, cycle store, vegetable store. *Duka* for selling milk in,' he explained.

'Any money in milk hereabouts?'

Fakhru said it wasn't the milk, it was the agency for American goods that would bring Fong a profit. 'He sells milk, yes – but he takes orders for all sorts of things you see listed on that chit. He will be doing very well. He might even get – *rich*!' Fakhru giggled. He hated himself. He knew he was behaving like an ass. Talking to Americans always threw him off balance; he could not prevent himself from acting foolish or talking too much. From this provocation to foolishness, which he felt when he faced most Europeans or Americans, came his contempt for these people, shared by nearly his whole community. What sometimes made it worse was when he remembered Gupta's warning: 'In the eyes of the white man you are as black as these Africans and more dangerous.'

Fakhru was still talking about Fong ('You have nothing to worry about; I will keep him well stocked with American goods, ha-ha'), but Mel was not listening. He stared at the badly printed, mis-spelled handbill of unbleached newsprint paper and shook his head. These mothers have a long way to go, he thought. Such thoughts crossed his mind only when he was confronted by definite evidence of the simplicity and smallness of the lives and ambitions in East Africa. At other times (he might be showing someone how to thread a film projector or stack pamphlets) the hopelessness of the whole place would leave him and he would laugh, sometimes too loudly, and think: I'm getting twenty grand a year for this! (He once said this to a stranger in a nightclub in Addis Ababa as they watched a very thin Negress remove her clothes to the *pong* of a wooden xylophone.) In the same way the hopelessness of the Fong scheme left him. He took another look at the handbill and laughed.

'Yes?' asked Fakhru, tilting his head.

'Supposin – just supposin we send someone in that there milk store to buy somethin, spend a little money, know what I mean?'

'You mean tell someone to go to the milk store and buy goods?' Fakhru looked puzzled.

'Well, I'm just spit-ballin – this ain't no *idea* or anythin like *that*!' Mel laughed. 'I jess thought this'd be a hell of a lot simpler if we sent a couple of people in there to juice up the whole operation, spearhead it, so to speak. What do you think of that?'

Fakhru stared at Mel. He said nothing.

Mel continued. 'I mean we pay some people to go in there and buy from the Chinaman. Simple as pie.'

'Pay someone? To buy?' Fakhru twitched.

'Yeah. That's it.' Mel bobbed his head and said 'Yeah' again. He was thinking of his salary and smiling.

Fakhru shaped his lips. At first no sound came out, but soon there was a noise, a dry one, something like, '*Vhai?*'

'What's that?'

Fakhru tried very hard. '*Vhai* are you saying this?'

'Whah?'

'Yesss, please.'

''Cause we think it's a good idea, that's whah!' said Mel, wondering if it was a good idea. 'Anyway, it wouldn't do no harm now, would it?'

'No,' said Fakhru. 'No harm, certainly.' Good heavens, thought Fakhru, and turned grey.

'So what's the objection?'

Fakhru's face stayed grey. 'It might be dear,' he finally said.

'*Dear?*'

'Costive. It might be costive, isn't it?'

'So what?' Mel stared at Fakhru, as if Fakhru had said 'It might be blue' to someone who was colour-blind.

'Needless ... expense, maybe no profit, just ... throwing money ... As we say, business is busin ...'

'Shit, man, you can't measure good will in dollars and cents! What kinda cheap bastards you think we Americans are? Sure, I agree, bidnis is bidnis, but *this here* ain't bidnis! This here's good will, *frinship*!' Mel set his face close to Fakhru's and said, 'Besides, you yourself said it won't do no harm and, brother, if it don't do no harm what difference does it make *how* much it gonna cost?'

Fakhru wanted to say, 'If you Americans were not so rich I would say you are crazy and quite dangerous,' but good manners prevented him. He said simply, 'Indeed,' and let it go at that.

Mel sensed Fakhru's bewilderment. But the more awed and bewildered Fakhru became, the more convinced Mel was that he was doing the right thing, that his plan could not miss. Briefly, it would require making Fong rich without actually handing him the money. He would discover fun, broads, greed, throwing money around, putting people to work, all the bonuses of capitalism, the corruption of comfort and so forth. Mel told Fakhru how a man becomes a Communist: just like a drowning man he will grab anything. He told Fakhru about Communists he had known, about their crummy teeth, rotten health, awful clothes, Barney Oldfield caps, joyless lives. The object was to make Fong happy, content, preferably rich, and with a strong suspicion that America made him that way. After that he would be useful in telling the world the truth about Communism. He said that Fong had proved to be a tough nut to crack.

'When he is cracked you will be heppy?'

'Not me necessarily,' said Mel. 'But the world'll be a better place, know what I mean?'

'No.'

'Take Africa. You take your average underdeveloped African country and your average gutfull of growing pains. Then you stick in a Chi-com and, brother, you've got trouble, don't think you haven't.'

'I am not understanding.'

'What *are* you, a Communist? Here I am explaining the whole thing to you. The trouble with you, Fakra, is you jess don't *wanna* understand, that's all. You want me to spell it out for you ABC? *Jesus.*' Mel rolled his head.

'You mean this fellow Fong? You think he's annoying the blecks?'

'Annoying? No *sir*. Killin, screwin up, burnin, *yes*! I tell you,

he's –' Mel leaned closer to Fakhru '– he's the one that's responsible for this here emergency thing, sure as shootin. Why you think
the Old Man's so het up for?'

Fakhru tittered.

'You laffin? I tell you we *know* that guy's messin around. We got
him watched, don't ask me by who. We know everyone that's
messin around here.'

'The blecks, no?'

'No. The yallers.'

'Fong?'

'Right. Fong. That's our man.'

Fakhru sighed. 'Let me just say I have lived almost my whole life
here in East Africa. My father traded in cashews on the coast. I
know the blecks. If there is trouble here, it is the blecks. The
trouble is never serious because the blecks cannot do very much.
They are as lazy in breaking down as they are in building up. You
see, there was what they called emergency here where any poor
fellow could be arrested *kabisa* for no reason at all. That simple
chap Fong had nothing to do with that – it was the blecks, I know
them very well indeed . . .' Fakhru continued to explain, first using
his experience and talking about the deportations; he told how,
using a simple trick at the airport, he had singlehandedly convinced all the politicians, and especially the Old Man, that the
Asians 'were good cheps'. He acted out his airport trick and
showed how the money had dropped out of his pockets. Mel did
not seem convinced. Fakhru told his jokes, the one about the
sahib's houseboy and another about the banks taking on African
members of staff and making them 'branch managers'. Finally he
said, 'You have not been here very long. You will see. Yes, it is true,
all men are brothers – but the blecks are our younger brothers. You
do not fully understand the blecks . . .'

While Fakhru was speaking Mel had risen out of his chair. He
was now facing Fakhru.

'Now don't tell me the so-called blacks did *that*!' said Mel.

'I am telling you, sir. The blecks run this country. They make the
laws. They raped Sheth's daughter. They break our shop-windows

and deport us. The blecks want to kill us all. If they had more arrows they would do it.'

'No, they *wouldn't*!'

'How do you know, if you please?' Fakhru said saucily.

''Cause *I'm* black and *I know*.'

Fakhru did not speak. He simply folded his hands and took a good look at Mel. He knew something was going wrong.

'Now *back up!*' Mel said loudly. 'For your information, buddy-boy, *I'm a black!* You see that skin?' He held his huge forearm in Fakhru's face. 'That's *black* skin.'

'No, it's not,' said Fakhru in polite correction. 'It's brown, like . . . like *mine*.' He smiled.

'It ain't like yours. It's *black*!'

In this rare moment, when the words of persecution that Mel had always suspected were being whispered were actually spoken, Mel was at one with the Africans. It was 'These are my people' once again, and not because he had changed his mind about them (they still pissed in broad daylight against the side of National and Grindlay's), but because of Sam Fong, the menace who was responsible for the emergency, and Hassanali Fakhru, who represented, in his brown contempt, all the insult that Mel had endured, real or imagined; and in this loveless chaos which the impoverished Africans endured it was clear to Mel why the embassy took no notice of Asians. Mel was also very happy. Again he was a person, no longer a perfect stranger. He was scoring.

Fakhru backed up. He continued to look at Mel's arm (Mel was rolling up his sleeve). He thinks he is black, thought Fakhru.

'What you're saying is plain racial prejudice. It's nothing new to me – I'm used to it,' Mel said with pain in his voice. 'But, Fakra, I thought you and me were frins . . .'

'We *are* friends,' said Fakhru. 'I had no idea . . .'

'Don't you *see*? I'm an Afro-American.'

'You are?'

'You bet,' said Mel. 'And I can tell you it ain't the Africans screwin up this country. It's the Commies. I tell you, Fong's our man.'

Even as much as Fakhru hated Gupta, the Hindu meddler, he could not blame him for the trouble. And the idea that the incompetent Fong could be responsible for the near overthrow of the government when he obviously had problems with his own small *duka* – it was so ridiculous that Fakhru almost laughed. He would have laughed, but he knew that somehow he had offended Mel ('I'm *black*, I tell you!') and so he kept his mouth shut. He let Mel tell him about what the Chinese had done in a dozen countries, making it look as if the Africans could not run their own affairs, buying and selling people left and right like cans in a grocery store. And while Mel spoke, Fakhru, who was after all a business man, put two and two together, thought of Fong and said to himself: So that is why . . .

There was not much more. The conversation hit a definite slump when Mel sided with the Africans, but Fakhru managed to say, 'Indeed, if we give them a chance . . . multiracial society . . . build the nation . . . *harambee* . . . let bygones be bygones . . .'

And at the very end Mel explained that they were throwing a party for Fong, a big splash. ('We're gonna use psychological warfare on him . . .') As he said this, explained the party, he sadly realized that only Fakhru could get Fong to the party. And Fakhru himself, of Hassanali Fakhru Enterprises Ltd, had this very thought the moment it crossed Mel's mind. Mel reflected that however honky and big-mouth biased and two-assed about race relations Fakhru was, he was more or less indispensable. While the friendship was certainly at an end, Fakhru would continue to act as a middleman; without affection and even without understanding and definitely without sympathy the plot against Fong would continue, and from both points of view – it saddened Mel a great deal to think this since he was now sure he hated Fakhru's guts – business was booming.

19

You are a running dog, Mr Chen had said. It was the prologue to a torrent of abuse, all of which Fong bore in silence, the large counter his only protection against Mr Chen and his partner. First one, then the other harangued him, told him he was a lackey, a leech, a disgrace to China.

Fong said nothing; he had started to object but was silenced by more abuse. The men did not look harmful, though they were certainly impolite. Still, they were Chinese, and their accent was good – thirty-five years of speaking Swahili had taken the edge off Fong's. He wondered why they chose him to insult; the insults were most odd. *A disgrace to China?* It reminded Fong vaguely of one of his first dealings with Fakhru in which Fakhru accused Fong of 'giving Asia a bad name'. That remark bemused Fong at the time, and he was further bemused when Mr Chen said something similar, for China, indeed, all of Asia in his mind, was nothing more than one muddy little hillside paddy with three huts, all leaky, some naked children, his playmates and two oxen. There was also a bridge which washed away every year and some wildflowers. The two Chinese in the shop hissing like snakes rapped against this vision and disturbed Fong's reverie. They said they had seen the Americans in his shop many times, and Indians too, bloodsuckers all of them, weakening the country and causing chaos. Fong had dealings with them, had sold out to them; he was a jackal in Marxist clothing, a puppet, a fascist octopus who would soon sing his swansong because he was pursuing a revisionist line. They knew; they had watched him. They knew every move he made. 'You are never out of our sight,' said Mr Chen.

Their harangue had not gone on long. But it was non-stop; one got his breath while the other hissed. At the end they reached into briefcases and withdrew bundles of magazines and clean new books: *The Quotations of Chairman Mao Tse-tung*, with a red washable plastic cover, *China Reconstructs, China Pictorial, Peking Review, The Selected Military Writings of Mao Tse-tung* in a boxed edition with a silk ribbon bookmark sewn to the binding and *The People's Songbook* which, when thrown on Fong's counter, opened unaccountably to 'As a Paddy Field is Ploughed the Afro-Asians Will Dig Up All the Shackles of Colonialism and Imperialism While Chairman Mao Shines Like a Red Sun in Our Hearts'. They screeched again, this time in unison, and said that Sam Fong should carry the revolution to the end, that he should stop being a tool of the Yankee imperialists and that he would see them again.

The Chinese had skulked in and accused. They left the store unseen. Mel Francey arrived in the embassy Chevy with Fakhru, a mob of Africans running alongside the car. No secrecy, no skulking was involved. Secrecy was out of the question; it would not have been psychological warfare. The aim was to make Fong feel wanted.

It was the long, shiny, unblemished car, the two American flags attached to chrome posts on the huge fenders, the licence plate USA-32 and also Mel, a large, clean man, that drew the hostile crowd. (Everything large and new has the fascination of arrogance in a poor country, where things are little, usually dirty and are not seen; or if they are large are invariably in disrepair.) Mel was wearing his straw hat, a light-coloured jacket with matching shorts instead of trousers and sandals. The outfit, and the fact that he was sitting in the back seat – the car driven by an old man – made Mel look like a large silly child in his father's car. He got out and walked towards SAM FONG FRIEND MILK STORE FOR ALL YOUR MILK NEEDS. Fakhru followed.

The crowd gathered to stare. The driver snapped insolently at them, but they refused to disperse. Mel smiled, oblivious of the hostility, and shook a few moist hands saying, '*Jambo!* Howsa boy ... *Jambo!* Howsit goin, buddy-boy!' etc. He was met by reproachful gazes; no one spoke except Mel, and before he came anywhere near the entrance to Fong's *duka* both American flags were pinched from the fenders. The flags, passed from hand to hand, ended up at the doorway, where two small boys wagged them in Mel's face.

Mel was delighted. He snapped a picture with his pocket camera and murmured, 'Warm welcome in jungle outpost. We are loved everywhere,' as if supplying a title.

All Fakhru's anger was roused when he saw large crowds of Africans. He imagined them travelling in mobs, in herds which destroyed – ate, broke, defiled – everything in their path. While Mel grinned and winked at the hostile faces, Fakhru shouted, 'Go back to sleep, you bastards! *Toka!* Go away! Can't you see we have big business here? What are you looking at, you bugger! You never saw a white man before? What is the big *baraza* for? Piss off, *wananchi*, back to the trees and stop troubling ...'

From the crowd came a chorus: '*Muheendi mshenzil!* ... Indiani stupeedi ... Bloody Indiani ... *kondo!* ... Lobber! ... Blood sheet ... You beeg sheet *kabisa!* ...'

Mel smiled and continued waving.

Fong saw them coming. He was in the same position when, ten minutes previously, Mr Chen and the small fellow had harangued him. The pile of magazines lay on the counter, the *Peoples' Songbook* still open to the song about the Afro-Asians digging up colonial shackles.

Trained in such things, Mel was able to greet Fong warmly and mentally note the name of every pamphlet and book on the counter as soon as he entered the store. He was not surprised to see them there; he had read every one of them. The fact that they were in English did not trouble him in the least. The presence of the *Military Writings* confirmed what he had said about Fong; he reminded himself to tell Fakhru about it, Fakhru who had said, 'If there is trouble in this country, it is the blacks.'

'Buying nice milk?' Fong said to Mel. When he saw Fakhru his face fell and he said, '*Selling* nice milk?'

'We're not here to sell you a thing,' said Mel, taking out a large square envelope with an eagle embossed in gold on the flap. This he placed on top of the *People's Songbook*.

Fakhru translated. 'In this big-big envelope is a special discount chit, very cheap, you pay me later if you are interested. With this chit you are able to sell milk to all Americans.'

Mel looked eagerly at Fong, hoping for a smile.

Fong was confused. 'Look around. Look at all the goods. No money, just goods.' He gestured at the crates of milk, the cans on the shelf.

'The Americans are having a big *baraza* – buying and selling as well – at the big-big fancy embassy house. You can sell many cans there.'

'They want milk?'

'These people want everything. But to enter their *duka* you need this chit. *Bwana* here is asking do you want to buy.'

'How much for the chit?'

'Not much. Little-little. Hundred only. You don't have to pay me with real money. Say yes, finish. You owe me just the same. Take the chit and then you owe me an even five hundred.'

Fong looked at the envelope. It was pure white; the eagle gleamed on it. He picked it up.

'Too pretty this chit. Costing more than hundred only,' said Fakhru.

'What're you saying?' asked Mel impatiently. And before Fakhru could answer, he asked, 'What's *he* saying? He wanna come?'

'It appears he wants money, though he is reluctant to accept it here while his family watches. Note an exceeding number of faces in the doorway.'

'Tell him to name his price,' said Mel, looking around the shop.

Fakhru turned to Fong. 'He says he will sell you the chit for shillings seventy-five only, special today. Six months to pay, no *down payment* . . .'

'Yeah,' said Mel, hearing Fakhru's only English phrase, 'Whatever it is, tell him it's jess a down payment. There's a bundle more to come if he plays along.' He looked at Fakhru with pleasure.

'You know, Fakra, you sure are a sonofabitch, but you got a helluva good head for bidnis.'

Mel felt he had at last zeroed in on Fong; with the help of Fakhru, of course. Another success, a little sunlight let in through the bamboo curtain. It had not been easy, but in a world populated by Chinese saboteurs of Fong's ilk, racists like Fakhru with whom one had to do business both at home and abroad, and red tape – Bert's title for the report (or was it *red-handed*? He could not remember, though he knew it was catchy) – what *was* easy?

'I try my best, *bwana*,' said Fakhru, bowing. 'He wants shillings five hundred only.'

'Give him 600,' said Mel with enthusiasm.

'I offer sixty,' said Fong.

'He accepts it,' said Fakhru in English; and in Swahili, '*Anaiku-bali*, he accepts it.'

20

'Invite all your friends, Fakra,' said Mel, 'providing they're Africans.'

Fakhru had come to know that Mel was not joking. Using his own invitation as a model, he had his friend Bhimji print several dozen more, and these he hawked shamelessly to Africans around town at fifty shillings apiece. Shoogra did the inscriptions with a thick-nibbed pen.

The night of the embassy gala in Fong's honour, Fakhru drove to the *duka* in his grey van. Fong stood in the doorway, his invitation clutched tightly in his hand. Fong was not wearing his cork helmet as he usually did when he went out. He wore an old, pinstriped, grey woollen suit that was creased with a hundred little squares and angles as if it had been folded as small as it would go and then stored squashed under something heavy. His collar tips curled upwards, his wide, frayed tie hung outside his oversized jacket; on his feet were soiled tennis shoes, which his trouser cuffs covered completely. Shoogra was in a sari of gold brocade; Fakhru wore a clean set of pyjamas.

As they drove away Fong looked back. Soo was not sitting on her stool. She was standing behind the counter where, for well over four years, Fong had stood. Her neck was straight; she stared through the door.

The American Ambassador's residence was in the centre of town, across from Parliament. Formerly the house of a colonial officer, it had, in addition to a large veranda hung with vines, a private zoo in the back and terraced gardens extending to a postcolonial swimming pool with lights glowing inside it. A slum of grass-roofed shacks lay beyond the embassy fence ('You've got your

very own village!' a visitor had once remarked to the ambassador).
In Fong's honour, paper lanterns – they were Japanese – had been
strung along the driveway, across the veranda and even over lights
inside the house. A paper dragon and a paper tiger dangled from
the ceiling; on the walls were scrolls with oriental writing on them.
In plates around the room were fortune cookies, small Buddhas
and smouldering joss sticks. It was as if someone had collected a
bit of junk in every bazaar from Beirut to Tokyo and brought it all
intact to the ambassador's house. For balance, to compensate for
the farrago of oriental knick-knacks, American flags were everywhere: on a tall pole on the front lawn, over the fireplace and in
every corner of the house. There was a photograph of President
Kennedy chatting with the ambassador; under this picture the two
statesmen were identified, and there was a quotation under their
names to the effect that Africa was the last frontier and that the
'New World' would accept the challenge of this 'Newer World',
not because the Communists were doing a lot but because it was
the right thing to do. The house was large, the living room alone
held four huge sofas and a dozen chairs.

In spite of the many places to sit, when Fong entered with
Fakhru and Shoogra everyone was standing, and among these
standing people, at the entrance of the three Asians, there was a
hush which quickly became a dead silence. The silence lasted a
long time, and in fact was not broken by the ambassador introducing himself to Fong and saying that *his* name was Sam, too. It
was not broken by the ambassador's wife who, full of charm and
speaking idiotically slowly, said that she had deliberately decorated the place *à la mode Chinoise*, as she put it. It was not broken
by Mel or Bert's glad hand or by the cautious greeting of first one
and then another member of the embassy staff. And when the
ambassador said that he too was an Indian – at least his mother
was, though not an 'India Indian' like Fakhru, but rather a 'Red
Indian', a Comanche to be exact – the silence seemed heavier, more
intense, like the noiselessness at the airport whcn all the Asians
watched Fakhru kneeling before the Prime Minister and waited for
a signal, not knowing that the silence itself was a signal. The

silence in the ambassador's residence stopped time and made people conscious of their breathing, and most of all it made those in the room conscious of the little yellow man in their midst, flanked by Fakhru and the ambassador and backed up by Mel and Bert, like a rare trophy brought back alive from a jungly distant land everyone knew existed but which no one, save Mel and Bert, had visited. The little yellow man did not blink; he may not even have had his eyes open; he stood – the smallest person in the room – and held tight to the frayed cuffs of his jacket sleeves. His hair was carefully parted: it was pure white, for although his face was not lined, he was old. His certain age occurred to the people watching in silence, but it was his creased woollen suit and not his age that was as awesome and almost as damning as the fact of his race.

The ambassador's wife stirred again. All eyes followed her, waiting for relief. She put on a record. 'Slow Boat to China' was followed by 'My Little China Doll', songs from an LP entitled *Slant-eyed Symphony*. It did little to relieve; everyone listened in silence to the words and watched Sam Fong. They were people who were unaccustomed to silence, who were comforted by the racket of their own voices. Stillness made them nervous and jumpy, aware of the silence they dared not break, and ashamed of the noiseless fidgeting they considered unforgivably rude.

It was not until the Africans arrived that things got moving. The Africans who had bought invitations from Fakhru arrived first, with clamour, and made for the bar. The embassy personnel merrily pounced on them, like old friends, cornered them in twos and threes, filled their glasses, remarked on their bright shirts and even on their colour ('If I come back to earth a second time, I want to come back black, just like you,' said one of the embassy men to an African who replied, 'Sure, *bwana*, why not?'). With the arrival of the Africans the once silent embassy staff succeeded in raising the level of noise to a comfortable din. Shortly after, other Africans showed up, the politicians, members of parliament, the chairman of the Lint Marketing Board, a political scientist, a banker and a dentist.

These last were the regulars. They were invited to all embassy parties and were now thoroughly bored with them – bored with them to the extent that they made only the minimum conversation, greeted only the senior embassy officials and drank without pause. They resented the fact that they were continually invited to the parties and were unable to refuse. Now they viewed the invitations as a gross form of persecution about which they were frankly and quite openly critical. Out of spite, the regulars made a point of never reciprocating invitations. They took pride in the fact that an American had never set foot in their houses. But the American hostesses repeatedly said that in Africa no party was complete without at least a few African faces. And so the regulars were never dropped from the guest list, a kind of slavery they felt helpless to prevent. The regulars said that they were the most familiar of all with shackles and chains that enslaved, that could be felt but not seen, and were stronger than iron. It was foreign domination all over again.

With the arrival of the Africans Sam Fong moved – or rather, was pushed – to a corner. Fakhru had not been lying: it really was a big *baraza*. There were well over a hundred people in the room. A good chance to sell a little milk, buy a few tyres, make a little money and then go home to bed. Fong allowed a man to get him a drink. That is, he said yes to a man's incomprehensible question and seconds later found himself with a tall icy glass. It froze his hand. He looked for a place to put it down. Seeing a small table near the window he edged over, but as soon as he had placed the glass on the table something moved outside.

Cupping his hands to the sides of his eyes Fong peered out the window. Peering back through the glass, and wearing a seedy suit much like his own, was Mr Chen, moths settling on his face and other insects strafing him. 'Lackey!' yelled Mr Chen with incautious loudness, and then he disappeared.

Fong felt no emotion. Mr Chen represented only the tiny but very noisy number of troublemakers that began to appear in China shortly before he left. Fong knew they were anti-government and atheistic, that they burned churches and blew up bridges. What

Fong wondered was how this Chen fellow had gotten as far as Africa. Perhaps he had been driven out by the Christians. Fong was not disturbed by Chen's shrieking; he had few memories of the Chinese speaking softly to one another. It seemed they always shrieked. He gave Mr Chen no further thought.

From his place near the window Fong watched the First Secretary towering over Shoogra, who sipped at her Coca-Cola. 'I been all over the world,' said the First Secretary. 'Been to Hong Kong, Bangkok, Calcutta, Benares – your neck of the woods, right? – Agra, Delhi. Saw the Taj Mahal by night and then the next day, by day – Karachi, Rome, Athens, London, Shannon. And let me tell you – and India, *Christ*, I don't know *how* she's gonna, no offence, solve her problems sort of, with the high birth rate and all. But as I was saying, let me tell you: *people*, I don't know, *they're all the same*, you know what I mean?'

Shoogra stared. Her Coke had gone flat. She watched the First Secretary drain his glass and then purse his lips.

'Sure,' he went on, 'it takes a few drinks for people to become their real selves. There was this college professor, a bright little guy in Bangkok – no, Bangalore, I think it was Bangalore – we had a few and he loosened up, cut the sahib crap and he was telling me the same thing: they're all the same, regardless of the colour of a man's skin. And you know? I think that's just great.'

Shoogra did not react. Not because she was a Moslem and did not like the First Secretary saying, 'It takes a few drinks for people to become their real selves,' but because her English was faulty and she was not quite sure what he was saying. The First Secretary took her silence to mean disapproval of his sentiments. His tone turned to pleading.

'I know you Indians aren't crazy about Africans. But, Jesus, you gotta realize that Africans are just like everyone else, only darker.'

Fong went for his glass again. A man was standing near it. Fong approached him and said, '*Unajua kiswahili, bwana?*'

The man grinned and said, with gestures, 'Me. No. Speak Chi-nese. Me. Speak. Eng-lish.'

'Buying milk?' Fong took his crumpled invitation out of his jacket pocket and showed it to the man.

'Me. No. Speak.' The man began again. He raised his arms to gesture, but just as quickly dropped them to his sides and gave up. He walked away, muttering.

Fong picked up his glass and gulped it. He felt his bladder swell and then go taut.

'Africa. Big deal,' a voice to Fong's left whined. 'Mountains, trees, flowers, coons, unforgettable scenery. Man, I've had it up to here. If you ask me I'd say it's pretty god-damned forgettable. The other day I was saying to my wife, "Helen, everything you see in Africa – every last thing – you could see five miles out of Washing-ton, DC." That's what I said to her and she said, "Bob, honey, you're dead right." Africa, big deal!'

'There are nice zoos here,' was the rejoinder. The woman who spoke had the hard face of a barfly.

'Zoos! Don't talk to me about zoos! Ever seen the zoo in Damascus? Now *there's* a zoo.'

'There's a swell one in Caracas, now that you mention it.'

'And did you ever see the one in Kuala Lumpur? Near the what's-its-name?'

'The Esso station?'

'No. The . . . the . . . museum thing.'

'No, never saw it.'

'That's a shame. I think that one's tops.'

'When were you in Borneo?'

'Kuala Lumpur's not in Borneo, for Christ's sake. It's in thing, in Malaya. I was there three years. I'm an old Far East hand. Saigon, too. Boy, *there* was a city. No bananas in Saigon, you can bet your butt on that.'

'Saigon? Veetnam?'

'Oh, sure. You could *live* there. It's gone down a lot, though. The fucking Chinese have . . .' He did not finish the sentence. He apologized, not to the lady with whom he was talking, but to Sam Fong, whom he saw eying him.

Fong slipped away, and the man said, 'I've really done it now.

Just like when I was in Tokyo in forty-six and forgot the war was over.'

'You seem to have travelled quite extensively,' said the lady.

'In this racket you gotta keep moving,' the man said. He walked quickly to the bar where Mel and Bert, surrounded by listeners, told of the difficulties they had in winning over Fong. The party seemed more theirs than Fong's. For once, no one offered information about Communists he had known; no one, it seemed, had ever met one. 'It was a real bitch,' said Mel. 'He's tough as nails, that Red,' said Bert. 'Heartless. He'd sell his mother down the river . . .'

Fong went to the side door and looked for a toilet. He peeked into several corners, behind some potted ferns and into the hallway; he saw nothing that resembled a toilet, nowhere to relieve himself. He thought of going outside and pissing against the house, but he knew Mr Chen was there waiting for him. Mr Chen would corner him and begin yelling. Fong saw Fakhru talking to one of the embassy wives. Fakhru was saying that he had always wanted to visit the States; it was his one dream and one day he would do it. Hearing this, an African appeared. He had apparently misheard the conversation; he was under the impression that the woman Fakhru was talking to was interviewing Fakhru for a free trip to the States to go on a study-course. The African asked for a free ticket. When he made this request the woman turned away from Fakhru, ignored him totally (Fakhru was still speaking as the woman turned) and began talking to the African. Fong made a sign to Fakhru.

Fakhru came over. 'How is your milk selling?' he asked.

'No milk selling,' said Fong. 'I am searching for the *choo*. Where is pissing? I want to piss and then go home.'

'Not now. This is your fat chance. You will have a lot of *baraka* here, selling milk. First selling, then pissing.' He swung Fong around to the First Secretary and introduced Fong, then himself.

The First Secretary was drunk. He eyed Fong with suspicion and tried to hear what Fakhru was saying (in the centre of the room some Africans were demonstrating a native dance; they were hooting and clapping in rhythm).

'Very nice party,' said Fakhru. 'My esteemed friend Fong enjoys it very much.'

The First Secretary looked at Fong. Fong smiled. The First Secretary looked wildly into his glass and then drank.

'Oh, he is very happy indeed,' said Fakhru expectantly.

'Thass what we like to hear,' said the First Secretary, and he walked away.

'You've just sold three crates. I am authorized to pay you,' said Fakhru. He dragged Fong into the hallway and stuffed sixty shillings into Fong's side pocket saying, 'You're a lucky fellow selling this milk. You can't go home now.'

Fong looked at Fakhru. Beyond Fakhru's beaded cap, in the corner near a large carving, was Mr Chen, glowering.

'Do you know that *muntu*?' asked Fong.

'Which one?' Fakhru turned, but Mr Chen had disappeared.

'You have drunk too much *pombe*,' said Fakhru.

The ambassador appeared where Mr Chen had been, as if the wily oriental had changed himself into a paunchy half-breed with big square jowls and a shiny silk suit.

'You were saying,' said Fakhru to the ambassador, 'your mother was an Indian.'

'Sure was,' said the ambassador. 'And not only mine. Lots of people in this very room – Americans just like you and me' – the ambassador said this automatically, as though everyone he spoke to was an American – 'they've got tons of Indian blood in them. Mel Francey, you know Mel, claims his granddaddy was a Seminole from Tallahassee. Who'm I to say he's lying!' It was clear from the ambassador's tone, however, that Mel *had* lied about his grandfather.

'Such an interesting country you have, mixed up by immigrants just like East Africa.'

'The best,' the ambassador said. 'And we're hoping that our friend here' – he nodded towards Fong – 'will accept the invitation of the American people and pay us a visit.'

'I am sure he would be very happy to see your country,' Fakhru said. In Swahili he said, 'Three more cases of milk.'

Fong felt his bladder bulge up into his rib cage and harden. It was odd. For the first time in his life he was in a place where he could not urinate at will. But he had made 120 shillings, of which sixty was clear profit, since the price of admission had to be deducted. The pain of his full bladder put these thoughts out of his mind. 'Ask this *bwana* where is pissing,' he grunted to Fakhru.

'If you please,' said Fakhru, 'can you direct my friend to the latrine?'

'To the *what?*'

'Latrine. He want to peace.'

The ambassador made a sour face, as if he had just swallowed something foul. He pointed to a doorway at the end of the hall and walked in the opposite direction, his face set in the same sourly bloated expression.

Fakhru led Fong to the toilet. 'Here it is, American-style, *wazungu choo*. Do not fall in.'

Fong hopped inside and slammed the door.

Shoogra put her head into the hall and called Fakhru. She said it was almost midnight, time to go. The children were alone. She hinted that it was a bad hour to go back; the Africans who were getting drunk in the living room would start to leave any minute.

I have delivered the goods, thought Fakhru. He felt he had done his part. He had delivered Fong and also ensured that he would stay by faking a deal and giving Fong the sixty shillings. Fakhru did not like the idea of leaving Fong alone; there was always the chance that, as Fong's interpreter, he could make more money. Alone, Fong would stay out of trouble, for he did not speak English, and none of the embassy staff spoke Swahili. There would not be any misunderstandings. Tomorrow would bring fresh profit, and the day after. Fong was the best bit of merchandise Fakhru had seen for a long time, and it struck him, there in the hallway ringing with Shoogra's unpleasant voice, that Fong was, in his own way, like the rest of the valuable goods, also from the black market.

Shoogra's voice was getting urgent. Fakhru told her to shut up and, when she was silent, took a handful of peanuts from a plate and walked out to the van munching, his wife several steps behind.

Inside the toilet Fong looked at the large raised bowl. It looked like a Chinese vase, a fountain, nothing like the old familiar hole in the floor. His brain worked quickly. *How to do it?* He imagined various positions, but was not sure he would be on target. With his tongue between his teeth he climbed carefully on to the edge of the bowl where he stood, his feet on the rim, with one hand braced against the wall.

From his hiding place near the carving Mr Chen watched the bathroom door. He had seen Fong enter. Minutes passed and Mr Chen was seized with the fear that, for security reasons, Fong might be inside slashing his wrists. He looked around. There was no one in the hallway, but the laughter and loud singing inside were proof that he was not alone. Lifting the carving (it was of a man, slightly hydrocephalic, with popping eyes and an out-stretched arm holding a spear; conveniently, it was almost life-size, or roughly Mr Chen's height), Mr Chen crouched behind it and held it before himself for camouflage as he picked his way down the hall to the bathroom.

He had ten feet to go when he heard:

'Oh, *there* you are. I bin lookin for you *every*place.'

Mr Chen spun round and tried to disguise himself as a feature of the carving.

Mel faced him, looked irritated and said, 'I don't know what I'm gonna *do* with you, brother!' in mock motherly fashion, shaking his head.

Mr Chen went stiff. He stared Mel in the eye. He contemplated leaping out the window, but there was no window in the hallway. Mel was holding a brandy snifter with an inch of brandy in it. Mr Chen thought of dousing himself with Mel's brandy and setting himself alight (the whole embassy might go up with him), but he had not secured permission. It was enemy territory. The American stood and urged him. Now the American had him by the arm and was pulling him out from behind the carving. Mr Chen kept his hand near the revolver strapped under his baggy woollen suit and followed Mel.

When Sam Fong came out of the toilet he entered a silent hallway.

Fakhru was not there. Shoogra was gone. A large carving stood in the centre of the floor. In the living room the noise had stopped. Fong saw only a large group of people with their backs to him. He did not see that they were all drunk, that they were now drunk enough to speak and that they were speaking one at a time to Mr Chen, who stood at the centre of the group as Fong had done. Unlike Fong, and perhaps because he was a diplomat, Mr Chen had the good sense of timing to smile and say thank you when he was told that he, Sam Fong, was going to visit the United States of America free of charge, at the request of the American people.

Fong passed unnoticed through the front door of the embassy and went home. He told Soo of the evening, of the six sold crates and most of all of the odd gleaming fixture in the small closet. Before he went to bed he opened the door to the store and looked in. The stacks of milk crates, the cans of milk on the shelves, were silver in the moonlight that filtered through the shop-window. There was a lot of milk; it nearly filled the store. But Fong knew it would be sold and he repeated this to Soo that very night.

Part Three

21

Mr Chen could have been an undersized clothes post on which several thoughtless people had thrown a velour Tyrolean hat with a feather, a summer suit (so wrinkled and so large that it looked like two), a pre-knotted clip-on tie with the Washington Monument painted the length of it, two cameras and a tape recorder; the camera straps swung and everything bumped together as he walked. Mel Francey and Bert Newt carried the maps and brochures. They were deeply touched when the man they knew as Fong paused a few reverent moments before the Eternal Flame of the late President. They visited the Smithsonian Institution, the Pentagon, where Mr Chen tirelessly (and with special permission) snapped pictures; they stood before the stone gaze of Lincoln in his memorial, walked the wide avenues, chatted with some indignant sign-carrying mothers and youths with musical instruments who were picketing the White House; they drove to a small town in Maryland where not only Mr Chen, but also Mel, was refused service (Bert graciously said that it did not matter, he wasn't hungry anyway). In halting English Mr Chen said he wanted to see everything and to collect information, street maps and postcards for his family album.

Four moon-faced Onondaga Indians were flown in from Syracuse, New York, to dance for him. Mr Chen was delighted: he snapped pictures while the spools of the tape recorder turned slowly. After the dance Mr Chen spoke with the Indians. He gave one of them his velour hat in return for a large, feathered headdress with tassels, which he immediately put on. The oldest of the four, a man with squirrel pelts scarcely covering the soiled BVDs he wore beneath, refused to give Mr Chen his tomahawk (Chen admired it) but made him an honorary chief of the Onondaga tribe. The old man said that if Mr Chen ever happened to be in Syracuse he should give him a buzz. 'I will if I can find one,' said Chen. He did not know that he had made a joke until he saw Mel slapping his thigh and laughing. With the headline INJUNS FETE EX-RED IN DC POW-WOW ('*Just like A Film-show,' Says Chief Fong*) a picture showed Mr Chen in his floppy war-bonnet brandishing the old man's tomahawk.

He was denied nothing. For several weeks he lived with an American family in suburban New Jersey: he attended a church bazaar and cake sale with them, went to the local supermarket and marvelled at the frozen foods, helped their teenaged daughter with her geography homework and in all ways shared the simple comfortable life of middle-class Americans. When Mr Chen bade them farewell, the man of the house said it would be a great thing indeed if people like Mr Chen, whom he knew as Fong, foreigners and suchlike, could spend more time in the USA. It was one pathway to understanding. 'Foreign policy means people,' the man said with emotion. And to this, Mr Chen bowed. Later he visited high schools, where he read to the assembled students a text prepared by Bert, which began, 'I have lived warmly with your people; I have seen your tremendous vitality; I have sampled your delicious hot dogs . . .' and ended, 'Now I know what it means to be an American. I have, just as a bold Italian from Genoa many centuries ago, discovered America.' The speech was a huge success; it was quoted in scores of newspapers under the picture of the war-bonneted Chen.

It occurred to Mel and Bert that Fong had learned a lot of English in a very short time, but they were not surprised. They said he must have known English all along, but as he gained confidence in the Americans and became less obstinate he had discovered that it was not necessary to hide himself behind the gibberish of Swahili.

Mel and Bert were given promotions even before their recording of the programme that would tell the world with the speed of sound, better than any newspaper article, of the monstrous contradictions of Communism, of being a spy in East Africa and of seeing the Free World for the first time. From *Red-handed*, the name of the programme changed to *Red Tape, Red Herring, From Communist to Citizen* and *I was a Menace*, to its final title, *Fong and the Indians*, subtitled *The Odyssey of a Communist*. This played up, as Mel put it, 'not only your Onondaga angle, but lots of other stuff as well . . .' The story, in three voices, was one of disenchantment, desertion and discovery: on a spying mission to East Africa, Sam Fong, a Chinese secret agent masquerading as a grocer, succeeds in finding out everything that the Americans are doing – the aim of his mission; but after bugging the American Embassy and sneaking around snapping pictures and generally casing the embassy buildings, he discovers, to his immense confusion, that Yankees are really nice people and mean well; he is so taken by their simplicity and good will that he refuses to relay his intelligence work to Peking. Having spied so thoroughly on the Americans, he feels he knows them and understands them even better than he does his fellow Chinese, whom he has decided are worse than Nazis; and it is in the safety of this kindly embassy that he is granted asylum by two understanding and helpful information officers, Mr M. Francey and Mr B. G. Newt, Jr. He is quickly on a first-name basis (as he almost guessed he would be) with his new friends and he confesses that his one wish is to visit America. This, with the assistance of the American people and the staff of the American Embassy in East Africa, he does. Sitting in a Washington hotel room while four Onondaga Indians stamp on the floor and shake cans filled with beans, he discovers the rhythm and vitality of America, the meaning of freedom.

On a crisp fall day very recently this programme was recorded. Mel Francey, Bert Newt and the man they knew as Sam Fong sat in a recording studio of the Voice of America and watched the minute hand of a noiseless clock bump towards twelve. 'This is a dream come true,' said Bert. Mel agreed; so did the man known as Sam Fong. In the programme each man was to play himself, to relive the drama of those tense days in East Africa. The programme was in three parts: *Africa, America, Awake*.

The first part opened with drumming.

Mel spoke first: 'Africa! The *light* continent! Yes, in lightest Africa many new and wonderful things are happening every day of the year. Not the least of these is the heartwarming story of Fong and the Indians, the odyssey of a Communist, the awakening of Sam Fong, soon to become an American citizen . . .'

Then Fong: 'I was born in the year 1918 of poor but honest parents in Central China. At this time the brutality of the vicious Communist thugs was snowballing into cold-blooded savagery. I did not know what to do. I was confused and beguiled by the new words on everyone's lips, and little did I know . . .'

Behind large glass windows engineers looked on and twirled knobs. The three men in the studio spoke in turn, with the knowledge that now everything was fine, aware that it had taken them all great trouble – even some misunderstanding – before this fulfilment came to pass. Now they were relaxed; it was clear that each of the three had succeeded in his mission and was very happy.

And what of Fakhru? He had heard of the Fong–Chen mix-up the day after the embassy party from N. Bhikhu, the travel agent who issued Mel, Bert and the man known as Sam Fong the tickets. 'You seem to be losing a tenant,' said Bhikhu. 'I pray he is not jumping off your lease.' Fakhru had run to Fong's shop where he saw the Chinaman staring across the counter at the canned milk on the shelves opposite. Fakhru thought of going to the embassy to set the matter right but he waited a day to reflect and, after this reflection, decided that it would be an error to do anything. Mel and Bert had gone with their families; Bhikhu said they did not buy round-trip tickets. They would not be back. The understanding that Fakhru had reached with Mel and Bert did not extend to anyone else on the embassy staff. It would have been too much to explain, and there was always the chance that it would backfire, that they would want their money back. The marketing of Fong had taken place over many months, with each move and counter-move pushing the price up, increasing Fong's value, adding the compulsion of mystery to the deal. During these months, and taking into consideration the airport business which made Fakhru a salaried consultant on Asian affairs in East Africa, Fakhru had managed to make, and save, a tidy sum. The American money had bought him Patel's dry goods shop and coffee *shamba*, Mehboob's paint store, several more *dukas* and a warehouse full of merchandise, all foreign. Taxes on imports were going up. He would only need to sit quietly on his merchandise. He was rich.

Being rich was the same as being poor except that he was now less busy. There was no work to do. Fakhru felt out of touch with his business; he had set it all in motion and now there was not only no need to keep pushing, but also no way of stopping it. This thought warmed him. He now used money where he had once used his wit. It was a good chance to test proverbs. These he found false to the last; he had many good friends; he was able to intimidate anyone and buy almost anything, including love; and, contrary to the proverbs he knew, being rich pleased him – each digit to the left of the decimal point caused an added joy, a further refinement of happiness.

He missed Mel and Bert; this was his one sorrow. He missed being an interpreter for them, talking to them and turning their ignorance into money. The Americans were rich, earnest, harmless fellows and Fakhru felt it was a shame there were not more of them around. Life would be more pleasant with them. They would be trusting; they would leave important matters to people like himself; this would please everyone, even the Africans. African countries would tick over like General Motors. The British had done nothing except talk and make promises; when they tried to bargain they spoke in small figures. They were not honest, but they expected everyone else to be honest. The Americans were honest and assumed everyone else was honest. The British got nothing in return, deserved nothing; the Americans earned sympathy for their innocence, which was all they wanted. Fakhru no longer held the Americans' unbusinesslike attitude in contempt. They had made him rich.

There were the other Asians in East Africa. Most would stay, some would be deported, none would leave of his own accord: Fakhru knew this and there was never any need to form an Asian political party in order to bully the Africans. People were easy to buy; the Africans came cheapest of all. As for the Asians – they ate regularly, arranged their marriages, washed their feet, dressed well, bought cars, had swamis and betel nuts flown in; and there were enough women for everyone. Business might be slack, but it would never cease. There was unpleasantness, but in all the recrimination, all the abuse, all the nastiness and accusation, was the simple truth – proved by the abuse – that the Asians were needed. S. R. Patel's fear, that without persecution life was terrible, may have been real, but it was short-lived. A month after he phrased his fear ('I feel like a transistor radio, nice and shiny, new batteries, but . . . no programmes, just wires inside . . .') the Prime Minister viciously attacked the Asians, accused them of being 'big bosses, rich *bwanas* who pushing little poor countrymen all over the place . . .' Again Asians were openly hated; they were called dirty dogs, hypocrites and bloodsuckers as before, and with this a vigorous knowledge of identity was reborn in each Asian. Not protest – no one closed his shop – rather, they felt pain, the sting which told them they were alive, where and who they were; the abuse a reminder of their importance to East Africa. Not *bwanas* and bloodsuckers, but indispensable. Business had not really changed. Fakhru said that as he knew 'the black mind', he had expected a return of the abuse all along; the Africans would keep talking and accusing, but they would never get rid of the Asians. And even if they did, who would suffer? Only Africans (and people like Gupta), who had never made a shilling in their lives. Whether the Asians stayed or went elsewhere the Africans would be the only real losers. It was the same with everyone who came to East Africa. The visitors and immigrants seldom lost. For the Africans nothing would ever change.

The State of Emergency had been a bad thing for business. Everyone knew that. It was the Prime Minister's fault – all the trouble. He was a cruel man, he wanted to be king (whose idea was it to call him 'The Supreme Redeemer'?), but he had good business sense. It was this that kept him in power. Fakhru understood him. With many other property-owners Fakhru feared the passing of the Prime Minister. 'When the old man goes there will be trouble,' Fakhru said at the close of business deals. The Asian answer, delivered with a jerk of the head and the exploded consonant, was inevitably, 'Yes, please.' But the deal had been closed and the money had changed hands, and that was the point of it all.

Fakhru sat in his office, comforted by the portrait of His Highness the Aga Khan. He picked up a thick pair of cutting shears and trimmed a betel nut. There were certainties, few, but important ones. The Asians were lost. The Africans did not matter.

The British belched lies. The disorder and inconvenience of Africa killed charity and made profit possible. Fong still lived down the street. He owed. He had been used, but he was unworn, unsold. The Americans would stay; Africa was their green worm which, in all the childish innocence that their earnest stupidity was made up of, they valued more than treasure. The betel nut lay in slices on a white dish. Fakhru rubbed one smooth slice with his thumb and then placed the spotted nut slice on his protruding tongue. He smiled. Fong was still his.

23

Sam Fong counted the cans of milk and shouted numbers to Soo, who sat on her stool with the abacus on her lap. The filled shelves, the crates stacked near the counter, gave the store a look of prosperity; made Fong — with merchandise all around him — seem more a shopowner than ever. Six crates were stacked in the corner, awaiting delivery to the Americans. It was now only a week since the embassy party and Fong had seen Fakhru only once; he had bowed to Fakhru and not said anything. The two Americans had not been in the store at all. And just as well, Fong thought: he still owed money to Fakhru; the handbills advertising the American goods had brought no business. The retainer of ten shillings arrived every Monday; the debt to Fakhru was now over 400 shillings. Fong did not want to speak to Fakhru or the Americans until he had orders to fill, or news, or money.

But there was no money. Fong's poverty was unchanged. Sales were small, in the smallest combination of large mocking coins which filled the biscuit tin but added up to very little. Soo threaded the pennies through their centre holes; each heavy stack of twelve equalled one shilling. In the wooden box at the back of the store these threaded stacks of brown pennies looked like dog turds to Fong, reminders of his indignity.

Prices had gone up, rice was expensive and Fong had changed his diet. There were new foods, cheaper ones: sweet potatoes and peanut stew, boiled cassava and (it made him wince) bananas. They were all very recent to Fong; he had never tasted them before. Indeed, he associated their tastelessness with the dull sameness of life in Africa. The food was an indicator of why nothing had ever happened to the millions of East Africans: their country, their lives dominated by bananas. And now his own life as well. His loyalty to the Chinese diet, which had not flagged in thirty-five years in this strange land, was now at an end. Since opening the store things had altered a great deal for Fong, but now there was an almost explicit promise that nothing would change. He was certain of this when he looked at his plate. There was no rice on it. Locusts were heaped in a greasy mass next to a pale green lump of banana mush. Business could not worsen, but neither would it improve (the worst, the emergency, had already occurred and here he was, whole and unscarred by the events). There was the predictable weekly sum of ten shillings offset by the drabs of plugged pennies which did not equal ten shillings even at the end of the week. Except for the prayed for derailment of the train there could be no more unexpected profits; he had attempted a swindle, but it had failed. So the change in diet, from Chinese to African, had come of necessity; once the necessity for it had been established there could be no argument. Resigned to bananas, Fong ate them in silence, with chopsticks. It was clear after a period of eating the local food that there was no going back. The immigrant's last compromise is his diet. He would stay in Africa and not starve; he was strong but there was not much time left; he knew he was closer to death than to China.

It was late in the evening. A beggar with tiny hands and large swollen feet crouched in front of the store waiting for Fong to close. He wanted to curl up in the doorway for the night. He was patient. Fong looked at him. The beggar was black, homeless in his own country. Fong thought of the back room, warm with the steady breaths of Soo and the children. Fong would sleep soon and not be afraid. Africa did not frighten him: it was all accidental, and accidents could not be foreseen. The disordered slowness he knew existed in Africa was an assurance that the accidents would be small; he would not be harmed. He blew our the candle and locked the door. Even before he slid the bolt he heard the beggar fumbling with his rags, snorting, settling into position for the night.

Fong knelt in the darkness of the back room and said a prayer.

Soo wheezed; outside wild dogs were upsetting the trash cans and snarling. On the eaves bats squeaked like rusty wheels. Fong made the sign of the cross and then found his mat, where he lay on his back, his hands folded across his chest, his face turned straight up. Just before he went to sleep Fong had several lucid thoughts, captions vivid enough to be dreams, but not grotesque, not peopled by demons in pursuit. Here he was in a foreign country, on a reed mat littered with dirt grains; he had lost his trade and had learned a new one, an uncomfortable, uncertain profession. But it had not been a plot against him; this was accident, not design. He was alive and old, with healthy children and a store full of merchandise which would be sold if God willed the derailment. He was an immigrant, a stranger, and yet had been treated no differently from anyone else. For this he was grateful. He had not been harmed, although he knew he was outnumbered by the Africans and outfoxed by the Indians. By nature men were different (the Chinese were the easiest of all to understand), but however much the differences created upset or alarm, still there could not be deliberate evil, for man was good. And it was sometimes a discomfort, though seldom a misfortune, to be far from home.

While Fong slept, a train chugged through the Rift Valley in a rainstorm 300 miles from the store. The train clattered along, nosing through the unseasonable flood, its cowcatcher sending up huge streams of water to sizzle on its boiler. At two in the morning, near a village that was later to be widely photographed as the scene of rescue operations — tent hospitals and a wreckage of metal that was not cleared for months — the steam engine sagged on the unsupported tracks, the ties ripped away by the hillside torrents, and trembled in disjointed confusion down a gully. Its entire cargo of milk splashed out of the tank cars willy-nilly and mixed in puddles on the rain-sodden ground.

GIRLS AT PLAY

For my parents, with love

'*At my request we took a two hours' walk in the forest, following a very narrow and almost invisible path, while a native armed with a stick preceded us to clear the way. Interesting as this walk was, amongst the unfamiliar vegetation, I must confess I am a little disappointed with the forest. I hope to find better elsewhere. The trees are not very high; I expected more shade, more mystery and strangeness . . .*'

André Gide,
Travels in the Congo

I

The Playing Field

The flame trees enclosed the hockey field in a high leafy wall of bulging green; rotting orangey-red blossoms littered the moist grass. The setting sun, spattered over half the sky, made patches in the ordered field precisely gold. Beyond a straight row of blue gums, but out of sight, a bog with a stream cutting through it housed a motley orchestra of swamp-dwellers tuning up for the night. On all sides of the field were green juicy barriers; an African cage, comfortable and temporary.

If the fat black girls had not been there and playing, the order of this playing field in the highlands of East Africa would terrify. The order seemed both remote and unreasonable. Explorers have come upon abandoned buildings deep in Africa and suddenly felt despair, confronted by roofless walls, broken lizard-cluttered stairs, solid doorways opening on to dense ferns and dark towering trees. A discernible order in a place where there are no people (the dry mosque in the dunes) is a cause for alarm; it means failure; the decaying deserted order is a gravemarker.

The delighted squeals of the girls at their game, the whacking of sticks, the ball being cracked across the grass, gave the order a reason for existing. The playing field stayed a cage, and the sun moving down, drawing all its yolk with it, darkened it; but the girls were enjoying their two hours. For the black, large-buttocked girls at the school, there was nothing to worry about. In their green bloomers and grey jerseys, which showed their swinging unsupported breasts, they ran heavily hunched and held their sticks low, yelping cheerfully.

The game had just started; now the girls' voices were loud, the motion of their squat bodies was unusually vigorous in no specific direction. They were playing on a regulation-size hockey field, they had good equipment and wore uniforms, but the game was clearly chaotic and lacking in suspense. The game was an end; no one tried to score. It was not a question of the game going well – the game always went well. The motion was important, it allowed the girls a chaste outlet for their mindless energy. It was the reason for the orderly playing field hacked out of the bush. It gave the girls two hours of caged supervised play. This was Miss Poole's idea; it also gave the teachers a chance to have tea or a sundowner, to visit each other, have a siesta and generally forget that they were in the East African bush, over two hundred corrugated miles from Nairobi and not married.

Miss Verjee, the Games Mistress, worked these two hours. She watched the girls at play. An Indian (her father manufactured nails in Kampala), athletic except for her bowed Asian legs, she had a year before earned her teaching certificate from a rural teacher training college. She hated the girls, feared Miss Poole and was uncertain about her teaching. She knew she would not be at the school much longer; as she stood there on the playing field watching the hockey game, her parents were arranging a marriage for her.

Out of the corner of her eye Miss Verjee saw a small white figure nestled in the bushes on the far fringe of the playing field. The white figure did not move. It sat, ghostly in a still hedge, squinting at Miss Verjee.

Miss Verjee grasped at her whistle.

Like tired dancers the girls started to drop sighing to the field. Six lay on their backs in the grass. Miss Verjee commanded them to get up. One looked at her and then fell back heavily, flinging her hockey stick to the side. Miss Verjee blew her whistle and walked angrily towards those who had stopped playing and fallen down. As she approached the six she saw others at the far goal sit on their haunches and grin at her. She blew her whistle again and shouted for them to rise. Now all the girls flopped down and as they did Miss Verjee looked back once at the silent white figure, the dwarf at the far end of the field who, Miss Verjee knew, was taking it all in. In a strident voice which retained the Kutchi rhythms, rising and falling like a frantic prayer, Miss Verjee called, 'Get *up*, you *girls*! It is *not* the half-*time*!'

The girls did not move. On the field, patched gold and green, they could have been dark chess figures, checked into immobility by the ugly white queen squatting at the far end. The wind shushed in the flame trees, and then there was a voice.

'Thees woman ees useless.'

'Who *said* that?'

Miss Verjee took a girl by the arm and demanded to know if she had said it. The girl laughed, others laughed, and then from a group of hunched-over girls came a high excited yodelling, as from a tribal dance. Miss Verjee panicked. Holding the girl and drawing her up, Miss Verjee hit her hard across the face. The girl pulled away roughly, scrambled to her feet, and began running in the direction of Miss Poole's house.

'The rest of you *play*!' shrieked Miss Verjee, chasing the girl. None of the girls moved or spoke; they watched the bow-legged Indian chasing the short fat African across the green field, the steps making a moist squash-squash-squash in the grass. Miss Verjee caught the girl easily at the sideline and held her. 'Where do you think you are going?'

'You heet me,' said the girl, looking to the side sullenly. 'I weel tell Miss Poole.'

'Not now,' said Miss Verjee. She could not control her nervousness and was out of breath. 'You are supposed to be playing, don't you see?'

The girl said nothing. She folded her arms. Both teams, flat on the ground, stared at Miss Verjee who, facing the girl, blocked the path to Miss Poole's.

'What do you *want*? You disobeyed me. What shall I *do*? You know you can't see Miss Poole now. It's playtime.'

'I am going.'

'Miss Poole is expecting the new teacher. You can't see her.'

'Yes.' The girl tried to pull away but Miss Verjee held her fast.

'*Please*.' Miss Verjee had promised herself that she would not use that word. It came out quickly and she regretted it as soon as she heard it. 'Don't.'

The girl's smooth black face was expressionless. Even the eyes, brown-blotched and narrowed, revealed nothing. She turned without a word and walked back to where her friends lay like casualties.

Miss Verjee knew she had done more than she should. But it was worth it. Miss Poole would not be disturbed. She put her steel whistle in her mouth and blew a shrill *tweee*. Then in her high helpless voice called:

'*Half-time!*'

2

Miss Poole

Miss Poole was sitting in her room awaiting the vulgar knock of the intruder. She was alone with her prickly reverie: the same room for fifteen years. She quickly corrected the thought – not that particular room, but in that kind of room; and for the past seven years the room had been in East Africa. The previous eight, a sad pause, had been spent in a room in London and, before that, twenty-five happy years in the sun, in the highlands of East Africa. It had been a short life; now she thought of it as mostly over, only a few more years left: the surprise of ease and happiness at the beginning, now the close gloom of walls and the uncomfortable knowledge that she was about to be intruded upon.

She did not think of the years in numbers, seven years back in East Africa after an eight-year absence in England. Not in numbers – rather, in blocks of time made out of light and joy or darkness and strain, all of which created in her sensations she could phrase very simply. If someone asked her how long she had spent in England she replied, 'Too long,' and that was that. Sometimes she added, 'A shocking place. Absolutely shocking.' The length of time she had spent in East Africa she explained by saying, 'I was born here.' The simple statement was given a greater importance by her looks: she was forty but could easily have been taken for sixty. Her clear eyes were in queer contrast to her dry skin, her frumpy brown frocks and her hairstyle that appeared deliberately plain. She had no wish to look young, and her apparent creaking age was an advantage, for she knew that the old were not required to compete.

Nowadays people very seldom asked Miss Poole questions. It seemed as if the Americans were the only ones who had ever bothered to wonder, and there were few Americans around. They had asked in their curious way, 'You mean to say you were *born* here?'

Miss Poole preferred not to think about it.

But she could not ignore her room. What worried her was that from where she was sitting she could see that the room was slowly cracking, showing shrivelled rents, coming apart and falling away from her. Soon, she imagined, it would fall completely and leave her unprotected. Those on the outside, and not all Africans, had weakened it with their insistent knocks. The Africans ignored the fact, or did not care, that all doors had been open to them for the past seven years. Their revenge was not complete in the knowledge that they could enter anywhere and take over. They wanted to tear the whole place down.

They rattled the windows (Miss Poole heard them at night); they tapped on the walls in a threatening code (often Miss Poole had shone a flashlight out of the window and watched their shadowy figures disappearing with arrogant slowness into the trees, their knives flashing); they tried the doors, trampled the flowers, snatched underthings from the clothes-line and upset the trashcan grubbing for papers. They kicked at the cats and made gabbling noises at Julius in the kitchen. Once she had heard them creak across her tin roof, bumping their knees and toes on the rippled tin and making a fearful metallic juddering. The racket that accompanied this roof incident was horrible for Miss Poole lying face up and helpless on her bed, knowing that they were above her, probably naked, a few feet away, armed with machetes and trying to get in. She replaced the tin roof with tiles.

Miss Poole's one consolation was that the poor dears never seemed to be able to do anything right, not even burgle a house. But this was a small comfort, for when she heard them she did not stir, she lay in her bed malarial with fright. They usually went away. It was suicide to face them. She had seen a thief lunge at her father, who was holding a shotgun and fired into the thief's screaming mouth, opening his face up – a wet stringy hole – with the blast.

When intruders came she prayed, and fatigue's blessed mechanism would work on her and send her into unconsciousness before dawn. Long ago, in her youth, the sun had calmed her, but these past seven years had been awful. There were days when she refused to leave her room to go into other parts of the house, days when she did not go to the office or teach her classes, days when she could not bring herself to look out of the window, worn out from keeping awake the whole night, stiff, hot, anxious and awaiting the violent ripping of her knotted unvoiding bowels by the sharp tool of an intruder.

The night before had been like that and now she sat in her room, trying to rest in safe dusty daylight, squeezing her irritation between her palms. Her whole head was rigidly staring, her gaze was fixed on her office in the stone building across the hedged lawn of the compound. She knew why she had been scared and could not sleep: there had been a nightmare intruder, not an African, but a white woman.

That had been a nightmare; it had kept her from sleeping. Today the intruder would arrive. The previous day a letter had come from the Ministry of Education. Miss Poole had expected the usual ungrammatical circular ('It has came to my attention . . .') and so slit open the envelope with indifference. The envelope still read ON HER MAJESTY'S SERVICE, although East Africa had been independent for seven years. It was not a smudged circular; it was a letter from the Chief Education Officer.

Dear Madam,
> *Notice of transfer: Heather Monkhouse*

Ref your letter D/22/67 of 11th inst. requesting English teacher.

This is to inform you that as from 24 Jan., 1967, Miss H. Monkhouse, formerly of Lord Mainwaring Girls' School, Nairobi, is transferred to your employ. She is expected to take up her duties immediately and has been notified to arrive on the above date. Her subjects are English and drama.

Her Confidential File etc. has been sent via registered post.

Miss Poole was elated. She had not expected a prompt reply to her request; teachers were so hard to get up-country. No one wanted to come to the bush.

'Simon!'

'Madam.'

'Did a registered packet arrive this morning?'

'Yes, madam.'

'You might have had the good sense to bring it to me.'

'Madam?'

'*Leta* important *baruha pesi-pesi*,' demanded Miss Poole. The elation had worn off; such feelings did not survive the heat. Miss Poole prayed for simple patience; it was the middle of the morning – by noon the temperature would be in the nineties. Above her head bits of sawdust snowed down from the wooden roofbeams: white ants. The sawdust gathered on her blotter with ugly subtleness, like dandruff on a collar.

Simon placed a foolscap-size folder, fuzzed with rolls of lint from constant rubbing, over the whorls of dust. He left the office in silence.

Momentarily, Miss Poole's elation returned. The folder was unusually thick, filled with dog-eared letters, onion-skin carbons of directives, reports and ministry documents strung together on a frayed piece of green cord. She flipped through the bundle quickly, then placed the folder flat, opened to the top letter and read. She read only four pages before she slammed it shut (it huffed dust), kicked her chair back and called for Simon.

'Take this away,' she ordered stiffly. 'And unless you do something about those ants I shall be looking for a new clerk. Is that clear?'

'Madam?'

Miss Poole began impatiently repeating the same words in Swahili, but half-way through broke into English saying, 'Can't *any*one do *any*thing right!' and clopped out of her office to her house, her room, where she knew she would be safe. Her room was close with peace and fragrance, but this would not last; the woman was on her way.

3

Heather

Her lingering memory was of an elderly methodical gent in Croydon who had made love to her in the way a man might eat a soft-boiled egg. Heather had watched him do both. If there was a difference it was in frequency: he had an egg every day, but demanded her less often. Each time he took her (only fleshless verbs occurred to her: *had*, *took*, seldom *made love*) she watched him carefully, in silence. He picked at her with the tips of his fingers. He flaked off bits and rubbed them with his thumb. He peeled, prodded her smooth shell and all the while stared at what he was doing. For over three months Heather stared with him. Her metaphor never changed. She even worked out elaborate sexual imagery: the Male, spoon in hand, hunched over a warm egg; the shell picked slowly off with blunt fingers and broken nails, the membranous skin peeled and smoothed. He worked slowly and Heather was always amazed to discover that during this preliminary her desire heightened, she became hungry. And so did he: he cooed breathy nonsense, his eyes popped, his mouth fell open, his tongue protruded. Then the dunking of the spoon, the gooey yolky mass trembling.

The image of the soft-boiled egg, instead of diminishing the vividness of the act, made it seem more passionate and easier to recreate. It gave an acceptable form to something she looked upon in England with uncertainty. She liked doing it, but it seemed healthier not to think about it always in the same naked way. Most of all, her image was private, a guarded secret: it was all the privacy she had. She clung to this single perception as if to a fragile antique: she, the ravished egg, scraped clean, spooned of her juices, emptied in a cute little cup, with scraps of yolk, a soiled spoon and the remnants of broken shell littering a plate some distance from a still, satisfied man.

The jerky motion of her VW jouncing at sixty over the corrugated back roads always made her think of sex; it hurt her, and even the safe image gave her little relief. For days she had thought of nothing but her recent humiliation. The VW's sexy rhythms did not help matters, for driving she thought of love and how either party was able to turn the trust of love into violation and, in time, ridicule. At any moment, with something as simple as a careless gesture, a man could make a whore of his lover.

Heather winced. Well, she thought, wasn't it pleasant with that nice old man in Croydon? Such a dear he had been: quiet, considerate, discreet (before he pushed off he put his slippers, his toothbrush, his hot-water bottle and pyjamas in his briefcase and kissed her on the forehead: no harm done). He was nothing like the bastard in Nairobi – Heather refused to think of his name, but it came against her will – Colin. She had, after knowing him some while, made a joke about the name, the point of which was 'because you're so anal', but he had not found it very funny and replied angrily with something irrelevant and rude. Heather had never seen this in him before but it provided an explanation to something that had been bothering her. This rude impulse of Colin, just one random insult, seemed to explain his early marriage and now his excessive unhappiness at being married. When he was out with Heather and making love it was performed with the married man's directness, artlessly and in silence. He had never said much about his wife, but for that brief moment Heather had assumed the wife's taunting role, was insulted, and it became clear to her why the whole affair, like so many others (but excluding the kindly old egg-eater in Croydon), was hopeless. If she became the wife for a few mocking moments, Colin became the husband, and she knew as soon as he made the reply that she should break it off. She had said, 'Are you trying to tell me something?' He was silent. But it was a warning, and she knew humiliation would follow.

It had before. Heather thought of herself as a girl, and dressed like one, but she was a woman of thirty-six who had had on the average one and a half affairs every year since she was twenty-five. She had a capacity for disaster that was written bluntly in a cuneiform of small scars all over her body. Most of her affairs began just before Christmas when everyone seemed friendly, were consummated on New Year's Eve ('Let's start the New Year off right,' many of the men had said), and went completely to pieces in the spring. Those were the English ones, largely influenced by the foul weather and the difficulty of meeting people casually, or at all, except at large parties. Heather's job as a salesgirl in the 'Stork Shoppe' in the Croydon branch of an Oxford Street store made it impossible for her to meet men; she sold only maternity wear and when men did come into her department their most remote thought was of picking her up. Heather always considered it the worst place to be: none of the men even looked at her and she was aware that, because of her particular job, the men assumed that she was in the early stages of pregnancy herself. And instead of kindling an interest in motherhood, the job convinced Heather that children were the last thing she wanted. The distended women that shopped were flushed or blotched, vacant-eyed, flatulently lumbering among the clothes-racks, rubbing the flowered tent-like frocks between their cold fingers; their husbands looked away, distractedly praying. The few men that shopped alone ignored her; she had to wait for the Christmas parties, and she dreaded the coming of spring.

It was against all poetry, but poetry was rubbish. Love was two friends disembarrassing themselves in a bed, not handholding in Kew Gardens. In spite of all odes, love and the lies that went with it appeared in the winter, indoors, after dark. By spring the friendship was finished and, as with Colin, a signal was given, a futile rudeness which meant that it would all be over soon. The men had been rude, never Heather. And each time, Heather had asked a testing question to find out if the insult was intended. The men seldom replied, but Heather knew they had been trying to tell her something. She could not stand the thought that she would be left again; she always let the warning pass. But after two or three times she grew to recognize these hard scarring words which were uttered long before the actual parting; they made the last months terrible and the parting itself a predictable misery.

She had come to Africa five years before to get away from it all: the filthy crowded subways, the sooty church steeples, the wilted working-class faces she saw everywhere, the swollen women who shopped in her department. When the man in Croydon put his toothbrush and pyjamas into his briefcase, kissed her coolly on the forehead and said, 'Cheerio, my dear, keep your pecker up,' Heather looked into a mirror, detected signs of wear and decided to go to Spain. She needed a *fiesta*.

But with the English equivalent of only a few hundred pesetas the *fiesta* would not be a long one, she knew. A friend suggested a Mediterranean cruise because 'one never knows what might happen to one on a cruise'. The friend hinted at the unknowns and Heather calculated coldly all the possibilities in a little mental log: there would be sex, after a few days at sea everyone would be screaming for it, possibly on a moonsplashed deck, more likely assignations below deck ('We could go to my compartment – It's quieter there and I could slip into something more comfortable . . .'); there would be cocktail parties at the Captain's table, costume balls, games of shuffleboard and deck tennis, lots of vino and perhaps another go at *Anna Karenina*. Everyone knew what cruises were like. But Heather did not want a cruise, she wanted a life. Like Spain, the cruise would end and, even if it did not end disappointingly, depression would follow. After the holiday she would have no money; there would be a let-down, comfortless brooding, her heart and purse emptied out. Still she knew she had to leave England, and soon; the Christmas meeting, the inevitable New Year's episode and the spring collapse had been so regular – and now an almost glandless ritual – that Heather recoiled from the thought of December.

She did not send Christmas cards that year. She avoided the Christmas ads in the paper and, when holly appeared on the teller's cage, stopped going to the bank. Without being fully conscious of it she scanned the classifieds, and one day read a large framed ad about teachers being wanted in East Africa. The ad was half a plea and half a travel brochure. 'Teachers', it said, 'are sorely needed by the children of deprived farmers in the cool upland plateaux near the breathtaking slopes of the majestic volcanic mountains of East Africa. Struggling for an education the African child often must walk 15 or 20 miles through incredibly green meadows and thick pine forests in his bare feet. The fauna and flora are of a kind rarely seen outside the spectacular and seldom-visited . . .' Heather read on to the last sentence which ended, '. . . you would be rendering valuable service to East Africa, now on the threshold of independence.' Heather reflected on the ad. She was not a teacher, but the store had once sent her on a day-release course to study mothercraft and a little bit of domestic science; she had done well in the course and the manager even spoke of sending her to Bath for a diploma. She could supply reasonably good references; the old egg-eater would write an enthusiastic one. And she spoke English, an added advantage, since this would give her another subject to teach the poor people in the green upland plateaux. Heather wondered if it was East Africa where that exotic love story took place, the romance on the equatorial plantation between the wealthy tea planter with the Daimler and the girl that had just come out from England on a visit. 'I knew you were British,' the silver-haired planter had said to the girl; 'you have ice in your heart that wants thawing.' They had made love in a room smelling of blossoms. Outside, the roar of the monsoon.

After a strenuous physical (no one asked her about the mothercraft lessons) and many warnings (the friend who had recommended the cruise said, 'Don't come back with a black man'), Heather signed a four-year contract and boarded the *Prince of Wales* bound for Mombasa. It was in many ways the cruise she had reflected on earlier; there were costume balls, dance competitions and several proposals to go 'just below to my cabin' from unattached men. Heather turned down all but one. The man was insistent, very strong and rather slow-witted, and the most persuasive words he spoke were not about the delights of going below but that in a week's time the ship would be calling at Aden and he would be getting off: his wife and children were waiting for him there. It was the speedy, private, uncluttered affair Heather badly wanted. Calculating their movements with a precision she lyingly attributed to the man, she managed the whole business with elaborate secrecy and made the man believe in his heart that he had plotted it all. He gave Heather his elephant-hair bracelet as a souvenir and left at Aden as he said he would. Heather was happy. A little caution had made the trip pleasant and now she could arrive in East Africa alone and completely free, like the English girl in the exotic story.

As the *Prince of Wales* left Aden and drew closer to the East African coast, the passengers began drinking heavily, staying up later; and they became friendlier, closer, offering stories to testify to their good intentions. With her man gone, Heather had more free time and spent part of the day and much of the evening in the ship's bar. The men took an interest in her that was protective rather than romantic. They made an effort to let Heather listen to the stories because, as they told her, she had never been to Africa before and had not the slightest idea of what it was like to live in a country populated with savages. The stories were of unrelieved horror made even more horrible for Heather when she said, 'Oh, but I'm rather like that English girl in the Maugham story. Very lucky, you know. I'll meet a tea planter and he'll see me through!'

'I read that story,' a man put in. 'It wasn't about East Africa.'

'You must be mistaken,' said Heather. 'It was the tropics, and Nairobi was mentioned, I'm sure.'

'You're way off,' another man said. 'That was Singapore or somewhere in Malaya. There were *punkawallahs* mentioned in that book. We don't have *punkawallahs* in East Africa.'

'You don't?' Heather spoke in a tiny voice.

'Nope, not a one.' The man grinned.

'You see,' said a man sitting close to Heather, 'the Malayans have a reasonably interesting culture. They brought bananas to Africa – they had boats, they travelled. But I'll tell you something. Civilization started in East Africa, right in Olduvai Gorge, not far from my place.' The man swigged his beer and smacking his lips added, 'It started there, and that's where it stopped.'

'In the arsehole of the Empire,' said a man across the room into his frothy tankard.

Heather was crushed. They talked of East African brutality, a bloody outpouring of atrocity stories which trapped Heather in worry and made it impossible for her to stir. She began to hate herself for having signed the contract. She felt like a fool; she knew she could have stayed in London, continued working, and gone on as before. She thought with remorse of the missed opportunity for breaking the depressing pattern of loveless affairs. She might easily, she considered, have rid herself of it all. And even if she had gone back to the same thing, what the men in the ship's bar were describing was something much worse than any fear she had known: those June days in England were empty, but it was a familiar emptiness and, as bad as it had ever been, there were still memories of kindness. Another Christmas might have caused her unhappiness, she knew that; but she might have found a man as well.

Africa repelled her now. The *Prince of Wales* was three days out of Aden; Heather started throwing up. She did not let on that she was sick; she kept her aplomb by smiling at the drunks in the bar and saying, 'If you'll excuse me, I really must move off to the ladies' loo to spend a penny,' and then she would go to her cabin and retch violently. Sometimes she would be overcome by the heaving and spend the night gasping on her bunk, utterly exhausted, spewing green bile into her tin pail. Africa, the life she had thrown away, the decision she had made in a moment of foolish haste, the horrible stories – it all sickened her. Heather began to imagine Africa a huge black carcass, inert in the ocean, with evil at its centre, and all Africa's vastness radiating mishap off its shores in dark smelly eddies.

The sickening vision became fact. After one terrible night in her narrow compartment sensing the awful splashing, Heather went to the map outside the dining-room and saw that the red-knobbed pin which represented the ship had not moved. Every morning she had examined the map; every day the pin had moved closer to

Mombasa on a route of pin-hole punctures that had very nearly cut the map in half. But the pin had not moved; it was stuck in the Gulf of Aden where it had been the previous day. Her vision had been true. The ship was being repelled by Africa's plastic evil as Heather had been repelled by the stories of Africa's pointless brutality; the ship had stopped and was being thrust away. Heather lay on her bunk and puked into the pail.

The trip to Aden had been done in almost record time, but now less than 1,500 miles out of Mombasa the *Prince of Wales* developed trouble with the port screw. A typewritten notice tacked next to the map said there would be 'a slight but unavoidable delay due to engine difficulties . . .' No one seemed to mind. Instead of the horror stories there was now great mirth in the bar, as there had been at Gibraltar and Port Said, shouted exchanges about never getting to Mombasa, about being towed back to Aden and staying drunk. There were jokes about what could be wrong, which included the word screw in the punchline.

Heather listened to them all and smiled with the men. She did not want anyone to know of the fears that made her continually sick. Once she even added a screwing joke of her own (a limerick about the man from Timbuktu) and was yippeed. But after two days of joking about the varieties of screws, the horror stories began again, each one prefaced by, 'We're giving you the real Africa – not that shit you read about in poovey books.' With the ship listing uncomfortably Heather sat on a bar-stool licking her pink gin, not commenting, though encouraging the men by inquiring after details about Africans and frowning in genuine concern.

For a reason Heather at first could not even guess at, the returning settlers and expatriate civil servants suspected her of being sympathetic towards Africans. Heather was sorry they felt that way, embarrassed knowing this and also knowing the details of the stories about Africans they were telling her. She wanted to give the impression that she was not afraid and that she, like they, also disliked Africans; at the same time she knew with a deep private dread that she feared and hated Africa and Africans.

The suspicions of the people in the ship's bar were founded on an incident Heather had forgotten; it had been a very slight thing, but everyone knew about it. She had spoken to a soft-voiced African at Palermo who monotonously explained that he had bought a little crucifix and been cheated by the Italian at the side-walk stand. Heather put him wise to the Italians, whom she called 'Eye-ties', but as she said this word she realized that she would give a hundred blacks for one Italian – in fact, she had been loved by an Italian just a year before. The absurdity of describing a nationality she distrusted to a man she knew she loathed struck her at once. She giggled and told the African to watch out because 'the wogs start at Calais'. The African thanked her for her advice and went away with the crucifix in his hand. The conversation had not lasted a minute. The next day everyone seemed to know about it and several people in the bar asked Heather if she thought Africans were people in the same way the English were people. Heather answered quickly and truthfully, no, she didn't think they were. Nothing specific was said until, during the time the port screw was being replaced, she got on more than joshing terms with the men in the ship's bar; one evening a man said to her drily, 'The ones that carry books scare me more than the real savages. Like that black you were chatting up when we went ashore at Palermo . . .'

She knew she was not prepared for Africa; she knew she was a tense, frightened unmarried woman with less than half her looks left. The trip had not done anything for her: her hair was snarled from the salty wind; her elbows were hard and scaly; her eyebrows had grown out and a cold sore had started on her lower lip. She hated this ugliness and hated herself even more for her foolish weakness in going away from where she had been at least safe. Alone, so far away, among strangers there could be no comfort. Her throat ached from retching and over-drinking; her nostrils were filthy from chain-smoking. And just before the *Prince of Wales* docked in Mombasa she had a fleeting thought of the terrible mistake she had made in letting the strong dull man go back to his wife in Aden. She might have made promises, told lies, blackmailed him; she might have convinced him to come with her and make her safe. She walked down the clattering gangway trembling, into the humid reeking town, a sob stuck in her throat: she wanted that man back.

'Lots of rain,' the Major said. It was the first full sentence he had spoken all evening. He said it directly to Heather.

'It doesn't look that way,' said Heather. She smiled and sipped her gin. She knew no one at the table; she had come to the club with the Major, a tanned athletic man of about fifty whose only bad point, as far as Heather could tell, was the hair growing out of his ears. He had said he was a policeman and Heather had laughed, 'A *white* policeman in a *black* country.' The Major said there were stranger things in East Africa than that and chatted with her at her hotel before asking her politely if she would like to meet some of his friends. East Africa, he said, was a small place; she would get to know nearly everyone eventually. That was how things were. She had been in Mombasa only a day and had had a restful night (a sweeper had bowed and said, 'I will clean now, my ladyship,' in the morning; this she found reassuring). Now she found herself among strangers, but she was not unhappy. She felt almost relaxed and not very worried; it was night and, with the tropical foliage in darkness, like Cornwall in summer. The exactitude of this association gave the outpost a familiarity and calmed her even more. She drained her glass and saw the Major moving closer to her.

'No,' he said, 'a good eight inches more than last year.' He spoke quietly, as if he did not want the others to hear.

Heather was mildly confused. She did not know what he was talking about. The path to the club veranda was bone-dry; and even from where she sat she could hear the scrape and rattle of palm fronds rubbing. The grass near the hotel had been sparse and brown, the open drains full of dead leaves and dry scraps of paper.

'At the hotel I thought to myself: this must be the dry season they're always talking about,' said Heather.

'In Mombasa,' said the Major.

'Yes. But you say you're getting lots of rain?'

The Major's face emptied. He stared at Heather and said, 'Didn't you say you're English?'

'Heavens, *yes!*' Heather looked around. No one was paying any attention to her.

'Well, I heard on the wireless this morning that there's masses of rain in the South. Sussex alone got six inches.'

'I was on the,' Heather tossed her head, 'the ship, you know.'

'They're talking of doing something about better drainage if it keeps on like this,' said the Major with concern. '*Lots* of rain. Worst in years.'

Heather asked the Major when he had last gone on home leave.

'Eleven years ago. Went home to bury my mother, stayed three weeks. England – you can have it, love. A bloody *shenzi* place.' The Major drank for the rest of the evening without speaking.

Around midnight a radio was produced. After a great deal of knob-twirling and antenna-adjusting, a sputtering crackling cricket match issued from the torn cloth of the loudspeaker. The Major seemed interested in the match, but Heather suggested leaving.

They went to his house. It was near the ocean and Heather could hear the waves crashing on the reef from where she lay in the bed. The Major made love to her slowly, silently, as if committing incest with his daughter. Afterward, Heather sat up in the dark; she held his head against her belly and whispered, 'Tomorrow I have to go to Nairobi. I have to be posted to a school and all that rubbish. Such a nuisance. I'd rather stay here with you. But I can't. I really can't.' She paused and closed her eyes. 'I don't want you to think I'm promiscuous or anything like that. You'll visit me, won't you? You have a car – it won't be too awful to drive up to . . .' The Major's head was heavy. Heather turned it slightly and saw that he was fast asleep.

Nairobi helped her forget it all. She felt as if she had never feared anything. The brutal stories continued, people talked of nothing else, but Heather no longer minded. She had become young, upper-middle-class, desirable; men were good to her; her house in one of Nairobi's lovely suburbs was surrounded by flowers; there were servants. She felt confident, even wealthy; she never had to cook or clean. The nightmare of the ship, her fears and regrets, were forgotten in the ease of her present life. Her one sorrow was that she had not come sooner.

It was a fairy story, the gift of youth, with the same anxiety that fairy tales produce. Like the tale of the incredible longed-for wish, granted with a warning by the tall black genie, Heather's life in Nairobi came to have consequences which were more side effects than actual punishments. She had, a few weeks after arriving in East Africa, started using her outdated schoolgirl slang (she knew none other); often to her acute embarrassment she clowned; she began to drink heavily. But the gift was too great to let the few consequences matter.

The man in Croydon had once asked her what she wanted out of life.

'I want to be rich and famous, with men hounding me day and night. You know what I really want to be? A high-class call girl. Not a whore, you understand, but a paid girlfriend. I suppose that's every girl's dream. Which girl wouldn't trade places with Christine Keeler?'

In East Africa she got most of her wish. She was posted not to the cool upland plateaux but to a large girls' school in Nairobi. Nairobi was the most exciting city she had ever been in; she understood it, she felt she had a place there. Unlike London, it was filled with attractive people; no one was poor. There were bachelors everywhere, all doing exciting things (one of her lovers shot crocs, another had written the Five-year Plan). There were long gay parties which went on till dawn and finished with a dip in an embassy pool. The hairdressers, particularly one Italian lady who had come from Eritrea, were excellent – the best Heather had ever seen. She changed her hairstyle. She went out to eat nearly every evening and could open a menu and order with panache. Once in a while she sent food back to the kitchen and demanded to see the cook. She had wanted a new life; now she had one.

There was little to do at the school. She taught needlework, home management and did Drama Club one afternoon a week. Sometimes she had an English class: the pupils read out loud from their books; Heather corrected their pronunciation. The school was run on the lines of a girls' school in England of thirty years ago, emphasizing discipline, good grooming, religious knowledge, and charm. All other things, with the exception of Latin and British history, came last; in seven years Heather never marked a student's paper. When she got depressed she had her hair done, dressed in her best clothes and, with one of her girlfriends, sat in the Thorn Tree sidewalk café nursing a gin and let herself be cajoled into accepting a drink from a tourist. She was delighted just watching the beautiful people strolling by in their light clothes: the tanned hunters, the young slim-legged girls with long soft hair. Africans were all around her, but she never saw them; she found she did not even have to hate them; they kept their distance.

Heather knew that she would never leave East Africa, although she was also certain that she would not allow herself to die there. For the foreseeable future, there was nowhere else to go; there were no more decisions to be made. She knew that her fears could come back, the retching could return; she shored herself up against unhappiness by refusing to get involved with a man and, like the call girl of her dreams, was businesslike in her affairs. There were many men but she seldom lost control and never fell in love. Love would have made life unbearable. Sex for her became a small moment set in days of fun; it was a quick unsatisfying fumble on a bed that provided no relief but was over in a matter of seconds and almost forgotten in a week. She expected nothing from it. She only made love to a man after she had got all she wanted from him and, with one disastrous exception, made this plain to the man beforehand. Her love affairs ended with the act of love, which was how she wanted it.

But there were times when an ended affair produced violence in her. More than mere bitchery, it was frankly vicious, and for no apparent reason she would find herself at home after the man left, screaming, crying, smashing things. If her servant intruded on her weeping she fired him. But the next day, or sometimes the next hour, she would become very calm and write letters to old girl-friends describing the unhappy affair in a succession of cheerful half-truths. This reduced her unhappiness by creating for her a different personality, gay and mature, and found only in the letters. These selected fictions stayed with her and it was these versions of her affairs she remembered. Often she tried to mime the perfect emotions she wrote. After the letters she would get into her car and drive around Nairobi, down the wide, palm-lined avenues, past the race course or out to the airport, until she was tired of driving. Outside the city, where the huge green continent began, she parked and turned from the twinkling city lights to the darkness of the night's empty distances. She had everything except love and she knew that pursuing love she would lose everything.

Heather had reached that point in unmarried life where she tried not to think about what she was missing and would never have. She habitually consoled herself. Her dog, Rufus, was a bonus; she had not expected to like him: she had bought him on a whim three years before. She learned to take him seriously. His loyal affection, something she had taken for granted, now made her grateful. He had seemed a pointlessly gross hound, forever catching his tail in car doors and wounding his paws on stones. His size had conversational value, but except for that he had nothing: his eyes were rheumy, his tongue was raw and cracked, his teeth carious. Once or twice a year he had an attack of worms which made his ribs show and gave his jutting face an expression of listless panic, his eyes clouded, his jaw gaping. But none of this mattered to Heather. She had discovered in him a dumb sincerity she knew she lacked. This, with his stupid loyalty and his awkward maleness, she found touching. He was real; she knew she was not. She wondered whether Colin had been.

Only Rufus remained. There was no reason to think about Colin. She would never see him again. She was in her car, driving north with Rufus and everything she owned (many dresses, no furniture). Colin deserved nothing, not even a place in her memory, and she vowed out of bitterness not to think of the school she had just been forced to leave. The humiliation had been her own fault – bad timing, that was all. She had been telling herself lies. It didn't matter, nothing mattered, only the moving was important: now a new job, a distance, a different school. She could start again and not lose much. In East Africa it was not hard.

4

A Homecoming

The reverie of the room would not leave her: she was in a room and also imagining a tight box around her brain. The reality of one fed the despairing illusion of the other; it made her nightmare real. The cracked walls, the slumping shutters, the veils of cobwebs on the roof-beams, the plain decay of the room in which she was sitting caused that chamber of horrors in her imagination to become a hard image, a vision complete with discomfort and uncertainty, with dusty surfaces and loud noises, voices: a wall visibly cracking, the sound of a fist banging against the box, making it tremble. She could see herself, as if she were hovering above herself, staring down at the thin woman in the frayed chair, with her hands clasped prayerfully together and held against her sallow face, her elbows on her knees, her knees touching, feet some distance apart and pigeon-toed in brown thick-heeled shoes; the dress, an old dull cut, of fuzzy English wool; her hair held in a bun with wisps trailing down which, at intervals, she flicked back with her fingers.

She had bathed, but smelled strongly of her cats. In spite of bathing every day and often twice a day, she always smelled of cats. But she did not find animal odours unpleasant. They were honest and did no harm. Miss Poole reasoned that only a person who was pretentious and vain would be conscious of his own smell and find shame in nature. She was not a woman of the world and had never tried to impress on anyone that she was anything but a farm girl, plain and practical, with a mind of her own and a tolerance for roughnecks and dung smells. The thought had crossed her mind years ago that if she ever had a husband (now the thought made her cringe) he too would have to tolerate, and perhaps even enjoy, the odours of animals, the ferret smells in damp undergrowth, the grainy odours of hens and heavy hairiness of farm dogs. Miss Poole did not notice an odour until it ripened into a stink. And she had always had pets: in her youth, hens; later, horses, dogs, rabbits, grey monkeys, and now, near the end of her life (this phrase rather than the figure forty), cats. Animal smells for Miss Poole existed quite apart from the concept of cleanliness. A mouldy orange was thrown out immediately; a mangy scabbed hound might scratch and moan for days, inches from where Miss Poole sat and stared.

There was a kind of order in the room, and a smell lingered about this too, because the order had been imposed by a succession of household pets. On her return from England after her eight-year absence she bought three dogs of undistinguished breed. The dogs had decided on the decor: where the chairs should be, how high the shelves should be, where the books should be kept (the dogs pawed and growled at the books; Miss Poole put the books in a back room). Tablecloths that didn't overhang, hairy throw-rugs, even plastic dishes instead of china were chosen because of the dogs' inclinations and not Miss Poole's. So it was an order that was not order, simply a queer consistency of the unbreakable, the shatterproof, the bite-resistant. Miss Poole was only following instructions.

She was happy this way. There were moments when her terror of the Africans left her, moments when, after her arrival back in East Africa, she sat and read a *Reader's Digest* that was long out of date but clean, or times when she ate her bangers and mash – and these times she was happy that she had taken the risk and come back. While she read or ate or just sat in her chair the dogs sniffed at each other, pawed the carpet or sat beneath the dining table chewing hard at the fleas on the fur of their arse-flesh.

The cats a few years later made severe demands on her. The cats' insistence – particularly that of Sally, the oldest and largest – had been so firm that to obey their peculiar whim meant not only rearranging the sitting-room, but also getting rid of the dogs. Outside the house the cats played very well with the dogs. The girls at the school remarked on how well the beasts got along. Once inside the house there were snarls, glares; the cats hunched, bristling and hissing: the question of possession was raised. Miss Poole decided in favour of the cats, fixed up the room to suit them (clawing, kittens and soft sleeping places in corners had to be allowed for) and put the dogs in a house next to the servants' quarters where they terrorized the hens.

Miss Poole felt that her companionship with the animals was worthwhile because it was honest and predictable, and satisfying because it was not a substitute for human companionship (two canaries replacing one dead friend), but a satisfactory friendship that left humans out entirely. Miss Poole had no friends and seldom had visitors, except for the girls who came over occasionally for high tea. There was an absence of friends; but the animals with their smelly residues had not kept the friends away. She had always only had pets. As she grew older her pets had become progressively smaller (now she liked small cats). She could risk fairness with the pets and not be humiliated; she could stick to the rules and be rewarded for it. Animals obeyed and could be trained and would respond as humans never did, for she saw in these creatures a helpless innocence bordering on holiness which did not exist in humans. There were times when she herself felt this bewildered helplessness which small animals showed. Unlike most humans there was no malice in the cats; while there were the usual subtle responses – many more than most people thought – there was no evil. They had not fallen. Man had. Much more than the high-voiced and man-crazy female, maggoty in the head and committing sins, these meek creatures were God's own.

Until she returned from her sad pause in England Miss Poole felt exactly the same about Africans. She had fed them and they responded in a manner that was both savage and innocent. Their undirected savagery was occasional, always inspired by people who wanted to change them. In her youth she had heard others speak of red-eyed wildness and murderousness, but Miss Poole had seen few instances of it. These she did not talk about, for she was no more interested in retailing the vulgarities of Africans than she would have been in describing the unfortunate household defecations of her pets.

When the eight years of confusion began in 1952 the Africans on her father's farm, faced with uncertainty and fearing for their lives, sought the reassurance of their employer and stayed inside the farm enclosure. They were more loyal than ever and the cane was rarely used, not because of political pressure (the Colonial Government was investigating alleged abuses) but because there was now no necessity for it. The Africans on the farm hated and feared the terrorists' insolence and, when trouble came to the farm, it was not Miss Poole's father (clutching his shotgun) or brother (a round-shouldered, mean-faced nail-biter) who did battle with the six intruders – naked men, yelping through the geraniums in the front garden and throwing stones at the side of the house – but two of the African workers. The workers were unmercifully slaughtered and left bleeding in the flowerbeds. Her brother went to South Africa shortly after; her father followed six years later.

Miss Poole's eight-year visit to England began the day after the attack on the farm. She was driven at great speed to the Nairobi airport; she flew to England where she met each member of the family, sometimes for tea, sometimes staying the weekend. At the end of two months she received no invitation to live at any of their houses. Rejected, though not displeased (she had no feeling for her relatives, but hated England with a hate that chilled and grimed her), Miss Poole spent the next eight years sitting in a number of rooms, usually alone, reading the *Geographical Magazine* and her Bible, knitting mufflers, doing the crossword, and putting shillings in the gas-meter.

In these cold rooms, odd mausoleums with the grey corpses stirring slightly, she dreamed of the order her father had given to a wild patch of African bush. The fenced stretches of green stayed in her memory, the animals and (quiet and numerous) the black men who had lived in the round brick huts near the kennel. In her tiny English room with vulgarities everywhere, a soiled rug, crumbs on the table, fingerprints around the light-switch (she could remedy none of these; she had always lived with servants and was incapable of even the smallest household task), she saw the huge plan of the farm for the first time in her life: the many barns and stables, the straight red roads and taut wire fences that sang like harps when the wind blew. She saw the order of the blocks of buildings, and the reason behind the order; the shop her father provided for the Africans where soap, salt, tea, sugar and small quantities of gin could be bought more cheaply than in town. A whole community, safe and green, which came alive when the morning bell sounded, the Africans scampering like hounds, chattering among themselves, making dark trails in thick dewy grass in their bare feet. Her father had brought all this to people who had lived bunched in disorder. The name Concord Farm had been given to the twenty thousand acres and it had prospered.

These were her dreams in England: not dreams of old friends, but of a situation, her home, which was for the moment beyond her reach. In this English tomb Miss Poole stopped living but aged twice as fast, a consequence she attributed to the cold and damp, and which her relations attributed to her bitterness and inaction. She knew that her relations would have mocked her horribly if they had known that in these dull rooms the inert and silent Miss Poole thought constantly of equatorial foliage, her soft pets, the gigantic pattern of the farm, and her happy days as a young girl in a land where the sun did not die. And what would the cousins have said if Miss Poole had explained her nostalgia: the warm caresses of a fat nursemaid who spoke reassurances to Miss Poole in Swahili? The vision of the woman's huge arms persisted: soft, black protective arms. And the woman had smooth cheeks and hard yellow palms.

Miss Poole flew back to Africa in 1960 and, when she arrived, wept. Worse than being a stranger, she was an enemy. She had decided that she wanted only to be anonymous in the sun with her small comforts; but she was not anonymous and she was hated. Before, people had said the Africans had no memories at all; now they said Africans had long cruel memories. As she passed through Customs and Immigration in Nairobi she saw that there was no longer a white man at the desk and not even a clear-eyed Sikh (efficient rustics and, for Miss Poole, the cleanest and most tolerable of the Asians in East Africa). There was an African in dark glasses who scraped his thick fingers over every page of her passport, was idiotically slow, set his mouth at her and instead of handing her the passport, rudely flipped it in her direction. It slapped on the floor; the African pointed an oversize finger at another traveller waiting to be processed. Miss Poole bent over for the passport. Her handbag dropped, spilling most of the contents: a brush and comb, a ballpoint, a wad of toilet paper, a compact, a small worn address book and diary, a half-eaten tube of fruit pastilles, some large loud English pennies. While she crouched and put this in order a magazine dropped and splashed on the stone floor (she could not remember how she had been carrying it). Confused by the humiliation, with her chest heaving against her knees making breathing difficult, she felt her throat constrict, started quickly away and heard an Americanized African voice shouting from behind. "Hey, lady, you forgot dis." She turned and saw her passport still on the floor. She went back and retrieved it (everyone in the lounge had heard the African; everyone watched her). Afterwards, she went straight to the ladies' room and burst into tears.

There were other incidents: an African in the hotel elevator (she could not tell if he was drunk, she could never tell with Africans) insisted on shaking her hand and telling her there was nothing 'to be fearing of black people – everyone is the same now, isn't it?' Later, a misunderstanding with a waiter she tried to tip: he thought she had raised her hand to strike him; he pulled away; a cup slipped from his tray and smashed; the saucer stayed. Avoiding the stares of an Asian family in the hotel corridor, she bumped her head on a supporting post and broke her sunglasses; the Asian man, despite her protestations that it was really nothing, uselessly tried to comfort her while the rest of his family watched Miss Poole in dark-eyed silence. Each time she wept in her room. There had never been Africans in the hotel and now there were many, in dark suits, talking together, each one eyeing her through a small white slit in a smooth black half-turned face. The thought struck her that an African might have slept in her very bed the night before. It was midnight when this occurred to her and she spent the rest of the night in a chair with a blanket wrapped around her, not sleeping, but thinking with sadness and anger of the violation the whole country had undergone. It was being trampled. From the first moment at the Customs and Immigration desk at the airport she had had the uneasy feeling that something was wrong, and now she knew: it was proved by her aching head and trembling hands. The whole place was undeniably fouled; but there was another plain truth which was worse than this: she was home.

Concord Farm had been sold. Some of the land was parcelled out to friends of the President who were already quarrelling over it. The farm buildings were part of an agricultural institute staffed by Americans from the Middle West. As crass and unresourceful as Africans, the Americans were pulling down the buildings, planting uneconomic crops and importing expensive farm machinery from America. This she gathered from the newspapers. She had known for some time that her father had joined her brother in South Africa; they were in Durban. Her father had sent a letter, but it was only after she arrived back in East Africa and had wept five or six times that the words of her father's letter came back to her. She had received the letter while waiting for her sunless exile in the English room to end, and so anxious had she been to preserve her soul-warming dream that she had barely noticed it or did not dare understand it. In the hotel room it returned to her, this time real and in her father's own hoarse voice: '. . . Sold Concord to the blacks . . . good price . . . only a fool wouldn't . . . No place here for a white . . . Things are different now . . . About time I retired and wrote my memoirs, but there is so much to tell I probably won't bother . . . Isn't it bloody? . . .'

That was the second night in the hotel, the phrases running through her head, mocking her fear ('. . . Only a fool wouldn't . . .') and extending her sleeplessness and provoking tears in another unbearably bright day: her memory of the sun was not this white fatiguing heat which made a simple stroll a great effort. The crowds on the sidewalk, the many tourists (Germans, of all people) and all the Africans, who seemed to have money and certainly were dressed well and undoubtedly in charge, made the third day a nightmare. It was on the third day that she resolved to leave Nairobi and go up-country, anywhere green, where she could have flowers and pets, pray and, if God was willing, continue living. She could see the hills from the hotel window, the flatness which rose slowly and dropped sharply to a valley forty miles across where the earth had cracked and spewed up lava. There would be few people in the highlands; only those who had been born there could love it. The words of a hymn came to her, all the roaring voices of farmers in a rustic church singing in a children's service:

> Daisies are our silver,
> Buttercups our gold;
> This is all the treasure
> We can have or hold.
>
> These shall be our emeralds –
> Leaves so new and green;
> Roses make the reddest
> Rubies ever seen.

She could teach; a quiet mission station up-country would be glad to have her, she thought. The next day she hunted for a job. Though no mission schools existed – all had been taken over by the government – there were many teaching jobs available. She sat in the Ministry of Education and filled out forms. Each form demanded to know what she had been doing for the past eight years, where she had been, who would vouch for her. Many unhappinesses were described on those forms; she shuddered just writing those several outer London addresses. She was interviewed the same day and it went well, even though the African conducting the interview left the door to his office open and allowed many faces outside to see Miss Poole nervously stammer answers. When the

African asked her what job she thought she was most suited for, Miss Poole was surprised to hear herself say, 'I think a Headmistress – I would dearly love to head a girls' school up-country. Education is such a terribly important thing in East Africa, and I would consider it an honour . . .' She ran on. The African was no longer officious but helpful, totally beguiled and even saying that in his own district (Miss Poole recognized the name of the place: she had been in a jumping competition there in the forties with her favourite horse, and had won a ribbon) there was a girls' school which needed a Headmistress; would Miss Poole consider that? His younger sister was there, in Form Two. 'A very clever little chap,' he said.

Miss Poole smiled. Though she had not meant any affection by smiling and was only reacting to the word the African pronounced *clayver*, the African smiled back and shook her hand and grasped her thumb in the manner of a brother. Miss Poole said she would be most eager to take up her duties as soon as possible and added something to the effect that her lack of experience would be more than compensated for by her enthusiasm and, she said, 'zest'.

She had not thought of that for seven years, but for seven years there had been no serious intruders; there had been no need to reflect. In the bush, the school was out of danger, and changeless; the Ministry had always sent girls, and the girls had not stayed long. Today was different. Sitting in her chair, looking out of her window to the school compound, where the neatly pruned bougainvillaea divided the hacked-out bush in a labyrinthine hedge of pure flowers, she recalled the words that were running through her head when she left the Ministry with the carbon of her signed contract. They sounded different now, very childish: *there will be flowers there*.

Miss Poole looked up and began to pray. She implored God with her heart. She stopped when she realized that she was looking not into Heaven but at a crack in the curved groin of the roof-beam. It was a new one; she had never seen it before. As her prayer subsided, the crack seemed to open and lengthen deliberately into a dark smirk.

5

The Memory of a Bitch

A long smooth patch of road, air rushing untroubled through the side-window, cleared Heather's head. The VW hummed along without bumping her mind back to men. Along the roadside, feeble decrepit shacks poked out from sturdy green foliage, huts squatted fouling delicious grass; here and there a flock of skinny mewling goats, a gap-toothed tribeswoman with a bundle of sticks on her head, a terrified hen flapping for its life. She was in the bush and she knew it by the awed stares of men standing in waist-deep grass, she knew it by the stupidity of the flea-bitten dogs sleeping in the middle of the road; a hundred miles into the forest, a thousand years back in time, now among people who uttered magic, dug with small pointed sticks, and with shards of glass circumcised little girls spread on mats.

Perfect for Miss Poole and bloody awful for everyone else, Heather thought, narrowing her eyes at the road ahead. Heather had heard a great deal about Miss Poole, but had met her only once, though memorably enough, at a conference for teachers in Nairobi.

'Isn't this the perfectly dreariest dullest thing you've ever seen!' Heather had said passionately to Miss Poole after one session.

Miss Poole had turned her grey face on Heather and said curtly, 'No. I don't agree. I think it's extremely useful. Our teachers need this sort of thing.'

'It bores *me* to tears.'

All the conference participants wore nameplates. Miss Poole looked at Heather's; Heather looked at Miss Poole's.

'You're a teacher?' asked Miss Poole, zipping her briefcase.

'Yes, I am.' Heather's voice was cold.

Miss Poole started to walk away, her mouth set colourlessly in anger. She stopped, turned her head stiffly sideways and, not quite looking at Heather, said without emphasis, 'It's a good job you're not at my school, young lady.'

Bitch, thought Heather. Now, with all her belongings in boxes tied to the roofrack, she was on her way to see Miss Poole, her new Headmistress. Heather laughed. Women did not frighten her; she knew what helpless madness they all felt. She knew what they wanted. The old ones were the worst of all. But working for Miss Poole would not have been easy in any case, even if she had never spoken to Miss Poole at the conference. And that had not been a blunder; she would have said something like it eventually. She knew exactly where she stood, which was more than most people knew when they started a new job.

Everyone in Nairobi talked about Miss Poole. Some said she had slept with the Minister of Education in order to get her job. She could not have got it any other way, it was said. She was a failure, a ludicrously inefficient woman, a recluse at her own school. Many stories were told about her: having failed to collect fees one term, she had been accused of misappropriating funds and was forced to make up the difference from her own pocket; a hypochondriac, she spent days, weeks in her house moaning while a young Peace Corps girl acted as Headmistress; and there was the story, told with some variations, of how the visiting Prime Minister discovered the national flag to be flying upside-down on the school flagpole. Miss Poole had made a public apology, but this was not enough; the Young Pioneers, the government youth brigade, forced her to carry a whole stalk of bananas on her head through the village market. So many stupidities.

But the school was small, remote and unimportant. Stupidities in the bush did not matter. People would tell stories, just as they told of outrages in the prisons; like the outrages, the stories of bush stupidities ('bush fever', some called it) could only be verified with great inconvenience. No one in East Africa would wish to take the enjoyment out of the stories by disproving them. If people gossiped about her Heather would never hear it. Nairobi was too far away.

Heather knew she had arrived at the school when, at the brow of a hill, she looked across the valley to a square collection of brown stone buildings, a queer order in all that jungle; the red-tiled roofs were redder, odder in the setting sun. The incongruity of a flag flapping in the mown quadrangle at the centre. To the side Heather saw a corner of the playing field, a green patch with black girls darting in and out of it with sticks. A stream ran along the far side of the compound, beyond a neat row of trees and a light green area that could only have been a papyrus swamp. For Heather it was a kind of detention camp — it even looked like one, with natural barriers of trees and water instead of barbed-wire fences. Heather was not hurt by the comparison; she preferred, at least for a while, the seclusion of a bush school to the further humiliation of living observed by gossips in Nairobi. She might be infuriated by the sewing-circle boredom; but she would hear no ridicule. Everyone down there under those red roofs was an embarrassment or they would not have been sent to the bush, like her. Heather could not disgrace the school; it was already in disgrace, and that had happened in Miss Poole's seven years.

As Heather descended the hill Rufus awoke, barking and slavering in the back seat. Heather told him sharply to lie down, but Rufus paid no attention. His head was out of the side window and the wind rushing by blew into his gaping mouth, curling his tongue sideways and making his loose jowls flap.

The VW jounced on the rutted puddly driveway and splashed towards Miss Poole's signboard.

6

Cat and Dog

Rufus sniffed at Sally and followed her around the lawn, bristling, making a prolonged growl in his throat. Miss Poole was at the window; Heather stayed in the car, teasing and fluffing her hair in the rear-view mirror, her eyes glassy with all the driving, lids dusted blue, her lips pressing several hairpins tight. From where she parked she could not see Rufus and the cat. She had not planned to let Rufus out of the car – he sometimes trotted away and stayed hidden for hours. He had tried but failed to get his large body through the window. He wagged his tail as he leaped around the back seat, lashing Heather's hair into a nest. 'Oh, damn,' Heather muttered and she opened the door. Rufus had made directly for Sally.

He faced the hunching cat and continued growling with his head down, stepping sideways with his hind legs; he put the prune of his nose firmly against Sally, all the while drooling on her, nudging her across the grass. The growls rose in his throat and, as they rose, grew sharper and sharper until he was yelping against Sally's fur.

The cat first purred, a soft bubbling sound; with the weight of the dog's nose on her, the purring became a yowl, long and agonized. As the dog prodded and bumped her with his whole head the yowling turned to a shrill offended wail, harrowingly human in both pitch and attitude.

It was this wailing of Sally's that roused Miss Poole. The pugnacious sounds of the dog, whom she saw as a large unwelcome beast wetting her cat's soft fur with his slippery jowls angered her. It was the sort of intrusion she hated most.

For the moment Miss Poole forgot that it was Heather she was meeting. She was confronted by an unmannered dog; it might as well have been a person, though Miss Poole was usually more charitable with animals. She concentrated on the personality of the dog; she saw nastiness, intrusion, a bulky stranger terrorizing a small well-brushed cat, actually bullying the little thing, a stranger harassing a life-long resident! It infuriated her and, although she had thought of nothing else for the past day, Heather's face – the grinning, overpowdered mask with the silly voice – did not occur to Miss Poole at that moment. The dog was the intruder; the foolish woman did not exist. And Sally, the dear little cat with the bow and bell at her throat . . .

Miss Poole rushed out to the lawn; Sally spun round and leaped into Miss Poole's arms, curled up and squirted urine over her dress. This Miss Poole ignored. She turned to Rufus and shook her finger at him.

'Go away! You leave this poor thing alone, do you hear?' She spoke as if to a delinquent child. 'That's just about enough of that. Now off you go!' Miss Poole stamped on the grass.

Chastened, Rufus pawed a tuft of grass and barked. Holding Sally high and away from him, Miss Poole reached for Rufus's neck-fur to calm him.

'Don't you touch that dog.'

It was Heather; she spoke slowly, pausing after each word, with poison in her voice. She had appeared from an opening in the bougainvillaea at the far side of the garden.

Miss Poole straightened. Rufus ran to Heather and let himself be stroked.

'If this dog is yours,' said Miss Poole, 'I would suggest you keep it on a leash. My cats do not take kindly to strange dogs, even less to strange people. Strangers sometimes get scratched, you see.'

They faced each other: Miss Poole with her hair in a bun, in brown tweed darkened with a streak of cat-piss, flat-chested, yellow-grey in complexion with light feline tufts of facial hair, rocking her cat mechanically at her bosom as a mother does a small child; Heather, her blue dress wrinkled at the back from the hot drive, her blonde-streaked hair half-fixed, thick-calved, pudgy with drink, her lips a bright sticky red, a fleshy braceleted arm holding her dog's collar. The cat made her bubbly purr; the dog moaned, tugged forward. In the playing field beyond the trees, the whack of sticks, the fuguing screech of the girls at play; and on the other side of the compound, in the direction of the staff houses, past the bamboo grove to the boggy meadow, the swamp and stream, a racket of noise started up, as it always did just before dusk with almost industrial persistence: frogs scrooped and croaked like rough boards being planed, and hylas and bats squeaked like rusty nails being pounded. It was a vast carpentry shop in the bog beyond the staff houses, where many demon workers hammered and sawed near dusk but, for all the efficient-sounding noise, produced nothing more than a penetrating swamp smell.

'Heather Monkhouse, your new domestic science teacher.'

'Domestic science? The Ministry told me you do English and drama,' Miss Poole said with surprise. 'I teach domestic science and I think the girls have quite enough of that.'

'Well, I was told –'

'You will find, Miss Monkhouse, that in the East African civil service words mean nothing. People say a lot and do very little. We try to do things differently at this school.'

'I was told I would do needlework.' Heather was insistent.

'But that's impossible.' Miss Poole tried to laugh; she did not succeed; she cleared her throat. 'I do needlework, as well as cookery, mothercraft and flower arrangement. You may help with these, of course, but as far as we're concerned English and drama are your subjects. Some time soon there will be a staff meeting – you are required to attend. We can settle this matter at that time, as well as when you will teach, what your set books will be, and so forth. I like grammarians. I was rather hoping you would be a grammarian –'

'Well, I was told I would do needlework. That's all I know.' Heather tried to be as obtuse as she could.

Miss Poole went on, 'There are other odds and ends of school business. As English mistress you will have the school magazine, and I can tell you'll have to work jolly hard to make it as good as last year's magazine. The Christian Union, of course, the Bible study group which we're all expected to chair once a month – oh, masses of things. It may look a small school, but an enormous great deal is happening in our compound.'

'I don't see any girls,' said Heather, measuring her sarcasm carefully.

'They're at play,' said Miss Poole quickly, 'over there. Fortunately we have a games mistress who has charge of them after four. I can't promise you, but you can be reasonably certain of having your evenings free. It's our playtime too, so to speak. But you'll find you'll be well occupied.'

'But how super.'

'I think that will be all for the moment. I should remind you, though I'm told you've been in East Africa several years, um, the unit of time,' now Miss Poole was lecturing, 'the unit of time here is the month, often the year. I don't accept this. I try to make it the minute, minutes are golden. I tell my girls that. I like punctuality.'

'So I've heard.' Heather smiled.

'Rose will show you to your house.' She turned to go, but clucked and added, 'How foolish of me. *I* am Miss Poole.'

Heather muttered a reply and watched her go. When the door to Miss Poole's house banged, Rufus pulled away and trotted to the window. He put his forepaws on the window-sill and howled. Feeling an insect on her elbow, Heather stiffened, held her breath and slapped. Her palm hit the soft bulk of fingers.

There was a cry of pain. Heather turned, saw a figure and immediately took a step backward. The girl was short and wore a ragged ankle-length dress, a sun-faded beret pulled down over her ears and black plastic sunglasses. On her neck, uncovered by the beret, were dirty reddish-gold curls, very tiny and stiff. The girl's face and arms, which Heather first thought were white, were not white but pale and membranous, an eerie translucence which showed pink and blue threads just under the skin-surface. The exposed parts of the girl's body – face, arms, neck, ankles – were blotched and scabbed with violet sores. The girl's features were

African: a thick nose, a wide mouth; this mouth was an added ugliness – her thick pale lips hung in a heavy frown of pain.

'I am Rose,' said the girl. She dangled a key-ring in Heather's face.

7

B.J.

'Do you drink?'

'Sure thing.'

'You should do. In a place like this.'

'You just got here, right?'

'A few minutes ago. I left Nairobi this morning.'

'You been in Africa very long?'

'Seven years.'

'You're lucky.'

'*Lucky?* I don't quite understand.'

'If you came out seven years ago, then you were here at the time of independence. That must have been really exciting.'

'I never noticed.'

'Seven years,' said the girl. 'Golly, I've only been here a little over four months. But the Memsab – that's what we call Miss Poole – she was *born* here, for cry-eye.'

'What part of the States are you from?' asked Heather.

The girl's mouth dropped open. She looked dumbfounded for a few seconds, then began to giggle. 'How in heck,' she said, 'did you know I was from the States?'

'Just a wild guess.'

'Well, for Pete's sake,' said the girl, shaking her head and smiling broadly.

The girl had come in while Heather was unpacking; she had said hello and asked if she could help. It was then that Heather asked if she drank. Heather now showed the girl a gin bottle. The girl wagged her finger no; she accepted a warm lime squash. Heather poured an inch of gin into a glass and glanced at the girl: she wore plaid Bermuda shorts and a sweatshirt with markings on the front which Heather could not make out; her stockingless feet were in low scuffed sneakers. She was not fat, but would be in a few years. There was a look of deep serenity in her face as she held up her glass of lime squash, sloshed it and stared at the bubbles rising.

'Crazy, isn't it?' She smiled and focused her eyes from the bubbles to Heather.

'What do you mean?'

'I mean,' the girl sloshed the lime again, 'here we are in East Africa, in the boondocks. We're here and everyone else is some-where else. No, that's not what I mean. What I mean is, we're *no*place and everyone else is *some*place. Get it?'

'You've been to Nairobi?'

'Oh, yeah, Nairobi. Big deal,' said the girl. 'It's like Omaha. Ever been to Omaha?'

'No, but I've always wanted to visit the States –'

'Well, if you go to the States, *don't* go to Omaha. It's really cruddy, let me tell you. Like Nairobi, with lots of farm-types, people eating delicacies with big ugly hands and complaining. My father once . . . Hey!' The girl suddenly sat up. Heather noticed that she sat indelic-ately, knees apart, like a lewd fishwife or a small girl. 'I didn't even tell you my name – it's Bettyjean, only everyone calls me B.J., except the Memsab, who calls everyone Miss this and Miss that. I'm B.J. Lebow.'

'You Americans have such extraordinary names.'

'It's sort of Jewish. It used to be Lebowitz, I guess. You probably knew that, everybody does. But I'm no Jew. I went to Israel one summer. That cured me. What a bunch of boy scouts.'

'The Jews have a tragic history.'

'So do the Africans,' said the girl with a shrug. 'I know your name. Heather Monkhouse. Boy, Heather's a nice name.'

'I'm glad you like it.'

'We only heard you were coming yesterday, but we weren't sure you were arriving today. The Memsab refused to tell us, but we're sure she knew. She doesn't tell us *anything*.'

'No, I supposed not.'

'She's a settler, did I tell you that? At least her father was. I guess she's okay in her way, and all that.'

'Of course.' Heather finished her pink gin and made herself another. As drops of angostura fell slowly into the clear liquid and dispersed in small inverted explosions Heather asked lightly, 'Tell me, B.J., what have they been saying about me?'

B.J. flushed but did not pause. 'Nothing really. Just that you're coming, nobody knew when, and you're doing English and drama. You used to be in Nairobi, I think they said Nairobi, and you're from England etcetera. Nothing really.'

'They haven't been telling tales, have they?' Heather took a long swallow of the gin. 'People in Africa have an incredible knack for saying all sorts of outrageous things.'

'Like?'

'Oh, outrageous nasty things. I can't think of an example at the moment. Yes, I can. There was a widow in Nairobi I knew about. People said she went to bed with her houseboy. Pretty soon, no one would talk to her.'

'That's terrible,' said B.J. with feeling.

'Well, I'm only repeating what I heard. You know how people are.'

'Yeah,' said B.J., 'but suppose it was true. Let's say the widow *was* sleeping with an African. Is that any reason for not talking to the lady? Africans are people, too. I know the Memsab hates them, being born here like she was, but gee whizz,' she said, pained, 'they're *people*, you know.' B.J. wanted to say more; she muttered and added, 'So many people got this *thing* about black people.'

'Yes, of course,' Heather said. 'But what did people say about, ha-ha, *me*? Did they say anything embarrassing?'

'It all depends what you mean by embarrassing.'

'Look, B.J., you're a big girl, aren't you? I'm asking you quite simply what people have been saying about me. It would make things a lot easier if you came right out and told me. I don't care if it's unpleasant. I just like to know where I stand.'

B.J. looked at Heather with large long-lashed eyes. Her skin was clear, pinkish; she wore no make-up. Her lips were full, teeth perfect.

'Can I call you Heather?'

'By all means.' Heather took another swallow of the gin and braced herself.

'Okay, Heather.' B.J. tilted her head and continued. 'What you're asking me to do is repeat a rumour. I suppose some people might think it's a fair question, it being about you and everything like that. But I don't repeat rumours, not even *to* people about the *same* people. I wouldn't tell you what I heard because it's not fair to you and not fair – maybe you don't agree with this, I don't know – to the people who spread the rumours. What you do is your business, isn't that right? That's the way I look at it. So what do you care what people think about you? Man, I hate this gossip-gossip-gossip, especially here in Africa, you know what I mean?'

'You mean you're not going to tell me what people think of me, what they've been saying.'

'It's not that exactly.'

'It *is* that. Exactly that.' Heather lit a cigarette and huffed and puffed the smoke. She put her fist to her mouth and coughed, then said, 'Well, I don't care.'

'That's the spirit, Heather!' B.J. finished her lime squash.

Heather looked around the room. She said nothing for several minutes, then sighed and looked forlornly at B.J. 'It was awful, wasn't it? You don't have to answer. I didn't even have to ask. I know it was perfectly frightful. People are always saying frightful things about me. There was a particular incident I had in mind –'

'Please don't talk about it. I mean, when people talk about themselves I go all funny inside. I don't know what to say.'

'Try listening,' Heather said sharply. She was angry but realized she had spoken too quickly. The girl was young, she knew absolutely nothing. A typical American face, thought Heather: empty, without a trace of sin on it. Heather knew she had been needlessly sharp. She apologized.

'That's okay,' said B.J. 'You've had a long drive – you must be really tired.'

Jesus, thought Heather. She tried to change the subject. 'What do you think of East Africa? I don't mean Nairobi – I know what you think of that.'

'Africa's the sexiest place in the world,' said B.J. without hesitation.

'Well, that depends on what you know about sex,' said Heather. 'Or the world.'

'It really is.' B.J. grinned.

'What makes you say that?'

'I don't know. But it's sexy, the sun, the grass, all the naked people. It's smelly. It's really wild. Then there are other things, stupid things. Africa,' B.J. said, still smiling, 'I didn't expect it.'

'You knew you were coming –'

'Oh, yeah, I knew I was coming. I read the books and all that stuff. I did my homework,' said B.J. 'But there were things I didn't expect, like all the people in Nairobi getting dressed up. Men have to wear *ties* in the hotels, for criminy sake! And it's a hundred in the shade, not to mention in the African jungle.'

'Nairobi is hardly in the jungle,' said Heather.

'Well, you know what I mean. In Africa. All the yes-bwana, no-bwana. They even have fox-hunting, horse-riding with the velvet hats and red coats, like in the movies, jumping over fences . . .' B.J. seemed at a loss and then said, 'Here they are, in Africa of all places, and you see these guys in their crazy suits on horses, trotting through muddy villages blowing horns and shouting *Tally-ho!*'

'I'm sorry you feel that way.' Heather was abrupt. 'Personally I am a most frightful old snob. I am all for the aristocracy. I love to see them around the place, riding their horses, wearing ties, shooting in their tweeds. It's civilized. It's good. It's English, if you know what I mean.'

Her accent had changed, from the slow plea ('People are always saying frightful things about me') a moment earlier to a clipped tonelessness, each hard word frozen and bloodless, definite and confident, almost sneering. The change had come in a matter of minutes.

B.J. recognized the change; it had taken her nearly four months to see, but now she knew what was happening. She had on her arrival thought the English people in Africa to be the friendliest, warmest people on earth: they always inquired about the United States, they showed interest, they conducted conversations with ease and order. But something was missing, politeness maybe; although the inquiries were phrased nicely, the interest seemed like condescension. The order of the nice response in the end was an offence because it was all ready-made, as if contempt, stirred into a soup-mix of dry phrases, was being served up as instant Olde England. It was sad. The English practised and even admired dishonest cleverness. They were people who decided on a pose and, believing none of it, carried it off. In this they showed the greatest uncertainty; it was only playing. As soon as Heather said, 'I am a most frightful old snob,' B.J. knew it was a lie and was embarrassed for Heather. If she's only a teacher, then her father's not Lord So-and-so, and if she's like me, what's she got to be snobby about? B.J. thought. And what's so special about the English?

'My room-mate, Pamela Male, she's English,' said B.J. gamely.

'Yes?'

'She's quite interested in meeting you, being English herself.'

'You must bring her around.'

The going was hard. 'Oh, I will,' said B.J. 'You'll like her.'

Heather leaned towards B.J. 'Tell me, what was that perfectly dreadful *thing* that brought me here? That Rose person.' It was a command, not a question.

B.J. looked into her empty glass. 'The poor kid. She's an albino. I think you say albeeno. Funny, I never thought there could be African albinos. But that was stupid of me, wasn't it? If we – you know, white people – if we have albinos, why shouldn't Africans have them, too?'

'Quite.'

'The girls laugh at her. She's quite intelligent, but doesn't see so well. The Memsab took her in. She sort of helps around the place, doing I don't know what exactly. I feel for her, really I do. The sun must kill her. I'll bet she's unhappy.'

'Why should she be unhappy? All Africans want to be white. She's got her wish, hasn't she?' Heather laughed, tilting her head back and holding her throat with one hand.

'You shouldn't joke about things like that.' B.J. spoke slowly. 'How would you like it if you were like that?'

'Don't you see? I *am*. We're all of us albinos in East Africa, aren't we?'

'It's not the same thing.'

Heather relented. 'Suppose not. Bad joke.' She swirled her empty glass, tipped it up and gulped air. 'Well, I really must –'

'Oh, sure,' said B.J. standing brightly. 'Look, Heather, if there's anything at all I can do I'd be glad –'

'No, honestly, I wouldn't hear of it. You've been most kind.' Heather paused. 'Believe me, most kind. You must forgive my rudeness.' The accent was now gone. 'I'm too old to change. Sometimes I'm a horrible bitch. Please take no notice. You're a very sweet girl, B.J.'

'Gee.' B.J. flapped her arms helplessly and started to leave. Then she stopped and turned. 'Oh, *now* I know! I thought you were a good guesser. What an idiot I am!' She pointed to the markings on her sweatshirt which, when she pulled the bottom down, stretched and read *San Jose State College*. 'You *knew* all the time!'

How can someone so stupid get so far from home? Heather tried to put thoughts of B.J. out of her mind, but the image of B.J. remained, sitting awkwardly, knees apart, a lime squash in her hand, correcting Heather, contradicting her sweetly and stupidly. She is innocent, thought Heather, and, yes, I am a bitch. But innocence is a bigger bitchery.

Heather flung her empty glass at the wall. When it hit, and smashed, a lizard ran out from behind a picture, paused near an unshaded light protruding from the wall, flattened itself and turned white. Heather stared at the lizard for several minutes: it did not alter its colour and, although it was very white, it neither blended with the wall nor moved.

B.J. walked back to her house in the darkness. It was past six, she knew: she could not hear the girls. There was no human sound, only the flutter and intermittent screech of large birds, kites or ravens probably, flapping blindly for a perch, and from the swamp below the gulping rabble of frogs squatting in the murk, a sound which occasionally kept B.J. awake. It was a noise worse than traffic.

B.J. was pretty, she gave off perfumes, but she was dense. Her nerves lived deep in her sweet pink flesh. She had to be touched to be awakened, physically touched. Slapped, she got angry; caressed, she felt desire, and swallowed. The contempt Heather had just uttered perplexed rather than angered her. As she walked through the grass from Heather's house to the one she shared with Pamela Male, B.J. replayed the conversation; she objected to the blunt sounds Heather's words had made and deeply pitied Heather.

The photograph of the Indian child with the swollen belly, picking through Bombay garbage, the spectacular calendar sunset of Kodachrome Yosemite – these caused no quickening of recognition in B.J. She preferred to smell the garbage, swat the flies, hold and cuddle the child; she had to feel the setting sun on her face, roll on the grass, dampen her Bermudas with dew. Her denseness (which she was well aware of and pondered) prevented any pictured vision from awakening her. She hated movies and never read with any pleasure unless she either knew the director or author, or had been to the place. One of her reasons for coming to Africa was that she had seen all the films, read all the books; the descriptions and visions interested her (she had a huge catalogue of exotica in her head as a result), but were a long way from giving satisfaction. She wanted more than the two dimensions of pretty pictures, more than the garbled pidgin of kitchen natives. She wanted to touch, smell, *feel* the place deep in her where those nerves lived; she was dying to sink her teeth into a fresh equatorial orange and spray the pips into the tall grass.

She had once explained it to Miss Male: 'I have to plunge right in. Get it?' As a result of this passion for total immersion, which Miss Male saw as specifically American, B.J. had travelled extensively in her twenty-one years. She jetted to foreign places, touched things and smelled her fingers. She had hugged a Doric column on the Acropolis and stared straight up its pock-marked shaft to the blue Greek sky; she had put her hands into the Ganges where saddhus bathed, kissed the Blarney Stone, peeled a banana in Caracas, rubbed her cheek against the Vatican. It provided simple, useful information, but revealed no secrets. It was her way of knowing the world, the child's way, an international show and tell.

Her father indulged her, urged her on: 'Look at B.J., Mother. Now she wants to ride that mangy old camel!'

In Hong Kong, aged fifteen, she had sampled rat.

'You're not really gonna *eat* those awful things?'

'I want to see what they *taste* like,' said B.J. playfully. She had dysentery for a week. But B.J. could not help it. She knew she was dense, but was also curious, a wondering that was at times harmful, for no second-hand description, no matter how detailed, could satisfy it. It was this wondering insulated in layers of density that had led her to join the Peace Corps and come to Africa. For once, she was travelling alone; as her father said, she was a big girl now and would have to learn to find out things for herself.

A flashlight bobbed towards her. Miss Male.

'Is she here?'

'Who?' asked B.J. She had been thinking about peanut butter. She often thought of peanut butter. It seemed the one thing you could not get in East Africa, in spite of the gigantic peanut crop.

'The Mother of the Year,' said Miss Male.

'I wish you wouldn't call her that, Pam.'

'I thought you Americans liked that sort of thing.'

'Well, we do and we don't –'

'For heaven's sake, B.J., is she here or not?'

'If you mean Heather Monkhouse – yes, she's here. She's very sad.'

'I daresay she's got bags of things to be sad about.' Miss Male laughed and aimed her flashlight at Heather's house.

'Be kind to her,' said B.J. 'I told her you were dying to meet her, you being English.'

'You're a dear,' said Miss Male. 'Oh, by the way, you've got a caller. That chap from the Electricity Board. I'm off to the Staff Room – see you anon.'

'So long, Pam.'

A very short African in a dark suit scrambled to his feet when B.J. entered her house. The African breathed out, but said nothing; he wrung his hands and grinned.

'*Habari gani*, Wangi,' said B.J. cheerfully.

'*Mzuri*.' He tugged at his tie.

'My God, sit *down*. You Africans got better manners than the so-called English people around here!'

8

Wangi

'Boy, have *you* been brainwashed,' said B.J.

Wangi had come for tea.

'I mean, I thought only English people drank tea.'

'As you know,' said Wangi, 'the British were our masters.' He held his saucer in the air and, pursing his lips, stirred the tea with a rapid rotary motion of the spoon.

'You poor thing,' said B.J., screwing up one eye to show she was really sorry.

Wangi smiled as if he had scored a point. He made no reply, only stared. The staring was something B.J. had never liked about Africans; that, with a dark silence. They seemed to gape at her endlessly, their eyes flashing from her feet to her head, lingering on knees, arms, and breasts, without a word. She had been told that Africans loved to talk and tell long stories in front of the fire, or anywhere, which was why they had an oral history, nothing written down: talking was their real gift. They would walk miles to shoot the bull, that was how B.J. imagined it. And several of the lectures in her Peace Corps training said what chatter-boxes Africans were and how they loved to pull your leg.

That's what they said. But B.J. had not seen Africans do anything of the kind. They entered a room and produced agonizing silences by gazing watery-eyed at everything. One of these long silences, the African scrutinizing fabric and flesh, seemed to destroy conversation. Worse than this, she found that she could not sit still under the large eyes that never seemed to meet her own, eyes that fixed themselves (as Wangi's were at that moment) on her breasts and flashed from one to the other. B.J. poured more tea into Wangi's cup. Wangi stared first at the bulging *San* then the bulging *Jose*. She returned to her chair and, for no reason at all, giggled.

B.J. had been certain almost from the first that she did not like Africans very much. Their staring, their silence, their odd humour and poor English – all these taken into consideration with the great strength obvious under their lapels made them seem mysterious. They were not necessarily dangerous, but they possessed a secret B.J. had not yet learned.

At first she had assumed Africans were like American Negroes. But she was not really sure what Negroes were like. Her father distrusted Negroes and told B.J. to distrust them too: 'If you take one home you'll be breaking your Daddy's heart, and your Daddy loves you, remember.' B.J. admired her father's honesty nearly as much as she detested his sentiment. But it was understandable: he had been born in Pine Bluffs, orphaned at eleven, raised by relatives and educated haphazardly in Chicago. He had taken a number of menial jobs, waiting on table, lugging moulds in a tyre factory, cleaning spittoons; he had earned enough money to go to college. He loved to talk about the degrading jobs he had done; that his whole family had been illiterate and he had scrubbed spittoons were two of his greatest sources of pride.

Very late in life, bald with worry and eaten by a stomach ulcer, her father became a dentist. He married, moved to San Diego and in twenty-one years earned enough money so that he could swear that his kids would never have the rotten hardships he had; they'd have everything he'd never had. B.J. had once pressed him for reasons why he disliked Negroes. He began by describing his past, how his life had been as hard as any schwarz's; as he spoke, his words became more and more crude and finally shifted to a tirade of racial abuse so pointlessly vulgar, from someone B.J. thought of as the gentlest man in the world, that she resolved never to challenge him again on the race question and to date, in private, as many Negroes as she could.

She looked, but saw none, and had to settle for foreign students. She ran into them all over the campus: Jamaicans, Filipinos, Koreans, Thais, Nigerians, Indians in saris, Hungarians with

scraggly beards who had thrown rocks at Soviet tanks, and dozens
of other nationalities. All the foreign students sat together in the
Student Union, at the same table, exchanging heavily accented
platitudes. For a reason B.J. remained clueless about, every one of
them was studying agricultural economics. The foreign students
were easy to meet; they hungered for companionship. The slightest
word of greeting roused them to stand, bow graciously and offer a
cup of coffee. They taught B.J. their proverbs, how to say hello and
how-are-you in the popping labials of their vernaculars; they remin-
isced about their countries, which they said were nice and green
and poor. They were sick with loneliness; when they walked down
the college corridors they were jostled, for they were dark undersized people in a land of white giants. After classes they gathered
pathetically at their sticky table in the Union. For B.J. the foreign
students were all San Jose could claim of the exotic. Also they were
coloured, some of them in more ways than Negroes.

But there were no Negroes at the college and B.J. lived in the
wrong neighbourhood for Negroes to be easily accessible. She
lamented this: there was a certain something she liked about them,
she never knew what, maybe their tremendous vim.

Wangi had been staring (B.J. checked her watch) nearly fifteen
minutes. She had never known him to be so engrossed with her
body; but, then, she had not known Wangi very long. A week
previously she had met him at a party at the home of his cousin,
the District Education Officer, Wilbur something, who had just
been transferred from Nairobi. Wangi had what seemed to be a
good job with the Electricity Board and dressed in dark suits, his
shoes always shined. He used after-shave lotion and was scrubbed
to the point of being polished. His snazzy appearance had been
something of a disappointment for B.J., who expected skins, but
sitting there in her living room he seemed to her like a crouching
Congolese figurine, hard, glossy, black, representing something.
B.J. could stand his silence no longer. In desperation she said, 'Tell
me something about yourself.'

'My cousin is the District Education Officer.'

'You *told* me that already. Anyway I knew it. Tell me something else,' B.J. urged.

'I did my primary education in Nairobi.'

'I *know* that, silly. But what about before then – what about your village and like that?'

'My village is poor.'

'I'll bet,' B.J. clucked.

Wangi peered at her. 'Do you know,' he said, 'I didn't have a pair of shoes until I was twenty.'

'What a shame! Cripe, I've had shoes my whole life.'

'Village life is terrible,' sighed Wangi. 'That's why we killed the British. We had to. They wanted us to live in villages.'

'People still live in villages, don't they?'

'*I* don't,' said Wangi. 'The British are terrible. They hate you and they don't say it, but you know they hate you. It's terrible. You never know if they hate you, but you know if they're British they have to. That's the way the British are. So we killed them.'

'Were you in those gangs?'

'Oh, yes.'

'Wow,' said B.J. softly.

'No,' said Wangi, 'two of them: Mau-Mau.'

'You don't mean you actually . . .' B.J. swallowed, wondering whether to ask. 'You actually . . . ah . . . killed –'

'Oh, yes,' Wangi said, brightening. 'Everyone had to. That's how you get free. It's not easy. They used to call us natives and what-not –'

'Sure, but a native just means someone who lives in a particular –'

'That's what I used to hate, when they said "You bloody nat-ives". So I didn't mind joining up, and one night,' Wangi con-tinued, interspersing his story with little bursts of laughter, 'we went to a farm in Nyeri District. My uncle said that now we ha-ha just have to do this. These buggers have been ha-ha treating us too badly. I took my knife ha-ha and was creeping slowly ha-ha –'

'Please, Wangi. Tell me about your village.'

'Don't you want to hear the story? It's very interesting.'

'Tell me about your village. I'll bet it's great.'

'That's interesting too. I'll take you there some day. You can meet my father and his wives.'

'Wives? More than one?'

'Three,' said Wangi. 'He has more than twenty children.'

'Twenty! Goodness, no wonder you were poor!'

Wangi looked confused. 'No,' he said, 'children are good. Children didn't make us poor. The British did.'

B.J. was not sure what she should say. She knew that if she talked about the British she would be betraying Miss Poole and Heather. As much as they got on her nerves, still she could not bring herself to talk behind their backs. She noticed Wangi had started staring again. She began to think that perhaps village life was not so bad. But she had no way of telling, about that or poverty, and for a moment the thought crossed her mind that her children would have all the things she never had: misery, hardship, poverty, dirty jobs. She would not give them a thing. It would do them a lot of good.

'That's why we like you Americans,' Wangi said finally, his gaze resting on B.J.'s bare knee. 'You're kind people. You talk to us. You even like us, don't you?'

'Of course we do,' said B.J. She was glad of a chance to say it, but as soon as she did she had a feeling Wangi would be a regular visitor. She was not troubled by this; she knew she would go out with him. There were many reasons, a little bit of politics, maybe some guilt, and even if there were no love there would be sympathy and curiosity. He wasn't a bad guy. And even if he was (but he wasn't) life at the school was dull and why else had she gone all the way into Los Angeles to take the Peace Corps exam and put up with the Mickey Mouse of three months' training and come all the long way to Africa, if not to get to know Africans?

9

Rose

Crouched simian-fashion in the dark hollows of a giant bougain-villaea in the garden, Rose looked across the compound to the girls' dormitories. The buildings were lighted, but to Rose's scorched eyes the lights were fogged faintly luminous haloes, like bulbs underwater. They began to go out.

She waited until there was complete darkness and then crept towards the kitchen door where a small light burned; she saw it only as a small glow, no bigger than a firefly. It illuminated nothing for her, but she did not need it to find her way. As soon as she tapped on the door the glow was gone. A key clicked inside. The door creaked open an inch. Rose pushed the door open, making the hinges snarl, and felt her way through the kitchen, sniffing the familiar odours: bread, dust, soap, oranges, mangoes, flour, all permeated with the sharp stink of cat-piss. Ahead of her she heard slow steps, but there was no voice, no other sound. She saw nothing. She slid her bruised hand along the edge of the side-board, touched at the jamb of the door and entered the living-room. Now the softness of the rug under her bare feet, a small table brushing her thigh and, across the room, the large front window, all she could see, blurred round in the white glow of the moon.

She had not removed her dark glasses. She moved bent over, with agility, to a stool she could not see but whose place she was familiar with. The moon did not relieve the darkness for Rose. Like those fish that live deep in the ocean and glow, she had lived her whole life in darkness and gave off a similar pearly light. The dark glasses kept the sun out of her eyes, but she did not wear them to protect her eyes; the glasses were an opaque mask to prevent others from seeing the pink blistered slits beneath. She removed them only when she slept.

She touched the stool and sat, in her ears the slow rhythmic purring of the slumbering cats and the breathing of another person.

'*Nataka chai*, Rose?' asked Miss Poole softly. 'Do you want tea?' The Swahili was delivered with an English intonation, unaccented, the lips scarcely parted.

'Thank you, no.'

'*Iko hapa*,' said Miss Poole. '*Hapana iko njaa?*'

'Little bit,' whispered Rose, again in English.

'*Kitu gani*, Rose?' Miss Poole's voice was impatient. 'What's wrong?'

Rose paused and then said, 'I like talk Englis, madam.' She breathed heavily and nothing more was said in the room for several minutes. The darkness purred with cats. Rose was still; for a second the shiny plastic of her dark glasses caught a moonbeam from the window. The skin that in bright sunlight showed horrible mottle, dead blotches and threads of blood, in the moonlight seemed perfectly white and clear, a radiance Miss Poole loved.

'My poor Rose,' Miss Poole said in English, 'you are night-blooming.'

'Englis,' said Rose, satisfied. She bent forward and hugged her knees; on the stool, her profile forward, skin gleaming, she could have been a newly carved gargoyle about to be hoisted into position on the parapet of a cathedral. Now she spoke in Swahili: 'Yes, I will have tea.'

'Ah,' sighed Miss Poole. There was the clink of the spout against the cup, the *shuff* of the sugar being spooned from a bowl, three scoops; the cup tinkling on the saucer as it was placed on the floor. 'Here is good tea,' said Miss Poole in Swahili.

When Rose had lifted the cup and sipped, Miss Poole spoke again in Swahili. Rose replied. They continued this way: the dull tongue-flaps of Rose, the English consonants and open Bantu vowels which Miss Poole timidly voiced in low flat tones.

'With the American you say?'

'With the American.'

'For how long?'

'Less than one hour.'

'They talked?'

'Indeed.'

'As friends?'

'No.'

'How do you know?'

'Their voices were different. The new teacher was angry a little bit.'

'Why was she angry?'

'I don't know.'

'Did they talk about me?'

'Your name once. That was all.'

'They drank of course.'

'The American drank lime squash. The other *enguli*.'

'Is there anything else you remember well?'

In broken sentences, with many hesitations, Rose told of the glass being thrown against the wall. She hissed, simulating the smash and finished with, '*Pole*.'

Miss Poole was silent except for her angry breathing.

'Sorry,' said Rose, this time in English.

'And what did you see at the American's house?' asked Miss Poole in Swahili.

10

Carving a Joint

A week later, Miss Poole prayed: 'Our Father, we thank Thee for this delicious repast in full knowledge that there are those of our brethren who have naught. For our daily bread accept our praise and hear our prayer. By Thee all living souls are fed; Thy bounty and Thy loving care with all Thy children let us share. Make us obedient, kind and true, and Grant us strength, O Lord, to be grateful that we may serve Thee. Amen.'

'Amen,' said B.J. and Miss Male.

'And what,' asked Heather, reaching for the potatoes, 'do you plan to serve Him?'

'I beg your pardon, Miss Monkhouse.' Miss Poole jerked her head at Heather. She gave Heather's name a queer pronunciation, as if she were saying 'Mongoose'.

'You said we're . . .' Heather paused and glanced around the table. 'You said we're going to *serve* Him, ha-ha.' She dropped a potato on her plate with a stiff *bonk* and passed the dish.

No one moved to grasp the dish. Heather put it down beside her plate and folded her hands. The expressions on the faces of the women did not change. The women were motionless in intense postures, as if being sketched.

Miss Poole appeared calm. Only her hands, clasping the edge of the table, betrayed her rage. Her knuckles had gone white. When she spoke it seemed as if at any moment her voice would become a scream. 'That is blasphemy, Miss Monkhouse. This is a Christian school. *We* are Christians. I must ask you to apologize or leave the table.'

Heather nibbled at her lip. She stared at her plate, then looked up and, still expressionless, winked at B.J. and Miss Male, and said, 'I'm terribly sorry. I am a perfect fool, aren't I?'

There was another silence, this one timed, precise. The three women looked at Miss Poole or, rather, at Miss Poole's knuckles which had drained completely of blood and were turning a grey-blue, like ten agates. The food steamed untouched on the table; two moths staggered through the air and made for the light, which hung over the food on a thick fly-specked cord.

'Gee,' a voice began. Everyone turned towards B.J. The words tumbled out with a cheerful clatter that broke the silence like a lawnmower. 'I know this doesn't have anything to do with what we're talking about . . . I mean, see, I'm not a Christian, really. I'm a Jew. That is, my father's Jewish, a sort of conservative – I'm a reformed . . . So . . .' B.J. paused. There was no response. 'I just thought I'd tell you all that because you, ah, Miss Poole, you said we're all Christians and, ah, that's not really, ah, actually . . .' B.J.'s voice trailed off. When her voice had gone completely she filled her mouth with bread.

Miss Poole switched off her glare and moved slightly. Miss Male coughed nervously; she saw that Miss Poole was looking at her. In a low defeated voice Miss Poole said, 'Here you are, Miss Male. As our only biologist I'm sure you know more about these things than we do. I'm afraid it's none too sharp, but do your best.' She handed Miss Male a carving knife.

'Thank you,' said Miss Male solemnly. The joint, a sad-looking log that had fat stitched on it with white sodden string, was passed to Miss Male. She examined it with the tines of a long serving fork, said, 'Here goes,' and began sawing off large frayed chunks of juiceless meat.

The knife-blade was dull; it cut only because it was chipped in enough places for it to be saw-toothed, jagged. Miss Poole kept the knife dull on purpose, thinking that it would cut less meat from the joint if it were dull and leave more meat for the cats. In fact, the blade was only good for crudely sawing and hacking off pieces; consequently, Miss Poole's knife, because it was dull as a hoe, produced only large pieces. Miss Male cut incautiously. She had discovered, a short time before, Miss Poole's reason for keeping the knife dull. The table shook, the plates rattled as Miss Male sawed at the hard log of burned meat.

'You look like you're trying to kill it, Pam!' said B.J., bright-eyed.

Miss Poole gazed sadly at the mutilated joint and said, 'I think that will be just fine. You may pass the platter around.' When the meat was passed to Miss Poole, she said in a voice that had become suddenly gentle, 'Oh, there's a *delicious* one, and another one. Can you eat all that? You're a little piggy, aren't you? *More?* All right, but just one . . .' She forked hunks of meat into her lap, then put her fork on the table. As she did, there was a deep satisfied purr from her lap, where Sally was curled, her head stuck into a plate, licking at meat. Miss Poole removed the plate and placed it on the floor beside her chair. Sally followed, hitting the floor with a thump.

'I sure feel sorry for vegetarians,' said B.J., chewing her meat enthusiastically.

No one heard B.J. or replied; Miss Male and Heather were still watching the little scene at the head of the table; Miss Poole's eyes were on Sally lapping the meat and switching her big tail back and forth.

'Ooo, you're a *fat* pussycat,' said Miss Poole.

When Sally finished, Miss Poole tinkled a little bell; Julius, Miss Poole's aged cook, appeared at the door to the kitchen. Excusing himself in Swahili, he creaked over and took Sally's empty plate and, holding the plate in the air on the pedestal of five long fingers, went back to the kitchen.

B.J. was still chewing. 'Say, speaking of vegetarians, that reminds me – where's Miss Verjee? Couldn't she come?'

'I take it Miss Verjee is the Games Mistress,' said Heather to Miss Male.

'That's right,' said Miss Male. 'The Indian chap.'

Miss Poole spoke with caution. 'Miss Verjee is quite happy where she is.'

'Well, that's what I was wondering,' said B.J. 'Where is she?'

'At her quarters, one would presume,' said Heather.

'No,' said Miss Poole. 'She is a member of staff and, like us all, has duties to perform. At the moment she is refereeing the netball match over at the playing field. She'll see the girls to their dormitories after evening meal.'

'While we're here?'

'What's wrong with that, B.J.?' asked Heather.

B.J. put down her knife and fork. 'You mean to say it doesn't bother you that while you're sitting here eating, Miss Verjee is over there on duty, working like a dog?'

'Interesting simile,' said Heather slicing her meat. She chewed, swallowed and added, 'If she wasn't invited here, then why should *you* get upset about it?'

'It doesn't seem fair,' said B.J. 'Anyway, what gives you the idea I'm upset? I'm not upset. I'm just –'

'Someone has to watch the girls until lights-out,' said Miss Poole, opening her mouth very wide and then closing it on a forkful of stringy meat.

'Why is the *someone* always Fatima Amirlal Verjee, is all I'm saying.'

'You *do* have a gift for these difficult Asian names,' said Miss Poole, working her jaws on the wad of meat-sinew.

'I think B.J. has a point,' said Miss Male.

'I don't see any point at all,' said Heather.

'The point,' said B.J., facing Heather, 'is I've never seen her in this house. And she works here, is the point.'

'Now really,' fluttered Miss Poole, 'I fail to see what the argument is. Miss Verjee is doing her job. Each of us does her job, only we never seem to be doing our jobs when Miss Verjee is doing hers. Let's not make an issue of it. I know *I* shan't say any more about it.'

'But we're here stuffing ourselves and she's there working, the poor kid.'

All had stopped eating; in the silence that followed B.J.'s words, all the women except Heather resumed. B.J. poked at peas. Heather was still looking at B.J.

'Why is it,' inquired Heather, 'that Americans hate to see people happy? Americans act as if it's a horrible old *sin* for people to enjoy themselves.'

'That's not entirely true,' said Miss Male. 'We English —'

'Let me finish,' said Heather sharply. 'We're here eating and for all I know enjoying ourselves. Miss Verjee isn't here – she's working, in point of fact. But immediately our American friend detects Miss Verjee's absence she decides there's something sinister in it. I do believe she thinks it's racial prejudice.'

'That's absurd,' said Miss Poole. 'How could it be racial prejudice? We're all of us educated women, aren't we? We can have anyone we want in our house – that's not racial prejudice, it's the privilege of the house-owner. I know some people say that we're racially prejudiced, but my answer to them is, if I were racially prejudiced wouldn't I be living in Australia or some white country instead of Africa? I should think so, but we are here, in a black country. There are black faces everywhere –'

'Except at this table,' said B.J. in a whisper.

Heather leaned towards Miss Poole and said with sincerity, 'You're absolutely right.'

Miss Poole's eyes widened at Heather, stunned.

'It's these Americans that come here,' Heather went on, 'that's the only problem with East Africa. It's incredible. What does a Yank know about the lower classes and peasants? We English know they're different, but these Yanks – it really irks me – they think every bod in the world from top to bottom is the same. It's fantastic. Give every nig-nog from here to Kingdom Come some Coca-Cola, peanut butter, corn flakes, comic books, hamburgers, and the whole world will be all right.' Heather paused, screwed up her face and said in what was intended to be an American accent, '*No more prahblims!*' She laughed. 'It's fantastic. You act as if you have no problems in the States – that's what's really fantastic about Yanks. There are poor people in the good old USA, aren't there? You're bloody right, there are! I read somewhere that one-third of the people in the States live in hovels and wear rags, but *no*, you don't stay there and put things right – you come *here* and play the good sheriff, fighting for people's non-existent rights and all that rubbish. And what about your own nig-nogs? I once read –'

'I think you're being a bit unfair,' said Miss Male, folding and unfolding her napkin.

'Well, there's something in what Miss Monkhouse is saying,' said Miss Poole. Again she said 'Mongoose'; it had not been a slip of the tongue the first two times. 'Racial prejudice is jolly difficult to define.'

B.J. looked first at Miss Poole, then at Heather. She spoke, shifting her gaze from one to the other. 'I know Americans aren't perfect. I never said we were. I know poverty's a big hang-up for lots of people. But that's not what we're talking about. At least I'm not. I'm talking about Miss Verjee who isn't here because she's an Indian. She eats with her hands and licks her fingers and her English is bad and things like that. Africans don't like Indians, neither do white people. We all know that, so why don't we just come out and say it, huh?'

'I told you,' said Heather, scraping her loose food together in a little heap with the side of her fork, 'you can't stand to see people enjoying themselves. You always have to ruin it with your bloody self-righteousness.'

'Does anyone want more meat or vegetables?' asked Miss Poole loudly. 'If not, I'll give them to the cats.'

Heather was breathless, B.J. angry, Miss Male hurt and confused. No one replied to Miss Poole and so all the dishes of food were placed on the floor for the cats. B.J.'s downcast eyes caught the swarming cats, fighting for the food, licking the plates with their small pink tongues, plates that she would herself eat from when she came again.

Miss Male cleared her throat. 'How are you finding it here?' she asked Heather.

'Frightful, perfectly frightful,' said Heather. She lit a cigarette and looked at the light-bulb over the table. 'I had forgotten how terrible it is to be among women. It's nothing personal against you chaps, except that you're not men. They say men are bad – and that's true of course, men can be bloody awful. But there's nothing worse than a bunch of women together. It must be our predatory instincts or somesuch. We're all so damned bloodthirsty, we women. When I read in the papers about some bloke murdering his wife I say to myself, "I'll bet it was her own fault." In a group men are pretty jolly, but we're like some breed of ghastly bird, always pecking and clawing –'

Miss Poole had gripped the table-edge, but kept her eyes hard on Heather.

Heather glanced at Miss Poole, saw the knuckles whitening and said quickly, 'I'm sure I'll adjust to it. It takes time, doesn't it?'

'I must say it doesn't take much adjusting to live here in the *bundu*. I rather prefer life here to that awful Nairobi,' said Miss Poole.

Heather threw her head back and gave a stage laugh, loud and brief; Miss Poole was still talking, not to Heather, but to Miss Male.

'– The Africans here are really quite sweet, don't you think so? I find the Africans in Nairobi rather aggressive – bullies, to be frank.'

'Quite,' said Miss Male uneasily. She could add nothing more. Miss Male had been only three months in East Africa. She preferred not to talk about Africans; she usually said that she had nothing against them.

'I've never heard such a thing,' said Heather, exasperated. 'When I was in Nairobi I took no notice of the blacks. I thought they were all the same. Now I see there are differences, those chaps in Nairobi had something after all. They're cheeky, I suppose – that's what we get for spoonfeeding them – but they know how to dress. Not like the *watu* here, dashing about in rags and stinking to high heaven. The typist in our school was a keen little chappie, always neat.' Heather looked at Miss Poole and shook her head from side to side. 'You prefer life here, you say. I don't. These people . . . *smell*. Full stop.'

'To you they smell,' B.J. broke in. 'I read somewhere that black people consider whites very unclean because we don't bathe in running water.'

'Isn't it the Indians who feel that way,' said Miss Male, 'not the Africans?'

'Back to Miss Verjee,' said Heather disgustedly.

'Well, Africans *are* very clean,' said B.J.

'You're sure of that?' asked Miss Poole.

'Sure I am.'

'Well, I know I'm hardly an authority —'

'You see, I read somewhere that Africans are very careful about washing. They wash every day,' said B.J.

Heather laughed, again too loudly. 'That's rubbish. I'll bet it was written by a Yank.'

'Of course, Julius may be an exception,' said Miss Poole.

B.J. was silent.

Miss Poole seemed agitated. Sally had crept back on to her lap, and Miss Poole calmed herself by stroking Sally's fur. Now there was silence all around. Miss Poole continued to stroke the cat, saying, 'I've heard all this before a thousand times. Do they wash, don't they wash? Who is cheeky and who isn't. This doesn't make a particle of difference. I said I prefer life here and I mean it. I can handle my Africans – they don't mind if one is firm as long as one is fair. The Africans here are reasonably honest. They have the tribe and the chief. They are living with their own people. Even the English and the Americans go a bit mad when they're away from their own people, there's no denying that.' Miss Poole glanced at B.J. and then continued. 'The Africans lie of course, and steal little things. That's their way. I know Julius is constantly in the sugar, but he doesn't take much, and he does an honest job of work. But I get perfectly ill when I think of those people in Nairobi driving around in their long American cars, having their fiddles at the Maize Marketing Board, spending our hard-earned tax money —'

'I beg your pardon,' said Heather haughtily. 'While these people sit in the mud and beat their bongos, the Africans in Nairobi show a bit of initiative —'

'It's bribery and corruption and you know it,' said Miss Poole matter-of-factly.

B.J. looked at Miss Male, who stared straight ahead, at nothing.

She hoped Miss Male would say something. She was English and, in B.J.'s eyes, had a right to speak. In the course of the meal B.J. had heard her own voice; she knew it sounded foolish and American and unlike the other refined, correct English ones at the table; but she could not speak differently. If she said something they would laugh; she had become acutely aware, with an awareness that dumbed her, that she pronounced her *t*'s likc *d*'s, as in 'running wadder' and 'Miss Verjee's on doody' (Howdy Doody, thought B.J., grimly: what a stupe I am).

'I grew up with these people,' Miss Poole was saying. 'I know them. They don't belong in big strange cities where all manner of horrible things can happen to them. They need their tribe, the air, the sun –'

'They need to be bloody-minded, that's all. But mind you,' Heather said, dithering, 'I wouldn't give you a shilling for the lot of them. If I had my choice –'

'In Nairobi they are immoral. Drunkards. It's shocking,' said Miss Poole.

'I don't even *care* about Africans. It's fantastic. I don't know why I'm talking like this, but since coming up-country a week ago I've seen nothing but lazy *watu* sitting under trees doing damn-all.'

'There is goodness in them. What would *you* know about that? Yes,' said Miss Poole, with tears in her eyes, 'still some goodness –'

'That's rubbish! Now you sound like an American.' Heather's voice sweetened. 'How does it go? I remember a man in Nairobi telling me, "In East Africa the birds have no song, the flowers have no fragrance, the women have no virtue." So true.'

Heather looked around the table for a reaction. There was only an offended silencc. She went on placidly, 'Goodness? *Here?* Not bloody likely, I'd say. I recall a white woman, as white as any of us, was killed by an African not far from where we're sitting. That was a few years ago. She was also, they say,' she paused for effect, 'molested in the most savage way.'

Miss Male looked worriedly at Heather. 'Did it happen here at the school?'

'Oh,' said Heather lightly, '*somewhere* near here. Strangled with her own brassière, they say. Among other things.'

'Did they catch him?' Miss Male seemed oblivious of the others. Her hand touched at her throat.

'I suppose not, I forget. But it's something to think about, isn't it? Especially when you use big words like goodness and suchlike.'

B.J. stiffened. 'Well, how would you like it if someone spit at you and called you names, like the British did to the Africans here? Yeah,' said B.J., 'and made you live in a village and treated you like dirt. *You* wouldn't like it.'

'I neglected to mention,' said Heather. 'This was *after* independence. The blacks were in power.'

'Some people have long memories,' said B.J. quickly. On the word *people* she spat a small bubble of spittle into Heather's face.

'Some people possibly,' said Heather, wiping at the spittle. 'Not these people.'

'You didn't —'

'No. They're savages, pure and simple. When you realize that, as I did — and I was just like you, B.J., when I arrived, full of idealism and let's give the chaps a fair chance — when you realize that, you're content and you stop fighting people's battles for them. You wait and see. You'll change.'

'You didn't answer my question,' said B.J. 'How would you like it —'

Heather whipped around and looked B.J. full in the face. 'How would you like it if someone called you a dirty Jew? Would you wrap your bra around his neck and strangle him? *Would you?*'

'It's not quite the same thing,' said Miss Male attempting to calm Heather. 'Anti-semitism is hardly —'

'It's close,' said Heather. 'It's ruddy close. Human life means nothing here. I lock my doors here, I can tell you that. Who knows, some dirty great spade might take it into his head —'

Miss Poole scraped her chair back; she was trembling with suppressed rage. She helped Sally to the floor. Sally yowled while Miss Poole swayed cobra-like at Heather and said, 'My Africans can be trusted, they work hard, they respect me. My Africans . . . my Africans are better than your Africans.'

She did not speak loudly but she spoke with conviction, her voice steady, even if her body was not. When she finished Heather opened her mouth to say something, but she had only said one word when from the kitchen there was a terrific crash which sent all the cats, led by Sally, looping over chairs and into the bedroom. The crash did not end at once; it tapered off with the splinter, shatter and tinkle of glass. Heather said nothing more; Miss Poole jumped up and ran to the kitchen. As soon as the door flapped shut, Heather's lips curled slowly into a smile.

Now they sat in the living room, holding coffee cups on their laps. They spoke politely in turn, their voices growing softer and softer. Julius had dropped the chocolate mousse and had broken Miss Poole's heavy crystal bowl. His penitent sighing, as he mopped the pieces of glass on the floor, was audible even in the living-room. Neither the dessert nor the breakage was mentioned by any of the women.

'Fruit?' asked Miss Poole coldly.

B.J. said she would like a banana, but she had no sooner said it than she realized she had mispronounced it, given it a short *a*. To make matters worse she added, 'As we say back home.'

Miss Male's head was in her hands. The cats had returned from the bedroom and were squabbling for room on Miss Poole's narrow lap. When B.J. finished her banana she looked for a place to put the large damp peel; seeing no receptacle, she cradled it in her hands. She felt bites on her legs. There were cat fleas in her chair; she dangled the banana peel by its hard tip and with her free hand rubbed her thighs and calves, squashing the grey fleas and leaving small streaks of juice on her skin.

Their talking had now stopped altogether; the only sounds came from outside the room – frogs, whining locusts, bats; bugs pattered on the screened windows. Heather puffed her cigarette and, expelling the smoke loudly to get everyone's attention, glanced around the room.

'I know what you're all thinking,' she said. 'But as bad as we are – and I *know* we're bad; I don't need Americans to tell me that – we're the best they'll ever get. Who wants to live in Africa, what white people? Only cranks, fools, failures . . .'

Before anyone could respond, Heather said again, 'We're the best they'll get. The best,' she added almost with malice.

11

Games

Heather knew she had talked too much at Miss Poole's, and hated
herself for having spoken sincerely; she felt she had given them a
chance to know her doubt. She regretted the evening. Strangers had
called out to her from a distance; their indistinct intentions and
her own loneliness had eased her into their company, but only
when she was near did she recognize them as strangers. They had
duped her and looted her of her sincerity. It was not new to her
and this made her feel worse. There was a further humiliation:
they had watched her; they would be next to her for a whole term,
reminding her of this loss.

Miss Poole, because she seemed pathetic, had won. Where there
were sentimental witnesses the old, the ugly and the inept always
came out best. On leaving Miss Poole's house, Heather resolved
that she would not say another word socially to her again. But
there were several other things to consider: another humiliating
defeat, sourly sitting in her throat; there was the fact that an invitation had been extended and she had accepted. The invitation
would have to be returned; the school was too small and tightly
balanced for safe rituals to falter into irregularity; chaos would
follow. The week after Miss Poole's dinner, Heather handed a note
to her cook and told him to take it to the Memsab and to wait for
a reply. Miss Poole initialled the note and the next day joined B.J.
and Miss Male at Heather's house for a meal. That evening Miss
Male invited Heather and Miss Poole for a meal with her and B.J.
And so it went, in rotation, with all the women always present; a
pattern had formed. Attendance at the weekly dinners was obligatory, for this was the bush; with the exception of the Horse and
Hunter, a rustic hotel fifteen miles up the road, there was nowhere

else to go, nothing else to do. They were all unmarried white women, living together in a remote post, in a black country. In the absence of privacy lay their safety; an assertion of privacy by any of them would have meant threat. Even if B.J. and Miss Male had not yet caught on, they would soon realize this necessity as, in her five years, Heather had. There could be no excuse for not playing along with the others.

With sadness Heather sent the second invitation to Miss Poole. She knew the drill: the dinner would start with a 'sundowner' at four when the girls went out to the playing field, and would continue through the evening, moving from the veranda to the sitting-room to the dining-room and then back to the veranda for the last drink. Heather hated the idea of the intrusion, inescapable, possibly humiliating. But after getting the initialled invitation back, she realized that Miss Poole was similarly inconvenienced and maybe even annoyed by the fraudulent gesture of hospitality. When Heather considered it she grew absolutely pleased to be giving the second dinner; she could get back at Miss Poole and, if everything went well, she could do what she wanted to the hag at the head of the table who had served burned meat and said, 'My Africans are better than your Africans.'

Miss Poole arrived at Heather's on time.

'I wasn't sure you were coming,' said Heather blandly. 'I couldn't make out your initials on the note. Did you use a quill?'

Rufus barked, interrupting Miss Poole's reply, but when Miss Poole took her place on the veranda she spoke to Rufus softly, scratched behind his ear and even fearlessly held his lower jaw while she examined his teeth; the dog wagged his tail, grunted and flopped beside her.

'He has a spot of caries,' said Miss Poole.

'It must be this poxy place,' said Heather.

'Hi, all!' called B.J. from the grass. Miss Male was next to her. B.J. held something in her hands; one hand was clasped over the other. 'We got a hurt bug here. I hope you have a first-aid kit.'

'Drink?' asked Heather, ignoring B.J.

Miss Poole asked for sherry, the others beer. When it was

brought B.J. opened her hands a crack and showed the insect: it was a small praying mantis, green, and one of its long legs (B.J. said) was missing. B.J. reached for her drink, but in taking it she let the praying mantis slip to the veranda floor, near Heather. B.J. went for it, but when she came close Heather tipped her glass and let loose a stream of gin on the back of the thing, dousing it. The praying mantis twitched one of its legs, made a feeble half-spin with its body and then was still.

'Look what you did!'

'Shame,' said Miss Poole.

'They eat other insects,' said Miss Male, 'but I think you've killed it.'

'Sorry about that,' said Heather. 'I hate *dudus*.'

Miss Poole sipped at her drink and spat. 'What *is* this?'

'Why, it's cherry brandy,' said Heather. 'Isn't that what you said you wanted?'

'The poor thing's croaked,' said B.J. still looking at the dead insect. She plucked it by one leg and took it to the bed of African violets, where she scooped a tiny grave and dropped it in.

'You're a sentimental thing,' said Heather to B.J. 'It was just a *dudu*, after all.'

'They're quite beneficial,' said Miss Male. 'They eat other insects.'

'I think you did that on purpose,' said Miss Poole.

'I did,' said Heather. 'I hate *dudus*.'

At dinner, oil swam on the surface of the cold oxtail soup, the toast was burnt and looked like slices of coke, the butter was frozen solid, the meat bloody, sinewy goat, the potatoes crisply uncooked. Heather, who had clocked each bit with her egg-timer so that it was certain to be underdone, filled all the plates and took great delight in giving Miss Poole large inedible portions of the stuff.

B.J. mentioned the praying mantis again ('The poor thing didn't have a chance'), but none of the women responded or commented on the meal or called attention to the fact that the corpses of several flies were floating in the soup tureen. Heather had planned to fuss and blame the cook if the subject of the food was raised; no one mentioned it. The three guests ate slowly, with disgust and incredulity, and Heather even managed to force seconds on everyone by saying, 'I'll have to throw this away if you don't clean it right up. I hate to throw good food away, especially here where so many Africans go hungry.'

Plates were passed and filled.

An added, unplanned, but to Heather delicious discomfort occurred over coffee when, without warning and just after nightfall, the electricity failed.

'I think I should pop over to the school and see that the girls are all right,' said Miss Poole, rising.

'Surely,' said Heather to Miss Male, 'that Miss Verjee can deal with this. It's simply a power failure.'

'Miss Verjee gets all the donkey work,' said Miss Male.

'Yeah,' said B.J. 'Coolie labour.'

'Did you say *coolie*?' laughed Heather.

'I mean she's always left holding the bag,' said B.J., 'while we're eating and having a good time.'

Heather, who was lighting her cigarette, laughed loudly, then coughed and finally seemed to choke into her fingers.

'We all do our jobs,' said Miss Poole quickly. 'Each of us carries a fair share of the load. Miss Verjee does no more or less than any of us.'

Miss Poole looked from face to face, realized she was standing in the darkness, muttered, and seated herself again. Two flashlights were produced, switched on and placed upright on their ends. They lighted the cobwebbed ceiling of Heather's living-room but little else. The four women sat in shadowy cricket-haunted darkness, grumbled about the Electricity Board and felt for their coffee-cups.

'Do you know anything about this, Miss Lebow?' Miss Poole asked at one point. She gave B.J.'s name a French pronunciation, Lebeau, which B.J. liked.

'No, how should I know anything about the electricity situation?' B.J. giggled. She added, 'Gee whizz, Americans get blamed for everything around this place!'

'Please don't be offended,' said Miss Poole. 'I just thought you might know. You have dealings with them, haven't you?'

'We all do, don't we?' B.J. asked. She swivelled her head at Miss Poole, trying to make her out in the darkened room, and repeated, 'Don't we?'

'Well, I was thinking . . .' Miss Poole paused. 'Oh, never mind, Miss Lebow. I don't know *what* I was thinking.'

'How absolutely mysterious,' said Heather. She offered a second cup of coffee and, filling Miss Poole's cup, succeeded in pouring some squarely on to Miss Poole's foot.

One of the flashlights dimmed, grew orange and then faded out completely; Miss Male managed to revive the flagging conversation by commenting on the dead flashlight: she gave them all a little spiel on leakproof batteries which, she claimed, were not leakproof at all. B.J. and Heather both had flashlight-battery stories. Heather's was pointless, but B.J.'s, which was about being in Piraeus late at night with only a flashlight and using this to find her way to the hotel, caused the others to murmur with interest. B.J. said that she had always wanted to sell the story as a true-life adventure to the EverReady company to use on their ads, 'but they weren't EverReady batteries. I'm not sure what kind they were, to tell the truth.' Inevitably, the conversation turned to servants' foibles. Heather told a story about her cook in Nairobi whom she had told that she was going right next door for lunch; when she returned she found him standing sullenly amid the brooms, the floor polish and canned food, in the store-room. He had thought she had told him to stand in the store for lunch. The others offered stories: Miss Poole's was about Julius's inability to distinguish *r* and *l*, B.J.'s was about her gardener's amazing ability to tell the time of day to the minute by aiming his forearm at the sun and gauging the angle of his elbow. Heather sneaked gin into her coffee-cup and became drunk. By the end of the evening she was puffing her cigarette and blowing the smoke at Miss Poole in the darkness.

The score was even, Heather felt.

The following week B.J. and Miss Male gave their dinner party. Heather beamed when B.J. entered the room wearing a barkcloth sarong and carrying a large platter of grey porridge and smaller dishes of pumpkin leaves and hard red beans.

'We're going to eat African style,' B.J. announced, passing the porridge. 'Something different for a change.'

African beer was brought, a thick, bitter liquid, lumpy with crushed kernels of corn and served warm in sticky gourds. B.J. sat on the floor, drank with relish and scooped up the beans with a ball of porridge which she held in her right hand. Miss Poole sipped at the beer, nibbled at the beans and fell silent.

'This was B.J.'s idea,' explained Miss Male.

'It's bloody marvellous,' said Heather, who was pleased to find the meal revolting. She glanced at Miss Poole, who was delicately holding the gourd of beer but no longer sipping. Her lips were pursed; her porridge was untouched.

'Mood music, anyone?' asked B.J. She put on an African record of drumming, chanting and rattling bells, a Congolese funeral ceremony she said she had picked up in the States.

'Did you say *funeral*?' asked Heather. 'They don't sound as if they're in mourning to *me*!'

'What do you expect?' asked B.J. 'They're Africans, aren't they? They have their own way of doing things.'

'Last week you were telling us that Africans are the same as everyone else. *You* said it, not me.'

'Well, they are,' said B.J. 'It's just that –'

'Why don't you join us?' asked Miss Male. B.J. was still squatting on the floor, bent over her bowls of food.

'It tastes better like this,' said B.J., smiling and tucking the top of her slipping sarong into her brassière.

'In-credible,' said Heather softly; in a louder voice she inquired, 'Do I understand that all Africans up-country eat this? I mean, your common or garden nig.'

'They wouldn't eat anything else!' said B.J.

'It's lacking in certain essential vitamins,' Miss Male put in.

'Which accounts for the lethargy in Africans, sometimes mistaken for laziness –'

'You read that in an American book, am I right?'

'It happens to be a scientific –'

'Oh, I don't mean to be nasty, Pam,' said Heather. 'I just never agree with these simple theories. Africans *do* have such disgusting tastes. Ants, monkeys, fish-heads – have you ever heard anything so sick-making?'

'There's a lot of nutrition in fish-heads,' said Miss Male.

'You tell 'em, Pam!' said B.J. from the floor.

'It seems an uninspired fare. In Nairobi, of course, the diet is quite different, but then so are the people. I must say I'm not mad keen on this mush.'

Feeling personally challenged, Miss Poole ate her entire helping and drank her gourd of beer. When she tipped up the gourd she saw a small cockroach inside, clinging to the wet wall and flicking his antennae. She put the gourd down, said she felt unwell, and left.

'Do you think she's going to puke?' asked Heather after Miss Poole had gone.

'I hope it's not the food,' said B.J. 'I really tried hard –'

'Surely it's not the food. No,' said Heather, 'there's something wrong with that woman.'

A week later it was Miss Poole's turn to give the dinner. Heather wondered at first whether Miss Poole would dare; it would be asking for a rematch. The invitations were typed by Simon and sent out. On the appointed evening all the women were present and chatting cheerfully about the new school badge Miss Poole had designed, with its motto lettered in a flapping scroll at the top, *Daisies Are Our Silver*. Miss Poole served a stew made of vegetables and fish-heads. The fish-heads floated at the top, their scaly jaws agog, eye-sockets empty.

The dinners continued without let-up, B.J. and Miss Male's sometimes very pleasant, Heather's and Miss Poole's always made painful by cold-blooded bitchery and booby traps: ants in the sugar bowl, collapsing chairs ('Was that caused by white ants or bore beetles, do you suppose?' Heather had asked Miss Male while Miss Poole sprawled in tumbled disarray on the floor), knives and forks horny with old dried food, glasses with lip-rending chips in their rims. The invitations went out regularly every week; now the score was never settled.

What Heather considered her most successful move was the evening she paid her gardener and his brother to beat on the walls and roof while the women ate their dinner. One crawled on the roof and thumped with a hoe, loosening the soot and cobwebs from the ceiling, sending it into plates and on to heads. The other boy walked around the house poking the walls with a thick pole. Once he poked the wall behind a picture; the picture flew off its hook and smashed. The noises were as regular and persistent as a poltergeist's. Only B.J. mentioned the sounds; Heather ignored her. 'Possibly an earth tremor,' ventured Miss Male. But nothing more was said.

The uncanny thudding, the batterings from the blackness outside, shook Miss Poole terribly. Banging and knocking in the night had always given her bad dreams or kept her anxiously awake; now she felt that somehow Heather had discovered this, her most private and nagging fear. That evening she had to be taken home by Miss Male and B.J., one girl on each of Miss Poole's limp arms.

In her turn Miss Poole invited the three over. They had their usual pre-dinner sherry on the veranda and then entered the dining-room. There was something irregular about the table, B.J. thought; she studied the places and saw that it was set for five. When they sat and were served (it was 'toad in the hole', sausages in Yorkshire pudding, one of Julius's specialties) the extra chair, the silver, the plates were in order (next to Heather), but stayed empty. The extra place at the table caused the women to bunch together, bumping elbows. B.J. found the collection of clean plates maddening.

'Are you expecting someone?' she said.

Miss Poole looked surprised. 'I beg your pardon?'

'I mean, there's a . . .' B.J. had a mouthful of sausage and could not speak. She grinned sheepishly and jabbed her fork at the plate, the silver, the napkin, the empty chair.

'Oh, *that*,' said Miss Poole. 'Yes . . . um . . . he said he'd not be early, but he told me we shouldn't wait for him. He'll be along directly.'

'*He?* So it's a *man*, ha-ha!' B.J. had swallowed her sausage. She showed her perfect teeth. 'How *about* that!'

Miss Poole saw that she had the floor. She twiddled their curiosity. 'Yes . . . he's . . . well, one does even at this age have the occasional male friend,' Miss Poole lied. 'Of course, he doesn't get all the way up here very often. That frightful road. They should do something about that road. It's a positive disgrace.'

'Mmmm,' murmured B.J. impatiently. 'But the man?'

Heather forked food into her mouth and appeared not to be listening.

'The man?' Miss Poole's brow furrowed. 'What man?'

B.J. tossed her head at the empty place.

'Yes, I see. He's from . . .' Now Miss Poole stopped speaking and plastered mashed potato on her fork, broke two peas over that and wiped it with gravy from her knife. She chewed the potato carefully, working her jaws in what appeared to be an exaggeration of eating, then said, 'What was I saying?'

'He's from —' Both B.J. and Miss Male spoke, their voices rising together earnestly.

'Well, he's from Nairobi of course. A teacher.' Miss Poole looked at Heather and said lightly, 'In point of fact, your former . . . um . . . school, Miss Monkhouse.'

Heather pressed her lips together and turned pale. With her mouth shut her face seemed to shrink. She put her knife and fork down; she ate nothing more. For the rest of the evening she smoked nervously, said nothing, and glanced furtively at the front door. But the man from her school never showed up.

Both Miss Poole and Heather quickly realized that it was impossible for them to have a showdown without involving B.J. and Miss Male in it. This worried them somewhat, for they now made no secret of their tactics, and the tactics were growing cruder and more obvious. At times, B.J. and Miss Male suffered nearly as much discomfort as Miss Poole and Heather. B.J. once sat in one of Heather's prepared chairs; Miss Male got a roach in her bouillon at Miss Poole's. But nothing could be done about it; all four had to be present or there could be no assault. And, while still realizing the unpleasantness the squirming girls had to endure, Miss Poole and Heather were extremely upset one particular day when Miss Male had a jigger in her toe and could not come. The dinner party at Heather's that evening was angrily cancelled. Miss Male, like B.J., was needed as a witness.

In their own time, when they were alone in the house they shared, B.J. and Miss Male calmed themselves by inventing games of their own. Whist, bridge and other games gave way to the building of intricate structures – houses, bridges, castles – with the deck of cards. There were late-night quiz contests in which Miss Male learned that Helena was the capital of Montana, P. T. Barnum said 'There's a sucker born every minute', and George Herman 'Babe' Ruth (b. 1895–d. 1948) hit a record seven hundred and fourteen homers while he was in major league baseball; B.J. learned the names of the Home Counties, the two beasts on the British coat of arms and the breed of the Queen's dogs. With the help of one of Miss Male's dish-towels printed with a map of the London underground, B.J. also learned the names of all tube stations on the Northern Line. Miss Male tried but failed to teach B.J. chess. B.J. said they could use the chessboard just the same and she proposed a version of bingo. She cut the chessboard into two sections, each one containing eight squares across and four down.

The game was called Gecko and they played it with passion, all through the empty East African nights. The far wall of the living-room lacked a window, and this was perfect: large squares, five across and five down, were blocked out in pencil on the wall; two chairs and a table were set up in front of the squares. The lights were switched off and the room left in darkness for several minutes. When the lights were turned on, the wall was quickly scrutinized for geckoes, the small lizards that lived in the crannies of the house. The first girl to spot a gecko and correctly give its position placed a button on the corresponding square of her Gecko board.

'Lights out,' B.J. would say.

They would sit in the darkness and then, 'That's enough! Lights on!'

When the lights came on (they took turns flicking the switch) they would crane their necks towards the wall and shout the position of the hapless gecko.

'G-Three!'

'No, it's on the line! G-Four!'

'It's moving!'

'G-Four. It's still G-Four!'

'I saw it first, B.J. Don't cheat.'

'Oh, fooey.'

Sometimes there were arguments, often there were no geckoes, and cockroaches had to be used – big dark ones from the open drain outside the kitchen door. According to the rules the game could be played at any time of the day. If Miss Male came to the house alone for morning coffee and happened to see a gecko hovering on one of the pencilled squares on the wall, she was at liberty to place a button on the appropriate square of her board. It was not uncommon for a game to last for days, and one game played during a dry spell lasted three weeks. B.J. said it was the greatest game ever invented; it was not, she said, just any old way of killing time, but a way of killing time that had East Africa written all over it. Sitting in their house for hours at a stretch, each girl with a drink in her hand, bowls of peanuts and potato chips near by, they watched for geckoes and talked about themselves, about interesting men they had known and about things they had always wanted to do if they had a pile of money all their own. B.J. listened horror-struck as Miss Male told her about the war years, the bombings and air raids in London; Miss Male listened in amusement as B.J. told her about Disneyland, the fake castles and pink elephants, Los Angeles, the time she saw Ava Gardner on Sunset Strip. Miss Male confessed that she had always wanted to visit the States; B.J. said that she would not mind staying a while in England, seeing the Queen and her corgis, walking on a foggy day in London town while candles burned in holly-hung windows and groups of cassocked choristers sang old English carols.

Late one night, tipsy on two lagers, Miss Male told B.J. that her name was really Malinowski. B.J., who had refrained from telling Miss Male what her real name was (telling Heather was one thing, but you never knew how your room-mate would react if you told her you were a Jew), said, 'Lebowitz here. *Shalom.*'

'*Shalom,*' said Miss Male. 'Isn't that a giggle?'

They swore that they would invite each other for a visit to their homes after they left Africa, just to see what their countries were really like. They avoided talking about Miss Poole or Heather and dreaded going to the weekly dinner parties. But the dinner parties, if nothing else, made B.J. and Miss Male grateful for each other's good humour; the more bitchy the parties were, the closer B.J. and Miss Male became.

In the way that a sportsman playing an unusually difficult game briefs the critics beforehand on his own skill and his opponent's crooked strategy, Miss Poole gave special teas and excluded Heather, Heather gave special lunches and excluded Miss Poole; and each took it as an opportunity to slander the other. The teas and lunches were failures partly because the girls were uncooperative, but mostly because the vulgar slanders were not being uttered according to the agreed rules, in the presence of the opponent. Miss Poole hinted at alcoholism, nicotine-poisoning and nymphomania in Heather; Heather, whose imagination and experience exceeded that of Miss Poole, suggested baldly that Miss Poole's appetites ranged from the bestial with her cats to the lesbian with Rose. To both hosts B.J. said, as she had once said to Heather, 'I don't repeat rumours, not even *to* people about the *same* people. I wouldn't tell you what I heard, because it's not fair to you . . . I hate gossip, especially here, you know . . .' Miss Male concurred with B.J., although she added that she might be tempted to phrase it differently. And they would both, B.J. and Miss Male, troop home across the grass, and calm themselves with a drink, a talk and a game of Gecko.

Miss Poole's teas continued, but in stony silence. And Heather developed a special way of inviting B.J. and Miss Male to her house. She would jump out from the hedge of bougainvillaea as they walked back from their noon class, act surprised to see them and say, '*Lunch?*'

Urgency, need was in her voice, but not kindness. The first time she did it, B.J. shrieked she was so frightened. Heather persisted; she wanted their company as witnesses to her own suffering and to Miss Poole's perversity. At the same time she did not want to appear disappointed by the girls' refusal. She could only do this by pretending that the well planned lunch invitation was extended on the spur of the moment, simply a bush courtesy. Slowly Heather learned a habit of abruptness which bordered on ritual, almost not an invitation, more the uttering of an aggressive formula. It seldom worked. Heather's lunch invitations were usually turned down.

There was no way Miss Poole or Heather could make the lunches and teas compulsory for the girls. They contented themselves with their attendance at the weekly dinner parties and it was plain that everyone was involved in the feud: the girls were witnesses, but close enough to the action to be harmed.

For a time, Miss Poole and Heather left slander and gossip and used new tactics. The thought of pestering Heather outside the dining-room came to Miss Poole by chance when, one day after asking Heather if her cook could help pick the coffee in the school garden (it was ripening fast; some of the berries had already dropped and rotted), Heather replied indignantly, '*Hapana*, no! Jacko is not going to help the girls with their chores. He's a cook, not a *fundi* on coffee. I won't allow it!'

'Everyone has to do his share. Julius was out there this morning –'

'If Julius wants to pick coffee that's his *shauri*,' said Heather. Whenever she talked about Africans she interlarded her speech with Swahili words. 'Jacko has *kazi mingi sana*, masses of work to do –' Heather continued to rant.

Miss Poole watched Heather reddening in anger, and she

decided that there were simpler ways to get at her than giving a dinner party.

And at the same time, seeing how she had let herself be riled by Miss Poole, Heather made a similar deduction.

They were possessive about their servants. If there was any privacy at all in the school compound it was in the kitchen, where the women and their servants carried on an exclusive exchange. Bush custom forbade anyone listening in on one of these conversations or interfering with the servants' duties. Practically everything in the compound was shared: Dutch ovens, electric kettles, hairdryers, typewriters, three-way plugs, phonographs, sewing materials and even, in times of real need, clothes. The servants were not common property; each was expected to be loyal, to maintain silence about what went on in his employer's house and to take orders from no one except the woman he worked for. Servants were seldom loaned. Although the women did not treat them particularly kindly (B.J. and Miss Male did not count; their gardener was a schoolboy, their cleaning woman was simply a part-time char), no one was allowed to talk to another's servant, much less give him an order.

It was with enormous anger therefore that a week after asking Heather if Jacko could help with the coffee-picking Miss Poole saw, from her office window, Julius staggering across the grass to the library, laden with a set of encyclopaedias, followed by Heather, whose hands held only a sprig of jacaranda. Miss Poole wanted to rush out of her office and scream at Heather (and tear the blossoms out of her hands: Miss Poole had planted that jacaranda herself and this was the first year it had given forth flowers). She had a more rational thought.

The next day, on her way to class, Heather saw Jacko high on a ladder against an unused building which Miss Poole intended for conversion into a library annexe and reading-room. Jacko was painting the wooden window frames green.

'Jacko, come down here this instant!' Heather cried in English. One of the schoolgirls was passing. Heather did not like to speak Swahili to her servants while the girls were around; if the girls showed no signs of going away Heather spoke Swahili in her coolest British accent. Jacko hesitated. 'Do you hear me? I said, come down straight away!'

Heather made a sign with her finger. Jacko understood. He placed his large brush over the hanging bucket and climbed slowly down the ladder to where Heather stood.

'What the devil are you doing?' The schoolgirl had now passed. Heather repeated her demand in Swahili.

Jacko faced his curling toes. Spots of green paint glistened on his muscular forearms and torn shirt. 'The *memsab* say to me paint this house, Jacko.'

'Which *memsab*?'

'*Mzee*,' said Jacko, 'the old one. Missa Poor.'

'The bloody cheek,' muttered Heather. She thought a moment, then said, 'Well, you're not doing it right. You go ahead, but paint the windows. I see you haven't done the windows.'

'Windows, madam?' Jacko's eyes opened.

'The glass, everything! The windows, the walls, even the roof!' Now she spoke slowly in English, with gestures and a big smile, as if to an imbecile. 'Go up ladder quick-quick. Take brush and paint. This paint. Paint whole house nice. Then paint, paint, paint' (she swished her hand), 'paint, paint. Make house all green. Aaaaalllll greeeeeeeeen.'

'Aaaaalllllll greeeeeeeeen,' echoed Jacko. Now he had his real orders, from his own *memsab*; he ascended the ladder happily.

Miss Poole stopped him, but not before he had painted the entire end of the building: the window-glass dripped, the door was streaked, the gutters, the brick walls, the threshold – everything gleamed a bright green. Jacko had been furiously lashing paint on the roof tiles when he upset the bucket, his last can of paint. He went to Miss Poole to ask for more.

'Let's have a look,' Miss Poole had said.

'No,' she whimpered, shamelessly and piteously, when she saw the huge green end of the building. Her shoulders shook, her mouth compressed; she knotted her fingers and squeezed the blood out of them. She knew she could not punish Jacko; she stood helpless before the building, wondering how many gallons of turpentine it would take to scrub the paint from the porous brick. The paint dripped in steady plops from the green roof to the wide green leaves below, making the stalks nod a mocking yes yes yes.

'That will be all, Jacko. *Kazi kwisha*,' she said sadly, 'no more work.' She gave him a shilling, sent him home, and a short period of mercenary activity had begun.

When the wind was right, Julius burned rubbish near Heather's house. The stinking, choking fumes permeated Heather's clothes on the line, lingered in the kitchen, fouled her bedroom and made Jacko's eyes water.

Jacko pitched lighted matches at the cats and coaxed Sally into eating a dead mouse, green with mould.

Julius, tiny, adept at stealing, jacked up Heather's VW and pilfered all four wheels, leaving the car aloft on wooden blocks. Heather fretted, accused, threatened to call the police; Julius replaced the wheels, but let out the air.

Jacko dropped a twist of his own excrement on the front steps of Miss Poole's house. Miss Poole stepped in it. Julius disgustedly cleaned it from her shoe with a stick. When he finished the chore he collected some bees in a paper bag and lobbed it through Heather's bedroom window. Heather was stung on the lip, Jacko on the neck.

Jacko stuck the swollen discoloured head of a colobus monkey on Miss Poole's front gatepost.

Julius slipped a bull's pizzle into Heather's meat-safe.

It had all started with a suggestion from Miss Poole: 'The wind is just right, and there is plenty of room to burn rubbish over there.' Then no suggestions were necessary. Jacko and Julius were of different tribes; in addition, their loyalties to their employers were strong, their identification with the separate households complete. They had been longing to get at each other and, with the consent of their *memsabs*, had their chance at last. It went on two weeks, from the burning of the rubbish to the secreting of the bull's pizzle; at the end of two weeks it verged on the tribal, a

personal feuding which at first did not involve Miss Poole or
Heather. The servants fought with each other, sabotaged each
other's bicycle and cooking pot, and from the kitchen windows
shouted insults: each accused the other's mother of having
copulated with a hyena to produce him.

The women had complained vehemently. Miss Poole brought
Sally to Heather's house and demanded to know why the cat was
ill; there had been no reply from Heather but, happily for Miss
Poole, Sally vomited the digested remnants of the mouse, and a
few other meals, on to Heather's carpet. Heather had dragged
Jacko to Miss Poole's and shown her the bee-bite on his neck
(Heather claimed that she had not been bitten, but Rose had seen
her applying alcohol to a bite and had reported this to Miss Poole).
Then the attacks stopped, the servants were battling each other in
private and the situation lurched into a new dimension. Heather
and Miss Poole knew the games had changed when briefly,
one afternoon, there was nearly violence. There had never been
violence before. It was not supposed to be part of the game.

B.J. had seen it. She described it to Miss Male as 'crazy, weird,
awful really'. In the field between Heather's and Miss Poole's, near
a dusty fat-limbed frangipani, B.J. saw Julius squaring off with
Jacko. Heather stood at some distance behind Jacko, Miss Poole
and Rose behind Julius. B.J. heard Heather screech, 'Don't just
stand there, Jacko. *Hit* him!' Jacko closed his eyes and slapped
Julius across the face, his loosely made fist hitting sideways. When
Jacko opened his eyes and saw what he had done, saw Julius
gaping dumbfounded and pained at him, he turned and ran. Julius
looked mournfully at Miss Poole, who said, '*Napenda?* Did you
like that?' Julius shook his head no and then dashed after Jacko.
B.J. started to hurry away. At the edge of her garden she looked
back and saw the women still facing each other, shooting glares,
motionless, their arms folded. Rose's body was inclined towards
Heather, as if at any moment she would rush up to Heather and
nip at her furiously like a maddened hound. The cooks had
bounded through the hedge (broken twigs drooped) and were now
out of sight.

They never came back. Their relatives carted away their bicycles and paraffin lamps. Without cooks, Miss Poole and Heather began buying expensive packaged soup, canned meat and (in a country which grew oranges, pineapples, avocados, paw-paws, guavas) fruit juice canned in Israel. Neither woman, in her whole time in East Africa, had ever squeezed an orange. They cursed the foolishness in their cooks that had made them desert. The women now knew they could expect no help from anyone, though each had privately nursed the unworded hope that her cook, venting tribal hatred, would permanently disable the other's cook, forcing her to buy canned fruit juice.

The showdown marked the end of the games, for it was violent and could have ended in actual harm to the women, a fist-fight, hairpulling or worse, as the cooks ran off leaving them to face each other. As it was, the women simply went back to their houses and sulked. The games had turned from a ritual of hateful play to hate itself; the symbolic gesture of dislike was now explicitly violent. The figged fist of the early harassment had become a fist.

No new cooks were taken on. Miss Poole and Heather stopped speaking. The weekly dinner parties, the teas and lunches ceased. B.J. and Miss Male had suffered through the meals and now they worried because there were none. Classes continued at the school as always, in ordered hours of mindless play, and at four o'clock, when the girls bounded on to the playing fields, each woman disappeared into her house, camouflaged in a clutter of dense African foliage and flowers. With this silence, the games froze into motionless hatred.

Silence

'She's a bitch, she hates me and she's dangerous. Apart from that I know sweet blow-all about the Memsab. Maybe she's out haunting a house.' Heather wrung a pencil as she spoke. She was in Miss Poole's office, sitting in Miss Poole's chair. B.J. stood at the doorway. She had asked where Miss Poole was.

'She might be sick,' B.J. said.

'Let's hope so.'

'That's not a very nice thing to say.'

'I think you'll find,' Heather said angrily, 'that *life* isn't very nice. For anyone. It's worse for women.' She changed her tone. 'Besides, you Americans say sick when you mean ill. When we say sick we mean puking. I didn't mean any harm to the old bitch – puking's not so bad, is it?'

'Who knows?' said B.J., hunching. 'Sometimes I wish I was born a man. They don't seem to have problems like ours, do they? I mean, you once said so yourself.'

Heather stared at B.J. 'That's an odd thing to say. You wish you had been born a man.' Heather continued to stare. After a pause she said softly, 'But if you *were* a man, I think I'd marry you.' Again she paused and turned her eyes to the window. 'I'd marry anyone.'

B.J. blushed. 'I think I'd better be going. Boy, I sure hope Miss Poole's okay.' She ducked out, wiggling her shoulders, pulling her sweatshirt down so that it fit snugly around her bottom.

Miss Poole was not well. She had told Rose, who conveyed the information to B.J. and Miss Male, that her chest hurt. She thought it was her heart. She claimed to have had two heart attacks since the day Jacko slapped Julius, three weeks previous, when the silence started. She had been absent from the school for both periods, each about a week long. During these absences she stayed in her house and sent Rose to the office with a note containing instructions for the teachers and saying in a P.S. that her chest pains had come back and only rest and tea would relieve them. On these days she could be seen through her front window, sitting in her chair, her elbows on her knees, hands clasped under her chin. When she appeared at the office she looked older, thinner, her skin deathly pale; and her dress stained and creased with sitting. This shabbiness and age was enhanced by a dryness in her face, as if she were dying not from a weak heart but by being slowly dried out.

During Miss Poole's absences, Heather acted as Headmistress. She tried to change as much of the school routine as possible before Miss Poole doddered back. She shuffled schedules of duties, took the mothercraft and flower-arrangement, gave Miss Male drama and some English, ordered different sets of books, fitted new locks to the file cabinets and generally horned in on everything that concerned the administration of the school. She purged 'Daisies Are Our Silver' from the morning assembly and ordered the girls to sing (which they did in grating harmony) 'Land of Hope and Glory'. Heather lied that the 'Land' referred to in the song was East Africa; she knew, with a certainty that gave her joy, that Miss Poole sitting in her room across the empty compound could hear the girls singing. She was sure Miss Poole hated the song.

After the song, Heather used the little inspirational talk to slander Miss Poole. Miss Poole had always taken as her subjects 'Our Friends the Earthworms' or 'Consider the Ant'. Heather spoke to the girls in a confidential, conspiratorial way.

'I must announce once again that Miss Poole says she is ill. Of course, there is very little we can do about this. We have prayed to God for her speedy recovery and, you see, nothing at all has happened. God will make her well when He sees fit, for He is all-knowing and knows all the nasty thoughts that a person thinks. He usually has good reasons for doing things, or not doing things, as you know. For my part, I am here and doing my level best, and I hope you appreciate how things have improved since I began acting as Headmistress . . .'

'Bosh,' Miss Male would whisper to B.J. in the back of the room.

'She's got her nerve,' B.J. would reply.

But Heather wanted to be friends. She used Miss Poole's absences to make friends with Miss Male and B.J. She told them about herself, what a madcap she was; she chirped that she was glad Miss Poole was ill because this might convince the Memsab that she should give up teaching; and then, in a fit of depression she would say that they all should pack up and go home. 'She's a bitch,' Heather said one day; she added, 'I'm a bitch, too. We're all bitches, aren't we?' 'On the other hand,' Heather said later the same day, 'she might still be playing games with us.' Excessive clowning was also part of her gesture of friendship to B.J. and Miss Male; unfunny and often painful, it embarrassed them both. One day she carried a tall moulting sunflower into the Staff Room. Holding it with her elbow up, she hummed and pretended to waltz with it.

'What's that?' asked B.J., looking up from a pile of exercise books she was marking.

'It's my new lover. Isn't he *gorgeous*!' Heather laughed and went on humming.

Heather's hair, usually blonde-streaked, had started to go white. Miss Male said this was simple neglect: Heather had stopped colouring it. B.J. insisted that it was a case of nerves. Her hair was turning white with madness. Miss Male said pooh. B.J. was so angry at Miss Male's contradiction that she guiltily broke her non-gossiping vow and repeated, to prove her point, a conversation she had had with Heather the day Heather wore a cardboard ape-mask to a staff meeting Miss Male had not attended. Miss Poole had just returned to work after one of her heart seizures and called the meeting to reverse all the decisions Heather had made in her absence. Heather had cut out the mask from the back of a cornflakes box and wore it throughout the meeting, in protest. It grinned while Miss Poole spoke of treachery, appealing to B.J. and Miss Verjee to stand by her.

After the meeting B.J. had said, 'That mask just kills me, Heather. You're a riot!'

'That's only the outside you see. You can't see the awful heartache I have in here,' said Heather solemnly through the grinning mouth.

'I hate to say this, but I think Heather's going nutty,' said B.J. to Miss Male. And there was no way of helping her because the two older women refused to speak to each other: the games were over, there was silence.

This truculent silence was much more worrying for B.J. than any of the games had been. The dead flies in the soup, the chair collapsing, the bad food, the cooks' desertion – these appeared silly, girlish, now hardly hurtful. B.J. said the silence was 'crummy for the school and the craziest thing I've ever seen'. Miss Male said that something had to be done to prevent the women from killing each other. The dead silence made contact impossible. In the stillness, even with the sun shining on the flowers every day, both girls sensed violence hiding.

The stillness threatened violence, but what made this even more upsetting for B.J. was that she had discovered contentment. What she thought intolerable was that people could hate each other in a silly, pointless place where peace was possible. She had successfully passed through her weeks of confusion and anger at the same time as Heather and Miss Poole had their games, before the silence. B.J. knew she had achieved a personal peace when, late one night, she said to herself desperately, *What the heck am I doing here?* She sipped at her warm beer and replied calmly, *I am sitting on the Equator with my Gecko board, watching two geckoes creeping across the squares on the wall.* B.J. was fine and, because of this, she was all the more worried about Heather. She felt something terrible was going to happen.

B.J. had suffered through the games; so had Miss Male. B.J. had suffered embarrassed anger, Miss Male abdominal pains. Miss

Male's ills could be traced directly to the bad food and the discomfort of her weekly dinners. B.J.'s anger was more complicated, and she was glad it had ended. While she was angry she had thought of quitting Africa and going straight back to San Diego.

It had started with the first dinner at Miss Poole's when Miss Male had carved the joint and Heather had argued and shouted, and when Julius had dropped the chocolate mousse. She had noticed it at the time, but the evening had altered her. She had passed through six weeks of denial.

She was at the Horse and Hunter with Wangi. The owner, a seedy alcoholic named Fitch, was behind the bar. B.J. bought Fitch a drink and he returned the favour by chatting to B.J. He said that he had seen her in there before; he asked her name. B.J. told him, adding that it was 'sort of German'.

'But you're a Yank –'

'Not really,' said B.J. and as she said it she realized that the denial was starting in earnest. She had never lied before in her life. But once she had said that she was not really an American, Fitch's curiosity was aroused.

'You *sound* like a Yank, if you don't mind my saying so. A certain bloody clankety-clank, if you know what I mean.'

'Well, I *studied* there. I suppose I picked up the lingo,' B.J. said. 'The *lingua franca*, ha-ha.'

'So you went to school in the States?' Fitch showed no signs of giving up.

'Oh, a year here, a year there.'

'What about San Jose?' Fitch stared at B.J.'s sweatshirt. He pronounced the *J*.

'That? Yeah, I was there a little while,' B.J. lied. She fidgeted. Fitch looked suspicious. B.J. explained by fabricating a tale about having studied abroad. In her confusion, Wittenberg was the only European university she could think of. Hamlet had gone there. 'It was very nice at Wittenberg. Very neat and clean. You know the Germans.'

B.J. pleaded with herself, *Why am I lying like this?*

'So you're not a Yank,' Fitch said.

'My mother is. My father – he's –'

'Yes?' Fitch was interested.

'He's actually a Russian *émigré*. Really. Named Lebowitz. He had to leave Russia when the revolution came.'

'He must be a pretty old geezer.'

'*Nein*. Not very,' said B.J., 'not terribly.'

'The revolution was in 1917, am I right? Let's suppose your father was twenty when –'

'He's not young,' said B.J., groaning inwardly. Lying about dates was impossible; one date was always connected to another. They had to fit. *What's wrong with me? Why am I saying this? Daddy's not from Russia – he's from Pine Bluffs! Oh shoot.*

'Anyway,' said Fitch, 'I hate the Jerries worse than the Yanks. Too bad you're half-kraut –'

'Well, what difference do nationalities make? We're all the same, aren't we?'

'No bloody fear,' said Fitch. 'I fought Jerries for years. Hate 'em.' He got himself a drink. 'Half-yank, half-kraut,' he said, eyeing B.J. 'Blimey, you Yanks are a fooking mixed lot. Now me, I'm English right through. Bugger the lot of them.' He drank.

'I'm an African,' said Wangi. He had trouble following the conversation. He said nothing else.

'I guess I'm a little bit of everything,' said B.J., thinking, *And I'm a little liar, too.*

Afterward, B.J. examined her lies. They saddened her. The only explanation she could think of for her strange behaviour was that she was tired of being an American. She was sick of English people pointing out niggling differences between England and America. She had always looked for similarities and expected everyone else to do the same. Now she was denying everything; she blamed Heather for it mostly, all of Heather's remarks which began, 'You Americans ...' She had once understood Heather and all other English people. She had pitied them. Now she could not recapture the understanding; she felt oppressed. She was certain of this when she heard herself say to Heather one day, 'I forget if I'm supposed to be teaching third period. I've not seen the shed-jewel.'

'You're doing the geography then,' said Heather with her finger on the teaching schedule.

B.J. thanked her and, as she walked away, thought, *I've not seen the shed-jewel. My God!*

On other occasions she actually heard herself say petrol, poss-port, the gulls are doncing, biscuits and tea, the boot and bonnet of the VW, a spanner in the works, tomahtoes, the hot-water tap, I tore my knickers, jolly good, sticky wicket and a dozen others. It wasn't American. B.J. wasn't even sure if it was English. She hated herself even more than when she had, to her horror, heard herself say *running wadder* and *on doody*.

Largely she hated herself because she had discovered why she was doing it. Over five months of bitchery, inquiries, nasty com-ments, explanations, arrogance, without an American in sight had upset her. It had changed her and she wondered how she could ever change back. She was a chameleon, out on a limb, and had chosen a difficult camouflage. It had been just talk, idle chatter, but the effect was definite: 'I've not seen the shed-jewel.' And that, she decided, was what Africa was for everyone: a lot of talk. Nothing more. It was darned unfair.

She had been cheated. She remembered her first thoughts of Africa, standing in the oval-domed lobby of the airport in New York with thirty other Peace Corps Volunteers (serious little bug-gers with sunglasses and handbooks and rucksacks, greeting each other in too-loud Swahili). She was about to board the plane for East Africa, but she took no notice of the others. Images of Africa had come to her in a rushing flood: drums, dancing, gaiety, Hum-phrey Bogart bars, fly-blown, the ceiling fans slowly revolving, the sweating settler faces, one man in an immaculate white suit playing with his gin and tonic; the lush forests overgrown with vines that obscured the forest paths; women naked from the waist up, their firm black melon breasts gleaming in the flakes of sun that filtered through the leafy trees; the shriek and tattoo of fantastic-tailed birds in the dense jungle where no white foot had trod; the blazing heat and mosquitoes and she, B.J. Lebow, lying in her tiny cot in a mud hut under the ripped mosquito netting, trembling with malarial chills, her faithful servant making tea on the Primus and saying, 'You nice *mzungu* help us and teach white man's tongue'; intrigue, mystery, the uncanny tales of the native, ghouls limping out of graveyards, heads shrunken and dangling from the straw eaves of huts; the peevish British boozehound in his up-country post, drinking the days away and plotting to strike a blow for merry old England, his thin angular wife gagging on her sixtieth cigarette of the day, the dry hacking cough of the woman ('Let's get out of this godforsaken place.' Cough, cough. 'I don't know why you stay here year after year, you bloody Welsh bastard . . . If only we were back in Clapham now . . .') and the benign but murderous planter ('Come back here, you black devil, and fetch me a drink . . .'), long afternoons on the veranda looking at the ploughed fields, the sun setting on the Empire, the strong noble faces of the Africans bent over their work, naked children gambolling in the sparkling creek; and, oh Heavens, yes, the drought, the disease, the attacks on the manor farm, the throats of mission docs cut and the blood running on to their oriental carpet, the one they haggled for in Port Sudan on their last home leave; the all-night throbbing of the jungle drums. And where were they, Mistah Kurz, Allnutt and Rose, Cecil Rhodes, Stewart Granger, Burton and Speke, Stanley and Livingstone, the Sultan of Zanzibar, Karen Blixen on a lion-hunt, torchlit and horrifying, anthropologists living for years in a village studying the movements of tribes and raising their nut-brown children on mangoes and Spengler, the oily Portugee plying his trade in used tommy-guns up and down the Zambezi and drinking sparkling wines in quaint Mozambican cafés, Arabs with long knives hidden under their cloaks who'll slash you for a piastre and pry the gold out of your teeth, the white hunters with sombreros and leopard-skin sweat-bands, Papa Hemingway bushwhacking through lion-country and swigging out of flasks ('There's a damned fine set of horns on that gazelle . . .'), and the delicious *veldt* stretching for miles under the eye, the lovely road that runs from Xtopo into the hills, the snows of Kilimanjaro, *The African Queen, The Heart of Darkness*, Nairobi, the hordes of pygmies and their pygmy king crowding up against your ankles,

the revolutions, revolutionaries, counter-insurgents, freedom
fighters drawing a bead on a caravan of Land-Rovers . . . *Safari* . . .
simba . . . *Watusi* . . . *bundolo* . . . *voodoo* . . . *ungawa* . . . *ungawa* . . .

It was not Africa. It was a lot of baloney. It existed only in
movies, books and people's crazy imaginations. B.J. looked hard
for it all, for just a teeny trace of it, and when she was sure none of
it existed she made plans to go home. It was, after all, the best
place to go: Hollywood was a shortish drive up the freeway and
that is where most of Africa was. She had to go home, for not only
did none of the romance exist, but also nothing of Africa held
fascination. Africa ('savage, wild, dark, spectacular, mysterious')
was the dullest place B.J. had ever been, the biggest zero on the
globe (and B.J. had drawn some pretty big blanks: everybody in
Spain lisped, Greece was queersville, and a dark little man in San
Juan, offering her a bunch of flowers he held waist-high, had displayed his poorly concealed and tumescently rosy member in the
bouquet – '*El sabor lo dice todo*,' he had urged). The Africans
were the limit, the most predictable, reactionary, sentimental
drunks she had ever met. The famous big game – elephant herds,
rhinos, prides of lions, all the beasts that the travel agencies
bragged about, were in game parks or zoos, a great disappointment, mainly because it was no different from Southern Cal. Who
wanted to go to the Snake Park in Nairobi and pay two shillings
just to see a python? B.J. had expected the exotic, the mysterious at
least. It was not asking much – mystery was easy. But Africa was
not mysterious, only disorganized, slow and dull. If there was a
secret, it was that there was really none. And the sun in Africa, the
blazing heat? It had been hotter in San Diego.

She had brought with her a little notebook, an old-fashioned
one with a shiny black cover, unlined white paper sewn to the
binding, and a red cloth spine. She had planned to write impressions of Africa, sights and scenes that moved her, fragments of
conversations, maybe even a few poems. The notebook was, five
months after her arrival in East Africa, empty; the blank white
pages were going limp and mossy in the humidity. On page one
there was a date; beside that, the beginning of an entry: *Africa*

is . . . The entry was unfinished, and there was nothing else in
the notebook except her name and on the cover, framed in a little
label, the title, *African Impressions*.

Africa so far was only the endless staring of Wangi, the bitchery
of Heather and Miss Poole and the noisy aimlessness of the girls at
play. And what really galled B.J. was the fact that the dull bitchy
things were happening there, in East Africa. It would not have been
so bad in San Diego or LA where those things were supposed to
happen. But East Africa! And this pettiness made the place even
more ordinary, no different from the plainest sleepiest hick town in
the Mid-West. The pettiness would have robbed Africa of exoti-
cism, if indeed Africa had ever been exotic. It would have been
mean to write all that down in *African Impressions*. The whole
hick aspect and the nasty women would pass into nothingness as
they had passed into silence. There would be no violence. Violence
needed motives; there were none in Africa. Several times, B.J. tried
to write in her book, tried to finish her little entry, to give a
definition to the place. It was no use. Africa was dull, boring and
sometimes people in Africa were pointlessly cruel. When this all
became apparent, she had no desire to write it down or even tell
her father in a letter; she just wanted to go home.

And then it came to her: *I'm going home eventually. It doesn't
matter. I only have another year here and then I cop out!*

Shortly after, she asked herself the question, *What the heck am I
doing here?* and gave her calm reply, *I am sitting on the Equator
with my Gecko board*, and so forth. She knew she was at peace.
There was no point in dropping everything and quitting. She
would never be able to explain to the Peace Corps how she had
been cheated. The fantasies that had flooded her in the New York
airport, all those Hollywood images of Africa, now deeply embarrassed her. On the plus side, Miss Male was nice, the weather
wasn't bad, the job was simple; she might even, she thought, be
doing her own thing, making a little contribution that would give
the East African gross national product a boost. It would not be
hard to stay, only a pain in the neck.

Something she found hard to believe, and had never thought

would happen, was that she occasionally forgot where she was. It happened a number of times, too often for B.J. to write it off as simple absentmindedness. She might be just opening her eyes in the morning or engrossed in one of the high-minded magazines the Peace Corps mailed her constantly or making herself a jelly sandwich. For those minutes, sometimes as many as five, she could have been on a little family vacation, with her father and mother out of earshot, reading the *Los Angeles Times* on the grass.

Eventually she remembered where she was, but it was not the drumming or the wildebeest or the lions (where the heck *were* they anyway?) that suggested the reality of her distance. It was, in fact, her Zenith Transoceanic radio that made her know that she was not in San Diego. After the snack or magazine she would flick it on and get horrible static: wheeling shrieks, Morse code, wobbling unfathomable music or gibberish from somewhere in the Indian Ocean. When a station did come in, it was an awful reminder of how far out you could be: Big Ben booming an intro to a BBC quiz, a crackling news broadcast from All-India Radio, vowelly Portuguese from God-knows-where, nasal French from Rwanda or the Congo, the platitudes of the gospel radio station in Ethiopia, an unmistakably Negro voice talking about the rising standard of living on the Voice of America, the familiar harridan screeching the thoughts of Mao on Radio Peking, or a loudmouth on what B.J. privately thought of as the Foice of Chermany. All the broadcasts said they were being beamed to Africa and the Far East, and it was painfully obvious to her that she was not in the Far East. All the broadcasts talked about Africa's achievements in development schemes, some even (ha-ha!) spoke of Africa's dark mystery. B.J. listened once to the BBC's 'Book at Bedtime' which, that evening, was a story about Africa by Joe Conrad, read in a Peter Lorre voice. During the entire broadcast B.J. was in stitches.

It was the radio that shocked B.J. into reality, but the reality was a dull outpost that she knew she would be leaving soon. The year would go quickly. When she shut off the radio and sat in silence, as she did after twenty minutes of searching the short-wave band for

Frank Sinatra, she knew where she was. The silence was heavy. But there were worse things than silence.

What if, she thought, there *were* murderous Arabs and yelling, spear-throwing Ubangis? What then? It might have been much worse than the silence. It might have been dangerous instead of dull. *If I can stand the silence I've got it licked.* And remembering that she was going home, that indeed unlike Miss Poole and maybe Heather she *had* a home to go to, was enough reassurance to wipe out the weeks of lying and denial, and the embarrassment at having been cheated in a big way. She dropped her English accent and Russo-German heritage and stopped saying 'shed-jewel'. She was an American. The more she thought of this the prouder she became. She loved America. She would never have a bad word for it again. America was a comfortable place crammed with invention and ease. The silence in Africa simply did not matter. She had made a big mistake, the biggest lulu of her life. She would correct it when she went home. Calmness came to her at the same time that agony came to Miss Poole and Heather; it was a certain satisfaction, deeply pleasing, in having realized how wrong she had been about Africa and how she was now right. Her good humour returned and she made jokes about Africa, not nasty ones, but ones that showed that she did not belong. And one day she said to Miss Male, 'Really, Pam, you should visit the States. It's the greatest place on earth. We've invented so many things. You know, *we* invented Africa.'

Wangi remained, B.J.'s only contact with the real Africa. She continued to date him – that also in silence, since he seldom had anything to say. She dated him more out of a sense of obligation to the Peace Corps than out of any affection for the man himself. She often thought of breaking it off, not seeing him any more, but she knew that this would be a mistake. For one thing, Wangi was what the Peace Corps laughingly called a 'host country national' and had to be known and understood. To stop seeing Wangi would mean a complete withdrawal from Africa, a withdrawal that would make her no better than Miss Poole or Heather or any of the other unpleasant white people who lived in East Africa and who never had anything to do with Africans. And she knew it was possible that without male company she would develop the same symptoms of bitchiness that Heather had. A husband or a male friend would cure Heather; she had almost said as much when she said, 'I'd marry anyone.' So seeing Wangi every week was necessary, first, because he was an African and B.J. was a Peace Corps Volunteer in Africa; and second, because he was a man. Women needed men, if only to get out of the company of other women.

Wangi was not dangerous. He was Africa, with all of Africa's dullness, simplicity and emptiness, with all of Africa's pretensions to order, the tribesman with puffy ornamental scars hidden (she was almost sure) by his dark suit and neat shirt. B.J. had at first pitied him, listened to his stories of terrorism with nervous impatience. He would mumble and brag and, as he went on, grow drunk. His speech became thick, barely coherent as he swigged gin. In the middle of a slow sentence he would slump in his chair and go to sleep. B.J. would rouse him with a poking finger in his cheek and help him out the door, say good night and *kwaheri*. For a few moments she would hear him stumbling in the dark outside, groping his way to the road. The next week he would return and apologize. He was harmless.

But the stumbling in the dark worked on B.J. She often thought of it: the black man muttering, stumbling through the flowerbeds at midnight, not even bothering to ask for a light – then silence, he was away. She thought of this pathetic image and wanted to help him. She wrote to her former teachers at San Jose and asked if there were any scholarships available for an African student. The teachers wrote promptly; they also wanted to help; they replied in long sympathetic letters asking about Wangi's qualifications. There might be something for him, they said.

Excited at the prospect of getting Wangi into a university, B.J. quickly wrote a letter on Wangi's behalf. He was, she wrote, from the poorest country on earth; he had not even owned a pair of shoes until he was twenty years old and he had had a hard life in the village. But he had good potential: he was very (B.J. searched for an honest word) *curious*, she finally wrote. Before she sent the letter, she talked to Wangi, whose eyes filled with tears when B.J. told him of her plan.

'You just have to qualify and you're in,' she said.

Wangi gazed, no longer tearful. 'But you said the scholarship was for an African.'

'Sure,' B.J. said. 'But if you want to go to college you have to qualify. You know, take tests, finish school, study, ha-ha.' Wangi's habit of giggling was infectious; now whenever she talked to him she laughed, she did not know why.

Wangi's face clouded over. He lowered his eyes. 'Write those people a letter. Tell them my cousin Wilbur is the District Education Officer. They'll take me.'

An emptiness grew in B.J.: there were airy sighs where hope had been. Wangi had done nothing in his life. He had been nowhere. The only book he could remember having read was *Coral Island*, abridged for overseas students with a vocabulary of a thousand words; he had forgotten the author's name. The application form to San Jose State would be entirely empty, a silence on the page representing the silence in the country: darkness, people stumbling drunkenly through the flowerbeds and muttering softly – not even the noise of curses breaking the silence. B.J. had not really thought much about him until the teachers in San Jose asked. She did not send her letter. She told Wangi he would have to wait a year. She did not have the heart to tell him that in a year she would be in the Golden West.

13

Orders

There were fleas in Sally's fur, small winged specks which could have been mistaken for dark grains of dirt. After Miss Poole had stared at them for several minutes she saw that the specks were moving; they were alive and crawling from hair to hair.

She could not kill them, although she had that afternoon bought a can of flea-powder from the Indian *duka* down the road.

'The best thing known for *dudus*. Wery scientific,' the Indian had said, overcharging her.

Miss Poole had watched him wipe his mouth on his shirt-front and began to have doubts. She looked at the Indian and saw a killer.

'Tell me, isn't it true that Hindus don't kill flies? I thought they didn't kill anything, in point of fact.'

'Jain. You know Jain? They are even not killing small *dudu*. They are letting mice wander quite free in their compounds,' said the Indian. 'They are being wery foolish, not modern. It is modern to rid food and body of all crawling insects and *dudus*. Isn't it?'

Miss Poole took the flea-powder but doubts nagged at her. The Indian was too eager to kill. By the time she reached her house she had almost given up the idea of dusting the fleas.

She continued to stare at the fleas, cradling Sally in her left arm and holding the can of flea-powder in her right hand like an over-size salt-shaker (it had a circle of holes punched in the top). The words of the Indian came back to her, and she began to hate him, nearly as much as she hated Heather. With these feelings of hatred awake in her she thought, *There is too much killing and cruelty in the world*, and hated Heather all the more. The worst thing about killing was not the savagery it betrayed, but the effect the killing

281

had: death upset the order of things when the death was unexpected. Cruelty made men stupid. These were Africa's misfortunes: sudden death and cruelty produced by intruders. First the migrations, the hordes of little black people trekking like a column of ants down from Ethiopia, across from West Africa, what the map-makers called Negroland, converging in the Congo basin and around the Great Lakes to squabble over territories they claimed for themselves. Similar in temperament were the Arabs, the Portuguese, the Indians; Miss Poole saw it as a great wog onslaught, killing, plundering a jungle and a jumble of ant-people that had never known order. It was a deathly bloody process that only the people like her father had attempted to reverse. These far-sighted people, the only men she could respect, had imposed a humane order on East Africa. For a brief period there were farms and, on those farms, people and animals; the people and animals lived in harmonious candour, not very different from Miss Poole herself, in her house in the highlands, with Sally on her lap and the fleas in Sally's fur. There was stability and she saw it all in a little parable on her lap. As soon as one of those living things was killed, the order was disturbed, death had begun and the jungle moved closer, a fat vine-tendril snaked into the schoolhouse window. Miss Poole put the flea-powder down and stroked Sally.

There were still intruders, as selfish as Arabs, and as sensual. But no one saw that while some people in Africa were intruders, others belonged and did no harm; these last considered East Africa their home. They behaved as Christians. God's little fleas did not intrude; they were part of the order, gentle, small, harmless, and at the mercy of the loud and the large, the corrupt, the blasphemers.

Heather was a killer, her intrusion could only mean murder. Miss Poole was sure of this. But she had no idea of what Heather's precise plans were. Until Heather arrived everything had gone smoothly at the school. Miss Poole was proud of the record: only three pregnancies, good discipline, a well-trained hockey team, no student strikes or complaints about the food, a successful parents' day and tree-planting. The school, except for the inevitable white ants and bore-beetles, was in good repair; the coffee yield had been high. And the teachers seemed to get along well.

With Heather it had all changed. Miss Poole saw her as a demon-figure, corrupt, lustful, lower-class with a put-on accent and falsely trilled r's. Her arrival had coincided with the onset of Miss Poole's debilitating illnesses. This made sense, for at one level corruption was physical and germ-ridden. Miss Poole went over her illnesses as if touching cautiously at scabbed wounds. Since Heather's arrival her heart trouble had worsened, the dull ache had become a sharp stabbing pain in her breast; she could feel a wad of blood constricted in an artery, leaking like an old faucet, each drop causing pain as it hit into the dry hollows of her heart. A large soft carbuncle had formed behind her ear, the size of a florin; Rose had lanced it with a heated needle: black goo had shot out and hit the wall. There was an almost weekly bout of malaria: chills, flushes, a searing headache that went on for days, scarcely relieved by quinine; her fevers had never been so bad. Waking with a start one night Miss Poole had felt for the lamp-cord and grasped a long furry caterpillar which bit her, it seemed, with the length of its body: red pustules were raised on her palm; these took a week to heal and the whole thing looked like an ogre's bite, each fang-mark gone septic. She had had prickly heat, rashes, heat-stroke and muscle fatigue made worse by chronic insomnia. At every turn she encountered fierce pain or discomfort. Roaches scrabbled from between bread-slices on the table. A bat dropped from a roof-eave into her window box and turned green; other dead bats turned up in cupboards, linen closets and market baskets. Julius was far away and could not help. Only Rose was left to witness the ordered bewitchment of all the creatures that had lived so peacefully before. The germs had obviously multiplied, the little beasts had run amuck; even the cats were contaminated. Sally had scratched Miss Poole on the neck; the wound had festered.

It was a restlessness which Miss Poole saw as devilish, inspired by Heather. Heather had brought the disorder, cruelty and death which Miss Poole associated with all the intruders that had ever plagued Africa. Because of Miss Poole's cursed illnesses and absences, the school had run down: indiscipline was common, bills were unpaid, a roof beam in the science laboratory was chewed to bits by white ants (again a diabolical order from Heather carried out; the ants had nested in, but never chewed through a beam before). The beam collapsed, sending thick roof-tiles into a cupboard of glassware, smashing everything. The coffee bushes were coated with fungus, the corn stalks with fuzzy brown smut. And all this in the short time Heather had been at the school, most of it during the silence that followed the painful dinner parties. Miss Poole had thought Heather an intruder from the first, but she did not grasp the full malevolence of the woman from Nairobi until she read an article called 'The Power of Love'. She had found the article in a *Reader's Digest* that had been donated with some used books to the school. It was an old issue, Miss Poole thought, but the message was timeless. The article spoke of a certain vicar from a village in Somerset who could make plants blossom and grow through the power of his love. Conversely, by not loving (hate was beyond him) he could make a plant wither; exercising this lovelessness, he could make a dog grow wild and bite his master, he could make petals drop or sturdy animals keel over. It seemed unearthly, but there were witnesses to the vicar's powers. And Miss Poole was convinced that, better than the vicar, she knew how vile emanations could work on lovely things, on simple folk.

In the single school term, now almost over, that Heather had been at the school, Miss Poole had watched the merciless sabotage of all her hard-won order. In addition to the unpaid bills, the smashed glassware and the infected crops, the girls had grown wild. They adopted Heather's high silly voice and idiotically italicized speech; they dressed like slatterns; they yoo-hooed, gobbled and used skin-lightener and blotch cream; they spent hours pulling their kinky hair into nests glistening with greasy bubbles of Vaseline. The rock gardens and terraces were in a shambles. The domestic staff was threatening a strike. And one night, without a word of warning, the building that Miss Poole intended for conversion to a library and reading room, the one Jacko had painted green, burned to the ground. The day before the fire the workmen had succeeded in removing all Jacko's green paint. Miss Poole knew it was an act of Heather's godless will and she fearfully concluded that Heather was a witch. Heather would have to go.

Miss Poole covered her face with her hands; she moaned into her palms. She felt her viscera freeze, and shuddered. She saw Heather's design: Heather wanted to be Headmistress – it was simple, so bluntly cruel, Miss Poole had not thought of it before this moment. Why else had Heather willed Miss Poole's illnesses and then taken over the school, occupied it like an invading Arab? If the stories told about her were correct (and they probably were: there was always a grain of truth in the East African gossip), then this was not the first time Heather had resorted to a fiendish means to get what she wanted. The stories from Nairobi were inconceivably grotesque. Miss Poole tried to stem her moaning by biting her hand. It was no good; when she bit, the moans came louder. Sally yowled and hopped to the floor where she stood with her back arched, her fur spiky with terror.

It was night, noisy with the swamp-dwellers tuning up. Miss Poole sat in the darkness of her living-room, the cats slumbering on chairs and draped in sleep on the floor. Rose squatted near the window. When Miss Poole spoke, Rose crept closer.

'You like me, don't you?' Miss Poole spoke in her heavily accented Swahili.

'Yes, very much,' said Rose in a low voice. Her head was reverently bent down.

'Am I a good woman?'

'You are good.'

'When I am here you are happy?'

Rose emitted a long *aahhhhhh*. She pressed her dry hands together and rubbed them. In the dark it sounded like leaves rustling, a strange sound since in that lush place the leaves seldom rustled.

'Am I good to you?'

'You are good. You give us food to eat.'

'And clothes.'

285

'Such beautiful clothes,' murmured Rose, feeling the hem of her long soiled dress.

'The flowers in my garden, my food, my house, everything I have belongs to you. It is all yours.'

'You are my mother,' said Rose. 'You took me into your house and cared for me when everyone called me bad names and said they wanted to kill me.'

'You are safe here.'

'Yes.'

'Rose,' Miss Poole said, 'have you ever felt a white person's hand?'

Rose uttered the verb in amazement. When she said it again, Miss Poole remembered that the only word she knew for feel was the same as for smell and taste.

'Have you ever held a white person's hand with your hand?' said Miss Poole. She had not realized how difficult this was to say in Swahili.

'Not in my life,' said Rose softly.

'Here. Take my hand,' said Miss Poole, lifting her hand from the arm of the chair and holding it out. 'Here.'

'I can't see.'

'Come here.'

Rose crawled slowly towards Miss Poole. She woke two cats that were snoozing on the floor; they pattered into the corner, hushing with surprise.

'Closer.'

Rose did not take the extended hand at once. She felt for it; when her fingers struck it she drew back. Shyly she teased the darkness again with her fingers and touched the hand, tapped the soft flesh with her forefinger, felt the slack skin, the thin birdbones of the fingers. She could have been caressing a sleeping chick. She worked her fingers around it and then clasped it with two hands, frantically; she sobbed, a phlegmy choking deep in her throat that shook her hands and the hand they held.

'You mustn't be afraid,' said Miss Poole. 'I'm not afraid. I know you love me.'

286

'Yes, I love you.'

'Can you feel my hand?'

Rose continued to sob. 'It is beautiful. So soft.'

'Hold it tightly,' said Miss Poole, her voice growing hard. 'And listen to me. Are you listening?'

Rose whimpered yes. She nodded: Miss Poole saw the flash of her dark glasses, the shadow of her queer beret bobbing up and down.

'Someone here wants to kill me,' Miss Poole said coldly, giving the word kill, *kufisha*, a snarling sibilance.

Rose shrieked. She let go of Miss Poole's hand and rolled on the floor, her shriek dying to a slow agonized wail. There was a crash in the darkness, a cat upsetting a vase; the bump of padded cats' paws on the floor.

'Rose! Stop it! Listen, Rose!'

Rose put her face against the carpet and continued wailing through clenched teeth, now softly, prostrate before Miss Poole in her armchair.

'We must be very, very quiet or someone will hear us. I will repeat: someone wants to kill me. This person wants to live in this house and be Headmistress. If that happens you know what will become of you.'

'We will die,' Rose moaned.

Miss Poole was pleased with the reply. Rose saw that if the order was disturbed, death would be the result; the fallen tree, cut by the intruder's axe, crushed the life out of small ground-dwelling creatures. Rose understood. It was the kind of logic only the innocent could comprehend: they knew of the kind balance, the calm order, that love caused. And Africa was the last stronghold of this order; everywhere else death and iron, people crouched in cold sewers, the air poisoned by filthy machines. Africa breathed peace, not a skull-shape on the map, but the head of God, Christ brooding over the rest of the threatening world.

'You don't want to die, do you?'

'No, madam.'

'I can help you, can't I?'

'Yes, madam. Only you.'

'Will you help me?'

'Yes, anything. Who wants to do this bad thing?'

'I don't know –'

Rose sighed.

'–but I know how we can find out.'

'Tell me.'

'The secret is in the new *memsab*'s house –'

'Madam Hethala,' said Rose, giving the name a Swahili shape.

'Yes. That one. You must go to her house when there is no one around. Make sure her dog is away – perhaps you can lock it in one of the sheds. Don't be in a hurry. Go next week, when we are busy with exams. Look in the drawers, on the tables, everywhere, and bring me letters, chits, notebooks, anything with writing on it. Tell me everything you see in that house. Be quick and don't let anyone see you. If someone sees you, leave immediately. I think there is something in that woman's house that will tell me who the murderer is. When we know, we will be safe.' Miss Poole took a deep breath. The strain of saying all this in Swahili was too much for her; she had searched for words that would not craze the girl – the excitement might drive Rose mad, and Miss Poole did not want that. She wanted help. In English she added, 'Whatever you find will be valuable. I am sure she is hiding something from us.'

Miss Poole was weary. She yawned and felt a tug at her ankle. Rose was on the floor, with her hands curled around Miss Poole's foot, like a village girl paying homage to an elder. Rose held on tightly, her arms gleaming white.

14

A Banana Peel

B.J. decided to give Wangi until the end of the term. After that, she could drop him and make friends with the clerk at the school, the vegetable-sellers, possibly even the Indians down at the shops. Face-to-face, the Peace Corps called it; getting to know the host country nationals. She would be seeing the Peace Corps rep in Nairobi after the term ended; he would be sure to ask how she had been spending her time. B.J. had a lot to tell him and was glad the end of the term was only a little over two weeks away.

But there was still what B.J. called 'the village bit' that remained undone. When she knew that she could do nothing for Wangi's further education, since his only qualification for being a foreign student was the fact that he was foreign (and you couldn't get much more foreign than plain ignorant), she agreed to go with Wangi to visit his village. Wangi borrowed his cousin's car and picked her up early on a Sunday morning at the school.

It started raining as soon as they left the main road, and the rain seemed to come down harder and harder as they travelled farther into the bush on the rutted back road. The car swerved; Wangi fought to keep it on the firm grassy hump in the centre. On both sides of the road, creeks had formed; the bare gleaming tyre-tracks had reddened in the rain in a way which, contrasted with the freshly doused green of the plants at the side, made the road seem almost diabolical, winding like the road to Oz where Judy Garland met those crazy animals. The sky was so grey and low that B.J. felt she could reach out of the window and snatch a handful of it.

There were few trees that B.J. could see, for the view on both sides was blocked by tall elephant-grass. Heavy now with rain, the grass curled towards the road and made a long fringed awning which brushed both sides of the car. Wangi drove in silence.

They had been on the road for half an hour when, without warning, the vast peeling face of a bus, its eyes orange, appeared from out of the awning of grass twenty feet ahead, in the centre of the road. Wangi slammed on the brakes; the car skidded; Wangi spun the steering wheel as if it was the handlebar of a careening bicycle. The car became light and rose to let the bus roar past, flopped with a crunch and came to rest, still on its four wheels, in the grass at the left side of the road.

B.J. screamed and held the dashboard. At once the windows steamed grey, opaque.

Wangi slapped the steering wheel, making it vibrate. 'Sheet,' he said, 'look at us!' He grinned.

'Let's *go*,' said B.J. 'We can't stay *here*.' She felt pain but could not identify it as injury or tell where it was. She wanted to get out of the car to see if she had been hurt.

'Yes,' said Wangi. 'When it stops raining. Then we go.' Wangi sat back and smiled at the steering wheel.

'How far is it to your village?'

'Maybe more than a mile, maybe two.'

'We can walk,' said B.J. decisively, yanking the door-handle. The door did not open. She pushed the door with her shoulder, while jerking the handle. 'I don't get it. How the heck –'

Wangi put his hand on B.J.'s wrist and lifted her whole arm away from the door-handle. He slid beside her and then put his other arm around her neck.

B.J. froze. It was the first time Wangi had ever touched her. She didn't like it. Her senses were jarred by the surprise of the on-coming bus, the shock of the car leaving the road, the clouded windows. She wanted to get out of the car and flex her arms, search for bruises. Her wrist was being squeezed; her neck hurt from the pressure of Wangi's arm which was forcing her head forward.

'Come on!' she said. But Wangi did not let go. The rain pattered on the roof of the car, gently, innocently; and all around the car,

showing in droplets on the steamed windows, were the dripping
tapes of glass, most of them squashed and bent from the car's
impact.

'I said, *come on!*' B.J. muttered through tensed lips.

Wangi seemed to grip harder; but she was not sure. And then
she heard herself saying '*Come on, come on,*' and realized what it
meant to Wangi, for as she said it he was coming on, holding her
more tightly, hugging her in a half-nelson.

'*Cut that out!*'

Wangi released his grip and drew back slowly towards the
steering wheel, his eye widening, his hands slipping to his knees.

'Thank you,' B.J. said firmly, fixing her hair, squirming slightly.
She did not look at Wangi. Once again, she tried the door, this
time with determination, shoving it with her shoulder. The door
creaked and slumped open against the grass. B.J. wriggled out,
stepped in mud and then pushed the door back into place. With
her hands in front of her face, she parted the grass; it scratched her
as it brushed her arms and legs, but still she struggled through its
abrasive wetness like a breast-stroking swimmer, until she splashed
into the road. She stood in soggy sneakers, soaked and aching. She
began to cry, an infant's blubbering, her face wet with rain and
tears. Her hair had gone ropy; she tasted bitter strands of it in her
mouth.

Ten feet down the road the grass swayed, then parted like a
curtain. Wangi broke through, agitatedly wiping his face with his
handkerchief.

When B.J. looked at him she stopped crying. His wet suit was
wrinkled and shapeless; there were green seeds stuck to his collar
and hair; his cuffs were spattered, his shoes large with gooey mud.
He looked pathetic, like an orphan turfed out into a rainstorm in
his Sunday best. B.J. felt curiously guilty and ashamed; she was
certain she had said the wrong thing. *Come on,* she had said; only
an American could be expected to understand that, and only an
American would. Wangi had touched her (her neck and wrist still
ached), but had made no suggestion. It was she who had unthinkingly urged him. He had said nothing; he had remained silent the

whole time, as he was now silent, eyeing her from his distance down the rainy road. In the silence was all of Africa's cruel ambiguity, what people took for mystery; it was not mystery, B.J. reminded herself, simply an overpowering silence in which nothing really moved, no one stirred, where there could be no bad intentions because there were no intentions period. It was a huge bluff, as in a poker game where the man keeping the inscrutable poker-face held blank cards: they were not winning cards, but empty, frayed bits of cardboard. If there had been malice (but of course there hadn't), it was the pathetic malice of the inept pretender. She stared at Wangi wiping his face and hands with the shrivelled handkerchief (he did it fecklessly; it was still raining), picking the green seeds from his collar, and the panic that she had felt left her completely. Her head cleared. She could not remember anything that happened in the car.

'We can walk,' she said calmly.

Wangi was surprised, but he took the hand she offered him and in the rain, their feet sucking in the mud, they squelched up the road.

After the first mile the rain stopped. B.J. was soaked; when the sun came out her drying clothes chilled and chafed her. The little cuts from the grass on her legs and arms rose into red welts. Her wet sneakers were heavy with mud. She felt miserable and longed for a dry spot, anywhere to sit down. She wanted to bathe, be alone, rest between clean dry sheets, eat something . . . A pain shot through her belly.

'I'm hungry,' she said to Wangi.

Wangi sighed. 'I'm sorry,' he said after a while; he looked down in mournful terror.

B.J. screwed up her face. 'Sorry? For what?'

'You're hangry.'

'Not *angry*, silly, *hungry. Hun. Hun*-gry.'

Wangi smiled, looked around and, seeing what he wanted, dashed into the grass, punching the broad blades away from his face. He returned after several minutes, his arms full of bright green balls. He said they were oranges.

'*Green* oranges?'

Wangi nodded.

'But oranges are supposed to be *orange*. That's why they're called oranges,' said B.J.

'Is it?'

'Yes. I mean, these things probably aren't ripe. They're the wrong colour.'

'No, this is the only colour. They're always green, even when they're ripe.'

'That's why they call them oranges, right?' B.J. smiled.

'You call them oranges, we call them *machungwa*.'

'Okay, hand one over. I'm game.'

B.J. regretted the green orange almost as soon as she started peeling it. The rind got wedged under her fingernails; the bitter juice stung her open cuts and soured her mouth and squirted into her eyes. She sucked; the juice dribbled down her arm and into a sore near her elbow she had not noticed before. Her hands became sticky and that discomfort, with the dampness and wet clothes, the chafing and searing pain of fruit juice on her cuts, made her all the more anxious to go back to the school. She had never in her life felt so miserable. She spat pips with a disgusted *pah*; half of them landed, in a long amoeba of yellow saliva, on her sweatshirt.

Wangi stopped sucking his orange. 'There,' he said. He sprayed a juicy mouthful of seeds in the direction of some small grass-roofed huts just off the road. To B.J. they looked like haystacks, and badly piled haystacks at that. About twenty feet away, a gaggle of small naked children dawdling in a mud puddle looked up and stared in disbelief at Wangi and B.J. The children cautiously approached and then followed behind, trooping like filthy elves. They held bunches of mud-spattered grass which they shook ceremoniously and, because they saw a white person, chanted '*Mzungu, mzungu, mzungu*' in squeaking voices.

The whole village seemed to sag from the strength of the rain that had just passed. Flameless fires billowed smoke into the clearing while women languidly fanned the smoke with squares of tin. A mangy narrow-jawed hound with fly-specked sores showing over a basket of skinny ribs limped from behind a hut and began barking at B.J. Then the women fanning the smoke looked up and saw Wangi and B.J. The women were dwarfish, with gremlin wrinkles around their faces, their ear-lobes stretched into jiggling loops; they wore long muddy skirts. They shrieked in a chorus of short high caws and shuffled towards the visitors, a flock of flightless birds. One came forward and took B.J.'s hand. The rest gathered around, shyly picking at B.J.'s seed-stained sweatshirt, feeling the thick softness of her damp hair and all the while making their insistent crowing.

The old woman holding B.J.'s hand greeted her in Swahili.

'Missouri,' said B.J. It was her new Swahili, a practised American-type; the name of the Show-Me state was close to the Swahili word for good, *mzuri*. And 'Missouri sinner' was like the Swahili, 'Very good'. The joke was her own, private and satisfying.

The women were pleased that B.J. was well; they clapped their tiny hands and grinned broken teeth at her. One gestured for her to come and sit down in front of a hut. A rickety wooden chair was brought. B.J. sat gingerly. It groaned but miraculously did not break.

There was another groan, not from the chair this time, but from inside the hut. The women babbled and stepped back from the hut. The groaning turned to wheezing which grew louder: an old man hobbled through the hut door on a stick. He was tiny, bent and wrinkled like the women, with tightly kinked grey hair cropped close. He stood before B.J. and stared; his whole body seemed to breathe woodsmoke at her.

'My father,' said Wangi. The women murmured their approval and, some distance away, the small naked boys hooted and wagged their grass whisks.

'Tell him I'm very pleased to meet him,' said B.J., fighting off an urge to scratch a nagging itch that ran like a coarse zipper from her head to her feet.

Wangi translated. The old man said, '*Habari gani?*'

'Missouri,' said B.J.

The women yelped and tossed their heads, making their loose

ear-lobes dance. The skinny dog pawed his way past the gleeful women; he startled B.J. by nipping hungrily at her hand. B.J. pulled her hand away and the dog leaped at her, but was caught in the ribs, mid-flight, by the toe of Wangi's shoe. The dog howled, flopped at B.J.'s feet and then trotted clumsily away.

'What's his name?' B.J. asked. The dog had frightened her. She tried to regain her composure. 'The dog,' she asked again. 'What's his name?'

Wangi said something quickly to his father in a vernacular that was not Swahili. The old man croaked a reply to Wangi which was greeted with laughter from the women.

'He said it's a dog,' Wangi explained. 'And he asks that don't you have dogs in England?'

'Tell him I'm an American.'

Wangi spoke again to his father.

This time the old man faced B.J. He grunted something, a heavy guttural which he repeated again and again.

'He's saying Coca-Cola.'

B.J. then listened closely to the old man again and realized that he was saying, 'Drink Coca-Cola.'

'He likes to talk English,' said Wangi.

'He does?'

The old man grinned.

'Coca-Cola Missouri,' said B.J.

The old man understood. He looked pleased.

'Where did you get your stick?'

Wangi muttered, pointing to the stick. Again there was laughter when the old man replied.

'He says from a tree.'

Gobbling, the old man thrust it at B.J. It was shiny from being handled; on the top end there was a knob, the rough carving of a monkey's head; at the other end, emerging from the gnarled shaft, was a battered simian paw.

'He wants you to have it.'

'Oh, no,' said B.J. 'That's *his*. I couldn't take his walking stick.' She shook her head at the old man and said very clearly, '*No*.'

The stick was withdrawn; the old man mumbled and looked sad. The women fell silent.

'What's wrong? Did I do something wrong?'

'You refused his gift. He says it is not good enough for a *mzungu* and that he is poor. You're supposed to take it if he offers. That's African hospitality.'

B.J. smiled at the old man and took the stick. The women clapped. The old man nodded and spoke to Wangi.

'He says you're his daughter now and you have to eat with him.'

'Why not?'

Food was brought, greasy stew and thick mush, which B.J., Wangi and the old man ate while the women and naked children watched. To the delight of the women, B.J. ate with her right hand and smiled after each mouthful. She wolfed the food down only because she was hungry – the food was awful; her own African meal had tasted much better.

'They think it is funny. They never saw a woman eating with a man before.'

'Where do *they* eat, for goodness sake?'

'Not with the men.'

When B.J. finished she felt as if her belly was full of rags; she felt dirty, sloppy, sick to her stomach. She wanted to lie down in a warm white room and be scrubbed with a large soapy loofah.

'What do they do here all day?' she asked Wangi wearily.

'Nothing.'

'Nothing at all?'

'They drink and waste their time,' said Wangi. 'Nothing happens here. Sometimes there isn't any food and they have to send a lorry with mealies from Nairobi. It's all rubbish. That's why we hate the British.'

B.J. had stopped listening to Wangi and was now listening to her rumbling stomach.

The old man muttered.

'He's telling a proverb,' said Wangi.

'Oh, I *like* proverbs. What does he say?'

'It's hard to translate. Lazy man tree, busy chicken. That's what he says.'

'Yes, but what does it . . .'

'It means, I think, it's better to be like a chicken that always pecks the ground than like the lazy person who is like –'

'A tree?'

'No. Like a giraffe, because giraffes look like trees.'

'But there aren't any giraffes around here.'

'There used to be. The British killed them all, like they killed us.'

'Tell him I like his proverb.'

Wangi turned to the old man, but saw that he had dragged himself to the side of the hut where he swayed, stickless, pissing.

'How will we get back to the school?'

'We can stay here. There is a bus tomorrow morning.'

B.J. panicked. 'I can't. I have a class.'

'It doesn't matter.' Wangi shrugged.

'Miss Poole will call the police if I don't show up. She'll think something's happened to me – I'll be in trouble. So will you, Wangi.'

'That car is stuck. How can I –'

'There are lots of people around here not doing anything. They'll help you pull it out of the mud,' B.J. pleaded. She changed her tone. 'I'm telling you, Wangi. I'm not staying in this place. I'll *walk* back to the school if I have to, I really will.'

Wangi rose slowly and called to some boys who were idling around a hut at the far side of the clearing. 'You stay here,' he said to B.J. 'We'll get the car out and I'll come and pick you.' He explained this to his father, who had returned to his low stool; the old man nodded and went on staring at B.J.

The women had squatted in a circle around B.J.; the old man faced her. She saw none of them. On the ground, embedded in the mud near her chair, she saw a small broken spear with a rusty blade. Where were the drums, the dancers with the lion-mane head-dresses, the fantastic-tailed birds? She had not really expected to find them near the school, but here she was in an authentic village and there was no sign of them. Perhaps they had been there before and this is what it had all come to: a small spear-blade rusting in a tropical slum. Near the hut there were sodden cigarette wrappers, a Coke bottle, crumpled boxes of tea, dog-turds. And all through the smoky compound, dirt and silence. One by one the women left, until there was only B.J. and the old man, soot blowing into their faces, flies gathering on their hands and arms and on the remains of the food in the cracked enamel bowls. Where the women had been squatting there was a pile of garbage: orange rinds, the frothy-sinewed spittings of chewed sugar-cane, limp banana peels. In this ripe pile of garbage was the image. Not drums, dancers or exotic birds, but a special laughable silence. Completing her unfinished journal-entry B.J. mumbled to herself, 'Africa is a banana peel.'

Her laughter startled the old man.

At dusk, the headlights of the car veered into the compound. B.J. walked stiffly to it. She was chilled to the bone. Her back hurt from sitting on the slumping chair; her legs ached from the chafing Bermuda shorts; her skin felt patched and stitched with stinging scratches. She knew her hair was a sight: it felt thick and greasy. Her hands were dirty, for even though it was dark and she could not see it, she could feel the filth clinging to her hands like gloves. She yanked the door open. Before she got in she turned away from the headlights to the old man's little haystack hut and said softly, '*Kwaheri*, good-bye.' She thought she heard a small troll's voice, as if speaking from under a large stone, returning her farewell. She knew she was imagining it, for she paused and listened. There was silence in the sodden village. If there had been a sound, it must have been the wind in the broken grass.

She felt dirty, but free. Now she knew how explorers must have felt, coming upon muddy ruins deep in Africa after a year's trek. Filthy and tired and standing in silence, they looked beyond the ruins and the clutter of rusting spears to dense grass; they were hermits in the desert searching for the evidence of faith. Like hermits they were assailed by images which mocked and tempted: savage warriors, slim black girls, the lustful rumble of drums, fearsome yelling and, all around them, wet dripping trees and lovely birds. In these imagined scenes the explorers found release in faith, and a literature was born. It was understandable; they could not have reported the silence or the decaying deserted order. And they could not be blamed for their imaginings – sailors had once thought the piggish dugong to be a shapely swimming woman.

And B.J. selected her own image, more honest than the explorers', more comic than anyone had ever associated with Africa. A cartoon sketched itself on her mind: there were two characters, a fat white huntress in a pith helmet and a feeble, chuckle-headed pygmy wearing only a bone in his nose. In a bubble near the lady's head was: 'I'm head over heels with Africa – wait till I tell the folks back home!' The pygmy was munching a banana. The banana peel was under the lady's raised boot; she was about to step on it . . .

'Why are you laughing?' asked Wangi.

'I was thinking I haven't washed my hands all day. This is the first time in my life that's happened.'

'We can stop at my house.'

'Oh, no you don't!' laughed B.J. and thinking, *You pygmy*. 'Take me straight home, and drive slow or you'll kill us both. I've got papers to mark.'

A banana peel, a banana peel. The words tumbled in B.J.'s head. She felt happy. She would bring one back in a box and present it to the San Diego Museum of Natural History and say, 'Here, get a good taxidermist and stuff it!' She would tell Heather; that would cheer up the old sourpuss. Heather. B.J. had not thought about her or Miss Poole or the school all day; now she imagined Heather in the cartoon saying, 'I'm head over heels with this place.' *Poor Heather*, thought B.J. *She's just lonely*.

When they arrived at the school, B.J. turned in the seat and said, 'You want to go out again, don't you?'

'Yes, I do want,' said Wangi.

'Missouri. Well, if you promise to behave yourself, I will. But only on one condition. You have to get a date for my friend Heather Monkhouse. She's very sad these days. She doesn't see many men.'

'Yes,' said Wangi.

B.J. got out of the car. 'One other thing. Heather's very hard to please, so get your cousin, the Education Officer. Then she *can't* refuse. She'll like him, won't she?'

'She'll like Wilbur. He's an important man,' said Wangi with respect. 'We'll go on Friday to the Horse and Hunter.'

'Sounds real good,' said B.J. and, twirling her new walking stick like a majorette, crossed the grass to her house.

'My God!' exclaimed Miss Male when B.J. entered. 'If you weren't smiling I'd say you've just been rogered in a swamp. Where in heaven's name have you *been*?'

'I've *been*,' said B.J. imitating Miss Male's English vowel, 'to Africa. That's where I've *been*.'

'You're keen on it of course,' laughed Miss Male.

'Of course,' said B.J. 'I'm mad about it.' She looked at her hands with disgust; shaking her head sadly from side to side, she said, 'Pam, really it was horrible.' She tried to say more, but she could not find words to describe the ugliness; it was a vocabulary she seldom used.

In bed, the peace she had felt before came again. This time it did not come from a recognition of what Africa was; it came from perceiving America; she dreamed of her father, a tub full of bubble bath, the San Diego Central Sophomore Hop, gleaming cars on the freeway, the twenty-foot plastic doughnut in Pasadena, Frank Sinatra, pizza, IBM machines and (laughing softly in her sleep), See ya later, alligator.

15

The Horse and Hunter

Sometimes people drove all the way from Nairobi simply to look at the signboard of the Horse and Hunter. It was a large creaking board, the sort found in front of an English country pub, symmetrically scalloped on its edges, worm-eaten, and hinged to a rusting iron bracket over the door. On it, a man togged out in hunting garb – peaked velvet helmet, scarlet riding coat, jodhpurs, high boots – crouched on a galloping horse. A curved hunting horn was strapped to the narrow saddle.

Before East Africa's independence, a white face showed under the hunter's helmet; the horse was a gleaming black. Two years after independence the local party officials gave the owner of the pub, Fitch, a choice: change the sign or close the place and leave the country. The sign, they said, was an offence to all Africans, a vestige of colonialism; it showed that Fitch hated black people. Muttering 'bloody minstrel show', Fitch re-painted the sign: the hunter's face was painted black and given thick red lips. The horse was painted white.

It was a much-publicized incident. The Nairobi papers featured stories on the re-painting and, under the headline *End of an Era*, printed pictures of Fitch glowering under the freshly touched-up sign. The Horse and Hunter achieved notoriety: a small dining room and several guest-rooms were added to it; it was now an inn, Fitch an innkeeper. Fitch became very popular with Africans. For the first time in twenty years, business was good. The Horse and Hunter now made money for the same reason it had lost money before. What was formerly dirt was now character. People drove up from Nairobi to have a look at the sign and see Fitch.

Fitch was filthy; he had always been filthy. Pig-faced, his lower lip protuberant under a stained moustache, stubby-armed and with fat hands, he was the sort of man who would have looked dirty even if he had washed. He had meant to marry; it was almost as if he had forgotten to, for he liked women. In his shack at the rear of the bar he kept a purplish-back Nilotic woman who, after the custom of her tribe, had all her lower teeth knocked out. He called her 'Auntie'. One month in 1956 all Fitch's hair fell out. It fell out in dandruff-spotted swatches; Auntie bought some gluey hair-grower from a village *mganga*, which she smeared on Fitch's pate. This did no good: in a week the few remaining hairs fell out. Fitch was left with a smooth knob, crusted with dirt and ridged with crescent-shaped scars. The rest of Fitch's body was hairy: the hair curled like sour weeds on his chest and back and, on the nape of his neck, spiralled above his collar in a pelt. The thick tangles of fur on his forearms held flakes of dirt and grains of grubby shape-less matter that appeared to be decaying, like apple-cores in deep grass. He scratched himself continually, four broken fingernails raking across his soiled paunch; the scratching was a kind of strum-ming, as if his belly were a banjo.

He was a drunkard living unwashed in the East African bush, per-spiring heavily, cursing in forces' slang ('the bugger shits through his teeth after two beers', 'I have to go drain my snake', etc.); he was known to the whites who visited the pub or stayed in the little hotel-annexe as 'a real Graham Greene character'. In fact, Fitch had read and enjoyed Graham Greene, and there was a time when he had consciously mod-elled his drinking and generally squalid appearance on the unhappy expatriates in the Greene books. He had always wanted to be 'a real character' and had worked at it, studied it at first, thinking that it would be good for business if he were grumpy, kept flea-bitten dogs in the garden and an African mistress in the bedroom, did not wash and refused service to what he called 'the fooking Yanks'. After several years of working at it, the character *was* Fitch; it was no longer a pose. He had become an authentic cranky drunkard, mean with money, evil-smelling, spitting tobacco into his moustache, scratching holes in his under-shirt, punching up Auntie, cursing Africa and hating England. Many people said they wanted to write books about him.

It was Friday night. There were no guests in the hotel, the last customer, a beard-pinching Sikh from the garage in town, had just left the bar. Fitch was angry. He had against his will, struck up a conversation with the Sikh in the hope that the Sikh would buy him a drink. The Sikh talked about shock-absorbers, praised the British and exhaled his rancid betel-breath on Fitch who stood close, scratching his belly in four-four time and praying for the Sikh to say, 'Hev a vishkey, Feech.' After four whiskies the Sikh had wiped droplets from his beard, crawled off the barstool and stumbled into his car. Before driving away he relieved himself in one of Fitch's flowerbeds, in the darkness, a loud spattering on the leaves. Fitch kicked the wastebasket across the bar and considered flinging the Sikh's lip-printed glass into the road when he remembered that it cost two shillings. He tossed the glass into the steaming sink and decided to buy himself a whisky.

He had uncorked the green bottle when a distant engine, like a fat horsefly, hummed in his ears. It sounded like a car. If it was, it would stop. There was nowhere else a car could be going at night: the Horse and Hunter was on the Great North Road; beyond it were rocky hills, scrubland stubbled with dusty broken bushes and cacti, then Ethiopia, which Fitch called Abyssinia. He slid the cork back, replaced the bottle on the narrow shelf and walked to the veranda, two of his dogs nipping at him, the third howling at the far side of the garden. Above him the signboard creaked. He stilled it with his hand and listened. Yes, it was a car.

As soon as the four people entered the bar, Fitch knew he would get a drink. Two African men and two white girls. The Africans would buy him a drink, to prove to the girls that they didn't hate whites. One of the white girls he recognized as having bought him a drink before. So there were three drinks for sure, possibly more.

'Evening, Chief, what's your pleasure?' said Fitch to the large bald African. Fitch spoke in a hearty, maty way. Because he hated Africans he always took special pains to ingratiate himself to them; he knew that if he did not do this his contempt would show. And this African, Wilbur, was a senior civil servant and had become, in the few months he had been in the district, a regular customer at the Horse and Hunter. Fitch had no choice but to be maty with him and, in fact, could only really afford to be grumpy with whites. He forced a laugh and set up four glasses.

'I say,' murmured Wilbur pompously, 'I do believe I'm going to have a whisky and soda. Black and White brand, if you please.' Wilbur looked at Heather and B.J. and winked. 'I'm all for integration!'

'Well, fancy that,' said Heather under her breath. Only B.J. heard.

'Ha-ha, very good,' said Fitch gamely. He had heard the joke a hundred times, had claimed to have brought it himself from Nairobi.

'What about the ladies, Wangi? Don't be a savage. Ask them.'

Wangi scrambled to his feet. He started to speak but was interrupted by B.J. saying, 'Beer for me.'

'Pink gin,' muttered Heather.

'I'll have a whisky,' said Wangi. 'Black and White, ha-ha.'

'Right you are,' said Fitch, fishing a beer bottle out of a tub of stagnant water.

'What are you having?' asked Wilbur.

'Me, sir? Oh, very kind of you, sir,' said Fitch gratefully, and hating the ungenerous Sikh even more. 'Whisky for me as well.'

Fitch passed the pink gin and the beer to Wilbur, who handed them to B.J. and Heather. Then he made the whiskies. 'Fook everybody in the bleeding world,' he toasted, with the drink already to his moustache. He lapped thirstily.

'Cheers,' said Wangi.

'Bottoms up,' said B.J.

Wilbur swirled his glass and watched the fizzing bubbles. 'Was that Schweppes soda you put in here?' he asked. 'You know I don't take anything else.'

'Schweppes it was,' said Fitch.

'Very good then.' He raised his glass. '*To the ancestors!*' he bellowed, and he poured the entire drink down his throat. When he had carefully unfolded his handkerchief, wiped his mouth and then replaced the handkerchief in his pocket so that three white points showed, he looked at B.J. and Heather. 'You're going to think I'm a rotter, but I don't know your names. Mine is Wilbur.'

'This is . . .' Wangi began.

'B.J. Lebow. Pleased to meet you.'

'We've met before, I believe.' Wilbur said this in sincerity to most white women.

'Yes,' said B.J. 'Well, I was at your house, I mean. The party you gave when you were transferred here. That's where I met Wangi.'

'I'll tell you something,' said Wilbur genially. 'Wangi works for the Electricity Board. Don't let him shock you!'

Wilbur doubled up with laughter. B.J. smiled. Wangi tittered uneasily. Fitch didn't laugh; he decided to be sullen unless he was bought another drink. Heather remained conspicuously silent.

'You think that's funny?' said Wilbur to Heather.

'Yes,' said Heather flatly. Her expression of unamused impatience was unchanged.

'Then why aren't you laughing?'

'I don't feel like it.'

Heather was there much against her will, though when B.J. had first asked her to come along for a drink she had gladly agreed.

'With pleasure, dearie. Where did you *find* him?'

'Right here,' B.J. had said. 'I mean, he's Wangi's cousin.'

'*Wangi?* That local?'

'Sure, he fixed it up.'

'He did, did he? Well you can tell him to bloody well *unfix* it. Count me out.' Heather barked a laugh. 'I've never heard of such a thing. Oh, you *are* fantastic.'

B.J. pouted, 'Come on, Heather. Be a sport.'

'I *am* a sport. Ask anyone. But I'm not desperate. I hope I'm not offending you, but I don't like Africans.'

'But this is an African country,' B.J. protested.

'Why? Because you see a lot of black faces around? Don't you believe it, ducky. *We* run this country; *we're* in charge, *we* pay the bills. If we pulled out there wouldn't be a virgin or a shilling left in East Africa.'

'*We?* You mean us teachers?'

'No,' said Heather, pulling the hem of her dress down to cover her fleshy knees, 'the Western Powers.'

B.J. stared at Heather's badly made-up face: the mascara was thick, the powder had missed a few sunburned patches on her jaw, the lipstick made a false bow-shape on her thin lips. Heather's hair, the streaks that had been dyed, had gone greenish in the humidity. The loose flesh on her arms jigged as she swished her glass to and fro to mix the bitters. B.J. was speechless.

'They told me this would happen,' Heather mumbled. 'The people in Nairobi told me there was a lot of this going on.'

'Come on,' B.J. said, now uncertainly. 'You'll have a good time.'

'No, I won't. If you want to take your chances, you can. I'm not a trade unionist and I don't like blacks. I'm not going to risk my life for a free drink. I don't trust these blacks one single bit. The term's over next week. I can wait – then I'm going to Mombasa and really have a dirty old time for myself.'

'I'll bet he's nice.'

'Who's nice?'

'Wangi's cousin.'

'You mean you don't even *know* him? What next!' Heather laughed. 'If you Yanks want to play with the blacks, go right ahead. You're welcome to them. But not me, Bettyjean.'

'Gee, he'll be disappointed.'

'That's hard cheese.' Heather drank to demonstrate the finality of her words. She smacked her lips. 'I'm not going out with a black and that's final.'

'He's not any old African, you know. He's the District Education Officer. *I* thought you'd be glad.'

Heather's smile slipped from her face. Her lips were wet with gin. 'The *District Education Officer?*'

B.J. nodded.

'Did you tell him I'd come?'

B.J. said yes with her eyebrows; she raised them once.

'You're an absolute bloody fool!'

Heather knew the insanity of refusing to see the DEO, especially after B.J. had promised. He was the only person who could make life difficult for her and she had already made up her mind that she would apply for a transfer back to Nairobi as soon as the term ended. The District Education Officer would have to approve that transfer.

And now in the bar of the Horse and Hunter Wilbur was looking at her closely and saying, 'I don't know *your* name either.'

His whole face was in sharp contrast to Heather's. It was more than a simple colour opposite; his tight thick skin shone in the unshaded bar-bulbs. It was perfectly smooth, his whole head rounded, the dome a tonsure edged with a thin wreath of black fuzz. His knobbed nose gaped hairlessly, while two ivory wedges of front tooth protruded into his wide soft lips. He stared hugely at Heather in a slightly crouching position (she was sitting), his neck shortened and swollen in almost tie-bursting tension. He seemed to Heather like a black rubber monster, life-sized, that some infantile practical joker had inflated and stuck with her in the small room.

Heather's sharp narrow-nostrilled beak trembled menacingly at Wilbur. Her lips were daubed in the usual red bow, but the red had rubbed from the place her lips met. The sutures of her bony forehead showed under the slack facial skin which, very pale, was covered with tiny blonde powder-caked hairs. She said, 'My name is Heather Monkhouse.'

'That's good,' said Wilbur, and he repeated to himself, 'Heather Monkhouse.' He went back to the bar and ordered more drinks for everyone, including Fitch. Then he turned towards Heather and said, 'Miss Heather Monkhouse, are you a teacher?'

'That is correct,' said Heather coldly, accepting her gin. 'I'm down the road at the girls' school.'

'At the girls' school,' said Wilbur thoughtfully, wrinkling his face.

'She teaches English and drama,' said B.J. 'They won't let us Americans teach English. On account of we ain't speaking it so hot!' she added comically.

'So you *are* a Yank,' said Fitch to B.J.

'Yes, I am,' said B.J. uneasily, sipping at her beer.

'But you said –'

'I had amnesia.'

'You had a fooking bad case of it, to my way of thinking,' said Fitch, scratching himself.

'Miss Heather,' said Wilbur, who had neither drunk his whisky nor taken his eyes off Heather, 'were you ever by any chance in Nairobi?'

Heather wondered whether she should answer, then remembered that she was talking to the District Education Officer. It was futile to lie; all the files were in his office. 'Yes,' she said, 'I was transferred here at the beginning of the term.'

'So was I,' said Wilbur, forming a smile. 'I was an Assistant DEO in Nairobi.'

'Nairobi is like Omaha,' said B.J. to Wangi.

'That's interesting,' Wangi replied, drunkenly stressing the third syllable. He swallowed the last watery drops of his whisky and handed his glass to Fitch for a refill.

'I liked Nairobi,' said Heather.

Frightening everyone, Wilbur burst out laughing. His rumbling laughter seemed to shake the black-framed watercolours of game fish that covered the bar walls. He woke the dogs, who immediately began howling, then stopped when he did. 'I know *you*,' he said to Heather. 'I remember *your* case.' He laughed again; giggle-borne tears welled in his eyes.

B.J. saw Heather stiffen; she feared Heather might do something nasty, call Wilbur an insulting name. Heather appeared to be thinking rapidly; her lips were moving as if going over all the possible alternatives. And then her whole body relaxed, she forced a smile, put her drink down and said, 'Why don't you come over here next to me, Wilbur?' She patted the bench with the tips of her fingers.

'Heather Monkhouse,' said Wilbur, pointing a large joshing finger into Heather's face, 'your case was a *good* one!'

'Come here,' said Heather almost seductively.

It worked like a charm. Wilbur sat down and put his left arm around Heather's neck. His whisky was in his left hand. When he drank he bumped Heather's face with his forearm. Heather smiled bravely.

'Do they know?' asked Wilbur, tossing his head in the direction of B.J. and Wangi.

'Shh,' Heather hushed; she whispered, 'Not here. We'll talk about it later.' She affectionately pinched the mischief out of Wilbur's face and rose. 'The same for everyone – a double for Wilbur,' she called to Fitch.

Wilbur grinned and shook his head from side to side.

'I'll never understand you fooking lot,' Fitch muttered across the bar at Heather.

Heather passed the drinks and returned to her seat next to Wilbur. She told a long story in the BBC voice that she had learned since coming to Africa, shushing interruptions as she proceeded by saying, 'You said you were all for integration, so let me finish.' The story was of a marriage that had taken place two years before between a former teacher at Miss Poole's school, an English-woman, and the Provincial Commissioner, an African. They married shortly after the woman arrived in East Africa; she was said to have learned Swahili in record time; she wore wax-print sarongs, ate local stews and had amassed a huge collection of drums and digging sticks in her house. She had met the Provincial Commissioner at a native *baraza* (he had just returned from a short course in England). They fell in love and were married in a village cere-mony: there was much feasting and drumming. She resigned her job at the school and took to pounding peanuts in a mortar at the back of the house. Less than six months later the African an-nounced that he had quit his job in the civil service and was making plans to emigrate to England. The woman was distressed; she refused to go. There were arguments that ended in fistfights. The woman was admitted to the local hospital with a broken wrist and severe bruises on her face. A divorce followed. The woman moved farther up-country, nearly to the frontier where she lived in a village with an illiterate tribesman, gave birth to a coffee-coloured child and let herself grow fat. The ex-husband, the African who had beat her, left for England. It was said that he had just married – this, the latest instalment – a woman of his own tribe who lived in Ealing.

B.J. said that the Englishwoman would eventually go back to England. 'She *has* to. Her family's there, aren't they?'

'Suppose she had no family?' Heather asked. 'Suppose they're all dead?'

'England is bloody dead,' said Fitch. 'What with the beastly bloody cold and the fooking socialists and the dirty great factories and the queers and fairies and what-not, England is bloody dead.'

'Yeah, but she can't stay here, can she?' said B.J. 'I mean, she's English, isn't she?'

'Are you planning to stay here?' Wilbur asked Heather.

'You want teachers, don't you? Who would teach the girls at the school if I went? Africans don't like being teachers. They want to be Prime Ministers, ha-ha. Of course I'm staying,' said Heather smiling, her head swaying, heavy with gin.

'Are *you*?' Wilbur turned to B.J.

'No *sir*!' said B.J. emphatically. And then she remembered Wangi. He sighed into his glass. 'That is,' she swallowed, 'I don't *think* I am. It's not that I don't like it here – it's great, really. But, well, to be perfectly honest, I thought Africa was different. Or something like that. But that's not why I'm going. Even if Africa was like what I thought it was, but it wasn't, I'd still be going back . . . golly, everybody's got to go home some time, haven't they?'

She looked at Wangi. His face was impassive. 'Haven't they?' she asked again. Wangi looked away. Heather smirked.

'Drink up,' said Fitch thickly. 'It's time.'

16

Blackmail

A moonscape appeared: crippled, twisted cacti, ant-hills, dry crater basins, and round bare mounds like inverted bowls, all of these frosted with ghostly silver and hard and darkened at ground level. On the far horizon was a black irregular fence of mountains. It was as if they were bumping across the moon in an old-fashioned rocket-ship; B.J. imagined the Africans two dark streamlined moonmen, one at the controls, the other seated silently next to her as the rickety machine was guided through the dramatic bareness in the unearthly gleam. Africa was much weirder at night.

The car plunged down a grade full-tilt and shot into a forest, leaving the moonscape behind. Desert turns to forest in East Africa without warning, arid plains become dank swamp, and sometimes snowy peaks show over the banana groves. Now a rotting dampness chilled the car; all the deep-green trees and vines seemed soaked, dense with lushness and oozing jungly waters. From the thick shadows, glowing animal eyes appeared, shone for seconds and then were gone. And owls, perched in the centre of the road, flushed noisily into the air with a wind-rush of big slow wings as the car passed, the beating wings brushing the upper part of the windshield. The headlights of the rocking car made all the great boulders, tree-trunks and ferns dance past in a frantic conga of rubbery twitching shapes.

When they reached the asphalt road, Wilbur speeded up; the tyres crackled, popping open the fallen jacaranda blossoms which quilted the road. Inside the school compound Wilbur slowed the car to a crawl. He drove cautiously past Miss Poole's to Heather's, where he coasted to a halt and cranked up the hand-brake, leaving the engine still ticking.

'Thank you so much,' said Heather. 'It's been fun.'

'It sure has,' said B.J., sitting up in the back seat.

Heather started to lift the door-handle.

'Miss Heather,' said Wilbur, 'would you mind if I used your *facilities*? I think I'm going to burst if I don't find a latrine.' He chuckled softly.

'I'd rather you didn't,' said Heather.

'I *will* burst!'

'I'd rather you didn't come in.'

'Are you afraid I'll stand on the seat?'

'It's late,' said Heather impatiently. 'Couldn't you just do it in the garden?'

'You think I'm a savage, don't you?' The joviality had left Wilbur. His eyes flashed white at Heather in the darkness of the car. A panel light illuminated his large hand, nothing more.

'Of course not,' Heather protested. 'I just –'

Wilbur jerked his door open and got out. 'Take this little girl to her house, Wangi,' he said. Then he walked to Heather's side of the car and, with an effort, got her door open; it had not been fixed since the time Wangi went off the back road. Wangi got out and made his way to the driver's seat.

Before Heather got out of the car B.J. leaned forward and touched her shoulder. In a whisper she said, 'I don't think Wangi's too crazy about my leaving and everything. He hasn't said one word since we left the bar – hey, do you think he's okay?'

'I wouldn't know,' said Heather with a coldness in her voice that B.J. had never heard before.

'Look, I know this was my idea, but I think I said the wrong – please, Heather, *wait* –' The door slammed. Heather disappeared.

B.J. got into the front seat. Wangi shifted the car roughly into gear and drove up the road, past the servants' quarters, to the small school bungalow where B.J. lived with Miss Male. What alarmed B.J. was that there were no lights burning in the house.

'It's through there,' said Heather in the living-room, pointing vaguely to a darkened hallway. She did not look at Wilbur. 'First door on the left.'

She sat on the edge of the sofa and pressed her hands to her eyes. She tried not to hear the relentless cataract bubbling grossly into the bowl, then the dripping, a hawking of phlegm, the silly tinkle of the chain, the loud flush and glug. But she heard it all, her drunkenness amplifying and distorting the ugly sounds, as if it was happening three feet away. She wanted to rush into her bedroom and lock the door, to hide until Wilbur discovered her gone and went away himself. She rose to do this – she could not think of anything else to do – but as she did, Wilbur entered the room buttoning the jacket of his suit across his pot belly.

'Miss Heather Monkhouse,' said Wilbur with a crooked smile, looking Heather straight in the eye.

'I wish you'd stop saying that,' said Heather. She walked to the front door and stood with her hand on the door-knob. Delicate white moths had collected on the outside of the screen; they crept around in circles, fluttering their wings, watching the light with large eyes.

'Why, Miss Heather Monkhouse?'

'I'm sick of hearing you say it. I don't think you're very amusing.'

'It's your name, isn't it?'

Heather did not respond.

'I said, it's your name –'

'Yes, it's my bloody name. So what?'

'Monkhouse,' said Wilbur. 'Is that English?'

'Stop it. Of course it is.'

'I was in England, you know. Aberystwyth.'

'That's in Wales.'

'Yes, Wales. You English are more tribal than we Africans.'

'Rubbish,' said Heather. 'Wales is a different place.'

'So is Africa.'

'So it is.'

'You like it here?'

'What if I do?'

'I'm simply asking.'

'Sometimes I like it. But you –' She paused; she wondered

whether she should say *blacks* or *Africans* '– you Africans think you own the whole place.'

'We do own it. It's our country.'

'Then you come to England and think you own England, too. What a cheeky lot!'

'We paid for England. You exploited us and stole –'

'We *worked* here and built this country and you damned well better believe it. This was all ours once, all of this –'

'Miss Heather Monkhouse,' Wilbur sneered.

'Stop saying my name!' The African was mocking her, an African mouth saying her name over and over again. She wanted to crush his insolent face.

'A very neat little house,' said Wilbur fingering an ashtray that had been made from the hoof of an animal. He strolled casually around the living-room picking up magazines, looking at the spines of books on the shelf, the framed photograph on the desk. 'Nice things. From England?'

'Isn't it time you went home?' Heather said, as rudely as she could.

'No. I'm not ready yet. I want to talk to you.' Wilbur glanced up from a magazine he had been leafing through and leered at Heather.

'I don't want to talk to *you*. Don't think you can barge in here and insult me just because you're an education officer and I'm a teacher. You have no right. I can call the police.'

'Call them,' Wilbur said. 'Do you think they'll believe anything you say? Don't forget, we Africans are all brothers.'

'You Africans cut each other's throats, don't tell me you don't.'

'Your throat maybe,' Wilbur said, 'but not my brother's.' He played with an ivory letter-opener.

Heather became frightened: he *could* cut her throat, very easily. She changed her tone. 'I'm very tired. Please go. I have to work tomorrow.'

'Tomorrow is Saturday.'

'This is a boarding school. We have to work every day. You should know that. You're an education officer.'

'Yes, I am,' said Wilbur. 'I was an education officer in Nairobi, too.'

Heather glanced at her wrist-watch. 'See here,' she said, 'it's after twelve –'

'When you were in Nairobi, that's when I was there,' Wilbur cackled. He grinned as he had done in the Horse and Hunter when he first learned her name, and again he said, 'I remember your case.'

Heather crouched in a chair some distance from Wilbur, who had seated himself on the sofa. She took a breath and then spoke. 'That's quite enough,' she said. 'I've had enough of this. It was damned inconsiderate of you to bring that up while we were there at the bar with those others listening. What happened in Nairobi is over and done with. In any case, it's my affair, not yours. I don't want to hear about it again and I don't want the people here to start talking about it. You should be thankful I didn't row with you in the bar when you brought it up, but if you insist on taunting me with my name and gloating over what you know about me, I shall make a scene here and you'll be sorry. Mark me, you'll regret ever talking to me and you'll rue the bloody day you came here to piss. Your superiors wouldn't like it if they knew you were in my house making my life a misery –'

Wilbur interrupted her harangue by shouting, 'What would *your* superiors,' he gasped, 'your superiors say if they knew about you?' Wilbur was rattled.

'I daresay they bloody well know!' Heather brayed.

'I'll tell them about the police station. I was there at the police station after you made that big *shauri* at that fellow's house –'

'Shut your mouth! Leave my house this instant,' Heather said through clenched teeth.

'I'll leave when I feel like it,' said Wilbur. He walked heavily towards Heather. 'You're a Boer. This isn't your country. You have no business –'

'Get out, you insolent bastard. You filthy . . .' Heather choked; racial abuse, every vile name she could think of, welled in her throat; the words trembled there, already formed. Now she would let him have it; she wanted him to know how much she hated him. She tried to select the most offensive words, but Wilbur had already started shouting back.

'Don't talk to me that way – I'm not your houseboy. I know a lot about you. If you make me angry I could just go ahead and tell anyone about you.'

'That's blackmail!'

'Don't say that to me,' Wilbur hissed. He started for her, but Heather stepped back. 'I'll get you and no one will know about it. You can't scream loud enough. You're not in Nairobi now.'

'Stay where you are!' Heather snatched a large glass ashtray and flung it; it sang past Wilbur's head and hit the far wall. It did not break, but the clang it made stopped Wilbur. He was near the desk, huge with rage. He slammed his fist down on the desk so hard that the framed photograph flew off and tumbled to the floor.

'You're a blackmailer!'

'Shut up!' snarled Wilbur. 'What have you got against black people?'

'I hate you, I hate you,' Heather said in sincere, almost prayerful ejaculations, as she backed towards the opening to the hallway. She saw that Wilbur had misunderstood, and she was glad; it could not have been better if she had actually said all the words that had run through her mind a few moments earlier. He faced her, raging, his mouth hanging open.

'We're as good as you are. I've had English girls, plenty of them –'

'*Welsh* girls, more likely!' Heather laughed hysterically and stepped back again.

'They loved me,' Wilbur said, crossing the floor, stooped and swaying like a drunken bear. 'They loved me.'

'I *hate* you!' Heather saw the words wound him; Wilbur made two large black fists and lifted them at her. Heather spun, skidded down the hallway to her room, banged the door and locked it. At the last click of the key she heard a muffled thump in the living room, as if Wilbur's body was hitting the solid floor. Then there was a deep sigh.

In the darkness of her bedroom, Heather's heart pounded; she could feel it pulsing hatefully against her throat. She pressed the side of her head to the door to hear Wilbur, but heard only herself, all the pumping noises of fear and anger from her own body, her heart, her blood, her rapid breath. She stayed in the room for what seemed to her a long while. Still hearing nothing, she went to the window and looked out. She could see some tall silvery trees, the glistening grass, some neat rows of flowerbeds; there was no movement, although she suspected that she might be startled by Wilbur clawing at her window. Nothing outside moved: it could have been a winter scene, the whole landscape frozen into stillness by the cold moon.

She went to the door again and listened, her ear against the wood. Her heart had slowed and she was no longer panting; several minutes passed in the fuzzy faraway engine-hum of the deep silence. Turning the key slowly so that it would not click, she unlocked the door, twisted the knob and edged the door noiselessly open. When she peeked into the hallway, she could see one of Wilbur's feet, toes pointing upward, protruding into the hallway. She tiptoed towards him and took a long look: Wilbur was stretched out, mouth gaping open, on his back; his belly swelled obscenely, arms in a welcoming gesture of either lust or anger. Beside him lay the small framed photograph (Heather in a straw hat at Brighton, aged six); the glass was cracked where Wilbur's heel had crushed it and slipped.

At that moment, with the photograph in her hand, Heather heard a sharp sound at the front door. She turned quickly in panic and saw Rufus, his nose pressed into the screen, pawing the doorframe and growling softly.

'This is a fine time to show up,' Heather said with a shiver. Rufus howled when he saw Wilbur. Heather pulled him by the collar into her bedroom; with Rufus there she knew she would be perfectly safe.

Heather could not tell if Wilbur was breathing, she could not bear to put her face close enough to find out – a whisky-reek hung about his head that, worse than suggesting drunkenness, made him seem a dead monster shot with the alcoholic preservative that keeps large specimens whole. She lifted out a piece of the shattered picture-glass from the little frame and held this shard across his lips. A small moist cloud collected on the glass.

The swine, Heather thought. And with this thought came a feeling of terrible remoteness and smallness: she was trapped in a little house with a black unconscious man, in a little post, late at night, as far away from help and sanity as one could ever get. There was nothing to do but to lock him in the spare bedroom; in the morning, gagged with a hangover, in blinding sunlight, he would weakly go away, she hoped.

From her bedroom Heather got a rectangular carpet. She spread it beside the body and, by twisting his legs, rolled Wilbur on to the carpet on his face. The floor was smooth waxed concrete under the sisal mats; Heather kicked the mats aside and with a great effort tugged the carpet – Wilbur lying the length of it – into the spare-room.

Heather was in bed when she remembered Wangi. She had to go all the way to her front door, with Rufus in tow, to get a glimpse of B.J.'s house. Across the moon-silvered meadow she could just make out the car. It was parked under a tree, dead-still and gleaming with starry dew. There were no lights on in the car or in B.J.'s house.

'Stupid girl,' muttered Heather. She put out all the lights, locked all the doors and went to bed, remembering to lock her own bedroom door and wedge a chairback against the knob. She was aware of Wilbur's presence two locked rooms away, as if he were giving off a sickening odour of decay. He was there in her small house, inert on his back, a huge dark carcass, like the image of the putrefying black devil she had once had of the whole continent.

17

'Can I See You?'

Heather blundered into troubled sleep and towards dawn had a nightmare. She was on a photographic safari in a Congo forest with several other women she thought she knew. They had all been warned against going so deep into the forest without a male guide; all the women were afraid except Heather, who mocked their fear by parodying their whining voices. After dinner the women sat around a fire and talked about the giant gorillas that lived in the area. As they spoke, Heather looked up and in the flickering of the fire saw five rubber-faced creatures, as big as houses, lumbering erect into the clearing. The women screamed and ran in all directions, upsetting pots and spilling water on the fire. Heather could not move at first; the gorillas were bearing down on her. She rose from her canvas chair in slow motion and grasped the trunk of a tall tree which she climbed with aching delay, looking down at the gorillas at the bottom. When she reached the tree-top she clung breathlessly to a flimsy branch and sensed a shadow moving across her, blocking the starlight. Craning her neck back she saw, towering above her, a sixth slavering gorilla, a King Kong hundreds of feet tall, his arms stretched wide, fingers apart, about to embrace her.

There was a stiff rapping at the front door. Sunlight dispersed the nightmare like flames destroying a photograph. Heather jumped out of bed. As she put on her robe she glanced at her watch: five past eight. Rufus snored in the corner. Still dazed with the terror of the nightmare, she clumsily unlocked the bedroom door and stumbled in the direction of the knocking. With the bedroom door open, the knocking was very loud; it woke Rufus, who began barking at the door of the spare-room, then leaping and scratching at it.

'Quiet *down*, Rufus,' Heather said. To the rapping door Heather called, 'All *right*, I'm coming.'

She slid the bolt and saw the faded woollen beret, the blotched face; Rose was standing close to the threshold as an intrusive salesman or beggar might do. In the sunlight Heather could pick out every vein in the pale skin; Rose's snub nose was sunburned, white skin-flakes peeled petal-like from her face and arms, exposing thin chafed skin. The dark eyeless goggles faced Heather and mirrored Heather's blue robe. Rose stuck her hand out.

'Letter from Memsab.'

Heather took the letter and closed the door on Rose's face. She ripped a thin strip from the side of the envelope and took out a small sheet of paper. There was very little writing on it, without a signature but in Miss Poole's hand: *Please come to my office at once. Urgent matter to discuss.*

'Damn her,' Heather said aloud; she crumpled the letter into a ball and flung it at the wastebasket. And then she heard Rufus barking in the hall. She rushed to the door of the spare-room and listened, as if all at once there would be a roar inside the room or the thumping of Wilbur's fists on the door. There was no sound except Rufus moaning and scratching.

'You'll wake him up, won't you?' Heather whispered to the dog. She took him by the collar and dragged him out of the house; Rufus continued to strain in the direction of the spare-room, imploring with his moans, his shuttling body and waggling tail. 'Better come with me, old boy.' Heather locked the front door.

'Please take a pew, Miss Monkhouse,' said Miss Poole. She spoke lightly, but seemed nervous; she was shuffling papers on her desk to disguise the trembling of her hands. 'There is something I wish to discuss with you.'

'I gathered as much,' said Heather. She was not interested in annoying Miss Poole and was not even aware that for the first time ever Miss Poole was speaking courteously to her. Even the thought of Wilbur left her momentarily, for as soon as she had spoken and looked at Miss Poole's face, the details of her dream returned. Miss Poole, Heather now realized, had been one of the women in the camp and had been the first to run when the hairy creatures entered the clearing. Miss Poole had run quickly; she seemed to know an escape-route, but of course she had been running deeper into the jungle. Like most dreams, Heather decided, it was about sex. She had read her Freud; with D. H. Lawrence he was one of the two male writers Heather took seriously. Both had 'terrifying insight' — the phrase was a reviewer's, Heather had seen it on a Lawrence paperback — into women's desires and, curiously, both had the woman's gift of frank sensitivity. And they both wrote about sex. Heather believed that any writer who was concerned with women and ignored sex was a fool, for there was no race, no nation or person who had normal sex. Her dream was clear to her and it contained a warning: the tumescent male apes, the women scattering, screaming into the tall trees. The warning would have to be heeded. Heather searched the dream for further phallicism and resolved to get herself laid at the earliest opportunity, either anonymously or for old times' sake, with a good friend.

Miss Poole was talking about the school, rambling on about duties, the Head Girl, what the prefects were saying about the hockey team — all of it without malice. But Heather was not listening; she was thinking of a hotel on the beach at Mombasa: she was naked in a darkened room, near a window which opened on to palm trees and surf; she was joking with a bare-chested man who sat on the edge of a four-poster untying his shoes. She would do it. If any arguments were needed for doing it, they could be read on the face of the woman gabbing aimlessly behind the desk. Miss Poole's was a face illustrating extreme fatigue, paranoia, bush-fever, and other symptoms of dry anxiety; it was the unretouched photograph of the *News of the World* crackpot, blurred somewhat by the bad lighting but otherwise described fully in the caption: note heavy lids, compressed lips, dull hair, vacant eyes set in dark circles, sallow malnourished complexion, shrivelled neck. Sitting there talking to Heather in pointless syllables, staring while nervously fidgeting, arranging loose papers into neat piles with her fingertips, Miss Poole looked to Heather as if she were being gnawed at from within by a large worm.

'This is the end of term,' Miss Poole was saying.

'I am aware of that,' said Heather, thinking, *A real dirty time I'll have for myself, some swimming, the sun, a man. If I can't have a husband, I'll have the next best thing; and who knows, it might be better than a husband?*

'I've been doing quite a bit of work, sorting out schedules and so forth. The exams, um ...' Miss Poole continued, almost as if she were purposely delaying Heather, glancing past Heather to the door as she prattled on. 'The exams will be in about a week's time –'

'Exams,' said Heather coming awake and thinking, for the first time since she entered the office, thoughts of Wilbur. 'Yes. Well,' said Heather distractedly, 'if you're asking my opinion I'd say flatly no, don't bother.'

'No? I don't think you understand –'

'It is *because* I understand that I'm saying no. Exams for these girls can't possibly do any earthly good. Now I really must be off ...'

Miss Poole stopped arranging papers on her desk and drew back from Heather. The movement made Heather pause; Miss Poole's face continued to remind Heather of a woman with a grave illness. Miss Poole said, 'May I ask what you mean by that?'

'Tell me, Miss Poole, if one of the girls fails her exams, will you send her back to her village?'

'If a girl fails, she'll have to pull her socks up, and smartly. You know that.'

'I know that I've been through these so-called exams hundreds of times. They're a bloody farce – we had them in Nairobi at Mainwaring and I know we'll have them here. But if you're asking my opinion on the matter, as I believe you are doing, then I will tell you how useless I think they are. Girls who fail their exams stay on at the school like everyone else, like a bunch of bloody –'

'You mean to say that you're concerned about the academic standards at this school?'

'In my way,' said Heather curtly.

'I would hardly have thought so from your behaviour.'

'My behaviour, as you call it, is my business.'

'We were talking about exams,' said Miss Poole.

'See here,' said Heather, raising her voice, 'I am a teacher, whatever you may think of me, and I feel every responsibility for what happens at this filthy school. Or *fails* to happen. I have never in my life –'

'I would have thought differently,' said Miss Poole, a cold angry light coming into her eyes.

'Oh, you would, would you?' Heather chattered, but her mind was on Wilbur. Each time she thought of him and jerked forward to leave, Miss Poole delayed her. 'You've spent a good part of the school term on sick leave, Miss Poole. You forget that I have had a great deal to do with the day-to-day running of this place in your absence.'

'I haven't forgotten that,' Miss Poole said with hatred.

'I'm pleased to hear –'

'Oh, yes,' Miss Poole went on, 'I see what you've done. I have noted our numerous disasters.'

'Disasters? *Which* disasters?'

'You know very well what I mean,' said Miss Poole, touching at her sallow face as if she had become conscious that there was something wrong with it, as if she was developing a defensive mannerism to hide it, like the person with bad teeth who learns not to grin.

'I have no idea what you're talking about.'

Miss Poole itemized in a high voice: 'The girls' utter disregard for authority, the chronic lateness and lack of discipline, the wanton destruction of the laboratory and the library annexe. And many other things, all terrible, all since you arrived at this compound.'

Heather's eyes widened. 'I do believe you're mad, Miss Poole. I used to think you were a nasty-minded old bitch, but you're not – you're stark staring bonkers!'

'I know you want to think that,' said Miss Poole, her voice

breaking. 'You want to think that and you've been telling everyone around here –'

'Everyone? There's *no one* around here!'

'You've been spreading lies about me so that I'll be forced to resign. And I know why – you want to be me!'

'*That's a bloody lie,*' Heather blurted, rising from her chair. She was frightened by the words; they were a kind of truthful prophecy, based on logic, as the dream had been, reversible but also possible. Heather knew that in a few years, if she took no precautions and let herself be guided by Africa's bestial nudges, it could very easily come about: she, Heather, would be the mad Headmistress rotting away in the bush girls' school. With venom, as if to poison Miss Poole's words, she spat out, 'I don't want to be *you!*'

'I didn't mean that,' said Miss Poole sadly. 'I meant that you want to be Headmistress. I know you do.'

'I most certainly do not,' Heather said disgustedly. She walked to the door and said, 'I had planned to tell you this week, but you might as well know it now. This is the bush, as far as I'm concerned, and it's going to stay that way. I'm leaving. I intend to leave this school as soon as the term ends and never come back. Good day.' She banged the door.

From her cool stone office Miss Poole peered out of the window at Heather crossing the grass. The sun beat down and whitened Heather's skin to a ghostliness that in East Africa gave the expatriates a look of special strangeness. Heather's whole being bleached and seemed to lighten and get nastier from the sun's intense rays; when she reached the road to her house she sent up a puff of dust with each step – such an odd figure, so unearthly among the emerald green of the grass and trees, the wild reds and yellows of the flowers, a devilish intruder with shapeless ectoplasmic body, moving across the fresh green like a slug on a track of slime. '*Liar,*' said Miss Poole.

When the word settled on her tongue there was a *clank* at the office door. Miss Poole spun around but became calm when she saw who it was stepping over the threshold: Rose, head tilted shyly down, one arm extended, and in her scabby hand a bunch of keys.

'I want to talk to you,' called Miss Male. She hurried rubber-sandalled across the grass towards Heather.

Heather had placed her hand on the door-knob, but withdrew it quickly when she heard the voice. She did not want to invite Miss Male in; she could imagine the scene: a loud banging on the spare-room door while Miss Male sat bewildered in the living-room, then shouting from the locked-in Wilbur, accusations possibly, howling, a noisy row. She put her back to the door and, like a sentry, faced Miss Male.

'What is it?' He might be shuffling around the locked room, he could be forcing the door or prising the burglar bars from the windows. Fortunately – as far as Heather could make out it was the only fortunate thing in a morning of misfortune – the spare-room was at the back of the house.

'Can I see you? It's rather urgent.' Miss Male was out of breath.

'I've just had a frightful *shauri* with the Memsab. I'm on my way back to bed – don't tell me you've got problems, too.' Heather tried to be gay, but her gaiety missed and she sounded even more gruff than she was.

'Not me,' said Miss Male, shielding the sun from her eyes with her hand cupped to the side of her head. She proceeded, squinting gravely, 'It's B.J. I'm terribly worried about her. I think she's poorly.'

'I'm sure it's nothing. Now if you'll excuse me –'

'Listen, please,' Miss Male begged. 'She's been sobbing in her room since early this morning. She refuses to talk to me or get out of bed.'

'Why should she get up? It's Saturday. If I hadn't got an urgent note from that bitch this morning I'd be in bed, too, I can tell you.'

'But it's not *like* her to go on this way. Please help me – I don't know what to do.'

'Don't do a thing,' said Heather. She made a gesture with her shoulders to signal that the subject was closed as far as she was concerned. Miss Male did not move.

'I'm very worried. I –'

'If you don't mind my saying so, Pam, you're not being very sporting about this.'

'You don't seem to realize that this is a serious –'

'I realize *perfectly*,' Heather exploded. She stopped and resumed in a softer tone, calmly and reasonably, as if talking to a child: 'I realize perfectly what has happened.'

'I don't think you do, Heather.'

'No one,' said Heather, 'gives me credit for knowing anything that goes on around here. It's fantastic. I've been at this school nearly a whole term and I am putting it to you – and mind you, I said the same thing to the Memsab ten minutes ago – that I *do* know, about B.J. and everything else in this bloody compound. My advice is to leave the girl alone.' Again Heather reached for the door-knob, again Miss Male stood firm.

'She's been crying her heart out.'

'And so she should,' said Heather crossly.

Miss Male looked at Heather as if at a stranger. 'You don't know what you're saying.'

'Oh, I *do*!' Heather laughed mirthlessly.

'That's cruel of you, Heather. That poor girl –'

'That poor girl,' Heather mocked. 'That poor girl – Pamela, isn't it about time you learned the facts of life?'

'I would like to know what you mean by that remark,' said Miss Male, blushing in anger.

'Just that. You're getting upset for nothing. Do you by any chance know where your Yankee friend was last night?'

'I didn't see her. I went to bed.'

'Didn't she tell you where she was going?'

'She said for a drink.'

'For a drink. Shall I tell you where she was, what she did?'

Miss Male pressed her lips together. She watched Heather.

'Well, I'll tell you. She had a date with her silent little African friend, the piccanin from the Electricity Board. I went along to see they stayed out of trouble, but of course I can't be everywhere. At about midnight they dropped me here. Just before I went to bed I happened to look out the window and saw a car parked near your house – not too close, you understand, but near enough. Now you tell me she's in bed weeping – this, the morning after I saw the car. I put one and one together and decide that your friend B.J. was getting thoroughly screwed, pardon my French, in the back seat –'

Miss Male bit her lip and frowned, as if she was the one who had been speaking and had abruptly stopped. 'If I had only stayed up and waited for her.'

'If you had stayed up I doubt that you could have done a thing.'

'Why, you act as if she *wanted* to do that . . . that –'

'Don't be a fool – of course she wanted to. These things don't have to happen. Rape is biologically impossible, don't you know that?' As Heather spoke she thought again of Wilbur, apishly caged in the spare-room, preparing to bellow wildly through his rubber mouth or, bulked against the frail door, about to break it noisily to splinters.

'He looks quite a strong chap.'

'Who does?' Heather saw only Wilbur.

'B.J.'s friend.'

'Rubbish. Tell me honestly, Pam, have you ever been raped?'

'No, in fact I never –'

'I haven't either and I've been in Africa for some little time. I don't believe in rape. There's no such thing. Oh, there were lots of times when I wanted desperately to believe that it had been rape – with me, you know. But it wasn't, it couldn't have been. The odds are against the rapist.'

'Are you saying –'

'I am saying that I have seen these girls before. They come here looking for it – it's the big liberal thing, you know, opening your legs in Africa. Talk to the drivers in the tour-buses, ask them, *they* know. Did you know that these American tourists, those old hags you see dressed up in topees and bush jackets – did you know that at night they crawl into the buses and bed down with the drivers? It's true. I have a friend in Nairobi who's a travel agent. He told me. The drivers love it.'

'That doesn't explain B.J. Whatever you may think of her, I can tell you she isn't mad on Africans. She's dying to leave.'

'It doesn't make any difference. You forget that we're free, we girls. We can do anything we want. Look,' said Heather, gesturing around the garden and flapping her hand in the direction of the boggy meadow, the clumps of shiny bamboos with their sprays of narrow leaves, 'we're single, and here we are in Africa. We came all this distance alone – the whole place is ours. And that's what's wrong with us. We're as bad as Africans – we're ashamed to admit that we want something simple.'

'Something simple?'

'A man,' Heather said, 'a husband. What fool wants to be single? I'd take any man I could lay my hands on, providing he was white.'

Miss Male kicked at a lump of dirt near her feet, a small mound; the top of the mound crumbled and revealed a black smooth-sided hole swarming with fleeing ants.

'Poor B.J.,' said Miss Male. She had taken her hand from the side of her face and was letting the sun shine into her eyes, into her whole helpless face.

'She'll get over it. Oh, she'll moan for a few days, but she'll sort things out. She got what she wanted. Now I must go.'

Miss Male said nothing more. She turned and walked away, across the grass, towards her house. She walked slowly, dejectedly hunched, watching her sandals flap. She did not look back.

The front door was unlocked, but Heather could not remember if she had locked it when she went out or, indeed, if she had unlocked it before Miss Male held her up. She entered the house and, the moment she did, sensed something was wrong; things seemed out of place enough to nudge the senses without being absolutely scattered. When she entered the hall she saw the door to the spare room half-open. The room was empty, sunshine streamed through the window. Where Wilbur had been lying there was a damp stain, a gamy odour of stale breath. Then Rufus appeared – from nowhere with a bound, his tongue drooping – and began barking. But he was barking only at the odour, for the house was empty.

18

Incubus

It was so dark, the girl's voice was so soft: she appeared, a figment in a rag of light, at the far corner of B.J.'s bedroom. Not B.J. herself, but a girl B.J. seemed to know well, one she thought she recognized, had seen many times before and was on the point of naming when, distracted by the girl's helplessness, the girl's identity became unimportant. She did not need a name. She was being raped.

It seemed a cramped waste-area of edges and moony light there in the corner of the room; the girl was on her back, twisted uncomfortably and softly pleading. It went on all Saturday and then into Sunday, the blinds drawn in her room, the girl appearing at a distance which made all B.J.'s efforts to dispel the vision futile, like the nagging dirty beggar who will not go away, who keeps his distance and wails open-faced, motioning towards his mouth, asking for bread. The awful repeating vision of the girl being attacked seemed provoked by the aches in B.J.'s body; her own pain induced pain.

On Sunday night the bodies and voices came again, as they had come a hundred times, all the words now familiar, ordered, shaping themselves in an aching pattern. This insistent rehearsal of shadow and panic shuddering there on the wall made B.J. moan, for the more times she heard it and saw it, the clearer the separate actions became; she anticipated each violent gesture. The girl's pain hurt B.J., and the only way B.J. could get relief from it was to sob as loudly as she could. At times she managed to freeze the progress of the vision by yelling, '*Stop!*' And she found she could slow it by crying. But when she was silent, it began again with dreadful sameness, proceeding with horrifying and deliberate efficiency, increasing in clarity as the rag of light spread over the wall; now it was two people, a girl and a silvery black man occupying the far wall of her room.

'Now what?' The girl spoke in what appeared to be the stuffy darkness of a car's front seat.

The black man said nothing. His head was unsteady; he slowly swung it around to face the girl.

'Look, I've got to go,' the girl drawled.

The black man placed his hand on the girl's shoulder. When the girl shuddered and pulled away, the black man slid close and held her with two hands.

'Stop it,' the girl said, but she did not say it loudly; it was a teacher's reprimand. She tried to get loose; she squirmed; there was not enough room on the front seat to move about in. The black man was close, like an insect in a hairy suit, bulbous-eyed, with long flicking arms and sticky gripping fingers. He did not speak; he held the girl and pressed himself against her.

'Would you please cut it out!' The girl got one of her arms free and reached for the door-handle.

Without taking his face away from her neck the black man seized her arm roughly and, when he felt it, punched down hard against her forearm, knocking it limp.

'Ow, that *hurt*!' The pain was unexpected; it worried the girl and made her examine what was happening to her. The black man was holding her tightly; his weight pressed her down on the seat; her legs seemed to be sliding forward and she could not move her left arm, which was wedged at her side by the pressure of the black man's body. The musky smell of sweat and breath crowded into her nose and mouth; and then, as the smell grew stronger, the girl felt a hand on top of her head, fingers reaching as far down as her ears like a grotesque cap, shoving her down.

Here B.J. screamed, but she was weak and could not make the vision pause. She hated this part of it; it terrified her as nothing else had ever done, and in this terror she was flooded with nausea which made it impossible to end the vision or escape it. For this fleeting moment B.J. felt everything the girl felt, each sensation of touch, the black fingers pinioning the girl, the breath on her, the weight of the man. B.J. crouched in her bed with her face against her knees: again it was happening.

It was this. A soft strand in the girl's body refused to resist the man; she thought of giving up, surrendering herself to the black man's weight and letting him do what he wanted. It was, in all the density of the girl's unwilling flesh, a small warm spasm of real desire, a pang of hunger produced by the heat of close struggle. This was a wrestler's passion which came savagely, suddenly, when the black man rubbed her breasts, squeezed the loose flesh along the girl's side and then rammed his hand between her legs and forced them apart. The spasm grew, paralysed her, a sweet cramp – almost welcome – weakening her will to fight back. It was more than a surrender of will; it was heat, unmistakably sexual, something the girl thought could not occur against her will. But it was happening and, as all the times before, B.J. whimpered, felt the vision seize and shake her. As the black man stroked the girl and slobbered at her neck, disgust rose in B.J.'s throat and weakened her. It was not rancid hatred; it was the wet reality of animal desire mixing with the knowledge of this weakness, for while her mind was made up, her body was not. The outraged mind and unde-cided body were two separate things: a wisp of will and caution fluttering over a bundle of pawed muscles. It made B.J. ache and the girl sob, 'Don't, please don't.'

'Yes,' whispered the black man. He repeated this over and over, rubbing the word into the girl's ear as he rubbed his hands over her body.

In a pulsing silence made alive and ugly with the twisted face of the girl disappearing under the dark shadow of the man, B.J. fell back, captive to the vision. The black man clapped his hand over the girl's face, hiding her the more and forcing her flat on the seat until her head was caught under the thick arm-rest on the car-door. This made B.J.'s forehead smart; all the girl's useless squirming caused pain and so roused sympathy and pity in B.J. The girl's legs were tangled in the black man's, she tasted bitter acid on his heavy palm and panicked, struggled with her free arm and tried to sit up; but the arm-rest over her forehead prevented her from moving. The black man gripped the side of her shorts; there was a binding tightness at her waist, then the release of this tension on her flesh as the shorts ripped free. They passed over her knees like liquid as the black man freed his legs and pushed the shorts past her ankles.

The man's hand was heavy; it smothered and sickened the girl. When the girl tried to shout, the thick part of the palm sagged into her mouth. The man's other hand fumbled with her legs, a rough fondling of her naked skin, while the hand in her mouth opened her jaws and moved between her teeth. The first pain began in her belly and she bit at the hard palm-flesh, as if at a sour fruit, her saliva running on to the palm and down her chin. Still she bit and moaned, harder and harder, as her head was bumped against the car-door in a brutal rhythm. Her teeth were pressed deeply into the palm. Several minutes later the bumping stopped, the hand slackened. The hand was gone, the girl's mouth empty, running with drool, her body no longer constricted. The girl was motionless.

B.J. drew a deep, deep breath. There was no pain in her body: she was completely exhausted and alone, a cool breeze lapping her legs. She felt weightless and lifted her head dreamily; in half-sleep she looked down at her two white legs, now far apart, like those of a large doll, one flat along the bed, the other raised, bent slightly. Between these, the wall where the girl had sobbed was uncluttered by the shapes that had terrified her. The rag of light was gone.

But something remained, a small figure, shadowy as an incubus, near the bed, at the far edge of the white loop the sprawling legs made.

'Who is it?' B.J. was dizzy; she tried to focus on the figure but could not. It stood, mute and indistinct. B.J. called out again, fearfully, raising herself up on one elbow.

The figure spoke: the voice was soft as the darkness, as if it were being uttered through a curtain of dense cloth.

'What do you want?' B.J.'s voice broke.

The figure glowered, but there was no movement. It was simply a lump, with certain edges that suggested human features. It seemed to crouch in the room like a fly, twitching its mandibles, jerking its head left and right, its whole dark body smeared with filth.

B.J. heard 'No' echoing in her head, but she could not tell if she were thinking it or screaming it. She slid from her bed and ran to the door, pulled at it, all the while her head drumming *No, No, No!* The figure made no move, only stood as B.J. fumbled with the key; its shape had altered and now it seemed to be smiling, gloating with powerfully evil confidence. B.J. dashed into the darkened hallway and out of the house; feeling the strong presence of the thing at her back, she pounded across the garden, swished into the grass to where the slope of the boggy meadow carried her easily down, faster and faster. She heard the rushing of stream-water and ran to it, knowing the water would make her safe. The grass became longer, running was difficult, and then there were bamboo stalks bumping; she pushed the bamboo aside, but they snapped back at her and tore into her flesh. Beyond them were reeds and papyrus that brushed and scraped her face as she fought through them towards the roar of the water. And as each thing touched her – the deep grass, the bamboo stalks, the reeds, the hairy tufts of papyrus – it was as if those black arms pursuing her had reached out to embrace her and, as she pulled away, clawed her.

Her feet sank in the soft bog and sucked as she panted forward; water dribbled through her toes and a peculiar weightlessness came over her – her breath leaving her in a gasp – as she shot downward into water shoulder-deep. Her legs were stuck in mud and went deeper as she thrashed her arms, struggling to float.

B.J. looked up one last time before the mud gave way: she was in churning blackness, being sucked breathlessly down from the black air to the black swamp. The incubus had pursued her, embraced her, engulfed her in sensational black folds. In her ears a riot of liquid voices started, an annoying roar of bubbles that increased in volume as she gulped the poisonous blackness; she swallowed again, and again her mouth was filled with a demon's sour fingers. Her body became stupid with heaviness, like the water around it.

19

Police

Exhausted with worry, Miss Male had gone to bed early on Sunday evening and had been awakened only once in the night: there were sounds from B.J.'s room; a door had clicked open; a busy mumbling and movement was quickly drowned in the hubbub of night noises. Miss Male had listened; she heard locusts scraping tunelessly on broken instruments, bats hurrying through the sky like nimble marks of punctuation and emitting ear-splitting squeals, the frogs and hylas hammering and sawing in the boggy meadow and a steady giggling down where the stream splashed. Miss Male drowsily muttered, 'Good,' thinking that B.J. had pulled out of her shock and was now quietly asleep.

On Monday morning the silence in the house startled and sobered Miss Male as the crying had the previous day. She got out of bed and saw that B.J.'s bedroom door was ajar and that B.J. was not in the rumpled bed or anywhere in the room. The room was scattered with dropped clothes and swirls of dirty laundry; it looked as if a struggle had taken place in it – contradictory evidence, for the disorder could have meant that it had been occupied by lovers or enemies. Miss Male hurried to the school but saw no one except – as she crossed the lawn and made her way along the hedge of bougainvillaea to the Staff Room – Miss Poole in her car flashing at top speed down the driveway and into the main road, throwing up dust.

Heather arrived at eight and found Miss Male dejectedly searching the buildings, opening this door, peeking in that window. Heather said she knew nothing; she had no idea where B.J. could have gone and had heard nothing strange in the night. She said that she had spent the evening writing letters; something, she added, as if revealing the substance of a dark secret, she had not done in a very long while. Miss Male looked puzzled and Heather added, 'They were letters to old girlfriends – women always reply, that's why I think twice about writing to them. But that's how bad things are.' Heather put her lips together softly, thoughtfully, then said, 'As if there aren't enough women here. It's a bloody free-for-all, this bitchery.'

In Miss Poole's absence, Heather agreed to conduct the girls' morning prayers which, that week, were a series of veiled demands for God to help them pass their end-of-term exams. The girls were pathetically pious; several in the back of the room keened in piercing misery like pilgrims at a shrine. All knelt and with heads bent intoned the wooden prayer, 'Guide my hand and heart and head, O Lord, in this decisive moment. Make me steadfast and strong . . . etc.' With gusto, as if it were a magical incantation, they ended the morning prayers with all the stanzas of 'Land of Hope and Glory'. Heather conducted the singing with a knitting needle and hoped desperately that Miss Poole would turn up in time to hear the song.

Milky, heavily sugared coffee was served at ten in the Staff Room, but only Miss Male and Heather were there to drink it. While they sat thoughtfully stirring the tinkling cups, the door swung open abruptly. Miss Male dropped her spoon; Heather held her coffee in her mouth and could not swallow it. But it was not B.J. It was Miss Verjee looking for the netball. She said she had not seen B.J. for nearly a week.

When Miss Verjee left, Heather imitated her saying, 'I hev not zeen her for nearly a veek.'

'I'm going to tell the police,' said Miss Male. She cradled her coffee cup in two hands near her face, like a crystal ball.

'Whatever for?'

'It's the proper drill, isn't it? You can never –'

Heather was about to say 'rubbish', but she noticed that there were tears forming in Miss Male's eyes. She said, 'If it'll make you feel better, by all means go to the police and report it. Cheer up, Pam, everything's going to be all right. Take my car if you want.'

'I think you'd better keep it here. If B.J. turns up you might have to take her to the hospital.'

'What did you say?' Heather looked at Miss Male as if at a lunatic.

'To the hospital. I know this is silly, but I think something is terribly wrong. Something terrible's happened to B.J., I'm sure of it.'

'You're jumping to conclusions,' said Heather.

'I wouldn't say that. I always think about your story, the one about the woman who was strangled near here. It was so horrible –'

'Pam, I'm afraid I exaggerated that one a bit,' said Heather sheepishly. 'But Miss Poole made me so bloody angry –'

'You mean it didn't happen?' Miss Male started to smile.

'Not here – that is, not in East Africa. I think it happened in . . . was it Nigeria? One of those countries. I read about it in the *News of the World*.'

'Then you lied.'

'I suppose I did then, didn't I? But that's rather a bald way of putting it.' Heather tried to laugh. 'Anyway, take my car and for goodness sake stop worrying about B.J.'

Miss Male closed her eyes and sighed; there was a smile of relief on her lips. 'I feel much better,' she said. She smiled at Heather, then lifted her arm, squeezed her watch and said, 'It's after ten. I'd better run. I won't have any trouble getting a lift.'

On the main road, Miss Male inhaled the fragrance of the flowering trees and stretched the worry out of her arms. A few minutes later, a Land-Rover approached on the main road; it rattled to a halt next to her. A plastic side window was slid back. An African policeman stuck his head out.

'You are a teacher here?' The African's tongue was pure pink, a lovely bubble-gum colour, with white chiclets of teeth pressing it lightly.

'Yes, I am,' said Miss Male. 'I'm on my way to the police station, as a matter of fact. I wonder if you'd –'

'Get in, please.'

'You see,' said Miss Male in the back seat, 'I'm rather worried about my friend.' The engine of the Land-Rover whined; Miss Male's seat jogged up and down. 'She seems to have been away all night.'

The African twisted his neck so that he was watching the road with one eye and shouting to Miss Male in the back with part of his face. 'I served in Burma Campaign in King's African Rifles. British liked me. Got ribbons, too, nice ones, man. Rangoon, Bombay, Aden, even India, myself I've been there. Give me cigarette.'

20

Confidential

'It's a pity,' Wilbur said, scraping his chair up to the desk and tugging a stack of fat files towards him. 'We education officers don't see the schools as much as we would like. But I'm sure you realize that we're very busy with one thing and another.'

'Yes, yes, of course,' said Miss Poole. She had been waiting in the office since eight, the official opening time of government offices; it was now past ten and already breathlessly hot. It would be a scorching day; Miss Poole did not like to think of what the heat would do to her tar patches on the roof tiles. The last hot spell had caused many of them to bubble and drip through to the desks.

Rumpled, though with dignity, Miss Poole stood in Wilbur's office clutching an old handbag of flaking snakeskin; she was stiff, but this was not nervousness so much as good posture. Her raised chin, head tilted back, revealed a considerable amount of her scrawny neck. She wore sunglasses very similar to Rose's and a wide straw hat with a faded pink ribbon band, the sort that might have been worn at a garden fête twenty years ago. Her long shapeless shoulder-padded dress was stained darkly at the armpits with perspiration. She was at attention. She watched Wilbur bury his face in his handkerchief and then wipe the sweat-slime that glistened on his neck.

'Please sit down. I'm sorry I wasn't here when you arrived. Monday morning.' Wilbur chuckled in embarrassment. 'It's the one day when everyone is late for work.'

Ordinarily Miss Poole would have replied, 'Not *quite* everyone,' but she had other things on her mind, and in fact was surprised that Wilbur had appeared at all. She had feared that she would have to tell her story to a junior officer. She sat stiffly on the edge of the wicker chair, her back straight. She placed the handbag on her lap and folded her hands over it tightly. 'I understand,' she said.

'Now what can I do for you?' Wilbur said pleasantly. He opened and shut one of the files, subtly fanning himself.

'It's rather urgent,' Miss Poole began uncertainly. 'I've come on a very urgent matter. It's one of the members of my staff. I know it's a bit irregular of me not to have brought her along, but I want you to understand that it's a rather delicate situation. I wanted to have your strictest confidence.'

Wilbur nodded approvingly. Humming in assent through his nose, he walked to the open door, peered outside, told the messenger to buzz off, and shut the door. The air in the room stirred when the door slammed, then was still, thick and hot with dusty office-odours. Wilbur returned to his chair behind the desk, leaned towards Miss Poole and said, 'Go on.'

'I hardly know where to begin,' said Miss Poole. She had planned to start by telling about the first dinner party and Heather's blasphemous remark, but instead, and without thinking, she told how the person in question (which was how she referred to Heather) showed up at the school and turned her vicious dog on a defenceless little cat. She described how the cat had been savaged and then went on to the blasphemy. Wilbur smiled; Miss Poole did not pause. She told him of the dinners, of the coffee that was poured on her foot and the smoke puffed into her face in the dark, the collapsing chairs, the nuisance Jacko made of himself, the wilful destruction of the science laboratory and the burning of the library annexe. Using one of the Form Four girls as a typical example, she described how in one term the girl's grades had worsened, how she had grown insolent and unmanageable and, were the situation to continue, would most probably end up on the streets. The other teachers, Miss Poole said, had been most pleasant, but even they were becoming strangely unruly. The person in question was against having exams and said the most horrible things about the school, the girls and the country in general. She was, not to put too fine a point on it, dangerous, and would have to go.

'Yes, that does sound very serious to me,' said Wilbur. 'But I'm sure you know that it's not easy to get transfers for people that have trouble adjusting.'

'She wants to be Headmistress, can you imagine such a thing? She's been trying her best, by lying and gossip, to discredit me. I believe she would use physical violence to get what she wants.' Miss Poole craned towards Wilbur and added, 'I am sure of that. She would do anything, anything at all.'

'But transfers –'

'I am suggesting that she be forced to resign,' Miss Poole interrupted, 'not transferred. She should leave the teaching profession completely and the Ministry should recommend her deportation as soon as possible. She is simply not fit to go on.'

Wilbur shook his head. 'I have the power to do this – I could do it today if I wanted to – but in my years in this Ministry I haven't known anyone that was forced to resign and then deported. We usually send these sticky cases to the bush and, well,' Wilbur cackled, '*this* is the bush!'

'I haven't told you everything,' Miss Poole said curtly.

'Please do,' Wilbur said. He now took out a pencil and a large piece of lined foolscap. He poised his pencil over the paper and looked across his desk at Miss Poole.

'In a girls' school,' Miss Poole began in her preaching tone, 'there is one thing we must always insist upon. That is morality. We try to teach our girls the highest standards of behaviour, and we cannot do this, we can never possibly do this,' Miss Poole said in churchy repetition, 'unless we practise this behaviour ourselves. If one girl notices that we are slackening, she will take advantage of it, and others will follow.' She clenched her bag tightly; translucent scales danced from the snakeskin. She continued: 'We teach by example. If our example is not of the very highest, discipline breaks down and there is chaos, moral and spiritual chaos. Morality to me, sir, means much more than good manners.'

'What exactly did this woman do?' asked Wilbur impatiently.

'I will come to the point. This is not simply a woman blotting her copybook. This is a clear-cut case of deliberate immorality.'

'How do you know she's immoral?'

'She has men spending the night with her,' Miss Poole said quickly, as if she were emptying her mouth of something vile. 'This is the sort of thing we cannot tolerate.'

'It's hard to prove these things. You need witnesses, people have to sign things and swear –'

'I have witnesses.'

'Well,' Wilbur fished for a question, 'maybe it was her boyfriend.'

'Boyfriends are one thing. I have often had the gentlemen friends of my staff members to tea. I encourage that. I enjoy meeting them and always had Julius make fresh cheese straws for them. But this is something else entirely. This is immorality.'

'I wish you would be more specific.'

'I shall. On Saturday last, a man was found in the house of the person in question. The man was dead drunk and reeking of alcohol, sleeping on her bedroom floor in a state of undress.'

'Sleeping on the floor you say?' Wilbur began doodling softly on the sheet of paper.

'On the floor. He was seen by my most trusted employee. I might add, with all respect, that he was an African.'

Wilbur dug the point of the pencil down through the paper and anchored it to the blotter. He twirled it and said, 'Yes, hm, I think I am in the picture now. Have you any idea who this . . . African is?'

'None whatever,' Miss Poole said promptly. 'But I am sure he can be found. People talk. I might add that I consider *him* just as guilty as the person in question. I was hoping you might ask about – there are no secrets here. It shouldn't be hard to find out who the man is.'

'You don't have any idea who it might be?'

'I haven't a clue.'

'I'll do what I can,' said Wilbur carefully. 'Now if you give me the teacher's name I'll get straight to work on this case.'

Miss Poole said the name in her usual way, pronouncing it again like the name of the furry ichneumon.

Before Wilbur could react, there was a knock at the door which

341

jerked the muscles in his face. He blinked and worked his mouth. Miss Poole turned her head towards the door and watched it.

'One moment!' Wilbur shouted.

The rapping continued, reminding Miss Poole of her old terror: as soon as a door closed in East Africa, someone was banging on it to be opened. Wilbur cursed and shoved his creaking chair back in anger, but by the time he had risen the door was open: coolness entered the room, the air stirred. Two huge policemen stood there, in sharply creased shorts, puttees and cork helmets. They saluted Wilbur, bowed to Miss Poole, and one spoke in a slushy vernacular that was not Swahili. Miss Poole sat with her back to the men and did not pay attention until, near the end of the gabbled monologue, she heard a strangled cluster of consonants, 'Fitch', and then a word she had once heard from Rose, 'Wangi'. The second was a common name in those parts, but the first she knew belonged to only one man.

21

Faces at the Window

There were about thirty Africans at the police station, some milling around in the sun, others watching silently from under the shady flame trees at the side. They gathered around the Land-Rover when it swerved up to the veranda. The engine shuddered off; as Miss Male climbed out, the Africans pressed around her, staring slack-mouthed with empty inquiring faces, like deprived tourists. The policemen pushed the crowd aside roughly and let Miss Male pass.

Inside the main door, sitting near a policeman on a wooden bench, was Fitch. Seeing Miss Male on the veranda, he scrambled to his feet. He was haggard, the stubble on his face soaked with bristly sweat droplets; he wore only an undershirt and trousers; there were torn sandals on his dusty, sockless feet; his hairy toes protruded. The undershirt was stained and damp, the trousers out at the knees. He sneezed shamelessly into Miss Male's face, then blew his nose into his fingers.

'Been up since four,' he said. 'Froze my flipping arse at four and now I'm sweating. Fooking big *shauri* with your friend.' He looked again at Miss Male and then shook his head. 'But *you're* not the one.'

'This way,' the policeman said. He walked into the building.

'I hope I haven't caused you any trouble,' Fitch said. 'You're not the one I had in mind, but all the same I'm glad to see you. They've been asking me a right lot of questions. My boys found the body on their way to work. They came and got me out of bed. She was undressed, mostly. They didn't want anyone to think they had anything to do with it. Thought I'd explain for them. Christ!' Fitch wiped his mouth on his hairy forearm. 'The way I see it, the body

343

must have floated a fair distance – pretty strong current in that stream. And she might have bloated up, you see. Well, I took one look at her and says to myself, I *know* her, she was with the fat bloke on Friday night she was, and the little chap from the Electricity Board and . . . bloody hell, when I reported it they started a great argy-bargy about who was she and when did I see her before . . .'

The policeman waved them forward and continued walking. Miss Male speeded up; Fitch followed behind, still explaining.

'. . . I couldn't lie. I got my business to think of. They could finish me, *kabisa* – take my licence away. I told them everything I knew. Saw her just last Friday, I says. She's a Yank, told me so herself. They called the Peace Corps chaps in Nairobi. They're on their way here now, flying in their own plane. Christ, there's no end to the money they got. I couldn't tell them anything except there was another *mzungu* along with her; from the school, I says. But I didn't know I'd get *you* mixed up in this, expected they'd get the other one, the noisy one that wears all the make-up on her face –'

'Heather,' said Miss Male softly, to show Fitch that she had been listening.

'That's the one. She'd know something about this, wouldn't she? They was friends, wasn't they? I hope you can straighten this thing out. These bleeding sods won't let me go home until someone identifies the body. I don't know her name, you see, though she told me once. I'm bloody glad you're here. Maybe I can go now. Hope I haven't caused you any trouble. Thought you was the other one, the noisy one.'

They were now outside a large door at the far end of the corridor. The policeman took a key-ring and inserted a jangling key in the lock. It was medieval; the black man in the gloomy corridor, the long antique key, the thick scarred planks of the door. He pushed the heavy door in; it squeaked on rusty hinges. The dark room was cool and smelled of swamp water.

Miss Male had dreaded the moment. When the policeman flicked on the overhead light and lifted the blanket, it occurred to her that since early in the morning, when she awoke, she had seen a dozen blankets being lifted on a dozen slabs in her mind. And each had revealed exactly what she now saw before her: a damp face, bloodless and going blue, speckled with bits of petal and broken green leaf; the hair, thick, water-darkened, was spread on the table behind the head, exposing a broad chalky forehead. B.J. could not have been mistaken for a sleeper; she was rigid and dead, her eyes were staring up, her lips, tinged with blue, were open in a fishy O of stupefaction.

'Yes,' said Miss Male. She tried to say more, but could only utter gulps; she put her hands to her face and sobbed uncontrollably.

Stamping, Wilbur appeared at the door looking agitated. He called to Miss Male, 'Is that your friend, the American?' He pointed towards the corpse.

Miss Male did not answer; she walked to the musty wall, rested her forehead against it and wept, ignoring Wilbur.

'That's the Yank there,' said Fitch, tossing his head. 'And it's a right bloody shame, to my way of thinking.'

'Come here, Fitch,' said Wilbur urgently. 'I want to talk to you.'

Miss Male had been shown to a side-room by one of the policemen. The room was damp, with buntings of dirt-flecked cobwebs on the ceiling boards. On one wall, poked on a bent nail, was a picture of the Royal Family standing in a row on a lawn that had once showed green. Miss Male sat hunched over a blackened table with her fists against her eyes. She looked up and saw that she was in near-darkness; there were African faces at the window, peering at her through the dirty glass and thick bars, blocking the sunlight. The faces saddened and enraged her; she shivered in the coolness of the shaded room and wept again. She saw B.J. in her fists, frozen in many laughing poses, as if she were flipping through a pack of her snapshots. Miss Male was weary; it seemed days since she had woken up and sensed the silence, saw the swirls of clothes in the room and B.J.'s empty bed. In her belly she felt an emptiness, a forlorn hunger that nothing could satisfy. She whimpered. There were no more tears. Her arms were streaked where her tears had run through dust and dried.

The door opened; a man stood in the doorway. He was tall, pink, and wore a new bush shirt, shorts and alpine boots; his hair was burned blond. He hesitated, almost drew back, when Miss Male faced him. Her cheeks were lined, pale with shock. Her eyes puffed, red-rimmed; her nose was raw from being blown.

'The sergeant said you were here,' the man said uneasily. 'Sorry for busting in on you like this.'

Miss Male tried to speak, but found she could only mumble; she was frightened to hear her weak voice. She shrugged sadly and began again to cry.

'I know how you feel.' The man nodded. 'She was a great kid.'

New tears had started down Miss Male's cheeks where other tears had left dry trails. She dabbed at her eyes and pressed her lips together to prevent a repetition of her half-human mumbling. The man took her hand and she was comforted; the man was also trembling.

The man said that his name was Chuck and that he was on the Peace Corps staff. He had been sent to escort the body to Nairobi. The trouble was that the body could not be moved until a post-mortem was done on it, to determine the cause of death. A doctor was on his way in a van. As soon as the doctor said it was okay they would leave by road.

Miss Male found her voice. 'Take me with you, please. I want to go home. I can get my plane fare from the British Council.'

'Sure,' said Chuck, smiling. 'I'll take you. There's always room for one more.' He untwisted his grin; his face fell. 'Sorry. That didn't sound right.'

Miss Male had not heard. The thought of going relaxed her; tension left her body, deserting the sadness that stayed.

'Say, you don't look too hot.'

'I feel unwell. This has all been a great strain.'

'I'll bet,' said Chuck. 'It's a rotten thing to happen. Can I give you a lift back to your school?'

'I'd rather not see it just yet. I don't think I'm . . . ready.' Miss Male laughed weakly, then her face crumpled; she seemed on the point of tears again.

'Look,' said Chuck earnestly, 'I'm supposed to be staying up the road at a place called the Horse and Hunter. Why don't you come along with me and have lunch? I'll give you a ride back to your school later this afternoon. I'd be much obliged if you came. I guess I need company as much as you do.'

Miss Male rose; Chuck took her arm. They were at the door when the faces at the window disappeared; the room filled with light.

On the way to the Horse and Hunter Chuck tried to make conversation. He said the countryside was the prettiest he had ever laid eyes on, so green. There were sunbirds on the trees near the police station; they had lovely curved beaks, but made an awful racket. Still, it was a beautiful country.

'I used to think that,' said Miss Male to the window. Africa was green, even lush, but lushness made death possible. B.J. had died in a clutter of flowers; there were petals on her dead face.

'Any idea who did it?' Chuck did not take his eyes off the road.

Miss Male did not answer.

Fitch smelled trouble when he saw the stranger arrive with Miss Male. He knew he was being spied on and, after all Wilbur had said to him, regretted having reported the incident to the police. He vowed he would say nothing more. In silence he showed Chuck to the thatch-roofed hut. He got drinks – a beer for Chuck, an orange squash for Miss Male – then ducked behind the bar, downed a double whisky and fled for the day.

On the veranda Chuck whispered that Fitch looked like a real character. 'Right out of Graham Greene,' he said.

A waiter announced lunch.

Throughout lunch Miss Male maintained silence. She ate slowly, thoughtfully cutting and spearing meat and potatoes. A whole conversation came to her, but she felt too shy to begin. Americans always asked for definitions, explanations, and sometimes they misunderstood. She had wanted to ask Chuck why he was in Africa. She no longer knew why she had come.

Over dessert, Chuck said, as if reading her thoughts, 'Africa. I used to think –' He stopped spooning his custard and stared. His face had the pained incomprehension of someone who had just been robbed.

Late in the afternoon Chuck drove Miss Male back to the school compound. He dropped her at the driveway and said he'd see her in the morning. As Miss Male walked up the driveway she noticed there were no girls on the playing field, although it was past four. There seemed to be great activity over at the dorms, a bustle of girls sweeping, stacking boxes and suitcases, flapping and folding sheets and blankets on the grass.

Heather was standing in the driveway near Miss Poole's signboard. She did not speak until Miss Male started towards Miss Poole's house.

'She's gone,' Heather said. 'They took her away.'

Miss Male turned and looked closely at Heather. 'Miss Poole?'

'Gone,' Heather said simply. She wore no make-up and looked different, old; her lips were narrow and dry, her face cross-hatched with thin lines that powder had always covered. Without either eyebrows or lashes, her eyes – her whole face – was empty and expressionless, as Miss Poole's had been for most of the time Miss Male had known her. Her hair was discoloured and grey at the roots; one dry strand draped the side of her face.

'The police came for her with the education officer,' Heather said in the voice of a sleepwalker. She spoke without alarm, but as she did, Miss Male formed vivid pictures in her mind of what Heather described: the police Land-Rover arriving at noon and stopping at Miss Poole's front door, the policeman leaping out and ordering the old lady to get into the vehicle. Bewildered, Miss Poole had hesitated and gone stiff in her chair. She had to be dragged out, like a small girl being yanked off a playground by rough servants. She had stumbled on the steps, her legs had given way. One of the policemen thought she was trying to escape and in panic smacked her across the face with his riding crop.

'It was ghastly,' Heather droned, 'ghastly. They pushed her into the front seat. She went all pale and began to shake. She looked straight ahead through the windscreen and I knew she hated me.

I knew it. I wanted to say, "I didn't do this to you. I don't like you –"' Heather's voice began to implore an invisible figure on the grass. ' "I never liked you, but I'd never do this to you, not this. It was all fair until this, and I didn't do it." '

After a pause, during which the insects and frogs down at the stream and the swaying leaves on the flame-tree boughs near the playing field combined in the usual nightfall crackle and hush, a reminder of the drooping cables of wild vines that lay just beyond the compound, Miss Male said, 'You've heard about B.J.?'

'On the bush telegraph. One of the girls told me, after you'd gone. It's monstrous. Everything's gone wrong. They think Miss Poole had something to do with it. Indirectly, of course. They're hoping to hush it up by deporting her.'

Miss Male shook her head. She turned and looked across the empty playing field. 'How are the girls taking it?'

'I told them to pack up. Miss Verjee resigned when she heard about B.J. She thought it was an uprising. Terrorists, you know. I tried to explain, but she wouldn't listen. She was scared out of her wits. She must be in Nairobi by now, but she's all right, isn't she, getting married.' Heather lit a cigarette. 'The girls leave tomorrow on the school lorry. There won't be any exams.'

'I'm leaving,' said Miss Male without feeling. 'I'm going back to England.'

'That's definite?'

Miss Male nodded.

'You'd better put it in writing. Address the letter to me. After they took Miss Poole away, Wilbur made me Headmistress.'

22

The Last Girl

Miss Male was packing when Heather came over on Tuesday morning. At first Heather said nothing. She sat in a chair smoking, kicking a crossed leg up and down nervously. Miss Male went on with her packing; she had had a sleepless night and was doing a bad job of folding the curtains, sorting a vast accumulation of files and notes, and wrapping the crockery in newspapers. She worked haphazardly, at one thing, then another, when the disorder caught her eye; she stepped from the pile of folders to the bundle of unfolded cloth. A dish broke, she cursed under her breath. All the things she stuffed in a large black trunk which, on the front, gave her name, the school's address and the freight instruction *via Mombasa*. The name of the port made Heather think of her trip out, the horror stories in the ship's bar, the anxious retching in her cabin, the man who got off at Aden. It had happened long ago and, it seemed, to another woman.

'The girls have just left,' Heather said. 'There were a few complaints about the seating arrangements, but they'll sort themselves out.'

Miss Male looked up from a tangle of twine and brown paper. 'Sorry I didn't get a chance to say good-bye. But there's so much to pack. I'm doing B.J.'s as well. She had masses of things, poor dear.'

'Americans,' Heather said. 'I knew one who brought a year's supply of toilet rolls with him. Can you imagine?'

Miss Male turned away.

'Can I give you a hand?'

'Thanks no,' said Miss Male softly. 'I'm nearly done, thank goodness. I've just got to find space for these curios.' She stood surrounded by drums, an oval red-painted shield, a little spear, a pair of carved kudu. In her hand was a small ebony figurine, a naked crouching man with exaggerated features. She dropped it in a box which bore B.J.'s name.

'That's an interesting walking-stick,' said Heather. She pointed to the gnarled stick with the head and foot of a monkey that the old man had given to B.J.

'It was B.J.'s,' said Miss Male. 'Take it, if you'd like. I'm sure she would have given it to you. She was very generous, you know.'

Heather received the stick gladly. She would treasure it; like many plain things she owned, it had a story. Heather said, 'She was Jewish. I don't know what made me think of that.'

'Yes. She told me. She didn't take it too seriously, though. She wasn't a Golders Green type.'

'Her family must be heartbroken. Did anyone remember to send them a telegram?'

'The Peace Corps took care of that. I'm going to write to her father when I get to England. I think he'd be glad.'

'Yes,' said Heather, 'he'd like that.' She looked around the room, then said, 'Please sit down, Pam. There's just the two of us left. I never really knew you very well. I wish I had done. I think we could have been good friends, age differences aside. But you must know all about me—'

Miss Male, who had closed the trunk and seated herself on it, started to rise, protesting. She was silenced by Heather.

'No. Don't be polite. It's common knowledge, my whoring around. But I'm not bad, really I'm not. I used to think it was this place; of course, it's not. Women are — the word is *promiscuous*, I think — because sex is such a bloody let-down. You always think there's going to be more to it, you think you're missing out on something and so you — I suppose I should say *I* — keep trying. That's why women deep down trust the great greasy lovers and let themselves get seduced. They think it's going to be different. Only it's always the same. By the time you've done it twice you're promiscuous and you say what the hell, you don't have anything to lose.'

Heather lit another cigarette and, puffing smoke, said, 'I'll tell you a story. I'm sure you've heard it, but not the way it really happened. There's not much point in going over it again, but I want at least one person to know the truth.'

She told the story plainly; she wanted to be believed, without pity, only with the understanding that she was telling it the way it happened. She had gone out with Colin and liked him. He said all the things she too believed. They enjoyed a mutual vulgar mockery that appeared at times to be consuming their friendship. She tested him by saying she disagreed with him. He did not care. He came after her and she continued to see him and sleep with him. He loathed his wife and even suspected that one of his two children was not really his, though he had no proof. One Easter he took Heather to the coast. And then he was rude to her, insulting, only once, but that was enough and she knew it was over with him. The month they quarrelled her periods stopped. She had been off-schedule before, but this time not even hormone pills would start a flow. There could only be one explanation: she was pregnant and Colin was the father. She was surprised by her happiness at the prospect of motherhood. Colin refused to see her. She told her friends. The word got round to Colin's wife and there was a visit from the Headmistress of Mainwaring, who was escorted by a chaplain. They explained that as an unmarried mother-to-be she would have to resign and compensate the government. But the pregnancy had to be verified. She was sent to the government doctor; by then she had gained weight, her belly had swollen noticeably and she was having morning sickness. The doctor ordered an X-ray and this showed a small knob in the uterus, but not a foetus. There were vaginal discharges. An operation was performed and a uterine cyst, a ball of tissue the size of a strawberry, was removed. She could not face her friends and did not dare to talk to Colin. Also she could not be forced to resign. But Colin's wife was circulating stories about her and these she found unbearable. She went to Colin's house to explain. There was a scene. The police were called and Heather arrested for disturbing the peace. Colin's wife was threatening divorce. Heather was transferred.

'It was all nasty,' Heather said. 'There were bad jokes, anonymous letters saying "What got into you?" The rumours were much worse. I thought it might do me some good to come here. Obviously, it hasn't. But, you know, I've never spoken to anyone like this before. I know I have a long life ahead of me – if you know the truth, I can face things much more easily. I couldn't sleep last night because I knew I was going to tell you all this.'

Miss Male was moved by the story, by the frank way Heather told it, as if she were asking for absolution. The version Miss Male had heard had been much milder than Heather's truthful account. 'Why don't you go back to England?' Miss Male asked. 'At least you belong there.'

'I don't think I could stick England now. Besides, there are such a lot of wogs there. They're coming in by the thousands.'

'What were you doing before you came out here?'

'I was . . .' Heather saw a little corner of a shop; there were clothes-racks and large ugly women in old hats picked at dress-sleeves; a shop-assistant with a pencil in her hair, wearing a smock with a little round badge bearing the store's insignia, inquired about fabrics on a stained intercom. 'I was in women's fashions,' Heather said. 'I don't have to worry about a job, really. My father has pots of money.'

'Then you don't have any problems, do you?' said Miss Male. But she only said it to calm Heather; Miss Male (Cheltenham, St Anne's, heiress to a brewery) was certain she was lying. Heather, she guessed, was lower-middle and it was a pity, for the people in the lower-middle classes lived long and never had money. 'Weren't you talking about going to the coast?'

'Oh, that's out now. It's funny. I feel like a hag. As if I've just let go of all my sex. I don't have any now. When I heard B.J. was dead I got scared; then they roughed up Miss Poole. My sex all leaked out. I don't have any instincts any more. I'm an old woman –'

'Don't be silly,' said Miss Male. 'I'll bet you have a lot of friends.'

Heather lowered her voice. 'I used to know a very kind man in Croydon, a funny old thing, kind of sexy and not-sexy at the same time. I don't know why I'm telling you all this. I sometimes wonder where he is. I'd like to find him, or someone like him. Not to have any children, I'm probably beyond that. But just someone who's kind, to live with, go for walks –'

She did look years older. And as she looked at her, Miss Male was saddened by all that had happened. For six months Miss Male had been happy; in one fearful weekend she had seen sadness, cruelty and death close up, and now she knew she could never be happy again. She had once envied Heather; Heather had seemed tough, gay, with a looseness about her mouth and a decisiveness about saying 'rubbish' that only very free women have. That was gone now. Heather was old, her face was lined, her mouth drawn tight.

In that moment Miss Male wanted to ask, 'Who did it?' as Chuck had asked. But B.J. was dead, it was over, and finding the culprit did not matter. There were many culprits in Africa; and there could be no justice because B.J. had been among strangers and had no business there. There were risks in coming to Africa; Miss Male had taken them; she knew she could expect nothing better than the dead girl in the morgue, the terrorized old lady, the chainsmoker in her parlour. Exiles, they had elected to live alone as girls, unmarried among bananas. It was cruel to think, but they had asked for it.

Chuck came shortly afterwards. He insisted on packing the things in the back of the van while Heather and Miss Male shared a Coke on the grass. Chuck had not wanted them to see the coffin; it was an ugly thing, just a box; an American deserved better.

'I'll write you a letter,' said Miss Male when she was in the van.

'Don't send it to *this* address,' Heather laughed. She waved good-bye with the walking-stick Miss Male had given her.

Heather remained staring until the red dust raised by the van sifted slowly down through the windless air to the road. The school compound was deserted and empty, looked to Heather less like a school than it ever had. It was a garden, once formal, now overgrown with lush green, pulpous fruit, heavy blossoms; the buildings were scarcely visible without the girls running around them. Some sleek green birds shot from tree to bush, gave a short whistle, then flew on. The weavers in their bunched nests in the bamboos near the driveway twittered crazily, a sound Heather heard for the first time, though they had been there a long while. It was noon, the sun blasted everywhere.

The police would come in the afternoon. In spite of Wilbur's bribe in promoting her, she had sent a note to the police. Practising her new thoughtfulness, she had kept this fact from Miss Male; she did not want Miss Male involved as a witness in a court case. Heather wanted to be alone in testifying; she would tell everything, every last detail of the Friday night and all Miss Male had related. Some people came to Africa and wrote books about their experiences; she would have the witness stand, a court packed with listeners, a stenographer noting it all down for the newspapers. Wilbur's feeble bribe angered her. '*She's* the cause of all this,' Wilbur had said when Miss Poole was still in the Land-Rover. 'This is the end of it, isn't it? Now you can run the school right. She was a settler, you know.' Proof of connivance (and this she longed to tell), Wilbur had winked. He would get what he deserved, as, cruelly, she always had. Heather spat air.

Before she went into her house Heather walked around the school grounds to make sure the dorms were locked, the classrooms and office in order. All the buildings were neat, with a one-day accumulation of powdery wood-dust which had filtered down from the ants and bore-beetles in their rafter holes. She bent to blow a smear of it from a desk when she heard a faint sound, a soft shuffle, like something being dragged across the gritty cement of the veranda.

'Is there anyone here?' Her voice sounded silly to her, echoing in the empty classroom. It died out and then the hot room trilled with insects. She felt embarrassed to have called out to no one. It might have been Rufus who, having disappeared the night of B.J.'s death, had not come back. Trudging pointlessly through bush, following endless taunting odours, he ate fieldmice; he was often away for days, and then he would show up, almost apologetic, with a cut paw, burrs and seeds clinging to his knotted coat, like an errant husband.

There was little food in the pantry. Heather found a tomato with crow's feet, part of a crumpled envelope of dried Swiss soup, a half-box of biscuits which had gone soft, and two heavily freckled bananas. In a fit of stubborn melancholy she wished that Jacko was still with her. He would have made something of the pitiful fragments and served it on a starched white tablecloth; there would be fresh scones for tea. But he had never come back.

She ate off the sideboard, standing up, to save carrying the dishes to the sink. When she had finished she rinsed the pan and dropped the spattered soup-bowl, the spoon and knife into it to wash up later. Leaving the kitchen, she faced the full sun streaming into the living room and went faint in the heat; she had to touch the wall for balance: the room swam with tropical light, white and dizzying. The moment passed. She drew the blinds on all the windows, locked the doors and went to her bedroom to lie down. Her VW was in the driveway; the police were not cretins, they would see it and knock.

She stirred slightly when the lock clicked in the kitchen door, but rolled over and, as always, grasped the spongey pillow around her ears. A rhinoceros beetle droned outside, strafing and bouncing off a window-pane where it saw the garden reflected. Heather snored, asleep; she heard nothing.

The house was dark, but Rose did not need light to see where she was going; she knew the arrangement of rooms. All staff houses were built to one blueprint by government order. Making a scraping sound with her coarse feet dragging on the hard floor, Rose moved into the hallway and paused before the bedroom door. The air of the darkened house on her burned skin gave her relief; she breathed the coolness. In her hand was a carving knife; the cutting edge was jagged, saw-toothed; the point, seldom used, was needle-sharp. She tested it with her finger and, in her own darkness, was not even aware that she drew blood.

The bedroom door opened easily, noiselessly, only the bunch of keys making a clink as Rose slipped them into her apron pocket. Heather lay on the narrow bed with her back to the door. Rose leaned forward and peered, but saw only blocks of grey fuzz. The straining to see made her eyes itch; she removed the dark glasses, put them on the floor, and the room lightened, the rounded bulk of the sleeping woman swam in and out of focus. Rose shuffled closer, scraping left foot, right foot, left foot, until she was near the bed. Gripping the moist wooden handle of the knife in her two bruised hands, she raised it over Heather's neck, just below the thin jawbone. Heather opened her eyes when she heard Rose shriek, but by then the knife was less than an inch from her throat, Rose was stabbing down.

The first stroke glanced off Heather's neck; the second ripped a flap of skin, dug through ribbons of muscle and struck bone. Rose stabbed again, a morlock mewing over Heather's neck, and continued to stab until she weakened. The hard thrusts became a savage sawing with the jagged blade. She stopped when Heather arched her back. Realizing that she could not see or gulp air, Heather sobbed a spout of blood. Her face twisted; she tried to complain; as she sank back into the bed, her head lolled heavily to the side, sticky with blood.

Rose is off, the last girl. She drops the knife and, crunching her glasses, stumbles out of the house. She crosses Heather's garden, trampling the violets, barging into the fat-limbed frangipani. Raggedly, falling forwards, she hurries across the main lawn (bordered by bougainvillaea trimmed square) to the playing field (with its high fence of flame trees), knees pumping wildly, skirts flying, splay-mouthed. And then, for no reason at all, she stops running and simply stands as if discovering she is trapped, alone on the broad green field, a white mottled dwarf, one arm across her stricken eyes against the agony of the afternoon sun.

JUNGLE LOVERS

For Anne, and my sons Marcel and Louis

'*J'ai seul la clef de cette parade sauvage.*'

Arthur Rimbaud,
Les Illuminations

'*Now, galloping through Africa, he dreamed*
Of a new self, a son, an engineer,
His truth acceptable to lying men.'

W. H. Auden, 'Rimbaud'

Part One

On the day before Christmas – this was just a few years ago – in a dusty little dorp in up-country Malawi, which is in Central Africa, a young man sloped down the main road, alone. The dorp's name was Rumpi, and the young man's Calvin Mullet. He was from Hudson, Mass. The quaint raffia suitcase he lugged could have passed for a picnic hamper, but he was no picnicker.

He had been dropped at the *boma* by a banana truck. The truck's dust-cloud hung for a moment in the air, then was gathered into a murmuring whirlwind and hurried off the empty road and into the scraggy jungle, leaving behind a strong odour of fragrant patchouli. Rare patchouli grew wild in those parts. Calvin watched the whirlwind go.

Latterly divorced, Calvin was suffering the effects of paying alimony. He sold insurance (Homemakers' Mutual, Boston and New York, with fifty-six branches around the world) but all his goods and chattels so-called and half his salary had been awarded to his wife. He roomed in a whorehouse in the capital, Blantyre, and hitch-hiked to his several accounts: thus, the banana truck. He had sold his car. The marriage had been brief, unfriendly and faintly squalid, like the hunched-over gust of brown wind that had a moment before swept whispering past him. The divorce was a relief but something to regret.

He stopped walking. He wiped his face with a bunched hanky and read, DRINK LION – YOU WILL INJOY. Under that sign slumped a larger-than-usual native hut which gave the appearance of being supported by some six or seven Africans who leaned against it for shade. Their heads were stuck under the eaves of the overhanging brooms of roof thatch. In front there was a smaller

but more professional sign, GUINNESS FOR POWER – BIG DRUM
BAR, bearing the motif of a black fist punching jagged cartoon
lightning; a small scrawl on a pasted label warned, *No Hawking*.

Ropes of hanging beads were strung over the doorway. Calvin
pushed through them, dropped his creaking suitcase and, after
ordering a beer, fanned himself with his hat – once a fairly good
panama, now a wreck, with grubby crown and bitten brim (it was
turned down front and back like a spy's, but very dirty). The bar
was dark. When Calvin's eyes grew accustomed to the deep gloom
he saw a row of Africans staring at him. Ragged and with unsteady heads, the Africans squatted on the dirt floor. They had
wide machetes across their knees; each man balanced a pint of
Lion on his knifeblade. Calvin smiled at them. They nodded back
dark hellos.

Strangely, there was no picture of Dr Osbong in the bar. He was
the President of Malawi. It was against the law not to have his
picture in a conspicuous place in every building in the country.
Calvin had one in his office. There had been one in the bar; a nail
and a rectangle of cobwebs remained. Calvin did not mention its
absence; it was none of his business.

The bar floor gave off a ripe stable-smell and was spread with
looping rosaries of black ants. Almost immediately some ants loc-
ated Calvin's suitcase. They swarmed into the mesh of the raffia,
violating the contents. Calvin put his hat down. Leaning on the
counter's sticky rings, one fist pressed into his cheek to aim his
head at the ants, he gazed with that fatigued curiosity of strangers
to hot climates. He was gasping for breath, trickles of sweat were
running down the sides of his face, meeting at his chin and dripping on to his smudged shirtfront. A drop of sweat made its way
like an insect down his breastbone to nest in his navel.

The temperature was in the mid-eighties, but there was no sun:
it had risen and once off the ground disappeared into shapeless
grey haze. A dull sky made the day throb with sunless heat, a kind
of cookery worse than sunshine. The steamy air was a sickness;
there was no fan in the bar, no electricity in the dorp.

A dusty bottle of beer was brought and opened, so warm it spewed suds. The bartender – wearing a paper party-hat with a sweat-diluted Lion slogan on it – slipped a soda straw into the bottle.

'A glass, please.'

'No want straw?'

Straws were favoured, especially for drinking beer. Osbong said Malawi could take credit for the invention of the straw; in olden times it was a reed from a marsh, and still in the villages the common beer-pot was drunk out of by a circle of men with four-foot reed straws. 'He spits through his straw' was a local proverb. The row of squatting blacks sucking on straws, balancing their pints on their knives, lifted their eyes to Calvin.

'No want,' said Calvin. Straws gave him gas.

The bartender lifted out the straw and emptied it of beer by blowing through it hard. He replaced it in the cardboard box. Pouring Calvin a glass of beer he said, 'Happy Christmas, bwana.'

'Somehow,' said Calvin, 'it doesn't feel like Christmas. No offence intended.'

Propped on the counter a new ad from the Lion breweries showed a comical lion in a red stocking hat and white St Nick whiskers; the ad was edged in plastic holly. A small tinsel Christmas tree dangled from a twist of yellow fly-paper in the centre of the room. Dabs of cotton-wool had been carefully glued on to the smeared mirror at the back of the bar: snowflakes. Calvin wiped the creeks of sweat from his face with his hanky. Snowflakes!

He tipped his glass and drank. He enjoyed drinking; he liked the bitter sting of warm beer on his tongue, the small bubbles needling his gullet, the taste of pickled nuts, a wash of foam, and so on to yeasty fullness; four pints was a square meal. He wasn't an alcoholic; he believed beer-drinkers never were. But he was almost certainly a drunkard. It was his choice, not an affliction; it gave pleasure.

'How far to Lilongwe?' He smacked his lips.

The dozing bartender stirred. 'Lilongwe. Three–four days on bicycle.'

'How many miles?'

'Two hundred-so.' The African shrugged. 'You going that side?'

'Today, I hope. I want to get the night bus to Blantyre.' Calvin sipped his beer. 'This is my first trip north.'

'You like?'

'Very nice,' said Calvin. 'You got a nice place here.'

'Not like south,' said the African. 'No Osbong here.'

'You mean no money?' Coins the value of a shilling were called osbongs, after the head they bore.

'I am meaning,' said the African, 'no *Doctor* Osbong bastard.' He said it like the bird, 'bustard'.

Calvin went silent. He didn't talk politics, not there.

The African was staring at Calvin's glasses. 'Good goggles,' he said. 'You buying here?'

'No, I got them from the States.'

'America?'

'Yup.'

'We hate Americans,' said the African calmly. 'They kill black Negroes. Start trouble. Spy on us. Hate us too much. Just big gangsters and cowboys up to now. That their badness. Doctor Osbong say it good to trust Yankees. Myself I don't trust at all. Osbong is' – the African squinted – 'how you say *fisi* in English?'

'Hyena,' said Calvin. He put a ten-osbong note on the counter. 'Have a beer.'

'Eh!' the African kecked gratefully. 'Happy Christmas, bwana. You with those soldiers?'

'Which soldiers?'

'In the trees,' the African said.

'I'm an American,' said Calvin. 'I sell insurance – or, as you say in this neck of the woods, *assurance*.'

'God,' said the African, 'made everyone the same. I take Guinness.' He got himself a brown bottle and inserted a straw; and slurping, his lower lip rolled down showing bright pink, added, 'For power, ha-ha.'

'It's a good brew,' said Calvin. He watched the African empty the bottle.

'Good goggles,' said the African.

'Thanks.'

He had six pairs altogether, the other five in his suitcase being trodden upon by ants. Calvin dreaded losing them, breaking the pair he was wearing and not having an extra. Being in Africa heightened his fear; he had bought three pairs since arriving in Malawi a year previous (Don, the Hudson oculist, said it thrilled him to send the specs all that way). But the glasses were all he had bought. The tan wash-and-wear suit he had picked up cheap in Filene's Basement; a year of dust and sun, rain and mildew had not been kind to it. It was wrinkled, it sagged, the cuff stitches had given away, the right elbow of the jacket was torn, the knees were swollen and the kneebacks creased like accordions. The seat was dark and dead with wear, mainly the friction of sliding in and out of rides he thumbed. He wore suede shoes because they didn't need polishing; they collected stains like blotters. Calvin had a habit, when drunk, of pissing on his toes. He had worn the suit on his trip north because he thought he might get a lift more easily; but the vehicles were few, the banana truck from the frontier to Rumpi was a stroke of luck. The suit had made little difference. If anything, in the heat and now-frequent rain, it made him look less respectable. In his panama hat and grimy suit he looked like a stricken preacher. He was, of a sort: his belief was life-insurance. He was pale, tall, a stringbean.

'Merry Christmas.'

He turned. An African at the far end of the bar smiled a white mouthful of greetings. The African nodded pleasantly, revealing at his side the small head of a woman, and she was smiling too. Their clothes made Calvin feel faintly ashamed of his own. The man's shirt was clean, his collar stiff, the creases on his sleeves sharp. He wore glasses, but Calvin could tell they were fakes, the plain flat windowglass ones that were sold for five osbongs at market stalls. The young woman wore a pink dress, with ribbons and lacy borders. Man and woman crouched on stools, elbows on the bar, faces level with the straws that sprouted from their bottles: postures of alcoholic unease.

Calvin smiled back, finished his beer, and then began brushing ants from his suitcase, preparatory to leaving. The bartender appeared before him with a pint of Lion. 'Bwana? That bwana and dona saying happy Christmas to you.'

The African at the end of the bar shyly twiddled his straw and said, 'Cheers.'

Calvin walked over to him and said, 'Look, merry Christmas to you, pal, but I've got to get to Lilongwe. I'm bumming, hitching. The night bus leaves at –'

'African custom,' said the man, waving Calvin to a stool. 'Drink. Be happy. No worry.'

The smile left Calvin's face. He looked straight into the lenses of the man's toy spectacles and said softly, 'Friend, do you ever ask yourself, "Where am I going to be in ten years or so"?'

'No,' said the man.

'But I'll bet there are plenty of times when you wake up at night and ask, "What the heck am I going to do for ready cash when I'm too old to work"?'

'No work,' said the man. 'After ten years pass I still here drinking, enjoying. Why not, eh?' He smiled at the woman. She nodded.

'Let me put it another way,' said Calvin. Rephrasing had to be the insurance agent's forte. 'How would you like to have a lot of money – about, say, five hundred pounds?'

'I like,' said the man.

'You like,' said Calvin. 'Good. Now, look at this bottle of beer. It costs two osbongs. For *four* osbongs a week, the price of two of these bottles' – Calvin flicked the beer-bottle twice with his finger – 'you can take out an insurance policy that will guarantee you hundreds of pounds after ten years. Stick it out for twenty and you get five hundred, cash on the barrelhead. If nothing happens to you in the meantime. What do you say to that?'

'I get couple hundred quid,' mused the man. 'I have to work?'

'Absolutely not.'

The man smiles, his lips stretching slowly, opening to reveal a set of hard clean teeth in a perfect row.

'All you have to do,' Calvin went on, 'is pay four osbongs a week. Now let's suppose that instead of buying this beer for me you had put two osbongs here. Go ahead, put two down.'

The man pressed two coins on the counter next to the bottle. Each showed the President in profile, with a laurel branch collar.

'All right, watch me. I'm putting an osbong down next to yours. You see?' Calvin stacked the coins. 'That's the way we operate. For every *two* osbongs *you* put in *we* give you *one*. You can't lose. We help you, just like I'm doing here. It's creative saving, and the surrender value of the policy is high. Plus full protection. Are you interested?'

'In what?'

Calvin took the man hard by the upper arm and said, 'Are you interested in getting hundreds of pounds at the end of ten years, yes or no?'

'Yes,' said the man eagerly.

'Okay,' said Calvin, 'now you're talking. Put your John Hancock right here.' He took a punched card out of his inside pocket and, indicating the dotted line with an X, passed the card and a ballpoint to the man.

The man adjusted his glasses deftly, a precise but pointless gesture. He studied the card and then signed with a flourish, a large spiral, then a squiggle, several strokes and numerous dots above and below the squiggle. He underscored it boldly. It was a handsome signature.

'Now your address. There, right underneath.'

The African's face went slack. He handed the pen back to Calvin. 'Cannot.'

'What do you mean? You've got an address, haven't you?'

'Got an address, sure.' He told Calvin his box number at the dorp's post office.

'P.O. Rumpi,' said Calvin. 'Here's the pen. Write it down.'

'Cannot write.'

'Well, what the hell,' Calvin tapped the signature, 'is that?'

'My name,' said the man.

'That,' the woman spoke up. She was very pretty, very young,

371

with a small round head and a cap of short hair. She wrinkled her nose and smiled and continued. 'That not name. That just –' She lifted long fingers and fluttered them to signify aimless writing. 'It look like name. But,' she smiled and dropped her eyes, 'that not name. That *signature*.'

'I see, I see, I see.' said Calvin. He filled in the man's address and printed the man's name in block letters, Ogilvie Nirenda. He grinned at his client, Ogilvie. 'Now you leave everything to me. I'll send you envelopes, reminders and the whole policy. But for God's sake remember,' Calvin preached, 'instead of buying that beer or that pack of cigarettes, or that new tie or whatever, put those osbongs aside. You'll be a rich man if you do. If you find yourself wanting a beer – *resist! resist!*' Calvin grasped the man's hand and shook it twice. 'Welcome to Homemakers',' he said. Calvin was pleased; and it wasn't the thought of the commish.

'Have a beer,' said the African.

It was ungracious to refuse the drink. It was dangerous not to buy the man a drink in return; people were killed for less. The man insisted on filling Calvin's glass. Calvin, the man reminded him, was a guest, not in the bar, but in the country. Dr Osbong was a socialist, and socialism was sharing beer. 'So,' Ogilvie smiled gently, 'don't go away. Buy me a drink.'

2

Two miles south of Rumpi a cool soldier named Marais watched the road through a pair of binoculars. He crouched hidden in tussocks of grass and dusty bushes on a high shelf-like bluff of red laterite. Behind him a dozen soldiers, black men in khaki, were dug in, flopped in formation on their stomachs like a stranded school of fish. A car passed below on the road. Dust-clouds pouring from the back wheels hovered just behind it in a high curling swell, threatening to engulf the vehicle.

'I give him a puncture yes,' said Brother Chimanga, who lay close to Marais. He peered seriously into the eyepiece of the telescopic sight on his carbine.

'Leave it,' said Marais. 'It's not him. It's the Indian. We know where he's going.'

'Small puncture, so he not forget.' Brother Chimanga locked a shell into the chamber and took aim.

Letting his binoculars fall, Marais grasped the tubular sight and used it as a handle to wrench the rifle from the African. With his right hand he hammered the African on the neck, forcing his face into the red dust; and when the African could not see or move – he was pinned to the ground – Marais took his knife away.

'No,' said Marais, coughing on the dust he had raised, 'don't be stupid.' He let the African up.

They knelt before each other, breathing deeply. The African, Brother Chimanga, humiliated in front of the others, flexed his fists and spat. Dust was sprinkled on his long eyelashes and it powdered his cheeks. Glaring at each other in confounded anger, they did not see the car disappear over a hill, though they heard the puttering engine shut out by the trees. Neither did they see that the sun was setting, the car plunging with a buzz distantly into it. It was half-past six, the spectacle of the sun rehearsing its disappearance usual in Malawi: the sun did not drop whole and round behind the earth, but rather broke like an egg low in the sky and slipped apart, making a fiery bloody omelette at the sharp rim of the sky's base. It was this wide thing – not the sun – that set, scrap by bright scrap.

Marais ejected the live shell from the carbine and tossed the empty rifle back to Brother Chimanga, saying, 'Don't ever do that again.'

Brother Chimanga did not reply. He brushed the dust from the oily wood of the stock with stiffened fingers.

'Brother George, you stay behind. If you see him, give us a whistle.' Marais found his cap. He clapped the dust from it and put it on, pulling the peak down. And surveying the road again casually, he lit a cigar. 'Let's go,' he said finally. 'Everyone up.'

They trooped through the stunted trees along a sandy path, Marais in the lead wiping the dust from his binoculars with a red pocket-handkerchief. Two men stayed at Marais's sides, the rest followed behind in a single column. They were all sizes, some very small, quick-marching to keep up with the long strides of the others, with shirt-cuffs doubled over thickly and oversized trousers drawn together in bunched folds at their waists with knotted rope, like sack-tops, and wearing clomping boots to their knees which fitted only because they were padded with balled-up newspaper. The two soldiers near Marais were tall and powerfully built, in close-fitting uniforms, their rifles propped menacingly forward as they strode along the path. All the men wore a red daisy in the buttonhole of their shirt pocket. Brother Chimanga's daisy drooped.

At the rough thornbush fence that marked the edge of the encampment they were met by a young sentry. He dragged his boots together, pounded his rifle butt on the ground and saluted, his forearm horizontal across his stomach, fingers touching the muzzle.

Marais stopped. He said, 'Do that again.'

The sentry saluted again, now with doubting slowness, sucking his lower lip as he did so. His large eyes were fixed on Marais.

'Who taught you to do that?' Marais walked up to the sentry whose arm trembled uncertainly and fell to his side. Marais spoke angrily to the men. 'Who taught him to do that?'

'What he do?' asked one of the tall soldiers.

'He saluted, goddamit!' Marais rubbed his moustache with the back of his fist. He straightened his shoulders. 'That man,' he said, shaking his cigar at the sentry, 'that man saluted to me! I want to know where he learned to do it.'

'Is coming night and we —'

'Shut up,' said Marais, 'this is serious. Somebody here is teaching these men to salute, and I don't like it.' Marais leaned close to the bewildered sentry and said, '*Don't salute!* Don't do this.' He demonstrated a foolish salute. 'You understand? Nobody salutes in this army. We don't have any officers. You're the same as him and him. If anyone tells you to do that you tell him *voetsak!* You hear?'

The sentry nodded uncertainly.

'I don't think he understands,' said Marais. 'Brother Mussa, translate what I said.'

Marais walked on to a shelter at the centre of the clearing, cursing the sentry under his breath and biting on his cigar. A hundred times he had told them: no insignia, no promotions, therefore no saluting. They were all equals; the fighting was done by everyone; everything was shared. It was a people's army, they fought together. Only loyalty mattered; the country was to be liberated, Osbong and his henchmen killed. The men needed no orders to shoot the corrupt, certainly no commands to act together. It was natural and inevitable that they should revolt.

On these principles three months previous in a camp on the Songwe River, in the far north of Malawi, Marais had armed his men and started marching south. The principles had proved assumptions: they needed correction. Unexpected things were happening, of which the sentry's salute was only one instance;

Chimanga's impulse to shoot the tyres of the Indian's car was another. And there were more, slight but disturbing. The younger men reported bullying. The men who habitually marched beside Marais asked for special insignia, and they complained because they had to eat with the youths. As it was, at meal-time they separated into age-groups.

'This not happen in village,' one of the older men said when Marais ordered them to eat together.

'You're not in a village now,' Marais had replied. 'If you want to live like that you have no business here.' And Mussa had translated to them all.

They competed for privilege, there were quarrels, and some men tried to dominate. At the same time, possibly because these few sought domination, others disclaimed all responsibility and lately at night had begun terrorizing the villagers in Rumpi. There were beatings and thefts. Marais had found the culprits and had them locked up. But he was hesitant to order a whipping: giving the order indicated a degree of authority he did not want to assume. It was not his intention to boss them.

Terrorism was part of Marais's programme. It was to be swift, selective, instructive – always against politicians and party hacks, never villagers, no matter how loyal to Osbong they seemed. They could be convinced. Local villagers were invited to join the terrorism with his men; they were welcomed in the camp. But the policy of violence, which was an extreme measure, was as difficult to explain to the villagers as to his men. Violence for them was a problem's complete solution; it had no limits. They saw it in terms of an ordeal: death was the proof of guilt, and was its own punishment.

In the first month Marais mistook their recklessness for courage. They had seemed brave: ignoring all risks they had rushed police stations, capturing weapons and a stock of gelignite, and they had sacked and burned the customs post at Fort Hill, on the northern frontier. A truck was commandeered and so was one party chairman's new French car. But that, Marais decided, was far from courage: it was simple thoughtlessness. It was the confusion of the shy egomaniac, one who is paralysed by reflection. Their strength was subject to changes of mood. Marais had seen them ponder a move and then shrink back. They refused to fight alone; they would only scout in numbers. They took no conscious risks. Acting out of ignorance, they ridiculed the discipline of strategy; without meeting resistance their attacks had deteriorated into fanaticism, nothing more.

That they had over-run the entire northern province as far as Rumpi had made them irresponsible; the possibility of power had intensified their bullying. Some had taken lovers at knife-point. Others had looted shops and cached the goods for themselves. Their whims with this new power became obsessions and, ungenerous, they killed or crippled. They were traced and made to explain. But they had not been punished severely. It had been enough, Marais had thought, for them to see their wrong. He had hoped to awaken the slumbering conscience. He had come a long way by a painful route to set these people free. He found it intolerable that all the risks were his.

He pumped and lighted his pressure lamp and carried it across the camp to a low hut. A soldier sitting cross-legged at the locked hut door stood when Marais spoke to him.

'Open it up,' said Marais.

Inside, a wick burned in a dish of kerosene, illuminating the faces of the thieves on the floor. Marais beckoned them out.

The men were barefoot, their uniforms were wrinkled and stank of kerosene. Their belts had been taken away. They stood before Marais holding their trousers in place with their hands. Marais raised his lamp. They squinted at its brightness, then glanced at the guard and at Marais suspiciously. Two weeks' detention in the hut hadn't changed them much. One yawned into his shoulder like a cat, still holding his trousers. Far from punished, they looked fed and content and, though stupefied by the fumes, well-rested.

'Give them their rifles,' said Marais. He walked away quickly, leaving his lamp and avoiding the cooking fires so that no one would see his anger.

Drink was traded for drink. The African had begun it, only the African could end it. Calvin was a guest. In the evening, in smoky lantern light, Calvin became uneasy, and his unease, his impatience and panic made him rude. Ogilvie was talking to him, blah-blah-blah, but Calvin wasn't listening and wasn't even looking at the fellow or his wife. He drank desperately, quickly, looking into his glass and at his watch and into the little cotton blizzard on the mirror at the back of the bar, his tired and drunkenly lip-smacking face showing through the phoney flakes like a sick phantom perspiring in a snowstorm. He missed his turn buying the beers, Ogilvie paid twice in a row; and then in what was simple panic he turned his back on Ogilvie, threw the bead-strings aside and looked out the bar door.

He felt woe deeper than dread.

He saw blackness, pure jungly blackness, thick and woolly. It did not stop after a mile or two. It extended for two hundred miles where it was pierced by a few lamps in Lilongwe; it continued for another hundred to Blantyre and a few more lamps, and it wasn't interrupted by light again until somewhere in Mozambique or Swaziland. Night had fallen while they had been drinking. The darkness was a net, flung over willing victims. Somewhere near the bar the dark night was being celebrated with a thumpy-thumpy of drums. But no one bothered to disperse it with a bulb. There was no juice.

And there was no place to stay in the dorp. It was Calvin's second night on the road. The first he had spent on the frontier, which was a burned-out shambles, not a soul in sight. He had slept under a table, wrapped in a big canvas wall map, and had shivered until dawn. Calvin still stood with his back to his hosts; he peered into the darkness. There were huts beyond the road, he knew. There always were. He knew those huts: windowless, stuffed with urchins, and stinking of woodsmoke, old food and damp clothes, worm turds and dog hairs littering the earthen hut floor between the crush of sleeping places. In a country filled with sun in the daytime and cool air in the evening, people crawled into huts and decrepit little bars, curling up in the dirt. It was not a recent impulse. These places were cool, but that was not the point. It was resignation; they were uninsured.

Calvin sensed his panic leave; the bird which had been flapping on his shoulder took wing. He felt eased, lighter, unworried all of a sudden. His nerves had been rinsed by the warm suds of the beer. He was fully drunk now (he tottered in the doorway): reason left his hands and feet, they felt like large turnips. Now he was out of the bar, swaying in the middle of the main street of the dorp, under the stars, pissing on his toes. He did not have the foggiest idea of what was going to happen next, and he did not care. He went inside, then thought, parted the bead-strings and spat. He was happy. He loved being in a place where you could spit where you pleased and piss by the door.

With silly vigour he clinked Ogilvie's glass with his own, hitting unnecessarily hard and shouting 'Merry Christmas, merry Christmas' much too loudly and finally smashing his glass to bits. He stood there in the half-gloom of the bar, sweating booze, holding only the bottom half of his glass, a little crazy cup of up-turned teeth, while all the beer ran down into his sleeve and collected in a slurpy puddle inside the elbow of his jacket.

'Oh my God, I'm sorry,' said Calvin, so drunk and so polite that he sounded like someone new to English. He was so extremely attentive to his slow apology that in his contrition he stepped on Ogilvie's foot and knocked the lady's glass into her lap.

'Christ Almighty, look what I've done to your wife!'

Ogilvie insisted it was nothing and signalled to the bartender to bring another bottle.

Abjectly, Calvin put his finger into his mouth and bit down hard, all the while uttering hurried apologies through the finger as if through a flute. This calmed him and he said, 'I'm sorry about this, Ogilvie, but I'm drunk as a skunk. I should have been out of here hours ago.' He picked up his suitcase and began dragging it to the door. 'Don't worry about a thing. I'll be sending you reminders about your premiums and so forth. Tell your wife I'm sorry. I couldn't look her in the eye after what I've just done to her, really I couldn't –'

'Please,' said Ogilvie, 'wait.'

Calvin gently fought him off with his free hand, but it was no good. He was in the road outside and Ogilvie was still with him, hugging him and being dragged along, bumping against the raffia suitcase. Calvin tried to run; it was like struggling underwater.

'Get off, sir,' said Calvin, hitting Ogilvie gingerly on the shoulder with the flat of his hand. 'You got your insurance. You're all set. I'm going now – good-bye and good luck.'

'You cannot,' said Ogilvie. 'You have to stay. Lilongweside too far, and listen,' he said earnestly, snatching at Calvin's hand, 'that lady not my dona. That my sister, same mother, same father, and –'

'Yes?' Calvin stopped. He saw that he had gained only ten feet with Ogilvie attached to his leg.

'She *like* you, sir.'

'She does?' Calvin put down his suitcase and turned his back on the jungle.

'Oh, yes, too much! She want you come home with her, enjoy and what-not. You like, sir?'

Calvin looked up. She was standing there in the doorway, holding the bead-strings open. The lantern behind her, just that feeble light, shone through what could only have been a very thin dress, for Calvin could see the girl's dark uncluttered shape sharply defined, with a light frock thrown around it. One hand was on her hip, which was slung sideways in a pose of impatience, and her feet were apart.

4

Calvin stepped on a soft pillow-shaped thing. It let out a little squawk of protest and shifted sideways. The girl said it was her brother and that there were more in the room. She did not say how many more. But Calvin discovered there were three little boys sleeping on the floor of the room: after a short time one asked in the darkness why his sister was making so much noise and if she was all right. And when the sister, at that question, became quiet – held her breath, in fact – one boy struck a match. He held it, his eyes goggling, in Calvin's white face even after his sister screamed for him to blow it out.

In the morning when Calvin woke the little boys were gone. There were three stained flour sacks where they had been. The girl snored beside him on the narrow cot, curled up, sleeping with her arms folded across her breasts, her legs poised like a cyclist's. The room, half the hut, was a low oven of musty odours, crammed with broken crates and poor blankets and misshapen clothes. A small prison window which was not square had been cut high on one wall; a rag was tacked over it. Calvin shifted himself to a sitting position. The girl groaned, stopped snoring, but did not wake. On the far wall was a calendar, a year out of date, with a highly coloured picture of a little blonde girl in a party dress playing with a fluffy kitten in a studio garden. The calendar advertised Jaganathy's Madras Bazaar and listed provisions.

That calendar picture on the mud wall of the hut annoyed Calvin even more than the other picture in the room, Dr Osbong, nailed to the door. It was the official picture of the President, the kind missing in the Big Drum Bar; it was sold by the local party branches. It showed Osbong in a fur hat bristling with rat-tails, a carefully beaded collar, tinted glasses and his old school tie (Fort Hare, '21). The business end of a fly-whisk was visible in the lower left of the picture. One side of Osbong's mouth drooped in what seemed to be a snarl. It was not a snarl, but a facial tic caught in a wild contraction by a quick camera, the side of the lower lip drawn down to reveal a sharp yellow tooth. It was the picture taken in the States on the occasion of Brandeis University awarding him the honorary degree of Doctor of Humane Letters. Before then he had been called *Ngwazi*, conqueror, because he had negotiated Malawi's independence. After Brandeis he was Doctor. He was the country's first and only president. He was seldom seen except through the thick windows of his Rolls. The legend under the picture read, *They call me a Dictator! If I am, then I am a Dictator for the People, by the People and of the People – Hon. Dr Hastings K. Osbong.*

In a year Calvin had seen him twice, once speeding past his office behind a raucous sound-truck and a lorryload of police, once at a political rally. Calvin had heard him often blustering over the radio about foreign aid ('I would go to the Devil himself to get help'), about Malawi ('What did we Africans do to deserve such a poor place to live?'), about the whites ('One white man can do the work of ten Africans, as you know very well, my people'), about a cabinet minister who attempted a *coup* two months after independence ('I want him brought back alive. If not alive, then any other way'). Any success, a big peanut harvest or a generous loan, pleased him to the extent that he would sing five verses of 'Bringing in the Sheaves' over Malawi Radio. Failure made his facial tic very severe. Local settlers called him 'the twitch doctor'. He was an elder of the Church of Scotland and hated by every other African president; he knew his way around *Debrett's Peerage*, and in the group photograph at the annual Commonwealth Conference he was always seated next to the Queen.

The face in the official photograph suggested a man eating. But it was black and battered, and it seemed appropriate in the little mud room. The chubby little blonde girl on Jaganathy's calendar offended Calvin. He felt pity for the Africans, the little black boys crouching on their flour sacks in the hut looking up at it, probably envying her and her fat pet. He pitied them all in their huts, snoring on their dusty beds, crawling tediously through a rubble of damp rags in a little jungle slum. Only the thought of insurance kept him from despair, as it would keep them.

He swung his legs over the side of the cot and looked for his trousers and shoes. It was only a little after eight, but already he had broken out into a heavy mucky sweat. His neck ached, his ankles were stung with mosquito bites. When he stood and stretched the girl woke up. She looked sleepily at him, then shook her head and said fiercely, 'Where you going?'

'Outside,' said Calvin, picking his undershirt from his sticky skin. 'What's wrong with that?'

The girl shouted something to the door. There was a knock. The door creaked open and one of the small boys entered on his knees. Drawing the sheet across her nakedness, the girl spoke to the kneeling boy in a bark incomprehensible to Calvin. He knew few words of Chinyanja, the national language: mostly greetings, and the words for money, good and beer. The girl said to Calvin, 'Go him.'

Calvin found his trousers knotted at the foot of the cot where he had leaped out of them; and under them his shoes. One sock was missing. He felt too sweaty to grovel around looking for it. He slipped on his suedes without socks but with great care: once in a hut he had found mice nesting in his shoes. And there were stories of scorpions.

The little boy beckoned him outside and led him to a narrow stall of bamboo secured with bits of string. Calvin entered; the little boy stood outside. The smell in the latrine was so powerful that in the blast of early-morning sun Calvin felt faint. He slapped at the large flies which, strafing the rocky floor, were making a buzz as loud as an electric shaver. Calvin left with his bladder still full and headed for a clump of high grass. Again the little boy stood guard, his back to Calvin.

The boy's presence inhibited what was usually a pleasure, but with determination Calvin let fly, bending the blades with his jet. When he finished he said, 'Do you speak English?'

'Yes, bwana.'

'Don't call me bwana.'

'Yes, master.'

'How are you?' Calvin spoke slowly.

'And I am quite well, sir, and hoping you,' said the little boy in a hoarse nervous voice.

'I don't believe you know English,' said Calvin.

'I do know and speak,' said the little boy.

'All right then, what's your name?'

'My name,' said the little boy, 'is Richard.'

'And what's your sister's name?'

'My sister name Mira.'

Calvin repeated the name and thanked the boy; he had found out what he wanted, the name of the girl he had made love to.

Later he was brought an enamel bowl with a cake of yellow soap in it. He tried the name; it was not challenged. Mira poured tepid water from a pitcher while Calvin splashed his face. It was ritual washing: the water was brown, the process turned grit into slime. Calvin felt filthy when he was done. He wiped his face with his shirt and without preliminaries asked, 'Why did you tell your brother to follow me?'

'Bad people here,' said Mira.

'So what?'

'My English not –' She smiled and called Ogilvie.

'Bad people here?' Calvin asked Ogilvie.

'In the trees,' said Ogilvie with authority. 'It not good walking here alone. Make trouble and noonsense.'

'Soldiers?'

'Some soldiers. With *bunduki*, pistoli, what-not. They are saving us,' said Ogilvie.

There had been talk in Blantyre; Calvin had been warned to take care. But he had checked with the Ministry of Information and they had denied everything. The *Time* magazine was late; it was hard to know what the rumours were without it. Trouble, some people said; and one man had said, 'The north is a complete shambles.'

'What are they saving you from?'

Ogilvie did not know.

'They kill people?'

'Sometimes,' said Ogilvie.

'Their leader,' said Calvin, 'he's an African?'

Ogilvie smiled and winked through his fake glasses. He wore a striped sarong, which he adjusted as he spoke, and an undershirt and plastic sandals. 'He is a white man, like you. Tough. Eats fruit from the bush and small animals and sleeps just under trees or anywhere. But he can go with no eating food or sleeping. Bullets do this, *pung*!' Ogilvie slapped his chest imitating a bullet bouncing off. 'He is going to kill Osbong, people say. He will kill you too, anybody.'

'Well, that's too bad,' said Calvin, 'because I'm leaving here.'

'And me,' said Ogilvie, 'I am leaving here. It is a nice place to leave.'

'Not live,' said Calvin, 'leave. I'm going.'

'No go,' said Ogilvie, becoming truculent. 'You stay.'

'I have to get to Lilongwe –'

'No bus. It Christmas. Stay here.'

'He no like us,' said Mira, pouting.

'No!' Calvin looked at her and shook his head. 'That's not true. I like you both, but I can't stay. I have business to do.'

'It Christmas,' said Ogilvie.

'I *know* it's Christmas,' said Calvin. But he hadn't known until Ogilvie reminded him. He said angrily, 'Merry Christmas.'

'Give us Christmas present,' said Ogilvie.

Calvin was being watched: the three little boys, another taller goofy-looking one standing at the side and taking licks at a dish, and an old woman who seemed to be wearing two or three long dresses, one over the other. All their heads were shaved. They stared at Calvin, with Mira and Ogilvie.

Calvin took out his wallet. That was a mistake, but it was too late to conceal it. They watched him flick off a beetle; they watched him part it to reveal folded bills. Calvin attempted to extract a single bill without disturbing the others; they seemed to understand. Calvin tugged impatiently to get it over with, but too hard: all the bills came loose and fluttered to the ground at the feet of the Africans like the dead petals from a large blossom. The dishlicker dropped his dish. The boy called Richard knelt, gathered them up and, still kneeling before Calvin, crumpled them into a ball and handed the ball to Calvin.

They settled for one apiece, although Mira and Ogilvie thought they should get more. Calvin tried to be firm; Ogilvie insisted on more; Calvin promised him another gift in the afternoon. The whole operation cost four pounds, ten osbongs, or roughly (Calvin figured rapidly) thirteen bucks. He had never spent that much on his wife on either of the two Christmases they were together. That thought pleased him: it was a charitable way of getting even with her.

And they gave Calvin a present: a fur hat, much like Dr Osbong's, but with fewer rat-tails (the number denoted rank). Calvin wore it for their Christmas drink, a yellow quart-sized Shell Oil-can brimful of local beer. They passed it from mouth to mouth. The beer was thick, soupy, very bitter, an alcoholic porridge which could have been consumed with a fork. Calvin was allowed to finish it after everyone had had a swig. He did so with a leaden feeling in his feet. Then had another.

They all drank. They drank for breakfast and lunch. They drank, they said, because Calvin had arrived and given them cash and it was Christmas. Calvin, sweating in his fur hat, remarked on the heat but said, 'It's a dry kind of heat.' They drank on that. They drank to make themselves sleepy, and slept. They awoke and drank to alert themselves. They sang and drank some more. Other villagers dropped by and drank a good deal out of nervousness for the white man who was quite drunk and pretty dirty, but friendly. They drank out of the common beer-pot, drooling through their straws.

The local brew was gone in the afternoon and they switched to local gin, *kachasu* unrefined, which (poisonous, colourless, viscous) looked and tasted like witch-hazel. It passed down Calvin's gullet like razorblades, leaving slashes in his throat. Calvin's belly had been sourly filled by the beer; now it was on fire with the gin. Gulping the gin in tots from a tumbler, they praised drink, America and Dr Osbong ('To Hastings!' Calvin said incautiously). There was an argument about Osbong, and a fight. Two men rolled on the ground, kicking and punching wildly, but soon they rolled away and the drinking went on. Late in the afternoon the drink was gone. Ogilvie appeared beside Calvin; he grinned and pulled the cork out of a bottle of crimson cough mixture.

'What I need,' said Calvin, 'is a couple of pints of Lion to fix me up.' Mira and the old lady were sent to the Big Drum Bar for some bottles. Drunkenly wagging his finger in their faces, Calvin said they should buy the beer with his Christmas present. They hurried off with baskets.

Calvin faced Ogilvie and discovered himself speechless and slightly panicky. Without a drink there was nothing to say. Calvin felt as if someone had ripped out all his bones, leaving sick flesh. It would be dark soon, another day gone. The feelings of pity he had experienced in the confined hut, in the narrow cot, were being crowded by thoughts of flight. He felt captive and watched; they apparently did not want him to leave. It could go on for days. His wallet was almost empty and he had few valuables. They thought he was rich. He had little more than his six pairs of glasses.

'I have a present for you, Ogilvie,' Calvin slurred.

The raffia suitcase was shoved under the cot. Calvin rummaged through it and found his darkest pair of prescription sunglasses. Perhaps suspecting a trick, Ogilvie lingered in the doorway. He grunted and sat heavily on the ground when Calvin leaned toward him.

'Merry Christmas,' said Calvin, grinning. 'Straight from the USA. Here it is.' He offered the glasses in an imitation alligator-hide case, snapped shut. 'Have a look, you lucky dog.'

Ogilvie thumped and bashed the case, but found it impossible to open. There was not much time. Calvin pulled it away and fought with the little button.

'Beautiful,' cooed Calvin, finally popping the case open.

They were expensive ones, with French frames and dark lenses for the equatorial sun, and thick for Calvin's astigmatic eyes. The lenses had cost thirty dollars alone, the frames with the wide bows another twenty-five.

'Nice goggles,' said Ogilvie. He caressed them and put them on, and stumbled.

'Look in the mirror,' said Calvin.

Ogilvie entered the hut by the door on the right. Calvin sprang through the left-hand door, snatched up his panama and his jacket, grabbed his suitcase and dashed outside.

Ogilvie was also outside. Calvin had not counted on a portable mirror. But there it was, Ogilvie was holding it before his sightless eyes.

'Cannot see,' he murmured.

'Hold it closer,' said Calvin, tip-toeing to the edge of the clearing. Cupping his hands around his mouth and shouting, thinking it would make him sound near, he called, *'Closer!'*

The mirror was against his captor's nose.

Calvin ran, the suitcase banging against his legs. He charged headlong into dense bush, crashed against trees and lost his hat. He changed direction. He crossed a little bare patch, a compound with two tired huts and a dozing family. Their dog tore after him. The family awoke to see in the twilight a tall *mzungu* in a grubby suit and goggles flinging himself past their hut.

The bush thinned out. Calvin was certain the road was close and with the road a bus, a car, another banana truck. Or he could walk. He wanted only to be away, and he knew that in a matter of minutes (his bejesused mind whirred) he could be. He found a path and followed it. Running became easier. He jogged, and all at once his glasses steamed up.

He slapped to a halt, took them off and wiped them with his sleeve and his fingers. When he put them back on he saw through the streaks two figures standing before him on the path. One was Mira. She had a pint of Lion in her hand which she raised. Calvin could not lift his arms quickly enough to stop her; they were drunk and slow. He said no, loudly.

Mira was not tall. She could not reach the top of Calvin's skull. She slammed the bottle against the side, just behind his ear and he fell, sat rather, on the path. The bottle didn't break, but it knocked his glasses off; Mira whispered, 'We want you,' and he was defeated.

'Today,' said Ogilvie, lowering his head through the doorway and peering over the top of his new sunglasses, 'it Boxing Day.'

'Who's fighting?' asked Calvin. He was groggy, barely awake; he felt the painful throb of his pulse in the bump behind his ear. He rolled over on to his side, nearly shaking the cot to pieces and squeezing the other sleeper – she who had raised the bump – against the mud-daubed wall.

'No one fighting,' was Ogilvie's answer.

Calvin looked up. Ogilvie's hand was out, palm upward, fingers scratching the air avariciously.

'Give him box,' came a whisper from the wall.

'I'm leaving,' said Calvin without feeling. 'Have to get that bus.' He yawned and rubbed his eyes.

'Boxing Day. No buses on Boxing Day,' said Ogilvie. 'Give me box, bwana.'

'I gave you a Christmas present – *two* Christmas presents!'

'For Christmas. But today,' Ogilvie smiled, 'today Boxing Day. Give.' His scratching fingers beckoned.

Calvin shook a pound out of his wallet and handed it without rising from the cot to Ogilvie, who saluted his thanks by touching a finger to the side of his sunglasses. Before he left, Ogilvie smacked Mira's ankle and said, 'She pretty, eh? She like you too much. And me, I like English people.'

'I'm not English.'

'No? Too bad.' Ogilvie's good humour was renewed by the money. He became helpful. 'You want to pass water? I go with you to the latrine. You want?'

'Get out,' said Calvin. 'And close the door.'

Ogilvie smiled, saluted again, and was gone.

'Give me,' said Mira, 'give me.'

With speed, his head rapping, Calvin turned Mira on to her back, lifted and parted her legs, cupped her cool bottom and entered her snugness in a single thrust. Mira arched; her slim arms reached in a praise-gesture for his hair, as if she was making an offering to a hut spirit. Calvin took her by the wrists, rode her for seconds, until his loins sneezed and he fell. She had scarcely realized what was happening when Calvin handed her twenty osbongs and asked her quietly to go. She did so, dazed, wrapping herself in a long cloth and shutting the door after her.

Word got out that Calvin was distributing cash. The rest came and got theirs, the three little boys, the tall goofy one, the old lady: they entered the hut on their knees and took their money, heads bowed, with two hands. Calvin told them to stand up. They wouldn't; each left shuffling backwards awkwardly, still kneeling. Calvin bolted the door when the old lady left.

There was more knocking, villagers, relatives perhaps, looking for presents. But Calvin had paid off the immediate family; he did not feel obliged to pay the whole village. He wanted desperately to leave. For the time being he knew he could not. Before he had assumed that to do so would have been impolite, offensive to their hospitality: they would be hurt. Now he knew it was dangerous; he would be hurt: they would savage him if he tried to leave.

He could stay. Lying in the cot he had a vision of how it would be if he did stay a few more days. He would drink with them, learn a little bit of their language, settle into their life. After weeks passed in this way his clothes would fall off his back and he would change those rags for a sarong, his suedes for plastic sandals. Mira would work in the fields. If the crops failed they would force him to buy bags of mealies. He would father a few children, not as black as Mira nor as white as he, but probably the colour of Mister Bones, the minstrel, a browny glow. He would insure them all and set up an agency in Rumpi for Homemakers' Mutual. All the while the whole extended family would be extracting money; but they would consult him on village decisions. He would die there, of drink or fever, and they would scrape a shallow hole under a tree, roll him in and heap up the mound with rocks and plant a little cross. Later they would spin yarns about him, in their homely droning fashion, making that long visit a simplicity: Once there was a white man who passed this way. And he gave us much money and fell in love with the beautiful Mira who bore him three strong . . .

Or were they making him their slave?

Calvin was not sure. He was positive he wasn't exploiting them. They seemed to need a chief very badly. They were treating him well. But he was paying, and they were making up excuses for him to stay: holidays, villains in the trees. A chief was at the mercy of his subjects; their pain was his suffering.

He dressed, went outside and was accompanied by Ogilvie and Richard to the high grass. Then he drank, sitting with his fur hat on, in the place of honour, in the only chair (a stuffed but badly bruised settee), while the others squatted around him and sat at his feet. They stole for him: a glass from the Big Drum Bar, an umbrella from a neighbouring hut (it rained at noon), a hen because he asked for something to eat and they had nothing. They found his panama hat and returned it. Mira had washed his shirt in a wifely way. She buttoned it on him. Calvin, with the Shell Oil-can full of beer in his hand, watched her fussing over him and decided it was cruel to stay. He would escape and leave no trace. It was enough to insure and go; he had done them some good; staying would undo it. His presence misled them: he didn't want to be their chief.

With more drink the mood that afternoon became by turns polite and threatening, one embarrassing, the other scary, for they made no bones about demanding money from him. They put their hands out and bulged their eyes at him in a belligerent way: and they began calling him *nduna*, chief. Twice during the afternoon of Boxing Day Ogilvie promised Calvin bodily harm; once he did so with a rusty dagger. He swished at the air blindly with the weapon, his sunglasses obscuring his vision. Calvin was terrified and ran to a tree. His mind knitted the several possibilities of escape; the question of being an ungrateful guest no longer troubled him, their anger would have to be faced. It was dangerous to go, but it was death to stay. Ogilvie clung to his dagger. Calvin decided to duck out at nightfall.

'Wait!' Calvin called out from behind the tree. He fully intended to climb it if Ogilvie's aim improved. He forced a ghastly laugh. 'I have an idea. Let's all celebrate – get back, Ogilvie, put your knife down – celebrate Boxing Day at the Big Drum. I'll buy some beer, we'll get some straws –'

Ogilvie dropped his dagger.

'Go Big Drum?'

'Why not?' said Calvin. He held his breath; his eyes asked for assurance.

'Why not, why not,' said Ogilvie. He kicked off his sandals and ran into his side of the hut to change his clothes. Mira did likewise. Somewhere in the hut mice and mildew did not reach. There Ogilvie and Mira kept their Sunday best. Ogilvie's shirt was spotless, his collar stiff, his silk tie in a thick neat knot. Mira's dress was the same, the pink wrapper with lace which in sunlight gave glimpses of her body's angles. She wore a turban around her head, a gay one, with enough pink to match the dress. Her gold earrings were large gypsy hoops which jangled and promised pleasure. Calvin noticed her eyes were hooded, almost Chinese. She held her slim neck perfectly straight, her excellent posture from a girlhood of carrying hefty objects on her head in marked contrast to Ogilvie's. He had carried nothing, and slouched.

Calvin's suit was in an advanced state of decay; on his sockless feet were mildewed suedes; the weaving ravelled on the brim of his panama; his lenses were specked. He had not shaved for three days. His hands were clean because he had eaten wet, rather abrasive food with them. In one trouser pocket he had the price of three beers, no more; in the others his remaining pairs of glasses, a toothbrush, five nicked anti-malaria tablets. His shirt was stuffed with insurance leaflets, some brochures and the details of another new account, whose quarterly premium had been extorted over the two holidays. He knew he could not flee encumbered. He left his raffia suitcase behind and in it a twisted tube of toothpaste, a hairy razor, one sock, some dirty laundry and a very dirty Michelin map of Central and Southern Africa.

There was trouble at the Big Drum when they arrived. A tall African who had been standing outside under the eaves of the building followed Calvin in and demanded a Boxing Day present. He put an empty glass in front of Calvin. He said, 'Fill up.'

'You no give him,' said Mira.

Calvin wanted to calm the man. He started to fill the man's glass. Mira knocked the bottle away, spilling the beer down the front of Calvin's suit jacket. She turned to the man and told him sharply in the vernacular to get stuffed.

And 'You noonsense,' said Ogilvie to the man.

The man leaned over and spat into Mira's beerglass.

Calvin quickly exchanged glasses with Mira. He said, 'He didn't mean it,' hopefully.

The man growled.

'Hit him!' said Mira to Calvin. 'He did spit! Beat him!'

'I couldn't do a thing like that,' said Calvin. He tried to smile at the man, but his smile was that squinting grimace of a person swallowing hard: it threatened. He put his hand out in friendship. The man gripped himself about the stomach where he guessed Calvin was going to land his punch, and he backed away and out of the bar.

'Tough guy,' said Ogilvie.

Calvin nodded and then uttered the sentence he had been rehearsing since they left the little hut, 'I have to pass water.'

The sun was dropping. Every evening, just after sunset, there was an hour of complete darkness; it ended when the moon rose and the stars blinked on, but while it lasted it was perfect and hid even the ground beneath one's feet. Calvin planned to flee into that darkness and hope for the best; he could crouch in it until the night bus passed. As long as he had an extra pair of glasses he needed no busfare.

'Okay,' said Ogilvie. 'I go with you.'

Calvin could not look Ogilvie in the eye. His trick was a cheap one; Ogilvie was a sucker for theatrics. He looked instead at Mira, so lovely, here in a place where love was simple. What had he done to her? *We want you*, she had said; how was he to explain that it was not fair to them, that he had business?

'Listen. I am going to pass water,' said Calvin, uncomfortable to hear two foreigners speak to each other in poor English for his benefit.

'There are people here,' Ogilvie said to Mira. 'They kill him.'

'I'm a tough guy,' said Calvin, removing his jacket. 'Just going out back, you see? To make water.' Calvin pointed through the beaded doorway to a black tangle of trees in which the last of the sunset was snared; an orange beam lingered. 'And to prove it, here's my jacket.' He shook the jacket out and folded it on the bar. Then he took off his glasses. 'And my glasses. I can't run away without my glasses, ha-ha, can I?'

'Watch too,' said Ogilvie.

'Not the watch,' said Calvin quickly. 'But how about a nice toothbrush?' He placed that with his glasses on the jacket. He was glad to be rid of the toothbrush, a Portuguese one he had bought in Blantyre, pig's bristles set in yellow bone.

Ogilvie grunted.

'This is what we call security in the insurance game. You keep this stuff just to make sure I'm coming back. I have to come back to get it, see?' Calvin spoke, backing to the door. 'And when I come back you have to give them to me, right? So don't think you can keep them. Bartender, three more beers! I'll be right back!'

Calvin went outside and listened to the bottles being opened. He walked to the corner of the building, zipped down, turned to see if anyone had followed, zipped up, and ran.

6

Single, commuting from Hudson to the Worcester branch of Homemakers' Mutual, Calvin had not been able to look at any girl without idly considering marriage; and thoughts of marriage produced more serious ones of divorce. This had made him shy with women; but his behaviour seemed to him natural for an insurance man, concerned with risks: a bad investment was worse than none. Marriage was a risk. A married couple could be an awful thing, with two heads and eight limbs, a monstrous octopus really, with a huge appetite and a short life.

In the leatherette album titled 'Wedding Bells', a volume Calvin had often browsed through in unbelief, and now in his ex-wife's keeping, there had been a professional photograph of the woman, taken before he married her. She gazed out of the pebble-grained picture through large unfocused eyes, her little fingers lightly twined, making a gentle support for her chin, her face forward, as if at an open window. She was cute, her earrings small pearls, the tiny buttons on the front of her thin blouse neatly fastened – they could only have been fastened by those dainty fingers. The posies on her fancy bra showed faintly where the blouse was snug. She pouted slightly, the lips ripely full and dewy. Pert little curls, the sort that are seen only in good photographs, wound toward her cheeks in springy tendrils, suggesting that she was gay and, probably, vivacious.

Lies. That album (it had cost a fortune) was mostly lies, with the exception of one snapped on the front steps of the Hudson Baptist Church, too soon for a pose and yet capturing all the truth of the marriage: his wife with wide-open lips berating the flower girl,

Calvin looking wildly in the opposite direction, towards the Assabet River, his hands crossed over his groin.

He preferred his own candid shots of the woman. He grimly considered these in the joyless solitude marriage had imposed on him, in the distracted regret of his divorce. His were mental pictures no court could award to his wife, with ironies, for they were what a single man might think of as sexy, showing a young woman naked, making unusual gestures. But they spoke to him; the malicious speech lived to infuriate. In Calvin's favourite, a memory that justified everything he had done and consoled him in his distraction, his wife stood before him stark naked; she cupped a breast lightly in one hand and with the deft fingertips of the other stroked the rosy nipple, watching its colour closely and harping in a voice that could have belonged to the crazy or cruel, 'Anyone who's not interested in me and my problems is a goodamned egotist.'

A fearless, bossy little woman, the instant they were married (they had met on a hayride organized by the sexton of the church; she said insurance fascinated her and that she was a college graduate, 'A small college in upstate Vermont – you've never heard of it,' she had said, laughing gaily, with the expressive poise that the third-rate grants as compensation) – the instant they were married she possessed everything she had ever wanted, and in that grasping she lost Calvin for ever. It did not matter very much to her that he was unhappy and not hers. She expected marriage to be unpleasant; she was not moved by what Calvin (who fancied bliss but would have settled for peace) came to think of as an unbearable swindle. Marriage had arrested him in his adventure, deprived him of companionship; he had never felt so lonely, so captive, as when married.

He had been shy with her and explored her gently; she mocked his pyjamas and flung off her nightie. In passion her personality altered for good, the sex masks were off, her face was hard in an expression of greed: she sought him the way a cloven monster might seek its lost half, and in seconds they were a thrashing octopus. Disengaged she was cold, her four limbs outstretched, and she developed the disquieting habit of referring to his penis in the third person. She spoke with such conviction that Calvin, hearing for the first time, 'He's getting a run for his money,' covered himself hastily with a pillow and turned to see if some stranger had slipped into the room, whom she was addressing.

She knew so much; she bought paperbacks and manuals with explanations so clinical they chilled Calvin into temporary impotence; her euphemisms appalled him. The word 'screwing' had implications of torture for him, 'fornication' was biblical, but 'fucking' had a finer edge, hinting as it did at a mutual enjoyable assault. Her phrase was 'having sex', a precise emphasis characteristic of her need, with a convenient balance of associations, suggesting appetite and regularity and a smattering of passion but not love. When it was over she leaped from the bed, dashed to the toilet, fitted herself with a hefty nozzle and a rubber bulb, and squirted a fatal concoction on Calvin's seed. Convinced she was purged of the slime, she returned to the bed and talked of the hell of having kids and how they would never have any. Calvin had at the first been impressed with her handy grasp of sexual matters. She liked to discuss it, sometimes using the sex manual euphemisms like foreplay, heavy petting and penetration; at other times hardly beguiling phrases like erectile tissue, erogenous zones, oral manipulation. She could talk this way at breakfast, chewing toast and spooning egg, and think nothing of it. She even thought they were well-matched; she encouraged Calvin to break a state law in bed. Calvin rued the hayride and the passivity he had felt at twenty-eight. And, childless, he felt the marriage a lonely conspiracy, almost as if he and his wife were a couple of queers.

And she was small-souled. Calvin could have put up with everything else if she had not been. She was bossy and demanding, his jailer; but millions of other men were in the same boat, Calvin knew. The fact of his marriage inspired discussions at lunchtime in Worcester with other salesmen. They compared agonies; one always claimed his wife was worse than the others'. Calvin, they said, had it easy; they winked and nudged. Marriage got worse: he would see. But Calvin had not told them everything.

Once he had tried. He began, 'The thing about my wife is she

hates everybody. I know women are supposed to be more conservative than men, but my wife is anti-Semitic. She hates Jews, she
hates Negroes, she hates –'

He stopped speaking. The others' silence was an interruption.
They gaped at Calvin, lowering their drinks. One, after a long
pause, worked his face into an expression of total incomprehension and said, 'What's wrong with that? So what if she hates Yids?
My wife *likes* them, she's always inviting them over. *I'm* the one
with problems!'

Calvin never mentioned his wife again to anyone. He had
known she was stupid, that her small nameless college was a
fiction; but he had not expected her to be cruel. Stupidity hum-
bled many people; it made them good listeners and easy to please.
For her, stupidity was privilege: it licensed her arrogance. She
could be blameless because of it. She took advantage of it and
talked loudly about the people Calvin insured: what she lacked
she imagined had been thieved and hidden by the minorities, each
of which she knew by a one syllable nickname. Calvin's defence
of each, at her attack, was ignorant simplicity, too; he saw her
bigotry make him stupid: she said Yids were crafty, he said intelligent; she said Wops were greasy, he said jolly; she said coons
were savages, he countered with jazz and baseball. He knew it
was not so simple. In ramshackle parlours, falling-down piazzas
and yellowing kitchens in wooden duplexes Calvin had seen them
studying the small print of numbered paragraphs on the back of a
policy. He knew more about them than their closest relatives; their
wonky lungs on X-rays, their explanations on health reports and
the reports of investigators and underwriters. *I have dizzy spells, I
shit blood, My eyes not so hot, Arthuritis in joint, Cold makes
my knee pain, Lump in my breast, Bridgework makes my gums
raw, Three doses of clap during the first war because I was young
and didn't know no better, My blood is tired and I sleep bad.* On
the long insistent forms they set down the pathetic details of their
lives. They were honest, most solemn when they were challenged;
they were shy. Most were black. No company on earth would insure
them. Calvin's heart twisted with their misery. They trusted him.

She hated them. Calvin did not hate even the customers who tried by various means to defraud Homemakers' Mutual: the insured who poured gasoline on their furnishings and set their homes alight, the ones who bombed their paid-up mothers out of the sky or who complained of an undiagnosable back injury after a minor accident and then made a deal with the garage mechanic, or the ones who lied on their forms or wrote to the general manager claiming compensation for bad service. The acts were mad, sometimes murderously backfiring; it was too desperate to hate. Calvin wondered how, if she hated so many, she could love him; but he saw hope for himself: if he could love that small-souled woman he could love anyone. He tried. She misunderstood. She thought he meant something else.

'I want to love you, I want to make it work out,' he said. 'I really do. We have a whole life left, but sometimes I get the feeling it's over. I don't think I like you now. But still.'

'What do you expect?'

'A baby, a divorce,' said Calvin, 'but not this.'

She replied in a voice she usually saved for minorities, 'Anyone who doesn't like being married to me can get the hell out.'

Calvin was given a new assignment at Homemakers' Mutual. It was, in a sense, the baby he said they needed, and for a while it looked as if it might save his marriage, not yet a year old.

He was called to the main office in Boston and spoken to by a director, a man whose name appeared on the letterhead. He said, 'I've been hearing good things about you from Worcester.' Calvin thanked him and the man said, 'Well, I like to hear good things from the branches.'

His name was Wilbur Parsons. He wrote poetry, which he sometimes included in the firm's newsletter. He also endowed poetry magazines and published in those; and he gave readings. He wrote about rustic things. He did a sonnet sequence about Cape Cod and then made a film of the Cape and hired a famous actor to speak his poems on the sound-track. He showed the film at his readings and sent prints of it to all the branches to be screened for employees.

The Worcester branch had privately jeered at the old man. Calvin stayed silent; he liked the poems, but even more liked the impulse in Patsons that made him write them, a civilized boldness, like playing the violin. And he did not despise Parsons' vanity. It was true the verse was not as ambitious as that of the late Vice-President of the Hartford Accident and Indemnity Company; none the less, it proved to Calvin that there was nothing in the insurance business that prevented anyone from setting down his thoughts in verse, and in his spare time Calvin often thought of writing himself. There was, in the process of insurance, a way of knowing what worried people: the insurance agent was as near to people's misery as a doctor or undertaker. And it was an encouragement to work for Parsons, a published author; it seemed to make the event of his own publication more likely: he imagined writing a warning novella, informed by what he had seen in shabby parlours, narrated by a man lamed by poverty, one only insurance could help. That, rather than poems about sugaring-off or fishing shacks.

Parsons said, 'I've got a dream, a kind of vision, call it anything you want.' He beckoned Calvin to the window.

Fifteen storeys down was Boyleston Street, aswarm with shoppers.

'Look there, Mullet. Look at them. *People*. Thousands and thousands of them. They're in a hurry. No one stops to pass the time of day. They're all going, going. But do they know where they're going? Do they know where they've *been*? Sometimes I stand here just like I'm doing now, and I look down at all those people. I say to myself, good God!' Parsons sighed in amazement and looked at Calvin. 'You know why I say this?'

'I think so, sir.'

'Tell me.'

'Maybe those people you see out there aren't insured.'

'You put your finger on it, Mullet. *People* – that's what insurance is. It's people, their hopes and dreams. And I'll tell you something: some of those folks don't have a dime's worth of coverage.' Parsons put his arm around Calvin, awkwardly – Calvin was tall. 'I'm sending you out there.'

Calvin nodded seriously. 'I'm out there already, sir.'

Parsons smiled and said, 'Not where I'm going to send you. How's your geography?'

But his wife said, 'If someone wants to sell insurance to black people why doesn't he go to Roxbury and do it?' Roxbury, a black ghetto, was Africa for Massachusetts.

Knowing her mind, Calvin said nothing about market possibilities or rising expectations. He told her he would be getting a hardship allowance, twenty per cent more than in Worcester, plus two round-trip air tickets. And he showed her brochures of Mozambique, Victoria Falls and one from Malawi which claimed it was 'the Switzerland of Africa'. Strangely, there were no black people in the pictures.

She agreed to go. Calvin was eager, and pleased. It would save the marriage; that was important, but not fundamental. Calvin was not escaping. On the contrary: it was a positive step, a mission, and though he said before he left, speaking of the cynics he worked with in Worcester and the Wasps in Hudson, 'I've had enough of those birds,' he was not fleeing an outrage or a weakness, not announcing defeat by going away. He was going to help.

The night before they left his wife said, 'The tropics – isn't that where everyone's marriage goes on the rocks?' She seemed almost giddy at the thought.

The plane stopped in London, but transit passengers were not allowed to get off. Calvin looked out: small yellow vehicles and little blue men were busy in the mist. At Rome they changed planes and had a *cappuccino*. It was one in the morning. They asked a man in a faded brown uniform where Gate Five was; the man replied '*Cosa?*' and smiled. So much for Italy.

Calvin's first view of Africa was from Benghazi, where the plane was delayed for an hour. It was dark, his wife crouched asleep on her seat. In the airport building Calvin drank a cup of heavily sugared tea, served by a shrouded male Arab, and then walked outside. A cold wind snatched at his jacket, the bright moon lighted the arid blasted place, the cactus and sharp stones. But Calvin was excited: he had arrived in Africa and felt, in an unlikely place to make promises – the edge of a desert – he would be staying a long time. They arrived in Malawi in late afternoon, in time for tea at their hotel. Buttering scones at a veranda table, they noticed a beggar walk out from a hedge and stand near, like a terrible angel. He wore rubber clogs cut from automobile tyres, and wings of rags, and a filthy skullcap.

'Tell him to go home,' Calvin's wife said.

The beggar stared: he made no gesture. His gaze penetrated to Calvin's innards. Calvin felt very white. The beggar looked fierce, strong even, a muscular man, capable of savagery. He could kill with his hands. Calvin knew the man hated him; he wanted to help him or at least tell the man that he was there to help. Calvin raised his hand, a timid salute. But a waiter took this as an annoyed signal and shooed the beggar away.

In the room they argued about the official photograph of Dr Osbong. It was hung over the bed, but Calvin's wife said, 'Even if it was in the john I'd take it down.'

'The President,' said Calvin. 'A nice way to talk.'

'Uncle Ben's Rice,' said his wife, and giggled mirthlessly.

'You insensitive bitch,' Calvin said. He took down the picture of Dr Osbong and banged it into a bureau drawer.

His wife locked herself into the bathroom and washed noisily. Calvin went to the window and threw back the curtains. It was still light, and it was cool. He peered down two storeys to the street, which was a side street, bordered by Hudson-like foliage: bushy-boughed trees, high hedges and even several tepees of pine-tops showing. A man in a wide felt hat pushed a bicycle out of sight. There were no more people. But Calvin knew there was a beggar in the hedge, and there were odours, of fresh grass, of flowering trees, of sweet decay; there was a high whine of locusts building to tea-kettle pitch, and a sky so blue he could have cried.

7

During his marriage Calvin had been able to look at any girl without worrying about marrying her. He stopped staring up the skirts of seated women or down their blouses in a bus queue; he could watch their shadowed parts, package-firm in tight clothes, and be tempted by no mystery or little challenge. It made him calm and gave him poise, useful to a young man who was too tall and too skinny, who sold insurance, who met strange women all the time alone in their homes. So many wives lounged half-dressed in parlours dreaming of laying the first salesman who knocked. Before his marriage Calvin had felt uneasy about confronting a housewife, lazy breasts loosely aswing in a flannel robe, giving his trousers a big moo-cow wink from inside the doorway and offering coffee. They seated Calvin on sofas and then sat beside him and leaned over the policies balanced on his knees; they squeezed him playfully and said their husbands were out of town and what bastards they were when they were home. Married, he was indifferent to what the flapping robes showed. His hesitancy had once been due to a guess; now, his wife a reminder of the dreary urge, he knew the risk. His was a frigid caution that made him a faithful husband and a good insurance man, all business; and he had stopped bumping into furniture and fumbling with his brochures when a lady idly drew a stocking up and hooked it.

And so it came as quite a shock to Calvin, after arriving in Malawi and moving into a Blantyre bungalow in the district called Sunnyside, to walk into the kitchen for matches one day, see the newly hired African girl fussing at the sink in her green uniform, and feel the old dread waking in him. But with this difference: his thought of marriage did not produce one of divorce. He could not keep his hands from plucking at that uniform. It seemed to have something to do with being so far from Hudson, at a great distance from anyone who would frown, in a place which was so green and simple, everything, even the risk of indiscretion, seemed possible and safe. The housewives in Worcester would have welcomed it; Calvin had been unwilling. He was prepared to loosen up for the Africans; they might appreciate the favour and receive it with gratitude. But he restrained himself.

He set up an office in town, on the top floor of a yellow wedge-shaped building, the only one of size, owned by a Goan named F. X. Agnello. His office window faced the clock-tower and the railway station. Downstairs was the British Council Library and a bar, the Highlife, at street level. Over on Fotheringham Road he bought office equipment, an adding machine, a typewriter, files and ledgers, and a ream of foolscap because he liked the name. He registered the company and had stationery printed with the Homemakers' letterhead.

For a month he stuffed envelopes, enclosing the Homemakers' Mutual brochure, the information about the easy payment plan (quarterly premiums) and a stamped postcard reading, 'I would like to have full details about your family coverage. Let's talk about it at your office/my home (delete one). I understand that I am under absolutely no obligation to take out a policy. My address is –' Calvin got names of potential clients from the slim Malawi phonebook and the voters' roll. His mailing, plus multilingual ads in the *Malawi News* and little taped inserts, with music, on Radio Malawi, produced eleven replies. Three of the replies asked for details but appended no names or addresses. Mr Agnello, who wore a rosary around his neck, told Calvin that it was a mistake to enclose stamps: people steamed them off and stuck them on their own letters. Calvin said it took time. He was only trying to sell them on the *idea* of insurance.

The second month he spent up-country, in the villages near Lilongwe and the lakeshore. Again, he had no plans to sell; he just wanted to get acquainted. He brought mechanical pencils and ball-points, little desk calendars and paperweights, letter openers and keyholders – all stamped in gold with Homemakers' Mutual name and *Your Agent: Cal Mullet*, abbreviated for the friendly sound. It was 'remembrance advertising', and it was accepted with thanks by people who couldn't write, or had no keys, or counted moons.

He would drive down a dirt track in his Austin and park before a collection of houses, and immediately begin handing out ball-points to the children who greeted him. The village men would follow and Calvin would order some warm beer for them if there was a shop nearby. And he chatted.

'That's a fine house you've got,' Calvin would say. 'Very nice little bundles of grass on the roof, too. You do that yourself?'

'Wife,' the man would say, and take a pull on his bottle.

'It'd be a real shame if it burned down, wouldn't it?'

'This hut, it will fall down, I think' – pausing, the African would count on his fingers – 'next year. Two rains will finish it. Then I think we move maybe that side.'

'But you could fix it up, put some more mud on and insure it.'

'Oh, yes, we mud it, but once in a blue moon only.' Calvin noticed they used phrases popular decades back: blue moon, blue lies, hot jazz, tough guy.

They expected their huts to collapse and so did not maintain them. They did not own anything worth insuring, except bicycles or radios; they denied possession of these in case Calvin asked to see licences they had never bothered to get. And they showed no interest in life insurance. 'But I still die, isn't it?' one had said.

One day at the end of that second month he lost himself in a labyrinth of roads near the lake. He drove and drove, trying to stay on cleared tracks, but always the tracks narrowed into a single path too small for his car. He reversed and was stuck in sand for hours. Toward nightfall, having used bundles of twigs for traction, he freed the car and climbed a hill on foot. He saw through the trees the brick steeple of a church.

It was a leper colony run by Dutch priests; they greeted Calvin warmly and gave him a bed. In the morning they showed him around the buildings, all of weathered red brick, some with ambitious arches and windows, and they invited him to mass. The altar was decorated with shards of broken glass set into cement: crosses and fishes and Latin mottoes. They pointed with pride to their generator, run by a paddle-wheel, and their dispensary. Draped everywhere, sleeping under trees and in the shade of round huts and even in the back pews of the church, were the lepers, dusty dozing souls with bandaged hands and feet.

The priests persuaded Calvin to stay for three days. He ate their food and found it unpalatable; he played whist; the lepers drummed. By candlelight (the generator was shut off at nine) Calvin read tattered magazines. An old priest, Father Euthyme, helped Calvin find his car and get his bearings on a map. Calvin offered him insurance. Father Euthyme smiled and touched the crucifix pinned to his stained cassock. 'Do I need more insurance than this?'

'I guess not,' said Calvin, and went on his way.

He should have been discouraged, but he was not. His was the only Homemakers' agency in Africa: it would take time to catch on. His fear was unconnected with insurance. It concerned Grace, the housegirl. He didn't trust himself. He was inclined to fire her, give her several months' pay and the sack, and hire a man. His wife wouldn't hear of it. She felt safe in Sunnyside, no black families lived there, and she refused to have a black man in the kitchen. She had started to call them 'kaffirs' (which she pronounced *car-fares*).

Ignoring the girl was out of the question. His wife criticized her, argued with her, claimed she couldn't understand her. Calvin, after nearly three months, was still finding his feet as an insurance agent; his wife in the same period of time had become a proper memsahib, a dona, a missis, and knew a dozen orders in the vernacular, a lingo known in Blantyre as kitchen kaffir.

Grace knew English cooking: boiled cabbage, fried pasty fish, stewed fruit, limp Yorkshire pudding and mince curry. 'Garbage,' said Calvin's wife. Grace used the English names for utensils, serviette for napkin, drying-up cloth for dish-towel, fish-slice for spatula, cooker for stove, geyser for water-heater. Her pronunciation was not perfect, and Calvin's wife took her speech to be a kind of pidgin, which she mocked, saying, 'What's your problem? Don't you speak Eng-lish?'

Calvin would look up from his chair and see them framed in the kitchen door. It wasn't as simple as black and white, one nice, the other awful, though that would have been a convenient contrast. Certainly the girl seemed innocent and pretty; but when Calvin was near her and alone and thought of marriage it was in his mind a sort of insurance, a good intention, to protect her ever after; it was one way of saving a poor person, hardly love. Which was why it was so hard to fight the urge: it seemed inhuman not to give her everything he had. And, alone, he didn't hate his wife. Seeing them together, his wife bullying Grace ('Don't just stand there like a bump on a log – say something!'), he was not inspired to hate one and love the other. It was something out of joint, something unfair and indecent he felt impelled to correct, even at the risk of being misunderstood. Not lust or a political attitude, his was a fragile sympathy, asking nothing in return, honest because it was not love, but kindness. He offered it to Grace in the same degree as his wife offered insult. When his wife was cruel, Calvin tried to be kind; his wife shrieked, he murmured apologies; Calvin gave private consolation when his wife humilated Grace publicly. He did his best to reassure; he took pains to be gentle; and had his wife simply left her alone and not slapped her Calvin might have spent months more in the bungalow, muddling along, and never attempted to make love to Grace.

There was nothing to eat that evening when Calvin came home. The cruets and sauce bottles that Grace habitually arranged on the table were not there. His wife did no cooking, did nothing in fact; she had been made redundant in every way except one, by Grace, and spent her days leafing through South African women's magazines, in a chaise-longue on the sunny lawn.

'Pickle?' She fished a gherkin out of a narrow-necked bottle with her fingers. Lights burned in the kitchen, but Grace was not there.

Calvin looked at the label and recognized the language as Afrikaans. He refused the pickle. He never used South African goods; it was a private embargo that deprived him sometimes of nutrition: the corn-flakes, peanut butter and ketchup in Malawi were all imported from South Africa. His wife, who declared no such embargo, said they were almost as good as the real thing and made life bearable: she went through a bottle of Koo Ketchup in a week.

'Where's the food?'

'Don't ask me.' She munched pickle.

'Grace?'

'I wouldn't know.'

Calvin found her sulking at her quarters, holding her stung cheek. She sat on the low steps of the hut. He sat beside her and talked softly to her; 'I know what you think. You think all white people are like my wife. I don't blame you. She's hateful. But please don't go away thinking that we're all exploiters. Take me for example. I sell insurance. I could have been pulling down a pretty good week's pay back home, but I figured . . . You don't understand, do you?'

Calvin moved closer and put his arm around her; his other hand trembled on her knee. 'We're not all like that,' he said, 'really we're not. Some of us are lovers.' He kissed her; it was a child's kiss, bumping heads, brushing lips. Grace tried to get away.

'No,' said Calvin. He held her; she tried to stand, and toppled into the hut where a candle flickered. 'Listen,' said Calvin. Grace resisted, kicking. The kicks made a loud thumping on the floor-planks and hiked up the skirt of her uniform. Around her naked waist was the loveliest beaded belt. Calvin touched it; it had the detail of wampum.

Grace whimpered, and squirmed out of Calvin's loose clasp. She leaped to her feet, her back to the wall; her hands were over her mouth, muffling her murmurs, and there was a look of mortal terror in her eyes.

Calvin left the hut and started back across the grass to the bungalow. On the rear veranda, her hair swarming with a corona of moths and sausage flies, stood his wife. She did not speak until

Calvin did. She silenced him with, 'You fucking bastard.' She repeated it and, unused to saying such a phrase, gave it a special clarity lacking in the slurred abuse of the experienced.

Later that evening Grace disappeared. Calvin's bedroom was barred to him. He spent the night on the floor of his office.

At nine the next morning Calvin was awakened by a knock. He thought it might be the police. It was a tall man with a briefcase, sucking an unlit pipe.

'I wonder if I might have a moment of your time?' asked the man. 'Saunders is the name. I'm a lawyer.'

Calvin stood barefoot in the doorway, in wrinkled trousers and undershirt. 'Having a little nap,' he said, gesturing to a blanket mussed on the floor.

'Right you are,' said Saunders. 'I'll come straight to the point. Your wife is suing you for divorce.'

'Go on,' said Calvin.

'The grounds seem to be adultery. The co-respondent's a Miss . . . a Miss . . . confound these names.'

'Adultery? It must have looked that way, but I never –'

'English law applies here, I'm afraid. The only grounds for a legal divorce are adultery and non-consummation. It's very sticky.'

'I'll take adultery,' said Calvin.

'You will? Good. In actual fact, the only matter I'm concerned with, as your wife's lawyer, is whether you plan to contest. It's awfully complicated, but you're entirely within your rights if you do. Now,' said Saunders heartily, 'are you in the picture, so to speak?'

'She's serious, I guess,' said Calvin.

'Hell hath no fury etcetera, etcetera,' said Saunders.

'I won't contest it.'

The hearing a month later was brief. Saunders had got Grace's signature (an X, a thumbprint, a witness), and Calvin was served with a summons but told he needn't show up at the hearing. His wife was there and so was much of Blantyre's white community. The details appeared the next day in the *Malawi News*, where, when, how many times Calvin had been adulterous. He had connived in the fabrications, but when he read them in the paper he felt warm towards Grace: he was stimulated to give them reality by marrying her. She was nowhere to be found. Calvin's goods and chattels so-called, and half his salary, were awarded to his wife. The day after the hearing she boarded a plane for Boston, and Calvin moved to Auntie Zeeba's Eating House, a brothel on the upper road, near the bus depot. He sold his car to pay for packing and shipping, and hitch-hiked to his several accounts.

8

Calvin dragged himself wheezing for a mile, his arms extended before him into the night like antennae. He stopped. Walking, he decided, was safer, if not a great deal healthier. His lungs could not keep pace with running strides, and his throat, harried by beer and gutted by cigarette smoke, gushed with deafening breath, constricted and burned. Going slowly he would be able to hear other sounds, those of Ogilvie for example. He was sure that if Ogilvie was chasing him, he would hear and would have time to take cover. He heard locusts and owls and certain shrieks he could not identify (from a hyena? a swindled host?). There were no quick noises of pursuit, though, no leaping steps; this was especially unnerving and made Calvin turn again and again from the darkness he was penetrating to face the darkness he was fleeing. Each time he turned he suspected Ogilvie of having crept swiftly after him on muffled feet, the angry man about to leap out of the ink to claw his face.

The repeated turning made him dizzy and once in the silliness of lost balance he stumbled into a ditch, believing as he fell that it was a boobytrap and letting out a yell. The yell died in the trees, silencing the night sounds. After the fall he shuffled backwards. It was slow work, and heartbreaking, for Calvin knew that if they caught him he would go back: he owed it to them for the dirty trick he had played ('Hold my jacket – I'll be right back!'). The poor things needed him, they had no chief, they didn't know any better. They were Africans: for years people had been bamboozling them.

It grew chilly; Calvin shivered without his jacket. He sniffed and for a minute or two thought he was crying. He felt the way he imagined the uninsured did, a sense of falling, falling, and getting colder and sadder as he fell. But he wasn't crying; it was the night chill, the gooseflesh on his arms, not sobbing but shuddering with cold. And the sadness; he had let so much slip through his fingers, no one had ever known him or his plans, his hand extended in friendship was taken for a punch, his height was a threat. Anticipating cruelty, no one had seen his kindness. If they had let him alone, let him get on with his insurance, if they had paid their premiums on time and trusted him and not expected his whole attention from a casual encounter, he would not have hurt a soul. But they had made him.

And then his back hit something cold with a clang. Calvin stiffened; it was smooth, dew-covered steel. He turned. The moon was rising, a neatly pruned orange peel, the colour the last splotches of sun had been. In this feeble light he could see the outlines of a low car, the sleek hood facing him.

A Citroën: Calvin could tell from its shape, the protruding beak-like hood, the slanting roof, the low foreshortened rear. He struck a match, but saw only the flare of the match: nothing was illuminated for him. There did not seem to be anyone in the car, there was no one around it. To steal it one had to jump the wires; car-thieves could do that with bits of silver foil from a cigarette pack. Calvin knew only the simple phrase, jump the wires. One of the rear doors was unlocked. Calvin jiggled the door-handle, then lifted the door slowly open. A light went on inside; it was empty.

'Don't move!'

Something hard and blunt pressed against Calvin's back, the nostril of a revolver snout, he was sure.

'Put your hands up and turn around.'

A powerful flashlight was switched on. It shone in Calvin's eyes. He heard boots crunching pebbles in the road, but saw no faces, heard no voices. There were more flashlights on him, playing on his baggy trousers, his shoes, over his shirt.

'Empty your pockets.'

Calvin pulled three pairs of glasses out, placed them on the ground, and heard a familiar word from behind one of the flashlights, 'Goggles.'

A black hand stretched out and tried to grasp them. A boot interfered and stomped on the glasses, grinding them into the road. The light had wavered and revealed a glove, an inch of white wrist.

'Take your shoes off.'

'Can I keep them?' asked Calvin, hating his pleading. 'They're the only ones I have. I lost my socks.'

'Tie the laces together and carry them around your neck.' That voice was American, the one giving all the orders. 'Blindfold him!'

9

The rag across Calvin's eyes stank, and the path – if it was a path – was strewn with boulders. They had taken a further precaution of tying a rope around his ankle which one man held and from time to time jerked, tripping him. When the blindfold was removed Calvin wondered why they had put it on in the first place: the night was still dark, his vision was no better with the rag off his eyes. He saw little more after his last pair of glasses was given back to him. He stood in skyless dark. A lantern was lit. He was towed inside a hut and left alone with the man who had done all the talking.

'Sit there,' said the man.

Calvin seated himself. He had never found it easy to be comfortable sitting upright in a straight-backed chair; he arranged his long arms and legs slowly, ineptly, as if he was folding the wooden lengths of a carpenter's collapsible ruler.

The man took a length of rope and, spoiling the careful arrangement of Calvin's limbs, tied his hands behind the chairback, his ankles to the legs. Knotting the rope, the man heard a rustle of papers, the sweaty bundle of policies and brochures filed away in Calvin's shirt. He tore open the shirt and peeled the papers from Calvin's hollow belly. He finished the knots on Calvin's wrists, then stood and said, before he began to read the papers, 'We've been expecting you.'

He was not tall, but he had an impressive compactness, broad shoulders and a solid head set on a thick sunburned neck. He was dressed like a soldier on bivouac. He wore military sunglasses, tinted green with gold bows; he removed these to read and Calvin saw his bright quick eyes. His khaki shirt was creased twice down the front where it had been folded for a suitcase or a pack; his peaked Castro cap was tinged with a dark band of sweat. His moustache drooped dramatically into two carefully waxed points, setting off his sunburned face, a young face with an eager muscle in the jaw. There were large flapped pockets on the sides of his trousers; the trousers ballooned at the knees where they were tucked into the tops of combat boots. Hooked to his wide belt was a bluish pistol in a shiny black holster. On the other side of the belt hung a machete in a canvas sheath. He wore no insignia except, in the buttonhole on the flap of his shirt pocket, a bright red African daisy, the wild variety. That flower gave Calvin curious hope.

Still reading, the man walked to a table beside Calvin and flipped open the lid of a cigar box. The box was gaily trimmed in green and white and stuck with an ornate stamp, a kind of seal the size and colour of a dollar bill. It read *República de Cuba*. On the end of the box in tall white letters was the brand name, *Romeo y Julieta*. The man took out a blunt aluminium tube, pulled off the cap and shook out a cigar and a thin slice of wood. Calvin expected a man with a pistol like that and in such a uniform to bite off the end and spit a chunk of tobacco into his prisoner's face, but he simply tapped it and drew out a small silver object which clicked open lengthwise. Thoughtfully, he circumcised the cigar, and with the long flame of a gas lighter, puffed it, turning the cigar in his mouth.

'Keeps off the mosquitoes,' he said and went back to the papers. 'You want one?' he asked after a while.

Calvin swallowed and pulled an appreciative face. 'No thanks, they give me a sore throat. You wouldn't have a beer around the place, would you?'

'Whisky?'

'Fire-water,' said Calvin. 'Never touch it.'

The man grunted, puffed, and said, 'All I see here is insurance.'

'Homemakers' Mutual,' said Calvin. The man stared. Calvin tried to point, but his hands jerked on knots. He went on, 'Fifty-six branches around the world, including,' he nodded at the papers, 'Malawi. That's my baby.'

'Like I say, we've been expecting you. What took you so long?'

'You knew I was coming?'

'There isn't much that goes on here that we don't know. But you were easy. One of the men gave you a ride. Don't you remember? He dropped you in Rumpi. We like to keep track of strangers.'

'The banana truck?' Calvin shook his head. 'Can you beat that!'

'Bananas on top, dynamite underneath. If you had run into something you would have been blown sky-high.'

'Dynamite,' said Calvin. 'What for?'

'There's a war on,' said the man. He puffed and twirled his cigar. 'We've liberated this area.'

'Oh, you have, eh? Well, you might tell the people up the road that. They'd be pleased to hear it.'

'They know it. We've been here a month.'

'Taking Osbong's picture down,' said Calvin. 'Whose are you putting up?'

The man did not reply. He looked at his cigar and picked off the slim brown band that circled it. 'It's a funny place,' he said. 'People here still have reactionary tendencies.'

'For shit sake!' said Calvin, sputtering. 'Who the hell gives you the right to come in here and throw your weight around? Yes, they know you're here. Soldiers in the trees, they keep saying. As if you ass-kickers really matter! Why don't you leave them alone, huh? Haven't they got enough to worry about?'

'We leave them alone,' said the man. 'Osbong's the one who squeezes them.'

'Osbong,' said Calvin, and laughed, recalling the official picture of the baffled snarling chief.

The man leaned towards Calvin, the peak of his cap almost touching Calvin's glasses. 'What's your game?'

'No game, just insurance. I told you. Read for yourself. You think I carry that stuff around in my shirt to keep myself warm?'

'Don't snap at me,' said the man slowly.

'Well, Jesus, what do you think I am, a spy?'

'You could be.'

'I'm not. Anyway, who would I be spying for?'

'We have enemies.'

'I don't doubt that,' said Calvin, looking around the room. A map was spread on the table. Near the cigar box was a steel case of bullets.

'You spent two days in that village. Why would a person like you stay there all that time?'

'Selling insurance. Look –'

'You travel pretty light. Where's your suitcase?'

'It's a long story,' said Calvin. The man was silent; he went on, 'Stopped for a beer up the road. I met a couple of people. They invited me to their house for Christmas, after I sold them a policy. Then I left. Without my suitcase. I guess it's not such a long story.' He felt the weight of fatigue on him, the itch of dirt, the frailty of three days of hard drinking.

'Sounds as if you were exploiting them.'

'That's a laugh,' said Calvin. '*They* were exploiting *me*!'

'We'll look into that,' said the man. 'The villagers around Rumpi have instructions to report strangers. You weren't reported.'

'You don't mind pestering people, do you?' said Calvin. 'They were very nice to me, those folks. And I fixed them up with a policy. I don't see why you should interfere. Are you going to do anything to them?'

The man blew smoke and watched it rise. 'We expect cooperation from these people. We got Osbong off their necks.'

'Yeah, sure. But they're Africans –'

'What have you got against Africans?' The man spoke through clenched teeth; it was his first show of anger.

'Nothing,' Calvin protested. 'What I mean is, no one ever gave them a shake. You know what I mean? They're kind of confused.'

'They're less confused than you are.'

'I agree,' said Calvin readily.

'You ethnocentric son of a bitch.' The man's mouth was clamped malevolently on his fat cigar. He strode to the other side of the room and seated himself on a crate. He puffed billows of smoke.

Calvin did not say anything for five minutes. He didn't feel, having been called an ethnocentric son of a bitch, there was any handy reply. He looked at the cigar box. On the lid the romantic couple embraced on a balcony, Romeo in blue tights on a rope ladder gazing into the white expanse of Juliet's bosom. There seemed to be much more in the picture, but in the bad light Calvin could not make out anything more. It was a warm little scene: it gave Calvin comfort, as the daisy in the soldier's pocket had done.

'Funny, the Cubans still making cigar boxes like that, isn't it? You don't expect it somehow.'

'They're for export,' said the man.

'I guess you're right.'

The man grunted. He seemed to be avoiding knocking the large ash from the cigar; he was gentle with it.

'Can I ask you a question?'

The man gave a barely perceptible nod.

'If you don't mind my saying so,' said Calvin, 'you're in a risky business, shipping high explosives, camping out and so forth. Now this is your business, don't think I'm crabbing – it's not for me to say you're right or wrong. I don't know anything about politics and I don't pretend to. But tell me something, did you ever stop to think what would happen to your loved ones if you suddenly passed on? Suppose your gun went off accidentally. What then?'

'What the hell are you talking about?'

'People that depend on you. Wife, kids, girlfriend – your mother, maybe. To put it in a nutshell – it would help if you untied me – do you ever ask where you're going to be in ten or fifteen years?'

The man smiled.

Calvin persisted. 'What about your men? Do you know that for a few dollars weekly you can take out an all-inclusive Homemakers' Mutual policy – don't let the name scare you, you don't have to be a homemaker to insure with us! When the policy matures you're guaranteed a very large sum, as much as fifteen or twenty grand if you reach the age of fifty-five. In the unfortunate event of your death anyone you name will get the money, as beneficiary. You know how it operates. Think it over. You can buy a hell of a lot of dynamite with twenty grand, and don't think you can't. Or look at it this way: you're not going to be here for ever –'

He was drowsy, he continued to speak without effort; the sales phrases came, they always did, like funky music out of a hand-organ. And then Calvin was awakened by panic; he realized where he was, where he had been for days. In a voice woozy with fatigue and kerosene fumes he pleaded, 'For God's sake, untie me! Let me go, please. I'm no spy, I haven't got a cent to my name. Have a heart! Spies don't hitch-hike! They kept bumming money off of me, they wouldn't let me go, I wanted to. You don't know what they *did* to me. Don't you have any feelings?' And went to sleep, his head down, his shirt torn open, his chin on his bony narrow chest.

Calvin's ropes were being loosened. It was still dark, the lamp low, the room close with cigar smoke. The man was undoing the knots, his daisy was wilted.

Calvin stood, immediately bending, a tall man's instinctive stoop. He was unsteady on his feet. He rubbed his wrists and said, 'You must think I'm a real jerk, crying like that. But you don't know how it is. I know you're an American. Where are you from? I'm from Hudson, Mass. Small world, eh? Who'd ever think,' said Calvin, stamping to get the circulation back into his legs, 'that in a place like this –'

'Don't you ever shut up?'

'It's my nerves. Normally I'm very quiet. When I'm balled-up I talk a lot. I'm balled-up now. Well, you should know.'

'Follow me,' said the man. He held the rope attached to Calvin's ankle and, keeping it taut, led him outside. The moon was bright, the sky a deep blue dotted with clusters of star buds. It was light enough to walk without a lantern. 'See those tents? Fifty soldiers. Fifty killers sleeping. Ammo there under that canvas, rifles, grenades, blasting powder, small arms.'

'Why are you telling me that?'

They passed low wooden buildings. 'Our kitchen. Blackboard for tactical instruction. Water supply. Workshop.'

Calvin asked for a drink of water. The water was cold in the tin cup. It revived him. He poured a second cup over his head.

'There isn't anything we don't have. See that tall tree? Radio transmitter at the foot, antenna up above.'

'It's very impressive,' said Calvin.

'Tell them that in Blantyre,' said the man. 'Tell them what you saw. Tell them you met Marais.'

'Any other name?' asked Calvin. 'Or –'

'Just Marais,' said the man.

'Like Mantovani,' said Calvin. The man didn't respond, and Calvin added, 'You know, the conductor. One name. Like Liberace. Like –' He gave up. 'My name's Mullet, Calvin Mullet. I take it you're letting me go.'

'You're clean,' said Marais. 'Stupid, but clean.'

'Thanks,' said Calvin. 'If you point me in the direction of the road I won't take any more of your time. I'll light out of here just as tight as I can jump. They say that back home.'

'Put on the blindfold. I'm driving you to Blantyre.'

Marais drove the Citroën like a maniac. Calvin forced himself to sleep, but woke on hairpin bends, sliding across the seat to see red laterite walls, scored with erosion, fly past. Marais went by a devious route, for Calvin had woken at regular intervals but did not see Lilongwe, or any town or roadblock. He mentioned insurance again.

'This is my insurance,' said Marais. He held his pistol in Calvin's face.

In the morning, outside Blantyre at the junction where the tar road began, Marais said, 'Know the name of that road?'

'Yes,' said Calvin. It was chilly; a light rain had started. He hugged himself and yawned. 'Isn't it Queen Elizabeth Drive or something like that?'

'No, it's Osbong Drive,' said Marais, 'all the way into town. But someday it's going to be Brother Jaja Drive. Tell them that. Now screw.'

Auntie Zeeba's Eating House ('*More than a bar . . .*'), a rambling tin-roofed brothel, had a wide covered veranda and deck chairs where, in slack hours, the girls sat, hooting amiably at passers-by.

Tonight it was raining. An elderly Englishman and two of the girls stood at the veranda rail, mutely watching the empty street awash in the rain. It had been raining most of the day, steady drizzle in the morning, windy beating in the afternoon, and now a straight heavy shower which poured ceaselessly from cold night. The dry season had been wet, and so the wet season was uncertain. For days the sun would shine, and then came the reminder that it was December. In other places rain gave life; this rain swelled rivers and washed out bridges, turned dust into muck, and moistened crumbling turf and made it slick; it inconvenienced and killed.

Major Beaglehole, the elderly Englishman, warmed a whisky and soda. The girls leaned on the rail; he stood some distance from it, as if watching an erupting ocean from a ship's bridge. He was stout, though dignified, and had a sparse square of moustache. His baldness emphasized his overlarge ears. He wore a hearing aid, a bulky cream-coloured plug in the right ear, with a wire looping down his starched bush-shirt to a small metal box hung from his neck on a harness. For the first time that day there was thunder. Major Beaglehole turned his hearing aid low and continued to gaze. A bolt split the sky very near in a blue electric crack. He yanked the plug from his ear. He believed the contraption would attract lightning. He claimed sometimes to hear morse code through the device, military messages in cypher. He liked that, and listened for the beeps, but he had the quaint fear of storms and machines of others who lived in Malawi.

Below the veranda, at the street's edge, the open drain frothed full of rotten water and flotsam. A cat, floating on its back, paws aloft, shot past, rigid in death.

'Bad luck,' said Major Beaglehole, 'a black cat crossing your path.'

The girls said nothing. The superstition was not theirs: their version was a snake on a path. They leaned and watched the street blister with the big raindrops.

'But it was dead, so that doesn't count, I should say. Possibly it only *looked* black. The fur was wet.' Major Beaglehole smiled tentatively and waited for a reply from the gods.

Another lightning bolt rent the sky, three-pronged. Even before the thunderclap reached the veranda the electricity failed. All the lights went out. Major Beaglehole took his whisky to one of the chairs. His curse was a very small voice in the thunder.

The girls groaned and slapped the railing. There were more groans from others within.

Pressure lamps were pumped, their cloth mantles lighted. In the over-brightness of one of these lamps an old woman appeared at the bar door. She hung the lamp she was carrying on a hook near Major Beaglehole.

'There you are, Major,' she said. She was chewing decisively; she nibbled as she spoke. 'Don't know what we pay our light bills for. Never any bloody lights. Gets my back up, it does.' She walked to the railing. 'Ain't it beastly?'

Major Beaglehole was retuning his hearing aid. He caught her last words and replied, 'Makes me want to spew, Bailey.'

'It would bloody well serve them right if we all went back to the UK. I don't know why we keep on like this.' She shifted slightly into the lamplight and saw that only a peel remained of the banana she had been eating. She tossed it into the darkness. 'What I'd give for a half of draught Guinness.' She looked into the night. It was totally dark, crackling with rain. Bitterly she said, 'The filthy sods.'

Several times a day Bailey stood on her veranda, looked at what she could see of Malawi, and threatened to leave. She had come to Malawi at the age of five with her parents, who were missionaries.

They were buried up at Monkey Bay. 'A fitting end,' as she said, 'for a mish.'

'Makes me want to spew,' repeated Major Beaglehole.

Bailey seemed to take it as a hint. She began coughing desperately, gasping for breath. She had a terrifying cough, fruity and full; she brought up juice and sauce and fragments of banana; she gagged, ruining the appetite of anyone within earshot.

Major Beaglehole hated her appearance, but enjoyed her rough moods; she was a good old stick. What was disconcerting about her was that while she did not smell bad, she looked as if she did. A diet of sodden fish and chips, which she ate lustily with her fingers from a copy of the *Malawi News*, had made her pox-pitted face fat and free of any expression. She blamed her bad complexion on the weather. She wore faded men's socks in hairy felt bedroom slippers. Over her shoulders was a shawl, greasy from her habitual clutchings. Overworked veins stood out on her calves. She had a heart condition, often went pale and flopped in a chair, looking horrible. She had diagnosed this as indigestion and, after a seizure, dosed herself with liver salts. She owned one dress; several buttons were missing from the front. She was Auntie Zeeba. In any other country she would have been jailed as a bawd.

Major Beaglehole burped at her. 'The wind's up,' he said. 'I'll have to get my UK woolly out one of these days. Didn't think I'd need it till May.'

'Ain't this weather a menace?' said Bailey. 'Had a shocking dry season, the *chiperoni* gave me my rheumatism back, then the thunder-rains were late. It's the atom bombs.' She made a move for the door, tugging at her soiled shawl. 'I've got the old wrap.'

Major Beaglehole looked away and spoke loudly, as if to a multitude, stopping Bailey in her tracks. 'This rain reminds me of a fearful storm we had in Alex in '43. Came hammering down in great buckets. My batman was pissing his bags with fright. Useless chap. Asked him for my handgun, and the damned fool,' Major Beaglehole turned again and raised his eyes to Bailey, 'the damned fool shot me in the leg.'

'You've had a life, Major.'

'I have indeed. The rain reminded me of that tale.' Major Beaglehole drank, and said, 'It's a pity I've forgotten all my Arabic. I used to speak it like a native.'

Bailey lit the butt of a cigarette she had put out earlier and kept in the pocket of her dress. There were not many more puffs in it. She screwed up her face, pinched the butt to her lips with her inefficient fingers, sucked twice and burned herself.

'Bugger it!' she said, tramping on the fag-end with her slipper. 'Think I'll go inside and put my feet up. It'll be quiet as a bloody grave tonight with no lights.'

Major Beaglehole said, 'My batman was a Gyppo.'

'A black,' said Bailey.

'A Gyppo,' said Major Beaglehole.

'They're all nig-nogs,' said Bailey, 'with arses for faces.'

'They're laughing at us now,' said Major Beaglehole. 'They're putting the Union Jack on their knickers. We're down and they're laughing. But we won't be down much longer. I tell you, Bailey, we're coming back in numbers and God help them then. You'll see a Union Jack flying over Government House.'

'They can have this bloody place, I say. It don't matter to me what happens, it's not my look-out. I got my house to see to.'

But Major Beaglehole had switched off his hearing aid. 'We'll have it all back, from the Cape to Cairo. We may have been wog-bashers, but by God we were fair.' He finished his whisky, 'Get me another peg, will you, Bailey? The damp's getting into my bones.'

Bailey took the glass.

'Where's the Yank?' asked Beaglehole, turning the volume knob.

'Still sleeping,' said Bailey, 'I haven't seen him about.'

'We might have to take it away from the Yanks, from the looks of it,' said Major Beaglehole, to himself.

Bailey went inside. The rubber blades of the ceiling fans drooped, the pressure lamps, pumped by the girls, spluttered and hissed, the glow of the mantles making giant shadows of the men standing at the bar. There was the tick-tick of the metal plungers, the hiss of the lamps, the sweep of rain on the tin roof. The only other sound was that of an Arab in an ankle-length *gallabieh* and sweaty skullcap, who fed osbongs into a one-armed bandit. He had chin-tufts of Abe Lincoln beard and held a glass of untouched orange squash in his left hand. He played the machine with his right, taking a lucky tango-step backwards and averting his eyes from the spinning symbols each time he pulled the crank. The rest of the gambling machines, the electric ones which on a normal evening would be buzzing and flashing lights, were silent.

Bailey handed Major Beaglehole's whisky to a fat waiter with a tray and directed him to the veranda. She took her usual place in an easy chair at a door near the back of the bar. Beyond were rooms, some rented for an hour or two, others for weeks or months, for she also took boarders. The room keys were on labelled hooks on a little board at her elbow.

The Arab kicked the fruit machine in disgust and walked over to one of the girls. He offered her his orange squash. She refused it and, seeing Bailey's eyes on her, asked him to buy her a beer.

'No beer! Beer bad!' He took the girl's hand and said amorously, 'If my penis could speak he would say "I love you, *habibi*."'

Bailey collected twenty osbongs. She passed a key to the couple and let them through the door.

Around nine there was a particularly intense flash of lightning. It illuminated the whole place, each beam, every cobweb, the broom in the corner, the official photograph of Dr Osbong, the amazed faces of the girls; it made a dog, driven indoors by the pelting storm, stiffen, and Bailey check a belch; it bathed in bluish light a sleek plump-backed rat making for the kitchen door. Every chair and bottle glowed, the tablecloths were crumb-free, for seconds all things were new, all the squalor gone, the spots gone from Bailey's face. Then just as quickly in the whoosh of sudden darkness, there was an earsplitting crack of thunder.

In a back bedroom of the eating house, Calvin Mullet sat bolt upright and listened to that last thunderclap fading, a thudding rumble, like a big piano being shoved on wooden castors. The rain drummed on the tin roof, the louvred shutters knocked together, clinking where they were loosely hooked. Calvin rattled the switch of his bedside lamp and saw there had been a power failure. He lit a candle.

By candlelight he took inventory. He examined his face in the dresser mirror (the dresser occupied a third of the small room, which was a cheap single of the sort the girls lived in when they were off duty). He wore a mask of shadowy blue stubble; his face seemed more pinched than the last time he had looked critically at it, his skin too white, a ghostliness that was sickly if not downright nasty. He had grit in his hair, and dust in his nostrils. The strain of the trip north showed. Tall people suffered more than most in an ordeal, and the suffering was conspicuous.

Marais had given him his papers back. The important ones were there, two do-not-spindle-or-fold cards with names and address, some damp brochures and monthly report forms which, folded carefully, became envelopes, needing no adhesive and no stamps if mailed in the United States or its Possessions. Five pairs of glasses were missing: one to Ogilvie for Christmas, one in the manoeuvre at the Big Drum Bar, three under Marais's boot. The sixth pair sat cross-legged on the dresser, mildly tinted tortoiseshells. On the floor where early that morning he had pulled them off were his baggy pants, his mudcaked suedes, his shirt – laundered by Mira, torn by Marais, dirtied by Calvin. And here in a stack his books: *Teach Yourself Chinyanja*, with a dog-ear at Chapter Two ('The rifles are rusty', 'My good bow has fallen'), the *Information Please Almanac*, ten *Time* magazines, *Principles of Selling*, a book of Parsons' poems (*The Muse and Mammon*) and two of the Vice-President of the Hartford Accident and Indemnity Company. And five novels, three in translation. He had brought the unwieldy paperbacks of these great works of fiction in the belief that Africa was the sort of place where among other things one had plenty of time for reading the classics, as on a sea voyage, a long illness or a summer vacation. He hadn't touched the novels, though paradoxically they had the look of having been read: the pages thickened by the dampness, the bindings curled and cracked. But he would read them eventually. Calvin had that sense of inadequate education, common among American graduates, that obsession to supplement what he felt sure must have been imperfect. He had continually bought dull difficult paperbacks in drugstores and forced himself to underline passages in them with a felt pen. He had attended night-classes on (was it?) The Disadvantaged Child, and still wished he had done more sociology, less sales and management.

In the top drawer of the dresser were odds and ends, can-opener, nail-file, band-aids, string, paperclips, mosquito-repellent, playing cards, mosquito coils, after-shave, passport and health card, one cuff-link, a tin of tightly rolled safes and an exhausted cigarette lighter. In other drawers bargains from Filene's, string vests from Jaganathy's Madras Bazaar, marriage certificate, divorce summons. This, plus a fifty dollar bill thumbtacked to the underside of a bottom drawer, a kind of primitive insurance, was all Calvin had: a small accumulation for thirty years on earth. There had been as much in Ogilvie's hut.

Standing skinny-legged in damp underpants, smoothing the stubble on his chin with one hand and fingering his worthless possessions with the other, Calvin felt a certain justice had been done; he did not feel guilty about Ogilvie and Mira; the only wrong was misunderstanding. The man whose insurance premium he had spent would never know. Calvin would make good the amount. He was no better off than any of them, and maybe worse.

But shortly after, having gorged himself on what was called in Bailey's menu, *Spaghetti Bolognaise* – a large knot of sticky noodles doused with ketchup and cheese – and two pints of warm Lion, Calvin was visited again by pangs of craven remorse. The pleading faces of Ogilvie and Mira ('We want you') and the smile of his own deception ('I'll be right back') scared and saddened him; even with his pistol stuck in Calvin's back and his leash tugging on Calvin's ankle, Marais had not affected him half so much. On a full stomach the memory of the Africans pained him terribly, particularly Mira, who at this distance seemed frail and very lovely. He could have been kinder; they hadn't wanted much. He had insured Ogilvie and slept with Mira, and run off. No wonder they hated whites. She lingered in his mind like a small bird circling.

'Power cut,' said Major Beaglehole, joining Calvin. He looked at the empty plate. 'God, how can you eat that stuff?'

'It's very filling,' said Calvin.

'You should ask for the rum omelette. Bailey does a good rum omelette. But you Yanks. Cranberry sauce. Marmalade on ham. Did I ever tell you about the Yank in Cairo who plastered marmalade on my ham?'

'Yes,' said Calvin.

'I could have fetched him one, I can tell you.' Major Beaglehole stopped speaking; he squinted, listening intently, with his head to the side, then straightened his head and said, 'Thought I was getting a message. They come about this time. But the storm gives me static. Been arsing about up-country?'

'So to speak,' said Calvin.

'You look a proper mess. Dirty weekend in the native quarter, what?'

'I went where you told me. There wasn't much traffic. The border post was burned down. I got stuck in Rumpi.'

'Saw you pitch up this morning, looking like the wrath of God. Bailey thought you were a burglar. I was up splashing my boots. "Go back to bed," I said to her. "It's only the Yank."'

'It was me all right.' Calvin wished Beaglehole would go away. He wanted to concentrate on Mira, in the lamplight, have a marrying reverie. But the bar had emptied, Bailey was asleep in her chair, snoring with her mouth open; she coughed without waking. Several girls lounged on chairs, Ameena, Rose, and a new one.

'Was that public house still there in Rumpi?'

'There was a bar,' said Calvin.

'The Izaak Walton. Run by a fat old chap, Dirty Dick. I know the place well. Dick's a rogue, he is.'

'I didn't see him.'

'Maybe he packed it up,' said Major Beaglehole. 'I could tell you stories about the Izaak Walton.'

'It's called the Big Drum Bar now.'

'*No!*' said Major Beaglehole in unbelief. 'Why, Dick must have flogged the place to a black.'

'There seemed to be an African running the place.'

'What about the dart-board, the bar billiards? Dick had every-thing, laid on. Even a paraffin refrigerator. It was always ice-cold at the Izaak.'

'They must have got rid of all that,' said Calvin. 'All I saw were ants.' In his confusion, trying to make the deaf Englishman under-stand, he said *aunts*.

'That's a shame,' said Major Beaglehole. 'But that's the blacks for you. Disaster. You meet any of the locals?'

'I made a couple of sales,' said Calvin.

'Used to be my old parish. Oh, almost forgot. A letter came for you.' Major Beaglehole drew a large white envelope out of his pocket and handed it across the table to Calvin.

The postmark was *Hudson, Mass.,* and *Mail Early.* It was a Christmas card from his wife, of the sort New Englanders liked to send: Yuletide on the farm, a red barn, snow-covered fields, a log fence in the foreground, a wreath on the farmhouse door, a hunter trudging through the snow with a rifle and a brace of pheasants.

Calvin ripped the card into little squares.

Major Beaglehole leaned forward and twisted the knob on his little metal box. 'Bad news?'

'Christmas card,' said Calvin. 'From my former wife.'

'Oh, her,' said Major Beaglehole. He had gone to the hearing.

How many times had he told Calvin what he had seen? Dozens. *You remember his case*, was the way he introduced Calvin to strangers.

'I think I'll go back to bed,' said Calvin. He yawned. 'I still feel crappy. What a Christmas.'

Major Beaglehole tilted his glass and saw that it was empty. He looked Calvin squarely in the eye and said, 'I killed my commanding officer, as sure as you're sitting there.'

Calvin had moved his chair back and had started to rise. He sat. 'What did you say, Major?'

'You heard me.'

He had. It was a familiar cue, Beaglehole's way of demanding a drink, startling revelation delivered with enough sincerity to be urgent, usually violent enough to make anyone pause. Only the heartless ignored Beaglehole's openings. He let these idlers pass on: they seldom refreshed him. The price of his candour was a whisky.

Calvin had not known Beaglehole long enough to be called a friend. For his friends Beaglehole abridged the stories, giving only the highlights and little dialogue. The tale he had told Bailey earlier in the evening, about his batman shooting him in the leg during a downpour, was with all its detail very long. Likewise the one about the American soldier slapping marmalade on the ham.

'A whisky for the Major,' Calvin called to the waiter.

The drink was brought, Calvin signed the chit, but Major Beaglehole did not speak.

'Now what's all this about?'

'I beg your pardon,' said Major Beaglehole. He was switching off his hearing aid. He was unlike most bores in that in his cadging of drinks he did not really enjoy listening to his own stories. Being stone deaf and a flawless lip-reader with the gift of total recall were advantages: he heard no interruptions or complaints. He spoke in a silence so fine that his shattered eardrums did not admit even the booming noise of his own voice.

'Your killing your C.O. What about it?'

'That,' said Major Beaglehole, 'is the truth. I'm not ashamed of it. He deserved it, the rogue.' He toyed with his drink and told the story at his own speed. 'It was in Cairo, just after the war, I was invited to a sort of officers' do over at Shepheard's. Now, among my own friends I was known as a character. I was famous for sleeping in my chair at important staff meetings. When called upon to speak I would open my eyes, make a trenchant remark and go promptly back to sleep.'

Calvin impatiently guzzled beer.

'I was not so well-known to the other brass, and so it came as something of a surprise to me, being introduced to one very tall colonel, to hear my name spoken by him. He interrupted the man introducing me and said my name. Then simply stood there, smiling at me, looking very pleased with himself.

' "I knew I should meet you sooner or later," he said. He had a double-barrelled name which I shall not divulge.

' "You know me, Colonel?" I asked.

' "Of course I do," he answered with a sneer, "I've seen your photograph on the mantelpiece many times."

'And with that he walked away, joking with the other senior staff and flexing his riding crop. It goes without saying that I had a suspicion as to which mantelpiece he was referring to. But to confirm it I wrote directly to my wife and put the question to her. Point-blank, you see. I thought I should never get a reply. A month passed, two months, three. In the fourth month I got her letter. She was not contrite. She admitted everything. The mantelpiece referred to by the colonel was my own, in my house at Broadstairs. Somehow this randy old colonel had met my wife, and while I was fighting in the Western Desert that chap was tupping my wife!'

'Have another drink,' said Calvin.

'Cheers,' said Major Beaglehole. 'It was crystal clear to me what my duty was. I was after all an officer in His Majesty's Own Fusiliers. I was a gentleman. What is more important, I was among people of colour, in a foreign land. I felt an especial responsibility. On Saturday mornings we had a full-dress parade, all the regiments out, the band playing. We did it partly for the Gyppos – showing the flag, as it were – and also for our own morale.

'I waited for one of these parades. It was one of those incredibly bright, sort of terribly Egyptian days. Blue sky, a slight breeze lifting the flags. And I saw the colonel, strutting about, and then standing, slapping his boot with his riding crop, watching everything in that rather sly way of his. The order was given to present arms. That was my signal. I stepped out of line and marched straight up to him. He looked a bit confused for a moment – what I had done was against all regulations, of course. Then he saluted.'

'What did *you* do? You shot him, right?'

Major Beaglehole saw Calvin's eagerness, and drank. 'I simply looked at him at first. I did not return his salute.

' "You're no gentleman," I said at last. Every eye on the parade ground was upon me, soldiers from every corner of the Empire. The band had stopped playing, but the drum-roll for the present arms was still going, and that steady beat heartened me.

' "You're off your chump, man," said the Colonel. "Get back to your regiment."

' "You swine," I said, "you filthy swine." I didn't take my eyes from his panicky face. Not for a second.'

'Then you shot him.' Calvin was nodding.

Major Beaglehole glared. His eyes were watery, his ears stuck out like jug handles. But his jaw was set. He made no move.

'Another drink?'

'Light on the soda,' said Major Beaglehole. With the drink in his hand he continued. 'Dash it all, I thought to myself. I've come this far. If I don't go through with it I won't be able to go near the Officers' Mess. I drew out my handgun and shot him twice in the face. He fell. The drums stopped. I threw the gun on his corpse, did a smart about-face, and marched off the parade ground.'

'Where did you march to?'

'To jail, you fool. Where else would I go? I had just killed my commanding officer.' Major Beaglehole swished his drink. 'They gave me life,' he said. 'After two months in the lock-up in Cairo, I was sent under guard to Gibraltar, and then to His Majesty's Military Prison in Kent, not far from my home. I was a model prisoner. Six years later I was released. They knew it was a *crime passionnel*. I was granted a full pension and came here to retire.

That was in late '51. I had aged ten years. They were surprised that I chose the colonies. They thought I was going to kill my wife.'

Beaglehole emptied his glass in one swig. Calvin did the same.

'I suppose I could have done,' said Major Beaglehole. 'Killed her somehow and collected on the insurance. But a gentleman doesn't do that sort of thing.'

'Depends on the policy,' said Calvin.

'You're mad. Of course I wouldn't.'

'If she had a comprehensive, with you as beneficiary, you might have.'

'Rubbish.'

'Or a double-indemnity that she countersigned.'

'Balls,' said Major Beaglehole. 'How do you know?'

'I've come across cases,' said Calvin. 'Homemakers' has had a few like that.'

Major Beaglehole attempted to shoot Calvin a withering glance. But he was too drunk; in the best of times his eyes were crapulous.

'I'm an Englishman,' said Major Beaglehole. 'Englishmen don't murder their wives. Wops, Dagoes, Yanks do that. We don't. We have a code and we obey it. It kept the Empire together. Dammit, it made these blackies respect us. They loved us for it, because we were British and stood no nonsense. Ask them, ask any one of these beggars. They'll tell you. That waiter there. If there's a jot of honesty in him he'll tell you that the British –'

'Why don't we just go ahead and ask him?'

Major Beaglehole thumped the table. 'Mark me, he'll say the British were our rulers and they cared. He'll say the British didn't keep us down – we kept ourselves down, he'll say. Which is the truth.'

'Let's ask him to choose,' said Calvin. 'The British or Doctor Osbong. If he says Osbong you buy me a beer. It's only fair.'

'Boy!' shouted Major Beaglehole.

The waiter stood at Major Beaglehole's elbow. He was a big man of about thirty, with a hunted look in his bloodshot eyes, and furtively hunched shoulders. His shirt was ventilated with long slashes, his shorts tattered. He was barefoot. He wore the red sash

Bailey required of all her waiters. He was nearly as tall as Calvin and uncommonly fat, the size of an old-time jazzman posing by an upright piano or holding a bugle, but without the jazzman's grin.

'Now,' said Major Beaglehole to the fat waiter, 'I want you to tell me who's the best ruler for this country. Tell me the truth, what you feel deep down. Take your time. Is it Osbong or the British Crown?'

The African looked at Major Beaglehole, then at Calvin; the hunted look left his bloodshot eyes. His jaw became defiant, his eyes wild; he straightened to his full height. 'They all exploit us,' he said.

'Go on,' said Major Beaglehole, 'choose one.'

'Brother Jaja!' roared the African, opening his mouth very wide and raising his fist in a stiff-armed salute. The sudden ferocity of it startled Calvin, but before he could respond the African had downed his tray and marched to a corner, where he continued to stare at Calvin and Major Beaglehole with that black half-mask of sullen defiance over his bridgeless nose.

'What did he say?' asked Calvin.

'I don't know,' grumbled Major Beaglehole. 'He's around the bloody bend like the rest of them. No different from Yanks, flogging life insurance.'

'Insurance is what they need,' said Calvin.

'There's where you're wrong. The black doesn't need anything. He's not like you or me. He's happy with whatever he's got. That waiter over there – if I gave him a bicycle he'd stop his nonsense right enough. That's the limit of his wanting, a bicycle, but he knows as well as I do that he doesn't *need* it.'

'They don't plan,' said Calvin. 'With insurance they begin to think about the future, they have something to look forward to. It's important.'

'It's a lot of cock,' said Major Beaglehole.

'You're a colonialist,' said Calvin.

'You're bloody right I am,' said Major Beaglehole. 'And this territory's going to be a colony again. We'll be back, just you wait and see!'

Calvin got up quickly and walked to the doorway, where Bailey dozed. He turned and shouted, 'You're a murderer! You killed your commanding officer!'

'You're just a fucking Yank who ran off with his black slut of a housegirl!' yelled Major Beaglehole across the room, wincing because he had not been able to see Calvin's lips and had turned up his hearing aid too high. 'What I did was for King and Country!'

At the word 'King' another bolt of lightning restored the lights, and during the ensuing thunder – a very mild crepitation this time – the fruit machines buzzed, the refrigerator behind the bar hummed, the fans started to spin, quacking crazily. Ameena, Rose, and the new girl hid their eyes, and the fat waiter put his broad hand over his brow, like a warrior watching for enemies. Major Beaglehole cursed as sincerely as he had when the lights had gone out. Bailey awoke, breathless, hacking and whinnying, and seized a black-handled switch on the wall. She swung it to *Off*, killing the lights. It was midnight, closing time.

Part Two

12

The morning after the storm, Blantyre was cool and had a sweet breath; it sparkled, the sun was gigantic in a cloudless sky. Brown kites and pied ravens swooped on the storm's leavings, and other birds soared so high they appeared motionless. All the dusty trees of the town had been renewed by the rain, the leaves washed green, the withered blossoms knocked off. The fresh branches still dripped. Overnight, the grey moss on the shady side of veranda posts had become lush and spongy. But there was a casualty. At a shopfront some children shovelling twigs – swept into twisted nests by the torrent of water in the storm drain – came upon the dead body of a man, apparently drowned.

On his way to Barclays Bank on Victoria Street, to collect his pay, Calvin had seen the crowd of people poking sticks at the corpse. It crouched in the narrow drain on all fours, as if it had drowned searching for something. A bystander took a mangrove pole and levered the body upright. It remained in the same stiff posture, its tongue sticking out of bared teeth. It was a grey-faced African, wearing a suit and a government necktie with the rooster motif, black cocks crowing at rising suns. The grooved handle of a bayonet protruded from the lower end of the tie like an awful black cross.

It was the closest Calvin had ever been to a dead man. He felt sick to his stomach, and a peculiar deadness dried his throat. But it was not the woeful look of horror on the corpse's face that bothered him; rather, the unfair surprise of being murdered, the indignity of dying uninsured in a dripping drain and being found, and poked, by a crowd of strangers.

He hurried away as the police arrived. At Barclays the nausea left him. A cable authorizing his December salary had come in that morning. In a corner of the bank, at a high desk, Calvin dunked the scratchy bank pen into an ink bottle, shook a drop from the nib, and made out the alimony cheque. At Jaganathy's, on the corner of St Andrew's Street and Osbong Drive (it *was* Osbong, as Marais had said, but when had they taken down the Queen Elizabeth sign?), Calvin bought a shirt of Japanese make, a razor, toothbrush (not pig bristles this time) and the rest of the essentials he lacked, including a new bottle of malaria pills.

'Time for new gap?' asked Jaganathy, smiling at Calvin's dirty panama. Jaganathy, a pin-headed Tamil, had close-set eyes, a huge nose and chin, and looked to Calvin like a Spaniard in black-face. He was as black as his African sweeper. He showed Calvin a plastic snap-brim hat.

'Not today,' said Calvin.

'Gristmas gards?' Jaganathy drew Calvin's attention to a dusty stack of festive Christmas cards, which he said Calvin could have cheap, Christmas being over. Calvin was on the point of refusing when one caught his eye: a card printed at the Stella Maris Mission in Kasupe. It depicted a nativity scene in a grass hut, with a black infant Jesus, black Mary, black Joseph, black Wise Men and, in the background, jungle foliage. He bought it, and sent it with the alimony cheque to his ex-wife.

Calvin wanted to avoid the crowd still gathered around the corpse at the upper end of Osbong. He detoured up Victoria Street, stopping at the bookshop next to the American Embassy for the new *Time* magazine. Back at the eating house he washed, shaved, changed into his Japanese shirt, and had a coffee on the veranda, reading the shortest letters to the editor, then the pictured items in the section headed 'People'.

One more detail remained before he could go to the office. He called the fat waiter.

'Sir?' The fat waiter sauntered over to Calvin, wiping his tin tray with a cloth. He was round-shouldered again, hardly defiant: this the man who had shouted and raised his fist in an aggressive salute!

'Anyone in the *chim*?'

'No,' said the fat waiter. He looked very tired; he wore his expression of fatigue with uncomfortable eyes, as if the heaviness was a poor fit.

'You're sure?'

'Sure.'

Calvin glanced at 'Milestones' and lit a cigarette. He sat very still. This first smoke of the day, and his quiet pause, made his heart patter and his breath short, but it helped to purge: it had a gently mollifying effect on his bowels. In the *chim* at the leper colony he had been cheated out of it. The wooden privy bench there had a splintery oval hole where two bats hung by their feet. He had not seen them immediately, but after he sat they had taken flight under him. They had flapped in circles in the deep cesspit, beating their wings, constipating him. He might have stayed at the leprosarium longer, but for that annoyance.

He inhaled the cigarette deeply and felt the weight of a heavy evacuation slipping on relaxed muscles. Everything hinged on that first dump of the day. If it was a success he was all right until the next morning. If not, he could not get the failure off his mind. It ruined his appetite and funked his digestion. It either happened at nine-thirty or not at all.

Calvin stubbed out the butt and locked himself in the toilet at the back of the bar. For the next fifteen minutes he sat, with the *Time* magazine on his knees, pleasurably crapping in spurts: the sound of beads spilling into a dish.

To complete Calvin's pleasure there was a short piece in *Time* about Malawi, titled '*Éminence Noire?*' Calvin read with interest.

In Malawi, Africa's peanut capital (half a million tons a year), the current slogan is 'Nuts to you'! So says dandified President and *éminence grise* of this pint-sized Republic, Doctor Hastings Kanyama Osbong, pooh-poohing the ugly rumour that the horse of his government is being shot out from under him by 100 Cuban-trained guerilla soldiers.

Black mischief is an old African story, of course, but Dr O.

441

has shown remarkable staying power for a sub-Saharan head of state. Malawi's per capita income is nothing to rave about: $20 a year – the lowest in Africa. But Osbong isn't alarmed in spite of . . .

The story went on to speak of rural unrest, 'parts of the country in turmoil', 'fear gripping the blacks who toil in peanut patches', and it finished, 'So there could be, after all, an armed *éminence noire* lurking in some jungle encampment.'

He's no more *noir* than I am, thought Calvin.

13

'Marais? Never heard of him,' said Major Beaglehole. He had dropped in at Calvin's office unexpectedly at noon, something he had never done before. He was not wearing his usual bush shirt and starched shorts, knee-socks and ox-blood brogues. He wore khaki breeches and puttees, a houndstooth jacket and a tweed peaked cap. He gave Calvin one of his very rare smiles, his old face like a loose cloth drawn up at the corners, making dozens of cheerful wrinkles.

'I think that's what he said. I was scared. He had a gun – did I tell you that?'

'Yes,' said Major Beaglehole. 'A gun. You didn't see what *sort* it was, did you? Type of weapon a man carries tells masses about his character.'

'Well, he stuck it in my guts. It was dark. Just a pistol, I guess. I don't know anything about guns.'

'Of course,' said Major Beaglehole. 'I told you before you left that the north was a shambles. My advice is don't say a word to anyone about it.'

'There was an article in *Time* magazine,' said Calvin. 'It's funny. When you read about a place you happen to be living in, it never sounds like the same place. It still sounds . . . I don't know, *foreign*, somehow,' Beaglehole wasn't listening. Calvin shuffled papers. 'You're not interested in taking out a policy by any chance?'

Major Beaglehole shook the merry wrinkles out of his face and became apologetic. 'No, nothing like that. I just popped in to say that I was a bit under the weather last night. Rotten of me to call you an effing Yank, old man.'

'No harm done,' said Calvin, and grinned.

In a low serious voice Major Beaglehole said, 'You're quite mistaken there. Don't you realize we were jawing in front of those African girls, and that waiter. That's very bad form. Encourages them to cheek us. You saw how that fat waiter got shirty with us. That's what happens.'

'He seemed okay this morning.'

'Oh, he's a nasty one. But Bailey won't hear a bad word about him. You know how it is: my Kaffirs are different from your Kaffirs.'

'That's a word I don't like,' said Calvin.

'Infidel,' said Major Beaglehole. 'Means infidel.'

Calvin saw that Major Beaglehole was staring at the mess of papers on his desk. Calvin clawed at them. 'Lots of work to catch up on,' he explained. On top were two policies, Nirenda Ogilvie and Mambo Goodson. 'New accounts.'

'I understand. Wheels of progress and all that, what?' Major Beaglehole drew out a gold pocket watch and pressed a button on the winding stem. Up popped a slim round lid, revealing the dial. 'Lunchtime,' he said. 'How about lunching with me at the Club? No hard feelings, eh?'

'Suits me fine,' said Calvin. 'I was just going to have a beer.'

'My bike's downstairs,' said Major Beaglehole.

Major Beaglehole had brought his motorcycle. He drove; Calvin sat on the pillion, his feet dragging.

The Moth's Club was on the Chikwawa Road, at the end of town, a white-washed building with a roof of red tiles, set in a clump of trees, in the centre of a ruined field. A Union Jack flew on a flag-pole, hidden by branchy camouflage.

A man stood on the veranda, watching the motorcycle bump up the driveway. He held a walking stick in one hand and in the other a drink. He shook the stick at Major Beaglehole and said gleefully, 'I *say*, Bunny, going ratting?'

'Aubrey, old man!' Major Beaglehole bellowed. He dismounted, with Calvin, and walked up to the veranda.

'What sort of kit is that, Bunny? I haven't seen a pair of those in donkey's years.'

444

'My old regimental puttees,' said Major Beaglehole, lifting a leg. 'Keeps the mud off. I always wear them when I'm using the bike. Where are the chaps?'

'Not a soul about. I came down for a game of darts. Had to settle for a whisky, ha-ha!'

'Aubrey, Calvin Mullet. You remember his case.'

'Pleased to make your acquaintance,' said Calvin.

'Case?'

'The housegirl,' said Major Beaglehole. 'You remember.'

'Well, actually,' Calvin began.

'Pleasure's mine,' said Aubrey. He winked at Calvin. He had two beaver's teeth sticking out from under a small immobile moustache. 'Well, I must press on. Wife waiting. Hip, hip!'

'Hip, hip!' said Major Beaglehole. Aubrey struck out across the ruined field.

'Seems like a nice guy,' said Calvin.

'Aubrey? Oh, he's frightfully good value,' said Major Beaglehole. 'How about a drink?'

'Beer for me,' said Calvin.

'Willy!' Major Beaglehole yelled, making Calvin jump. 'Beer for bwana, the usual for me.'

An old scarred waiter in a red fez brought the drinks. He flinched when Beaglehole reached for the whisky and soda.

'Frightfully good value,' said Major Beaglehole reflectively. 'But he's had a rough time of it, poor old chap.'

'Aubrey?' Calvin poured his beer. 'He seems very cheerful, and very, you know, very English.' He lifted his glass to his mouth, which was puckered into a chorister's 'O' to receive it.

'Yes, well, I suppose he does,' said Major Beaglehole. 'But his brother was carved up by the blacks. Then he had quite a time of it when his wife died. We reckoned here at the Club that he was taking it rather well on the whole. But —'

'Didn't he say,' said Calvin, 'his wife was, um, waiting for him?'

'Yes, dash it. Pathetic, isn't it?'

'She's not waiting?'

'She's dead,' said Major Beaglehole. 'How could she be waiting?'

'Then why –'

'One of Bailey's girls,' said Major Beaglehole. 'He takes them home.'

'I do that now and then,' said Calvin.

'Yes, I know,' said Major Beaglehole, and made a face into his glass. 'But Aubrey – well, you see, Aubrey takes them home and gets them to dress up in his wife's old clothes. Makes them stand in the scullery, you see, facing away from him. He talks to them, as if he's talking to his missis. Then he pays them, and they go. It's all very curious, very curious indeed.'

'He just talks? He doesn't do . . . anything else?'

'No,' said Major Beaglehole. 'He just talks, the poor beggar. Very upsetting really.'

'The last thing I'd do is have one of those girls dress up as my wife,' said Calvin.

'And me,' said Major Beaglehole. 'Still, Aubrey's quite a colourful character.'

Quite a colourful character, thought Calvin. It was what everyone said about Major Beaglehole. In Malawi it was the highest praise, and it was the reason no settler would take up arms against Osbong.

'Want to have a look around the place?'

'It's okay with me,' said Calvin. 'Where'd you get the name Moth's Club?'

'Memorable Order of Tin Hats,' said Major Beaglehole. 'This is Shell-hole Thirty-nine. See this badge?' On his lapel was a small gold helmet, the flat sort. 'Only the Old Bill is allowed to wear this – the President, you might call him. This year it's my privilege. Aubrey's the Wee Bill, the Vice-President, and there's also a Pay Bill and some others.' He explained that there was a British cartoonist who during the Great War immortalized the character Old Bill, a Tommy with a tin hat. Thus the names, thus the club. They met on the first Tuesday of the month.

'What if I wanted to join?' asked Calvin. Homemakers' encouraged its agents to be clubbable.

'Have you been fired at in anger?'

'In anger,' said Calvin. 'Let's see. What about that guy in Rumpi?'

'Did he take a shot at you?'

'No,' said Calvin.

'Bad luck,' said Major Beaglehole. 'You have to be shot at. In anger.'

Now they were outside, in the field, and between sips Major Beaglehole pointed out the crumbling brick squash court, the cricket pitch, bursting with weed clusters and stacked with rotting beams. 'And over here is the garden where we debagged Bobby Stallybrass back in '54.'

'What's that big thing?' asked Calvin. It seemed a large decrepit barn; branches billowed from a gaping hole in the roof.

'Stables,' said Major Beaglehole. 'For our ponies. Started with polo – that was the polo ground, beyond the tulip tree. Fever took most of the ponies. Switched to foxhunting. Enough ponies for that. Aubrey was Master of the Hounds.'

'I didn't think there were any foxes around here,' said Calvin.

'There aren't. Not one. But we had a fox pelt – a very nice one indeed. That steward you saw inside, that black chap, used to fit the pelt on his back and hare off through the bush, if you see what I mean. He was the fox, Old Willy, and very fast he was. It was a devil of a job catching him, I can tell you.'

'You chased that African,' Calvin said, 'on horses.'

'Oh, we had hounds, too. Can't have a proper hunt without hounds.' Major Beaglehole sipped his whisky and glanced sadly around at the rubble of broken buildings and the weed patches he had just identified as playing fields. 'All this was ours once. They took it all away from us.' He finished his drink, pursing his lips. 'No matter. We'll have it back soon.'

Lunch began with tepid chicken soup, topped with yellow oil-slick. A narrow wedge of fish followed. The main course, served in a quarter-inch of warm water, was a hunk of blackened meat, two boiled potatoes and pale soft peas.

'Just coffee for me,' said Calvin.

'Two coffees,' said Major Beaglehole to Old Willy.

Calvin scraped his chair back and looked around the room. On the wall were group photographs of men in cricket flannels, a large framed photograph of the Queen and one of a man holding a rifle, his boot on the mane of a small lion. Another showed a man hoisting up a fish nearly as big as himself. Nailed across one wall was a faded tigerskin, brown and striped with grey, with popping glass eyes and massive teeth enclosing a red plaster tongue. Calvin rose and went over to the skin to examine it. It was dusty and very shabby at the edges, but unmarked.

'That's *some* tiger.'

'Mine,' said Major Beaglehole. 'Shot him on a *shikari* in the Punjab in '32. I was born in India, you know. Spoke Urdu like a native. But I've forgotten it all now. Pity.'

Calvin brushed the pelt. 'Where'd you shoot him? I mean, I don't see any holes in the skin.'

'You won't find any bullet-holes in that tiger,' said Major Beaglehole. 'I shot him in the eye.'

After coffee, Calvin said, 'Did you hear about that man they found in the drain this morning – the African fellow?'

'Minister of Defence,' said Major Beaglehole. 'Knifed during the storm.'

'Terrible, isn't it?'

'It doesn't surprise me in the least. A few years ago we were getting knifed,' said Major Beaglehole. 'Someone's getting his own back.'

'Who? That's the question,' said Calvin.

'We ran this country once. It was taken away from us by the arse-creepers in London and handed over to the blacks, after Osbong made a fuss. I could quote you chapter, line and verse of that operation. It's only a matter of time before we have the whole place back. When I saw that dead black in the drain I said to myself, *This is only the beginning*.'

'I wonder who he was knifed by,' said Calvin.

'I can't say,' Major Beaglehole said very slowly. 'But remember, he wasn't knifed in the back. Only blacks do that. On the face of it he was killed by a gentleman.'

'The poor bastard,' said Calvin. He passed his hanky over his face, thinking of the dead man.

'That your first corpse?'

'Yes, I guess so,' said Calvin. 'And I hope it's my last.'

'I've seen masses,' said Major Beaglehole. 'And not blacks either.'

Calvin was folding his napkin. 'Duty calls,' he said. 'Look, Major, thanks for the lunch, but I have to –'

'Ever see a man hacked to death?' asked Major Beaglehole loudly.

'Can't say that I have,' said Calvin. He knew the opening; he ordered the whisky and soda.

'*I* have,' said Major Beaglehole. 'Hacked to bits. Thanks.' He took his drink. Calvin poured his beer.

The day, only half gone, was already wholly wasted. Calvin knew the progress of such days. It seemed that in the lifting of a glass, the staring at a tide of foam, the day flashed past: by the time the glass was set on the table, darkness had fallen.

'It was Aubrey's twin brother, Nigel,' said Major Beaglehole. 'Nigel was a prison governor on Livingstone Island in Lake Nyasa, a prison colony for the hard cases, rapists, murderers, what-have-you. But he was just like Aubrey – a wonderful *raconteur,* a fast bowler. Held his whisky like a gentleman. And Nigel had vision. He used to say, "What I want to see is a prison without bars or walls, warders without firearms, no flogging, no messing about." He was on that island for years, built a recreation hall and a cinema – very swish. Good quarters for the men. He even had classrooms put up. Started cottage industries. Everyone knew that Livingstone Prison Island sewed the best mailbags in the territory. First-class.'

Major Beaglehole grinned. 'But, you see, one can't treat them with kindness, can one?'

'That depends,' said Calvin.

'One can't,' Major Beaglehole said. 'They take advantage if they think you're weak, take the mickey out of you. Well, they tried that with Nigel; had a bit of a mess-up. Oh, the things he had to endure! One chap refused to work and started a sort of strike, you see. Said Nigel was overworking them and rot like that. Chap started a rumpus. Nigel handled that chap very well.

' "Don't want to work, is that it?" he said. "Off you go then." And he had the chappie transferred to another prison. Take the rotten apple out of the barrel, very sensible. But the others, being very largely bush types, thought that this chap's disappearance meant he was dead. Simple-minded, of course, but something Nigel hadn't reckoned on.' Seeing that his glass was empty, Major Beaglehole stopped speaking.

'Another whisky?'

Major Beaglehole closed his eyes, the subtlest of yeses. 'All the best,' he said, when the full glass appeared. 'So there was a riot on the island. All of them cock-a-hoop, screaming their heads off and waving sticks. Nigel came out of his quarters and saw them, all three hundred of them, black as the Earl of Hell's waistcoat and making a godawful racket. Incredibly off-putting.

'Nigel watched them closely. He understood the native mind, you see. Oh, he was a frightfully patient chap. He knew just how to handle them. He harangued them a bit from his veranda and said, "You have bad leaders who want to get you all killed. Don't believe these men. Go back to work – these men are misleading you!"

'Then quite unarmed he walked into the middle of this frightful mob of natives. He was cool. As tall as you, Mullet. He towered over them.

' "All right now," he said, "Rag Day's over – you've had your fun. We've all had a good laugh out of it. Now sort yourselves out, chaps, *sort yourselves out*!" '

Major Beaglehole put his empty glass on the table. He looked at Calvin severely. He said, 'And the bloody beggars hacked him to bits.'

Calvin whistled softly.

'I went with Aubrey to the island. Had to scoop up Nigel with a shovel. We put the bits and pieces in a mailbag. Naturally all the blacks had beetled off. Aubrey hasn't been the same since.'

'So you think Aubrey might have killed that African in the drain?'

'I can't say,' said Major Beaglehole. Then he gave Calvin an evil wink.

14

At tea-time Major Beaglehole suggested a game of darts but, angered by whisky, directed most of his darts at Old Willy and two or three at Calvin. The no-longer-nimble waiter ducked behind the bar. Major Beaglehole swore at him, dared him to show his face: 'Up with you! Defend your country!' Old Willy stayed out of sight; Major Beaglehole peppered the shelves and supporting posts above the quaking fez. Some darts stuck in the wood, others made tinkling glances off the bottles arrayed in rows at the back.

Fearing the public-spirited bravado that came over him in times of semi-drunkenness − five pints − Calvin cursed Major Beaglehole, staggered out of the Moth's Clubhouse and walked back to town. He chose the south sidewalk of Osbong Drive with the intention of drinking himself into a safe state of inertia. He stopped at the Goodmorning Panwallah, the Zambezi Bar, the New Safari Drinkhouse, the Victoria Club, the Highlife, each in spite of its name exactly alike: a damp musty-smelling room with a small fan, a few hard stools, Cinzano ashtrays, Lion beer ads, and not more than a handful of customers − men with banana knives. In the latrine enclosure at the back of the New Safari, a little girl of about fourteen, possibly out earning her school-fees, tapped Calvin on the leg (nearly knocking him, out of fright, forward into the pit), greeted him formally and asked, 'You want jig-jig?' She waggled her little bum. Calvin said, 'No thanks, sweetheart,' and gave her an osbong. Later, feeling perfectly drunk, fat and nerveless, he glided to his office to examine Ogilvie's policy.

He stared at the policy for a long while, holding it under the dim bulb. He was motionless, the paper trembled. He smoothed it flat on the desk and bent over to read it closely. A heavy yo-yo of drool dropped slowly from his gaping mouth on a string of spittle, and plopped on the policy. He brushed the droplet down with his sleeve, but it had already made a round wet blister on the page.

In handwriting unfamiliar to him Calvin made out a cheque covering the first three payments on Ogilvie's annual premium. He entered this amount beside Ogilvie's name in the ledger and saw that of the five other accounts listed there two were about to lapse, the period of grace gone. They were barely covered to begin with. Calvin wrote another cheque for these two.

Ogilvie had neither filled out a medical report nor named a beneficiary. A thorough medical wasn't necessary because of the small premium. Calvin got the proper forms from the file cabinet – so empty it thundered at him when he rolled out the steel drawer – and scrawled what he knew of Ogilvie, naming Mira beneficiary in case of death. In drunken candour, Calvin forged the short medical report, ticking boxes up one column and down another: *To the best of your knowledge and belief, have you ever had or been told you had or been treated for –*. In the space marked, *Any Additional Information? Attach Extra Sheets if Necessary*, Calvin wrote, 'I have dizzy spells, I shit blood. My eyes not so hot, authoritis in joint, I sleep bad . . .'

And before he could stop himself Calvin slid over the stack of foolscap paper and wrote passionately in his unfamiliar hand, *Would you insure me? I have been beaten, robbed and nearly killed a thousand times. I live at the worst end of a bad world where people drop dead every day from sickness, disease, tiredness, bugs, misery and drinking, and I live in a dirty hut without beds and food and it amazes me when I wake up alive but what do I see more misery more sickness leprosy that crucifixes can't help and a hut that leaks on me, like our proverb* (here Calvin thought a moment) *under the cabbage leaf of life we hang like hungry worms. The white man who we called Master and Bwana just threw darts at us and put us on prison island and beat us and made us wear clothes and took our land and the number one reason for this is I was born black and invisible because I am the colour of night.*

No, you would never insure me. I am a risk and I die easy. You say I am the colour of shit because my face is black, but you sit in the sun and read magazines from Nazi South Africa and get a tan and you think you are lovely brown, but you are the colour of my old granny who wears three dresses and shaves her head.

Someday soon I will rise up . . . Calvin wrote until the muscles in his hand stiffened, until he could not wag his thumb. At midnight he took a clean sheet of paper and in capital letters wrote THE UNINSURED. Underneath, he wrote, *By A. Jigololo.*

15

Calvin had been drunk and sad; he had begun the book, *The Uninsured*, on an impulse of fuddled despair; he had felt as misbegotten and slighted, as wasted and deceived as he pictured his jungle narrator, Mr A. Jigololo: squat, black, nearsighted, underfed and relentlessly screwed. Calvin had believed he was content until he had started writing; then on the page his anger was apparent. He had rushed into the book at night, in black-out and panic; but in sunlight, and sober, days later, he was no less eager to continue.

He continued in his own handwriting, sometimes altering the rambling paragraphs for effect, sometimes conveying the sense of oppression by using half-educated phrases, changing tenses and generally scrambling the grammar of the plea. The book's first pages were written in confusion, but the rest were thoughtful: it was a deliberate act – creation, rather than a valve for his idle misery. A. Jigololo had a past: born in a small rural village, he had never known his mother and was unsure that the man who drank and shared the hut and beat him regularly was his father: the man's paternity seemed essentially a rapist's, a mixture of pride and violence. A. Jigololo married a selfish girl; she was cruel and barren and he left her. He travelled, he met abuse at every turn; at thirty he was a houseboy, watching his white employers from the kitchen door, sweating in his uniform.

The Uninsured occupied Calvin's night hours, it was part of his daily routine. Each morning he awoke to the twittering of the birds and the clang of pots being shifted in the kitchen at the back of the eating house. After a coffee, a few items in *Time* and the four-page *Malawi News* (the Minister's stabbing was mentioned in neither) and the glorious dump that followed upon his carefully timed smoke, he went to his office to type envelopes for the Home-makers' Mutual brochures. At one he knocked off for lunch, had boiled cassava and fish kedgeree at a market stall, and started the day's drinking with a cool shandy, ginger ale slopped into beer. He gradually made his way, via the bars, back to the office, where he continued drinking, sending down to the Highlife for warm quarts which he gulped from a cracked coffee mug. For the remainder of the afternoon he dozed on his arms, drank, and typed envelopes.

As the afternoon wore on the clack of the typewriter slowed, and later, usually after dark, remembering he had but five clients, three of whom he kept up to date by paying their premiums out of his own pocket, he dragged out the pile of handwritten foolscap sheets and continued with his book. A. Jigololo was beside him, haranguing; he hung at the edges of Calvin's dreams; he was tire-less, he could be eloquent, he quoted scripture. The pages, written in black ink, were numbered in pencil for easy expansion of a thought by an added page (page-counting and renumbering was an obsessive activity, like the miser's, alone with his gold). On page two there was a morbid, depressing, but none the less true epigraph, from a poem by the late Vice-President of the Hartford Accident and Indemnity Company. It began, 'Death, only sits upon the serpent throne: Death, the herdsman of elephants . . .' and ended, after speaking of endless pursuit, 'Africa, basking in antiquest sun, contains for its children not a gill of sweet.' There were possible titles in it: *The Serpent Throne, Endless Pursuit, Not a Gill of Sweet*. But something austere was needed, the barbarous age demanded it. Calvin was going to use the word 'black' in the title, but decided against it as too stagey, too common (it abounded in American book titles): 'black' was losing its associations, like the word 'naked'. *The Uninsured* described the heart of the problem which was, after all, rooted in simple finance. Money made men.

He wrote until he was tired, then numbered the pages, punched holes in them and clipped them into a loose-leaf binder. Then he read, and corrected. Around midnight, flying ants and sausage flies found their way in noisy swarms to his lighted office. They came through the window and made for the light and the bright sheets of paper; they stuck on Calvin's arms and crawled up his leg. He could not kill one without making a mess, the white paste of insect guts on the swatted page. He went back to the eating house, ate some bananas and had a beer spiked with a soporific half of stout, took a reflective piss, slashing a tree in the air, and went to bed.

There were few replies to the mailed brochures, and some of his extra hours were taken up by the book, which gave him a sense of purpose and accomplishment, greater even than that afforded by making entries in a ledger or filing do-not-spindle-or-fold cards. But there were hours more, and still some loneliness.

It seemed a loneliness imposed by the solitary activity of writing – not during, but after: as if leaving the book was leaving good company, a crush of silence he had felt, single in Hudson and leaving a party alone, or that sense of falling he had experienced outside Rumpi after he had said 'I'll be right back!' and had run into the chilling darkness, the night against his face.

So nearly every night at the eating house, but always with the red eyes of the fat waiter upon him, Calvin took a girl to bed with him. They were the dregs, either schoolgirls or badly mauled hags, ignored by the regulars, the most lonely. If there was more than one in the bar when it closed for the night they quarrelled over Calvin, gabbling and pushing each other, holding to his arms, feebly protesting. They inspired dread and pity, they were awkward and fat and loaded with poisons. Some had ridiculous nicknames, Essy and Kitty, and others biblical names, Abishag and Zipporah (Abby and Zip), or names of troubling irony: Comfort, Grace, Chastity, the missions' legacy. All of them had bruises on their shins, a badge of the profession; their hands were lizard-textured. They were very shy; they giggled monotonously, they smelled, they snored. Calvin had seen men drag out their breasts and begin biting them.

'I love you, mister,' one whispered continually to Calvin. She was homely and had a cough like Bailey's. But if she seemed comfortably plain late at night in the frothy light of the bar, in the morning dead asleep in a faded dress, with sun streaming through the slit shutters, she had the alarming sadness of the very ugly. And her dry dusky arm was usually thrown across Calvin's narrow chest. On those mornings Calvin rose early, driven out of bed by the reek. He left money for them and hid outside under the window until he heard groans, bedsprings, water being slapped, a sigh, a banging door. He hated himself for ducking out: if anyone was uninsured it was them.

He felt responsible for these stragglers in the bar who turned his stomach with their guileless caresses. They said they liked him, in so many words ('You-Me-Bed,' was what they said). They had nothing. They were failures as prostitutes. And Calvin felt responsible; he wanted to help them. But there was little he could do except take them to bed and pay them, or make what sounded like wild promises, tell them to save, plan, beware, insure. Calvin tactfully defined the cause of their misery. They did not seem to care: they behaved as if it was his own misery he was describing. Calvin watched them with increasing dread. They killed time as heedlessly as queens, smoking *dagga* and *bhang* in newspaper tubes, making anonymous jungle love ('I love you, mister'); they lived hand-to-mouth, oblivious of risk, as if deathless. But they would die.

Some, not many, were lovely, and they eased Calvin of his loneliness. But what had begun as an exercise in ridding himself of loneliness became, after a time, an extension of selling insurance and writing *The Uninsured*, part of the activity of both. It was not a religious impulse. It bordered on guilt and made him ache, but it was not a sense of sin that drove him. What he felt was concern and, frustrated in his concern, acute regret. He would never be struck down blind on the road for going with the girls: he was not ashamed of his impulse. Vice was spending desire on the unworthy; but the objects of his desire were honest, they deserved kindness: there was no guilt.

Calvin wasn't offering salvation, as others had done in Malawi – only simple comfort, the possibility of a future with children, a little cash. The girls took their fees, but they did not seem interested in what Calvin said to them: the talk of bewaring and insuring. Even the Africans Calvin was personally insuring weren't interested. They never replied to Calvin's letters, they didn't seem to give a damn. Calvin continued to pay the premiums, and the longer he paid the clearer it became that to stop paying would be punishing them. And while all of this – the preaching, the wenching for charity, the paying of strangers' premiums – while all of it filled Calvin with a useful fury in adding to *The Uninsured*, it likewise depressed him, greatly; these additions, slanting with his mood, were a feverish polemic. Now, *I hate you* bulged in every line. Jigololo, a pseudonym chosen casually from a glossary of common nouns, became flesh and blood, a scary being (not near-sighted or weak). Calvin discovered impatient resentments in his narrator and gave them voice; he felt less a writer than a captive protector, helpless before his charge who, disguised as an orphan, had strayed into his life, and only at the moment of fond attachment did Calvin grasp that this was a soul-sucking child in whom it was impossible to eradicate the urge to growl and bite. Calvin was forced by fear to describe it. Such was the creation's cunning in revealing the creator's weakness. The oppressed brayings turned abusive. A. Jigololo raged.

And at last, indignantly, so did Major Beaglehole. He had watched Calvin throughout with growing disapproval. He had hoped to recruit the young chappie from Boston (for simplicity – who had ever heard of Hudson? – Calvin had given Boston as his home town; everyone from Massachusetts did when they were abroad). He believed Calvin to be a colourful character in small; he regretted calling him a fucking Yank and had confided, 'They say Bostonians are more English than the English,' which was a measure of Major Beaglehole's suspension of disbelief. He had lunched Calvin, the only American he had ever taken to the Moth's.

Major Beaglehole knew nothing of *The Uninsured*. And Calvin's beer-drinking habit didn't bother him, though he considered it working-class. Calvin's filthy clothes amused him, like Bailey's coarse threats. Major Beaglehole had one objection, but it loomed: he saw the makings of dementia (a humiliating and ineradicable blot on the copy book of every white man in Blantyre should the news get out) in what he took to be Calvin's mindless passion for the ugliest girls at the eating house. A character was made colourful by tasteless practices, but he had to understand the limits of excess.

He instructed Calvin with a story of a trek he had made his first year in Malawi, through the wildest bush. He had many such stories: he was the adventurer, setting out alone in bush jacket and topee. Each time, Calvin saw a solitary white man wrapped in jungle, and then Beaglehole would say, 'That day I lost thirty porters . . .' and dimension was given. Calvin would see the trek anew, not a little man alone in the green, but a huge caravan, half a mile long, hundreds of men with cases of whisky and kippers and HP Sauce on their heads, marching behind the Major.

And now Major Beaglehole was saying, 'At the first sign of a spot of bother all my bearers did a swan. We had sighted tribesmen on the road, certainly rather fierce, standing starkers, with their enormous great John Thomases hanging to their knees. I was left with only a knapsack, some tins of bully beef, my Webley revolver, field glasses and so forth. I offered those savages tinned food and spent some days among them.

'Weeks later I headed south, hacking my way through the thick undergrowth. And later one afternoon I burst into a clearing. There were scores of natives on their haunches muttering and dancing, a drinking party in progress – going full bore.

'They ceased their merry-making as soon as they saw me. They looked at me: fear was written all over their black faces. They were dead scared, of course. They had seen white men before, but never that close. I fancy I gave them a turn. They didn't know quite what to make of me.

'Well, I didn't pause. I've forgotten all my Chinyanja now, but at the time I spoke it like a native. I walked up to their chief, who was sitting in the centre of all those frightened fuzzy-wuzzies – he was on a throne, a sort of gilt toilet-bowl. I greeted him cordially. I told him I was a traveller and would not harm them.

' "I am British," I said. "I will share your drink."

'One thing led to another. Before I knew it we were chaffing each other and exchanging gifts. I gave the chief the last of my tinned food, drank myself silly and made a jackass of myself in front of the whole village. I had to be carried to bed.

'Late that night there was a knock at the hut door. It was the chief's envoy. He bowed low and said, "It is the chief's wish that you should have a woman." And I saw her there, standing shyly behind him, a woman with very full breasts and a blue stipple of tattoo, so to speak, around her eyes.

'If I could live through that moment again I would have shot that man and ran. But I didn't.

' "Tell the chief I am grateful, and I will use her well," I said. Which, to my eventual disgrace, I did.

'A month passed. There were holidays and festivals, and masses of drink. I told them that I really had to press on, but they wouldn't let me. I tried to bribe the chief with my pistol – I gave it to him with fifty shells. But all that came of it was that he shot one of his subjects to see if it worked. He said he would shoot me if I tried to go. I kept on with the black woman.'

Calvin knew the rest of the story: the casual encounter, leading to capture, had to end in escape, and its final feeling had to be regret. Major Beaglehole's disappearance was a more brutal matter than Calvin's ('A guard stopped me, but I told him quite plainly that if he continued to annoy me I would kill him, and with that I came back to Blantyre'), but it was a story so like his own. The principal difference was in emphasis: Major Beaglehole's shame was in going to the village, Calvin's in having deserted; Major Beaglehole spoke of the woman's ugliness ('but it's true that you don't look at the mantelpiece when you poke the fire'), Calvin thought of Mira's beauty: the hooded eyes watching for him to return. Beaglehole's was a colonial tale; and so, Calvin realized, was his own. It was not fair to insure and go. Insurance wasn't a business; it was a whole way of life.

Major Beaglehole's story should have been enough; but it was Calvin's fright on the street that decided him. It was an indulgence in terror Calvin did not believe possible in a person with as much coverage as he had. It was late. He had just left his office; he was drunk and felt the weakening effects of A. Jigololo's intimidation. He stepped off the sidewalk, holding tight to his briefcase, and vaulted the storm drain; then he paused.

The main road, once Queen Elizabeth, now Osbong, had been made broad enough (this, in 1910) for a large horse-drawn wagon to make a complete turn-about on it without having to back up. It was a long crossing. Fugitive cars whickered down it with the small pupils of their parking lights aglow. People snoozed at its edges, next to the drains. Calvin had to cross it: Auntie Zeeba's Eating House was on a back street, beyond the opposite side. But, unlit, Osbong Drive seemed to have no opposite side.

Calvin began to pick his way across, his heart sinking with each step. Bats menaced him; he waved his free arm to beat them off. A rising whicker signalled the approach of a jalopy. Calvin dashed, and felt the jalopy's breeze at his back. But he still had not gained the other sidewalk; he was breathless. Boozed, burdened by a case of envelopes to be posted, and slowed by the night heat, he wondered if he would make it. He could be run down in the darkness, flattened in an instant – and none of the girls at the eating house would lament: they didn't know his last name. He struggled toward the sidewalk. He felt like an enfeebled pensioner, a widower with no kin, caught out on a wild street at night, in his baggy pants, humping a heavy briefcase. It was not complicated fright: it was a drunken glimpse of jungle dark as he inched across the open street with the slowness of a dream cripple. He felt overwhelmed by his intentions. He didn't want to die childless, on all fours, alone in a monsoon drain.

Here was his simple hope: Mira had left birdprints on his mad heart, funny fragile tracks stitched all over it. The illiterate black girl had left her X on him; he had run from her, but still she touched him. He made it to the far sidewalk with the kind of vow on his lips that men make in storms at sea: as soon as the rains eased off he would go back to Rumpi, to the little dorp, to remind Ogilvie that he was safely insured, and to persuade Mira to come to Blantyre and live with him. He needed her.

16

'Eat!' said Mr Harry. 'Go on, eat! It's good for you.'

In the garage behind Auntie Zeeba's, a rough table – a door across two sawhorses covered with a checkered cloth – was laden with plates of food. A Tilly lamp hung from a rafter, lighting the meat and the two diners' eager faces: the fat waiter's and Mr Harry's. The fat waiter wore collarless black pyjamas, and heavy boots to his knees. He watched Mr Harry expectantly. Mr Harry's pomaded hair glistened; he had a thick black brush of a moustache which twisted as he spoke. He picked up a whole roast chicken and passed it to the fat waiter.

The fat waiter gathered the chicken up in his hands and tore it in half. It oozed grease where his thumbs gripped it. The bones splintered, making the sound of a basket being rent.

'Now,' said Mr Harry, tugging at the tablecloth with his damp fingers, 'eat it.'

Holding the chicken breast in one hand, sideways, like a harmonica, the fat waiter raised it to his mouth and lapped at the crisply varnished skin. Then he nibbled, loosening an underdone piece of skin, which shook as he ate. He put the whole piece in his jaws and tore at it by jerking his head back.

Mr Harry listened with satisfaction. The fat waiter was grinding bones and meat in his mouth.

'Excellent,' said the fat waiter, one full cheek a gleaming bubble. He smiled at Mr Harry; the black twig of a burnt bone stuck out of a notch in his front teeth. He plucked it out and used it as a toothpick.

'You like?' asked Mr Harry, eyeing a block of beef. 'Eat,' he said, 'You deserve it.'

'You take good care of me,' said the fat waiter.

'It is an honour, believe me,' said Mr Harry, opening his jack-knife with a black thumbnail. He began slicing the beef. As soon as he pierced its crust it bled into a puddle of juices, ovals of brown blood in warm grease. He sliced deftly, holding the free end of the limp slice between thumb and forefinger, and working the knife up and down in short strokes. He cut four thin slices of beef and folded them on his plate.

'Such an honour,' repeated Mr Harry. He felt the sinewy plug of meat-scrap tight in his back teeth. 'What I like is the texture. That's the best part of eating. The nice . . . chewy . . .' He chewed. '. . . Texture of meat.' He swallowed and smacked his hand on his heart.

'In the Congo,' said the fat waiter, 'they cut out their enemies' hearts and eat them. It makes you strong. They said that in the Congo.'

'I have lived in a lotta countries,' said Mr Harry, 'but not in the Congo. It is one thing I don't like, eating people. In some places they eat dogs. That's my idea of disgusting.'

'What does Marais eat?'

'He doesn't eat much. I asked. It threw me off,' said Mr Harry. 'He worries about other things. Watch a man eat and you know a lot about that man. That's what *I* say. The soldiers eat like pigs.'

'Maybe they're hungry,' said the fat waiter.

'You're going to leave those chicken bones?'

The fat waiter shrugged.

'There's a whole meal there. You're leaving the best part.' Mr Harry selected a long pale bone from the fat waiter's plate. He bit off the knob and blew it on to the floor; then he placed the bitten end in his mouth and crunched it, and sucked. 'Marrow, soft and nice, like chicken paste,' he said, tossing the shattered bone over his shoulder. 'Try one.'

The fat waiter did as Mr Harry suggested.

Harry said, 'I like to hear the little snaps when the bone breaks.'

'Good food,' said the fat waiter.

'Rice,' said Mr Harry. 'Didn't I see some rice – ah!' He found the rice bowl, put his hand in and squelched some into a ball. He popped the white ball into his mouth. 'You need that. Plain food with greasy.'

They continued eating, saying little. Mr Harry amused the fat waiter by opening a plump green bottle of Tuborg and holding it upended in his teeth with his head thrown back. He drank it all, no hands. He smashed the bottle by flinging it to the wall with his teeth. The fat waiter opened the next bottle for Mr Harry: he lifted the bottle-cap off with his teeth.

'Wonderful,' said Mr Harry. He stuffed his mouth with greens. 'Nice texture. Crunchy radish. Crunchy lettuce. Onion. Nice.'

Slowly the food disappeared and was replaced by sucked bones, rinds, knots of masticated gristle. Rummaging through a plate of bones, Mr Harry came upon a whole fish. He picked off the belly flesh, leaving the head and tail joined by a spiny backbone.

'We eat the head,' said the fat waiter, and showed Mr Harry how.

'You can have it,' said Mr Harry. 'The best thing is to get soft meat from a cracky shell. Lobster. We had them in Angola. You open their claws with a nutcracker, *crunch*. Then you pick out the soft meat. Delicious.'

. . . *pick out the soft meat. Delicious.* Calvin listened at the door, with his eye against a crack. He stood in the early morning chill, his trouser cuffs fixed with bicycle clips, his arms folded.

'Later on today I have to go up there again,' Mr Harry was saying. 'But when I come back I'll try to get some nice lobsters. You'll like them. But you can do the same with the sheep's head. *Crack, crack*, you knock the skull with your knife handle. You take away the bits of bone and, la-la, there is the soft jelly of the brain, still cool. You eat with a spoon. *Very* nice.'

Mr Harry found a dish of oranges. He peeled one and began eating the juicy segments, spraying the seeds on to the table.

The garage door creaked open.

The fat waiter was saying, 'By the end of July, every part of the country will be –' He stopped and rose to his feet.

Calvin squinted in the bright light. He could not take in the whole table. It looked like a pile of garbage; the edges of plates showed beneath the heaped leavings.

'Drink, sir?' asked the fat waiter, wiping his hands on his black pyjama suit. He picked up a napkin and folded it over his arm.

'At five in the morning?' Calvin laughed. 'You must be out of your mind.' He noticed Mr Harry.

Mr Harry tilted his head politely and, still seated, made a sort of bow.

Calvin smiled. 'You eat a big breakfast.'

Mr Harry guffawed, very loudly. 'That's good!'

'It is Ramadan,' said the fat waiter. 'We are Moslems. We fast all day and eat at night.'

'Ramadan, true,' said Mr Harry. 'You might not think I'm a Moslem, but of course I am, of Lebanese origin.'

Calvin was drawing on a pair of gloves. 'I won't be a minute,' he said. He walked to a corner of the garage and threw a large tarpaulin off Major Beaglehole's motorcycle. He wheeled the motorcycle to the door, saying before he left, 'I sure wish I had your appetite.'

Mr Harry bowed again as the door closed. He listened to the kick-starter. Once, twice: the engine fluttered. A third time: it scraped and roared. Its puttering died away. 'He always gets up so early?'

The fat waiter watched the door Calvin had just passed through. He said no.

'This is the first time. Interesting. I find that interesting,' said Mr Harry, biting into the last orange segment. Juice dribbled down his chin. 'You find that interesting?'

The fat waiter said, 'Maybe.'

Mr Harry tore a hunk of bread from a long loaf. He chose a likely plate and scrubbed it with the bread. He ate the bread, with his eyes on the fat waiter. 'You should,' he said, chewing. 'Keep a close eye on that skinny fellow. You never know, do you, brother?'

17

It was a beautiful old Matchless. Major Beaglehole said he had
ridden it through the battle of Alamein; he had loaned it to Calvin
for a quart of whisky and had said, 'Don't disgrace us, Mullet. Be
a man. And don't scratch the machine.'

Olive green, it had a wide, well-soaped saddle slung low between
the large wheel humps and suspended on springy coils. The coils
oinked pleasantly when the motor-cycle jounced. Three dials with
lazy needles were clamped to the handlebars, their cables trailing
past a profusion of spokes to the chrome hub-caps. The mudguards were trimmed with looping gold tracery and curled up,
front and rear, like the visors of antique helmets.

Calvin snuggled down on it, hugging the curves of the gas tank
with his elbows and knees. He shot up Osbong Drive, rattling the
shop windows and waking the night watchmen, then skidded
around the flowerbeds at the base of the clock tower, and down the
Chileka Road, past Henry Henderson Institute and the Flamingo
Bar.

A signboard at the crossroads outside town listed the following
choices: *Power Station, Mozambique, Southern Rhodesia*, and on
a single arrow pointing down a dirt road, at right angles to the
three choices, the one word, *North*. Calvin turned on to the dirt
road, settled into one of the deep ruts of the car tracks, and
gunned the engine. The refined bap bap, the sharp pistol crack of
backfiring when he decelerated down the dirt hills made his
pleasure greater. He flew. An hour passed: the cool low clouds of
early morning veiled the grass and the flat-topped trees with
draperies of silver mist, and long before the sun came up the sky
was streaked pink and yellow with faint sequins of stars.

He had bought a new Michelin map, but a map was hardly necessary. Malawi was finger-shaped, with mountains for knuckles; Mozambique was on one side, Lake Nyasa on the other; at the top was southern Tanganyika. There was only one road north, a bad one, and at regular distances there were white posts with the name of a town abbreviated to two letters on them and its distance in miles. Near a town called Dedza the road veered around a mountain into Mozambique for several miles. Here was a collection of square white shops at the edge of a precipice. Their signs read *Associão Portuguêsa, A. DaSilva, Games Motors*. And there were several cafés. Calvin stopped, frightening some feeding goats, and had a pint of Manica beer – it was good *tipo de exportação* from Beira – and two hard-boiled eggs on a café veranda.

Salting an egg, he watched the sun rise over low hills at the farthest end of a yellow plain. In the foreground dusty cacti grew as tall as trees, and behind them were huge single boulders with the beginnings of sculpture at their edges. Scattered between cactus and boulder were large mounds, the shape of wormcasts. For a moment a feeling of deep contentment settled on Calvin; he watched the emptiness of the desert with the same calm he had felt outside Benghazi, a peaceful aridity of soul from the vast un-peopled stretch. He was about to say, 'Another *cerveja*' when it struck him that the wormcasts were huts and kraals, there were stirrings of goat flocks at the boulders' sides and near the cacti. There was movement, so slow he had taken it for stillness; he felt sad to have misunderstood it, and remembered that he was delaying.

The Portuguese shopkeeper, a short square man with the face of a Sioux, sold Calvin a pack of brown cigarettes from Lourenço Marques, thin sticks called Pueinte-Cinco, wrapped in sweet-tasting paper. Calvin decided against having one: he knew it would bring on a shit and he feared being led to an enclosure with a hole in the floor. One had to accept the constipation of travel. He bought a bottle of Casal Garcia, a near-sweet sparkling wine; the shopkeeper obligingly loosened the cork and packed it in the saddlebag so that it would not break. The man signalled, through his African servant, that he had something important to tell Calvin.

'He ask are you going that side?' The African pointed north.

'*Si*,' said Calvin to the Portuguese shopkeeper.

The shopkeeper spoke directly to Calvin, a flood of gutturals squeezed intermittently into sibilants.

'He say keep careful,' said the African.

'What's wrong?' asked Calvin.

'African dere,' said the African.

The shopkeeper spoke urgently to the African for a few moments.

'They stopping car. Troubling and beating. Maybe you buy a *kisu* here –' The African continued to speak; the shopkeeper drew out a knife and nodded.

Calvin laughed.

The Portuguese man's Red Indian face creased. He muttered and went back into the café, kicking the door shut.

'What did he say?'

'It bad to trust African. They chop you maybe.'

'Forget it,' said Calvin. 'I don't need a knife.' He set off again.

Riding down a long slope he had a view of thirty miles ahead, the narrow brown road winding into a thicket of bush to appear, a thin shaved streak, two balding hills later; and showing again beyond that, a narrow thread at the horizon. He saw smoke trailing up from packed clusters of huts, the greeny quilt of vegetable gardens and, above it all, a black witch-like cloud dragging a grey skirt of slanting rain from the east to the road.

Closer to the rain there was a fertile earthen odour in the air, damp grass and turf, and an odd breeze which blew in circles, lifting the leaves. He knew he was in for a heavy storm. He increased his speed, keeping his eyes on the rain's hem, which was fast approaching the road. After half an hour, in one of the thickets he had picked out earlier, thinking he had outdistanced the rain – though the earthen odour was still powerful, and the air was cool – a dozen boys in red shirts, carrying rifles, jumped out from wind-lashed trees.

They aimed their rifles at Calvin's head.

'Alt oo go dere!' shouted one wearing a beret. His lower jaw was fearsome, big with teeth. He shouted again and set his gun-stock against his shoulder. He peered down the barrel at Calvin.

Calvin braked. The rain roared on leaves, out of sight, like the rushing feet of riotous peasants, voices in the jungle: this rising sound and the chill darkness of the cloud-eclipsed sun always preceded a storm. The rain was now near; in the jungle one could hear it approach; it breathed and breathed.

The red-shirted boys surrounded Calvin, each of them only a barrel-length away. On each shirt was pinned an Osbong badge, like a campaign button: the official photo, the snarling one. They were Youth Wingers, though not all young. Curiously enough the smallest were very old, the biggest looked youthful; the one with the beret was not more than eighteen.

'What,' said Calvin in a voice not his own, 'can I do for you?'

'Dis loadbrock,' said the one with the beret, still with his face against the rear sight of his gun. 'Where you coming?'

'Blantyre,' said Calvin. His trembling tongue gave it four syllables. He twitched before the gun muzzles, blinking fiercely: he could see their fingers crooked around the triggers. 'Take it easy,' he said. 'Be careful with those things.'

The beret growled an order; a frizzy head appeared at Calvin's chest; he felt his pockets being slapped, the buckle on his saddle-bag tinkling. Calvin still held the handlebars of the Matchless. He said irrelevantly, 'I'm a resident of Blantyre,' and attempted a smile.

One boy reached over and unscrewed the chrome gas cap.

'Don't think I'm being nosey,' said Calvin, 'but what are you looking for? Maybe I can help you?'

'We looking,' said the boy putting his eye against the greasy hole to the gas tank, 'for a certain gentleman.' The gas fumes stung his eye. He wrenched his head away.

'What your name?' asked the boy, wiping his eye.

Calvin told him.

'It not you,' said the boy with the beret. None of the older wizened men had spoken; but they looked impatient to Calvin and still steadied their rifles on his face. The beret moved the muzzle of his gun to a spot just below Calvin's nose. The noise of the approaching rain grew very loud, the road turned black. The beret shouted '*You Chinese?*'

'No,' said Calvin trying to raise his voice. 'I'm not, I'm –'

'He Chinese,' said a high voice at Calvin's back. Several rifles rested on Calvin's spine.

'Sure, *he* Chinese.'

'I think he Chinese too,' said the beret.

'Look at me,' said Calvin 'Go ahead.' He took off his glasses. 'Do I look Chinese?'

'Do not know,' said the beret. 'I never see one. But I *think* you Chinese.'

The bottle of Casal Garcia blew its cork, soaking the red shirt with his hand in the saddlebag. The rest broke into mocking laughter, seeing bubbles on the boy's face and his soaked shirt. As they laughed – the laughter made their rifles shake and poke Calvin – the rain came, drenching them all and putting a stop to their merriment. They turned their wet faces up to the low spitting sky; their shirts were black.

'Take this bottle,' Calvin said, handing the wine to the boy with the beret. 'Drink-drink! Very good!'

The rain made deafening slaps.

The beret took a swig and grinned. The others mobbed him, cracking their rifles together, pleading for a drink. The beret swigged furiously, swinging the bottle up with one arm and holding the others off with his rifle butt.

Calvin saw a straggler standing near him, watching the others, idly licking raindrops from his lips. Calvin hissed to him. 'This,' he said, tapping the Osbong button on the boy's collar, 'for this' – he showed the boy a handful of coins. It was raining so hard Calvin's cupped hand splashed full of rainwater.

The boy smiled and quickly unpinned his badge. Seeing that the rest had run into the trees, he snatched the money and followed them.

Calvin pinned the badge to his own collar. He tromped on the kick-starter and took off into the driving rain.

For a mile the road was slippery, but passable. Then the soil loosened to a soft porridge of muck. Gobs shot into Calvin's face, layers of the sticky stuff accumulated on the heavy tyre treads, rubbed at the mudguards and slowed him. He could barely see through his spattered lenses. His toes ploughed the mud. He dismounted and pushed the machine up one hill, but at a second, very long hill, he gave up half-way and, leaning the motorcycle against a tree, put his head down and ran for shelter.

He found a dry spot in a grove of peeling blue-gums. He cleaned his glasses. He wrung the water from his cuffs. Then he looked up and sighed.

Ten yards away, huddled under a leafy fig tree, were more red shirts. Two braved the heavy sheets of rain that separated them from Calvin.

'Alt oo go dere,' said one, casually sticking his rifle into Calvin's stomach. Calvin's whole body went instantly numb. Another rifle muzzle rested in the hollow at the small of his back.

'Is this a roadblock?'

'Is,' said the voice at the rear.

'Well, the damn road –'

'Load over there,' said the one in front. He motioned with his rifle, sliding it across Calvin's belly to point to the road.

Calvin looked at the boy's face. The boy was staring at the badge on Calvin's collar, and smiling.

A moment later, with the blessings of the two red shirts and the eager approval of the others wagging their rifles from the dry spot under the fig tree, Calvin crawled back through dripping forest on to the road. He didn't want them to change their minds. The rain fell with no less vigour than before. Calvin found the motorcycle and laboured up the hill, pushing it, walking beside it, but keeping the engine running in first gear. He worked the throttle, the engine griped and strained. Calvin's shoes were huge with mud.

It was worth the struggle. At the top of the hill he passed through a wall of rain on to a dry sunlit road. It was like leaving a rainy room; the rain was just behind him, pelting on a dark road. He stood in light red dust, in warm sun. After an hour his clothes were dry. But his shoes stayed soggy: they slavered bubbles when he flexed his toes.

There were no more roadblocks, though Calvin expected them and prepared for them by slowing down at blind leafy bends – good ambush spots. Closer to Marais country he took off his Osbong badge, for he knew that if he was stopped again it would be by Marais's men. On the other hand, he was not afraid of Marais: he had passed through that ordeal and lost only three pairs of glasses. If Marais stopped him, Calvin planned to say, 'I told them everything you said, about your soldiers and your radio transmitter. You've got them scared shitless.'

What a place, thought Calvin. In what could have been the simplest country in the world, nothing at all was simple. Drunk, he had expressed a similar thought to Major Beaglehole: 'You always think it's going to be cheaper here, but somehow it's always more expensive.' He was not sure what he had meant by that, though Major Beaglehole said he agreed. 'It's a fine place, Mullet,' the Major had said. 'I've spent some happy days here, and some bloody awful ones. I can't say I like the natives, but there are some damned colourful characters here. It's just as you say, one doesn't expect it.'

Bumping along the road on the motorcycle, Calvin had a more lucid perception: Malawi was not a country, not in the most generous definition of the word. He had seen the figures; Home-makers' Mutual showed more of a profit with its insurance than Malawi did with a bumper harvest of peanuts. Even Osbong admitted it: 'What did we Africans do to deserve such a poor place to live?' Most countries had factories here and there sending up smoke, an occasional election or riot, paved roads and stop lights. Most countries made a little money. But Malawi was a political accident, an attempt at order foiled by lusty jungle; it was bankrupt. Its one factory, Chiperoni Blankets Ltd, had to import rags from Italy to make the blankets with. Calvin had heard it with astonishment: *You have to import rags?* When Wilbur Parsons told Calvin where he was being sent, Calvin hadn't been able to locate it on a map. It seemed not to exist.

It had a president, a clownish Papa Doc defended by a *tonton macoute* of giggling Youth Wingers who, during the day or when it wasn't raining, put up roadblocks and searched for spying Chinese. It had a seat at the United Nations, a national flag, and a national anthem. But no, it wasn't a country. Calvin thought of Mira's words: 'That not name . . . That *signature*.' It was something like that; not a country, but a situation, a patch of jungle in Central Africa, so little a man on an old motorcycle could travel most of its length in one day and in doing so see no dwelling higher than one storey and, except for the Dodge City place of Lilongwe, no town larger than ten huts and two shops – see nothing in fact more significant than bags of peanuts decaying in uncollected mould-green stacks by the roadside, the one roadside.

Yet so much of it was lovely: the air charged with ozone, the fields of wild flowers and wide jug forests of baobabs, the sky's serious blueness, the faces of rocks; it was a dense beauty that made everything seem edible, the jungle was a salad, the bamboo looked succulent, the mountains were muffins.

Its prettiness was circumscribed by poverty, and though there was nothing newsworthy in either, the *National Geographic* had once taken photographs in colour: crocodiles and dik-diks, toothy and titsome black ladies carrying bundles of sticks on their noggins, ballocky black men paddling hollow logs down a coursing river. But that could have been any nameless jungle. *Time* magazine's notice was particular; it spoke of riot and intrusion, an infant war: it named Malawi. So Malawi was important. Murder, the equatorial commonplace, mattered to the world; a rumour of death had put Malawi on the American projection of the map, as tulips had done for Holland. That was its claim to statehood: the possibility of its being attacked. Though it had never existed seriously in print before, now it had a name; and the use of the name seemed to burden it with an importance it never needed and couldn't pay for.

Calvin arrived at the Big Drum Bar late in the afternoon. He decided to stop for a drink, hoping he would meet Ogilvie and

Mira. That would be appropriate: he had kept his word about coming back. The Christmas decorations were tattered, the bar was empty. Calvin called out, 'Anyone here?'

The bartender showed his head. Scaly bruises on his face were painted purple. He had a square of gauze taped over one ear.

'Remember me?' asked Calvin. 'The guy selling insurance?' He put money on the counter. 'A beer – and have one yourself. You look like you could use one.'

'No beer,' said the bartender. He touched at a purple bump. 'They took it away.'

'What do you mean? *Who* took it away?'

'Soldiers. In the trees.'

'The ones with that *mzungu* leader?'

The bartender said yes, them.

'What a bunch of bastards,' said Calvin. 'When did they do it to you?'

'Last night they come, drink beer, whisky, just taking like that. Beat some people here. I hate them too much.' The bartender looked at Calvin, as if he had just recognized him; he said with force, 'Your friends! Yes, yes – they troubled your friends!'

A dying fire smouldered in front of Ogilvie's hut. The compound was empty, the aimless trickle of smoke and the unimpeded shafts of sunlight giving it an aspect of abandonment. The two hut doors were closed. Calvin killed the engine and propped the motorcycle on its kickstand.

'Mira!'

His voice sounded helpless in the silence. It stopped the birds chirping and made a fluting locust pause. The place seemed deserted. Near to the fire, pots had been overturned; they leaked stiff gruel. The Shell Oil-can was on its side.

Calvin tried the left-hand door. To his surprise it swung open, exposing the dark room where he had made love to Mira on that first night. It was so still and shadowy it appeared empty. But flies buzzed, and a figure lay on the little cot, in a stained undershirt and sarong and wearing one plastic sandal. Calvin started forward with a greeting; but he quickly checked himself and turned, fanning at the flies, when he saw that the figure – it could only have been Ogilvie – had no head.

He did not open the right-hand door as he had the left. He rapped on it, holding it shut, afraid to see what was inside. He went on knocking persistently, in anger; and after a while, between knocks, he heard someone inside burst into tears.

18

'Here he comes,' said Marais. 'And she's with him. What did I tell you?' He lay on his belly, his elbows dug into the soil, and squinted through a heavy pair of binoculars. While he spoke, he spun the grooved focusing wheel, beckoning into sharpness with his forefinger the image of the two people on the motorcycle, the insurance agent, the village girl.

Marais moved to a sitting position and watched the motorcycle disappear, leaving a red dust-cloud on the brow of a hill. Marais was impressed by the fast driving, by the guts it took to start on a long journey at nightfall. He pushed his dusty cap on to the back of his head. In his left hand was a plump cigar: a jewel of a glowing spark was set into the coal of the blunt black tip. 'He didn't waste any time. I was right, wasn't I?'

The African soldier next to Marais was silent. He worked the bolt on his rifle, preoccupied.

'Wasn't I?' Marais insisted.

The African muttered and slid the bolt, slapping it down.

'Maybe you'll listen to me now,' said Marais. 'Let's get back to camp.'

In the babble of the camp at dusk a group of men stood around two prisoners tied to posts. Although the two men were tied, they spoke loudly and laughed often; the conversation was a relaxed one.

Marais had started towards them when he heard this note of cheerfulness in the talk. He paused momentarily and thought, They only understand pain. They had to be hurt themselves. Pain taught reliable humility. In the art of revolt there were more lessons in failure than in victory, and if the enemy was not strong enough to make a man beat a retreat into discipline, the punishing would have to take place in his own camp.

That morning, after the prisoners had been caught, Marais had searched through his books, and he had copied into his notebook: *The punishment of putting a soldier in jail for ten days constitutes for the guerilla fighter a magnificent period of rest, ten days with nothing to do but eat, no marching, no work, no standing the customary guard, sleeping at will, resting, reading . . . From this it can be deduced that deprivation of liberty ought not to be the only punishment available in the guerilla situation.* They were not his own words, but they were justification enough for what he planned.

'Get away from the prisoners,' Marais said. He never shouted; he didn't have to: his voice had an edge that was always heard. 'Make a circle, and bring the first prisoner forward.'

An African was released from his pole and led over to Marais. He stood before Marais unsteadily, wearing only a pair of khaki shorts, and in an exaggerated posture of attention, for his hands and arms were tied tightly behind his back. Roped as he was, with his chest out, he appeared smugly defiant. He picked out a friend in the crowd of watching soldiers and broke into a chuckling smile. It was for a few seconds the only sound in the camp, this assured cluck.

There had been four previous trials. Marais had always spoken eloquently. He had listed the qualities of a good guerilla soldier and then asked the prisoner to explain what he had done. It was a public confession. If the confession and apologies came too readily, as they often did, Marais humorously ridiculed the offender and allowed the others to jeer. His words were translated by a comical soldier named Brother Yatu, who screeched the mockery like a mad bird and worked himself into a frenzy of abuse, as Marais' words became his. The others shouted 'Shame!' 'No, no!' and laughed. And after a week in jail the humiliated prisoner was released and allowed to rejoin his patrol. It was no punishment at all.

Brother Yatu took his usual place, next to Marais.

'We won't need you tonight,' said Marais, waving him off.

Marais looked at the prisoner's bare feet: they were like roots ripped out of the ground, dusty, tuberous, with small yellow nails on the mangled toes.

The prisoner was still smiling into the circle of men.

'For murder,' said Marais.

The prisoner uttered a wordless yes; he closed his eyes and thrust out his lower lip.

'Yes! Yes!' shrieked the others. 'He's a dog!' They stopped abruptly to let Marais start his harangue.

Marais said simply, 'Where are the witnesses?'

Two boys, each about fifteen, with large eyes and long adolescent legs, marched over to Marais. They yawned nervously. Their cloth caps sagged over their ears, the peaks askew; their shirt sleeves were pushed up, bunched under their arms. They rocked back and forth in their large boots. They were dressed absurdly, but they were not absurd; their faces were small, fragile with childish concern; their hands were fine, their wrists almost feminine. They plucked at their trousers with their fingers.

'You are to punish the prisoner,' said Marais. 'You were brave enough to report to me what happened last night in the village. Take this pistol.'

The prisoner bumped his head questioningly at the translator, Brother Yatu. Brother Yatu shook his head; he understood English, but he did not understand what Marais was doing. He shrugged and folded his arms.

'This is how we forgive a murderer,' said Marais, motioning to the boy with the pistol. 'You are to shoot him through the right foot, the top of it.' Marais demonstrated. He took the revolver and pointed it at his own instep and said, *Pah*, here, you see?'

The prisoner saw Marais's demonstration; he threw his head back and yelled horribly. He continued yelling as he was tied to his post and wound with rope from his neck to his ankles. The young boy approached, the revolver so heavy in his small hand that it aimed down, testing his wrist. The prisoner rolled his head from side to side and, when the boy aimed the revolver, picking out a spot on the naked veined instep of the rootlike foot, the prisoner tried to dance. The muzzle was an inch away.

In fear the African's nose grew very small, his open mouth quite square, his face tight and slick, like a striking snake. He spat clumsily on the boy's uniform.

A loud report, a ringing bang, silenced the prisoner's screamings. Blue smoke mingled with a puff of dust. The prisoner's mouth was stretched open, his eyes shut, his face tensed in the expression of a scream; but the face did not relax into simple horror again or utter another noise. The second boy, holding the revolver awkwardly in two hands, fired a bullet through the left foot. The prisoner fainted, went limp on his ropes. He was dragged to a tent to be bandaged. At the base of the post was a scuffle of shifting footprints, and most of those hollows were bloody.

The second prisoner had already started to cry. It was Brother Mussa, the Yao translator, the rapist. Over the sound of Brother Mussa's blubbering Marais ordered a hole to be dug, just in front of the post. Marais had not finished speaking, but already the men had started to dig. He was indicating the size of the proposed pit with a vague circling of his cigar; he was saying, 'Right here, at his feet. You see what I mean –' Five men stripped off their shirts; they hacked at the spot with mattocks and spades.

The face of Brother Mussa was toffee, pulling and stretching. His mouth and eyes widened as the hole widened, the wails grew shrill as the hole deepened. With each gravelly crunch of the mattocks, stray pebbles flew up at Mussa's face, making him gulp and shout at the hole in broken English, for Marais: '. . . big picture Osbong in the room. They spies! I know spies! . . . These women are ever liars . . .' He denied the rape, he accused several of the watching men of doing it, he battled with his knots, and he wailed his appeal to the scroop of the spades in the hole.

Now two men stood back to back, waist-deep in the hole, shovelling dirt cakes into baskets and bumping each other with hurrying elbows.

It had gone dark, moonless; night had obscured all the landmarks of the camp and made the diggers invisible. But they could be heard: they gasped, hacked, chucked dirt in a steady three-beat rhythm. Brother Mussa whimpered; he could hear the hole being dug at his feet.

'Lights,' said Marais. Instantly, lamps were brought, and the clearing filled with light, making it seem the dusty chamber of a high-ceilinged cave. A grim soldier's face showed over each lantern; the face of Brother Mussa shone.

Marais regarded the tamed faces of the men; they obeyed now, he had not been wrong. Discipline had to be one of the bases of action of the guerilla force; even Che had said, *Punish him drastically in a way that hurts.* Brother Mussa was still shouting; the shovels obediently scraped the bottom of the hole.

'That's enough,' said Marais. The men stopped digging after Marais repeated it. Brother Mussa was making a racket; he had been a trusted man, the chief translator – what had he said to the men? It had to be worse for him; Marais had valued him. And the rape: *drastically in a way that hurts.* Marais pointed a finger at the shouting man, held it a moment, then let the finger bend and fall slowly, the nail describing an arrow's path into the hole. The men understood: it was the order chiefs gave when they wanted subjects to kneel.

Brother Mussa was trundled into the hole up to his armpits and held in place. The loose earth in the baskets was dumped back and tamped around his body. Only Brother Mussa's head and arms were free; the rest of his body was sunk into the ground. His breathing was troubled, his lungs were pressed by the earth. It was an eerie sight, Brother Mussa's large angry head with two limbs attached, like a piteously beached sea animal – head fitted neatly to arms – making fishmouths, scrabbling and clawing at the sandy soil.

Marais turned and looked around. He saw what he wanted, an egg-sized stone; he picked it up and weighed it thoughtfully with a bouncing hand as if he was considering whether to bite it. For a minute the only movement in the circle of men was Marais's filled hand, rising and falling, the arm-shadow truncated and made numerous by the hissing lamps. Worried into silence, Brother

481

Mussa watched Marais with anxious curiosity, his arms flat on the ground, his head back, no longer a stranded sea animal but a man in quicksand.

All at once the limp hands of Brother Mussa rose and produced a yellow palm-and-finger butterfly; it clung and fluttered before his squawking face. Marais was winding up, crooking his arm behind his head. He pitched the stone thirty feet, contorting the butterfly in a spasm of panic (here a smack of stone on bone) into two black fists. Brother Mussa hammered on his eyes.

The lamps were set down, a clamour of light. With a shout the men stooped for stones and began to pelt the head and arms rooted in the centre of the clearing. The men bumped each other, as if they were relearning an old ritual and were practising it in a poorly lighted place.

'What if he dies?' whispered a voice behind Marais.

'If he dies,' Marais said – but he did not have to take his eyes from the torn face and whirling arms of Brother Mussa to know that the voice was Mr Harry's – 'If he dies, then it means he's guilty, doesn't it?'

19

'This beece of gloth,' said Jaganathy, bumping the bolt along the counter and snapping a few feet of material with deft fingers, 'it was brinted in Holland. Observe golours: so bright. Battern: so glear. Nice imported style all ladies want.' Jaganathy regarded his two customers, Mira and Calvin.

Filing a claim for a bereaved family, Calvin had often wondered where the money went. It was no substitute for grief, naturally death made people cry. But Calvin had guessed that the cash, now where mournful loss had been, gave their lives a hopeful nudge and helped them start all over. It was not the insurance agent's job to go back and make sure the money was well spent; Calvin knew that nothing blotted tears like money. All insurance could be reduced to that. Calvin had always computed the amounts due and sent it with a note offering his condolences. He had given Mira Ogilvie's endowment when they arrived in Blantyre and had said, 'I don't know what to say.'

'Six-seven yards this,' Mira was saying to Jaganathy. 'Think of Ogilvie,' said Calvin. The first item had been a coffin for Ogilvie: mahogany, with chrome handles and lined with cushions of black silk. Jaganathy was frank in his disapproval; he recommended cremation. 'It is better to burn. Cheap, quick, no trouble.' But during the course of the morning the coffin proved useful. Jaganathy put it on the floor of his Madras Bazaar and filled it with Mira's purchases.

Calvin stood to the side, watching the coffin fill: a pair of sunglasses in a sequined case, a dozen Portuguese bras, a crate of scented soap, two pairs of gold quilted slippers, ten yards of raw silk, a clock.

'And what else?' asked Jaganthy, totting up the amount in the margin of a newspaper.

Mira ran her eyes over the shelves. She smiled. 'Comb and blush.'

'*Nice* gomb and brush set, *matching*, made in Great Britain.' Jaganathy tossed it in the coffin and turned to Calvin. 'You are very lucky chap, Mr Calvin. Our brices they are still modest. But next week they will be —' He closed his eyes and threw his head back, a crafty agony.

'That's what you always say.'

'Pomade,' said Mira.

'Quart jar, year's supply.' Jaganathy leaned forward and cupped his hand over his mouth. 'We are getting nationalice,' he whispered hoarsely. He grinned, but there was no pleasure in the grin.

'Tea caddy.'

'Nationalized?'

'*Collapsible* tea caddy. I throw in nice tea cosy half-brice,' said Jaganathy. 'Nationalice. You have not heard? Osbong is taking over all retail businesses in town, drygoods shops. Just,' he pulled the tassels of the tea cosy with his long fingers, 'like that.'

'He can't do that. It's against the law.'

'Blandy bottle.'

'South African, one case VSOP, aged on the train from Capetown, ha-ha!' Jaganathy wedged the case into the coffin, groaning. He straightened his back. 'The law, the law! He will nationalice law, too! They will nationalice our backsides and tax our shit.' He turned to Mira, 'Wireless from Japan? Radiogram?'

Mira said yes.

'Nice tunes with these,' he panted, heaving them. 'I tell you Osbong has no money. Trouble all over. Chaps want to kill him. He is vexed. What to do? He needs cash so he takes over my trading gompany. I am obliged to work for him. I am baid,' Jaganathy gave Calvin another mirthless grin, 'a *salary*, if you blease.' He spat.

Mira bought a Jim Reeves album, a Mildred Mafuya record, a watch made in Hong Kong, five Indian bangles, a book.

Jaganathy wheezed. 'Watch out, Mr Calvin. They will nationalice your business, too.'

'They won't make any money on me,' said Calvin. 'I'm running at a loss.' As soon as he said it he thought of Ogilvie's endowment and looked at Mira.

Mira bought a tennis racket, some earrings, five headscarves, a nickel-plated fountain pen.

'Osbong can do anything. Formerly, it was difficult. Now it is, *ptah*, simple,' said Jaganathy. 'Super handbag made of blastic. Bocket mirror.'

'Two,' said Mira.

'If they tried that in the States there'd be trouble,' said Calvin. 'They'd never get away with it.'

'This is not States, thank you,' said Jaganathy. He wrapped two handbags, two pocket mirrors.

'Well, I don't know anything about politics. I suppose they've got some reason for doing it.'

'Reasons! Of course, blenty reasons! They need money so they steal from us. Bathing towels? Shower cap? Ladies gloves?'

'They're not stealing – they're nationalizing your business.'

Jaganathy looked angrily at Calvin. 'You Europeans give these blacks such big words. I speak Chinyanja very well. In this language there is no word nationalice. They get from you. Tomorrow you give them another one, and they will rob us another way. They are goons. Girdles fresh from Liverpool? Sockings?'

'So you're blaming us for your problems?'

The coffin was full. A tea chest was brought, and the items for which Mira had nodded assent – the girdles, the stockings – were dropped in. Mira took out a stocking and started to examine it. Jaganathy took it from her and stretched it before her face as if he was working a concertina. He spoke to Calvin. 'I blame no one. But I tell you one thing. At one time, not many years before this, beeple here were so timid. They stole nothing. They liked to smile at we Indians. Hello, bwana, good morning, bwana, cheerio, *muli bwanji*. You leave the door to your godown unlocked. Your house. Bantry, larder. Many imported goods inside, wireless berhaps. These Africans see no locks, but they do not blace a finger on anything. This is true. They were mice. Little mice. Now,' said

Jaganathy, 'they want to kill us. I ask you one question – why?' He snapped the stocking into the tea chest.

'Big teddy bear.'

'Look,' said Calvin, 'whose country is this?'

'I agree it's not mine,' said Jaganathy. 'But is it theirs?' He wrapped the teddy bear and put it in the tea chest.

'Of course it's their country,' said Calvin.

'Necklace, with gold beads.'

'Excellent choice, madam,' said Jaganathy. He turned to Calvin. 'Monkey swings on tree. He eats nice fruit there. He is jolly. He sits on branches. He likes tree very much. But,' said Jaganathy, poking a sharp finger into Calvin's face, 'does tree *belong* to monkey?' He shrugged, sheathing his finger in his trouser pocket. 'That happens in countries also.'

'I think you're being pretty rotten,' said Calvin. 'Pretty rotten.'

'It's true I am a simple man, just a foolish trader. I am sorry to upset you and your wife, but –'

'She's not my wife,' said Calvin. 'She's an African! And she's got as much right to be here as you do.'

'She is welcome,' said Jaganathy. 'I thought she was your wife.'

'Me wife,' said Mira. 'This *mwamuna wanga*, my husband.'

'Not yet, sweetheart,' said Calvin. 'In a week or so –'

'No,' said Mira.

'I take your word for it, Mr Calvin. She owes me pounds one hundred and twenty-one, osbongs sixteen only.' He smiled at Mira and added, 'Gash.'

Calvin had filed the claims before; but he was unprepared for what had happened in the three days since Ogilvie had been beheaded in Rumpi. Here was Mira counting bills into Jaganathy's open hand. Virtually a waif, Mira was paying half of Ogilvie's endowment to the doomed Indian for a load of junk. Calvin could not look. There was no wisdom, nobody prospered; there hadn't been much grief, only fear, for Mira refused to tell Calvin why the soldiers had killed Ogilvie, and now she didn't remember. The event was lost, like any event that takes place in a jungle: Ogilvie was turned into money, and the money into junk and discarded. Perhaps that was what all insurance could be reduced to.

Witnessed by Major Beaglehole and Bailey, the marriage between Calvin Mullet (condition: divorced) and Mira Nirenda (condition: spinster) was performed in the Office of the Government Agent, Blantyre, in the last week of February. The dingy office was decorated with faded views of the lake and some of wild obtuse-looking animals, a mop-maned lion staring at his paws, a glabrous hippo kneeling at a puddle's edge, his bristly chin resting in the water, his armoured buttocks aloft.

Calvin and Mira stood; Major Beaglehole and Bailey sat on camp chairs, tacky things with woven plastic backs and seats. A worn blotter on a dented table was imprinted with an almost Arabic configuration of reversed signatures, one over the other, spidery and black, all sloping the wrong way. The ceremony was performed by an aged African in a threadbare double-breasted suit with broad winglike lapels. He read out of a leatherbound lawbook, turning from dog-ear to dog-ear. In ten minutes it was all over, the signatures were appended to the perforated marriage certificate. Beaglehole prefaced his name with three initials; Bailey licked the ballpoint, stifled a whiffling belch, and wrote her name laboriously, smudging the certificate with her thumbs.

It was a dry legal ritual, brief, ordinary, final until divorce. The bride and groom did not kiss; the elderly black man shook them by the hand and wished them good luck. He had a kind smile. Calvin smiled back. This was joy. Love required a kind of genius Calvin knew he did not have. It was a vertigo of mortal loneliness he had felt. Fortunately it was loneliness and not desire: her simple presence was a satisfaction. It was all he needed; she was safe. He had once desired the tender knowing body of his small-souled former wife. But they had not shared anything; they had only conspired to live together and she had made him more lonely, for desire, like appetite, was temporary: it was whisked away with a grunt. Loneliness endured without desire's hungry initiative; it was weak, it whined, wanting company. This, with black Mrs Mira Mullet,

Calvin had. Married, Calvin felt as if a warm sunset had been gathered from the black branches of a distant grove of trees and cleverly squeezed into his belly.

Part Three

20

Marais was dead. He had been gunned down on a city street, shot in the back while crossing the wide Rua da Boa Vista in Beira, Mozambique. The Portuguese secret police had pounced on him; his capture was announced in a thick headline in the *Noticias da Beira*. He was placed immediately in solitary confinement; torture was rumoured. The South African government asked for his extradition, to stand trial for the Post Office bomb in Johannesburg. But he was not extradited. There was a brief closed trial in Lourenço Marques. Marais was found guilty of treason and condemned to death. He was swiftly hanged.

As the days passed, detail was added. The authorities said he had pleaded for mercy and died a coward's death; he had given the names of all his lieutenants. An unmailed letter was found among his effects, in his own handwriting, in which he said that every man, woman and child of Portuguese origin would be killed, and that at night you would hear their blood running in the drains and choking the sewers. Much was made of the phrase, 'hear their blood'. Privately it was whispered that Marais had been brave at the moment of death, his last words, 'Now I will show you how a man dies.' He had leaped on the rope and broken his own neck before the hangman could mask him or spring the trap.

In his name a farm was attacked and burned, the owner murdered. Five Africans were picked up; they readily confessed, were sentenced and put to death, and their last words were that they would die as Marais had, bravely. They were shot, in public, in a bullring just outside Beira.

Marais heard of the execution of the five men in September. He was in a café in Vila Cabral, wearing a brown Franciscan cassock and fingering a rosary; a helpful planter translated the Portuguese article into French, bought Marais a glass of port, and asked to be blessed. Marais made the sign of the cross at table level and piously moved his lips. Then he raised the cowl of his cassock and pulled it over his head; he boarded the train for the lake.

He had reason to doubt the story of the five Africans, for he had read of his own hanging three weeks before in the *Noticias*, and he knew the PIDE had faked it. But he was heartened by the power of the lie: he was now convinced that when he did die it would matter. The planter had believed both stories and so, he said, did his tenants and their Africans.

The shooting was true. Three or four hard inches of his spine still gave pain. Using two mirrors he had looked at the scar where the bullet had gouged muscle and nicked several vertebrae, a roughened purplish bruise on an awkward part of his back. He felt the wound tugging at him when he ran or lifted something; he imagined it would hurt if he made love, but with the Franciscan habit he had taken a vow of celibacy. He looked at the scar only once; the one look killed his interest. But others could see it. It had silenced the mission priest who cauterized it and sponged it with alcohol. It was important to Marais that others were moved by it. It was proof he had been shot. And he knew what people would say: 'Marais was shot . . . in the back.'

Sheepishly he went first-class, intending disguise, not comfort. But when he got out at Metangula he saw three white-clad priests emerge from a third-class compartment. At the rail-head he took the lake steamer to Karonga, where he set out on foot for the prearranged spot on the Songwe River, at the northern frontier of Malawi, where he was to meet his men, who were marching from Dar es Salaam. He wondered if they had read of his death; they were already a week overdue.

Hope came unexpectedly one night, eight days after his arrival. He saw some nearby hills burning: snakes of flame wriggled side-ways to the summits of the hills, and the low forest around him also took fire. Where the stems were thick and the blades below dry there was a crackling like the rattling of muskets. Some old trunks of trees slowly lit and continued to burn all night. The fire passed on behind his camp and along the ridge parallel to the river. All around him the flames devoured old grass, with the violent appetite of passion. It was the burning season he had read about; everything in Africa was burned once a year or nothing new would grow. Marais watched with excitement, his clothes, his face were heated by the flames. He was alone, the only witness to the fire, and soon the shelter he had made of branches burned. All night he stood on the road, watching the flames, like the eager poet in love who waits sleeplessly for dawn. He threw the hooded cassock and the rosary beads into the flames. He saw himself a fireraiser bringing his own torch to decay.

By morning the fire was out; Marais woke to black hills and fields spiked by charred tree trunks. It was through this, across the smouldering turf of a black meadow, that his men came, a file of fifty, in sooty uniforms. They stopped when they saw Marais. The white man at the head of the column brightened and came forward with his hand out.

'They think you're a stiff,' the new leader said, offering Marais a clammy hand.

The men looked at Marais as if at a zombie – a familiar demon to them, but none the less scary: it was deathless and drank human blood and could assume the shape of any animal. Nothing could kill it. None of the men would speak to Marais. They stood uneasily in the black meadow, with their rifles and packs still slung over their shoulders.

'Dead, see? We read about that business in L.M. You're the last person I expected to see, but I'm goddamned glad you're here. It's been sheer fucking hell. The food is lousy. I've got things in my hair, I've been *walking* ever since Mbeya. And you can't get a cold beer in this banana republic either.' The man shook his head and smiled gratefully in relief. 'Anyway, this is your show now. They're pretty stupid but they're itching to taste blood. You won't have any trouble. Oh, by the way, my name's Harry.'

'Where's the van?'

'We ditched it,' said Mr Harry. He pointed behind him, without looking back at the black hills, the black tree spikes. 'Somewhere back there. They ganged up on me, wouldn't let me drive. Jesus, are they stubborn! One of them drove. I said take it easy, but they drive like loons. They knocked the sump off somehow, probably on a sticking-up rock. The engine seized, the radiator got disconnected, everything went wrong, don't ask me how. It's a Czech van or, I don't know, maybe Bulgarian. No spares. Don't talk to me about the van. Believe me, it was a problem.'

'You were supposed to be carrying ammo and blasting powder in it. And guns – what about the extra rifles that were in the van?'

'Some we took with us,' said Mr Harry. 'And some we left.' Mr Harry smiled. 'I thought you didn't need anything fancy like that. In Dar they say, "Oh, Marais. He can make a bomb out of an old alarm clock and a couple of boxes of match-heads. Too bad they knocked him off," they said. So what's the problem?'

'You left live ammo in the bush,' said Marais. 'You know what will happen if someone finds that stuff? Did you think about that?'

'The engine seized, they were all bitching and moaning. I told them to take what they could carry and leave the rest. I wanted to stick to the schedule.'

'You're two weeks late.'

'The fires held us up. These people burn everything! And I was sick, I didn't feel –' Mr Harry broke off suddenly and looked around. He saw that the soldiers were still in the field, out of earshot, watching. He put his face close to Marais. 'Don't talk to me that way,' he said in a rapid whisper, twisting his face. 'Understand? I don't like to be talked to like that. I get crazy. I hate it, see? So cut it out! If you want to give orders you can hustle over there and give them. But don't give *me* that crap. I busted my ass getting down here. They told me to come, "Marais's dead," they said, "it's your show, Harry." I started getting crazy with all their do-this and do-that. "I'm in the political section," I said. "We don't walk in the political section, we don't camp out in the rain, we don't eat shit." But they told me to come. So I came. So fuck you and get off my back.'

Marais stared at Mr Harry, whose shirt was unbuttoned to the navel, whose boozy gasping and low-slung paunch indicated a heavy drinker. He looked hungry, and glumly out of his element. His boot-laces were in knots, his neck burned red, his dark loose lips threatened drool. His hair fell in straight oily blades, parted in the middle, to frame his sweating face. He was obviously suffering, but Marais did not like the craziness of his feeble panic.

'You lost the van,' said Marais coldly.

'I'm telling you I didn't lose no van,' said Mr Harry. 'It's there, in the boondocks. We put it in a hut. Ask them where it is, they're a bunch of geniuses. They'll tell you.'

'Okay,' said Marais. 'Now you listen to me. I don't know you. I don't know where they found you. I've never heard of you. But let's get one thing straight. This is an army. As long as you stay with us you take orders, just like everyone else. If that doesn't suit you, you can clear out.'

Mr Harry smiled. He nodded and examined Marais's face. Then he asked, 'How old are you, sonny?'

'What difference does it make?'

'You ashamed of it?'

'No,' said Marais. 'I'm twenty-seven.'

Mr Harry laughed loudly, opening his mouth in Marais's face. He had a cracked laugh; he pumped it, then said, 'Twenty-seven! Twenty-seven years old! Jesus Christ, do you know how old *I* am? Go ahead, wise-ass, take a guess.'

Marais shook his head at Mr Harry's white-flecked moustache, his dirty shirt, the loose slick neck, the clotted nostrils, the dead grey eyes. 'I don't guess,' he said. He walked past Mr Harry and went over to the soldiers, watching them fade back as he approached. He told them to line up, but as soon as he opened his mouth two men broke into a run.

'They think you're a stiff!' Mr Harry called, and he laughed again. Marais sprinted after the men and coaxed them back. Mr Harry was in the road taking off his boots when he looked up and saw all the men standing in the black smoking meadow, in files of ten. There was not a green thing anywhere, and even the sun was hidden in smoke-haze.

After dinner that evening Marais explained in detail his

three-month journey, from Leopoldville to Luanda, to Johannesburg and Beira. Angola, Mozambique and South Africa all had to be fought; but there were better ways than Mondlane's. Osbong was collaborating with these racist governments; he had captured Mondlane's men and locked them up because he wanted to stay on friendly terms with the Portuguese who let him use the port of Beira, and the South Africans who promised financial aid. Malawi was a crucial country, a corridor into all the white-controlled countries. Once it was in sympathetic hands the other places would be easy. Malawi gave access to Tanganyika; it had a railroad, a big airport outside Blantyre, planes. And Malawi was the easiest place to take; the landscape was mountainous, heavily forested, excellent terrain to hide in. There were only three points to capture: the border post in the north, Lilongwe, and Blantyre.

The men listened in silence; they sat rigidly, staring as if at a ghost. None had spoken.

'You're wondering how I got away from the Portuguese and how I came here. Okay, I'll tell you.' Marais explained the shooting in the Beira street, how he had scrambled into a tenement and eluded the police, staying for weeks in a township of half-castes and then disguising himself as a priest. 'They lied about catching me – they wanted to demoralize Mondlane.'

He could not tell if the men accepted his explanation; he was not sure they spoke English. Later, Harry brought Marais a box. Marais removed his shirt to prise the cover off. He caught sight of the men staring at his strangely lunar bruise in the firelight. They whispered.

Marais removed the contents from the box, a .45 calibre pistol, greasy clips of shells, a first-aid kit wrapped in cloth, a stack of neatly folded shirts, eight boxes of cigars, a coil of green fuse.

'There was a bottle of whisky in there. I put it in myself,' said Marais. 'Where is it?'

The men looked down. They had seen the scar and now, with Marais close to them, asking about his whisky, they saw the collar of raw skin around his neck where the hangman's rope had strangled him. He was dead. Their leader was a *mfiti*, a demon.

'What happened to that bottle?'

Mr Harry spoke up. 'We didn't know you were gonna be here, did we? You were supposed to be dead, right? So we drank the whisky. I mean, *I* drank it. I didn't want any drunks around the place. They were bad enough when they were sober.'

'You opened that box,' said Marais; 'I gave orders that my box should brought from Dar *unopened*.'

'You don't look like a drinking man,' said Mr Harry. 'What are you worried about?'

'I don't care about the whisky. But I wanted that box kept shut.'

'We thought you were dead,' said Mr Harry. He appealed to the men. 'We didn't know he was alive, did we? We thought he was dead, didn't we? Go on, tell him.'

The men stared. For them he was still dead.

'What else did you touch?'

'Nothing. The whisky that was all. Have a look for yourself.'

Marais felt in the bottom of the box and took out a plastic bag with notebooks sealed inside, three slim copybooks.

'So that's what you're bothered about!' laughed Mr Harry.

'Did you mess around with these?' asked Marais. The edge of his voice intimidated.

'What would I want with them? I'm no bookworm.' He wiped his mouth. 'I wish there was a drink around this place. I'm leaving for Blantyre tomorrow.'

Marais peeled off the tape which sealed the notebooks. He asked for a lantern. With the men before him, reluctantly squatting close, near the embers of the fire and the remains of food on tin plates, Marais opened one notebook to the first page and read in a slow reasonable voice, 'A revolution is not a dinner party, or writing an essay, or painting a picture, or doing embroidery. It cannot be so refined, so leisurely and gentle, so temperate, kind, courteous, restrained and magnanimous.' He paused and said, 'Magnanimous – it means big-hearted.' The men watched him white-eyed, knotting their fingers. Marais stopped reading in a teaching voice. He exhorted now, in a voice tinged with excitement, 'A revolution is an insurrection! It is an act of violence by which one class overthrows another.' He snapped the book shut and placed it on the ground.

Mr Harry squinted at the neatly printed label on the cover. It read *Principles of Revolt.* He nudged Marais, who was looking from face to face for a reaction, and he whispered, 'I used to write stuff like that, when I was about your age.' He smirked.

'Do you understand?' Marais faced the men across the fire; their faces were lighted by the flames.

'You gotta do better than that,' said Mr Harry. 'They don't speak English too hot. I used a translator.'

Marais stood up and peered at them. He punched his palm and said, 'I'm asking you, do you understand? A revolution is an act of violence! It means killing!'

The men were startled by the sudden change in his voice. They looked around. One began to clap, slowly, with cupped hands. Another took it up, and another, in the same rhythm; and soon they were all clapping. It was not applause; it was the slapping of respect that was accorded to chiefs and elders. Now it was very loud, and several men gave an approving tongue-yodelling howl. The clapping increased its rhythm to a quick cracking, and with such loudness that Mr Harry slid back from the fire into the shadows and unsheathed the black bayonet that was strapped to his belt.

That was their first meeting. Marais did not see Mr Harry again until the slaughterous day in February when the two men were tortured, the murderer, the rapist. In four months Mr Harry had become fatter, his loose flesh had filled, he wore a flowered shirt; in his trouser pocket there was the obvious bulge of a pistol. He had knelt behind Marais, watching Brother Mussa struggling against the hail of stones; he had seen Marais give the order to stop, which was unheard by the men, forcing Marais to run over to Brother Mussa and cover him with his arms, ending the torture. Brother Mussa was dragged out of the hole.

Marais supervised the bandaging and ordered the hole to be filled in. Mr Harry waited for Marais, and later in the evening, when Marais returned to his square tent, Mr Harry showed him a bottle of whisky. 'I owe you this.'

'Come inside,' said Marais, entering the tent and hanging a lantern from the centre pole. The walls of the tent were stacked high with crates of liquor. 'We have plenty. They've looted every bar from here to the border.'

Mr Harry eyed the crates and swallowed thirstily. He whistled, the old way of showing surprise, and said, 'It looks okay to me. You could have a real booze-up if you wanted. But you don't sound too happy about it.'

'They stole this stuff,' said Marais. He looked at the wet rope-end of his cigar and added, 'I wish that was all they had done.' He sighed and looked again at Harry. 'You saw the punishments. I was trying to avoid that, but they had to be taught a lesson.'

'Tough lesson,' said Mr Harry. 'All I did was pull a knife on them when they got out of line.'

'I had to show them that I meant what I said.'

'Don't explain to *me*,' said Mr Harry.

Marais threw the damaged cigar on the floor and shook a new one from a metal tube. Lighting it he said, 'They had to be punished.'

'Maybe so,' said Mr Harry. He found a glass and wiped the inside of the rim with his finger, then settled into a chair and polished the glass on his sleeve. He poured some whisky in, sloshed it, and sipped. With a wet half-smile he said, 'They'll kill you for that.'

'They'll be lucky if they can walk.'

'I don't mean the guys you tortured –'

'Punished,' said Marais.

'Punished,' smiled Mr Harry. He sipped again and licked his lips. 'I mean the others. Now it's you against them. They hate your guts for that. Some day, when you think everything's rosy, they're gonna surprise you. They'll jump all over you and wham wham-o.' He drank again. 'I seen it happen before. Jungle bunnies,' said Mr Harry. 'Jungle bunnies.'

'How did you get up here?' asked Marais.

'I got me a nice car now,' said Mr Harry. 'There was a lot of dummies on the road. I've marked the roadblocks on my map. They tried to give me lip. They didn't reckon on old Harry pulling rank on them. I brought them some crates of food, cans of stuff, cookies and crap like that. I'm your mess officer, I says, just delivering this to you boys – you're doing a fine job. Naturally they believed it. They believe anything. They don't even have passwords. It's pathetic.'

'You hate them, don't you?'

'Me? I don't hate anyone. I got a wife and kids,' said Mr Harry. He said it with feeling, as if claiming a disability, like a gammy leg. 'I just don't trust people like you do. But I think you're learning. I watched that poor bastard getting the rocks on his nut and I said to myself, yup, Marais don't trust them either these days.' Harry grinned. 'You think I'm an old fart, but I'll tell you something. The trouble with you is you trusted them before. So when they let you down you hate them. Me, I *expect* them to let me down. I keep an eye on the loyal ones, the ones that are always doing what they're told. I figure they must have an angle or why would they be so nice. Anyway, I suppose it don't matter.'

'It matters,' said Marais. 'They know when you don't trust them. They can sense it.'

'They can't sense shit,' said Mr Harry. He poured himself another whisky. 'As long as they get theirs they don't care what we think. They care if you kick their asses, though, like you just did. Call it punishment if you want. We used to have other names for it. Whatever you call it they don't like it any better. So don't say I didn't warn you, okay?'

'We can't have them pushing people around,' said Marais.

'I heard all that before. It's natural. Who cares?'

'I care. I'm not going to be here long. As soon as we take Blantyre I'm moving back to Dar. I gave myself a year and I'm sticking to it. It's their show after that.'

'The Lone Ranger,' said Mr Harry. He pushed his hair back, accentuating the white parting down the middle of his head. 'So what do you want me to do?'

'What you've been doing. Sit in Blantyre and keep smiling. We hit Lilongwe in six weeks and bring it to a halt. We'll try to recruit some more men there to hold it. Then we'll move into Blantyre.'

'Like shit through a tin horn,' said Mr Harry. 'It sounds nice. But I figure you're a little behind schedule.'

'We'll make it up. What about your end?'

'We got it married. You could crash into Blantyre tomorrow if you wanted. I know my job. Everything's staked out.'

'Just remember, we do it quick. I don't like sloppy revolts. They don't work — you make enemies that way. If you can't do it quick, then don't do it. That's what —'

'They're still fighting in Angola,' said Mr Harry, patting his moustache.

'I talked to Holden in Leo. I told him he's wasting his time.'

'I got some buddies there,' said Mr Harry. 'They've had some terrific strikes in the mines. They know what they're doing.'

Marais snorted. 'They don't know the first thing about it.'

'Says you.'

Marais put his arms on the table and leaned towards Mr Harry. 'They don't know the first thing about it,' he said, drumming his knuckles on the map. The map was spattered with cigar ash; inked crosses, marking roadblocks, ran where they had been splashed with whisky.

'But *you* know, don't you?' said Mr Harry. 'Twenty-seven years old and you got all the answers. It's lots of fun, isn't it? All the glory-boys marching in and beating up the simps at the road-blocks! You make me laugh. A tin-pot little place like this with a tin-pot dictator who doesn't know his ass from a hole in the ground. It's a push-over! I've seen places like this taken in a week, a lousy *week*!'

'We're doing it right,' said Marais.

'Don't give me that,' said Mr Harry. 'You're enjoying yourself the same as me. Only you make a big deal out of it and I don't.'

'We're both in this together,' said Marais.

'You think so. But there's a difference between you and me, pal. For one thing, I do it for the money and you don't. As long as they pay up I'm working. But you – you make it into a big scientific study. Sure, I heard all your Chairman Mao bullshit. That's the way they talk in Dar, passing out books, having meetings, this and that. It's enough to drive you nuts. Give me the plane fare to Blantyre, I told them; I'll find a trigger and get Osbong knocked off. Then we see what happens. No, they said, we're doing it Marais's way, as if you have all the answers. They almost pissed their pants when they read about your bomb in Jo'burg. He just messed up some letters and killed an old lady, I said. They wouldn't listen. So I come all the way down here and see you bouncing rocks off your own men. Wow, do you give me cramps.'

'I know what the score is,' said Marais.

'Sure you do,' said Mr Harry. 'But I'll tell you something. To those jungle bunnies out there you're just another fucking *mzungu* bastard looking for a little action.'

'I think you've had too much to drink,' said Marais. He took the whisky bottle off the table and placed it beside his chair. He smoothed the map and said, 'Now give me a run-down on the roadblocks from here to Lilongwe. What kind of rifles do they have? What kind of cover?'

Mr Harry glared at Marais. 'You're writing some kind of book, aren't you?' He spoke with contempt.

'That's my business,' said Marais.

'Chapter one,' Mr Harry mocked, holding his glass up. 'How we beat up the simps at the roadblocks and raised the flag –'

'It's not like that,' said Marais.

'Yes, it is,' said Mr Harry. 'I read all those books. I know what you're doing. Big scientific Chairman Mao bullshit, with bells ringing and all the flags waving. Nobody gets dirty –'

Marais reached quickly across the table and pinched Mr Harry's windpipe, shutting off Mr Harry's gagging voice and making his eyes pop.

'Revolution is rape,' said Marais. 'I don't enjoy it. It's vicious, but it's quick, and no one ever forgets it. You won't forget this one, Harry, I promise you.'

Mr Harry pushed Marais's hand away from his throat. He swallowed painfully and rubbed at the spot Marais had pinched. 'You'd do that to them,' said Mr Harry. 'They're gonna kill you, sonny.'

'No,' said Marais. 'They're going to thank all of us, because when it's all over they'll realize that we've been raping a whore. That's what revolution is.'

Mr Harry started to reply, but voices outside the tent stopped him. He listened and crooked his head. Marais got up and flung the flap of the door back. Three men stood before him.

'What do you want?'

'*Achimwene* Mussa,' said one. '*Wafa.*'

Marais walked over to the table again and sat. The three men remained at the door, waiting for an answer.

'What's up?' asked Mr Harry.

'The man we stoned,' said Marais softly. 'He's dead.'

Mr Harry closed his eyes in concentration, studied forcefully for a few moments, pursed his lips, and then brought up a honking belch. He directed it at Marais as if it was a reflection, and when he finished he said. 'That's one son of a bitch who's not gonna thank you.'

21

The wedding presents were two: Bailey gave the couple her best double room, rent-free for two months; Major Beaglehole gave them his Matchless motorcycle and a full tank of gas. And no one at the eating house found it unusual that the day after his marriage Calvin slept late and didn't go to the office. There were jokes in the bar; as witnesses to the ceremony, as the only gift-givers, Bailey and Beaglehole took a kindly proprietorial interest in the couple and spoke for them: 'Honeymooners,' said Bailey. 'Not wasting a minute,' said Beaglehole. 'He'll be back to the office soon.' After a week there were no more jokes, but there was talk. Calvin was seen every afternoon on the veranda, with his long legs braced against the rail, with a bottle of beer clenched between his knees. He had stopped going to the office. Major Beaglehole wondered if something wasn't, as he put it, 'profoundly the matter'.

'Nothing's wrong,' said Calvin to the Major. 'I just don't sell insurance any more, that's all.' Calvin did not tell Beaglehole, but his interest in insuring people had died with Ogilvie (fully protected and paid up); he resolved not to delude any more Africans by offering the false hope of a policy.

But his concern for Africans, undiminished, took other forms. Instead of calling attention to the future he repeated the Chinyanja proverb, 'What comes doesn't beat a drum' and reminded the Africans of how lucky they were to live in a simple country where poinsettias grew wild and no one starved. He pointed out the greenery of the jungle salad, and indicated (from the veranda, where he sat and drank) the dozens of people stretched out in the free shade of the trees. He warned against complication, he smiled at their alarm.

The alarm was recent, and not more than a month old, acute. For some reason the Africans in Blantyre were plagued by intimations of disaster. In a chaotic way they petitioned Calvin for help. The Homemakers' Mutual brochures, sent months previously and all but forgotten by Calvin, were having a marked effect: many people wanted policies.

'Wanting inner-surance,' an African would say, with a new worrying wheedle in his voice and a stammering of the body, hand-wringing and glancing around the veranda where Calvin sat with Mira and a bottle of beer.

'What's the rush?' was Calvin's usual reply.

'Wanting money,' the African would go on, then, pausing as if to single out the worst verb, 'to achieve wireless set.'

'Simple as pie,' Calvin's new formula ran. 'Instead of paying us four osbongs a week, put that money under your bed. In a couple of months you'll have enough to buy a very nice radio. Now, how about a beer?'

It was soon the end of March; the rains were less frequent, there was a good breeze. Calvin's marriage to Mira was completion, he was convinced of his happiness, and only once since his marriage had he agreed to insure someone: a very old lady.

She had come to him with a paper bag full of money. She could not bank it – the Barclays Bank had recently been nationalized and all the strongboxes in the vault emptied by Osbong's men.

'Go,' said Calvin, 'and dig a hole in the ground, inside your hut. Put the money there. It will be very safe.'

The old lady did as she was told, but after a few weeks she disinterred the paper bag to count the money again, and she discovered that termites had chewed the bills to shreds. Calvin insured her, accepting the confetti of her cash. But he ended her policy when he had a remedy for the termites. He refunded her money, giving her new bills for the shreds, and told her to sprinkle the bills with goat piss before she buried it. This would, he said, repel all insects and keep the money safe.

The sort of insurance Africans needed, Homemakers' Mutual did not sell. Ogilvie was dead, the Minister of Defence was dead;

there were rumours of worse. Extra money wouldn't help anyone – it would only make him more liable to theft. A person who appeared the least bit prosperous was nationalized and burgled; if he refused he got his skull cracked by the Youth Wingers. Insurance: there was no future in it; Africans needed it like a hole in the head. And the country (not a country, more a wild little parish) was bankrupt, underpopulated and shrinking like a cheap shirt. To Calvin it wasn't foreign any more; usually it was a broiling hot nothingness, sometimes it was unaccountably cold, it was doused occasionally by rain, a heavy mist obscured it in the early morning. The phenomena were friendly, the clouds of dust sifting back to the road in the wake of a jeep, the startling sameness of glorious sunsets, the flowering trees always in season: all very routine, usual, familiar – the beauty had a trustworthy permanence.

Understanding everything, Calvin was not contemptuous of the place. He stopped comparing Malawi to Massachusetts (though Malawi came out well in that comparison: there was no Mafia in Malawi, there was less craft on Chichiri Hill than on Beacon Hill, and the Brahmins in Blantyre were real ones, not descendants of bootleggers as in Boston); Calvin stopped sizing up the Africans. He was concerned about them, but this was no special feeling. Provoked, he defended them. The girls at the eating house were black, the customers never were. Calvin was seldom provoked: in whorehouses there was complete integration. For this Calvin was grateful. He had begun to realize that the defenders of the underdog were in that pose an unpleasant minority of all their own, but more vocal than the genuinely oppressed. Calvin had been touched by their apparently sincere accusation; he had once indulged in this himself. Now he was unmoved by them: with their bugles out and in their screeching simplicities they were a type of underdog themselves. But unworthy, they were unbearable, like the beggar who has more coins in his outstretched hand than you have in your pocket. They were always foreigners, they were big bores. It was a relief to be rid of that impulse to preach, that yen to save lives. For what?

The arrival of Mira seemed to sweeten Major Beaglehole's disposition: he stopped mentioning blacks with malice, and Bailey too exhausted her curses. They often drank together, inviting Mira inside to join them at their table. Calvin heard them from where he sat, the old man's voice rising to the climax of a story: '. . . seen your picture on the mantelpiece . . .', '. . . had to scoop him up with a shovel . . .', '. . . forgotten all my Urdu now . . .' There was always a fourth at their table, a man named Jack Mavity, who was married to an African woman and who dragged three bushy-haired yellow children with him wherever he went. The eldest was only six, the others much younger. They pissed on the bar floor and took turns slapping it.

Mavity always had news. It was he who reported seeing Mr Harry in town. He reported it in a way that caused Major Beaglehole discomfort. Mavity reached over one day, interrupting the old man in a story; he switched on Major Beaglehole's hearing aid and turned it to loud. Major Beaglehole, hearing the thunder of his own voice, stopped talking. 'There's a new face in town!' shouted Mavity, not into Major Beaglehole's ear but into the small enamel box which hung on the harness around Major Beaglehole's neck.

'Good God, Jack, don't do that!' Major Beaglehole winced at the ferocity of his words. He returned and said, 'What new face – who?'

'In the Zambezi,' said Mavity. 'He looks a drinker he does.'

'He's bound to turn up sooner or later,' said Major Beaglehole.

'We'll make him feel welcome when he does,' said Bailey.

Mavity watched the door, hoping the man would stop in for a drink. But all Mavity saw was Calvin, sitting in what used to be known as the Major's chair, with a bottle of beer in his lap and his legs propped against the veranda rails. Sometimes Mavity would stand near Calvin and stare at the street, and he would sigh and sigh until Calvin asked him what was wrong.

'Oh, God,' Mavity would say. 'I could tell you stories.'

'About the Africans.' Calvin disliked Mavity, but he could not refuse to talk to him. They both had black wives: Mavity took this as something like kinship. But because he was married to an African Mavity felt free to abuse them.

'Yes, about the Africans,' said Mavity. 'They wear bandages and sticking plasters on their legs. They all do. But the queer thing is – *there isn't a thing wrong with their legs*. Them bandages are for decoration. Yes, it's a fashion. Can you believe it?'

On occasion Mavity would be reading about Americans in the paper, the *Rhodesia Herald* or the *Bulawayo Chronicle*. He never explained what he read; he smashed the paper to the floor and walked out to the veranda and said accusingly to Calvin, 'Now you're giving them rockets' or 'So you think ten million quid isn't enough for a jackass of a dictator?' or 'You and your flipping computers!' Once Mavity said, looking over the top of the paper he was reading on the veranda, 'It says here you're going to the moon.'

Most of the time Mavity watched the door for the man he had seen at the Zambezi. And one day he said, 'There he is.'

Mr Harry was being carried by two Africans, one on each arm. He was blowing through his lips and spattering his moustache. The two Africans steered him up the stairs and through the swinging doors to the edge of the bar counter. Mavity watched, fascinated. The fat waiter eyed Mr Harry and poured out a tot of whisky. When Mr Harry raised his head and reached for the drink, Mavity recognized him, and winked.

'I think I know that man,' said Calvin, who had wandered inside to watch the drunken man supported by the two Africans. Everyone – Mira, Bailey, Major Beaglehole, the girls – watched.

But Mr Harry was guzzling whisky and did not see them; the drink was running down his chin. He had several more. He tottered and threatened to fall. The Africans gripped him and held him straight. Mr Harry cursed, and tried to focus on the winking Mavity. The fat waiter poured another drink. Mr Harry picked it up and touched it to his lips. But the little tot-glass slipped through his fingers and smashed. He was drowsy, his head heavy.

'Time!' shouted Bailey to the fat waiter.

The fat waiter corked the bottle.

The two Africans held Mr Harry tightly under the armpits and gently steered him out. They had trouble getting him through the door. One took him through, and Mavity went to the veranda and watched him being carried down the street, like an injured footballer, his ankles dragging.

'He didn't recognize me,' said Mavity. 'I don't think he saw me.'

'I've seen him someplace,' said Calvin, but gave the fat Mr Harry no further thought. Calvin swigged his beer and watched the street and learned to prefer rainy days. The weather report on Radio Malawi changed: mostly sunny, scattered clouds, the possibility of showers in the afternoon. They said that every day of the year, and most days were like that. But Calvin preferred the rain. Africans could smell the rain coming, sense the wind shifting; they ran in all directions as the sky blackened and the far-off patter of raindrops started. The rain was an event: it made steam rise from the heated street, and it flooded the drains. Often, trees were blown down in the storms. And it was during the storms that murders were committed and shops broken into. But the rain's sound was not what Calvin had thought on the trip north: not the sound of riotous peasants or crying voices in the jungle. It was a thin regular patter of drops, small-talk at a beer party, with a number of rising amused moments, wind-inspired, a kind of laughter. It made a change, and gave Calvin something to look forward to, for nowadays he never went to his office.

It was cruel to make those people there with plastic bags pulled over their heads, pedalling their bicycles out of the rain's path, or sitting under the eaves of shophouses, much like Calvin, and like Calvin waiting for the diversion of a crashing tree or a boiling flood – it was cruel to make them think that they could be saved by insurance. The Africans sat; they were clumsy and perishable; they had a very old but very narrow culture. Nothing could or did happen to them, except death. Only storms diverted them, but briefly, for the sun always returned to heat their heads. Nothing changed, not even a death in the family altered them, insurance never would. Some giant would have to snatch up the country like a clogged ketchup bottle and smack it violently on the bottom for it to change; but that would never happen either. And besides, the bottle might turn out to be empty.

In any case, it was not crucial. People missed the point about Africans. The alien hurried past, clucking at the Africans hunkered down in a bit of shade. All the goals of wealth and position, even the memory of slavery, and certainly the idea of so-called progress, were the alien's own. Strangers upset the African by making him ashamed and calling his harmonic sense of peace laziness. What the stranger never saw was the blank smooth shrug on the face of the hunkered-down father, the jaunty twinkle in the eyes of the wood-carrying crone, and the delight of the naked black children flinging mud and jumping in puddles, or sailing reed-woven boats along the soapy plops of grey sewage in the open drain.

'What's going to happen to those children?' Calvin had once asked. The Africans had no answers. It was not their question.

The plague of flying ants convinced Calvin.

After a heavy rain they pulled themselves out of the ground, and crawled and flew in a pulsing swarm around the veranda rails and wooden steps of the eating house. They had done the same at the bungalow in Sunnyside Calvin had shared with his first wife. 'Creepy-crawly,' she had said. She hated them. She thought they carried disease. There were too many to kill. They could not fly straight. They were fat, their wings dropped off in shiny flakes on the floor, they exhausted themselves pelting against the lights.

Mavity said, 'You're sending planes to dust the country with DDT.' It was not only flying ants that were a menace, but also sausage flies, locusts, and green grasshoppers. Calvin watched them swarm and waited for the planes. Sometimes the veranda was alive with them: they shinnied through the seams in the planks and held to the posts and banisters; they wiggled their bodies, and shook off their shiny wings; the coated wood rails seemed to move. The ants flew into Calvin's beerglass. It got so bad that he considered moving inside whenever the flying ants came.

On that day in March when there were so many flying ants on the veranda that Calvin skidded on them and forsook his insect-upholstered chair, he wondered whether instead of escaping into the bar he should go to the office and see what he could do about getting the ants destroyed. The UN might help; perhaps he should ask Mavity about the planes. A plague of insects was a biblical punishment; but a little planning could wipe it out. It occurred to him that for the first time in weeks he was thinking like an insurance man.

'Why you no sit on *khonde*?' one of the waiters asked.

'Ants,' said Calvin, who was standing just inside the door, still in two minds about going to the office. 'They're all over the place. I don't know how you put up with it.' Several ants clung to Calvin's sleeve.

The waiter closely observed Calvin picking them off.

'Where you find?'

Calvin motioned towards the veranda.

But the waiter had already started out of the bar, and now he was gathering them up in his hands, bending this way and that. Calvin watched. Pausing at Calvin's feet, the waiter looked up and nodded with enormous gratitude. Later the ants were fried and eaten; Calvin shared them, eating them with his hands off a square of newspaper. And the planes never came with the insecticide.

The flying ants, yellow beetles, the locusts, the sausage flies and *ngumbi* were not a plague, but a blessing, welcome as food and for the sport they afforded – the thrill of the chase. After that incident Calvin began noticing greasy sacks of them at the market; they had been there all along; but why had he not noticed them before? They were a treat, they had a nutty taste, not disagreeable at all.

From his shady veranda and primed with beer, Calvin saw angels in the black men's minds. He had spent more than a year trying to sell insurance. It was, like any stranger's, a charitable but deluded eagerness to help, like crop-spraying or reporting on literacy or asking solemnly, 'What's going to happen to those children?' Worse than simply pointless, it was, in a word, corruption. Industry polluted, crop-spraying made people hungry, tin roofs were hotter than thatch. And literacy simply frustrated and crazed: *The Uninsured* was proof of that. But did any stranger stay long enough to get the hang of the place? It was not that Calvin did not care; it was because he cared that he saw their angels and left them in peace and only spoke to alert them of a swarm of delicious insects. Calvin was married, complete, and happy; he was thirty;

he felt jungle vines in his skinny legs; he was (munching toasty fried ants) practically an African.

Eventually he had another look at *The Uninsured*. He was shopping with Mira (the endowment had dwindled to five hundred osbongs, but with all the shops nationalized there was little to buy) and looked up and saw the yellow wedge-shaped Agnello building and the Homemakers' Mutual sign. He sent Mira on her way and hurried upstairs. On the floor, amid dusty applications and empty ledgers and a progress chart neatly recording sales on a rising black line and stopping abruptly in the middle of February, Calvin found the manuscript.

It was thicker, bulkier than he remembered it. What a lot of work was in it! The pages were carefully numbered to eighty-three, with some pinned in or glued over messy paragraphs; it was a secure much-laboured-over bundle of foolscap in a loose-leaf binder with the title and *A. Jigololo* showing in a window on the spine. There were ovals of green mould on the covers of the binder. It had a quaint charm, like a newly discovered book, in the unknown author's own handwriting (cramped, concerned), found decaying in a trunk in a dusty attic, the Mullet Manuscript of the Jigololo Variorum, a credible forgery. If it had value it was the curiosity value that all irrelevant antiques have, washstands and flatirons: something bizarre rather than beautiful. But it embarrassed Calvin. What embarrassed him most was that no honest African could have written it. Only a fearfully unhappy white person could be the author of the distressed phrases Calvin saw as he flipped through it: *My heart is heavy, my face is dirty, I hate everybody ... I am slavishly aping the people who chained up my grandfather and sent him to Alabama ... I suffer, I worry ... I am the colour of night, just a little voice in the jungle ... We have an old proverb ... Would you insure me?*

Calvin's answer to that last question was no. Not you or anyone. Sentiment permitted him to put the manuscript into the top drawer of the desk. But he would add no more to the narrative. Now he knew the narrator.

22

The real narrator, in mood if not in fact, was not himself or the imaginary A. Jigololo, but that fat swart man, the waiter, whose name Calvin discovered was Jarvis Moore.

Calvin at first tried to avoid Jarvis. He was happy with Mira in the large room. But Mira was not the carefree person she had seemed at Christmas; she was more serious than the girl who had waved her hand in the Big Drum Bar and said, 'That not name . . . That signature.' She was for weeks after the marriage afraid of strangers, especially soldiers; and she jumped at loud noises. Calvin had once reached for a light-pull and she had drawn back and covered her face, as if she expected to be struck, like the bully at the Big Drum Calvin had cowed with a handshake. She was quiet, cat-like, purring beside him; he heard the fast thump of her heart. She would not leave Calvin's side.

Trust was harder than love, and Calvin was grateful for her loyalty; but he scarcely knew her. The few details he did know could not matter – that she had done two years of primary school and knew hymns and sums, that her parents were dead and now her brother, that she oiled her legs and cared about clothes, that she had, in the Hudson expression, a nice ass. She was still a girl, maybe seventeen, but in an even less recent youth she had learned what love was and not to trust it. It was plain that she had had lovers, for she knew how to be attentive to Calvin's passion: she looked on with feline wonder at Calvin's jungle antics, and did what she was told. It was also plain that her role had been victim, for she was indifferent to her own pleasure, apprehensive about his. To inquire any more into that was to be pitying, and pity was a mood of contempt Calvin tried now to avoid. In the village, at

Christmas, she had said, 'We want you.' Calvin translated the want as need, and though part of her interest undoubtedly was his type of colour, the notoriety of being white in that place, she meant him, she began to trust. In the jungle, safety was more urgent than love, and had to be love's beginning: they began not by knowing but by needing.

He knew her temper, but in his ignorance of everything else he could not predict anything in her: a bonus, the promise of surprise giving its own special glamour. To have known one of her jungle lovers would have been to deprive him of any surprise: the lover and the loved tattooed each other with the same marks, as Calvin's ex-wife had affected his sense. Lovers might be opposites, but duration always turned them into twins. What Calvin didn't know of Mira, all that soft darkness, drew him on. He was secure in that mystery; she was slim, busy with his body, and without any malice; she tasted of peaches, and she knew him as a protector.

That Calvin was kind in his possession was nothing new. He had been gentle with prostitutes to whom most men were brutal. He had pined away for little schoolgirls in shrunken uniforms and plastic sandals who passed by the eating house, and been jealous, too, when a bar waitress he had once slept with sat in another customer's lap a day later. He was made miserable by a girl who claimed that she had learned a particular pleasing trick from an Italian tea planter in Cholo: it was a reminder of her use.

Calvin drank with gusto. Purely for the sake of appearances he kept his office sign up, *Homemakers' Mutual – Full Protection – Insure & Save The Creative Way*. But he refused to sell anyone a policy. It was a racket, the worst on earth. People only bought insurance for good luck: if you were insured, so the folklore went, nothing bad happened to you. That was a big load of crap. Calvin was sure that insurance corrupted the next of kin. He told interested customers to save their money, and when they had a fair amount to spend it in one splurge. 'Eat, drink, get married,' Calvin advised. 'Have kids, enjoy yourselves. Insurance? Don't waste your money!'

He rose late these days. He stopped buying *Time* magazine. It insisted too cynically on the terrifying, with hundreds of laboured puns, scores of shrill stories, riots here, revolutions there, wars somewhere else, rigged elections, political strife. Calvin read the *Malawi News* instead. Everything was fine on the four over-inked pages of the unbleached *Malawi News*: Osbong praising the Women's Brigade, Osbong repeating that he was a dictator by the people, for the people and of the people, Osbong being referred to as 'Our Great *Chirombo* Saviour, Messiah, Founder and Father of the Republic of Malawi, Life President of the Malawi Congress Party, Doctor . . .' There were lovely little misprints: MESSIAH PLAN-NING STATE VISIT TO EAT AFRICA, one headline ran, describing Osbong's visit to Nairobi. There were poems, too: 'I sing of Doctor Osbong . . .' or 'O Africa! O Malawiland! Let me taste of your bounteous . . .' There was no foreign news in the paper, except for the odd scrap from a wire-service about fifty reindeer crashing through some Finnish ice during the early thaw. It was all perfect for the can. Calvin sat with his elbows on his knees, bent over, the *Malawi News* spread on the floor and held in place with his feet. He read and he shat; he was happy.

But Jarvis Moore, the fat waiter, sulked. Large and black, he entered the bar or lingered on the veranda, and just like the evil-favoured narrator of *The Uninsured* he cast a grouchy shadow over all. He was huge, the colour of raw liver, with powerful shirt-splitting shoulders and a thick neck. His horny fists suggested cudgels, and he had a zombie's insomniac eyes, set close and deep in his head. He could, and often did, pull the caps off beer bottles with his teeth. Once Calvin saw him spit a clam of dribbling saliva into a small child's face.

Calvin saw the cheerless man brooding over a beer-crate, working his angry jaws on a cud. 'How about a smile?' Calvin said.

Jarvis Moore told Calvin to drop dead.

'Just being bolshie,' said Bailey, when Calvin told her. 'Oh, he's a shocker, he is.' She smiled.

'I never did anything to him,' said Calvin.

'Course you didn't,' said Bailey. 'That one's a lad, though.

Dresses up at night, he does. Fancy black suit, teddy-boy boots. Carries a knife now and then.'

'Doesn't it worry you?'

'Just acting savage and bloody-minded. They all do it,' said Bailey. 'They don't mean any harm. Jarvy's very good with the accounts.'

'He does your accounts?'

'He's very clever, is Jarvy.'

'I think I'll buy him a drink,' said Calvin. 'That might make him brighten up.'

'Don't you do any such thing! I don't want him arse-creeping around. Don't take any notice of him.'

'He told me to drop dead,' said Calvin. 'He dresses up at night and carries a knife. He sulks, for God's sake.'

Bailey replied by saying she liked Africans that way. Politeness in anyone was a challenge to her; in an African it was a threat.

Calvin kept his distance. He saw Bailey encouraging the fat waiter to be beastly. She snarled at him; he snarled back. She swore; he took to stropping a meat cleaver on an oiled piece of leather tacked to the bar. He refused to serve Calvin. When Calvin asked for a drink Jarvis twisted his face, flashed his knife and stropped. Calvin got his own drinks, made out his own chits, initialled them and pressed them on the spike.

In the first week of April Jarvis was especially moody, stropping and spitting, kicking chairs and growling as he did so. He had tremendous feet. In the evenings the girls strolled in twos on the street or draped themselves on the veranda, shouting and hooting to passers-by; Calvin sat on a barstool (Mira turned in early) and drank a beer. Usually he watched the progress of the fruit machine players, but this evening he looked through the delicate lace of dried froth at the tip of his glass at the fat waiter fretting.

Seeing that Calvin's eyes were on him, Jarvis grunted and drew out his meat cleaver. He began slapping it, rocking from side to side as he swiped at the grease-dubbed strop.

Calvin moved three stools down the bar, across from Jarvis. They were so close to each other the blade passed back and forth under Calvin's chin. Jarvis gave off a strong vinegary smell that might have been sweat.

'What seems to be eating you?' asked Calvin.

'Bloody white men,' said Jarvis. 'Big so-called bwanas killing Africans. I am fed up of it.'

'So what?' Calvin grinned good-naturedly.

'I know you despise me. I don't care about that,' said Jarvis. 'I have travelled around. My father was a chief. You can see I speak English. Booker T. Washington – I have read this book.'

'A very impressive man, Booker T. Washington.'

'A sell-out,' said Jarvis.

Calvin smiled. 'Where'd you come across a word like that?'

'Lumumba. I have read Lumumba.'

'No offence,' said Calvin, 'but big deal.'

'Osbong is a sell-out, a big stooge for the Boers. He uses Ambi-Special.'

'Why worry about Osbong? All politicians are like that. Replace Osbong with someone else and you'll have the same thing all over again. I don't know anything about politics, but I know that's the way it always is.'

'You don't know anything about politics. Lumumba was murdered.'

'By Africans,' said Calvin. 'I read it in *Time* magazine.'

'Some Africans behave like white people,' said Jarvis. 'They are stupid.'

'Sure, but some white people behave like Africans,' said Calvin, and he thought of A. Jigololo.

'They are good ones if they do.' Jarvis stropped faster. 'I know very well you bloody foreign devils want to steal this country.'

Foreign devil? Calvin was crushed. He did not think of himself as a foreigner. He was surprised to hear Jarvis name him so. He thought of himself as a sincere friend; he had sold insurance and, finding it inadequate and bogus, stopped selling it. He cared. He liked the Africans and trusted their idleness; he had thought the feeling was mutual, for his own idleness was no different from theirs.

'I'm your friend. I'm no foreigner.'

'You're a white bloodsucker. You want to kill us.'

'I don't want to do anything,' Calvin protested. 'Besides, my wife is black.'

'You're stealing our women.'

'I'm married,' said Calvin, 'to one of them.'

'You want to take Malawi away from us, like Osbong.'

'Look,' said Calvin, picking a shelled peanut out of a bowl on the bar and cradling it in a wrinkle on his open palm which he held near Jarvis's face. 'See this? *This* is Malawi.'

Jarvis stared at the peanut.

'No offence intended,' said Calvin, 'but who wants it?'

Jarvis plucked the peanut out of Calvin's palm. He opened his mouth, put his whole hand inside, deposited the peanut on his back teeth and crunched it. 'You want to eat us like this,' said Jarvis, swallowing. 'Many people want to crush us.'

'I hate to disappoint you,' said Calvin, 'but I don't know any. Oh, I know how you feel —'

'I know them,' said Jarvis quickly. He smacked his cleaver. Saliva brimmed in the dark little trough behind his slack lower lip. 'Spies! Spies!'

'But who would want,' said Calvin, nodding, 'to spy on you?'

Jarvis tested the cleaver's edge with a moist thumb. He raised it high, then slammed it into the bar an inch from Calvin's fingers. The whole surface of the bar rang with the vibration of the blade. He glowered fiercely at Calvin. 'Plenty of people want to spy on us! Maybe you. I can't stick you.'

Now that was not so strange. It was always the ugly neglected spinster who was obsessed by the thought that she was being followed by a man, and who was always being exposed to fugitive genitals. Calvin wanted to reply to Jarvis's abuse, but he didn't want to hurt the man's feelings. Calvin found it odd to hear such things from a man so fat. The sentiments were all those of A. Jigololo, the narrator of *The Uninsured*, one of the brow-beaten oppressed. Somehow Calvin had pictured the oppressed as very small and sick, like the unemployed in Worcester, not Jarvis's size.

Calvin decided to say nothing. Some people just didn't want to be happy, but why give them another excuse to be miserable?

Jarvis gave Calvin a wintry sneer. He yanked the cleaver out of the splintered wood and resumed his stropping, a caricature of A. Jigololo, who was himself a caricature of one Wasp's unhappiness. Jarvis would, Calvin was sure, give that up and perhaps he would be as embarrassed by the memory of his fruitless anger as Calvin was by his own. Calvin understood Jarvis; he knew what made him tick, better than he knew Mira's worries or wants. That was the saddest part. And because he talked that way it showed Jarvis wasn't being honest. Jarvis's was a white liberal pose. He would change, of course he would; as Calvin had. It was only a matter of time before he would find out that life was worth living. He would meet a nice girl – maybe a white girl, what was the difference? – and give up his griping. Underneath it all Jarvis was probably a very sweet guy.

23

Kill them all, Brother Jaja had written in the tall narrow loops of his graceful mission-school hand, his last gruesome dispatch to Marais. It was insane. It reminded Marais of the demented killer who lingers to riddle his victim with bullets, or keeps stabbing a corpse. Perhaps Brother Jaja was exaggerating; Africans often did, but Marais had Harry's word that Jaja was unusually bright: he had been educated in Rhodesia, had received military training in Algiers and had fought in the north-eastern Congo with Gbenye Christophe. He had been born in Malawi but was unknown there, for he had left for Salisbury when he was fifteen and had assumed a number of different aliases. In Dar es Salaam, Gbenye had said to Marais, 'It wasn't Jaja's fault we lost. But if we had won Jaja would have been the first man I killed. He's dangerous.' It intrigued Marais that Gbenye intended to kill his best man, and it was then Marais decided Brother Jaja should head the new government.

But Brother Jaja's latest dispatches sounded madder than the first Marais had received from him. Even if it was not madness it was very bad judgement: the impulse was revenge – excited, irrational, easily detected. The revolutionary put one bullet in his enemy's head and let that kill him. Vengeance was wasteful, and not a revolutionary's motive but a cannibal's. *Kill them all*. Marais decided otherwise. Encircling every village and attacking every flimsy compound was unnecessary and inconvenient, and with only fifty men and no dependable supply lines, probably impossible. A show of arms might persuade; it never convinced; at best it frightened. Marais knew he did not have Brother Jaja's instincts – that much was clear from the stack of bluntly worded dispatches. But he avoided a direct reply.

Marais's strategy could be explained in a sentence: three key places in Malawi were to be either controlled or neutralized, the way Marais had seen the brushfire in October. A torch was thrown on a dry mountain, and soon a whole province was ablaze. Malawi was small, arms were concentrated in one customs post and in two large towns. The first tactical objective had been the customs post at Fort Hill on the northern frontier. It was attacked and taken one day in November. It was burned to the ground, but the position was not held. It would be retaken when the *coup* was announced. The two towns, Lilongwe and Blantyre, remained. Marais was camped a day's march from Lilongwe.

Holding Brother Jaja's dispatch in his hand, Marais wondered whether he should give a candid reply to the order *kill them all*. But he hesitated to describe the attacks in terms of a brushfire. He was about to write that the key places once taken would spread and enlarge like a brushfire. *Like a brushfire*. He didn't like that: it sounded as poetic and inexact as Brother Jaja's order sounded cannibalistic and exaggerated.

Marais's perceptions had not changed, but his imagery, with the action of one violent siege and the fatigue of many marches, had sharply altered. He noticed the change in himself as a practical, almost puritanical insistence on order and necessity. This was new. It was disturbing how, earlier, in thoughtful essays on revolt he had taken refuge from concrete detail and worked on imagery which ignored such necessities as drastic punishment. He had never thought that he would ever have to torture anyone – Harry was right: it *was* torture. Torture worked.

He was colder now. The image of the brushfire rubbed at him: it was unclear, it lacked detail, it was romance, convenient but misleading. It made the whole operation sound too easy. He had seized on such images from habit – a habit consistent with the spirit of the early chapters of his *Principles of Revolt*, where he had described tactics in parables. There he had spoken of weeds being uprooted, insurrection's vulcanism cracking open the landscape, the rotting corpse of the middle class stinking in the marketplace. It was a beginner's impractical rhetoric. The images had come to him in a closed room in a hotel in Bagamoyo, a slave port north of Dar. He had not been hurried – that much was evident in the style of the book. Here was the neat desk, and beyond a stack of copybooks the seafront framed by a carved window: a dhow moving noiselessly from one side of the frame to disappear at the other, at the quayside boys in beaded caps sloshing small fish into tureens, above Marais a steady fan beating, and there beside him a loaded pistol weighting loose notes and scribbled drafts, before him a clean sheet of paper, an ink bottle. In such a room he had written of revolt.

He flicked the pages of one copybook and was disgusted. All the wasted time, the pretence of ambiguities. His tactic of occupying strategic positions he had described with easy lyricism: *A stone is dropped into a pool; it makes rippling waves radiate from the place of impact, which splash the sides of the pool. Every action is felt.* It was not a poem, but it was trying to be. The aim was all wrong. Poetry was a clever reply, an illness of the ear, a lying substitute for a coarse truth. The subject was obscured by the poet's self-importance, and there were always symbols, in themselves primitive statements: symbols were bubbles, falsifying, making brutality into a lyric.

The little pimpled man wrote of love, the coward of battle, but not even a soldier's image could represent a broken man crying and pleading for his life, the shock of a bullet, the stink of a jungle camp. It was no wonder Rimbaud chucked his poems to come gun-running in Somalia. Only the unloveliest of textbooks could describe how to win a war.

Marais regretted all his earlier attempts to describe revolt at a distance; he was haunted and mocked by how wrong he had been. Abruptly his style changed. Now, camped within striking range of Lilongwe, he was writing, *All guerilla bands minimize the importance of suburban struggle. This should not be so. A proper manoeuvre of this type is worth a hundred battles. The target should be the centre of a strategic city. The attack must take the people by surprise, at dawn, and ideally should end at sunset the same day. [In Lilongwe on April 27th sunrise is at 0620 hrs., sunset at 19.35 hrs.] It can, if completed with thoroughness, totally para- lyse the commercial and industrial life of the city and place the whole urban population in an atmosphere of unrest. Bringing everything to a violent halt, it will make people impatient for devel- opment of more violent events, to relieve the period of suspense.*

Weapons must be light: carbines, sawed-off shotguns, pistols, machetes.

For sabotage: dynamite, picks and shovels, apparatus for lifting rails, crowbars, gasoline . . .

'Everything will stop so suddenly – it will be so quiet – that people will get nervous and want something more violent to happen,' Marais was saying. He stood before a street map of Lilongwe, chalked on a blackboard nailed to a tree. His men squatted on the ground and watched him closely. 'But we will be in charge. They will do anything we say.'

There was no response from the men. No one had volunteered to act as translator in Brother Mussa's place. Marais now spoke slowly, choosing his words; he repeated and asked questions. But out of impatience or fear the men were sunk in a restless silence. They had behaved strangely ever since they had broken camp at Rumpi and marched south. Marais had skirted all the roadblocks and travelled at night over secondary roads, leading his column of men in the fully loaded Citroën. To attack the roadblocks would have been to alert Lilongwe of their progress south. For over a month not one shot had been fired, and the only casualty was Brother Mussa, the rapist.

'All right,' said Marais, 'now let's go through the whole thing again.' He pointed to a man at the front with his cigar. 'At the signal, where are you?'

The man got to his feet, walked to the map and pressed his finger against a white chalk-line, leaving a moist dark fingerprint. He said, 'Heah.'

'And you?' Marais pointed to another man.

'Power plant,' said the man, leaving a wet mark on the left side of the map.

Marais spent the next half-hour questioning the men about their duties, making them describe the sequence of the attack by showing their positions on the map. When he finished, the map was obliterated; all the chalk-lines of the landmarks, the roads, the carefully drawn positions and converging arrows were smeared and rubbed with the damp fingerprints of the men. Each had touched it; it was destroyed.

'Fine,' said Marais. 'Now what's the signal? Brother Eddy, when are you going to begin tearing up the railroad tracks?'

'When I heah a big bang,' said Brother Eddy mechanically, 'I take jack and lift up tracks.'

'Okay, you,' Marais indicated another man. 'What's the big bang?'

'Da big bang,' the man recited, 'is da car esplodin.'

'Right. I park it on the main street, here –' Marais referred to the map and chalked an X over a faintly marked line. 'It will be filled with dynamite. The timing device is set for seven. By then you should all be in your places. When you hear that dynamite explode, get to work as fast as you can.' Marais looked at the men. 'Brother George, where is the car parked?'

'Police headquarters,' said Brother George, speaking as he rose.

'Brother Chimanga,' said Marais, 'why am I parking the car there?'

'Cause at six-something police reporting for duty. They line up at seven near door. We blow them,' said Brother Chimanga.

'And at the same time we blow the front of the building,' said Marais. 'There's no cover, they'll be confused – very easy targets. Once we capture the building we have all their guns –' Marais stopped. He noticed that Brother Chimanga was still standing.

'Do you have a question?'

'Yes,' said Brother Chimanga. 'I am wanting to know why you ever drive the car. You driving car from the north. You driving the car into Lilongwe. You driving. We all the time walking, footing. I am wanting to know why.'

Marais was surprised, not so much by the question as by Chimanga's tone of voice. It was a challenging, aggressive complaint, too loud, almost as if no reply was expected. Marais was unprepared for it. His driving the car seemed so trivial. But an attentive pause hushed the camp. Marais felt he was being judged. They watched him. They were not with him.

'Do you know how to drive that car?'

'Eddy is knowing,' said Brother Chimanga.

Marais glanced over at Eddy. Eddy busily scratched his ankle. 'Yatu is knowing,' said Brother Eddy.

'But what about you, Chimanga?'

'You can teach me,' muttered Brother Chimanga.

'I am asking you,' said Marais, in the tone Chimanga had used in his own challenge, 'do *you* know how to drive that car?'

'Nuh,' grunted Brother Chimanga.

'Brother George,' said Marais, 'put the dynamite in the car. In the back seat.'

'How many leebs?'

'Put in a hundred. Four cases of sticks.'

Brother George went to the sandbagged enclosure for the cases of dynamite. He carried the boxes slowly, picking his way to the Citroën, holding as one would hold a small infant. He slid each along the back seat, closing his eyes as he did so. The men watched nervously, in silence.

Marais walked over to Chimanga. 'Here are the keys. Let's have a lesson. I'm teaching you how to drive.' Marais swung the keys on his finger. 'Take them.'

Brother Chimanga's eyes moved with the keys, but he made no other move.

'You want to learn, don't you? I drove that dynamite down from Rumpi. Now it's your chance. But just remember, you only make one mistake in this lesson. If you hit something – *boom!* –' Brother Chimanga flinched '– the dynamite explodes. You die. And without dynamite we can't attack Lilongwe, can we?' Marais smiled. 'Take the keys.'

The expression on Brother Chimanga's face said nothing. The

muscles were slack. Marais said, '*Take the fucking keys*,' and slapped the keys on to Brother Chimanga's palm.

The keys did not rest on the palm. Brother Chimanga tilted his hand and let them slip down his fingers, and there was an innocent clink as they hit the ground. Brother Chimanga's head had not moved; he had not looked at the keys in his hand. He stared past Marais to the scrub jungle where locusts whined.

Marais stopped over and picked up the keys out of the dust. The hush of silence subsided to a babble of relaxed voices. To show he meant what he said, Marais drove the car loaded with dynamite three times around the camp. The men cheered him when he parked it and got out, but it struck Marais with a force that made his spine throb that in the stretched seconds of that challenge he could have fumbled and lost them all.

24

In the last week of April, on a Saturday night in Blantyre, the Miss Malawi Contest was held. Sponsored by Ambi Creams Ltd, a Rhodesian skin-lightening manufacturer, it was an annual affair: every year Miss Malawi won a cash prize and several cases of Ambi, and was flown to London in June to compete against Miss Gambia, Miss Pakistan and the others for the Miss Commonwealth crown. There was always the possibility, though it had never happened to a black girl, of being sent later to the Miss Universe Contest in Miami. But that eventuality was so remote it was not spoken about, and locally the contest was seen as a political struggle. It was invested with all the authority of folk tradition. 'What will happen when the old man goes?' was answered with 'Who was Miss Malawi last year?'

Before anyone had heard of Hastings Osbong, the girl who was crowned Miss Nyasaland Protectorate was seen being squired around Blantyre by a talkative little man with a facial tic and always in a natty suit. The white settlers took no notice; they had their own beauty queens, elected at the sports clubs and agricultural shows, Miss Rugger and Miss Groundnut. But most Africans guessed that, at independence, the Homburg-wearing companion of Miss Nyasaland Protectorate would be the first President. This augury confirmed, a tradition was born, and many of the cabinet ministers used the Miss Malawi competition to test their influence. Entering their girlfriends in it was regarded as something like fighting a by-election in a stubbornly mute constituency.

That was the talk. It was what Major Beaglehole told Calvin. Major Beaglehole went on to say that three former Miss Malawis worked at the eating house. To look at them was to be certain the contest was rigged. But Calvin was bored by the thought of beauty contests: Homemakers' Mutual had one at their annual outing at Nantasket Beach, and Calvin told Beaglehole, 'I didn't come nine thousand miles to watch a beauty contest.' He would have ignored the Miss Malawi Contest altogether had Mira not brought him an application form and asked him to fill it out for her.

'Come off it,' said Calvin. 'What do you want to enter that thing for?'

'Miss Malawi,' Mira pouted.

It was wrong. There was not the faintest bit of African culture in it. It was a reversal, offensive to Calvin. Africans were a proud race: why should they let themselves get involved in the publicity gimmick of a Rhodesian skin-lightening company?

'What's the point? African countries shouldn't have beauty contests. It's not right. It's not −' Not *traditional*, he thought. She didn't know the word. He said, 'No good.'

'Is good,' said Mira.

'No,' said Calvin. 'You don't want to be Miss Malawi.'

'Do,' said Mira.

'Mullet, you're talking like a black,' said Major Beaglehole. 'Of course it's a fiddle, everyone knows that. Osbong's favourite popsie won it back in '63. It's always the same, but that's no reason to talk like a black.'

'I'll talk the way I want,' said Calvin. 'I won't have my wife entering any beauty contests, and that's that.'

'Don't you listen to him,' said Bailey to Mira. 'I always say, just having them up there with their bums showing in their cute little frocks is good for trade.'

'It's a waste of time,' said Calvin.

'You're a fine one to talk about wasting time,' said Bailey. 'Stop nattering and fill up the form. There's a love.'

Grumbling, Calvin filled in the application and pinned a fifty-osbong note to it as a deposit. Only then, delaying and snapping the bill, did he notice that the dark face in the watermark was Osbong's.

Calvin was angry, because in spite of what everyone said about

528

the contest, he was sure Mira could win. The winners of beauty contests were driven foolish and they always seemed to end badly, as whorish starlets or hostesses in nightclubs. In Malawi their pictures were used in the Ambi posters.

Mira received the application with a smile. She flung her arms around Calvin's neck and kissed him. She was wearing one of her flowered headscarves and a toga of a silken sari drawn close to her body. One arm jangled with a whole sleeve of gold bracelets. In her, jungle genes were threaded on black necklaces of Central African chromosomes. She was hard and slim, her mouse ears were slightly larger than most women's ears, or perhaps seemed so because they were not hidden by hair. She had a long graceful neck, and hooded slanting eyes; she was not black, but a deep brown. From the waist up she was gently moulded, like the handle of a dagger; her breasts were small. Her legs were long for her size, and straight as two stiletto blades. She was his blackbird, his cat; she had sharp little teeth.

When she was dressed in smooth silk, the soft fabric slipping over her curves, Calvin desired her. He tantalized himself by sliding his hand under the silk sheath and caressing the flesh of her gloriously firm edges, so many angles and surprises. It verged on the perverse. She obliged Calvin by dressing this way, baited him by draping her bareness which, masked, provoked him, drove him wild. He groped up her thigh. She showed her teeth and helped his hand.

She was pretty, and though he had not married her for that (he would have settled for the company of her simple presence) it was welcome. She had her secrets, but her loveliness was unhidden. Of this, Calvin was positive. A week after their marriage they had had a little quarrel about washing. She washed a great deal; Calvin did not. He had washed and shaved for the wedding, and had glued his hair down, but after that he lost interest. He was not trying to impress anyone. He said that like an African he was happy dirty: filth relaxed him. There was something cosy and familiar in an undershirt that had been worn for a week or two. Mira told him to keep clean; she gave him soap. Calvin was hurt.

And scared: obsessive washing reminded him unpleasantly of his other wife. Now Mira, black Mira from a little dorp in Central Africa, was starting the same business. Calvin said it was stupid to spend so much time under a dripping barrel suspended in the air while Jarvis lugged buckets of hot water up a ladder, attempting to keep the punctured barrel filled. Mira caught at the word 'stupid' and cried. But this was not the end of it. That night she lay flat on the bed; Calvin bent over and spread his hands on her; one hand on the full boneless dumpling of a breast, the other fishing in the fuzzy nave of her thighs. He was first a blind man lightly translating the body's braille; then, with desire, an organist feeling for chords. Calvin crouched to pick her open with a kiss. 'Peeg!'

She jackknifed and slapped his face.

Calvin fled from the room, tumescent, and walked the streets searching for a girl to pick up. The eating house bar was empty. Calvin walked down St Andrew's Street to Osbong where he found the bars closed and shuttered. A girl in an alley off Henderson Street clicked her teeth at him. Calvin stopped and went closer to her. She was drunk, she held his sleeve and pursed her lips, trying to kiss. Calvin pulled away and ran up to Victoria Street where, at Barclays Bank and Kandodo Supermarket, nightwatchmen huddled around fires or were slung in *charpoys* in the doorways with bedclothes of newspaper. Two blocks up Victoria a pack of Youth Wingers appeared, armed with truncheons and knobkerries, and started towards Calvin. Calvin ducked down Fotheringham Road and saw several girls dispersing. He followed one, then another, back down to Osbong, avoiding the Youth Wingers, and almost reached Agnello's building and the junction when he saw a figure he first took to be a little young Sikh boy in a sarong. It was a girl. Calvin followed, led on by the busy bobbing of her likely bum. In Chinyanja there was a specific word of eight thumping syllables for the rotating movement of a woman's bottom when she walked. The girl moved swiftly, sixteen syllables to a step, and had almost reached the clocktower when Calvin, drawing close to her and on the point of making a kissing sound – the way one calls a cat: all the girls responded to it – and saying *muli bwanji*, saw the girl's face in the helpful blaze of a watchman's fire: Mira, yes.

So pretty, even from the back, in the dark, late at night, as a stranger. They hugged and brushed lips; jungle lovers. Mira plunged her hand down the top of his trousers and held his quickening shaft. She steered him back to the eating house, and much later she bathed him, soaping him by lantern light in Beaglehole's clawfoot bathtub.

'*Lays and german!*' called the Master of Ceremonies on the stage of the Rainbow Theatre, in a slurring attempt at an American accent. 'Wid yer permission lays and german, lemme interduce these luffly, luffly chicks!'

They were under the Ambi banner *Look Lovelier. Look Lighter – AMBI is for you.* The Ismaili brothel had sent a very thin one, the Groundnut Marketing Board sent two, the *Malawi News* one of their girl reporters, the League of Malawi Women one, and two each from the Goodmorning Panwallah, the Zambezi Bar, the New Safari Drinkhouse, the Victoria Club and the Highlife. There were three (Grace, Abby, Ameena) from Auntie Zeeba's Eating House. Five in special finery (feathered hats, trim dresses and long white gloves) were unsponsored: these were assumed to be the cabinet ministers' girlfriends. There was Mira in silk. And there was another.

'Look at that,' Major Beaglehole said. 'A ruddy Hottentot.'

She was a fat black woman with streaks of red ochre on her face. She wore a leopardskin, a necklace of yellow lion fangs and a civet cat peruke. Strings of little bells were tied around her ankles and wrists. She stamped and made swimming movements with her arms, sounding these bells. She was armed, a quiver of arrows at her back, a bow slung over her shoulder. In her hand was a limber spear, a trident, popular with the lakeshore tribes. A carving knife with a beaded handle, and a stone hatchet, were crammed into her belt. She was introduced as Zanama.

Each girl on being presented by the Master of Ceremonies had winked or salaciously adjusted her dress. Mira had smiled towards Calvin. Zanama had called out in a coarse village voice; a whole section of the audience had replied. Encouraged, Zanama hopped to the centre of the stage, shook her bells and waved her spear. Calvin thought she might nock an arrow and zing it into the audience: he slumped down in his seat. But no arrow was shot. The Master of Ceremonies persuaded Zanama to return to her place in line. She did so, scowling.

Only Mira and Zanama appeared to be their natural colour; Mira was chocolate, Zanama molasses. The rest, rubbed with Ambi, were shiny-faced in hues of glowing blue, the difference in shade due to the strength of lightening cream each had used – Ambi-Regular, Ambi-Extra or Ambi-Special. All the girls' arms were brown, and all their mouths were clowny with lipstick.

'Les give da judges time to look dese luffly chicks over and pick da nex Miss Malawi,' said the Master of Ceremonies. 'Now a little music to brighten things up!'

A penny-whistle band from Johannesburg, led by a man named Spokes (a short *tsotsi* in a pork-pie hat), played two numbers. Spokes danced an extravagant *kwela*.

Elvis Masooka followed with 'Jailhouse Rock' and 'Ooby-Dooby', accompanying himself on a cracked guitar.

Jim Malawi sang a pious rendition of 'This World Is Not My Home.'

The girls' choir from the Stella Maris Mission harmonized, to the tune of 'Santa Lucia', the Hastings Osbong song; they finished up with '*Zonse Zimene Za* H. K. Osbong' – 'Everything Belongs to H. K. Osbong'. Doctor O's picture was right above the Ambi sign, and tinted blue, giving credence to Jarvis Moore's charge that the President used it.

A judge in a white smock went among the girls at the back of the stage with a tape measure. He shouted numbers to a serious faced judge who jotted in a notebook. Another judge examined the girls with a magnifying glass (upstaging the girls' choir) when the measuring judge was finished.

Calvin sat between Major Beaglehole and Bailey. Jack Mavity had also come along; he sat next to Bailey with two of his children. Mavity said, 'You see that magnifying glass? Well, the Africans like shiny objects like that –' Major Beaglehole looked at Zanama and said, 'Makes me think of a rogue elephant.' Bailey coughed, and ate from a parcel in her lap, and coughed. Calvin chain-smoked. He was embarrassed on behalf of every performer and contestant; he tried to avert his eyes. There was something unnatural about it. It was wrong; he had known that as soon as Mira had shown him the application headed *Ambi Beauty Search*. He felt discomfort, he wanted to leave.

One perception held him. It dawned on him that he was watching a minstrel show in reverse, a negative rather than a photograph. Instead of Al Jolson in blackface, popping his eyes and crooning, 'Mandy, is there a minister handy?', black people wearing skin-lightener were cavorting around dressed as bwanas, memsahibs and white showgirls. They weren't making asses of themselves: they were reacting against years of mockery and insult. Calvin had never seen Al Jolson, but he had seen the Hudson Baptist Men's Club dressed as darkies – that was their word, darkies – balling the jack in 1951 at a church gala. It made his flesh creep to recall that sorry decade, when dreary people tried to strut, and middle-aged men in striped golliwog jackets tipped paper derbies and said, 'Hel-lo, Mistah Bones! Who was dat lady I seen you wid last night?'

'That was no bloody lady – that was my wife!' was the reply by Spokes, fifteen years later on the stage of the Rainbow Theatre in Blantyre, Malawi, Central Africa. Time had stood still. There were the Ambi-whitened girls instead of the burnt-cork-blackened men; there was Elvis Masooka, Jim Malinki, and even his own wife, and it was still the fifties. That other era sputtered back in grey haphazard recollection like an old TV warming up: the Andrews Sisters, Perry Como, Julius La Rosa, Ed Sullivan's 'Toast of the Town', Dave Garroway, all the cool hepcats in Hudson, Mass., barfing on a six-pack of Carling's and listening to Symphony Sid. It was the Miss Malawi Contest in Blantyre; but it was also the Sunday afternoon variety show on a Boston TV: 'Community Opticians' with your genial host Gene Jones singing, *Star of the day, who will it be* . . . Talent-time in snow flurries on a twelve-inch Muntz.

Fond memories at thirty, effortless reminiscences. Africa permitted such insights. No one could be nostalgic in America, the country was not designed for it: with gusto the past was erased. But here in Malawi the world had not turned. Here for Calvin were ghostly voices and signature tunes: The Green Hornet, Inspector Keene Tracer of Lost Persons, Mr and Mrs North, The Shadow, Lamont Cranston, the Quiz Kids, 20 Mule Team Borax, Quaker Oats Shot from Guns, Jack Armstrong the All-American Boy, Tonto, the Rosenbergs and Guildersleeve. For twelve cents at the Hudson Roxy you could see Jane Russell (a torn blouse, a haystack) in *The Outlaw*, Edmond O'Brien in *The Barefoot Contessa*, Jane Wyman (whatever happened to her?); Lex Barker was Tarzan. Those queer grey years you were a liberal if you had seen *The Jackie Robinson Story*, and there were minstrel shows, millions and millions of (Toot-Toot-Tootsie, Goodbye . . .) minstrel shows.

'Here is another musical sandwich to munch on. So gird up your loins and let this squeeze-box knock you off your feet!'

Onstage, out of the Rainbow wings, came a nervous accordionist, a gangling man with a bad haircut. His black face was neutralized with Ambi-Extra. On 'Community Opticians' he would have said, 'I'm a bus-boy at the Chelsea Waldorf, Gene – been playing this here thing since I was ten-eleven years old – I guess you might say I'm waiting for my big break –' But the gangling man with the bad haircut when asked, 'What are you gonna play for us?' said nothing in reply. He shook his bulky instrument, felt for the keys and chords, and swaying in the way all the accordionists used to, played – *My God*, thought Calvin, *am I dreaming this?* – 'Lady of Spain'.

Singing 'Old Black Joe' and 'Swanee River' the Hudson Baptist Men's Club must have known how ludicrous a spectacle they were, and so probably had Amos 'n' Andy known: 'Let's unlax, Brother Andy. Get dose feet up on de desk and unlax yo'self til Kingfish come de Mystic Knights of de Sea Lodge.' But did *they* know, up on the Rainbow stage – Elvis, Jim, the Ambi girls, the 'Lady of

Spain' accordion-player, his wife . . . *his wife*? For their sakes, and his own peace of mind, Calvin fervently hoped they did, and that theirs was mockery in the same manner, getting even with their white-faced minstrel show, a form of revolt. It was awful to consider that other thought, that if they believed in the mimicry of their names and masks it was a sad terrible dereliction.

A dereliction, that is, for everyone except Zanama. She had business there. She stuck out like a sore thumb. She was not trying to be white, she was not mocking: her black integrity did not permit her to play along with the others. If she had a counterpart in Hudson it was the white soprano from the church choir who every year sang 'Alice Blue Gown' and reminded those present that there existed under all that warpaint a jewless master race. But what about Zanama?

The music stopped.

'What in bloody hell is going on up there?' grumbled Mavity.

The judges were at a small table, doing arithmetic and comparing sums. Most of the girls smiled through running Ambi. Zanama beetled her ochre brows and looked fierce.

'Will they announce the winner right here?' Calvin asked.

'Always do,' said Bailey. She ate from the parcel in her lap, licked her fingers and said, 'But they take their time about it.'

'I don't know why I came here,' said Major Beaglehole.

'You could have stayed back at the bar,' said Calvin. 'No one forced you to come.'

'What's that?' Major Beaglehole squinted at Calvin.

Calvin allowed his lips to be read.

'I meant to Africa,' said Major Beaglehole.

'Ain't it beastly,' said Bailey.

'They wear bandages on their legs,' said Mavity 'And there ain't a thing wrong with them.'

'The sods,' said Bailey. She coughed.

'I'm the one who should wear bandages,' said Mavity.

'This place,' Major Beaglehole looked around and winced, '*ponks*.'

'Like a bleeding rubbish-dump,' said Bailey.

'It?' Calvin looked at Bailey.

'Stinks,' said Bailey.

The doors of the theatres were shut, there were no fans, every seat was taken. The body odour was overpowering, an acidic old fruit smell which, taken in a whiff, groped into the nose and burned; humid and sark, the noxious air sat on them. But Calvin was sure that it was the fact that he was sitting between Bailey and Beaglehole that occasioned the comment. He knew he smelled worse than anyone in the place.

'Then you shouldn't have come,' said Calvin. He meant to Africa.

The audience was in milling disarray. People had left their seats. There was a general hubbub, some were singing 'Ooby-Dooby', others 'This World Is Not My Home'. At Calvin's feet a woman in a knitted stocking cap suckled a kicking infant; other babies, bound up and slung like haversacks on their mothers, yowled. Groups of angry boys slouched around the theatre blowing through paper cones.

'Lays –'

The drone of voices, the shuffling of feet, the yip-yip of laughter, the stray shouts, all these noises drowned out the Master of Ceremonies.

'Lays and german –'

The woman huddled on the floor at Calvin's feet stopped suckling her child. She turned him over her knee and clapped him on the back.

'– your attention, please.'

But most of the attention was focused on Zanama who, mumbling aboriginal static, a rising and falling *wah-wah-wah*, rocked on her heels, swelling forward and back. Calvin expected a war-whoop, some kind of scream. But hers was a sullen menace, and all the more scary for the suspense it created. At first Calvin had thought she was smiling; now he knew it was a snarl, it had never been anything else.

'– great pleasure to announce the winner of dis year's Miss Malawi Contest –'

The Master of Ceremonies glanced down at the piece of paper in his hand. His expression was that of a man who after blowing his nose examines the wadded contents of his hanky before folding it into his pocket – satisfied, but slightly apprehensive. He took a breath and spoke. The name was not heard.

An arrow thwacked a roofbeam. Another. Another.

With the first arrow half a dozen girls fled on wobbly heels, and the second sent Elvis Masooka and the accordion-player scurrying for their instruments. Others pushed towards the exit. The third arrow stopped the Master of Ceremonies.

Zanama threw down her bow, and with her spear-tip jabbing at the MC's bowtie, snatched the hand-mike from him and cried, 'Black! Black! Black! I am the winner!'

Calvin gnawed his thumbs.

'Call the police,' said Bailey, gathering up her parcel of fried potatoes. 'Get a constable!'

'It's the Hottentot,' muttered Major Beaglehole. Even with the plug of his hearing aid torn out he heard the moan of the mob tickling the dead drums in his ears. He winced.

'Why doesn't Mira –' Calvin began. He was drowned out by Zanama shouting into the mike.

'– Bloody nonsense! This is all lubbish! I am an African. I am fat and strong! I have spaces between my teeth! I am black, *black*!'

For seconds while Zanama shouted Calvin was on her side. It was only right. She *was* black, she should win. He had been wrong about the others. They weren't mocking; they believed in Ambi and Elvis and pale hour-glass loveliness with ironed hair and big boobs. They needed to be prodded into sense with a spear. Calvin would have sat in his seat except that Zanama was beginning to terrorize the contestants, one of whom was his wife. Zanama slashed with her knife.

Calvin vaulted on to the stage and took Mira's hand and led her out of the theatre. At the same time, Mavity passed one of his yellow children to Major Beaglehole, and holding the other in his arms like a football retreated through the crowd with his head down.

The rest of the contestants, the Master of Ceremonies and all the performers left. Zanama had the stage to herself. She continued speaking. She proclaimed herself winner in the name of Brother Jaja and all that was black. She said in a loud voice that Africans were here to stay. The disruption was enjoyed by everyone, as if, after being deprived of such pleasure for so long, at last they were allowed it, the quaint activity of furious hollerings. It went on much longer than anyone expected. The police, it turned out, were somewhere else.

25

The object had been to bring Lilongwe to a halt. They had given themselves twelve hours; but by noon on Saturday the attack was over, Marais was on the flat roof of the Great Northern Hotel, a wooden five-storeyed structure with a large clock on the front. The town was theirs: a column of black smoke rose from the telephone exchange. A dozen policemen were padlocked in their own jail cells. A fleet of trucks had been taken over, the Party Headquarters burned, stocks of food and ammunition found. There were no casualties. By any reckoning the attack had been made with classic speed. The several things that had gone wrong Marais had turned to his advantage, and Lilongwe was taken in only a morning. It was a market day. The streets were packed with tipsy stalls and goat flocks; hens squawked in cages; fruits and vegetables were piled on mats. Most of the shops were open. People milled around, haggling and buying, seemingly oblivious of what had happened a few hours before. The town had been brought to a halt, and earlier some people had been terrified; but now it seemed as if no one cared. Except for the smoke, it could have been an ordinary Saturday in Lilongwe.

The men had brought furniture up to the roof of the Great Northern; the hotel served as headquarters for Marais. Marais told the protesting manager, a Scotsman, to get lost. The hotel was the highest building in town, and the roof afforded a view of miles around. Marais could see the activity, the roadblocks to the north and south of town being manned by his soldiers, gun emplacements being set up on some hills above a road junction in the south-west. To the west the aerodrome was visible, a light green patch of meadow with a small hangar; like the rooftop of the

Great Northern, the hangar at the aerodrome flew the black and red flag of Brother Jaja on the pole that held the windsock.

The table on the roof was sheltered by an umbrella taken from an ice-cream stand. *The Principles of Revolt* notebooks lay on the table, their pages turning and riffling in the breeze. Who would believe that a place could be captured so easily? Marais sat, found his place, and began writing, *27 April. Lilongwe is ours. The operation got underway at 0500. The patrols headed for their positions by a circular route. I took the car and drove from . . .*

Marais drove slowly down the main street in the Citroën with only the parking lights on. It was cold enough for the windshield to be fogged with his breath; the rest of the windows were painted black to conceal the four crates of dynamite sticks wired to a clock and two dry-cell batteries in the back seat. He was riding in a bomb; it lurched on hard corrugations in the road, the loaded springs groaned with the weight of the dynamite and the drum of gasoline that sat next to him like a passenger. Twice, without warning, the car bumped into pot-holes, and Marais shut his eyes and held the steering wheel with numbed fingers, expecting to be thumped by an explosion. Both times the dynamite was jarred, the gasoline drum shifted. There was no explosion, though Marais passed those moments in a sudden fever, the air from the side window chilling his drenched face. They would never piece his body back together; it would be scattered all over town. But they would know who it was. 'Marais,' they would say, 'riding a bomb. He was once shot in the back.'

It was a cowboy town, a set for a western movie even if such towns did not exist in the wild west; only stage coaches and hitching posts were missing. One wide treeless street ran into jungle at either end; the street was crowded with shops, and except for the hotel and the police headquarters, all the buildings were one-storey affairs, with false fronts and roofed verandas.

At the police headquarters, a cement cube of two storeys, most of the lights were on, the only lights in town. The sign in front was illuminated. Marais smiled at the thought that he had committed the map to memory. He pulled into the compound and shut off the engine; he rolled up the windows, covered the gasoline drum with a blanket, and locked the car. Zipping the front of his jacket he entered the building, noting the movement of three of his men in the shadowy alley next to the hotel, diagonally across the main street.

The duty officer snored face down on a canvas cot behind the high reception counter. The walls of the room were dirty, there were papers on the floor, a cat pawed at an overturned wastebasket. It looked as if it had already been attacked, the inert policeman one of the victims. A roster was chalked on a wall blackboard just above the sleeping man, thirty names, and beside them a schedule with *Assembly* noted for 0700. Mr Harry's information was correct, the timing device on the bomb did not have to be reset. Even the clock in the room synchronized with Marais's watch, ten past five, the wrong time, just as Harry had said. Chained to a rack on a side wall were twenty rifles; in a glass case mounted beside it a dozen pistols, some handcuffs and leg irons and a row of knobkerries.

Marais rapped on the counter.

The policeman awoke with a start, groaning and rubbing his head.

'Are you the duty officer?'

'Yes, sir,' and he added sheepishly, 'just fell asleep this minute.' He got up from the cot and came over to the desk. He found his cap and put it on. He smiled. 'It's quiet tonight – this morning. I must have been sleeping –'

'That's all right,' said Marais. 'I'm just passing through and –'

'Can I help you, sir?'

'My car,' said Marais. 'It's probably the generator. It keeps stalling. You see –'

'Oh, yes, sir. You want to park it here? No problem.'

The policeman seemed relieved the matter was so trivial. Marais' long explanation, carefully rehearsed for the policeman's possible refusal, was unnecessary; and the bribe Harry advised him to carry in its envelope. The policeman was helpful, polite and even – unexpected in that filthy littered room – efficient. You parked it already? Very good. Leave it right here, it's quite safe, sir. The garage opens about nine. They'll take care of you.'

'Nine?' said Marais. 'I thought it would open earlier than that.'

'Maybe earlier. Nothing happens on time here, ha-ha. Just a very small town. Not to worry. You can leave it unlocked, sure.'

'It won't be in the way?'

'Oh, no, plenty of room, plenty,' said the duty officer. 'You're coming from Blantyre?'

'That's right.'

'Going north?'

'As soon as the car's fixed.'

The duty officer shook his head. 'There's some trouble in the north, didn't you hear?'

'They said something about it in Blantyre.'

'Yes, some of our men reported shooting in Rumpi District. If you're going that way you need a special pass.'

'I do? Where do I get one?'

'Not to worry. I can issue one. Here,' said the duty officer. He wrote numbers on and dated a printed sheet of paper. He asked for the car's registration number and Marais's name, passport number and address. He stamped it and initialled it. 'Show this and they'll let you through. Up to now they haven't been troubling Europeans.' The pass was headed *For Travel In or Through a Disturbed Area*.

'I suppose I can wake them up at the hotel?'

'Yes, yes. They will wake up, there is a night watchman.'

Marais thanked the policeman and started out of the building.

'Sir?'

Marais turned and put his hands in his pockets, one on the pistol, one on the bribe.

'Do you have –' The policeman laughed quickly.

'Yes? What is it?'

'I ran out of cigarettes.'

'Have a cigar,' said Marias. 'Here, just a minute, I'll light it for you.'

The explosion came precisely at seven, several blasts, one after the other, as the Citroën blew apart and was flung in flaming chunks all over the street. The attack on Lilongwe had begun.

'Right on the button,' Marais said, fitting his pistol into a gun-stock. He was with three of his men, under the back fire escape of the Great Northern. He waited a moment for the flaming gasoline to settle and then dashed with the men around the building, four rifles level, ready to pick off the scattering policemen.

They halted at the front of the hotel and looked across the street.

'Where the hell –'

The blaze crackled in the empty early morning street. There was a powerful smell of cordite, there were clouds of blue powder-smoke; gaudy orange flames engulfed the compound of the police headquarters, but no one, not even the duty officer, was there to be killed. At that moment, after the blast, the street was as silent as it had been at five. Pieces of cement facing had been knocked off the front of the building, and all the front windows were broken; but the front door, which was to have been blown off its hinges, had been open at the time of the blast. The chainlink fence was torn and stretched open; a sizeable crater had been dug in the compound. In the crater was lodged the black under-chassis of the car.

Marais waved his men back.

The exploding car had had the opposite effect from the one Marais intended. It was to have killed the policemen when they assembled at seven, the day shift for inspection, the night shift for filing their reports; but at seven ('Nothing happens on time here') the compound was empty. Instead of killing them, it put them on the alert, waking them in little huts all over Lilongwe. It made them sit up and yawn and remember that they were late for assembly; it made them wonder what all the noise was about.

It woke everyone up, for at seven-fifteen, as Marais and his men were ripping rifles down from the wall and smashing the glass case that held the pistols, a score of market women gathered outside to look at the ruined building and the big hole in the ground. Marais told two men to stand guard out back. He took one man upstairs where, in a toilet, they found the duty officer cowering. From an upper window they watched the crowd gather. Everyone went to see where the bomb had gone off: the staff from the power station, the radio operator from the aerodrome, the night shift from the telephone exchange, the Youth Wingers who were supposed to be manning the roadblocks outside town, some guests from the hotel, and a bus full of people from Blantyre. And there they all stood, until the police arrived, marvelling at the big hole and the damage.

At the sound of the explosion a patrol of Marais's men had seen the whole telephone exchange empty, and the people run towards the blast. Two of the men entered the building, sprinkled it with gasoline and gunpowder and set it alight. Several switchboards sounded futile buzzes in the flames, but this cricket echo was soon gone.

The power station, the pump house and the aerodrome, deserted by curious employees at the sound of the explosion, were easily occupied and left intact, though water and electricity were shut off for the day. The bus depot was taken over by one man, the hotel by two. At the roadblocks Marais's men simply changed places with the Youth Wingers who had run off.

The police tried to restore order in the ruined compound. The ground floor of the building was still burning, while Marais watched from the upper window. The police saw a mob of people and, unable to fight a fire, but trained to deal with mobs, they joined hands, encircled it and pushed it into the street; then the police dropped back and threatened the people with batons.

Three of Marais's men leaped from the still-smoking front entrance of the police headquarters, surprising them in their rear, and yelled for the police to lie down. The police turned, saw the rifles, and sat in the dust. Before the crowd of delighted people they pulled off their shoes and let themselves be handcuffed. They were led to the cells and locked up.

'Look! Look!' The smoke rising from the telephone exchange was noticed, the flag on the hotel, the flames at the Party Headquarters. The crowd dispersed. It was just after eight o'clock.

Before noon the excitement had died down. A few people lingered around the crater in front of the police headquarters, a small crowd watched the last of the telephone exchange burn. Stalls were set up, and goats were tethered to the blasted fence. Children played with fragments of the Citroën, doorhandles and ornaments. Most people shopped.

Marais, at his rooftop desk shaded by the ice-cream umbrella, was writing *The elements of surprise and dispersal in a largely undefended town must never be under-estimated. A bored populace watches the attack with interest, the fires fascinate them. And, as our experience has shown . . .*

Marais heard steps. He put down his pen and saw Brother George covered in sweat, panting towards him. Brother George's boot-soles squelched the softened tar of the roof, making a gum-chewer's snap.

'Come,' Brother George said. 'They are shooting. Come quick!'

Marais shut his notebook. He did not rise. He hooked his elbow on the chairback and crossed his legs. He nodded for Brother George to explain.

Blurting phrases between gasps, Brother George told Marais what he had seen. Just after eleven he heard shots at the railway station and had gone over to have a look. Entering the railroad yard he saw a man face down in some cinders, bleeding from his back. The station appeared empty, but when he called out the code word several men came to the windows and shot at him. He was not close enough to see who they were and, alone, did not dare to return fire. He found cover and slid away.

'How many men altogether?'

Brother George's eyes were pickled in fear. 'Three, four. Maybe five.'

'Not more?'

'Maybe more.'

'They might be police – we haven't got them all. They might be anyone.'

'They have guns. They shot at me.'

'You said that already. Don't get excited, George. Round up a few men. I'll be waiting for you downstairs.'

A mainline station, it was roomy but low, of sooty brick, with a weathervane cupola and tiny black spikes along the ridges of the brown tiled roof. To the left, just across the tracks, stood a water tower, its slack canvas cock upraised on a pulley. It should have been the easiest place to capture, Marais thought, watching with three men from behind a coal pile. There was much more cover than had been shown on the map, and Harry had said there were only two rifles in the place. There was no sign of the men he had sent to take it, no evidence that the tracks had been torn up.

The dead man was still on the ground between the station building and the goods shed. Even at that distance Marais could tell it was not one of his own men; he wore the white shirt and black trousers of a petty official, a ticket agent or a telegrapher. One of his shoes was missing.

There was cover everywhere. Two coal piles were conveniently placed, and a flatcar was overturned in such a way that it was a natural barricade. There were many stacks of oily ties and lengths of track, pyramids of steel drums, all bulletproof and affording good access to the station.

'You could have done this alone,' said Marais. 'Here, Brother George, go back to the hotel. Get the camera, the sawed-off shotgun and a bottle of gasoline.'

Brother George repeated the items, questioning the camera; he backed away.

'We can get pictures of this,' said Marais. 'We'll make copies and send them to Osbong.'

There was some movement in the building. Two men peeped over a window-sill, and another watched from a doorway. They did not show their faces long; they looked at the dead man and then disappeared inside.

'Keep your eye on me,' said Marais to Brother George when he returned. 'I'm crossing over to that pile of logs, then to the flatcar. Take a picture each time I move. If you see them shooting back, take one of them. When I'm up to the building, move close and keep clicking. You got it?'

'Who going with you?'

'I'm doing this alone. Watch me – you'll learn something. The three of you stay put.' Marais slung the carbine over his shoulder, and taking the shotgun in one hand and the bandaged bottle of gasoline in the other, he ran, keeping his head down, to the pile of railroad ties.

Brother George raised the camera and clicked.

Marais did not make a move to shoot. There was no target; the men were out of sight. He ran to the overturned flatcar. Just as he ducked behind it, a bullet banged it and ricocheted into the air. Marais got on to his stomach and aimed the carbine from ground level through a clump of grass at the far end of the car. A spray of shots burst from the station window nearest to Marais. Marais did not shoot back immediately; he waited, studying the window. The squashed head and shoulders of a man appeared, hunched over a rifle. Marais shot at the lump of rifle; there was a cry.

At the sound of the man's voice – it was a surprised groan, unusually loud – the shooting stopped for a few moments. Marais sprinted to some steel drums. He was positive there were only three men in the station. If there had been more there would not have been a pause when one was hit.

Brother George snapped a picture of Marais fixing the bottle of gasoline to a cylindrical stick extending from the muzzle of the shotgun: a catapult for his Molotov cocktail.

The firing started again. The bullets rang on the flatcar. They had not seen him move to the drums.

Marais lit the soaked bandage on the bottle. He stood, took aim, and shot. The bottle was an ungainly missile; it sailed, spinning wildly in a smoky spiralling arc, end over end, a trajectory which led through the near window of the railway station. The smash was barely audible, it was a gentle pop. Flames shot up, making rippling heat waves, and the building became plastic and seemed to shudder.

A dark figure flashed before the window. Marais had rested his carbine on the steel drums; he fired, and instantly there was a shout of protest. It was a healthy deliberate yell, not from the man

Marais had hit but from the remaining man who, still grizzling loudly, chucked his rifle and a belt of ammunition through the fiery doorway. He staggered out with his arms over his head in surrender. Once in the sun, he stopped his protest and began coughing violently.

Brother George raised his camera.

Marais aimed his carbine.

But neither did more than that. The man coughing on the cinder path of the railway station was Brother Chimanga, wearing sunglasses and a tan wash-and-wear jacket.

Marais leaned his carbine against the steel drums and signalled for Brother George to come over.

'Tie him up and tell the others to put out the fire. If the ones inside are dead, bury them here. If not, bring them along. Get the tracks torn up and,' Marais put his hand out, 'give me the camera.'

'Yatu and Eddy are inside,' Marais heard Chimanga saying. Marais walked behind the overturned flatcar; he stripped the leather holder from the camera and pinched open the back. He pulled out the length of bright yellow film and showed it to the sun.

26

'Calvin, I want you to meet my mate,' said Jack Mavity. 'Here he is, Harry, the chap I was telling you about. Where's the missis, Calvin?'

'In bed,' said Calvin. 'Pleased to make your acquaintance.'

'Hi,' said Mr Harry. 'Call me Harry.'

'You American?' asked Calvin.

'That depends,' said Mr Harry. He looked around, sniffed, then half-heartedly hiked up his trousertops with his wrists, a fat man's gesture.

'The reason I ask,' said Calvin, 'is *I* am.'

'Go ahead, Harry,' said Mavity, 'tell him what you told me.'

'How about a beer?' asked Calvin.

'I like a man who drinks beer in the middle of the morning,' said Mr Harry. 'Cold one for me.'

'Well,' said Calvin, 'it's Sunday. There's nothing else to do except drink on Sunday. Or any other day.' Calvin looked at Harry and added, 'I'm not complaining.'

'Tell him,' said Mavity. 'He'll be interested.'

'Okay,' said Mr Harry.

'Two beers,' Calvin called to Jarvis.

Jarvis, at the doorway to the veranda, fanned himself with his tin tray. He shrugged and looked away.

'Two beers,' growled Mavity. 'And step on it.'

Jarvis brought his shoulders together again and dropped them. He fanned faster. The meat cleaver hung on a thong from his leather belt.

'He doesn't like us much,' Calvin explained to Mr Harry. 'I'll get the beers myself.'

'Sit where you are,' said Mavity. 'I'll boot him up the arse if he doesn't –'

'Jack, for Christ's sake,' said Calvin.

'You're using the wrong approach,' said Mr Harry. 'You gotta know how to talk to the jungle bunnies.' Mr Harry waited for Jarvis to turn. He said 'Two beers' to Jarvis.

Jarvis nodded and went to fetch the beers.

'See?' said Mr Harry.

'Tell him now,' said Mavity. 'Go on.'

Calvin squinted at Mr Harry. 'I've seen you someplace.'

'Ever been to Rio?'

'Never,' said Calvin. 'You?'

'Twice,' said Mr Harry. 'Manila?'

'No,' said Calvin. 'It was somewhere around here. I could almost swear I have.'

'I've never seen you,' said Mr Harry.

'I didn't say you had,' said Calvin. 'I said *I've* seen *you*.'

'Smart guy,' said Mr Harry. 'Ever been to Algeria?'

'Harry's quite the traveller,' said Mavity. 'You name it, he's been there.'

'I'll think of it,' said Calvin. 'It'll come back to me.'

'Tell him what you told me,' said Mavity.

'The Algerian story?'

'No, no. Lilongwe,' said Mavity. 'Wait till you hear this, Calvin.'

Jarvis returned with the tray of beers. He poured into dented pewter mugs.

'Oh, Lilongwe,' said Mr Harry. 'Yeah, well, Jack here tells me you sell insurance.'

'Not exactly,' said Calvin. 'I used to. But people aren't very insurance conscious these days.'

'That's news to me,' said Mr Harry. 'Anyhow, Jack said you make trips now and then up-country. And I said to him, "That guy better watch his step if he knows what's good for him. Sure," I said –'

Mavity caught Harry's attention. He darted his eyes sideways at Jarvis, then rolled them ominously back. Harry puckered his mouth and shook his head. He said to Calvin in a loud voice, 'Don't go near Lilongwe.'

Mavity glanced at Jarvis and winced. 'Well, there it is,' he said quickly. 'You told him the important part. You can tell him the rest later in private.'

'Why? What's going on in Lilongwe?' asked Calvin.

'Not much,' said Mavity with another glance at Jarvis. Jarvis stared at Harry.

'Plenty,' said Mr Harry. 'Rebel soldiers captured the town yesterday. People dead all over the place, buildings burned down, bombs going off –'

'It probably don't mean a thing,' said Mavity. 'That's the way I see it.' He tossed his head in Jarvis's direction and rolled his eyes again.

'Oh, it's serious all right,' said Mr Harry. 'I figure if you sell insurance you better sell it around here and forget about Lilongwe. There's some mighty strange things happening there.'

'Was one of those soldiers a white fellow with a funny moustache and sunglasses? About so high?' Calvin demonstrated with his hand.

This information of Calvin's seemed to surprise Jarvis and Harry. They stared, Mavity fidgeted.

'I couldn't tell you,' said Mr Harry. 'I didn't get close enough to see. I took one look at the smoke and all the dead bodies, and got my ass out of there.'

'Imagine that,' said Calvin. 'There wasn't anything in the paper about it this morning.'

'You must be kidding! You think they'd put *this* in the paper? There'd be a full-scale revolt if they did.'

Mavity stamped one foot, and cursed, and tugged his ear.

'I suppose Osbong will send in the troops and mop up the whole mess. They've got a pretty good army, you know.'

'Not a chance of the army doing anything,' said Mr Harry. 'They might surround Lilongwe or something like that, but they'd never attack it.'

'You never can tell,' said Calvin.

'I can tell,' said Mr Harry. 'Those rebels in Lilongwe are sitting on the water supply for Blantyre. The water-pipes from the lake, see, run straight through Lilongwe.'

'So if they want they can shut off the water,' said Calvin. 'Is that it?'

Mr Harry smiled. 'Blow up the pump house,' he said. 'They can blow those water-pipes to Kingdom Come. Or they can poison the water.'

'I don't drink it,' said Calvin. He thought a moment. 'Osbong's Youth Wingers can't get in?'

'Nope.'

'Well, how do the rebel soldiers get *out* then?'

'I hadn't thought of that,' said Mr Harry. 'Anyway, Jack thought you might like to know. I've got a wife and kids myself.'

'Thanks,' said Calvin. 'I appreciate it. But I don't sell insurance.'

'Just thought you might be interested.'

'I'm interested,' said Calvin. 'But it doesn't matter. I'm not going anywhere.'

'You should watch what you're saying when there's locals around,' said Mavity reproachfully. But he was more fearful than angry.

'Which locals?' asked Mr Harry.

They looked around. Jarvis had gone.

'There was one here just a minute ago,' said Mavity. 'You should have told him to eff off.'

'That fat guy?' Mr Harry laughed. 'Forget it.' He turned to Calvin and said, 'Well, if you don't sell insurance, what *do* you do?'

'Nothing,' said Calvin. 'What about you?'

'Nothing,' said Mr Harry. 'So you might say we're in the same racket!'

'You got the right time, by any chance?' asked Calvin. 'My watch isn't working.'

Mr Harry pushed his sleeve up. On his hairy wrist was a silver watch with a heavy crystal face. Mavity and Calvin moved close for a better look. Under the crystal, in addition to the big disc clock, were four dials fitted into the clock's quarters, two black, two red, all with luminous green numbers. The watch itself had a rotating bezel and several winding stems.

'The astronauts have ones like this,' said Mr Harry. 'It's eleven-oh-five.'

'I'm not going anywhere,' said Mr Harry, raising glass.

'Like I said, neither am I,' said Calvin.

Mira was still asleep when Calvin entered. The room was stuffy with warm morning odours, the humid air that is generated by a naked person slumbering in a closed room. The latched shutters threw down two washboards of light, awhirr with dust specks. A fly was busy on the ceiling. In a dish on the floor next to the bed a smouldering mosquito coil released a thin vertical string of scented smoke. Calvin sat on a stool and picked up a little battery-operated fan, the shape of a flashlight, with a small pink propeller. He clicked it on and played it over his face.

Bailey considered this room the brothel's love nest. So much more classy, she said, than the filthy little knocking-shops down the hall. It had a brass bed and more mirrors than a barber shop, and it was trimmed in gilt and mauve. But it was littered, cluttered. This was Mira's doing. She was a collector, and this instinct of hers was apparent. All her things were heaped in the room. Several chairs were mounded with her dresses (closet space was always lacking in a brothel), and there were deposits of other things everywhere, string, shells, ribbons, Calvin's empties, fancy ashtrays, records out of their sleeves. Calvin wondered if this collecting was an assertion of her existence, all the junk as proof.

In February, Calvin carried a box of the Homemakers' Mutual 'remembrance advertising' out to the back of the eating house to be burned. He had met Mavity on the stairs, and Mavity had looked in and seen the plastic wallets, the key rings and calendars, the mechanical pencils and ballpoints.

'Where are you going with all that stuff?' Mavity had asked.

'It's just a lot of cheap crap,' Calvin had replied. 'I'm chucking it out.'

553

Mavity had picked out a few of the items. He looked at Calvin and said, 'Your missis would like that stuff. They love shiny things, the blacks. Little shiny objects. They save them.'

Testing Mavity's prejudice, Calvin offered Mira the box. She was pleased. She wanted it all. Calvin couldn't explain why.

More curious than this was her habit of tacking nude pictures to the wall and taping them to the mirrors. They were big-bosomed girls, ripped from the pages of such magazines as were stocked by the local bookstore. All had blemishless pendulous paw-paw breasts with pale dilated areolas. Most knelt, dimpled buttocks to camera, head thrown back; some lay on their stomachs, pillowed on their paw-paws, one leg crooked back and dangling. Some were preoccupied. They looked out of windows, they splashed in surf, they washed in bubbly tubs, they unzipped their dungarees or felt for buttons on soaked and clinging blouses, they pouted sleepily on rumpled beds.

They made Calvin uncomfortable, at first because they were white, but later more rationally because they were unnecessary. In the room Mira was usually naked, and her breasts were more manageable, her skin and angles finer and smoother than any of those in the pictures. Often she crouched and invited buggery in the same way as that kneeling girl. She lazed more temptingly, she bathed more candidly. It was Mira and not those girls who Calvin, busy, busy, wanted to tattoo with kisses and bites. The pictures were pointless. They did not arouse, yet they called attention to themselves, from size if not from nakedness. Calvin asked her to take them down. Mira refused.

Calvin's instinct was to discard, and while he only guessed that Mira's reason for saving was to prove that she lived and owned, he knew his motive for discarding was to destroy every trace of his existence. When Mira wasn't looking he packed the wastebasket and chucked things out of the window. But it was no good. Mira always won. She tipped out the wastebasket, and if Calvin broke or ripped something she saved the pieces.

Calvin continued to play the little fan over his face. The room was a pigsty, but he forgave Mira her collecting. He needed her.

Stronger than love, it was something which made him more thoughtful, more passionate than any lover, and he had none of the lover's selfish hunger. He watched his wife. She slept in the bed under a cone of mosquito netting, a wigwam of billowing gauze, soft and white, suspended from a rafter hook, the bottom edge tucked under the mattress. Her dark smooth shape, nude inside the tent, stretched slowly; she complained in a drowsy yawn, 'Let we shift.'

'What did you say, honey?' Calvin clicked off the fan and set it down.

'Let we go other place else,' said Mira.

'Shopping?'

'No shopping. Shifting.' Calvin strained to hear.

'Here is no good. Girls all time watching you.'

Calvin feared conversations with Mira. She was fluent, if illiterate, in two vernaculars, one of which Calvin could understand, though not reproduce. She insisted on English, and Calvin's own English suffered when he talked to her; in order to be understood he used verbs wrongly or sometimes invented new ones, he made Italianate gestures, he simplified, and occasionally, grunting for clarity, he was apt to overdo it. His reply was, 'Girls all time watching me who?'

'In bar, one with big bottoms. She looking you.'

'She looking *me*?'

'She saying, sure, you promise give baby her.'

'I no promise,' Calvin said firmly. 'Understand?' He stabbed himself in the chest with his thumb. '*Me no promise!*'

It was possible. Calvin had slept at one time or another – but always it had been out of pity and charity: it was the only way to get them to accept a few osbongs – with nearly every girl who hung around the bar. One day he entered the bar and looked at the twenty girls who sat in the chairs or played the fruit machines, and he realized he had made love to every one of them – some more than once. But since his marriage he had tried to ignore them. They eyed him from their chairs, they brushed by as he was drinking with Mira; they winked without subtlety, they sucked their teeth and said in the matey hoarseness of familiar greeting, '*Hey Carving!*' Recently, taking an evening walk, he had heard 'I love you, mister' – he was not sure whether it was he who was being addressed. It was embarrassing. They were not ordinarily homely, but truly horrible scratching beasts. Several looked like men. And they caused Calvin the discomfort that men who frequent prostitutes always fear, of meeting them constantly on the street in the daytime and forgetting their names.

Calvin bent close to the bed. 'Me not,' he started. Pig English had its limitations. He continued on as tender a note as the primitive syntax allowed. 'Me not promise give baby her.'

'You not?'

'Me not,' said Calvin sincerely. 'No kidding.'

Mira pondered this, then said decisively, 'You give baby me.'

Quailing at the sentence, Calvin clutched at the mosquito netting and asked Mira to repeat it. She did so, without varying her intonation.

'Do you mean . . .' said Calvin; then he paused. He had carefully thought out the sentence, but as soon as he started delivering it he panicked, and lapsed into standard English. 'You mean you want me to give a baby? Or,' he grinned as if with heartburn and clapped his hands on his stomach, 'or have you already got one?'

'Got one,' drawled Mira. But this might mean anything. In a verbal fog she groped for the familiar. Calvin's hurried sentences had bewildered her and made her echo his final words.

'*Have* you? I mean, are you preg-nant?'

'Preg-nant.'

'Because if you are,' Calvin attempted a chuckle, 'we'll have to make plans –'

'Plans.'

'– and *do* something, won't we?'

'We,' said Mira.

Now she sat cross-legged in the gauze tent, like an idol in a neglected shrine. Her loveliness bordered on error it was so generous. But they were barely able to communicate. Even after all Calvin's questions he could not establish whether her gnomic 'You give baby me' was a request or a statement of fact. Time would tell, time would tell.

'Guess what happened in Lilongwe,' said Calvin.

'Um?' queried Mira.

Calvin looked at her. She was the blackbird, he the grass snake – cousins, but bearing little resemblance. He started to describe what Mr Harry had told him. Then he broke off. What was the point?

'Bah,' said Mira. 'Me dress now.'

'Me go drink,' said Calvin. But he did not rise. He picked up the little battery-operated fan and with a painting motion, as if the fan was a brush, cooled his face. He continued to sit by the bed and look fondly upon his wife.

27

Marais sat solemnly at the bedside of Brother Yatu in a heavily guarded wing of the Lilongwe dispensary. It was late afternoon, the dust of the day was beginning to settle and thicken just above the ground in a tide of pale purple. Marais had been sitting staring in the room since before dawn; he had seen the day flash into brightness and felt the room dry out at mid-day.

Once in the morning, Brother Yatu had gasped and clenched his fists. But for the whole afternoon he had lain motionless, and it was hard to tell if he was breathing. His fists stayed stiffly clenched. His arms were strapped flat to the bed; in each, a needle and tube was stuck, feeding liquid – in the right plasma, in the left saline solution. Throughout the day the bottles emptied and were changed by the medical assistant, a short studious-looking African who ran the dispensary and who had spoken to Marais earlier. Marais took the emptying bottles as a sign of life in Yatu. What he could see of the body was burned, all the black skin had been scorched off, grey peels revealed bright pink underneath, some patches were raised with pale blisters. He had been swabbed with ointment, but it was not a medicinal odour that reached Marais – it was roasted flesh and burned cloth. The attitude of the body on the bed, the needles and gauze, only heightened the impression that this was not a human but a luckless animal, a side of singed meat swathed in sheets.

In the hot part of the day Marais closed the shutters to keep the sun out. Now the shutters were open, and Marais looked across the bed and out of the window to where a streak of sunlight on the road was losing its wattage. At the roadside some men were hammering on what looked like a wooden cart. Marais watched them

for a long time. They were huddled around it and knocking errat-
ically at it. Two of the men were his own; Marais studied their
movements especially – they were less busy than the rest. Marais
had a creeping notion of futility: it was impossible for him to say
from its shape or their random bangings what they were doing to
it. Most were busy. They levered boards up and clawed out nails,
making a sharp hen-screech sound; they tossed slats on top and
pounded at them. At five they dropped their tools and drifted away,
trailing good-byes after them. Marais looked again at the cart-like
thing on the street. It was not whole, nor was it dismantled; it
seemed in disrepair. All around it were woodshards and splinters,
the shadows of footprints. It did not have a name, but that was
unimportant. What troubled Marais was the knowledge that he
had watched the men closely for so long, more than an hour, and
still was unable to determine whether they had been trying to build
or destroy something. He did not understand.

It grew dark, and in the darkness of the small sickroom the
smells were stronger. There were unfinished shapes, the heavy bars
of the head-board, the lyre of a chairback, the small cluttered
tabletop with its jug of water and tumbler. The rest was shadow,
the furniture appeared legless, and the darkness was dense with the
smells of paint and floorwax, dust and soap, and that awful pre-
dominating smell of burned flesh. Marais lit a cigar stub and
inhaled it, refreshing himself with the smoke as if it was pure air.
Then he let the cigar go out. He had promised himself one puff,
that was all, he did not want to risk gagging Brother Yatu. No
smoking, or as little as possible – it was one of his rules.

The suspense had made him superstitious. All day he had been
framing rules for himself. He was not to leave the room, or look
too hard at Yatu's blistery face, or ignore him; no loud noises, no
direct sunlight, no sudden movement. Patience was needed, and
caution. Marais picked out omens everywhere: in a point of sun
sliding up the wall, in a twitching cockroach that sniffed at the legs
of the bed, in the angles of the cracks in the plaster. Watching that
wooden thing in the street he had said in a rushed whisper as if to
dispel a bad omen, 'Much too big for a coffin.'

'Bad burn and bullet wound, too,' the medical assistant had said. 'My, my.' He was young, but Marais felt curiously reassured by his starched white smock, the clean thermometer, the stethoscope coiled in the ample front pocket, ear-pieces showing. He said that in severe burn cases there was little to be done.

'Can't you graft skin on to him?' Marais asked. He showed the medical assistant his arm. 'Here, take some of this if you need it.'

'We don't do that here,' the man said. He looked at Marais's white forearm; it was very near Yatu's face. 'Also from you it would reject. They have to take the graft from the same patient, from his back or thigh. They do this in Salisbury.'

'Reject?' Marais pinched the pale hairless skin on the underside of his forearm; he held the flap. 'It would reject this?'

'Yes, I think.' The bullet wound in Yatu's upper arm was not serious, he said, but the burn covered most of his body and he had lost a lot of blood. And there was always the chance of pneumonia. 'Pneumonia. It is terrible,' he said. 'We always have successful surgery, then *bam* the patient dies of pneumonia. It is hopeless. We need a doctor. We had one but he went away.'

'Osbong probably chased him away.'

'Maybe. I know he didn't like Osbong. But Osbong never comes here. I think our doctor just got tired. He got tired and went away, back to England.'

The medical assistant began to tuck in the sheets at the foot of the bed.

'They say you are the man who captured the town.'

'Not only me,' said Marais. 'There were others, almost fifty men.'

'Our electricity was off yesterday. I asked one of your soldiers to please turn it on –'

'They're not all –'

'– and he said no. We had to operate. Strangulated hernia, very serious. No lanterns, no telephone to call the doctor from Blantyre. The man died.'

'I'm sorry,' said Marais. 'If you had asked me I would have given you some help.'

The medical assistant smiled. 'I thought your soldiers would help. Fifty soldiers,' he said, touching the bed. 'But not this one, isn't it?'

'What do you mean?'

'It is not me, but some people are saying this one and two others tried to stop you from killing us.'

'That's a lie.'

'So you found them at the station and killed one, and burned this one, and put the other one in jail, the one they call Mr Chimanga.'

'Who told you that?'

'People are saying.'

'We didn't come here to kill you,' said Marais. 'We captured this town because we wanted to get it away from Osbong. This man here disobeyed my orders. He was in the railway station shooting at us. He killed the ticket agent.'

'The people say you killed the ticket agent,' said the medical assistant. He did not challenge Marais; he simply stated the rumour.

'They, whoever *they* are, have it all wrong,' said Marais. He nodded at Brother Yatu. 'This man killed the ticket agent. He would have killed you too if you had been in his way.'

'He is not from Lilongwe?'

'No,' said Marais, 'he's not from Lilongwe. Don't you understand? He's *my* man, one of my soldiers. Didn't you see his uniform there?'

The uniform, what was left of it, a mass of burned and bloody rags, lay in a corner of the room next to a torn pair of boots that had been scissored from Brother Yatu's feet.

'He is your soldier?' The medical assistant began taking Yatu's pulse.

'Yes,' said Marais.

'He knows you?'

'We've been together for the past seven months. He was my friend.'

'Then why did he shoot at you?'

'I don't know,' said Marais. 'Maybe he didn't understand.'

'Pulse is very slow. Very faint. Almost cannot feel it.'

'Do you think he's going to be all right?'

The medical assistant frowned. Marais thought he was going to say no. He said, 'Wait and see.'

That was in the morning. Marais kept a fastidious vigil and made his rules from the little phrase, wait and see. He imagined that Brother Yatu's life depended on his attention; if Marais left the room or watched too closely or made a wrong move, Yatu would die.

His cigar had gone out. He slipped it into his pocket. Outside a radio began to blare. He rose quietly, swung the shutters together and hooked them. Then he sat in complete darkness and tilted his head back until it rested against the wall. He had caught Brother Yatu with his second shot. The first had hit Brother Eddy in the face – he was dead before he fell. Chimanga had taken cover. Yatu was shot after the fire started; he had run past the window and been winged in the arm. Reconstructing it, Marais saw their panic. It had been a mistake to shoot. He had done it for the camera; he had not guessed they were his own men. Had he known he would have smoked them out with the Molotov cocktail. All three could have stood trial and been forced to explain why they mutinied. While dead men were riddles and corpses had to be interpreted, the evidence was always in their favour: the dead always looked innocent, the death itself seemed proof of that. He had been wrong about the trial by ordeal. It was forgotten that Mussa had raped: his death, his smashed head were remembered. Eddy's body was hidden in the coal pile: what were they saying about him or Chimanga? The bottle soared out of Marais's cocktail launcher and through the large window; there were flames, and a frightened shadow leaping past them. Marais fired, driving the shadow back. The sun bore down, and there was shouting.

The sickroom light was on, an unshaded light over the bed. The medical assistant was lifting Brother Yatu's eyelids and shining a small flashlight into his eyes.

Marais had been dozing. He woke quickly, looked across the room and said, 'He's dead.'

'Yes.'

'Goddamn,' said Marais. 'What do we do now?'

He had looked at the door when he said it, and it was a sighing whisper; but the medical assistant replied to it.

'Now we must make out a death certificate. You can sign it. He has to be buried and –'

'No death certificate,' said Marais. 'He's not going to be buried yet.'

'Government regulations,' the man shrugged. 'Have to keep records.'

'You have a new government now,' said Marais severely. 'We'll put him in the morgue. Keep this room locked – I'll post a man here. You have a morgue?'

'A small one, but,' the man looked concerned, 'it's not so cold. It is just for the temporary. The body will rot. Smell bad. Even now, you see.' He sniffed and made a face. 'To bury is better.'

'Not now. I'll help you get him ready. We'll move into the morgue after I send my men off duty. If anyone asks you about Yatu say he's alive.'

'No one will ask. They will say he is dead. They know.'

'But he's *not* dead,' Marais protested. He grasped the lapel of the white smock and drew the assistant towards him, 'He's not dead, is he?'

'No, he is alive, sir. Alive.'

Much later, after midnight, Marais left the dispensary and headed for his hotel. The town seemed ridiculously small and silent. The map was deceptive: it had shown Lilongwe as important, the name had been printed as large as Blantyre, streets were drawn on it that did not exist. But, then, the other places, Rumpi and Fon Hill, had seemed important until they were captured. After the attacks they were hardly towns at all. Lilongwe was one poorly paved street.

Brother George was waiting in Marais's room. He stood when Marais entered.

'What is it?'

'Reporting,' said Brother George. 'Everything quiet. Men at posts.'

'Any sign of trouble?'

'No sign. Radio call from Harry. He says okay. Osbong still doesn't know how many we are, and he will not attack unless we stop the water. Harry says the rumours are going okay. Everyone believes.'

'What about the locals?'

'People here?' Brother George laughed. 'They don't care. I met one man who didn't know we captured. He was sleeping when we did it. Silly man.'

'They'll know pretty soon. We're having a parade, just to wake everyone up. Find some boys who know how to play the drum – maybe there's a police band. We can put them to work. Everyone will wear a clean uniform. We'll get as many of the locals to march as we can. Indians, too. We're got enough rifles –'

Brother George shifted his feet and sighed.

'What's wrong?'

'Parade,' said Brother George. 'The men will not like it. They are not,' he paused, 'they are not happy so much.'

'You said there was no trouble.'

'No trouble. Just – I went out to the roadblock tonight. The ones at the roadblock – asleep. I wake them up and tell them keep awake. But they walk slow-slow, you see? They say to me that *Where is Brother Yatu? What you do to Yatu?* He is okay, I say, but he shot to us. *We want to see Yatu. You killed him and Eddy.*' Brother George looked at Marais for assurance. 'Yatu – he's okay?'

'Yes, he's okay. He's much better.' Saying so, Marais thought, I don't trust George. He had not known that until he had told the lie.

'Good,' said Brother George with relief. 'Sometimes it is very bad, burns. My cousin burned. Dead very fast. The men don't –'

'Get this straight,' said Marais. 'I want any man who makes trouble or drags his feet reported to me. Everyone's going to march in that parade.'

'Yatu?'

'Yes,' said Marais, 'Yatu's going to march if he's feeling better. So is Chimanga.'

'Chimanga,' said Brother George. 'He want to see you. He was troublesome making noise. We had to beat him.'

'I'll see him tomorrow. But you tell the men this. I don't want any fucking around. We've got to get organized before we leave here. We can't march on Blantyre like this. Tell them I said we're not going anywhere until we get organized. I said we were staying here a week, but I'm changing that now. I want discipline, and I'll get it. I'll stay here six months if I have to.'

In the compound outside police headquarters the next morning the prisoners' women were cooking over wood fires and passing tin cups of food through the barred windows. It was nine, but already so bright that the cooking fires appeared to be flameless.

The ground floor cells were full. Most of the prisoners were policemen, some Youth Wingers who had been rounded up the day before, several Party officials and a number of worried-looking men who had been arrested as counter-revolutionaries – stooges, Marais's men called them. The stout Government Agent was alone in a cell. He wore a shiny green suit, but was shirtless, his jacket over a naked torso; he mopped his neck with a hanky and stalked the cell in his bare feet. During the night he had been removed from a crowded cell when three of his fellow prisoners tried – no one knew why – to garrotte him with a shoelace. An Indian family of six lolled abjectly in another cubicle. The morning of the attack their shop had been looted and they asked Marais's men for protection. They had brought their own food and spices in sacks; the sunken-eyed wife squatted before a kerosene stove stirring a pot of fragrant vegetables.

Striding into the compound Marais was besieged by appeals from bystanders, the women who were cooking and others who stood as soon as they saw Marais's stocky figure leave the hotel. They knelt and pleaded, beseeching him for the release of their relatives; one tugged at him and offered a bribe, a plug of tightly folded bills. They were like chickens disturbed in a coop, they beat the dust and fluttered and clucked at Marais.

He brushed them aside and hurried into the building, stepping carefully over the rubble of broken glass and the blackened timbers and chunks of cement that littered the entryway. Brother Jaja's name had been daubed large in thick dripping strokes on a discoloured rectangle of wall once covered by the guncase which lay shattered on the floor. Behind the counter, on the cot next to the wall, where early on that Saturday morning the obliging duty officer had been sleeping, Brother Henry lay askew, his feet stuck off the end of the cot, his shirt was open, his peaked cap over his face.

'Wake up!' Marais banged his fist on the counter. Bits of glass on the countertop tinkled.

Brother Henry groaned and sat up, letting his cap fall. He rubbed his eyes and sleepily tasted his tongue, running it over his teeth.

'What the hell are you doing? Get off your ass! What's that *smell* – has the toilet backed up?' Marais looked around in disgust. 'This place is a mess! Get out front and make some explanations to those people – and look smart, for Christ's sake. Do you want a riot on your hands? I want to know who they are, some are offering bribes. Write down their names and their complaints. If they don't have a reasonable gripe send them the hell out of here.' He kicked at a tin can, then lit a cigar and puffed it to drive out the smell. There were flies everywhere.

Brother Henry made no explanation. He sluggishly responded, slowly buttoning his shirt – yawning a roar as he did so – before getting up from the cot. It seemed deliberate provocation.

'Those people,' he said; he sampled his tongue again, looked displeased, and spat. 'Too troublesome.'

Marais was looking at the littered entryway. He said, 'And clean this goddamned place up. Sweep up that glass. What's that big puddle out front?'

'Big puddle,' said Brother Henry. 'Where the car esplode. Water come.'

'Drain it,' said Marais. 'Scoop it out.' He looked at Brother Henry. 'What's wrong with you?'

Brother Henry snorted, flipped his cap on and fitted a pair of sunglasses over his eyes. 'Chimanga out there,' he said, crunching through the broken glass in his heavy boots, his long laces trailing. 'Want to talk to you.'

Chimanga's was a low narrow cell at the back, sheltered by a makeshift roof of thatch bundles. It had originally been a kennel where the Royal Nyasaland Constabulary kept their Alsatians. Chimanga sat on the floor hunched over, talking to a group of children who crouched before the cell door hugging their knees. They were listening intently to Chimanga. Seeing Marais they got up and – sheepishly, Marais thought – backed away into the sunlight until Chimanga shouted for them to stop.

'You scare them,' said Chimanga. 'They are fearing Europeans.' He laughed and extended his left hand through the bars in a rude greeting.

The children covered their mouths and muffled embarrassed giggles.

'You refusing to shake me?' said Chimanga, smiling at his own hand. 'Well . . . You thinking I am a dog? Putting me in the dirty place?'

'There's no room inside headquarters.'

'The Indians will come here. I go inside. No good here, just sitting.'

'You'll stay here.'

'Uh,' Chimanga nodded, 'like a dog.' He called to the children in Chinyanja. 'He thinks I am a dog – woof! woof!'

Marais eyed Chimanga. 'What were you telling them when I came?'

Chimanga returned Marais's stare. His face was bruised, his mouth torn, the flesh around his eyes puffed up. There was a welt on his neck, as dark and thick as a leech. He held the bars with both hands, showing roughened, lacerated knuckles.

'Little story,' he said, and smiled.

'Telling them a little story? What story?'

'About General Bang-Bang. You knowing him?'

'No.'

'You knowing Livingstone Island, eh?'

'The prison. In the lake.'

'Mm. In the lake, Salima side,' said Chimanga. 'Before, six-seven years before, was a prison on island, and General Bang-Bang, European man like you, he was the in-charge of prison. A bad man. Had to wake up African prisoners in night when they sleeping and just telling them work-work. In night, eh. Sometimes they saying that we not working in night, and Bang-Bang he saying that okay I cane you twenty-thirty stroke. Too much he cane poor African, all time he cane-cane-cane with bamboos and *sjamboko* too. He like caning African too much. For Bang-Bang it is better.'

'You can tell me in Chinyanja,' said Marais.

Chimanga looked insulted. 'I speaking English.' He slid his hands down the bars and nodded. The children had crept closer; they seemed to be listening, understanding. Marais smoked.

'Oh, Bang-Bang was a bad man – *too* bad. He finished those African, kill them, bang-bang-bang with *sjamboko*. That why they name him. And some he take their cloths and make them running about just naked. Sure. Always when the government – *British* Government – asking that what you doing to these chaps, Bang-Bang he refusing that he finishing them and saying that, well, they all just bloody kaffir shit. Some caught with fever and some they had to fall down from paining.'

'That's the story you're telling these little kids!'

'That not the end of story.' Chimanga wet his lips. 'The end of story is that African prisoners they all hoping, sure, Bang-Bang he too devil and we just have to finish him for God sake, he sinning on us too much.' He smiled at Marais. 'So one night they making a hell of noise, all African jumping and doing *ngoma*. Bang-Bang he wake up and foot over to prison house and say that, okay, you all have to work just now. And all men saying that, yes we will work digging, so forth. And they take big *kisu*, shovel, stick, what-not, and they *cut* him in pieces, and they fire all houses, everything and singing –'

The children were very close to Chimanga now, fixed by his steady voice. He looked directly at them and started speaking in Chinyanja. Perhaps, Marais thought, he had interrupted at this point in the story and frightened the children away.

Marais listened, translating to himself.

Chimanga said, 'The police in Salima saw smoke rising up from the island and they went in boats. But the African men were not there. The islands and all the houses were burning and mocking the police. They could not find the white man, Bang-Bang. They looked very hard and saw blood, then *ah!* They found a piece here, and over there a piece. All little pieces with blood dripping. A dog was eating his leg and he liked it. The white man's head was off, his arm, his foot –'

'Stop it!' snapped Marais.

At his shout the children jerked their heads around and looked at Marais with startled faces. They jumped a few steps back and lifted their puny arms. Then they ran, stamping in the dust, scattering in four directions. Marais turned and saw them regrouping under a yellow thorn tree fifty yards away. He saw them dance; they spun in their loose rags like imps, lifting their legs high and holding their arms above their heads and calling out in bursts. 'Bang-Bang! Bang-Bang! Bang-Bang!'

Chimanga smiled, deeply satisfied. He said, 'They are knowing your name, eh.'

Part Four

28

It might have helped if they spoke the same language, but they didn't. Calvin patted his tummy, put his grin close to Mira's face and grunted, 'Unh? Unh?' He cradled an invisible infant in his arms and (saying goo-goo in sing-song) pretended to cuddle and burp it. None of this got through to Mira. She buffed her nails and looked blank. Her pregnancy remained unconfirmed.

And yet they were always together, either sitting on the veranda, or shopping in town, or taking an evening walk down Osbong to the clocktower. Her silences did not keep Calvin from talking, particularly in friendly sentences which began, 'Did you ever notice how –'

He noticed how whenever there was a grassy plot there were little footpaths criss-crossing it: Africans always trampled their own paths and detours, and after Calvin saw his second one he saw hundreds. Or the clocktower. This was a cement cube on the top of a slightly inclined steel post which grew out of a flowerbed. It was (with Osbong's Presidential Palace, Parliament House, Market Day, Lakeside Dwelling With Dhow and Queen's View – the hilly view south from the top of the escarpment) a favourite postcard subject. Calvin noticed the four clockfaces on the cube's vertical sides each showed a different time. The difference in hours shown was so great they could have told the time in four parts of the world. But that was not the intention. They showed the wrong time in Blantyre four times over. Calvin said, 'Did you ever notice how those clocks –' Mira looked away. She hadn't noticed. No one had. Calvin still began his questions in the same way, but now he knew that the reply would always be no. Sometimes Mira said 'Yah' but this meant no as often as yes. She was not a communicative person. They didn't speak the same language; most of the time she was silent.

The silence made their sex a wholly anonymous pleasure. Calvin locked the bedroom door and tied up the mosquito net; they usually made love in the dark, and except for her 'yah' did not speak. But it seemed to Calvin that most sex was anonymous anyway – though in the dark with his first wife it had felt like queerness or incest because it was, or so it felt, a cosy conspiracy of white people that left him feeling guilty and sullen. With Mira, the one time lightning flashed and lit up the bedroom, Calvin saw in the spacious barbershop mirrors a dozen skinny Americans in their undershirts, each hunched in a tense gymnastic with a pair of brown cycling legs. This sight, in the lightning's tumbling instant, took all the starch out of Calvin. It was better not to see or speak, and the very invisibility of it made them adventurous: the bird beating her wings in the heat swallowed the snake in gulps. It all bolstered Calvin's confidence, for he had a recurring feeling, fortified every time he made love to Mira, that he would never go home, ever.

It was strongest on rainy afternoons, with a thrum of drops on the tin roof of the eating house. People disappeared indoors, the empty street steamed; all work stopped and would not begin again until the rain was past. It gave Calvin a sense of well-being and in this hot place where there was little privacy, a cool stretch of undisturbed reflection. It was a calming he needed, for by the middle of the afternoon his head was full of fizzy beer-gas, and with the seven or eight pints he had put away since morning he felt a sick tingle at the ends of his unreliable limbs. His head was swollen, his temples balloon-tight. Drinking in sunlight took him that way; it tired him but would not let him sleep; it made his eyes boil and his head ache and swell like a football straining against its laces. He feared his head might explode.

But a spray of rain from a black sky eased everything: the temperature dropped, Calvin's head cleared. He got up from his veranda chair and passed through the bar, touching Mira lightly on the shoulder as he passed by her. In the bedroom he lay and waited, listening to the rain's splash on the leaves and the roof and in the gurgling gutter. Mira understood. She entered the room, active, kicking off her sandals, one arm twisted behind her back, unzipping, the other unwinding her headscarf. And soon, smoothly, still braceleted, she was beside him – so speedily from her chair that waffles from the cane seat were deeply imprinted on her buttocks – pulling his clothes off. These rainy afternoons there was no hurry; they made love slowly in the storm's twilight with amazed sighs, as if each moment of the way had to be invented, and everything they did happened to be new. Afterwards there was all that warmth; they lay in the rain-enclosed room, in a mist of love. No, he would never go home. He would stay and not fret: his silent sex, like any other passion, like politics, like revolt, had a pattern which comforted – a beginning, a middle, and an end.

This was maybe the middle. After the 'You give me baby' discussion Calvin saw a new dimension to his marriage. Speculating on the possibility of Mira's pregnancy, he decided that the most remarkable thing about children and the whole idea of parenthood was that it had nothing whatever to do with sex. After all (Calvin's reflection went), sex was fundamentally an embrace, and a brief one at that – though people tried to lengthen its duration by devising tricksy preliminaries, believing that, prolonged, it was more voluptuous. Naturally they failed: sex had explicit contours, and touching all these peripheries it had to repeat and so, finally, bored. The manageable variations were limited. Invention failed. And man was a sexual weakling – that was the first fact of life; it worried man sick and made him brood sadly over his body. Still man persevered, but not because of lust only. It was something else; it was a kind of intrigue. A love affair was as close as anyone in his square house got to real cloak and dagger suspense, to plotting, conspiring, defeating, to intentional mystification. Most got no closer to mystery; but what people called love was pretty close – almost a complete plot, that rainy afternoon in the bedroom. Parenthood was different, much more serious and companionable than sex, and like insurance in that it made promises, it took luck and it was vaguely morbid.

He hoped Mira was pregnant, or, as the vernacular put it, 'had something on her person'. The childless were paupers – children were insurance in its purest form. Your small deposit, given with thanks and allowed to mature undisturbed, guaranteed a residue of your flesh for ever on earth, a kind of immortality for people who found it hard to get through an afternoon. It was possible that your children might fetch and carry for you; more likely they would do nothing. But after your death they had no choice: they were deputized in your image to pass on to other generations that waspish pallor, that yen to laze and drink in the morning, those toothgaps and long bones, that nailless little toe. Your whole style was bequeathed. In your child, the squat simian version of you, was your death – the child was the mortician of man: but this deadly elf, probably less than half human, charmed you with his undertaker's eye, beguiled you with a dimple or a foible of your own endowment, buried you and then carried on, helping you to outlast your death. It was insurance, but no policy could guarantee the drama of those certainties. An example of Homemakers' Mutual futility, the folly of all insurance, was the feeble memory of poor dead Ogilvie living on in the tarnished bangles that Mira kept on the neck of a beerbottle; Ogilvie lived in the clutter of merchandise in the bedroom, the heaps of clothes, the silly pictures. In his way, Ogilvie had paid for it all. And so many other clients had simply piffled off into death without leaving so much as a brat behind. The Africans were right in valuing children. They trampled their paths and ignored the clocktower; they weren't bothered by Osbong, they saw no landscape and had no faith in anything except their children. It was right. Barrenness was the only poverty.

Weeks passed. Mira varied her utterances. One day it was 'Let we shift', the next day the ambiguous 'You give baby me', both sentences either preceded or followed by 'Yah'. She spoke without alarm or hurry, her mood was constant, she did not urge. She said, over and over again, 'Let we shift' and 'You give baby me'. Calvin said okay, fine, very good, if you say so.

A month after that first discussion there was a distinct swelling in Mira's stomach, the half-globe of a heavy meal. It stayed. It grew. Now there was no doubt.

'I rather fancied she had a bun in the oven,' said Major Beaglehole when Calvin broke the news to him. 'I'm glad you didn't do the dirty on her.'

'No,' said Calvin. 'I wouldn't do that.'

'You did the decent thing.'

'I married her.'

'You married her,' said Major Beaglehole. 'I say we drink on it. Where is that bloody waiter!'

'There he is,' said Calvin, 'talking to – say, did Jack introduce you to that guy Harry?'

'A swine,' said Major Beaglehole. 'He chats up the blacks. Pay no attention to him.' The Major looked at Harry talking to Jarvis. 'Chap could do with a haircut.'

It was now May, the wedding present of the double room – the love nest – ceased to be a present: it would have to be vacated or rented. This, Calvin considered, was as good a time as any to shift and have the baby. It was not a question of money – if anything there was too much of that, more than Calvin wanted or needed. There was plenty. Mira's spending had still not exhausted Ogilvie's endowment; her brand-loyalty prevented her from squandering it all. She deprived herself when her brands were out of stock: she smoked only tipped Matinées in yellow boxes of fifty, drank only Manica *cerveja* (*tipo de exportaçao*) and chewed only Double-Bubble (smoothing and saving the waxy cartoons). Calvin's own paycheque was still cabled every month from the National Shawmut Bank in Boston to the Barclays Bank in Blantyre.

What had he done to deserve any of it? He had not filed a report to the home office or sold a cent's worth of insurance since February. He had persuaded people *not* to buy. The honest thing to do was to resign and stop paying that farcical alimony, to close up shop, sell what Homemakers' called the hard furnishings and ship the files back to Boston, and then shift himself and his swelling wife into the lush cushions of secondary jungle in the highlands south of Blantyre. They could live in a sturdy little hut, tangled and hidden in the high skirtlike roots of the trees that grew there. He could raise chickens, do a little fishing, farm a few acres of peanuts, ride on the motorcycle, go for walks and wait for Mira to pip. Life was simple, death was inevitable, only the children had meaning; and there was no inconvenience except pain, despair the only calamity.

'We're moving,' Calvin told Bailey. 'But I want you to know that room meant a hell of a lot to Mira and me. Be seeing you.'

'Wait half a tick,' said Bailey. She drew her greasy shawl tight and examined Calvin. 'You mean to say you're vacating that room there?'

'That's right,' said Calvin.

'That cute little room? You're packing it up?'

'Yes. We're shifting.' He didn't want to say *into a hut*. 'Out of town.'

'Haven't you heard?'

'Heard what?'

Bailey spluttered. 'Why there's a ruddy *war* going on! You can't go a half-mile out of town without some black sod stopping you and getting you into a punch-up.'

'I heard there was a little trouble in Lilongwe –'

'A little trouble in Lilongwe!' Bailey showed her spotted teeth. 'They blew the bloody place up! All the white people have moved across the border to Fort Jameson – they ran for their lives. The blacks went buzeek. Ask anyone.'

'They're not all black,' said Calvin. 'I know that.'

'You know so much, don't you?' Bailey sneered.

'Their leader is a white man. I saw him. He's worse than any of them.'

'What's a nice European bloke like that getting mixed up with Kaffirs for?'

'He's not such a nice bloke, really. I admit he seems sincere, but he killed Mira's brother. Or his soldiers did – but that's the same thing. Anyway, before that, he showed me around the camp in Rumpi. He's white all right.'

'You're quite the pleasure-tripper, aren't you now?'

'I was up there – that was Christmas – seeing some clients.'

'I've seen your *clients*,' said Bailey. 'Ha!'

Calvin frowned. 'Well, I've seen your clients, too, and *they* don't win any prizes.'

'Don't be sarky,' said Bailey. 'I keep a clean house.'

'Right,' said Calvin. 'I didn't mean to be nasty. I just want to move for personal reasons.'

'But you know about this here war, don't you?'

'I've heard the talk,' said Calvin. At the Zambezi, a week before, the bartender had said *bloodyshed and boochery*, and other listeners had chimed in; but all had returned serenely to their drinks. They didn't care. Late at night they blamed Calvin for the trouble in Lilongwe, as Mavity blamed him for American space travel. All the Africans in Blantyre seemed to know that it was a white man who led the soldiers.

'So I'm right, aren't I?'

'Yup,' said Calvin.

'They're going to kill the old man,' said Bailey. She tossed her head at the picture of Osbong (*If I am a Dictator, then I am a Dictator by the People . . .*).

'That's what they say.'

'And take over this whole bally place.'

'So they say.'

'There,' said Bailey, and threw her shoulders back and smiled as if she had just baked a cake and was holding it up for Calvin to admire.

Calvin lifted his glass and drank. He said, 'But we're still moving out of town.'

'Oh, bloody hell!' said Bailey.

'It's cheaper for one thing. But that's not the reason.'

'It's gormless, that's what it is. You're better off here in the house,' said Bailey. 'You may pig it here, but it's safe. You don't have a lot of kaffirs shaking knives at you.'

'I wish you wouldn't use that word,' said Calvin.

'Which word?'

579

'Kaffir,' said Calvin. 'It's disagreeable.'

'Listen to *him*!' said Bailey. She put her head down in a butting position. 'They was kaffirs before '63, and as far as I'm concerned they're still kaffirs. Maybe it's just my habit, maybe not. But it'll be a long time before they're anything but kaffirs to me.'

Calvin felt uncomfortable. He had made her say the word three more times. 'You don't like Africans shaking knives,' he said. 'But Jarvis has a knife.'

'Jarvy wouldn't hurt a flea,' said Bailey.

'I don't think he likes me,' said Calvin.

'Course he don't like you,' said Bailey. 'He don't like anyone except the bloke in fifteen.'

'Harry,' said Calvin. 'I thought he looked familiar. Now I remember where I saw him. It was out in the garage, they were eating like two cannibals, Harry and Jarvis. I felt like puking. And you want me to stay here!'

'Not good enough for you, eh?' said Bailey. 'Well, I'll have you know the UK High Commissioner came here once with his dolly. It was good enough for *him*. That don't happen to every house, I can tell you.'

'We're moving,' said Calvin wearily. 'And that's final.'

'There's a bloody revolution —'

'Fuck the revolution,' said Calvin. 'Nobody cares.'

'That's a fine way to talk,' said Bailey. 'And here you are grousing about the way people eat and thinking you're the bee's knees.'

'Sorry,' said Calvin. 'Now I think I'll have one more beer and then go in there and start packing my stuff.'

'I'll give it to you for fifty osbongs a month,' said Bailey. 'Take it or leave it.'

'Look,' Calvin began.

'Twenty,' said Bailey, helplessly.

'It's not the money.'

'Take it for bugger-all,' said Bailey. She turned away. 'I don't need it.'

'But that's your best room,' said Calvin. 'Everyone wants to stay in that room. It's got mirrors.'

'Used to be number one,' said Bailey. This was nostalgia. 'Oh, it was very lardy-dardy before the mess-up. The UK High Commissioner stayed there, and lots of government bods. We had a nice class of gent, I can tell you. Used to hide their cars out back in the garage. Everything was laid on, cheese and biscuits, a little Portugee plonk, the sparkly or that *rosé* in baskets. I had hopes, I did.'

'Before the mess-up.'

'Before the, yes, the mess-up,' said Bailey. 'Not much call for that room since. Might as well be frank.'

'Since the mess-up.'

'That's right. You see, round about the new year, must have been about then, we, you might say lost one of the gents, you see.'

'You lost one.'

Bailey puckered and coughed. She splashed a little gin into her tankard of beer and said, 'I could use a little rain about now to cool things off.'

'You *lost* one?'

'Correct,' said Bailey. 'Lost one. He you might say dropped dead on us.'

'Who *might say*?'

'You, the police, lots of people might. You know how people are. There was some talk.'

'I never heard it,' said Calvin.

'*You* don't hear anything, do you? Just go your own way – bugger you, I'm all right Jack. Well, I suppose, that's your lookout.'

'Let's get back to this guy that dropped dead, okay?' said Calvin. His fourth pint always made him methodical. 'No one . . . ah . . . no one *helped* him drop dead, did they?'

'There was a few what you might call clues. But it don't make tuppence worth of difference now. Because after the mess-up none of them politicians wanted to use the room, if you see my meaning. They was scared and such-like. And they're the only ones with two tickeys to rub together. So I says to myself, I says, as no one's going to use that nice little room, might as well give it to the kids, I says. And you got it, God help us. It ain't much, but –'

'Which clues?'

'Well, there was a sort of knife, if you see what I mean.'

'You found a knife?'

'Yes, we did,' said Bailey. 'Mavity did, that is.'

'Whereabouts did you find –'

'Point of fact, it was right in that room, the knife was.'

'In the room,' said Calvin. 'On the floor?'

'Yes, right on the floor.'

'Just lying on the floor, right?'

'Not lying. It was what you might call sticking up in the air.'

'I see,' said Calvin.

Here, Bailey became very positive: 'Yes that there clue was sticking right in that kaffir's shit-bag. It was in so bloody far we couldn't yank it out.'

'So you didn't. You left it there and dragged him out and wedged him in a drain during the storm.'

'You might say that,' said Bailey. 'Gives the house a bad name if they find dead corpses inside. They found him the next day, of course. Funny, though. It still gave the house a bad name. Didn't make no difference at all.'

'He was the Minister of Defence.'

'So they said.'

'Maybe the murderer's still around.' Calvin looked around.

'Won't be the first,' said Bailey.

'But that guy was killed right here, right in my room!'

'Not so loud,' said Bailey. 'What are you complaining about anyway? You got a free room out of it, didn't you?'

Calvin started to reply. He was going to call them all pigs and fling his glass at the mirror over the bar. But he had not said two words when he felt something warm pressing against his leg. He saw a gold woolly head. It was one of Mavity's children, a little girl; her face was smeared with ice-cream. He scooped her up and wanted to kiss her, but he thought he had better not. He was known as a drunk, and drunks were excused for many things; but they were blamed for more. After a minute or so the little girl wriggled off his lap and ran to her father.

'Everything,' Calvin said, sweeping a pile of papers from the desk with the side of his hand, 'put everything in these boxes. Don't leave a scrap behind. We're clearing out.'

Hired for the day, Jarvis slouched about the office flipping wrapped parcels of brochures into crates. He crushed sheaves of paper into file-boxes which he bound with string.

Most of the office papers were set aside to be burned. Some had to be shipped with the adding machine (rust erupting in bubbles under the blue lacquer), the gummed up typewriter with a piece of headed paper in it and the beginnings of a message (*Dear Sir I regret to inform you that I haven't done a stroke of work since the middle of February this year, and furthermore I don't think* ...), stocks of pens, ornate policy blanks with gold stickers on them, a stack of papers headed *Table of Values Per Each 1000 Face Amount*. Thompson's *Ready Reckoner* in plastic, empty ledgers and gift calendars (Samuel Chamberlain's scenes of rural New England with Season's Greetings from Homemakers' Mutual). Everything was coated in a gritty layer of red dust. Termites had nested in the receipt books.

'All this shit is going back,' said Calvin indicating a pile of papers. But he would have preferred to destroy it all.

Jarvis tidied the pile by nudging it with his toe.

At twelve-thirty Calvin went downstairs to the Highlife for a beer. He was hunched over his glass and thoughtfully blowing a hole into the inch of warm foam when Jarvis appeared beside him.

'Upstairs,' said Jarvis, rolling his eyes up to emphasize the direction. 'Man says he wants you.'

'You might know,' said Calvin. 'Just when I decide to have a beer. Here, you want to finish it?'

'If I want a beer I will buy one,' said Jarvis, petulantly. 'I don't want your germs.'

'Germs,' said Calvin. 'Jesus, I haven't heard that word in ages.'

He drank up quickly, gagging on the foam, then wiped his mouth on his sleeve and they went upstairs.

An African man was sitting behind Calvin's desk, leafing through a Homemakers' Mutual appointment book, the Samuel Chamberlain one. He was in Calvin's swivel chair and working it around in squeaking circles. He wore a dark suit, a striped tie, large gold cuff-links and sunglasses. His hair was stylishly uncut, very bushy, a kind of hairy helmet. He did not rise.

'Boy!' he called. 'Get over here.'

Calvin walked to the desk and said angrily, 'Don't you talk to my assistant like that. He's not your slave.'

'I'm talking,' the African flipped the page of birch trees to one of a covered bridge, then looked up, 'I'm talking to you. Boy.'

'Well, that's better,' said Calvin.

'You don't care?'

'If it makes you happy,' said Calvin, 'why should I spoil your fun?' Calvin saw that pinned to the African's collar was a Doctor Osbong badge. 'Now, if you don't mind, we're busy.'

'Doing a little spring-cleaning?'

'Nope,' said Calvin, 'closing up shop. I'm giving up the whole works. Leaving.' He saw a clearing in the jungle, dappled by sun.

'No, you're not.'

'Yes, I am.'

The African smiled and shook his head. 'You're not going anywhere, boy. You've just been nationalized.'

29

Two weeks ago – Marais wrote – I buried Yatu, taking every possible precaution. I used to be able to make people disappear without a trace. It's a revolutionist's most useful talent, better than bomb-making or a good aim. The art of kidnapping, the murder with no corpse, the vanishing act. I'm sure the PIDE never found the man they sent to hunt me – even on the run I was able to send him into thin air! I know they're still looking for me. The South Africans are still looking for the man who cancelled all their letters with a bomb.

I was going to take Brother George along. There was a marginal risk, but I was willing to take it to find out whose side G. is on. There would be digging. G. would insist on doing it, and then resent the fact that he worked while I watched. I decided to go alone and be done with it. Most of the men seemed to sense a month ago when I hid the body in the morgue that he was dead, that I killed him unfairly and that he'd already been buried. So there weren't any suspicions. I put the body in the van before dawn and drove into the bush pretty far. No one followed. It was still not light when I finished digging the hole. Afterwards I covered the freshly turned dirt with boughs and took a round-about route back to town. Today, out of curiosity, I went back. Had no trouble finding it. The grave was piled a foot high with a mound of boulders. There was a hefty spear wedged upright in the rocks, probably showing that he had been a warrior. In a little clay pot next to the grave there were fresh flowers.

I think it is that shock that made me turn this textbook into a diary. That and the fact that for five weeks we haven't moved. We seem to have lost whatever momentum we had, and I know I'm alone.

They remember incidents with terrifying inaccuracy. Their version of the march from Rumpi is a slave caravan being stalked by Mussa's ghost, with me as a slaver riding comfortably at the lead. A simple manoeuvre becomes a death-march, a gesture a threat. Today three came to me drunk and said that all along I've been hindering them. I got up to explain. They thought I was going to chase them, and ran out of the room.

There's no one to talk to. They don't trust me. I'm not sure if I trust them. George sulks whenever I ask him about their sneaking treason. He was never much company, none of them was. But I thought it would be all over by now: this was the week I was supposed to go back to Dar. I told G. that I never expected them to be loyal to me, only to each other.

They fight. Fist-fights among themselves and with the towns-people. They don't punch; they close their eyes and slap wildly, missing, spinning around, kicking out. They've looted most of the shops. And there's some kind of sloppy, bullying protection racket going on. Yesterday one of them tried to screw some money out of an Indian tailor. The Indian gave him all he had. It wasn't enough, apparently. He was shot in front of his kids. The other day it was an African they killed. I tried to find out what was going on. 'Leave us alone,' they said. 'He's an African – this is our business.' They had beaten him to death. The beating victim is the most mangled corpse; they keep at it, never quite sure when he's dead. I have no control over them now. If I have any it's negative. I've threatened to track down and shoot anyone who starts for Blantyre. This has some effect, though they don't seem organized enough to do any-thing together, if I could kill Chimanga and get away with it I think I could get them into fighting shape. But I'd never get away with that, and now it's impossible to put him in solitary. They won't let me near him. If they weren't so heavily armed I'd leave. They're dangerous with all those rifles. Tonight I saw two having a smoke next to some gasoline drums.

*

Sometimes they talk to me, a stupid kind of needling that wears me out. If I talk in English they reply in Chinyanja, or vice versa. I can't win. They tell me not to interfere. When I ignore them for a whole day they say I don't care what happens to them. They accuse me of delaying ('You don't want to kill all those whites in Blantyre!'). They don't know anything about my bomb in Jo'burg. I suppose I should stand there and tell them how many white people I've killed; but that would be foolishness as bad as theirs. I never thought about it that way. It was always political. But these bastards are making me into a racist.

'It's not racial,' I want to say. 'Don't you see it's not?' Perhaps they have no respect for me because I trusted them so much, and they know they were never worth it. It's bad when they accuse me, but it's much worse when they're silent. There are times when I want to wake up black, anonymous, and then seat myself at one of their tables. Maybe Chimanga was right when he said, 'No white man can ever be friends with an African. Look at your skin.' The only thing that gives me hope is that I know him to be a liar.

It used to be We, Us; now it's Them and They. This bothers me, but I can't write it any other way. We is a lie. Lately I've caught myself thinking: maybe there's nothing there when they're silent, maybe they're not thinking anything at all. Maybe they don't care because they can't. I begin to hate them and wonder if it was hate or a kind of revenge that made me torture those prisoners and shoot Yatu and Eddy. In which case they were right to distrust me. Analysing it is no good. The process of analysing it makes me guilty, and my guilt in the end makes me easier on them. Then, after these feelings, I walk out of my room ashamed and I accept their abuse. I seem almost to ask for it. I know I'm to blame for most of it.

It's not one complaint. For some it's that I'm not black, for others that they're not white. A few haven't got over the feeling that I'm a zombie; some can't forgive me for being half-American. Most object, in a very unusual way, to the fact that I led them here. All are unanswerable, but the complaint about leadership is the only one I've looked into.

They insist that they were forced to follow me and to do things against their will. Their major grievance was this persuasion. They could not mutiny in Rumpi because I had 'medicinized' them, put a spell on them. There was nothing they could do to prevent it: 'So we had to kill our brothers.' The blame was all mine because I gave the order and worked the spell. I am an enemy, a witch; I gave this power, and they see themselves as powerless. But it's a paradox because I'm still with them, still powerful. They hate and accept my power at the same time. They can't do anything except complain. All the while they obeyed my orders they were building up a resentment for obeying them. To them this is a form of exploitation higher than Osbong's. I thought that I was any white man to them, no different from the American from Blantyre we picked up who tried to sell me insurance.

Their racial mutiny might be as simple as this: they needed me; they hated the thought that they needed me and so hated me; but this did not make them need me less.

So they have their own demonology which they obey, and still they keep a kind of order in town. They know it has to be defended. (It is failure that makes them superstitious. They stumble and then see the witch.) They've set up scanning posts on the hills outside town. A few days ago a beat-up Dakota tried to land. Probably the journalist I was told to expect. They let it come in low – I was watching from the roof of the hotel – and then peppered it from all sides. It banked sharply, nosed up and sort of peeled off. They already have a song about this. Tradition seems to come easy.

Today they woke me up early. I had my hand on my revolver as soon as I heard the knock. Told them to come in with their hands in the air. A half-dozen of them, all shouting like hell. 'Come see – a spy!' I went expecting to be jumped. They took me to the jail, one of the basement cells: a white man. From the amount of blood on the floor it looked as if they locked him up first, then shot him through the bars. A spy, they kept repeating. I'm sure he wasn't. And not a missionary from the look of his tattoos. They had taken all his valuables, papers, etc. He was about thirty-five to forty, not tall, had some old scars, probably from combat. Almost certainly a mercenary looking for work. No idea how he got here. I hate the mercenary code – never shoot at another white man, even if he's on the enemy side. But I felt sorry for this guy. I must be weakening; I think I might have taken him on, if only for someone to talk to. They were very cheerful about the murder, bragging and so forth. They refused to bury him. Dumped him in a field to let the kites pick his bones. There are so many voices they hear that I don't.

There are several alternatives. I can leave or I can sit it out and wait for their own leaders, whoever they are, to let them down. I've threatened to leave a dozen times already, this is the only thing that brings them around. They don't want me to leave, but the threat produces an odd reaction: they want me to stay and yet the threat itself intimidates. They're dependent on me; I still somehow represent their ambition. But in their eyes I'm still an enemy. They hate me more and depend on me more when I say I'm leaving them.

Another possibility: they really don't trust each other any more than they trust me. Their accusations are excuses. After a certain period of time they'll reject whatever leaders they have. But we've been here two months. Another: I can kill myself.

People have started to disappear from town. It's emptier during the day, most of the cars are in disrepair, the drains are blocked. The shopfronts aren't as beat-up as I thought before – some are in good shape. But practically all the shops are empty, either looted or locked. I don't think they're secretly massacring people. I'm pretty sure that most of the townsfolk have snuck off into the bush at night. I remember the day of the attack, a market day, the streets were full of people. There was even a kind of euphoria, excitement, with the flags flying and lots of people talking together in groups, wondering what had happened.

The emptiness is not gloomy: it's desertion, and it's made this already small town seem even smaller. Most of the people in the street during the day are in uniform. But I don't recognize them. They're townspeople mostly, young boys and old men in khakis they've found. They are not armed, but at a slight distance they look like a formidable army.

The men have a cowboy image of themselves. They complete the impression I first had of Lilongwe: a cowboy town, the main street with wild-west covered sidewalks and false-fronted shops. The men dress up in extravagant stolen clothes – bright shirts and blue jeans, sombreros, scarves, boots etc., with beads and bracelets. And they all wear shades – dark wrap-around sunglasses. They swagger along, clomping their boots, with their hands jammed into their front pockets. Some take pot-shots at cats or stray dogs. Most of them wear pistols slung low on their hips, with full ammo belts criss-crossed on their chests. A lot of them carry shotguns, at slope arms on their shoulders – very casual. Mad black cowboys.

It's almost comic, and safer now that the townspeople have left them to their masquerade. They live by these fantasies, they like this cowboy image. Almost the first thing they asked me was whether I had ever seen a real cowboy. I thought they were joking then. A lot of them have set up house with local girls. Most were billeted in this hotel, but now they've moved out. I think I'm the only one left. From time to time the wind slams a door. I notice its emptiness when I walk down a creaking corridor. The carpet is rucked up. Outside some rooms there are shoes which were put out to be shined on the day of the attack and left behind when the guests ran off. This is the only wooden building in town. I'm on the top floor at my desk most of the day. With a little planning they could burn it down. I don't think I could get out in time. But they won't do that, and I feel safer knowing I'm able to hear them climb the stairs.

*

She came today for the second time. But when she left she said she would not come any more. She is afraid they'll find out and kill her for it. I gave her some money.

I thought Osbong was a fool when he didn't rush his army here. We have no strategic advantage. The town is in a kind of depression, enclosed by thick jungle which makes tracking impossible. We have no heavy arms, and after the second day had no discipline. During that first week I expected to be woken by bombs and to hear tanks rattling down the main street. They could have been on top of us before we laced our boots. I was tense then and didn't sleep.

I should have guessed that it's really unnecessary for Osbong to attack us. Osbong knew it all along. He knows these people better than I do. He's leaving us alone on purpose – he never put up a fight. He let us capture our positions. He's probably laughing up his sleeve. Once in a while he sends his old French jets; vintage Mirages, I think. We haven't got anything to hit them with: I can see the pilots – probably Israelis – looking down at this pitiful little place.

It was a mistake to try and start a popular revolt here. No one cares. The biggest error was arming fifty men. I made them dangerous; I made the mutiny possible. The town, like the exploitation, was imaginary. This is just jungle, with a few buildings and some voices, all dispensable to Osbong. The image of order was mine. What I didn't see before was that the order is tribal, chiefs and headmen, ancestor-worship and bride-prices. And no one is angry about that. Politics never got to this level, I don't think there was any exploitation here. No one mentions Osbong: he was my demon. It's still a tribal village, and all we've done is to uproot it and scatter it temporarily. When we leave, as we must, it will go back to being a village, slightly scarred with the memory of deaths. It was always cows and children. Osbong knew that.

I thought it was a rape, but it was a love affair. And now we're at the worst stage: knowing we don't love, we see only the worst and we know what hate is. We select the worst to prove that the decision not to love is the right one. Indifference isn't strong enough to justify our parting.

I spent most of the afternoon looking for her. Some bad weather has started, dull chilly days and a driving wind, filled with sleet, that blows sideways into your face. They call it *chiperoni*. I was caught out in it this afternoon, *chiperoni* and thunder, and decided to wait in a shed for it to let up before I pushed on. I knew she lived in the area. The sleet whipped the shed and spat through the straw walls. I looked out and saw a small boy running along the road, dodging puddles, with his head down. He ran into my shed. He was wearing a long yellow shirt drooping sodden to his knees. There was a thundercrack just as he entered. He grimaced and stuck his fingers into his ears, shuddering under his soaked shirt. Then he saw me and shrank frightened into a corner. There were raindrops beaded on his face. I tried the Chinyanja greeting, saying it softly so as not to scare him. He recoiled when I spoke, but did not take his eyes off me. After several moments he slipped a finger into each ear, carefully, one at a time, and then darted out into the rain and thunder. I watched him go. His dancing yellow shirt bulged and twisted as he ran.

30

Major Beaglehole and Calvin stood elbow to elbow at the sputtering two-stall urinal in what was called the Gents at the eating house.

'You're up early,' said Major Beaglehole.

'Yup,' said Calvin.

Each was, splashing, intent on his task. Calvin crowded his place, his eyes fixed on a space high on the mossy wall.

'Off to work?'

'Right,' said Calvin.

'Bastards,' said Major Beaglehole. 'I was just starting to trust them.'

'No choice,' said Calvin. Having acknowledged Beaglehole's presence with the usual polite but brief lavatory exchanges, he fell silent.

Then Beaglehole sighed and said, 'Oh Christ, have a look at this.'

'What's that?' Calvin spoke to the wall over the urinal.

'Look over here.' Still Beaglehole splashed.

Calvin could not look.

'Here, have a squint.'

Calvin's bladder seized, his jet petered out. Beaglehole spattered on, and urged.

'I'm off,' said Calvin. 'Work.'

'Look here.' Again Beaglehole sighed.

Out of the corner of his eye Calvin saw Beaglehole nodding downward.

'What have you got there?' said Calvin. He did not want to see. But he took a breath, squinted and leaned.

'That,' said Major Beaglehole. He pointed with his free hand.

'I don't see anything,' said Calvin.

Major Beaglehole touched the porcelain on the upper part of his stall. Just above his finger, near a leaking pipe, a blue tattoo-like emblem showed under sticky grime.

'See that? It's a Twyford Adamant,' said Major Beaglehole. 'Made in UK. Christ, do I get homesick when I read that? Don't you?'

'Never saw that brand in the States,' said Calvin. 'But even if I had,' he went on, stepping back and zipping, 'I don't think it would make me homesick. Excuse me, I'm late for work.'

'Off you go,' said Major Beaglehole, looking at the Twyford emblem. 'They'll nationalize Bailey next, the bastards.'

Calvin walked unsteadily down the street in powerful sunlight, his shirt pocket full of ballpoints. Swinging his new cardboard briefcase, he headed for the Agnello building and his office. He had been back on the job for over two weeks and felt some frustration. Osbong's takeover of Homemakers' had surprised him, as if out of the blue, and just as Calvin had started to sprint away, a dark hand had awkwardly grasped one of his ankles and was holding it. He would not have minded going back to his old routine of rising with the kitchen clatter of pots and spoons, reading the paper in the toilet and perhaps soothing himself with a warm pint of beer in the empty bar before going off to work at ten or eleven. But this was denied him. Nationalized, he was a civil servant and had to keep government hours, nine to four-thirty, with a coffee-break in the morning, a tea-break in the afternoon, and an hour off for lunch. He missed his session in the toilet, his paper and his beer; he missed napping with Mira on rainy afternoons.

The Homemakers' Mutual sign had been taken down. The new one, a homely signboard from the Ministry of Works, read *AFSURE, The African National Assurance Company*. The Commission to Nationalize Vital Industries had thought up that detestable name as well as the testimonial on the Afsure stationery: 'The only assurance company in Central Africa owned and staffed *by* Africans *for* Africans.' It was partly true: the Commission had given Calvin an African trainee.

A peanut-vendor had set up his boxes of shelled nuts and paper cones on the stairs of Agnello House; he dozed, his head against the handrail. Calvin stepped carefully over the boxes and went up to his office.

The once-vacant office across the hall from Calvin's was now occupied. A man in white shorts and kneesocks stood at the door and greeted Calvin with a snort. He asked, 'Any post?'

'I don't know,' said Calvin. He unlocked his office door and pushed it open. Some letters lay on the floor where they had fallen from the letterslot.

Seeing the letters the man said ruefully, 'The stupid bugger didn't bring *me* any post.'

'Maybe tomorrow,' said Calvin. 'The mail's slow.'

'Not a hope,' said the man. 'I think the post-boy's pinching them. I'd report him, but that wouldn't do any good. They're all the same, aren't they? They raised the rent on the British Council downstairs. They nailed you right enough, I heard.'

'I'm training someone to take over the business,' said Calvin. 'After that I'm cutting out.'

'Back to the States?'

'I don't know,' said Calvin. 'Some quiet place.'

'I've had it. I'm packing it up and going back to the Republic. They're turning communist here, and when the old man goes –'

There were footsteps in the hall: Mwase, Calvin's trainee. The man in the white shorts looked at Mwase, cursed, and entered his office. The pane of glass on his office door was still rattling from the slam when Mwase said good morning to Calvin.

'Hi,' said Calvin. 'How's every little thing?'

'I'm late,' said Mwase gloomily. 'I was getting that hawker off the stairs.'

'The peanut man?'

'He was in the way,' said Mwase. 'Hawking.'

'You shouldn't have done that,' said Calvin. 'He's been here for years.'

'It looks bad, selling groundnuts there.'

'I don't mind,' said Calvin. 'He doesn't bother me.'

'Others will come, selling sweet potatoes, maize cobs, cigarettes, what-not. You don't know Africans. If you give them an inch they take more.'

'Let me ask you something,' said Calvin. 'How would you like to be out there selling peanuts on the street?'

Mwase shrugged and put his briefcase on a side table. It was a Japanese briefcase, fibreglass, with a plastic nametag. Mwase said, 'I've done my O-Levels.'

'You've done your O-Levels,' said Calvin. 'So no peanut-selling for you! You mind if I ask you another question? No? Okay, who got you this trainee job?'

Mwase unsnapped the briefcase. 'I applied,' he said.

'A pig's ass you applied! Who was it, your uncle? Brother? Second cousin?'

'I applied,' said Mwase. 'I've done my O-Levels.'

'You know what?' said Calvin. 'I'm going to check on that. Yes I am. I don't have anything against you personally, Mwase – I know all about extended families. But the least you can do is be honest about it.'

'I am not telling lies.'

'We'll see,' said Calvin. 'I'm going to check. If I find out you got this job because of family connections or something, I'm going to put that peanut man right at your desk, right there.'

Mwase opened the briefcase. It was empty except for one small pamphlet, a correspondence lesson perhaps, which he took out and placed on the blotter. He snapped the briefcase again and seated himself. With his fists clamped over his ears and his elbows on the blotter he studied the pamphlet.

Calvin phoned the Commission to Nationalize Vital Industries and asked to speak to the head of the personnel section. There was a buzz and then a British voice: 'Harris here.'

'This is Calvin Mullet of . . . Afsure,' said Calvin. He hated the name so much he could not say it well. 'I've got a question, so I thought I'd call you up and ask you. It's about my trainee.'

'Go right ahead, Mr Mullet.'

'Well, what I was wondering,' said Calvin, 'is how do you go about picking them?'

'Is he making a nuisance of himself? Because if he is, you can send him straight –'

'No,' said Calvin, 'he's okay. But how did he get picked? I was just wondering.'

'Yes. We have an absolutely rigid selection board a written examination and an interview. Your chap has his O-Levels, which is more than most of them have. It's a pretty ropy lot.'

'Thanks,' said Calvin. 'That's all I was wondering.' He replaced the receiver and said softly, 'Mwase, how would you like a beer?'

'I'm not supposed to drink on duty,' said Mwase, looking up briefly from his pamphlet.

'You're the boss,' said Calvin. He found an airmail envelope in the stack of mail and slit it. He pulled out the letter, unfolded it, and held it up and snapped it several times.

'Mr Calvin?'

'Yes?'

'I am thirsty.'

'*That's* the spirit!' said Calvin. He threw down the letter and got up from his desk. 'There's a bar right downstairs.'

They stayed in the Highlife until after lunch. At one-fifteen Mwase struggled up from the table and said to Calvin, 'I cannot stand it. I must refresh myself with that pleasant girl,' and he disappeared out back with the waitress. Calvin waited, drinking, until three, and when he was certain Mwase would not return, went upstairs to read the letter he had opened at nine-thirty.

He was sweating, three-quarters drunk, and had to pinion the letter to his desk with his two palms in order to read it. It was from Homemakers', regretting the nationalization but giving in to it. Calvin was offered his plane fare back to Boston. In the previous weeks several letters and cables had been exchanged between Homemakers' and the Nationalization Commission, and all had been cross-copied to Calvin. He opened the file.

The Commission had notified Homemakers' of the decision to

nationalize the agency. The value was being assessed so that full compensation could be made. It was hoped that Mr Mullet would stay on long enough to train someone to take over.

Homemakers' wrote a shocked reply to the Commission saying that it had been promised that there would be no nationalization. A great deal of capital had been invested in setting up the agency. But, the letter said, it looked as if they were being offered no alternative. They wanted compensation in American dollars and not in osbongs. On Calvin's copy of that letter, Wilbur Parsons wrote in a PS that he was sorry it had to happen like this but that maybe everything would turn out all right: 'We were forewarned. Reliable sources say the Malawi Government is going to be overthrown in the very near future, and the thrust of our information is a very real possibility that the new regime will take more kindly to an HM agency, allowing normal operation to resume. Are you interested in playing ball?'

Calvin wrote to Parsons. He didn't, he said, know where HM got their information, but the so-called new regime was just a bunch of bullies kicking the slats out of a little town in the Central Province. He had already tried but failed to sell these creeps a policy. He wouldn't make a deal with them even if he was paid to do same.

The Commission wrote again to Homemakers' informing them that Mr Mullet had agreed to stay on and that assessment had shown the agency to be heavily in debt; no compensation could be made.

Calvin clipped the latest letter from Homemakers' into the file marked *Nationalization Correspondence*. Then he wrote to Parsons: 'I wasn't given much choice but I'm staying here just the same to train the new man whose name is Mwase. I forget if I told you I got married again and she's having a baby and I'm sorry if I put you to any trouble. Longer letter follows.' But he knew as he wrote the last sentence that there would be no more letters. He wrote his letter again, improving the punctuation and omitting the last sentence.

And the next day, with Mwase's approval, the peanut-vendor returned to his place on the stairs.

31

His absorbed secretiveness with his little pamphlet and his occasional fits of melancholy aside, Mwase was a busy, usually cheery soul, and once Calvin was certain Mwase had forgiven him his blunt accusation of having used pull to get the trainee job, became a good friend; though for many days Calvin repeated his apologies. Their chief pleasures were drinking beer during the breaks and reading *Boom* comics. *Boom* was a weekly magazine of photographic sequences illustrating the serial adventures of The Lance, a half-caste detective in Johannesburg, in one section, and a Zulu Tarzan named Samson in another. Samson loped through jungle and low veldt in a leopard skin, doing good and shouting gibberish to wild animals. For a while Calvin was The Lance because he owned a hat; Mwase was Samson. This was the way they introduced themselves to the girls in the bar downstairs. Mwase said to Calvin, 'I like you. You are not the same with other Europeans.'

On the last page of *Boom* there was a pen-pal corner, thumbnail sketched, with photographs and addresses. Mwase wrote to the girls who advertised and, while still keeping his pamphlet to himself, showed his letters to Calvin for correction. They usually opened, 'Well, here I am writing to you this missive,' and went on, 'I am a strong healthy boy of 22 years, brown of complexion, Chewa by tribe, and I collect stamps, coins and Elvis records. I like dancing, sports and games of all kinds.' He offered visits, promised vigour, and hinted broadly at marriage. He ended each letter, 'Hoping for your prompt and favourable reply . . .' He was an industrious letter-writer. He had won a two Rand prize for a letter condemning spitting; it was published in *Boom*. Much of the morning mail which so irritated the man across the hall was Mwase's. He used the Afsure stationery and diligently taught himself to type with the office portable; he frowned down at the keys, hovering and selecting like a berry-picker, licking his lips when he was successful, sucking his teeth when he bungled a key.

Over his desk Mwase hung his framed O-Level certificates, a pale green diploma from the Emmaus Bible Correspondence College in Salisbury, and a first-aid certificate issued on the completion of a course given by the St John Ambulance Brigade. He added an old photograph of a very black man wearing wire spectacles and a suit buttoned to the knot of his cravat. He was seated outdoors in a stuffed chair, and he had a Bible on his knee.

'Looks like a clergyman,' said Calvin, wondering who the man might be.

'My father,' said Mwase. 'A good preacher, but a stooge of the British.'

'You shouldn't say that about your father,' said Calvin.

'Crucifixes can't help us,' said Mwase. 'You don't know him.'

On Mwase's birthday Calvin presented him with an Afsure policy, paid up for a year. It was the large Homemakers' Mutual policy certificate with that firm's name smudged out by a block of ink and *Afsure* overprinted at the top. This, Mwase framed and hung.

Mwase's policy was the only one Afsure sold for some time. The interest in insurance which Calvin had noted months back had fallen off. Mwase had an explanation: no one trusted the government, no one liked Doctor Osbong, so no one would insure with a company that had been nationalized. It was a boycott. There had already been, Mwase said, two go-slow strikes, Posts and Telegraphs, and Public Works.

'The Post Office was on a go-slow strike?'

'Oh, yes,' said Mwase, 'for a month. Didn't you know?'

'I didn't notice,' said Calvin, 'no.'

Other strikes were planned, said Mwase. Everyone knew that the government was going to be overthrown by the soldiers who were in Lilongwe.

'If everyone knows that,' said Calvin, 'how come *I* don't?'

'You don't eat rice,' said Mwase.

'No,' said Calvin, 'I don't eat much of anything.'

'Because if you ate rice you would know that there hasn't been any for three months – anyway no number one, just cracked. Most of the rice comes from the northern region, but it has to pass through Lilongwe to get here. No rice has come to this side.'

'So what?'

'That means the soldiers are strong. They cut off the supply. It always happens. When the Portuguese raid their villages hungry people escape and start a famine in our side. It's the same. If you cannot buy a stick of cassava you know there is trouble somewhere.'

'So you ran out of rice and you guessed there was a revolution? Maybe it was just a bad harvest – ever think of that?'

'Not only rice. At first it was maize. That grows in Fort Hill. Maize was short in November. Trouble in Fort Hill. Then a shortage of sweet potatoes. That's Rumpi. Trouble in Rumpi District.'

'I had a little trouble in Rumpi myself,' said Calvin.

'December.'

'Right,' said Calvin. 'Around last Christmas.'

'The rice stopped in April. Trouble in Lilongwe. Each town is closer, so we know the soldiers are coming this way. Their leader is a European. They say he is as strong as Samson in *Boom*. He talks to animals, too, and he can even just change himself into an animal if he wishes. He can sleep under trees or go for a month without eating. He can –'

'Stop,' said Calvin. 'Don't believe that. I know the guy you mean. He wears shades and carries a gun. He's just a bully, a tough guy with a big cigar. He picked me up in Rumpi. I wasn't afraid.'

'Some people are afraid,' said Mwase. 'Bullets bounce off his head.'

'Mwase, who tells you this crap?'

'It's true,' said Mwase. 'People know.'

'It's not true.'

'You think I am telling lies, Mr Calvin?'

'No, of course not. But, look, it's just a bunch of soldiers. I saw them myself. Just some troublemakers in Lilongwe.'

'They are not all in Lilongwe,' said Mwase, forcing mystery into his voice. 'Some are here.'

That day Mwase did not drink with Calvin. He sat in the office and said he had work to do. But Calvin knew there was no work. Mwase had withdrawn into melancholy; he studied his pamphlet, holding his ears.

It was June, cold in Blantyre; the flower petals rotted on the grass, and a stiff wind blew down from Soche Hill and rattled the eating house shutters. The days were misty. For much of the time the hill was hidden from view. Some days whole bluey-white clouds sat on the town. In the Gents on one of these chilly June mornings Major Beaglehole said to Calvin, 'Queen's Birthday tomorrow. We're having a little do at the Moth's. Like to come along?'

'Sure,' said Calvin. 'No objections if I bring an African?'

'Certainly not,' said Beaglehole. 'We're multiracial now.' He chuckled and nudged Calvin's elbow with his own.

'What's *he* doing here?' demanded Beaglehole in a loud voice the next night. Mwase stood petrified by the silence created by his entering the Moth's Club with Calvin and Mira and his own girl-friend. Many eyes were upon them; a song was in progress when the four appeared on the veranda. The song ceased as suddenly, as awkwardly, as an interrupted adultery.

'You said it was all right,' whispered Calvin, hoping that Beaglehole would whisper too, and that the music would start.

'Balls,' said Beaglehole. 'I thought you meant your wife.'

'He could join. I bet he's been shot at in anger,' said Calvin.

The people in the Moth's Clubhouse, among them Mavity, Bailey and Mr Harry, started singing again, joylessly and with some defiance. Major Beaglehole joined them.

'He hates me,' said Mwase.

'No, he doesn't,' said Calvin. 'Here, let's find a seat and have a beer. What does your girlfriend want to drink?'

The girl did not speak English. She was not like the other girls Calvin had seen Mwase with. She was from a village; she might have spent the day in a cornfield, hoeing; she had a dusty brown face. She kept her head lowered and did not seem comfortable in her chair. She squirmed and cracked her finger joints, the sound of twigs snapping. She had a gin, and gulped it, and had another. Perhaps she was Mwase's reproach to Calvin, as Mwase himself was Calvin's reproach to Major Beaglehole and the Moths.

Mira did not take to her; Beaglehole and Mavity eyed her severely. Mavity had left his own wife at home. Bailey ignored the girl, but Mr Harry, who was standing with Bailey near the tiger-skin, smiled at her and came up to Calvin and Mwase and murmured, 'You know what? I bet she's hiding a fantastic front porch under that get-up.' He offered Calvin and Mwase cheroots, and winked at the girl.

She wore a faded blouse with old-fashioned puffed ruffled sleeves trimmed with a carelessly stitched border of white wiggly ribbon. A washed-out sarong was drawn up and tied tightly at her midriff. She kicked at yellow plastic sandals. She had fine ears, her hair was knotted into narrow plaits, her skin was smooth and seemed an inch thick. She ventured to speak only once. She asked Mira in Chinyanja, 'How many months?'

'September-October,' said Mira, and sniffed.

A record was put on; the machine was cranked. Everyone stood and sang. Calvin knew the tune and sang 'My Country 'Tis of Thee', the rest sang 'God Save the Queen'. When it was over, Aubrey stood on a chair and rapped for silence. He raised his glass to a picture of the Queen, bemedalled and wearing a blue sash and a diamond tiara. Aubrey shouted once, 'The Queen!'

'The Queen!' shouted everyone in reply. And they all drank.

Mira sat back into her chair; her knees were apart, her big arms folded over her baby. Pregnancy, ruinous to some women, had given Mira a peaceful glow. She was rounder, and when she walked did so with a slow flat-footed gait, considering her steps, one hand on her hip, the other pinching a hanky. The heavy-meal bulge in her stomach had swelled to the size of a pumpkin, and her face, arms, and ankles had grown too. Her yen was for Settler's Oats with melted margarine, sprinkled with sugar. She was solid, and the motherly roundness of her new size made her seem very reliable, with a look of serene content in her eyes. Calvin was proud of her. He said, 'If it's a boy we'll call him Mwase.'

Mwase nodded.

'No,' said Mira.

'She's right,' said Mwase. 'The midwife has to name the baby. That is how we do it.'

'No midwife,' said Mira. She raised a trembling arm and said, 'Doc-tor, hospital!'

Major Beaglehole came over. He looked at Calvin as if Calvin had behaved traitorously and said, 'Well, you're here, dammit. Take a pew. You're going to see a very old tradition. Keep your eyes on that door.'

Seated beside Mwase at a long banquet table, Calvin asked, 'By the way, what colour are African babies when they're born?'

'Some are almost white or grey,' said Mwase. 'But after you wash them,' he said sipping at his water, 'after you wash them they turn . . . black.'

'Interesting,' said Calvin.

Mwase was watching the door gloomily. A man appeared in the doorway dressed in a velvet hat and a cape, knee-breeches, and square-toed shoes with silver buckles. Mwase's girlfriend said '*Eee*' when the man blew his trumpet. He stood aside.

Wine was poured. Two Africans, one of them Old Willy, carried a large plank through the door. There was a side of beef on the plank, roasted black, basted shiny.

'Before you drink,' said Calvin to Mwase, 'there's just one thing I want to say. All that business about the soldiers sleeping under trees and the bullets bouncing off them – let's forget it, okay? You got a girlfriend here, and I've got my wife. That's the important thing, isn't it?' He smiled, hoping to inspire a smile in Mwase.

Mwase did not drink, or smile.

Aubrey got to his feet and thumped the table with his

knife-handle. Cupping his hand to his mouth he shouted very loudly. '*What ho! Is that the meat?*'

'Isn't it the important thing?' repeated Calvin.

'We have worries,' said Mwase. He looked at the carcass on the plank.

'Yes! It *is* the meat!' the man with the trumpet was shouting back to Aubrey.

The Africans tottered with their burden; the side of meat swayed.

'We suffer,' said Mwase. 'You can leave if you wish and go back to America. But where can we go? Even Osbong says it. God punished us with this useless country. God hates us, everyone does. These people here. You have chances. We have no chances. We are hopeless. Hobbies – have you read Thomas Hobbies? He was right, life in Africa is nasty, British and short.'

'And is it good meat?' shouted Aubrey.

'Indeed!' said the man with the trumpet. '*It is the baron of beef!*' He picked up a carving knife from the plank and slashed off a hunk of meat. He nibbled it. 'And it is a *good* baron, m'lud!'

'You don't know,' said Mwase. He put his wine to his lips and drank. He said ominously in words he might once have used in a school debate, 'But I put it to you, Mr Calvin, that I do know and I do possess information. Not one information, but many. I like you, Mr Calvin, but you are a white man and you do not know what is going in my black head. I have worries.'

'Serve it to all and sundry,' yelled Aubrey. 'Let not a scrap be wasted. God save the Queen!'

The side of beef was carved and dished out.

'You think I don't have worries?'

'Not like mine,' said Mwase. 'I am a prisoner. This country is a jail and Osbong is the in-charge. These people want to kill me and cut me up like they cut their roasted meat.'

'It's the Queen's Birthday,' said Calvin.

'Not for black people,' said Mwase. 'I will tell you something I learned. Yellow is a colour, so is red. White is *all* colours. But black

– it is not a colour at all.' He paused, groping for something more. Finally, he said, 'You think my girlfriend is a savage.'

'No, I don't,' said Calvin.

'But she is,' said Mwase. 'That's the trouble.'

After the banquet, on the pretext of showing them the cricket pitch, Calvin fled with his guests.

Calvin scratched on his blotter with a sharp pencil, pretending to write. Through his very dark sunglasses, with growing curiosity and diminishing patience, he watched Mwase studying his pamphlet. It was not a correspondence lesson. Mwase did no writing. He read, and what he read caused gloom. He remained bent over the booklet, regarded closely by Calvin. At ten Mwase shifted his feet and looked up at his framed certificates. Calvin continued scratching with his pencil. They did not break for beer.

At half-past twelve Calvin dropped his pencil into his plastic pen-tray and said, 'How about lunch?'

Mwase shut the pamphlet and put it in his briefcase, snapping and locking the chrome hasps. Lately, Calvin noticed, Mwase had taken to eating with his hands. He went to wash them.

Calvin heard the washroom door click shut, heard the bolt shot and water being run. In a flash the briefcase was under his arm, and he was prising off the hasps with a scissor blade. They came off easily, the case was open, the pamphlet was in his hands.

The title, ketchup-coloured, was UNITE, BROTHERS! Calvin riffled through the pages; it was badly printed in a tiny antique typeface, unevenly inked, with faulty margins and blots. It was bound with one staple which had worked loose, freeing the centre pages. No author's name was given, and for a moment, holding the stained pamphlet and standing over the damaged briefcase, Calvin felt all his curiosity disappear. Wearily he thought of a bad excuse for his prying – no! he would take all the blame.

His eye fell on the first sentence. *Would you insure me? I have been beaten, robbed, and nearly killed a thousand times. I live at the worst end of a bad world.* Calvin flipped to the last page. The ending was unchanged: *never hold my head up high,* even to the trailing dot-dot-dot. The epigraph from the poem by the late Vice President of the Hartford Accident and Indemnity Company had been expunged, and so had the name Jigololo.

Presently, Mwase returned from the washroom. Wiping his fingers with his hanky, he walked only part of the way into the office. It was not the broken briefcase gaping open on the floor, the hasps twisted off – though that gave him pause, he had valued it and had saved to buy it; it was not the disorder which had visited the room, but that was new. What made him freeze in his tracks was the look on the face of Calvin who stood with big accusing bwana's eyes, and who held the pamphlet out to him, a ripped half in each raised fist.

32

At the Rumpi camp, the men had told Marais of a lunatic in the hills, an old Portuguese, who, marooned by a failed love affair, went about naked in a pair of ragged sandals. He brandished an ancient shotgun at strangers. He had lost the gift of speech; he was dirty, and his hair was wild. He would have starved long ago but for some African women in a neighbouring village who regularly left food at his hut door, the way they left pennies on the gnarled roots of witch-trees, a token against the possibility of wrath.

Marais thought of that poor man whenever he strapped on his pistol and went for a walk. He heard his men whispering behind him. Often he heard laughter. No one spoke to him. Many watched; he felt their curious eyes. Perhaps they had decided that whatever powers he had were now dispersed. He wasn't feared, he knew. He was left alone. He had not heard from Harry or Brother Jaja for months, which was unusual, but no disappointment. The men might have been intercepting messages and keeping them from him. Or maybe Harry and Brother Jaja had changed, like the men; or maybe they were dead. Marais did not know. He seldom thought of them. He had privately resigned his command: he did not think of revolt any more.

In that captured town he felt slightly absurd, as if in walking he was acting out a meaningless routine, like the man gone foolish, the local figure of fun who is allowed his eccentricity because he is harmless. The town had been his, and he had made the whole place tremble with a bomb. But the eccentric often made those claims. 'Do you know who I am? See that deep crater in the street and those burned-out buildings? I did that. I am Marais.' He had said that to puzzled strangers in Lilongwe, speaking in English, though he was not sure they understood. One man had walked away before Marais told his name.

He spent less time walking in the town. Normally, feeling watched, he turned off the main street – named Brother Jaja – and took deserted paths. On wet misty days he looked for landcrabs, glossy black and touched with scarlet, scuttling on high legs and holding pincers – so odd there, a thousand miles from the ocean. At dusk flocks of small wild hens nested on the sun-warmed paths: he saw men on speeding motorcycles hunting them by running them down. If a figure approached on the path Marais hid himself. He did not want to be seen. It was said that the naked man in the hills preferred solitude and in his own mad way was armed. Marais understood. He felt as naked and as hunted. A person gliding easily through grass intimidated him; another presence seemed a judgement on his sanity, or a jeer. He wondered what version they knew of his failure. They made him uneasy. But in solitude there was no madness; alone, the lunatic was just a naked man who had been loved once.

He wanted to go on with his diary. He sat with it open before him. The only whole thoughts that came to him were of ingratitude and mutinous betrayal. He hated: he thought of revenge, of a punishment so elaborate it required help and apparatus. One evening he scratched in his notebook, making small doodles; he shaded and enlarged them. He began to write with a word hinged to a doodle. He darkened the word, tracing and retracing the letters, as if waiting for dictation. Then anger broke over him and shook a sentence out of him: he cancelled the first halting words and his handwriting quickened and changed character as his mood turned. He wrote for hours, the sentences sloping into abuse, the wavering candle-flame making his pages jump as he stabbed excitedly at them. He stopped, exhausted, but slept badly. His half-ignited brain still smouldered behind his eyes, composing, erasing, appealing. He fingered pages in his dreams.

In the morning his pages accused. There was a time, not distant, when he killed men who wrote such things. There was no anguish in the handwriting; it had all been written easily, speaking with eagerness of vendetta. Marais tore them out and burned them, noticing that as he did so a handful of corresponding leaves at the front of the notebook, some details of revolt scribbled somewhere else, fell free. He burned those, too.

He wrote no more. On rising, he crossed that day off the calendar. (Once he had habitually done this at the end of the day; now he knew in advance that the day held nothing for him.) He opened his notebook to a clean page, but he did not write. He felt something savage in him, something unlovely that stank, like a rat in his room. Always with a sigh he slammed the notebook shut, and he walked. Walking was all he could do; it simulated action and helped the time pass.

But he came to fear even that.

On a walk late in July, the clammy month, he saw small boys huddled in grass, smoking mice out of holes in the ground. Some roasted them skewered over fires. The mice sizzled and burst like sausages. To Marais it was a moment from prehistory: naked black children carrying embers from fires and cramming them into holes, driving the mice out and killing them by tramping on them or swatting them with sticks. He watched one boy chase a mouse and kick it to death against a stump, and peel its skin off and begin to cook it. Busily they hunted and ate. The crude method worked, but that was not so frightening to Marais as the boys themselves. They were not playing at cruelty any more than their fathers who in brown ragged overcoats hunted bushpigs with torches; locating a bushpig the men scattered and lit the grass, building by degrees an encircling fire. They waited scowling at the fire's fringe and when the pig stumbled through the flames, all its bristles alight and sparking, they clubbed it to death. Marais had seen them. They were hungry.

It was hunger that made the boys so busy they did not notice Marais at first. They mutely tended their fires. Marais was fascinated: the sight revived much of his old disgust, and for a moment he understood all his bombs – it was this degraded hunger he had tried to eliminate, though he had not imagined it so bad. Those boys, forced to practise savagery, justified all revolt. Marais was composing a new paragraph, finding words for what he saw, after three idle months feeling his despair diminish and blur in his surge of indignant longing to make another bomb.

He got no further with that paragraph; it collapsed in his head and his despair came back and cloaked him with a chill. The scene he was witnessing – the naked boys hunting mice in a windy field – was happening in what he used to call a liberated area. The children, like those men hunting pigs with torches, lived within sight of the bombed police headquarters and the room on the top floor of the hotel where he slept. They had been free since April. He watched them eating the mice and he realized that he was speaking his thoughts, narrating the scene in a distressed whisper.

The children looked up, but they did not move away from their fires. Their bodies were streaked with dust and grey ashes, and they knelt, hiding their penises. They were not cowering or begging for mercy; discovered in their meal, they were protecting their food, a small pile of limp rodents.

Marais took a step towards them. One muttered and picked up a stone and showed it. The wind shifted, blowing smoke into the boys' faces, then into Marais's. It whirled an ungainly acrid cloud about and gave the illusion that the little boys squatting in it – headless in one gust, disembodied heads in another – were actually moving about in jerks and hops, and swinging their arms. Marais thought he felt a sting on his thigh, a pain that could have been a stone or his unsettled imagination: it may have been the deception of the wind-whirled smoke, or the uncomfortable itch of its bitter smell. Another stone seemed to strike his boot. But he was uncertain. He saw nothing thrown. He backed into the grass rubbing his eyes, and he turned down the path. A moment later five black boys ran before him clutching their food. While Marais watched them a sixth dashed by, bumping and startling Marais as he passed. This one swung a glowing stick he had dragged from the fire.

For a time (he did not know how long, he was impatient in crossing days off the calendar) Marais stayed in the hotel and kept himself busy. He did not want to see those children again and, even more, did not want to be seen by anyone. He was the jilted lover, to whom people can be as cruel in their indifference as in their curiosity, and who knows enough of hurt to keep to himself and not risk hitting back. He shined his boots and took his pistol apart and cleaned it; he noted temperature changes and weather in his diary, and did his tiny dark drawings. He did not move out, not even when one day his window was shattered by a shotgun slug; he swept up the glass and moved his desk away from the window to the centre of the room. Most days he cooked his meals in the room on his Primus. Occasionally he used the wood-burning one, a black cast-iron stove in the hotel kitchen; and on those days he rummaged through the larder. He found gallon cans without paper labels, though each was stencilled with the name of what it contained, baked beans, pineapples, syrup, cooking oil, soup. They had been left untouched by his men, who opened a can only when the label pictured the contents, assuming all else was motor oil.

Marais carried the cans he could use up to his room, saying nothing to the men who sat drinking, dressed in cowboy clothes, in the broken chairs of the hotel lobby. Earlier he had looked through all the rooms. The walls were pissed on and scorched, there was shit in the corners of some, and broken bottles and crockery; in others there was mouldy food that even the rats that infested the place refused to touch. (At night Marais heard rats pattering across the top of his ceiling, vaulting the rafters.) He never looked in the hotel bedrooms again. The men seldom came upstairs; having fouled a room once they did not return to it, a habit of village hygiene that demanded space. What hours Marais did not spend on the roof searching the town and the surrounding jungle with his binoculars, he spent in his bare room – orderly because it was so empty – at his desk, facing the door, with his loaded pistol and his notebook.

He did not fire the gun, or write. He thought constantly of doing both; but each was so final.

Stocking up on cans in the larder one afternoon he caught sight of a dog outside the kitchen door. It pawed a pile of rubbish and lapped at papers. A wild mongrel, very skinny, with a patch of mange on its neck, it fumbled and glanced nervously around, shaking its broken tail, as Marais walked to the doorway. He wanted the dog, he felt pity for the scavenging outcast. He had some spare food to fatten the dog; it would keep him company. He opened a tin of stew and splashed some at it, pitching it with a spoon.

The sound of the stew hitting the ground scared the dog; but it turned, moaning, and looked at the food and at Marais.

'Here, boy,' Marais coaxed. He displayed the open can. The dog appeared interested. Marais walked a few feet, edging towards the dog, and said, 'Take it.'

There was a loud bang behind Marais, a gunshot. He winced, stunned by it, feeling his brain wither; he started to fall. But the dog's piteous howl checked him. The dog jerked forward, as if kicked, and fell on its side. It struggled, its eyes popping, and rolled and whimpered, leaking blood. Then painfully it rose to its forelegs and dragged its dead hind-end into the tall grass.

'Where you going?'

Brother George, in cowboy hat and bright shirt, leaned against the grey clapboards of the hotel, holding his rifle waist-high, aimed at Marais.

'You shot that dog,' said Marais, walking up to Brother George. The gunshot had deafened him: he did not recognize his own voice. Brother George stopped Marais with the rifle muzzle; he pushed it into Marais' stomach and nudged. Marais said, 'If I had my gun with me I'd kill you,' and he slapped Brother George's face hard.

Marais ignored the rifle stuck against his stomach, which made him slap at arm's length. Brother George slid away from the wall and back to the kitchen steps, Marais stayed with him, a rifle's length away, and slapped Brother George on one side of his face, then the other, saying, 'Stupid, stupid,' with each slap. Brother George squinted and made his smarting jaw big, and he prodded Marais with the rifle and fumbled with the bolt; but he did not shoot. His nose began to bleed.

'He tried to escape!' Brother George said suddenly, looking behind Marais.

Marais turned and saw four men behind him with rifles levelled at him. They were silent, and looked not ugly – though they could repel – brutish, their faces clumsy and unfinished. It was something in their features Marais had never seen before. Chimanga stood at the head of the group.

'Who let you out of prison?' Marais asked. Marais had blood on his fingers. He wiped them on his shirt.

'I have been out of prison for long time,' said Chimanga. 'You in prison now, bwana.'

'What do you mean?'

'We arrested you last week.'

'You're crazy. I've been going for walks anywhere I pleased.'

'But not outside hotel, eh. Not for one week,' said Chimanga. 'We know. We guarding. Special orders.'

'Jaja wouldn't tell you to do this. Who gave the order – Harry?'

'Secret,' said Chimanga, and he laughed, opening his mouth and unrolling his wide tongue and wagging it, stuck out, as he laughed.

'I have a gun,' said Marais.

'One only,' said Chimanga. 'We having plenty guns. If you try to escape we kill you.' He laughed again.

'Why don't you kill me now?'

'We wanting you,' said Brother George.

'You are my prisoner,' said Brother Henry in Chinyanja, '*Iwe wam' jigololo wanga.*'

'We not your monkeys now!' said Chimanga.

'You're not Lumumba,' said Marais.

'Take him upstairs!' said Chimanga. 'Bye-bye, Bang-Bang!'

Three of the men accompanied Marais to his room. They nailed the door shut, but badly, all but splintering a door-panel with a wild swing of the hammer. Marais heard two men descend the stairs.

The door was frail; he knew he could kick it in pieces, or cut through the wall into the next room and sail down the stairwell on a rope. There were half a dozen exits in the hotel, and on two sides fire-ladders that ran from the roof to the ground. He knew he could get out; he had known it all along, and so he had kept it unconsidered.

For Marais, escape was ingenuity, always simple; it was staying that pressed him, because that measured his hope. But in the time he had stayed willingly, they had declared him their prisoner: *Iwe wam' jigololo wanga*. He had been satisfied to stay and test himself and them; and he might have done for weeks more if they had said nothing. Now everything was changed. With the knowledge that he was their captive he thought only of escape.

33

In the end Calvin decided against going to the police about Mwase. You didn't report someone for stealing your porn or your zip-gun, so why make a fuss about the theft of your subversive literature? Malawi had an instructive precedent. In Calvin's first month in the country a case was heard at the High Court of a man suing for breach of contract. The man (his name was Odrick Chipandale) was a witch-doctor. He had been hired for a fee of four pounds, ten osbongs to turn into a crocodile and kill a bewitched girl who was provoking a drought in a village near Blantyre. Half the money was paid in advance. Shortly after payment the dead girl was found by a riverbank; she was punctured with long rows of teeth. It rained for days. Satisfied with the deluge the villages saw no need to pay the balance. The witch-doctor Chipandale took them to court. He was awarded the two pounds, five osbongs, tried for murder, and hanged.

Calvin heeded that lesson. He would get his pamphlet back, but he would be shot for treason or imprisoned with the three thousand others in the political detainees' camp on the lower river. Osbong was not gentle. But Calvin's decision gave no assurance of safety. What if Mwase turned *him* in? The manuscript in Calvin's incriminating handwriting was missing. Mwase had all the evidence. Calvin would swing for treason. Osbong had hanged one man publicly in Zomba.

Mwase was no help. He went remote again and demanded his copy of the pamphlet from Calvin, with swallowed insults. He stuck the torn pages together with tape and, as before, studied it at his desk.

Calvin got plastered for courage. He winked, and said as

light-heartedly as he could, in a joshing sing-song voice, 'I know where you got that thing.'

'I don't care,' said Mwase. His eyes were red, troubled.

Calvin saw criminal arrogance, the killer witch-doctor. But he attempted conciliation. 'Shall we have a beer and talk it over? We'll kick it around for a while – what do you say?'

'There is nothing to talk. I want a new briefcase.'

'Take mine,' said Calvin eagerly.

'It is cardboard. Mine was fibreglass, washable, Japanese model.'

'I'll get you a nice one, really. But, Mwase, the pamphlet,' said Calvin. 'It's all lies.'

'Of course you think so.'

'I *know* so! And I know where you got it. Not that one,' said Calvin, 'but *another* one, right? Written in black ink, by hand. Huh?'

'It was given.' Mwase wouldn't budge.

'You stole it!' said Calvin, his anger released. 'I know you did. You can't kid me. That's the trouble with you people – you think everything is public property.'

'I know you hate us.'

'I don't,' said Calvin. 'Anyway, what do you mean *us*?'

'Well, we hate you,' said Mwase. He glared and said, 'Would you insure me?'

'I would, I *did*!' said Calvin. 'You know I did – there's the certificate on the wall, all framed. I gave it –'

'I have been beaten and robbed,' Mwase went on. 'The white man treats me like rubbish because I am black. I am poor.'

'You have your O-Levels,' said Calvin. 'And this job. You're going to be the fucking manager of this agency!'

'I slave.'

'Bullshit! There's no business, no one wants insurance. You don't do a thing here.'

'I go to meetings,' said Mwase mysteriously. 'You don't know.'

'You write letters to pen-pals, I know that.'

'Not at night. At night we are invisible because we are the colour of night.'

'I know where you read that.'

'Someday we will rise up.'

'Please,' said Calvin, 'stop saying that.' Words he had scribbled on boozy evenings were being shoved down his throat. They choked him. He pleaded, 'I'll make a deal with you.'

'No deals with white men.'

'Just one?' Calvin's voice was small.

'None. You hate us.' Mwase turned and looked past Calvin to the window and intoned, 'On the banana leaf of life we hang like hungry worms.'

'Cabbage leaf! That's in the book.'

'It's our old proverb.'

'It's not, it's a fake.'

'Our old fathers taught us this wisdom.'

It was impossible. Mwase knew the pamphlet by heart. Calvin tried again, with care, in a soothing voice, 'Mwase, the whole thing's forgotten. I'm not going to tell anyone about this. You don't have to worry.'

'I do worry,' said Mwase. 'And suffer.'

Calvin continued, conceding: 'What you steal is your business. Just like,' he implored assent, 'what I do is my business. Right? So . . . everything . . . is okay . . . isn't it?'

Mwase did not reply. He sat at his little desk before his certificates, with his smashed briefcase and his patched pamphlet, holding his ears. He was undersized, quite black; and lately, probably because of meetings or doings at night, he had begun to look frazzled. His name could have been A. Jigololo.

'What are you going to do?' Calvin asked at last.

'Rise up,' said Mwase, without taking his eyes from the pamphlet.

The mood in town had changed, with Mwase's. Africans sidled up to Calvin and abused him with unexpected malice. The malice was new; it was uninformed, a raw kind and full of fright. It pinched Calvin's heart. The Africans followed him, prancing. They cawed at him and honked him off the road. They knocked off his panama hat and called him 'the giraffe'. It happened everywhere in Blantyre, on the side streets, St George's, St Andrew's, St David's, and at the market, on Osbong and Livingstone and Hanover. The baggers at Kandodo Supermarket were rude and dented his purchases, pressing their thumbs into the items Mira had a yen for, *naartjies* nut-bars, slabs of chocolate. In the drink-shops and the post office, blacks jumped the queues, crowded him, assaulted him with bone-sharp elbows; he was shoved aside. It happened to other white people, too: the Greek brothers who ran the coffee shop, the tea planters and their children, the queer Maltese barber on Henderson Street, the fat Rhodesian ladies from the bookshop – people he had never taken any notice of before. Now Calvin saw them, confused foreigners who had stopped in the wrong place to trade, who didn't belong, and whose faces were damaged, set in new and not natural expressions by the strain of humiliation which, in addition to altering their faces, made them grovel or bluster unreasonably. Calvin thought he disliked them, but he felt sorry for them. They moved slowly, these old expatriates, not comprehending the city, as if the place had overnight become populous and strange with villains; they were often rude to the Africans, and for this provocation, at night, they were jumped and struck with clubs, and they got their shins kicked. For sarcasm and their funny colour they were hit: the violence was the African's reply, the savagery his denial that he was a savage.

Returning one evening to the eating house after a film at the Rainbow (*On Moonlight Bay* – he had last seen it in the early fifties at the Hudson Roxy, but not with Afrikaans subtitles) he was stampeded by a dozen black boys, and one had whispered hotly, 'You a white sheet!' Calvin tried to protest, but there were so many of them and they were so angry. He said nothing, lest they be pushed to murder. He even allowed one to claw the inside pocket of his jacket.

You a white sheet. Calvin didn't mind being called that. But later the veil fell from the mild abuse. 'Keel new boat,' a black man had said to Calvin and Mira, nowhere near a shipyard. Mira hurried Calvin away to translate, 'Kill you both.' On other occasions he was a bloody sheet, a useless sheet, a stewpeed sheet. The

Africans were sinisterly equipped for abuse; their English was no good, but their mood was dark. Calvin was worried. It was as if all of them had read his awful little book. And after a time he saw loose copies of it in town; the ketchup-coloured title was unmistakable.

His unborn child worried him most. The place was becoming unsafe for children: what would they do to a half-caste child, a brown and gold one with green eyes? At night he lay beside his large wife. Threatening noises and shouts kept him awake. He feared arrest, and worse, mob violence – feared it most because it was just: a mob inflamed and inspired by his own words. He wanted to throttle Mwase. Each time he dozed the pamphlet was shaken in his face, and once in a dream he was made to eat it. He dreamed of the prison island Major Beaglehole had described to him. Calvin was the governor, Aubrey's brother. He looked up from his desk and saw a pack of muttering inmates trotting towards him, armed with shivs and machetes. 'Stop! Sort yourselves out, chaps!' Calvin screamed. 'I will insure every one of you!' He woke himself with his pleading.

But that night the muttering jungle voices did not stop when he woke. He sat up in bed and listened. He heard grunts rising to a bawl of accusation, and dropping low in threats that seemed to scratch the bedroom wall. Calvin wondered for a moment if he was deranged. But no: Mira murmured, she shifted to her side and protected her big belly with her arms; she heard.

Calvin got out from under the mosquito net. It was like so many other voices. Everything in Malawi spoke: the little scurrying whirl-winds, the rain on the leaves, the breezes patting and smoothing the grass; drains grumbled and belched when they were full, cooking fires munched branches. And now the house itself was alive and gabbing in what sounded like English.

He put on his clothes and crept into the hall. The sounds were loudest in the bar. Calvin entered on all fours, by the side entrance, his teeth clenched for fear of noise. He slid behind a stack of beer-crates, pulling his knees after him. The beer-crates obstructed his view of the bar and the men.

'Wait, wait!' said a bass voice. 'That's all you can say.'

Calvin snared his face in a cobweb and immediately began wondering if it was a spider web, and if so where was the spider now? He picked strands of web from his eyes and mouth and unthinkingly sucked some of the dusty filaments into his nose.

'It's not my fault. He's delaying, I told you. You want me to sing it?'

'Every week you say that. It's late. Osbong should be dead by now, but he's not!'

'Not so loud. You wanna wake everybody up?'

There were only those two voices; both were thick, drunken. They argued in the dark.

Calvin tried to identify the voices. There was something in the conscious grammar and finished word-endings of the bass voice that indicated a person who had learned English late; a slur in the other's disclosed the impatient familiarity of the native speaker. But Calvin was so close that it distorted instead of clarified, and he could not link the voices to the faces.

'It is not the job of the President to fight,' said the bass voice slowly. 'If I have no choice, of course I will fight beside my men.'

'You're not the President yet, don't forget that.'

'Don't threaten me. You have not been paid yet; remember that.'

'That's another thing. If you want action you gotta pay for it. Nothing for nothing.' Liquid was poured, the bottleneck chinking the rim of the glass twice. After a breathy swallow, the same voice continued, 'I have to do all the dirty work.'

'You expect me to perform all the dirty work?'

'I didn't say that.'

'Who stabbed the minister? That was a big job. He had a gun.'

'I said thanks, didn't I?'

'I do not want your thanks. I want Osbong dead. I want this country.'

'You drive me nuts with all your "I want".'

'I want results.'

'You got some.'

'We have been fighting for almost a year. You tell me what results.'

'For Christ's sake, half the country is ours.'

'I don't want half!'

Someone was slapped, someone muttered.

'Slaps, that's all I get.'

'You deserve worse.'

Worse? Calvin tried to leave. He wiped what remained of the web from his face, and started to back out. There was a noise at his heel. The plump-backed bar rat was nibbling at sawdust in a pool of moonlight. Calvin drew his legs up and made himself as small as possible. He had to sit it out. The rat was stupid and moved noisily; to scare it was to give himself away.

'I deserve a medal for all the shit I've been through,' the slurring voice said. 'Who sends all your messages? Who runs his ass off around town delivering your pamphlet? Who *printed* the lousy thing! I had to set the whole thing up by hand. Damn near went blind doing that.'

'So you think it is a lousy pamphlet? Do you realize that my pamphlet is the only thing we have to show for a year's struggle. The people read it and now they listen to us.'

'It was a corny title. I could have done a better one.'

'You are wrong. No white man could have written that.'

The thief. And it wasn't Mwase.

'I did a nice little book in Angola. It was called *Now*, but in Portuguese. Give us our land, take off our chains, listen to our crying voices, and so forth and so on.'

'They're still fighting in Angola.'

'Marais said the same thing.'

'Because they don't know anything about revolution. You don't know yourself.'

'Revolution! Don't talk to *me* about revolution, you twerp. I know the old way, a few bombs, a few arrests, some snipers on the roof. Riot, strike, riot, strike. You don't have to start a whole goddamn war against one man. You want a big army to come here and blow the place to bits. That's not a revolution, you fat-head, and I told Marais that, too. You're both new to this game. So don't tell me what I know.'

'It will happen here whether you help us or not.'

'When it's supposed to happen, it happens. You don't have to push all the time. People help. If they don't help you, it's no go.'

'It sounds to me as if you don't want to work for us any more.'

'I look and what do I see? A couple of people knocked off. No one cares. A little town captured. No one cares. You have a strike and no one notices. Just a few black people turning nasty, but no riots, nothing like that. Sometimes I figure why not go back to Addis or Dar and have a cold beer and forget the whole shebang. No one gives a shit, why should I?'

'That's what you think!'

Feet scraped.

'Get your hands offa me! If you're so full of piss and vinegar why don't you go kill Osbong?'

'I will!'

'I mean, why should I? I got a wife and kids.'

'Bugger your wife and kids.'

'You get so British all of a sudden.'

Someone spat, a table was bumped. Calvin pressed himself between the wall and the beer-crates and hoped that they wouldn't chase into him. Or shoot! What if they began shooting? He put his head between his knees and tried to shut out the noise of the two men cursing each other in the dark.

'This is a knife.'

'So is this. Now back off!'

There was a scuffle; chairs were cracked and tipped over, and Calvin could hear the men panting and dragging their feet sideways.

'I'm going to kill you first, then him in Lilongwe. Then Osbong. I don't need any of you.'

'Yes, you do, you gutless bastard. You need us to fight your battles.'

'We were doing all right before you came.'

'Sure you were! Shitting in the grass —'

A crash of glass. One swore.

'Come one step more, jungle bunny, and you'll be so much dead meat.'

Quick steps were followed by a short pause, then a thump. Calvin imagined a lunge. He closed his eyes and heard bodies rolling on the floor, upsetting the wooden furniture in the bar and smashing glass. Then the hurrying bumps of a person crawling swiftly on hands and knees. This stopped with another struggle, puffing and blowing, and an insistent but muffled punching, each punch producing a groan. One was dying, making the sounds of a mourner, sighing down the scale in a kind of grief. That slowed, and soon was gone; one man breathed heavily, making snore-like sounds.

Calvin opened his eyes. Through the bottles in the beer-crates he saw a feeble swinging light at the far end of the bar-room.

'Get out of here or I'll ring for the police!' This voice was Bailey's. 'And take him with you. If he's dead I don't want to hear about it. Filthy bloody sods,' she gasped, and then the light was gone.

34

After that night Mira produced some early pains. Calvin thought they might be her response to the fright of all that noise: idle trees in Hudson orchards sometimes blossomed and bore fruit when their trunks were thwacked by a big farmhand swinging a pick-shaft.

She woke, turning with cramps. They went away for minutes and she got up; then they surged back, and she had to sit. Calvin put her back to bed. She started to tell about them in her halting English when the pains were gone, but when they were on her she switched into her own language: she remembered it in her distress. Calvin didn't know a word of it.

They had shared everything before and had managed tenderness without speaking. From the pain Calvin was excluded. It was private, she laboured with it alone. He wheeled the tea-trolley into Bailey's kitchen and piled it with food, bananas and boiled eggs, oatmeal and a jug of orange squash. The sight of it seemed to make Mira dyspeptic and knotted her cramps. Calvin got on the Matchless and flew to the Queen Elizabeth Hospital; he reported the pain and the cause to the Israeli doctor in Emergency. The doctor put a few extra tools in his black satchel and rode cheerfully on the groaning rear saddle of the motorcycle, still wearing his white coat. He said as they crackled over leaves near a vast fence of gum trees what a lovely day it was, so fresh.

At the eating house the doctor wrinkled his nose. 'This place give us a lot of headique.'

'She's in the back,' said Calvin.

They passed through the bar. The furniture was still tipped over from the night before; the room looked bombed. On the bar counter stood a tray of dull unwashed glasses. The doctor regarded them. He said, '*Lot* of wee-dee.'

Mira crouched on the edge of the bed at the raised fly of the mosquito tent. Her arms were folded, dismay made her face small.

The doctor picked his way through the untidy room. He was white-haired and plump and had rosy cheeks, and he looked to Calvin like a benign mayor visiting a slum.

'And here is the little mother,' he said, and smiled.

The exclamation was a comfort to Calvin. He thought of Mwase; he owed Mwase an apology; he would find him and explain.

The doctor felt Mira's forehead with the back of his fingers. He timed her pulse and tapped her back and took her blood pressure.

'Tell me where is the pain?'

'She doesn't speak —'

The doctor bent and elaborately cradled her belly, the whole harvest in his hands. He pressed gently with his thumbs and inquired, 'Here? . . . Here? . . .'

Mira shook her head.

'They come and go,' said Calvin. 'Maybe they're gone.'

The doctor asked Calvin to leave the room for the rest of the examination. Calvin shuffled into the hall. The eating house was strangely quiet. It was just past nine and usually at this hour rumpled clients would be slipping out, Bailey would be cursing the cooks, Beaglehole spattering the Gents, Jarvis polishing glasses. But there was no stir. Without movement and people the eating house seemed very squalid.

Mira dozed on the bed, tucked in neatly, when Calvin was recalled to the room.

'My diagnosis is false alarum,' said the doctor. 'If they come back, give me a tinkle, yes?'

'There's no phone,' said Calvin. 'I'll come and get you if she has pains again.'

'Best thing is to time contractions,' said the doctor pushing up his sleeve. 'How many minutes pain, how many minutes no pain. Like that.'

Calvin was staring at the doctor's wrist. 'Pardon me for asking, but why two watches?'

'You remind me!' said the doctor appreciatively, slipping off the large silver one. 'This morning I must go to the police and give this.'

'Can I see that watch?'

The doctor handed it over. It was still ticking.

'Astronauts have ones like this.'

'Was the property of a man they bring in this morning dead. Poor fellow, full of wounds. No identification, only this niche vache.'

'African?'

'No,' said the doctor.

The office door was unlocked, but Mwase was not inside. Calvin searched the hall and the washroom and even the broom cupboard, preparing his introduction and detailed apology each time he flung a door open. He looked everywhere; he found the peanut-vendor sneaking a drink. But no Mwase. Entering his office a second time, he noticed the doorknob was loose. The lock had been yanked out.

'Come in and shut the door.' The voice came from behind the file cabinet.

Calvin pushed the door shut.

The man appeared. Calvin recognized him instantly as Marais. He wore the same khaki fatigues, but they were faded; his hair was longer and it was pushed, rather than combed, straight back over his ears and showed the round indent of a cap. His sunglasses were the same and so, Calvin thought, were his boots; but the boots were chafed and covered with mud. His face was thinner and very sunburned, his moustache ragged, and on his chin was the sun-bleached stubble of a week's beard.

'What do *you* want?' It was meant to be sharp, but it caught in Calvin's throat.

He was shorter than Calvin remembered him. Calvin towered over him, feeling awkward and badly arranged. He tried to do something with his hands that would not alarm Marais. But he could think of nothing; he let them wander.

'Just want to talk to you,' said Marais. There was no threat in his voice. It was, if anything, apologetic.

'Where's your gun?'

Marais patted a lump under his shirt.

'You the President now?' asked Calvin, giving the sarcasm a cautious edge.

Marais shook his head slowly. 'Let's sit down,' he said. 'My back aches. I walked from Lilongwe.'

'What happened to your fancy car?'

'I want some life insurance,' Marais said, ignoring Calvin's taunt. He sat in Mwase's chair and took a taped block of bills from a haversack at his feet. He placed the money on Calvin's desk. 'I'm willing to pay.'

'Why come to me?' asked Calvin, seating himself at his desk but not looking at the money. 'There are lots of insurance companies in town.'

'I've got reasons,' said Marais. 'I want it from you.'

'Well, you're wasting your time. So you can walk back to Lilongwe for all I care. I'm not going to insure you.'

Marais moved his chair closer to Calvin's desk. He said, 'Here's the money.'

'I see it,' said Calvin. 'Stick it.'

'What more do you want?' Marais asked quietly.

'I don't want anything from you,' said Calvin. 'You killed my brother-in-law.'

Marais looked at the floor, then at his palms. He nodded. 'I'm sorry.'

'*Sorry! Sorry!*' Calvin repeated in unbelief. He rapped the desk. 'That's what you say when you bump into someone – not when you kill him! Do you know the difference, pal? He was a harmless little guy, he didn't give a sweet shit for politics, and you knifed him in his own house. Sorry! Jesus Christ, you got a big nerve.'

'The men were punished,' said Marais. 'What do you want me to say?'

'Nothing,' said Calvin, 'but don't tell me you're sorry when I know you're not. I don't want to see you. Get out of here and leave me alone.' A sob dragged itself through Calvin and he thought he might cry. He didn't want to cry in front of Marais.

'A favour –' Marais started to say.

'Wait a sec,' said Calvin. The sob passed and left him lucid. 'You called me an exploiter, you remember? And I used to worry about that. But I don't worry any more, because you know what I think now? I think *you're* a fucking exploiter! You and all those ass-kicking bastards of yours! You killed my brother-in-law and you scared the hell out of my wife! You cheesy two-bit bastards –' Calvin had risen and was shouting down at Marais. 'All the lies I've had to listen to! You're bullet-proof, you're big and strong, you're going to save everybody –'

Calvin was still burbling and blinking, but he was not saying words. Marais had removed his sunglasses. He faced Calvin, who stood over him.

Marais's faded clothes and muddy boots had suggested effort, and the voice out of his thin face had been strained; his eyes confirmed that and said more. They were the eyes of a casualty, lifeless, sunken in patches of yellow flesh the shape of lenses, set off and framed by the sunburn. The hollow eyes were on Calvin but did not focus or register his presence. It was as if they had seen something terrible and had been stunned and emptied by that sight. The sunglasses had masked them. The doomed had those eyes.

A tirade had been building in Calvin for months, and he wanted to continue, to make up for the anger and shame at the thought of his stolen book being passed around and crazing the Africans, for Ogilvie beheaded in his hut, the rumours of attack, Mwase's accusing fantasies and the still-vivid memory of the knife-fight in the darkened bar. He wanted to shake Marais, spit threats at him, wound him.

The eyes revealed hurt deeper than any he could inflict. They had suffered the calamity of despair. Calvin could accuse, but he knew that whatever he said, whatever abuse he offered, would be accepted. The murderer was wounded and was himself a victim. Calvin saw this and forgave.

'Please leave,' Calvin said at last. 'And don't ask me to insure you. Look at me –'

The ruined gaze was terrifying.

'– I sell the stuff and I'm not even insured myself. That sounds nutty, I know, because I'm an insurance man and if I don't have it, who does? I used to have a lot of coverage, but after we got nationalized I let my policies lapse and said screw it, it's no use. I mean what's the sense?'

'Who nationalized you?'

'Who else?'

'Did he rough you up?'

'Osbong doesn't rough people up,' said Calvin. He was about to add *not like you do* but he stopped himself. 'He just nationalizes them. You never see the guy – he might be out of the country. You never know. I'm not saying I like him. He wrecked my plans. I suppose I should complain, but who to? I'm not ambitious, and this isn't my country. Jesus, I don't even think it's a country.'

'No?' The voice was empty, like the eyes. 'What is it, then?'

'It's a little parish, sort of,' said Calvin. He thought a moment. 'If you got the faith it's okay. If not, not.'

'The only thing worse than having it,' said Marais, with fatigue, 'is losing it.'

'I used to have it,' said Calvin. He was surprised to hear himself say it. But he meant it. 'Now . . . I don't see the same things or hear them. They still do. I guess I don't really fit in.'

'I don't either,' said Marais. 'But I envy you.'

'Come off it,' said Calvin. 'You're in *charge* of them, for Christ's sake.'

'Not any more,' said Marais. 'I gave it up.'

'Really? You gave it up?' Calvin smiled briefly, then asked, 'But what about *them*?'

'They're still at it.'

'That's worse, you know that? Why the hell didn't you stop them?'

'I couldn't,' said Marais. 'I didn't try.'

'That's worse,' said Calvin again. But he had no blame for Marais. He thought of his book, his little pamphlet: it screamed at him. He had given that up, but men studied it. It was a voice he would always hear.

'I know.'

'What are they going to do?'

'Everything I taught them,' said Marais bitterly.

Calvin rose and went to the door. He fought with the bolt, jiggling it, and finally, by lifting the door, shot it. He pulled the shade down over the frosted pane of lettered glass.

'I wasn't going to tell you this,' said Calvin, seating himself. 'But last night I heard a thing or two. My wife and I live –'

'At the hotel on the upper road,' said Marais. 'I know.'

'Well, it's a cat-house, really.' Calvin went on, 'Late last night, after midnight, I was having a bad dream. I woke up and heard these noises in the bar. I got scared. The thing is, if I hear something like shouting at night and I don't see the person actually doing it, I start to think *maybe he's shouting at me*. So I went to have a look . . .' Calvin described what he heard, the voices, the threats, the brawl.

Marais did not ask Calvin to repeat anything, and when Calvin said, 'I think one was an African,' Marais accepted it with a grave nod.

'One was killed?' Marais asked. In his fatigue his concern sounded like pleading. 'Are you sure?'

'Positive,' said Calvin. 'I didn't see the body. I heard it hit the deck, though.'

Marais' face was anxious. 'One said he was going to Lilongwe, the other said he was giving up. But one was killed.' He looked away. 'It's hopeless.'

'You know who they are?'

Marais nodded.

'Tell me.'

'It doesn't make any difference to you,' said Marais. 'What matters is who died. If knew I could make a move.'

'Was one a man called Harry?' Calvin asked.

'I thought you said you didn't see them.'

'I didn't,' said Calvin. 'But a doctor at the QE did. See, my wife is going to have a baby pretty soon . . .' Calvin told about Mira's pains. He repeated the doctor's story and described the watch. Marais listened motionlessly, as if hearing of a great catastrophe, not a stabbing in a bar, but something perhaps as awful as that which had stunned his eyes. He folded his hands and seemed to pray.

'The other one was Brother Jaja,' said Marais in a strained voice. 'Harry and he were friends. I didn't think they'd ever fight. Besides, Harry was good with a knife.'

'But the other one killed the minister,' said Calvin.

'So you know about that, too.' Marais breathed deeply and said, 'I didn't count on Harry and Jaja fighting.'

'Like I said, they were fighting over a pamphlet of some kind,' said Calvin, his voice dropping.

Marais put on his sunglasses. 'I need a car.'

'Where are you going?'

'Lilongwe,' said Marais.

'To stop them?'

Marais waited, then said, 'I don't know.'

'I've got a motorcycle,' said Calvin. 'Take it.'

'How much do you want for it?'

'Nothing,' said Calvin. 'But bring it back.'

'Okay,' said Marais quickly. He grasped the block of bills. 'There's a grand here. How much insurance can I get for that?'

'For a thousand bucks?' Calvin snickered. 'A mint. If you died we'd be bankrupt I mean, not me, but Osbong.' Calvin smiled. 'We'd have to close the damn agency!'

'Make me out a policy,' said Marais.

'Are you serious?'

'That's what I came for.'

'But for that amount of cash you have to have a medical check-up. I mean, you don't look like the healthiest person I've ever seen. You've got to have a check-up. It's the rules.'

632

'You're the agent,' said Marais. 'You can fix that.'

'I can fix it,' said Calvin. He opened a drawer and took out a thick application. 'Okay, sign here where I make a checkmark. Just your name and address, date of birth and that stuff. I'll fake the rest.'

Marais signed the forms.

'Montreal,' said Calvin, looking over Marais's shoulder at the form. 'Well for Christ's sake!'

'You from Montreal too?'

'No,' said Calvin. 'But we've got a fantastic Homemakers' agency there. One of the fifty-six.' I'm still a company man, thought Calvin. 'Actually, I'm from Hudson, Mass. There are quite a few Canucks in Hudson – Hey, the beneficiary, you forgot that.'

'Did you say your wife was going to have a baby?'

'Yes, but –'

'When she has it, put the baby's name there.'

'*My* kid as *your* beneficiary?' Calvin started to smile, but Marais's frown stopped him. 'He's not even born yet.'

'Put your name there for the time being. Afterwards you can put your kid's.'

'What do you mean *afterwards*? After what?'

'After your wife has her baby.'

'I don't even believe in insurance,' said Calvin.

'No, but your kid might,' said Marais.

35

The night sky over Lilongwe glowed red. A deep lighted cloud appeared through a mesh of black branches as Marais came near. Holding the Matchless stiff-armed like a plough, he plunged off the road into grass and made a wide circle around the border of the town on narrow tracks, rocking the motorcycle over the knuckles of roots and entering the way he had escaped, in the dark, by the north end, where the roadblock was abandoned. He leaned the motorcycle into a ditch and walked the last half-mile.

Voices came towards him on the road – muttering, and hurrying feet. He pulled himself behind a tree and saw, in the red glow from the town, people – the first he had seen since before nightfall – families sneaking off. The men pushed squeaking wheelbarrows stacked with belongings, some women carried cloth bundles on their heads. Certain they were not soldiers Marais started again, and the line of people passed by him, walking in the rain-trough at the side of the road. They scuffed the gravel with invisible feet; most were merely shadowy torsos, the children were small heads, the bundles the women carried were highlighted pink. They fled like scared beasts from a blaze of grass, without looking back, calling out, crying to those ahead of them; the straggling line continued to pass Marais, and then the last lighted shirt vanished into the blackness.

Closer to the town the colour of the sky altered: the crimson cloud was laced with gold, sparks lifted and died in the dark after a wobbling flight, and buntings of blue smoke like yards rose slowly wrinkling as if unfolded from bolts on the ground. Not the lantern it had seemed from a distance, it was a ragged nimbus, and at its edges steady sheep, pink and orange, led off in flocks, becoming tiny lambs, then rose-coloured wisps, before they disappeared altogether.

It was fire, the dry season again; a whole year had passed since that first blaze on the frontier where the hills had been spectacularly alight, the whole province a furnace. Marais had stood alone, enclosed by fire; he had faced south down the dirt road, a lane of steaming dust which led through waves of sloping flame. He recalled the roar of the burning, the hot cloth of his shirt, the gusts of the sweeping draught, grass crackling and the sputtering hiss of sap. Some trees had fallen muffled, as if into fathoms of water, and he had woken to skeletons, the black spikes of trees, his black soldiers marching through the black meadow.

Lilongwe was burning. Marais hid at the corner of the last shop in town. A tall bonfire swayed in the middle of the street, about the place the bomb had gone off, near the police headquarters. It was a pyramid of flaming crates of the sort Marais had seen his men hammering in the street the day Yatu died; he had watched from the dispensary, unable to guess what the men were doing. But it seemed inconceivable that they planned the fire so far ahead – that was April. Or had he been unfair? He had charged them with never planning. Maybe, he thought, they've had their own plot all along and kept it from me.

Beyond the bonfire, on the far side of the street, a row of shops was alight. There were men near the shops in a long snaking line. Some held gallon jugs, others sticks and axes. Led by a big man with a thick four-foot torch, the line wound towards a shopfront. A broken sewing machine stood on the veranda. Men with axes smashed the shutters of the shop and broke the door down; they were followed by others with jugs who first sprinkled the liquid over the shutters, then threw full bottles into the shop. It was gasoline: the big man touched his torch to it and there was blossom of orange flame. When that shop was burning more gasoline was thrown. The men cheered and knocked their sticks together, and on their way to the next shop they sang.

They burned the shops one at a time, stopping at intervals to run back to the bonfire for fresh torches. Marais heard bells, and saw the men wore strings of them on their wrists and ankles; some blew low notes on gourd horns and others rattled shallow drums to a monotonous three-beat chant. Marais thought he heard his name screamed – but he was not sure, for the men were coming up the street and closer to him, and the roar of the burning shops drowned their words.

It should have been a devilish sight, or at least unusual, but it wasn't to Marais. It was methodical holocaust, an annual reflex. Every year in that season there were fires, Marais knew, for he had been in the country now a year and had been through the whole cycle of seasons. The Africans believed that unless every dead plant was burned and every field blackened nothing would grow. So they lit fires. They lost their dry houses sometimes, and always in those months the sun was shrouded in a haze of grey smoke which only the heavy rains dispersed. The soldiers were burning the town with the same ritual energy they used on acres of brown corn shucks. One season was finished; only fire could renew. Marais wondered who had given the order that night. It may have been just a coincidence, the bonfire and the hysteria prompted by his escape and the death of Harry; but if it was not an accident, it was genius.

He was surprised by their number. The people on the road leaving the town with their belongings had prepared him for a deserted place, for though fires were not unusual, people near them were. The burning frontier had been empty, no man stood nearby with a torch, Marais was the only witness. But here in the snaking line there were many more than fifty men – there were hundreds.

They wore the khaki uniform and visored cap; they wore cowboy hats and bright shirts and cartridge belts. Most were dressed in the baggy shorts and torn collarless shirts of the villager; a score were in clerk's garb, dark trousers and white long-sleeved shirt with the cuffs buttoned. The majority of these last wore ties. It was the only incongruity, these men in neat ties and billowing white sleeves pouring gasoline on shops and shrieking when it was lighted. Their ties flew to their shoulders when they ran to a new shop. Marais recognized some of his men: Brother

George, Henry and Chimanga were near the head of the line; they were busy, but not giving orders.

The leader was a man Marais had never seen before. He guessed it was Brother Jaja, the man Marais had avoided meeting personally. He fitted the description Harry and Gbenye had given. He was a fat giant, the biggest African Marais had ever seen, impressive not only for his height, but also for his broad shoulders, and with it all, his fatness, a rare bulk. He had a bellowing laugh that rang above the crackle of the fires, and he led the line with a big man's rolling walk, swinging the torch he held in his fist in wide circles. It was obviously heavy, but he twirled it like a matchstick, at times singeing his men and making them scatter about his legs like pygmies. He was agile, in a tight black suit of a material that glistened in the firelight, and he wore boots which reached to his knees and also gleamed. Around his waist was a waiter's red sash, but he wore it with casual pride, like a campaign ribbon.

Why didn't you stop them? Marais heard Calvin's question again. He watched the men; he was satisfied that his reply was true: he couldn't, he didn't try. And he began to think that there had never been a time when it was possible. He wished he had always known that. Now they were just across the street. Marais held a loaded pistol in one hand and a full clip in the other. He could kill a dozen or more right there, drop them in the line, and the others might pause. It was no good. Death and grief made men silent, but it never cowed; on the contrary, it waked their revenge: men smouldered with the memory of a death. Death was the beginning, grief was anger. And no less for his own death. He smiled at the illumination, the flames.

It was then, as Marais stood dreamily by the shopside watching the opposite building burn, that they saw him. His name was distinct, it stopped the chanting song. He turned to them.

Chimanga ran half-way across the street, fired two shots from his revolver, and hesitated. He had missed, but he seemed to understand it differently. He ran back to the line. Others left the line and pointed. There were more shots. Another man skittered into the street crying out at Marais, who remained, dazed, with his arms at his sides. All the men were shouting and blowing their horns, but they were still separated from Marais by the wide street. Except for the one man half-way across the street, wincing at Marais and trying to move forward, the men showed no inclination to mob him.

Brother Jaja roared at the men and stalked to the centre of the street, jabbing his torch at Marais. He waved the men on. The men held back.

Marais had not counted on their cowardice. They would have to move. He took a step towards Brother Jaja. Brother Jaja flung down his torch and pulled out a revolver, and still bellowing, he shot repeatedly at Marais. Marais took aim.

Brother Jaja screamed and fired at the ground near his feet. He shuddered, and held himself with his arms and sank to his knees, going down with a crack, as the shop behind him caved in and blew cinders and splinters of flaming wood on the men. He steadied himself with one arm, holding his heart with the other, and he screamed his angry disappointment not at Marais or at his men, but down the empty smoke-filled street.

'Kill him!' a shout went up, two voices, then many. The line of men broke and crowded past Brother Jaja.

Marais spun and ran behind the row of unburned shops on his side of the street. He knew where he was going. He saw the dull gleam of a trashcan lid and leaped in the dark, tripping and falling in a clatter of metal. He rolled, discarding his pistol and clip, and looked up. Torches bobbed towards him; he heard feet and shouts. But he saw no faces: they could have been any angry men.

'Shoot him! Shoot him!' the wall echoed. He climbed the high fire-ladder on the clap-board side of the Great Northern Hotel. They were in the yard, under him, shaking the ladder. A bullet hit the ladder and made the rungs vibrate in his hands. He continued climbing. He looked down one last time before he vaulted the lip of the roof. Now he could see their faces. They were shining at him.

Crossing the roof to the stairwell he got a glimpse of the single row of blazing shops. From the ground it had seemed the whole world was burning, and he had felt some exhilaration: the night sky red as a sun capsizing in it, heat against his face, and the whole town lighted. But at this new height he saw it differently, without the exaggerated distortion of closeness. From the roof the faces in the mob had no names; the bonfire was mostly black and flickering out, and on the opposite side of the street from the hotel the row of small shops was in flames. Long, but regular and narrow, from one end of the street to the other, it was like a row of children's toy blocks, set alight in an immense and darkened room.

It was a trivial blaze, it burned noiselessly and without spreading; beyond it was night and jungle, all of Africa, and stars he had not seen from the ground. The darkness confined the flames, and at one end it seemed to smother them.

Marais's room was brightened by the fire at the window. The room had been ransacked, the bed tipped over and the mattress torn apart. The desk was on its side, the drawers dumped out, the mirror over the dresser smashed. Marais went to a corner and lifted a floorboard; he removed his notebooks. He considered their covers, then broke their bindings. And his own face shining in the flames which brightly curtained the windows, he hurriedly dealt the loose pages on to the floor, like playing cards.

The following morning a charred skeleton was found in the smoking rubble of black beams and plaster that had collapsed into the basement. It was seated in a burned-out chair, but no one could tell whether, alive, it had righted and chosen the chair, or whether it had been dumped into it when the floor gave way. Even so, it may not have been Marais, the men digging had decided, for it was impossible to establish from what remained of the body if it had been white or African, man or woman.

36

The birth, Calvin thought, should have followed promptly upon Marais's death, or at least the news of it which Major Beaglehole, flustered, brought back from a stroll in town. It would have eased his grief, making a logical sequence of the sort that helps to compensate, a nice surprise coming after a bad shock, like the neat comfort insurance was supposed to be. It would have been a pattern achieved in all that outlandish confusion – celebration of success with a little lesson bringing a finish to all his suspense. The insurance money was no solace to him; he mistrusted that amount, it broke the agency, it wasn't his. He looked for relief. It happened in the smooth push-and-pull of popular fiction; and even the old ballad which claimed its hero in stanza eight produced a powerful infant in ten.

The death prepared him, but the birth didn't happen. The only events were disappearances: the girls decamped, the eating house emptied, Mavity went to Beira, the baby stopped kicking. There were closures, the bars and shops were shuttered. What a terrible place it was without drink. The weeks went in jerks and reverses, and Calvin lost track of time; but it was hot again, and cloudy with smoke-haze, so he knew it was the hot season, October perhaps, a month he hated.

In the evening noisy black soldiers came to play the fruit machines. They jammed them with flattened bottle-cap slugs and demanded beer from the diminished stock. Jarvis was gone; Bailey served. Mira and Calvin sat with Major Beaglehole, who had yarns and rumours. The most violent caused Mira pain, but it was always simulated labour, false alarm: they timed the pains now. Sometimes Bailey said, 'He was a lad, was Mavity,' and Beaglehole shushed her and turned up his hearing aid, raised his eyes to the plane he heard and said, 'It's them. They're coming, by God. I can hear them . . .' He meant the British, but it was usually the DC3 from Salisbury with the mail. Major Beaglehole was vulnerable with the volume up; one evening when it was on loud a soldier booted a fruit machine and knocked the old man to the floor.

Calvin's eyes were on Mira's bundle, so intensely that he saw nothing else: the periphery of his vision. He was jumpy in an agony of waiting. He offered no stories. He showed no surprise when told of Jarvis, Brother Jaja: the king of spades, as Bailey came to call him.

'I twigged it, you see, when he dressed up at night,' she whispered in a voice full of gravel. 'If he had taken over I'd have closed the place and got me one of those really swish knocking-shops in Bulawayo or Jo'burg.'

Aware that he too might have to leave soon, Major Beaglehole spoke of the discomfort in cold countries, and his feeble blood, thinned by a life in the tropics. He obsessively described the effects of English weather on his elderly body: 'It gets me in my toes and fingers. They ache and sort of die on me. And would you believe it,' he would say, grimacing and showing a finger, 'a frightful stabbing pain in the tip of my old man.' He had seen soldiers camped near the radio station, near the High Court at Chichiri, at the Queen Elizabeth Hospital and the clocktower and on the grounds of the Presidential Palace. Siege recalled to him many stories; he told them all, and said Durban was the place for him.

Calvin was with Mira all day now in the bare eating house. The office was closed: Mwase had left, seemingly for good – maybe, as he had warned, to rise up, though Calvin hoped not. Calvin's only consolation about *The Uninsured* was that if he had not written it, someone else would have done; but he was still annoyed by the thought that the someone would have had to be a stranger to the parish, like himself or Marais.

Mira was soulful, staring at the floor through her hooded eyes; and Calvin came to believe that the baby had died. Mira was terrified by the soldiers, of any man with a gun, as she had been just after the marriage. She held Calvin's arm when the soldiers were present, and she would not let go until they left.

But one night after the soldiers had all tramped out, Mira still held on. It was a loose grip; she was reassuring herself rather than enduring a pain. She looked across the empty bar with a wondering face, at the fruit machines, widening her eyes, then squinting, while Calvin looked at her.

She stood abruptly, as if inspired to march across to a machine, feed in an osbong and pull the lever for a jackpot. She murmured and held her dress and put her knees together and said, 'Goodness.'

She splashed from under her skirt. Beneath her chair was a small dune of flooded sawdust. The waters had broken. But there was no pain. She began to speak in her language, a familiar signal, but no more comprehensible to Calvin than the first time he had heard it. She tried to run.

'Get her to the bedroom!' Bailey cried. 'Quick!'

Mira was carried to her bed.

There was no motorcycle to reach the doctor with; and there were soldiers on the street watching for enemies. Calvin knew panic. But Bailey pushed him aside and brought a basin, and threw off her greasy shawl. She scrubbed her arms and then comforted Mira with a show of such gentleness that Calvin permitted it and stayed apart.

'Here?' he asked.

'Won't be the first,' said Bailey. She started to tell of the deliveries she had performed on her girls, right there in the eating house. 'Oh, I've delivered so many kids for my girls,' she said.

'Hosipital,' said Mira. 'Doc-tor.'

'Now you just lie there,' said Bailey. She handed Calvin a rag and told him to wipe Mira's perspiring face.

Major Beaglehole tidied the room, muttering about disorder. He found a chair and, overcome by tiredness, slept.

Bailey was nimble and clean; she spoke to Mira in Chinyanja and was busy in her midwifery. She calmed Mira and told her when and how to breathe and push. The baby was six hours coming. It arrived after a great struggle, in the darkest hour of the morning, giving a gasp and a yell as soon as its head protruded.

'Boy it is!' said Bailey, snipping the cord and swinging him up. It was a packed, colourless little child, covered in gore. Bailey laid him on the bed. He shrieked and shot out his arms, and immediately he took colour.

'A boy,' said Calvin, stunned. The infant was amazing: he had a full head of thick black hair, and a very wrinkled grey face. His fingers found his mouth, and he sucked them loudly.

Mira raised herself on her elbow and watched Bailey bathing it. It pissed a thread of spray in the air. Bailey washed it and said, 'That's funny,' and washed it again, and repeated her perplexed remark. She scrubbed it thoroughly and poured a pitcher of water over it. The baby started to cry. Bailey dabbed its pudgy face with a towel and looked puzzled. She closed one eye and studied the baby's face; she shook her head and tried to hand it to Mira.

Calvin intercepted it and wrapped it up. He cradled it carefully in his arms. And Bailey, with the expectant look of someone re-membering something, a look she often got before she coughed, left the room and closed the door.

Mira's hands were out. Her eyes pleaded. Calvin held on. The baby's chipmunk face was folded, his eyes were shut tightly. Calvin lifted him and kissed the wet wool of his head. The baby seemed very black. But Calvin's imagination had fooled him before: he had simulated miseries in his black book, and there had been times when he himself had felt black, like the king of spades of Mr P. Lumumba, grumbling under vines in the wet stillness of jungle. It had been an unusual feeling.

But Mr Bones was dead, and lately Calvin knew that he would surely go, now with a whole family. And he saw himself planted in Hudson or elsewhere, walking down a clean sidewalk in squirts of sunshine, a breeze stirring the poplars: he would stroll past hedges and lamp-posts, while people gawped amazed in cottage windows at the black woman he loved on his arm. He hoped they would be able to see, in the carriage he wheeled, the tar-baby kicking and gurgling, his son.

The baby woke and wailed again, furiously changing colour, going darker.

'I knew it,' Beaglehole said, without waking himself. 'It's them . . . they're . . . I can hear . . . '

Outside in the hall Bailey was breathing. The cough took her and held her. She hacked and panted and sawed the silence of the empty house with her sobbing cough. She coughed without a let-up again and again, as if she would drive out her very life.